W9-CDJ-038

Praise for S. M. Stirling

Conquistador

"A novel of complex landscapes, both moral and geographical."
—*Locus*

"The moral landscapes of this novel are intriguing, and the sight of an undeveloped West Coast is unforgettable." —SciFi.com

The Peshawar Lancers

"Lush backgrounds, tight research, lively characters, thoroughly nasty villains, a fascinating and plausible society—what more can anyone possibly want?" —Harry Turtledove

"Sure to please S. M. Stirling's legion of devoted fans . . . *The Peshawar Lancers* is a wonderfully evocative adventure, told by an absolute master."
—Mike Resnick, award-winning author of *The Outpost*

"Exciting." —*Santa Fe New Mexican*

"Complex and bloodthirsty . . . superlatively drawn action scenes and breakneck pacing . . . an irresistible read." —*Booklist*

"A remarkable alternate history. Stirling's impeccable research infuses both plot and characters with depth and verisimilitude, creating a tale of high adventure, romance, and intrigue." —*Library Journal*

"Aimed at readers who thrill to King, Empire, and the fluttering Union Jack . . . a nifty premise." —*Publishers Weekly*

"Stirling shows his ability to paint quite a vivid tale of intrigue."
—BookBrowser

continued . . .

Island in the Sea of Time

"A perfectly splendid story . . . endlessly fascinating . . . solidly convincing."
                                                    —Poul Anderson

"A compelling cast of characters . . . a fine job of conveying both a sense of loss and hope."   —*Science Fiction Chronicle*

"Quite a good book . . . definitely a winner."
                                        —*Aboriginal Science Fiction*

"Meticulous, imaginative . . . logical, inventive and full of richly imagined characters, this is Stirling's most deeply realized book yet."   —Susan Shwartz, author of *The Grail of Hearts*

"Utterly engaging. This is unquestionably Steve Stirling's best work to date, a page-turner that is certain to win the author legions of new readers and fans."
            —George R. R. Martin, author of *A Game of Thrones*

"One of the best time travel/alternative history stories I've ever read, period. Stirling combines complex, believable characters, meticulous research, and a fascinating setup to produce a book you won't want to—and won't be able to—put down. An outstanding piece of work."   —Harry Turtledove

"The adventure that unfolds, powered by Stirling's impressive stores of knowledge and extraordinary narrative skill, is an enormously entertaining read."   —Virtual North Woods Web site

Against the Tide of Years

"Fully lives up to the promises made in *Island in the Sea of Time*. It feels amazingly—often frighteningly—real. The research is impeccable, the writing excellent, the characters very strong. I can't wait to find out what happens next." —Harry Turtledove

"Mixing two parts historical fact with one part intelligent extrapolation, S. M. Stirling concocts another exciting and explosive tale of ambition, ingenuity, intrigue, and discovery. *Against the Tide of Years* is even more compelling than *Island in the Sea of Time*—but just as much fun."

—Jane Lindskold, author of *When the Gods Are Silent*

"*Against the Tide of Years* confirms what readers of the first book already knew: S. M. Stirling is writing some of the best straight-ahead science fiction the genre has ever seen." —*Amazing*

On the Oceans of Eternity

"Readers of this book's predecessors . . . will find the same strong characterizations, high historical scholarship, superior narrative technique, excellent battle scenes, and awareness of social and economic as well as technological factors in evidence again."

—*Booklist*

Other Books by S. M. Stirling

The Peshawar Lancers

Island in the Sea of Time

Against the Tide of Years

On the Oceans of Eternity

CONQUISTADOR

S. M. STIRLING

A ROC BOOK

ROC
Published by New American Library, a division of
Penguin Group (USA) Inc., 375 Hudson Street,
New York, New York 10014, U.S.A.
Penguin Books Ltd, 80 Strand,
London WC2R 0RL, England
Penguin Books Australia Ltd, 250 Camberwell Road,
Camberwell, Victoria 3124, Australia
Penguin Books Canada Ltd, 10 Alcorn Avenue,
Toronto, Ontario, Canada M4V 3B2
Penguin Books (N.Z.) Ltd, Cnr Rosedale and Airborne Roads,
Albany, Auckland 1310, New Zealand

Penguin Books Ltd, Registered Offices:
80 Strand, London WC2R 0RL, England

Published by Roc, an imprint of New American Library,
a division of Penguin Group (USA) Inc. Previously published in a
Roc hardcover edition.

First Roc Mass Market Printing, March 2004
10 9 8 7 6 5 4 3 2

Copyright © Steven M. Stirling, 2003
All rights reserved

Cover art by Jonathan Barkat

 REGISTERED TRADEMARK—MARCA REGISTRADA

Printed in the United States of America

Without limiting the rights under copyright reserved above, no part of this publication may
be reproduced, stored in or introduced into a retrieval system, or transmitted, in any form,
or by any means (electronic, mechanical, photocopying, recording, or otherwise), without
the prior written permission of both the copyright owner and the above publisher of this
book.

PUBLISHER'S NOTE
This is a work of fiction. Names, characters, places, and incidents either are the product of
the author's imagination or are used fictitiously, and any resemblance to actual persons,
living or dead, business establishments, events, or locales is entirely coincidental.

BOOKS ARE AVAILABLE AT QUANTITY DISCOUNTS WHEN USED TO PROMOTE PRODUCTS OR
SERVICES. FOR INFORMATION PLEASE WRITE TO PREMIUM MARKETING DIVISION, PENGUIN GROUP
(USA) INC., 375 HUDSON STREET, NEW YORK, NEW YORK 10014.

If you purchased this book without a cover you should be aware that this book is stolen
property. It was reported as "unsold and destroyed" to the publisher and neither the author
nor the publisher has received any payment for this "stripped book."

The scanning, uploading and distribution of this book via the Internet or via any other means
without the permission of the publisher is illegal and punishable by law. Please purchase only
authorized electronic editions, and do not participate in or encourage electronic piracy of
copyrighted materials. Your support of the author's rights is appreciated.

To Jan, forever

ACKNOWLEDGMENTS

To Jerry Pournelle, for advice and assistance; Giovanni Spinella and Mario Panzanelli, for help with Sicilian dialect; Steve Brady, for Afrikaans; Greg Saunders, for local knowledge of LA; to the Critical Mass, for continuing massively helpful criticism; and any others on the list.

All faults, errors, infelicities and lapses are my own.

And a special acknowledgment to the author of Niven's Law:

"There is a technical, literary term for those who mistake the opinions and beliefs of characters in a novel for those of the author.

"The term is 'idiot.'"

PROLOGUE

Oakland, California
April 17, 1946

FirstSide/New Virginia

John Rolfe had rented the house for seventy-five a month, which sounded extortionate but was something close to reasonable, given the way costs had gone crazy in the Bay Area since Pearl Harbor. The landlord was willing because Rolfe promised to do the badly needed repairs himself, and because he had a soft spot for soldiers—his son had died on Okinawa, where Rolfe had taken three rounds from a Nambu machine gun and gotten a Silver Star, a medical discharge and months on his back in a military hospital. The house was a solid three-bedroom piece of Victoriana, a little shabby and run-down like the area, shingle and dormers; what they called Carpenter Gothic hereabouts, but at least it had a basement. The previous owners had been Japanese-American, sent off to the relocation camps in 1942; then it had been rented out to workers in the shipyards to the north, part of the great wartime inrush, and they'd made a mess of it.

A whole house to himself was an indulgence anyway, since he was unmarried, but he'd spent too much of the last four years on troopships and in crowded bases and bivouacs, plus painful months in the crowded misery of a hospital. Solitude was restful.

He rubbed his thigh as he limped out to the porch, scooping up a bottle of milk, the mail and the newspaper. The mail included his monthly check from Uncle Sam, which was welcome; every little bit helped to stretch the modest legacy from his father, even though the house and land back in Virginia had gone for a surprising sum. There were also a few more no-thank-yous from prospective employers. The market for ex-captains wasn't all that brisk, not when their only other qualification was Virginia Military Institute. Being able to endure Beast Barracks, run an infantry company, and take out a Nip bunker complex . . . well, none of them were really salable skills in peacetime, particularly when they went with a slowly healing gimp leg. War heroes were a dime a dozen in the United States these days. He'd get something eventually. . . .

I'm still having better luck than my grandfather, he thought.

John Rolfe III had lost a leg at Second Manassas, leading a regiment of the Stonewall Brigade *against* the United States, under Jackson. That had turned out to be a bad decision, at least from the viewpoint of the family fortunes; though not as bad as Gramps' subsequent one to put everything he had into Confederate bonds as a patriotic gesture.

Of course, I'd have done exactly the same thing, but there's no denying it never pays to lose, he thought with a chuckle.

There was also a letter from Andy O'Brien, who'd been his top sergeant in Baker Company until he and Rolfe were invalided out on the same day. Enemy holdouts had infiltrated in the dark just before dawn and nearly overran them; it had come down to bayonets and clubbed rifles, boots and fists and teeth, with only the muzzle flashes to light chaos and terror and the stink of death.

For a moment his face froze under a film of cold sweat and the paper crumpled in his fist as a year vanished in an instant—he remembered the ugly crunching feel that shivered up the ruined weapon as the butt of his Garand splintered on a Nip's face, with a splash of blood that blinded him and ran salt and hot into his own open screaming mouth. He remembered the bayonet poised to kill him until O'Brien smashed it down and hacked the wielder's head half off with an entrenching tool, roaring in a berserker fury. That cut off suddenly as the bullets struck him like fists pounding on a block of beef and he toppled into the officer, pawing with arms gone flaccid.

He'd carried the big Irishman out on his back—until that slant-eyed bastard with the Nambu cut his left leg out from under him and broke the bone in three places; then he'd had to crawl. . . .

He gave a shuddering exhalation and wiped a hand over his face. It was very bad when the memories came like that, taking you back so you could feel and taste and touch, so you were *there* again.

Got to stop doing that. It's over, goddamn it, and you're alive.

The daytime memories weren't as bad as the dreams, but they were a lot more embarrassing; nobody was around at midnight to hear him screaming.

He opened the screen door with two fingers, kept it open with his elbow as he got his foot up on the doorsill, and let it bang behind him as he went into the kitchen, tossed the mail on the table and put the milk in the Frigidaire, taking out some cold fried chicken left over from last night and a couple of big juicy tomatoes. One of the advantages of living in California was that you could get fresh vegetables earlier than most places. Rolfe's housekeeping was painstakingly neat, a legacy of VMI and an inborn fastidiousness, but he didn't pretend to be able to cook beyond the can-opener-and-campfire level.

You're only twenty-four, he thought, eating and reading the paper. *Your life isn't over; it just feels that way sometimes.*

The postwar world was going to hell in a handbasket, according to the *Chronicle*. The Russians were cutting up ugly in Eastern Europe; half the people between England and the Ukraine were starving or dying of typhus or both; the Reds were making gains in China; the French were trying to get

Indochina back, and not having much luck; ditto the Dutch in Java; the Brits were having problems with the Jews in Palestine.

And MacArthur was lording it over the Nips, who were evidently worshiping him like a god or their own emperor. Which meant that Dugout Doug was finally getting what he thought he deserved.

He's almost *as good a general as he thinks he is,* Rolfe thought with a smile. *Which means he's pretty damned good. We may need him again, someday. Vanity's a small price to pay, and I don't believe in an end to wars.*

And closer to home, John Lewis was talking about taking the coal miners out on strike again. Rolfe ground his teeth slightly in fury. He was a Democrat, of course—it was virtually hereditary; where he was born they hadn't forgotten whose idea Reconstruction was or who went around waving the Bloody Shirt afterward, but . . .

But I'd have had Lewis taken out and shot for striking during the war, he thought, and tossed the folded newspaper aside, standing and stretching cautiously.

The leg made it difficult to sit comfortably when it stiffened up, and it reminded him each time that he was less than he'd been before the wound. He was naturally an active man, a little above average height and built like a greyhound, slim but deep-chested and lithe, with short-cropped hair the color of new bronze and leaf-green eyes in a narrow, straight-nosed face.

It was a fine April day, Bay Area style; that meant a bit chilly, with a cool ocean breeze out of the northwest coming in through the kitchen windows. The noontime haze over the bay was gone, and there were probably whitecaps out there on it—no ocean view here, of course, or the place would have been too expensive for him. A few planes were overhead from the naval air station farther north, adding the drone of their engines to a subdued hum of traffic, a ship's horn, the distant clang of electric trolley cars. Rolfe finished his sparse meal, washed the dishes and doggedly went through another of the exquisitely painful series of exercises the doctors said would help the damaged muscles and tendons heal. That done, he felt he deserved some fun.

The basement was clean and tidy now, big and dim, smelling of the cement mortar he'd used to patch cracks, and mostly empty except for tubs, scrub board and mangle. Or it had been until the shortwave set arrived; it was war surplus, of course, and he'd gotten it cheap through friends. He'd also fiddled with the insides a good deal, and he flattered himself he'd made some improvements—certainly he'd improved the reception, even if he'd nearly killed himself rigging the antenna on the roof. Engineering and math had been his best subjects at VMI, and he'd been thinking about using this G.I. Bill to get into one of the California universities— you could do that and convalesce at the same time. A field officer had to be able to sprint, but there were types of civilian engineer who didn't, and with luck he could still avoid being stuck behind a desk all the time.

One thing engineers didn't have to be either was poor. Genteel rural poverty was something he knew far too well from his Tidewater childhood to court willingly.

His fingers moved confidently over the exposed tubes and circuits as he thought. With a grunt of satisfaction he made the final connection, flipped the power switch and sat back to let the tubes warm up—

CRACK!

The sound was earsplitting, louder than thunder, accompanied by a dazzling flash. John Rolfe threw himself out of the chair with long-conditioned reflex, hitting the dirt and blinking the dazzle out of his eyes desperately, because if you couldn't see then you didn't get to go on breathing. . . .

It took a couple of extra blinks before he realized that he was really seeing what his eyes were showing him. The far wall of the basement—the long side to the right of his shortwave set—was . . . gone. Instead of a mortared fieldstone wall half-covered in rawly new pine-plank shelving, there was a sheet of something silvery, something that rippled very slightly, like the surface of a body of water set on its side, staying there in defiance of gravity.

No, not like water, he thought. It was too shiny; the overhead lights he'd put in above the workbench had turned pale, as if there were some diffuse internal glow from the surface of the whatever-it-was. *It's not like water. It's like a sheet of* mercury *standing on its side.*

He could smell his own sweat, and it felt cold and clammy down his flanks, and there was a liquid feeling south of his belly button, and his testicles were trying to crawl up to meet it, but he was used to functioning well while he ignored the physical sensations of fear. Once you got going, you were too busy to notice it. His eyes flickered back and forth, trying to catch details in something so strange that it slid away from the surface of his mind. Then he noticed the shelves he'd put up for tools, and storage for miscellaneous junk that his aunt Antonia had shipped out when he got out of the hospital; stuff that had been around since his father died in '41, and his mother moved in with her.

Now all he could see was the base; the upper nine-tenths of the shelving had toppled out *into* the whatever-it-was. He took a stiff step forward, then crouched and touched the rough wood; it felt completely normal, no hotter or colder than it should be, texture the same. Carefully bracing his foot against the flagstones of the cellar floor, he pulled on one section. It stuck for a moment, then slid back into the room with him, leaving the silvery nothingness undisturbed.

It was if he had pulled the shelf out of a mercury pond that neither wet it nor rippled as the wood went through its surface. His fingers found no damage, except where the backs of the shelves had splintered in a few places as if they'd fallen against rocks. And there was dirt, a little, and bits of grass and leaf caught in irregularities, and his hand darted out and closed on an insect. A perfectly ordinary insect, a beetle of some sort. He flicked it away, and it vanished through the silvery barrier.

"Well, I'll be damned," he whispered in the soft purring drawl of eastern Virginia. "Ah will be *eternally* damned."

Swallowing, he extended his hand. There was a momentary coolness as it slid through the surface, faint and fleeting, perhaps only his mind expecting the shock of water. Then nothing except wind on his fingers, which felt completely normal when he wiggled them, despite the arm *looking* as if it ended where the silvery surface began. There was no unusual sensation at all as he withdrew it, and wiggled the fingers again in front of his face.

Decision hardened. John Rolfe took a deep breath and leaned forward. For a moment he was dazzled, but that was only because the setting sun shone into his eyes. He gasped at that, and then again as he looked down, seeing his own head and shoulders emerging from a flat expanse of ever-so-slightly rippling silver. Because what he saw was certainly not his basement or anything in Oakland, California; and that meant the front half of him was a long way from the rear, joined only by the odd material of this gate to wherever. His swift-hammering heart must be pumping blood across some unimaginable gap.

The stones of his cellar wall were scattered before him down a low grassy slope, with the shelving and tools and boxes lying on top of them and above that a clear blue sky streaked with high cloud. Just beyond, perhaps twenty yards away, was a tree—a huge, gnarled, wide-spreading coast live oak, unmistakable to anyone who'd spent any time in California, blocking most of whatever lay beyond as the sun glistened on its new springtime leaves. He *could* see glimpses of vivid green salt marsh, and beyond it the blue glint of open water. Right where San Francisco Bay ought to be—if the city of Oakland weren't in the way. And between him and the live oak, a bear.

A grizzly. Old Eph himself, a big silvertip male, standing erect for a better view and weaving its long massive head in curiosity as it stared at him.

John Rolfe tumbled backward with a yell, landing on his backside on the unyielding stone of the basement's floor. For perhaps three minutes he lay there, the hard gritty surface cold under his palms, and then a long slow grin lit his face.

I don't know what's happening, he thought. *But whatever it is, I suspect my days of being bored are over.*

It took only a moment to go upstairs, change into jeans and flannel shirt and boots, and add a brown jacket and billed cap; they were his hunting clothes, bought for when he'd recovered enough to take up the sport again. He loved stalking deer, and an African safari had been his when-I-strike-it-rich daydream for years. He took down a rucksack and dumped in a few things from the kitchen, matches and canned beans, enough for an overnight camp if he wasn't picky and the weather wasn't too cold. The pain in his leg was distant, unimportant, as he clattered down into the basement and over to a tall steel footlocker he'd installed underneath the stairs that led up to the pantry. The lock was a combination model. He twisted the dial and then opened the door, hesitating for a second as he reached in.

His old webbing belt was folded on a top shelf; he swung it around his Levi-clad hips and buckled it with a sudden decisive movement. Checking the .45 was automatic; slide out the magazine, thumb the top round, slide it in with a snap and pull the action back. He buckled the holster flap down over the pistol and took the Garand rifle out of its rack, pushing in an eight-round clip and letting the bolt snick home.

He still had a deep affectionate respect for the Garand design, and had bought one from an accommodating supply sergeant as soon as he got out of the hospital; it hadn't been difficult in the freewheeling chaos that accompanied demobilization after V-J day. The .30-06 rounds ought to make even a grizzly sit up and take notice; he tossed a dozen clips into a pocket of the rucksack on general principle—you never had too much ammunition.

Now I know what John Rolfe the First *felt like,* Rolfe thought. *Wading onto the Virginia shore all those years ago, rapier in hand.*

Cradling the rifle in the crook of his left arm, John Rolfe VI stepped into the wall of silvery light.

Chapter One

Los Angeles
June 2009

FirstSide

I joined the Department of Fish and Game because I couldn't be a soldier anymore and I hate cities, Tom Christiansen thought, the Berretta cold and unforgiving in his hands. It didn't have the heft of an assault rifle, which would have been comforting right about now. *God is an ironist.*

He and his partner were crouched behind the rear door of a car not far from the SWAT team; the FBI agent was up beside the front wheel. It was a typical early-summer day in LA; the ozone was enough to fry the hairs out of your nostrils, his eyes hurt from the smog that left a ring of dirty brown around the horizon, and the nearest vegetation was a tired-looking palm a block away, if you didn't count weeds growing through cracks in the pavement. It was better than going after holdouts in the Hindu Kush, but that was about all you could say for it.

"Leave the 'Freeze!' and 'Hands up!' stuff to our esteemed colleagues of the LAPD, a.k.a. 'those fucking cowboy assholes,' Tom," the FBI agent said quietly, glancing over at him. She was a thin, hard-looking black woman named Sarah Perkins. "'Game wardens shot dead in LA bust' doesn't make a good headline."

Tom nodded, grinning; it was an expression that came

easily to his face. He was a broad-shouldered, thick-armed, long-legged man three inches over six feet, dressed in T-shirt, a Sacramento Kings jacket and jeans, with battered hiking boots on his feet. His short-cropped white-blond hair topped a tanned square-cut face and a straight nose that had been broken and healed very slightly crooked a long time ago. He looked every inch the east-Dakota Norski farm boy he'd been born thirty-two years ago, down to the pale gray of his eyes. A very slight trace of Scandinavian singsong underlay his flat Midwestern accent, despite the fact that his great-grandparents had left the shores of the Hardangerfjord a hundred and thirty years before. The wheat country north of Fargo hadn't attracted a whole lot of newcomers since then.

"Ever hear what happened when they sent the LAPD to find the rabbit that attacked President Carter, back when?" he said softly.

Just sitting and waiting before action let you get knotted up inside. Gallows humor was the only sort available on a battlefield, but that was when you needed to break the tension.

"I'll bite," Perkins said.

"Well, the LAPD went into the woods, and half an hour later they dragged out a grizzly bear by its hind feet; it didn't have any teeth left and both its eyes were swollen shut. And it was screaming over and over, 'All right! I'm a rabbit! I'm a rabbit!'"

She snorted laughter, quietly, and without taking her eyes off the target. Tom exchanged a silent glance with his partner, and Roy Tully grinned back. It wouldn't be tactful to mention the other part of the joke—the FBI burned down the whole wood and shot everything that came out on the grounds that "the rabbit had it coming."

And there was no real reason to complain, even if working for Fish and Game was more like soldiering than he'd anticipated; he *was* a cop, sort of—he was part of the Special Operations Unit; the SOU was the enforcement branch of the DFG. That made him smile a little too; SOU, DFG, FBI,

SWAT, LAPD, the alphabet soup of police bureaucracy. Still, guys like him were as necessary as the scientists and administrators; without them there wouldn't be any condors left, or eagles, or cougars, and Lake Tahoe would be ticky-tack *all* the way 'round, and the whole of California would look like *this*. If that meant he had to crouch here next to a crummy little warehouse of rusting sheet metal in South Central LA, hoping he wouldn't get shot and frying his sinuses when he could be hiking in the Sierras breathing air colder and cleaner than crystal, or canoeing in Glacier National Park, or even just taking a break to help out on his brother's farm back in North Dakota, then so be it.

The SWAT troopers' heads came up; something was going on, and they were getting the word through their ear mikes. He'd never liked the Imperial-Death-Star-Nazi look of the black uniforms they insisted on, like hanging out an "Oooooo, AIN'T WE BAD!" sign, but they had good gear.

There was a loud *whump* from within the warehouse. Flames shot out of windows at the rear—he could tell by the plumes of smoke—and the big sheet-metal doors at the front slammed outward as they were struck by an invisible fist of hot dense air; the clerestories on the roof shattered upward in a weirdly beautiful shower of broken glass, glinting in the harsh sunlight. Smoke followed seconds later. It wasn't a big explosion, but it had obviously been linked to incendiaries; flames were licking out as well.

Subtlety might be a problem with the LA cops, but firepower and straightforward kick-ass aggression were things they did well; they all charged forward, M-16s and machine pistols at their shoulders. The other teams would be going in from around the warehouse, and the snipers were ready on the flat roofs of the neighboring buildings. The troopers went through the doors, leaving them swinging and banging—and almost immediately there was a second explosion, the sound much lower and sharper.

"Shit!"

Tom wasn't sure if that was him or Tully or Perkins; they all reacted identically too, getting up and running toward the door. He found that comforting. Running toward trouble wasn't always the right thing to do, but people with that reflex were generally the ones you wanted around you when things got rough.

There were two policemen down just inside the door, one limp, the other putting a field bandage on his own leg.

"Fire set off something," he said. "Rodriguez is OK, I think."

"Good pulse, no bleeding, no concussion," Perkins confirmed, peeling back an eyelid and pressing her fingers to the man's throat.

She and Tully helped the man with the wounded leg, swinging arms over their shoulders and carrying his weight between them; they were about the same height, five-six or so. Tom stooped and lifted the unconscious officer in a fireman's carry, rising easily under the hundred and ninety pounds of man and gear—he was even stronger than he looked, and that load was fifty short of his own body weight. The waiting paramedics ran up to take the injured men, so that was all right; sirens of several types were screaming or yodeling nearby.

Tom scooped up a Colt Commando carbine someone had dropped as they went back in. This was the interior loading bay of the warehouse, with nothing in it but oil stains and orange paint on the concrete. There were two sets of stairs along the walls leading up to the higher interior floor, and two big orange-painted vertical sliding doors buckled and jammed in their frames. Smoke was coming out of those, but up near the top—that meant most of the fire was going out the roof for now. The dull roar was getting louder with every heartbeat, though, and the heat of the combustion was drying the sweat on his face faster than it could come out of his pores. Perkins nodded at him, and the three dashed through, ducking under the twisted sheet metal. There hadn't been any shooting, and he could hear the members of the SWAT teams calling to each other.

It took a few seconds for what he was seeing inside to sink in. Piles of crates, boxes and bales . . . And piles of tusks. Elephant tusks, a couple of hundred of them. Walrus tusks. The fire had the piles between him and them, but he pushed into the smoke, close enough to confirm what the heavy burnt-leather reek had told him. The skins were polar bear, and grizzly, and tiger, and sea otter—stacks of them, hundreds at least.

"Oh, my God!" he said, acutely aware of the utter inadequacy of the words. "Fuck! Fuck! *Fuck!*"

That wasn't up to the occasion either, but it did a better job of expressing how he felt. Tully's amazing flow of scatology and obscenity was a little better, and more sincere than usual the smaller man's Arkansas accent was notably thicker.

The SWAT team came back, coughing and crouching as the smoke grew heavier and came closer to the floor. One of them held a big cage, with an even bigger bird jammed into it, something like an enormous vulture, thrashing and screeching hoarsely. A *really* enormous vulture . . .

An adult California condor.

Tom felt his teeth show in an involuntary snarl of rage. There weren't more than a couple of hundred of those in the whole *world,* and only a captive breeding program had saved them from complete extinction. This one warehouse could have pushed a couple of species halfway to the brink! The rising shuddering roar of the fire, the rumble of sheet metal buckling and twisting, the *ptank!* as rivets gave way, all seemed to pale before the thunder of his own blood in his ears.

The officer in charge of the SWAT team grabbed him as he tried to push farther in; the offices were in a glassed-in enclosure up against the far wall, and it was there that any evidence would be found.

"No use!" he shouted, flipping up his face shield. "They must have had some warning—the charges there went off first. We took everything we could find, but I think there's thermite planted here that hasn't gone off yet, and sure as shit someone drenched the place in gasoline. Out of here before someone gets killed!"

They did, retreating before the billowing rankness of the smoke made by things not meant to burn. The leader of the SWAT team pulled off his helmet, coughing and rubbing at a gray-and-red mustache.

"Son of a bitch!" he said, as they dodged aside to let the first wave of firemen wrestle a hose forward. "I didn't think there was that much ivory in the *world*," he said, grinning through smoke-smuts. "These must be some seriously energetic smugglers you're after."

"There are only two hundred forty-seven condors in the world," Tom said grimly. "That one your people got out is one half of one percent of the entire goddamn *species*. Congratulations on that, by the way."

"Oh," the LA policeman said, then nodded to them and walked away.

"Also Known As," Perkins muttered.

"As the bear said, I'm a rabbit," Tully said, his grin making his face look even more like a garden gnome's than usual. "Guy must have been a marine." Perkins raised her brows, and Tully went on: "Marine—Muscles Are Required, Intelligence Not Essential."

Tom took a deep breath, not even minding the air much—or that Tully had stolen the Ranger joke. Anger seemed to burn the impurities out of his system. "You know what makes me *really* mad?"

"No, Tom, what makes you really mad?" Perkins said.

The evidence had been set up temporarily in the back of one of the LAPD vans; the condor was farther in, in shadow with an improvised cover thrown over the cage, and seemed to be all right except for being agitated. And rather smelly; condors were naturally carrion eaters, and messy diners at best. The rustling of the great bird's wings inside the confining cave gave a slithering undertone to the murmur of the growing crowd, the noise of the fire and the firefighters' machinery. The LAPD evidence team were at work with their Baggies and tweezers, making sure everything was preserved properly, and taking continuous video as they did.

"My father and the potholes, that's what makes me angry."

Perkins's thin eyebrows went up; she noticed that she still had her 9mm in her hand and put it back in the holster at the small of her back and let the thin polyester jacket fall over it again.

"Told you my dad farmed, didn't I?" Tom said; she nodded, and he went on: "Well, up in the Red River Valley, the land's flat as a pancake—a lot of it had to be tile-drained before it could carry a crop; it's naturally swampy all through the spring and fall. Some of it's still in these little isolated marshy lakes, we call 'em potholes. And it's on a big migratory bird flyway. *Millions* of birds depend on those potholes to get to and from their breeding grounds. Problem is, after you've drained them, those potholes are prime land . . . and there's not a farmer in the world who can afford to pass up another hundred acres, even if he's farming twenty sections, which Dad wasn't. The bigger you are the bigger your debts get. So we're coming back from duck hunting one fall; one of those sunny crisp days, with a little haze on the horizon, the wheat's in but some of the sunflowers are still nodding in the wind.

"And I'm on top of the world because it's the first time I've been allowed to take a shotgun out with Dad and my brother Lars and we've each gotten a couple of mallards, and it's been the best goddamned day in my life. And we stop at a crossroads and talk to a neighbor—who *did* farm twenty sections—and he says that if he was Dad, he'd have drained that pothole for his kids' sake, not wasted it on ducks."

Perkins looked at him a little oddly. "What did your father say?"

"Nothing, until the neighbor was on his way. Then he turned to us, Lars and me, and smiled, and said: 'And if I did drain it, you boys would never get to see the ducks going over in the fall, or go hunting with *your* kids. Better than getting a motorbike for Christmas, eh?'"

Tom kicked the wheel of the van, remembering the rough hand tousling his hair, and the smells of pipe tobacco and

Old Spice he'd always subliminally associated with his father.

"Dad worked himself to death keeping that farm going, but he wasn't going to steal that from his grandsons. And now some *son* of a bitch had that place stuffed to the rafters with the carcasses of animals maybe nobody will ever see again except on a recording, and for what? For money to shove candy up his nose, to give some hooker a diamond, to buy some three-a-dollar Third World politician."

He very carefully did not slam his fist into the side of the van, letting the fingers unclench one by one. "Sorry," he muttered, embarrassed by the outburst; he normally wasn't a very verbal man.

Perkins patted him on the shoulder as she came up to his side. "Hey, that's more emotion than has ever been shown in Sweden before," she said. "No, it's all right, Christiansen. Every good cop has got to have a little passion in them about *something* in the work, or they burn out. Your passion is critters and trees; that's OK. I like collaring scumbags: this bunch, terrorists back in the war, whatever. Our passions coincide." A grin. "Don't tell my husband I said that."

"Yah, you betcha," he said, with a relieved snort.

They moved over to the van, where the specialists had completed their work; the yellow tape was up, and uniformed police were keeping the crowds back. Tully took out a piece of the beef jerky he always kept in a pocket and tried to interest the condor in it; the big bird just cowered lower in his cage, which was quite an accomplishment, since he essentially filled it.

The evidentiary spoils set out on the van's floor were pathetically meager; the fire must have blown up like a volcano going off in the SWAT team's faces, leaving them only seconds to grab what they could. There were a few sheets of paper that might have been accounts, a few letters, a charred and battered computer unit that might have salvageable data on its hard drive. And one large glossy photograph, curled and discolored along one edge. Tom reached toward it, picking it up by the corners of the plastic bag it was sealed in.

"What the hell is this?" Perkins said, looking around him—she'd have had to stand on a chair to look over his shoulder.

"I think those are supposed to be Aztec priests," he said dubiously. "Some sort of re-creation, or a movie. But it doesn't look quite right."

The setting reminded him of things he'd seen in *National Geographic* articles; the top of a huge stepped pyramid, the edges of the stones carved in violently colored serpents and shapes even more arcane; the alien symbolism made it difficult to pick up the details. The men grouped around the altar were a little easier, despite the huge feathered headdresses, grotesque devil masks set with turquoise and silver, multicolored cloaks, elaborate loincloths. And blood, a great deal of it, flooding down from the gutters on the altar. Bodies lay around, their chests gaping open; another was stretched out across the altar block with a priest holding each limb and another holding up the severed heart and a broad dagger of polished obsidian with a dragonlike hilt.

"The idol he's offering the heart to, that's Huitzilopochtli," Tom said.

He'd dated a Mexican-American girl interested in ancient Mesoamerican art, back when he was in the Rangers and stationed in Texas. Personally he thought it was all sort of grotesque; this statue was indescribable, a tall multicolored stone nightmare of hearts, stylized spurting blood, knives, teeth, snakes, clutching hands and God knew what.

"Hooti Lipopki?" Tully said. "They're worshiping some Polack country-western star gone bad?"

Tom chuckled, and even the rather grim FBI agent was startled into a smile.

"It's in Nahuatl, the old Aztec language—he was their god of war—the name translates as 'Left-Handed Hummingbird' and 'The Shadow Behind the Shoulder,'" Tom said.

Perkins made a moue of distaste. "Maybe these scumbags were dealing in snuff films too?" she asked. "Or this might be a still from a horror movie."

"I don't know—the sets look awfully realistic and detailed; that costs." You couldn't live in California for years and not know *something* about "the Industry."

"I think a horror flick that elaborate would have gotten some publicity."

"Realistic except for one thing," Tully said with a guffaw, peering a little more closely and pointing out a detail that only became clear if you put your face close to the picture.

"Yeah," Tom said, with an answering chuckle. It was nice to have *some* comic relief in a day like this.

Above their loincloths, the "priests" were all wearing T-shirts, black ones, showing a dancing skeleton with a chaplet of red roses and more blossoms falling around it.

"Isn't that an album cover from one of those sixties rocker groups that kept on performing until they were shuffling around the stage in walkers with oxygen tubes up their noses?" Tom said.

Perkins got it first. "Grateful Dead. I didn't know they were touring Mexico *that* long ago."

They all laughed at that; it was odd how a picture of carnage that would make you faintly sick if it were real looked ludicrous when you knew it was fake, no matter how good the illusion.

"Well, that seems to be that for now," the FBI agent said. "Let's get our part of this ratfuck cleared up, at least."

She shook hands with the SOU wardens, and Tom Christiansen turned to go; he had to arrange to get the condor into the proper hands at the San Diego Zoo's captive-breeding program, and then they had to *catch* these smugglers and put them away for a long, long time. In a way this ratfuck would help—they could add arson and reckless negligence, possibly attempted homicide, to the count of crimes—but it meant that the bad guys were still one step ahead of them.

As he turned, he caught sight of something that stood out from the crowd, enough to stop him for an instant. Two men as tall as or taller than he was, one of them as big, which was rare; they were also white men, not common on the street in this part of South Central, and dressed in conservative narrow-stripe business suits. They were just turning away. Between them was a young woman who must be tall herself; he caught a glimpse of bright hair and then the trio were lost in the crowd.

Well, that's California, he thought. *Always surprises.*

Tully put a hand on his arm as he turned back, with a slight facial twitch that said *Hang around* and *Shhhhh!* Tom waited until the FBI agent had left before he raised a brow.

"Strikes me that there's one place we haven't looked, Kemosabe," Tully said. "The condor's cage."

Tom nodded, sighing a little. "It's a dirty job—" he began.

"No worse than shoveling out the chicken house back on the farm," Tully said, pulling out two pairs of disposable gloves.

"We were wheat farmers," Tom said, drawing the tight plastic over his fingers and keeping a wary eye on the bird. On the one hand, condors weren't very aggressive. On the other, they were very big, and so were their claws and beaks. "We got our chicken at the A and P, like everyone else."

"Not like us Arkies down in Dogpatch," Tully said. "Why, mah daddy tanned the leather fer our shoes! After he wrassled him the bar, 'n' rendered it down fer candles 'n' tanned the hide."

"Your father was a lawyer," Tom pointed out. "In Little Rock."

"Now *that's* a filthy job," Tully said, peeling back layers of sodden, droppings-laden paper. The acrid stench was heavy. "*Hel*-lo, what have we here?"

"Well, well, well!" Tom said. "The Oakland *Herald.* Looks like our bird wasn't LA-LA born. Closer to our neck of the woods, yah, you betcha. And what's this?"

One of the pungent linings at the bottom of the cage wasn't newspaper. It was some sort of corporate letterhead.

"'Bosco Holdings,'" Tom read out; a white splotch of condor feces obliterated most of the rest, but there was a San Francisco address. "Bay Area. So far we've been about as useful as an udder on a billy goat. Here's our chance."

✸ ✸ ✸

Adrienne Rolfe stood with her hands on her hips and frowned as the fire engines went past her. The warehouse was a bellowing pillar of fire now; the first firemen on the scene were just trying to keep it from spreading rather than trying to put it out. With any luck it would keep burning until nothing was left but ash. Ashes could tell a surprising amount with modern forensic techniques, but they didn't have the public-relations impact of intact pieces of dead animals—or, worse, living ones that shouldn't be here. There were limits to what even the Commission could hush up, but the fire had kept a number of headlines unprinted.

The crowd was growing now, mostly black with a scattering of Hispanics, watching the blinking lights of the police cars. The heat was dense, between the afternoon sun baking back from asphalt and walls and the thick crush, and the smell added to the normal throat-catching vileness of FirstSide city air to put her nerves on edge. That wasn't all bad; it kept you alert. She still didn't enjoy being jostled by strangers, or feeling this conspicuous.

Nor was she the only one. The tall, pale-eyed, lanky man beside her muttered, *"Verdonde kaffirs,"* under his breath. Then *"Varken hond!"* at one teenager in low-slung pants whose head was like a shaved black cannonball beneath a yellow bandanna, and who'd casually elbowed him.

Adrienne shifted, inconspicuously planting the low heel of her sensible leather walking shoe on her assistant's toe and leaning her weight onto it. She wasn't a small woman— five-nine and a hundred and thirty-five pounds—and there was a vicious expertise in the swift, painful grinding motion she used.

"Schalk, remember where you are," she said in a pleasant undertone as he yelped and staggered, distracted. "I'm not going to tell you again."

Freely translated, what he'd said meant *goddamned niggers* and *pig-dog* respectively. Those were not tactful expressions around here.

Schalk van der Merwe scowled, but muttered a brief: "Sorry, miss."

Beside him Piet Botha rumbled agreement—with Adrienne. He was as tall as his partner, but older; a dark, bullet-headed, massive man with hands like spades and the beginnings of a kettle belly over solid muscle. One joint of the middle finger was missing from his left hand, and there were white scars running up both hands into the cuffs of his suit. She had her suspicions about how both of them felt working under her on this assignment, she being a she and a good bit younger than either, but she'd been the only member of the Thirty Families available and remotely qualified. Something like this was too important not to have a member of the Commission's inner circle in charge. She strongly suspected that Piet was a lot calmer than his thinner colleague, which could be helpful in keeping Schalk in line.

And I know I'm not going to let either of them screw this up, she thought, giving the FirstSider operation one final careful glance.

Damn.

The FirstSiders had gotten some stuff out of the offices; reluctantly, she admitted that must have taken guts and presence of mind. Three plainclothes operatives were examining items set out in the back of a van: a black woman, a short white man in high-waisted green pants and suspenders, and a very tall, well-built blond man a few years older than herself. They talked together for a few minutes, laughing at some joke, and then held up a photograph. That would be very bad . . . except that nobody would believe it. Particularly when digital photography was so easy to modify. Everyone here was used to seeing convincing images of impossible things.

The Commission would have lost its secret long ago, if it weren't for the convenient fact that it was simply too wild. People didn't grasp it until they were shoved through, usually.

"Another half hour, and the fire would have started before anyone got in," Piet grumbled. "We should have set the timers shorter."

The tip had been so hot they'd come directly down from

the San Francisco office without even changing clothes. The result was that they were breaking the first rule of FirstSide operations, sticking out like sore thumbs—standing out even more than they would have in costumes that were tailored for a quasi-slum area of LA, rather than the Commission's outer-shell offices in the San Francisco financial district. So far no harm had been done, but when the news services began arriving—apart from the helicopter, which had been overhead since a few minutes after the police went in—and the cameras started panning across the crowd, they'd stand out like a Chumash shaman at a polo match. With a little bad luck, someone might stick a microphone in their faces and try to get a person-on-the-street reaction.

They turned casually and walked back toward where their van was parked. *Never get your face on a record if you could avoid it* was another rule, and one getting harder and harder to follow, what with surveillance cameras popping up everywhere.

They walked past more self-storage and then into streets of ordinary shops, seedy and many boarded up; they weren't far from Sepulveda Boulevard. Knots of men and boys lingered on doorsteps, or leaned against cars; she was conscious of eyes following her, and a palpable mist of hostility toward the affluent white girl. Schalk and Piet stood out too, although not in any way that would attract local predators. In their expensive Armani suits and thousand-dollar shoes, they looked to be exactly what they were—a pair of merciless hulking killers stuffed into Armani suits and thousand-dollar shoes. Anyone who might think of attacking them would also probably recognize that they were armed. She smiled slightly; all three of them actually had valid concealed-carry permits for the Belgian FiveseveN specials under their jackets.

Although not for the P90 machine pistols in the attaché cases, and some of the stuff in the vehicle would be right out of it. Semtex, timers, detonators, cans of gasoline and thermite bombs, for example. Even if the invoice reads "Cleaning supplies" back at HQ.

Still, it wasn't far to the van, and if they hadn't been along she might have had to hurt somebody, which would be more conspicuous still.

A couple of youths were lingering around the minivan; it was an inconspicuous Ford Windstar, several years old and externally a bit scuffed-up. That was ironic too. The Families were some of the richest people in the world—two worlds—and here, at least, they didn't dare show it. Getting your picture in *Town and Country* or the gossip pages was enough to have your Gate privileges revoked. You could show a certain degree of affluence, but not real status, whether you were working or on vacation; and that was under threat of dire penalty. It was an important reason why so few members of the Thirty Families lived FirstSide anymore.

Me, I just hate this place, she thought, as she clicked the little device on her key chain that unlocked the doors, turned off the alarms, and started the engine. *The stink, the ugliness, the crowding, the swarms of strangers, with the stress that puts on you every moment, the fact that you have to lock everything up . . . did I mention the stink? Just a small-town girl at heart, I suppose.*

Schalk went over to one of the young men who was standing too close to the driver's door and looked at him from an inch inside his personal space. After an instant, the would-be gangbanger took three steps backward, stumbling on the curb. Then the Afrikaner smiled and inclined his head. *"Danke, kleine maanetje,"* he said sardonically, and held the door open for her.

"We have a problem," she said, as they pulled away from the curb.

She drove conservatively, carefully, and rather slowly until they were northbound on the Harbor Freeway, on their way to the Santa Monica junction; they were staying at a hotel called La Montrose, which was quite tolerable. At midmorning on a Thursday, the traffic wasn't too bad—open enough for her to enjoy the trip a little. Driving fast on broad limited-access roads was one of the real pleasures of

FirstSide, like ballet and professional live theater. Of course, it was best with a sports car and an open stretch of desert, not this clunker in the midst of LA's hideous sprawl.

"*Ja,*" Piet said after a moment; he had checked that they weren't being tailed. "That was too close. *'N Moerse probleem;* we have to wrap this up quickly."

She nodded. Schalk was useful—she'd heard he once grabbed a bandit's neck and left wrist, and then pulled the arm right off at the shoulder—but Piet was actually capable of thought, too. *Well, they both earn their corn, each in his own way,* she thought, and went on aloud: "But that's not the real problem. The real problem is that we're working against *both* someone with Commonwealth connections who's managed to smuggle goods past Gate Security, *and* against First-Side law enforcement, this time. And the FirstSiders have a good lead they're working on; otherwise they wouldn't have known about the warehouse."

She paused for a moment. "It's like two birds eating a worm. We have the New Virginia end, they have the First-Side end; and we're in far too much danger of meeting in the middle. That would be very bad."

Piet frowned. "Yes, miss, that means we have to be quick."

"That means we have to find out what they know," she said. "Beyond what our usual pipelines can tell us. They don't know what we really are, and we don't want to give them ideas, either. Sometimes the questions you ask tell more than answers would."

Schalk looked a little baffled. Piet gave her a glance of surprised respect; she kept her own reaction to that politely concealed. He should have been smart enough to realize that the Commission wouldn't send a complete figurehead along on a field operation, even one with her bloodline. The Old Man was ready enough to indulge a grandchild's whim, but not where it could have a serious impact on business.

"And I've got the inkling of an idea about how," she said thoughtfully. "I need to do some research first. If things are the way I think . . . we'll still need permission to use it—authorization from the Committee, possibly from the Old Man."

Schalk muttered something in his native tongue. She didn't really speak Afrikaans—she had fluent Spanish, which was much more useful here FirstSide, plus French and Italian and a little German, which were sometimes handy in the Commonwealth of New Virginia. She *had* picked up a fair smattering of vocabulary in the past eighteen months, since these two were assigned to her as a combination of bodyguards, gofers and muscle.

"Yes, Operative van der Merwe, he *is* my grandfather," she said sweetly. Schalk flushed. "But that's going to make talking him into what I have in mind harder, not easier."

INTERLUDE
May 5, 1946
The Commonwealth of New Virginia

The flicker of the campfire cast unrestful red light on the faces of the five men who sat about it; a battered camp coffeepot bubbled away on three stones in the midst of the coals and low red flames, sending its good smell drifting along with the clean hot scent of burning oak wood, the tule elk steaks they'd grilled, and the briny smell of the bay not far to the west. An occasional pop sent red sparks drifting slowly skyward, up toward the shimmer of firelight on the leaves of the big coast live oak whose massive branches writhed above them, and toward the stars that frosted the sky in an arch above. Their simple campsite stood on the fringe of the circle of light, three army-surplus tents and a few bales and boxes; horses snorted nearby, stamping and pulling at their tethers as something big grunted and pushed its way through a thicket. Faint and far beyond that was the chanting of the Ohlone Indians in their village, where a shaman held a ceremony to decide the meaning of the strangers with their wonderful gifts and terrible weapons.

Closer to the fire was a neat stack of small tough canvas sacks, crimped tightly shut. There were ten of them, and each held an even hundred pounds of gold in nuggets and dust.

"Now, would any of you have believed a word of it before you saw it with your own eyes?" John Rolfe said.

He looked around as they shook their heads. His cousins Robert and Alan, Aunt Antonia's sons, alike as two peas in a pod, tall, lean young men just turned twenty-one, their long faces much like his but with the dirty-blond hair and blue eyes showing the Fitzmorton coloring of their father. They were just out of the service too. Rob had been running a tank-destroyer company in Italy, and Alan had been a B-17 pilot based out of England; they'd just finished picking flak shrapnel out of his butt. Then there was Andy O'Brien, the big beefy freckle-faced Boston Irishman who'd been top sergeant in Rolfe's unit—not to mention a notable shot even in a division known as the Deadeyes; and Salvatore Colletta, small and smart and with the best poker face Rolfe had ever come across. He'd been Rolfe's personal radioman, as well as an artist with a Thompson. He had a tommy gun lying against the log at his back, and his dark, thin features were utterly expressionless as he leaned forward to light his cigarette from a splinter. His cheeks hollowed as he inhaled, showing blue-black stubble; Salvatore was in his early twenties too, but the big black eyes were ancient in the thin Sicilian face.

"But are you sure this isn't our California, a long time ago?" O'Brien asked uneasily. "And we could all go . . . pop, like a soap bubble, if we changed the things that made us."

Rolfe shook his head. "The first time I came through, I carved numbers on rocks in places I could locate on both sides—boulders, cliff faces—carved them deep enough to last for thousands of years. There's no trace of them back on our side of the Gate, where we know it's 1946. I'm still going to get some astronomers to look at pictures of the night sky—the stars change with time, you know—but I'm pretty certain this is the same time as back there in California, the spring of 1946. It's just a world where somehow white men never showed up. A different past, a different history, but the moon and sun are exactly the same, and the shape of the land, and the plants and animals—everything except what men have done."

"That gives us a monopoly, then," Rob Fitzmorton said, and went on with a dreamy smile: "There's an awful lot of gold in them thar hills. Francesca is going to be pretty damned happy."

"We can't just go back and turn the gold into money," Rolfe went on. "Salvo? Fill them in."

"Yeah, you got that right, Cap'n," Colletta said; it sounded more like *youse got dat roit,* in a hard nasal big-city accent straight from the corner of Hester and Baxter in Manhattan. "For starters, that *figghi'e'bottana* Roosevelt, he made it against the law to own gold, back before the war."

O'Brien blinked in surprise. "What can we do with it, then?"

His voice was South Boston; not unlike the Italian's, but with a hint of a brogue in it now and then, and the odd stretched New England–style vowel.

Colletta chuckled and shrugged. "Nah, maybe—just maybe —I might know some guys who've got, like, a flexible attitude about that sort of stupid rule, for a reasonable little cut. Guys who got relatives in Los Angeles. Maybe the cap'n was thinking of that when he invites me on this little hunting trip."

His eye caught his ex-commander's, and they gave an imperceptible nod of perfect mutual understanding.

"Risky, though," Rob Fitzmorton said. "Not that I've got any objection to getting rich, and y'all can take that to the bank. Jail I could do without."

Rolfe reached out with a bandanna around his hand and poured more of the strong black coffee into his mug. There was something chill in his eyes, and his smile showed an edge of teeth.

"You're thinking small," he said. "All of you."

A snatch of poetry came to him: *breathless upon a peak in Darien.* And hadn't Francis Drake touched land near here, as he took the *Golden Hind* around the world? The thought went down like a jolt of fine bourbon, and the heat in his gut was better than that. They'd filled his dreams as a boy, the conquistadors and sea dogs, the buccaneers like Morgan, the frontiersmen and adventurers like Andy Jackson and Crockett and Boone who'd carved states out of wilderness. . . . *And no stingy monarch in Madrid or London to take the plunder and the glory, not this time. No Washington to answer to, either.*

He indicated the canvas sacks. "That's a little over half a million there, for a month's work and travel time. That isn't *rich.* That's *seed money;* what we need to fit out the next expedition and hire the help. Then there's no limit to what we could do. Centuries from now, there could be statues of us here, and generations learning our names in school—a new world waiting for us, the way it did for our ancestors."

"We'll be like the Pilgrim Fathers at Plymouth Rock, then?" O'Brien said, and chuckled at the scowls of the three Virginians. "In a manner of speaking, Captain."

Salvatore's voice kindled. "Yeah! We're the only people here on . . . on . . . what in hell, the Other Side . . ."

"I'm going to call it New Virginia," Rolfe cut in. "The Commonwealth of New Virginia."

"Right, Cap'n, we're the only ones in New Virginia who aren't bare-assed Injuns walking around with bones through their noses and gourds on their *ciollas.* To hell with just getting rich. This place is our oyster. *And* we get filthy stinking rich," Colletta said.

Rolfe nodded. So did his cousins, which didn't surprise him; he'd known both the Fitzmorton boys since they were in short pants, and the families had been related since about the time the first John Rolfe discovered Virginia was a good place to grow tobacco. Both were newly married with children on the way, and the family rumor mill said Rob's war bride was an impoverished Italian aristocrat with expensive tastes, at that.

Their father was a not-very-successful country lawyer; Rolfe's had been career army, until TB retired him to a miserly pension and a hopeless battle to support a son and two daughters on that and the remnant of the ancestral acres. Which were just about enough for a big kitchen garden, a cow and a tumbledown house two centuries old and three quarters boarded-up, with a few cannonballs from McClellan's gunboats still embedded in the brickwork. They were all men whose families had spent the last three-quarters of a century going downhill in a world less and less suited to their sort. The great days of the First Families of Virginia had been nostalgic memory *before* the War For Southron Independence, and since Appomattox they'd mostly been too poor to paint and too proud to whitewash, as the saying went, living on a thin gruel of memory spiced with glory.

This other-side California had a number of advantages over the James River swamps in Chief Powhatan's time, besides the climate. It really *did* have gold, and he could look up the exact location on a map before digging. The climate was better and the Indians less formidable, too. His hand caressed the Garand resting across his knees.

"Yeah, Cap'n, this place is our oyster *if* we can keep doggo about it," Salvatore went on. "Uncle Sam gets his sticky hands on that Gate, they'll stamp it Ultra Top Burn Before Reading Secret, and we'll get a pat on the fanny if we're lucky. Only ones who'll make anything off it are the ones who can already afford a congressman or three of their own."

O'Brien looked around at the darkling wilderness, full of mysterious night sounds and the distant chanting of the Indians; he wasn't a hunter or country-bred, like the three Virginians, and unlike Colletta he hadn't adapted well.

"My family got off the boat in South Boston and stayed right there," he said. "That was in the first famine. I can't see myself being the bold pioneer, Captain. I'm a city boy. I like pavement under my feet and a good bar on the corner, and working with machinery, not cows."

"The pioneers didn't have a big city right at their backs. Just a hop, skip and a jump away, whenever they needed something, with gold by the ton to pay for it," Rolfe said, jerking his chin back over his shoulder.

They'd rigged up a shelter of poles and tarpaulins to hide the silvery surface of the Gate on this side; it was hideously conspicuous at night, a beacon across the countryside. The Indians were terrified of it, and of the men and strange beasts who'd come out of it. Rolfe snorted at the memory of what it had been like smuggling horses into his basement without attracting attention, not to mention building the ramp without anyone suspecting. *And* getting his cousin-once-removed, Louisa—she was Aunt Antonia's husband's brother's daughter—to house-sit for him, with no questions asked. Her bribe had come with a ring, which was fair. She was a good kid, no Ava Gardner but pretty enough. Smart, too, and she'd hung around him since they were both toddlers. His mother had been dropping hints about grandchildren since the day he got out of the hospital, and anyway, he'd never planned on being the last Rolfe.

"With the Gate, we can bring in anything—anyone—we want," he said. "We'll have to buy the house in Oakland; buy up the block and the neighborhood, come to that, get it re-zoned. Start a company; trading to the Philippines, say, or Siam, and investing in some old mines there, to cover the gold—you can buy fake customs stamps cheap in Manila, or anything else for that matter. And . . . as I said, we need organization. That means someone has to provide the leadership. I think I'm the best man for the job. Anyone disagree?"

His cousins shook their heads.

So did O'Brien, grinning broadly and exaggerating the brogue a little: "You got me through Leyte and Okinawa alive, Captain," he said. "I'll keep backing you the now. You're still the Old Man." He shook his head in wonderment: "Mother O'Brien's little boy a lord! Mary and Patrick, you know, I like the sound of it!" Softly: "She'll be off her knees and washing no more floors on Beacon Hill the way she did to feed the six of us before the war, and that's the truth."

Colletta turned up his hands with a smile of melting sincerity that made Rolfe suspicious. . . .

But Salvo's trustworthy enough. You just have to watch him, and remember he's always figuring an angle.

That could be valuable; Colletta had been the best scrounger and fixer in Company B, plus he could charm a snake out of its skin when he decided to, plus he had a way with languages. And . . . most men had to get worked up to kill; O'Brien, for instance, who was a wild man once his blood was running hot, but squeamish otherwise. The little wop was a stone killer; dispassionately skillful, like a farmer's wife picking a chicken and wringing its neck. That could be very useful.

"OK, Cap'n, you're the *padrone,* no argument," the small, dark man said, with a massively expressive shrug. "There's enough here for everyone to be a boss—but we need a boss of bosses, yeah. *Capo di tutti capo,*" he went on, smiling at something that passed the other men by. "Yeah, or we'll lose it all to the thieves and politicians and police and the rest of them *minchioni.* We need a boss, and we need to keep our mouths shut."

"Right," Rolfe said easily. "The first thing is to turn that gold into money and put it somewhere safe; Tangier, maybe, or Switzerland. Then we can start buying up the land . . . we should incorporate, too. . . ."

Unexpectedly, O'Brien spoke up: "We need to get Sol Pearlmutter in on this, Captain."

Rolfe raised his eyebrows. "I didn't think you liked him, Andy," he said.

That was an understatement. They'd circled and sniffed and growled all the way through training and deployment, and nearly killed each other just before Leyte, when O'Brien made top sergeant—Rolfe had had to sweat blood and crack heads to keep it covered up, not wanting to lose two of his best men to the stockade just before they went into action.

And while they'd settled down to work together well enough after that, it had still been . . .

What's that journalese term? Rolfe thought. When two countries hated each other's guts and didn't quite dare to fight, the newspapers said the atmosphere at diplomatic meetings was . . . *correct.* The two men had been *correct* toward each other, in an icy fashion, after he'd threatened to bounce them out to other outfits, where they'd be strangers.

Pearlmutter was offensively smart, unbelievably well-read, and the only Jew in the outfit; he could also argue up down and black white, and loved doing it. Nobody could figure why he wasn't a technician or company clerk or at least in the Air Corps, but he'd been worth his weight in gold.

"I *don't* like Sol," the young man from South Boston said. "A mouthy Jew he is, and too clever by half. But the little Hebe *is* clever, and he's got balls enough for a big man too; I saw that with my own two eyes—remember Shuri?"

Rolfe and Colletta both nodded automatically. Disarming that fiendishly ingenious set of interlinked booby traps while the Japanese mortar shells dropped all around them had required a cold sort of courage. There were men alive today who'd have bled to death if Pearlmutter hadn't cleared the way for the stretcher party, with nothing but a bayonet, a pair of pliers, a screwdriver and an ability to outguess the Nip sapper who laid the trap.

O'Brien went on: "He's studying to be a lawyer, not run a shop like his old man—got into Harvard, I hear, where they like the Chosen People less than they do a mick, and not much better than they like a nigger. We could use a smart Jew with steady nerves, if we're playing for stakes like these. I don't think he'll dislike the pot of gold any more than meself, either."

Colletta gave a cold, thin smile. "And if we ever need to shut that flapping mouth of his, well . . ." He patted the Chicago typewriter by his side.

"Good idea, Andy," Rolfe said. "First thing tomorrow, Rob, Alan and I will take the gold back to the First Side"— he jerked a thumb over his shoulder—"and start work. Andy,

Salvo, you'll look after the camp here for awhile, until we can get someone in to spell you. Salvo, you write up those names—of the men I need to contact and anything I need to know about them—and keep working on the chief's daughter. Pick up some more of their lingo."

The New Yorker laughed and kissed the tips of his bunched fingers. "Hey, Cap'n, *dat* ain't *woikin'!*"

O'Brien nodded and sneezed.

CHAPTER TWO

Sacramento, California
June 2009

FirstSide

"OK, we know that the condor passed through Oakland," Tom said thoughtfully, pointing his ballpoint at the map on his computer screen and leaning back in a way that made the swivel chair creak threateningly.

The headquarters of the Fish and Game Department bustled around them, but they'd both had enough years in office cubicles to learn to ignore that. Tom sipped more of the vile office coffee from a big mug with a cougar painted around it. Where he came from, if you weren't doing something that required both hands, you got a cup of coffee, so you brewed it weak. That meant he had to drink decaf here, since Californians couldn't be brought to appreciate the properly diluted brew that the Norski favored. Consuming that much regular brewed at Californian strength would be like doing meth.

"Oakland's a big town, Kemosabe," Tully said meditatively, playing with the black-and-crimson necktie that fell past his belt. "Big bad town. They had a lot of problems there during the war, couple of near-miss bombings. Close to major airports. Lots of tourists, lots of through traffic on the Interstate. *And* it's a major seaport. Smuggler's paradise and a cop's nightmare."

Tom nodded, and worked the ball of the mouse, his long, thick fingers incongruously delicate. "But! Here's what I came up with for Bosco Holdings, and what the SEC people have."

"'San Francisco,'" Tully read. The address was not far from the intersection of California and Montgomery. "Financial district."

"Yah," Tom said. "If you dig a little deeper—"

"Subsidiary of Colletta Enterprises—which has cross-holdings with . . . mmm, Rolfe Mining and Minerals?"

"RM and M owns the building. *And* that address is also listed as corporate HQ for a good thirty-two other corporations," Tom said. "Nothing illegal, of course. Most of them seem to be sequentially numbered single rooms or suites on the upper floors. Plus, RM and M owns a big operation in . . . guess where . . . Oakland."

"Nothing illegal. But skanky. Definitely skanky," Tully said. "Shell corporations are just too damned useful for all sorts of not-goodness. . . . Do we want to talk to the SFPD or the Oakland cops?"

"Definitely not the Oakland cops," Tom said. "And not the SF people, not yet. Too much chance of something leaking."

Tully raised one eyebrow, an ability of which he was rather proud. "You think someone on the inside is dirty?"

"Not necessarily, but *something* blew the bust in LA," Tom said. "And we're not going to inform our good friends in the Bureau just yet either—same reason, you betcha. Not before we do some legwork. And . . ."

Tully nodded. "Why share the glory if you don't have to?"

✹ ✹ ✹

Rolfeston
June 2009

Commonwealth of New Virginia

Adrienne Rolfe sat across from her father; she'd changed into the black uniform and peaked cap of the Gate Security

Force to emphasize that this was official business; no makeup, and her hair scraped back into a bun at the back of her neck, too. Charles Rolfe was glaring at her over the polished ebony of his desk, and she forced herself not to glare back.

No sense in going through that *again,* she thought. *We had far too many entirely unproductive fights back when.*

"Sir," she said. This wasn't just her father, after all. He was the Chairman of the Commission, and the heir to the Rolfe Family. "We came far too close to seriously endangering the secret of the Gate this time, and the problem isn't over yet. I must respectfully request permission to pursue this matter further on FirstSide."

The Chairman's office faced west; it was in the northern wing of the Commission headquarters building, where the flat bayside plain began its rise. French doors lined that side of the office; the room was large, but not grandiose—smaller, she told herself with an inward wry smile, than the office of the Colletta Prime. A slight murmur of sound came through and caressed the back of her neck on the wings of the same mild bayside spring breeze that carried the scent of flowers and water; there was a park outside, and then the public plaza of Rolfeston.

Behind the desk was a wall of polished teak paneling. On that hung a great oil painting of the Founders, the first of the Families making their pact at the beginnings of New Virginia, with appropriate accompaniments—rifles, shovels, miner's basins for panning gold, rearing steeds, and a few women doing what she thought of as the Sturdy Pioneer Helpmeet Thing. The frame was flanked on either hand by the Commonwealth's flag, a black field with diagonally crossed red bars and thirty-two many-pointed golden stars.

The picture was conventional heroic art, but well done: She could recognize many of the faces, though her mind called them up with the wrinkles, bald patches and white-haired pates of old age. Tough, taciturn old men, most of them honorary granduncles, dying one by one as she grew toward adulthood.

It shocked her a little how old her own father looked today, as old as her childhood memories of the Founders; she hadn't seen him in person for several months. *His* hair was mostly gray now, at sixty-two, though still thick—the Rolfe men didn't lose theirs.

And when did he get those jowls? she thought. *He's putting on weight, too. All those years I changed and he seemed to go on just the same, and now it's the other way 'round. . . .*

The Chairman's desk bore little beyond a few pictures and a ceremonial pen and inkstand. It did have a number of hidden screens; two of them had risen, one facing her and one her father. The Commission bought only the best, and the image in them was crystal clear, almost three-dimensional—the face of a man precisely twenty-five years older than her father. John Rolfe VI, Chairman Emeritus and Founding Father; despite the snowy whiteness of his hair and the deep lines on his face, he looked scarcely older than his son. There was less harassed care and more amusement in the steady leaf-green eyes as well, and his belt measurement was the same as it had been when he left VMI. He would be looking at their paired images in a screen in his own sanctum, up north in Rolfe Manor, leaning back in the leather-cushioned chair.

"It is a bit shocking," the older man said, with an elegant gesture of one hand. "Thanks to Agent Rolfe's quick action, largely recouped. But still shocking. I fear we've grown a trifle complacent—not to mention divorced from the realities of FirstSide."

Another hand entered the pickup screen. It was slim and female; it handed him a cigarette in an ivory holder, and a glass frosty with ice. The old man took a deep draw and a sip of the bourbon and water.

"Thank you, my dear," he murmured, turning his head for an instant.

"We've had smuggling before, sir," Charles Rolfe replied.

The title of respect was ungrudging, despite his obvious irritation. While he lived, the Old Man was master of the nation he had founded, whatever the formal titles might say. More than law, it was custom, and "custom" was a word that carried a great deal of weight in the Commonwealth.

"But scarcely on this scale," said the man who had been soldier, adventurer, and king in all but name. "That was mostly a case of the occasional overshipment of precious stones or gold, and before we had Nostradamus to keep an exact running tally all the way through."

Charles Rolfe sighed. "As nearly as Gate Security can tell," he said, "it's barely smuggling, technically. None of the goods were on the prohibited list. They went through as bales of general cargo from various Families, through affiliated firms rather than directly—Nostradamus has the shipment records, of course—but they weren't going to ring any alarms. The Boscos seem to be involved, and they're Colletta collaterals, of course, but . . . finding out how it all got bulked into an embarrassing mass rather than being dispersed will be tricky politically. We've always paid more attention to keeping track of incoming freight, anyway."

"And we've always had a shortage of qualified personnel for Gate Security," John Rolfe said.

"Sirs," Adrienne said, dragging the conversation back to her concerns. "We've got to update that prohibited list. Immediately, and that just for starters. Yes, none of the species represented in the Los Angeles warehouse were extinct on FirstSide—not *completely* extinct. But those goods in those quantities were absolutely bound to cause dangerous publicity. Someone brought them through, moved them through commercial channels on FirstSide, and then sold them—or delivered them, anyhow—in a single mass."

Her father shrugged angrily. "Yes, yes, no doubt it was careless—and we should *discreetly* try to find out here in the Commonwealth who was responsible, and see that they get a reprimand if it was one of the Families, or a trip to the mines otherwise. However—"

The man in the screen raised the cigarette. "I think Agent Rolfe had something else to add."

"Yes, sir," Adrienne said gratefully. "Once attention *was*

drawn to the goods, the results could have been catastrophic. DNA scans are now extremely cheap, fast and accurate, and routine. With illegal animal products, they use them even where they've got no particular reason; if it's so easy, why not? When animals are down to a few hundred well-studied individuals, DNA from an unrelated population . . . we might as well hang out a 'From Another Universe!' sign. Once or twice we can tolerate. People disregard information that upsets their preconceptions. But if we rub their faces in facts they can't dodge, *somebody* is going to start connecting the dots."

"Individuals have stumbled on evidence of the Gate before," the Chairman snapped.

"Yes, sir. But it's also getting more suspicious when people disappear over on FirstSide, too. The crime rate's down there, and they tightened up on security a lot during the war, with identity cards and biometric scanners all over the place.

"Sirs," she went on earnestly, glancing from her father to her grandfather and back, "we *have* to tighten up too. We've got to put anything illegal—or just rare and unusual—on FirstSide on the prohibited list, and we've got to be more careful about bringing the American authorities down on us."

"We're not in the business of enforcing United States laws," her father said.

John Rolfe's upraised hand cut short her reply. He spoke instead: "We are when it's to our advantage, Charles," he said mildly. "The agent has a point. You and I can discuss it later. Now, back to the matter at hand: investigating the investigation on FirstSide. I agree that it has potential, albeit also risks."

"I don't like it," Charles said slowly.

"Neither do I, very much," his father said. "Is there anyone other than Agent Rolfe in a position to do the legwork? Or can you get the Commission to act quickly and decisively here in the Commonwealth, so that we need not move on FirstSide?"

"Not easily," Charles said, rubbing the fingertips of his right hand over his forehead. "Not without definite proof the Collettas are up to something. Not only would creating a stink be a godsend to the Imperialist faction, but I'd have to step on the corns of a lot of influential Settler business interests, restrict their trans-Gate exports and capacity to earn FirstSide dollars—and the Commission's monopolies are unpopular enough as it is. That would bring in the Families they're affiliated with—you know they can't afford to ignore their clients' complaints. Not if they don't want them looking for new patrons." There was a hint of frustrated anger in his voice.

His father grinned, not unsympathetically. "Well, I *did* set this place up with a more *decentralized* power structure than I might have if I'd had perfect precognition," he said. "Though efficiency isn't everything . . . but I think that does reinforce Adrienne's point."

Adrienne kept her face expressionless. *She* wouldn't have let the Commonwealth's government drift into the sort of sloppy, amorphous neofeudalism that had evolved here over the past couple of generations, but it suited the Old Man fine most of the time.

Keeps life interesting and colorful, was the way he put it: or mildly chaotic and dangerous, from another point of view. The Old Man was an inveterate romantic, when he thought he could afford it.

"Very well," Charles Rolfe said. "Sir, we'll discuss the whole matter when I return to Rolfe Manor this weekend, if that's agreeable." His eyes went back to his youngest daughter. "And I'm giving you an unrestricted authorization for FirstSide," he said. "Get results, Agent; get them quickly. I don't care how, within the Regulations."

"Yes, sir," she said, coming to her feet and saluting.

Handsomely done, Dad, she added to herself, as her father rose to see her out. The Regulations for FirstSide operations boiled down to "Don't get caught." *He may be a lot more ponderous than the Old Man, but he does have a certain style when he decides to do something.*

She took the hand he extended. *"Baciamo le mani,"* she said, bowing and kissing it.

"Be careful," he said gruffly, and rested the palm on her shoulder for an instant.

"I will," she said, and added with an urchin grin, "And I intend to have a good time doing it, too, Dad."

✳ ✳ ✳

San Francisco, California
June 2009

FirstSide

"Well, it's not much," Tully said, handing over a medium-thick folder of printout. "Just the public stuff."

"More than I've got so far," Tom said. "Bosco Holdings is a ghost, as far as the U.S. is concerned. They've got a bank account, and another in the Caymans; I couldn't get anything out of *them;* they'd never heard of California Fish and Game. That would take Perkins; she'd get results fast enough, but . . ."

"But they'd be *her* results."

Offshore banks were a lot less secretive these days, at least as far as U.S. government "requests" were concerned; there had been a couple of spectacular cases of strong-arming during the later mopping-up years of the war, and none of the little countries that specialized in no-questions-asked wanted a repeat while memories of Uncle Sam's heavy hand remained fresh.

"Let me take a look," the big man went on.

He skimmed the results of his partner's research; they were sitting on a bench outside the Civic Center, which was still the best area in San Francisco to do digging of this type—the big central library was nearby, and the morgue files of the newspapers. For a wonder it was neither foggy nor uncomfortably cool nor too windy, and the Civic Plaza area was a pleasant place to sit, especially since the area wasn't swarming with bums anymore, what they'd called "homeless" back in the twentieth century. The great Beaux-Arts pile of the city hall reared at their backs, a dome higher than the Capitol in Washington as solitary reminder of the plans made and discarded after the quake of 1906; before them were espaliered trees flanking a strip of grass, green with an intensity that only San Francisco and Ireland seemed able to produce.

"Rolfe" had produced a couple of historical articles dealing with early Virginia—he turned out to be the guy who'd married Pocahontas. *Funny, I always thought it was John Smith.* They'd had two sons before being killed in the Indian massacre of 1622; the children married into the ramifying families of the Virginian aristocracy and apparently did nothing much of note besides grow tobacco and breed like bunnies, thus making George Washington and Jimmy Carter descendants of the Powhatan chieftains; a politician or general here and there, declining into middle-class mediocrity after the Civil War.

The next reference was to a business-history site. Tully had printed that article out in full.

"This is strange," Tom said. "The mining business is too legit. There's nothing in these shell companies but mailboxes and bank accounts—most of them—but RM and M looks like a genuine business. Solid. Lots of assets, lots of employees. Lots of profits, too—according to this, their costs per ounce are half the industry average."

"No reason they couldn't be bent *and* have a legit side," Tully said dubiously.

Tom grunted and read, skimming with the ease of someone who'd been flipping through reports most of his adult life. Rolfe Mining and Minerals Inc. Founded by John Rolfe in 1946, and he'd been born in Virginia in 1922; apparently a real connection to the Pocahontas people. He scanned quickly down the article, but found no picture of the man.

"No visuals?" he said, looking up at Tully.

"Nothing," his partner replied. "Not in the back files of the newspapers, not in the society magazines, and not anywhere on the Web. Interesting, isn't it, for someone with that much money? I've got a request pending with the Pentagon—there might be something from WWII."

"It is interesting," Tom said cautiously: Tully had a tendency to leap to convictions. "But it's not illegal. By lots of money, you mean *lots* of money, I presume?"

"Read on, Kemosabe. Tonto think it maybe *too* quiet there."

Rolfe had a fairly impressive service record; commissioned out of VMI at twenty in '42, service with the Ninety-sixth Infantry in the Pacific, Purple Heart and field promotion on Letye, another Purple, a Silver Star and a serious wound on Okinawa, which was why he hadn't ended the war as a major at least.

Then the move to San Francisco, like so many veterans who'd shipped out through the Bay Area during the Great Unpleasantness. His company had gotten big fast in the postwar boom, diversifying in the sixties into real estate, banking and insurance, but staying a closely held private corporation; no more than the minimum SEC information. That meant no real idea of what they were worth, but it had to be immense, just from the publicly acknowledged holdings—a corporate headquarters in the San Francisco financial district, and a huge warehouse complex in Oakland. There were also offshore operations, theoretically independent: the Caymans, Hong Kong, Singapore, and Bermuda, which hinted at massive assets moved out of country for tax purposes, plus mining properties in Africa and Asia and odd corners of South America. And those odd subsidiaries, which didn't fit at all.

"I've got a bad feeling about this," Tom said, crossing an ankle over his knee and considering the documents in his lap. "A bad feeling that our promising lead is evaporating."

"Yeah, it smells funny," Tully said, fishing for cigarettes inside his jacket and then popping a stick of gum into his mouth instead. "There was what, maybe ten, fifteen million worth of stuff in that warehouse?"

"'Bout that." Tom nodded.

"Which is petite larceny to this crowd," Tully replied. "Cappuccino money."

"Yeah. People *that* rich don't do crime—not below the bribe-the-dictator-of-Corruptistan level when they need a pipeline concession. Hell, even the Italians went respectable when they made their pile. That's the way it works; you get into organized crime, make a bundle, and your kids or grandkids invest it and get out. Hell on a stick, RM and M is old money now by Californian standards. I'd expect them to be living off capital gains and making donations to worthy causes, maybe the third generation becoming art collectors or painters or living in cabins in the north woods."

"The Bad Things could be happening at a lower level," Tully said. "Someone *in* this ratfuck of corporations, rather than the top management themselves. But the condor *did* pass through Oakland, RM and M *does* have that big facility there and we *did* find the Bosco Holdings stationary in the cage."

Tom flipped back to the beginning and looked at who RM&M had done business with in its early days.

He transferred some data into his PDA. "All right, we'll split up and tackle it from both ends. I'll take this angle; we could use some firsthand background on RM and M in its early days. You go sniff around that complex of theirs in Oakland. It's a little odd, a company this big still doing the physical with warehouses and such rather than outsourcing."

"Will do, Kemosabe," Tully said. "Be careful."

"Aren't I always?"

"No," Tully answered bluntly. "You forget that stepping on toes can get you kicked in the balls. We're talking a really big, well-established California firm here. They're bound to have pull. Enough to get an investigation quashed, unless it's damn well grounded. I'd want to have something pretty solid before we go see our esteemed boss, and rock-solid before he goes public. Otherwise we're likely to end up in California's Siberia."

Tom watched him head for the BART station, then thought silently for a half hour or so; intently motionless, so much so that a couple of pigeons walked over his shoes, and a beat cop almost rousted him for sleeping on the benches—the SFPD were fanatics about that, since the big cleanups.

"Time to spend some shoe leather," he said to himself. "See how the facts jibe with the speculation."

❋ ❋ ❋

"Ms. Sorenson?" Tom said.

The house was in the lower part of Nob Hill, part of a row of beautifully restored Edwardian residences with Tiffany stained-glass fanlights over the doors—not quite the sort of home the silver kings and railroad barons had built from the plunder of the Comstock Lode and the Union Pacific, but certainly the upper management of a century or so ago. Then he realized this particular one wasn't restored: it had just been well kept all that time.

"I am Susan Sorenson," the owner said. "Mr. Christiansen?"

She was in her late seventies, but slender and what they used to call well preserved, with a burnished overall sheen, quietly expensive clothes, and a rope of thick silver hair falling down her back. Her eyes were pale blue and very clear; the Persian cat sitting at her feet was almost eerily similar. . . . When she invited him in, the house was similar too—perfectly polished antiques, some contemporary pieces, Isfahan carpets and a faint smell of lavender sachet. He perched uneasily on a settee, and accepted a Sevres china cup of extremely good coffee from a Filipino maid. There were a couple of family portraits on the sideboard: his hostess at various ages—she'd been quite a red-haired fox—and herself with friends, and a man who was probably her father. No husband or children, he noted.

Her smile was charming. "Now, Mr. Christiansen, you said you were interested in the history of my father's company, Sierra Consultants?"

"Yes, ma'am," he said. "There's surprisingly little in the public record. In fact, most of what I could find was in the course of looking into another firm—Rolfe Mining and Minerals."

The older woman's lips tightened slightly; in anger, he was pretty sure, although she was so achingly well-bred that reading her expression was difficult. *Roughly equivalent to throwing things and using the F-word in an ordinary person, I think.*

"Them," she said. "Perhaps it's unjust, but I blame them for the way Sierra went downhill."

"I understand your father did a number of contracts for Rolfe in the 1950s," he said.

"After a while, we did scarcely anything else!" she said. "I was working as my father's executive assistant about then, you understand. Beginning in about 1950."

"Ah," Tom said, thinking furiously. "They gave your father's firm a great deal of business, then?"

"Yes. By the mid-1950s it was most of the cash flow, and almost all of it before the end in 1962."

"And this damaged the company?"

The woman sighed. "I know that it sounds strange . . . but the work Rolfe had my father do wasn't . . . wasn't *real* somehow."

She stood and walked to an ebony sideboard, handing Tom a picture. "This was my father."

The man in the faded photograph was in his mid-thirties, ruggedly handsome, dressed in riding boots and jodhpurs and an open-necked shirt, a broad-brimmed hat in one hand and a .45 holstered at his waist. The background showed sun-faded rocky slopes and brush; it might have been anywhere in the tropics, or even one of the 'Stans.

Sort of like Indiana Jones, he thought, as she resumed her place in the chair across the table. Roy Tully had a taste for old movies and TV series; Tom occasionally sampled his vast collection.

No, he realized suddenly, *it's the kind of guy Indiana Jones was modeled on. Civil engineer, archaeologist, someone who went out to the hot-and-dangerous places.*

"My father was . . . he traveled everywhere as a young

man. The Caribbean, China, South America—that picture was taken in Bolivia in the 1930s, only a year after I was born, Mr. Christiansen. He *built* things. Bridges, dams, irrigation projects, support structures for mining operations. Sometimes he had to fight off bandits—Jivaro headhunters, once, in Peru. He was in the army engineers in Europe in 1918, and during the war—World War Two, that is—he was all over the Pacific."

"What did he do for RM and M?" Tom asked softly.

Living history, he thought: He was talking to someone whose father had fought in *both* the world wars, something he'd grown up thinking of as dusty antiquity.

"Nothing *serious,*" she said. "Nothing *real.*"

Tom leaned forward in the chair, his elbows on his knees and his eyebrows arched. There was an art to questioning, and a large part of it was encouraging without interrupting. Most people vastly preferred talking to listening, and a sympathetic and interested ear made them pour out surprising revelations.

"Consulting—after the war, he did feasibility studies for a great many projects here in California, and abroad. Then Rolfe came—oh, he was a charmer when he wanted to be, and he thought women should fall all over him. Which," she added with a sniff, "many did. And he . . . he wanted feasibility studies too. He was willing to pay for them, pay extravagantly and in cash. But none of them were ever actually *built.* None of them were for his overseas operations, the gold mines and alluvial diamond projects we heard about. They were *fantasies.*"

"Fantasies?" Tom prompted gently.

"Fantasies about projects here in California! About waterworks that had already been built, or . . . or geothermal generators in hot springs north of the Napa Valley, or mines in places where all the ore had been taken out a century ago! Replicas of the Palace of Fine Arts, of all foolish things. Or flood control in areas like Sacramento, where all the work was already done when my *grandfather* arrived in California from Sweden! My father was used to doing real work, and seeing what came of it. I'm convinced that the . . . the *futility* of it all drove him to retirement, and to dying before his time."

The elderly woman was a little flushed, and sat down. Tom made soothing noises and poured her another cup of the coffee, admiring the graceful way she picked up her cup and saucer; he was an ignore-the-handle-and-grab-the-mug type himself.

"Could you give me any details?" he said. *Something extremely odd is going on here.*

Sighing, she shook her head. "That was another thing. Rolfe always required—ordered—that *every* scrap of paper be handed over when a study was completed, with nothing for our records but the bare minimum of financial data for the tax people. But I remember. . . ."

INTERLUDE
June 7th, 1950
San Francisco
FirstSide

The chief engineer of Sierra Consultants was a little surprised when the chairman of Rolfe Mining and Minerals was shown into his office. Pearlmutter, RM&M's company lawyer, had been pure New York; bright, pushy, abrasive without even realizing it, and painfully young. Rolfe himself was . . .

Also too young, for starters, he thought. Then on a second look: *Or perhaps not, in experience if not years.*

He was sixty himself, but he remembered the godlike sense of immortality and infallibility he'd had four decades ago, before the Great War. *He'd* left it behind amid the stink of death in the shattered forests of the Argonne. Rolfe had a very slight limp in the left leg. Probably from a war wound; his eyes had the set of someone who'd seen the elephant, and encountered mortality firsthand. Rumor had it that RM&M had been started by a bunch of veterans clubbing together with their buddies . . .

Still . . . is the whole company composed of boys barely old enough to shave?

Rolfe stood about five-ten, lean and athletic, with short-cut bronze-colored hair and level leaf-green eyes, a straight-nosed, fine-boned face with that planes-and-angles look they called "chiseled," and was probably quite a success with the ladies. No more than thirty at the outside, maybe a bit younger; hard to tell with that weathered outdoorsman's tan.

Smooth, too.

Very expensive but conservative suit: Saville Row, the sort few Englishmen could afford in these days of shabby austerity in London. It contrasted with the hand that shook his, long pianist's fingers that were also callused and very strong, with a Virginia Military Institute class ring. Southern accent but not "hush-mah-mouf"; he'd have placed it somewhere south of the Mason-Dixon line but within fifty miles of the Chesapeake. Overall, this John Rolfe VI had a sheen like antique beechwood furniture.

Old money, or at least a family that had had money once. Not at all the type you expected to see at the head of a hungry young firm still clawing its way up the greasy pole in a notoriously rough-and-ready business like mining.

But RM&M *was* a new outfit, based out of the East Bay, specializing in buying up and refurbishing minerals properties in the Far East wrecked during the war, with sidelines in Persia, Angola and the Belgian Congo. That was risky with the political turmoil in Asia, but they'd been doing extremely well. He'd heard about some substantial purchases of dredging equipment for riverbed mining, some hard-rock gear, and great job lots of the sort of stuff you'd need for operating in the wilder and hairier parts of the world: bulldozers, heavy trucks, riverboat engines, drilling rigs, generators, fuel storage, construction machinery and prefab housing.

They'd been holding their cards extremely close to their chests, too, which was only to be expected; the engineer had started out as a roving mining consultant in some of the odder corners of the Earth, and he knew how the game was played. Apparently they didn't need to go to market for expansion capital, either, which argued that their returns were quick and rich.

But *this* . . .

He tapped the thick folder in front of him. "Mr. Rolfe, this proposal of yours is simply . . . *bizarre.*"

Rolfe nodded politely, reaching into his jacket and producing a silver cigarette case. He turned to Susan and raised a brow with old-fashioned good manners . . . and also revealed that he probably knew that she was his daughter, as well as his confidential secretary. A bit of an eccentric arrangement, but she'd worn him down, and he had to admit she was extremely competent.

Susan nodded frostily. "By all means, Mr. Rolfe," she said. "Mr. Sorenson smokes. I do not."

Rolfe gave a charming smile and flicked the case open with an elegant snap of his wrist; not cigarettes, but cigarillos.

"I assure you that our check for your firm's work will be entirely regular, though, Mr. Sorenson," he said, offering the case.

The engineer accepted one with a nod of thanks; they were Punch Claritos, about the best there were, and he'd acquired a taste for them a long time ago in Cuba, working on a project in Oriente province. He didn't let that distract him as he clipped the end, lit, and blew a cloud of fragrant smoke. The young man's tone had been perfectly polite . . . but there was an underlying amusement to it, as of a secret joke Rolfe didn't intend to share.

"Surveying and plans for a reservoir and hydroelectric project in, of all places, the Berkeley hills? Mr. Rolfe, you don't own that land; most of it is government property and not for sale. Such a project there would make no economic sense whatsoever and would stand no chance of approval by Sacramento . . . which I'm sure you know. Hell, a lot of that area's already occupied by the San Pablo and Briones reservoirs!"

"I'm fully aware of it," Rolfe said cheerfully; his smile didn't reach the cool green eyes. "Consider it . . . a trial run for a very similar project in an area not under the jurisdiction of the U.S., or the state of California."

"That doesn't make any sense either," the engineer said, baffled. "You *must* know that plans like that are extremely site-specific."

Rolfe's voice stayed level, but took on an edge of steel. "Then consider it a rich young fool's whim, sir," he said. "Consider it anything you wish. The question is, will you do this survey for us, or shall I walk over to one of your competitors?"

He waved a hand toward the window, and the harsh bustle of California Street below. The engineer ground his teeth. *On the one hand . . .*

The money was good—even in boom times, a project so close to home would be low-cost. He could get most of the data he needed out of the library, and most of the rest by taking the ferry and driving about; the ground check would be a matter of a couple of afternoons' hike for his subordinates. The fee, on the other hand, would be nearly as big as something requiring real work—core drillings and seismic soundings, for instance. It was simply too juicy a peach to pass up, even if it did taste a little off.

So there is no "on the other hand." It's not illegal to run a survey and estimates for an impossible project, and if Rolfe wants to waste his money, that's his lookout.

"We'll take it," he said aloud.

Rolfe smiled and drew on his Punch Clarito. "I'm sure you won't regret it," he said.

CHAPTER THREE

Sacramento, California
June 2009

FirstSide

Tom Christiansen finished the series and lifted the bar into the rest, sitting up on the bench and picking up his towel. Bad form to do it without someone spotting for him, but he wasn't pushing it—only two seventy-five on the weights, well below his maximum. He breathed deeply and easily as he wiped down his face and neck and the parts of his torso exposed by the muscle shirt, considering what he'd do next.

Some laps in the pool, he thought, rolling his neck as he glanced around the mirror-walled expanse of the gym's weight room. *Important to keep the aerobic side up.*

He'd always rather despised people who pumped iron just for cosmetic purposes without building endurance and heart health, and he always made time for a balanced program, including keeping his hand in at unarmed combat. He did it all because he liked having a well-conditioned body, because it had become a habit, because it was useful in his work, a lot of which was outdoors, and because he couldn't spend enough time canoeing and hiking and climbing to keep fit for the times he *could* get away. If you pushed yourself in the wilderness as hard as he liked to, you could end up dead or very, very miserable if the strength and endurance and flexibility weren't there to match the experience and skill.

And, he thought with wry honesty, looking at himself in the mirror, *you do it because of what you'd look like if you didn't.*

His elder brother Lars was still strong as an ox at forty—machinery or no, farming took a lot of hard-sweat work—but he had a belly on him like a fifty-gallon keg, and hams like a boar hog. That was the way the Christiansen men went once they were past thirty, if they let themselves, the hard muscle turning marbled with fat like a stall-fed bullock, the chest sagging down to the stomach and staying there, bull neck and jowls . . .

Thin wasn't an option with his genes and bones.

Plus it was a good way to get the tensions and fatigue-poisons of the office out of his system. That sort of work tricked the body into pumping fight-or-flight hormones into your bloodstream, without giving you a chance to purge them and sweat them out.

The big brightly lit room had a strong odor of sweat; nothing rank, because Grayson's Gym and Health Club was respectable if not fancy, but pretty strong. One reason he came here, besides the modest monthly fee, was that it wasn't tarted up with superefficient air scrubbers, acres of polished metal, or, God forbid, hanging plants and an on-site coffee bar. He had nothing much against gay people, but being hit on by guys got old fairly quickly even if it was polite, and a disconcerting proportion of the men who worked out at the fancier establishments *were* gay. The usual selection here was more eclectic, and included the members of an Okinawan-style karate club who time-shared part of the premises; Tom filled in as a substitute teacher occasionally for Sensi Hidoshi, in return for free sparring to keep his edge sharp.

The weight room was fairly busy, despite it being a Sunday afternoon—downtown Sacramento went fairly comatose on weekends, but the spillover from the weekend karate session just finished kept it full of grunts and whuffles and sharp exhalations, and there were a few people like him in after working irregular hours. He'd been subliminally conscious of a woman in one corner hanging head-down with her feet hooked through a set of padded bars while she did sit-ups with her hands linked behind her head, twisting to touch left elbow to right knee and vice versa. She'd finished a set of fifty, then dropped to her hands, stayed that way for a moment, and lowered her feet slowly to the floor. That was impressive, if a little showy, and gave him a chance to look at the legs and butt, which were extremely nice even through a loose set of sweatpants, which she was wearing over a body stocking. As she came erect, he got a look at the rest of her, and blinked.

Va-voom, he thought. *Thirty-six, twenty-five, thirty-six.*

A nice face too, if in a rather sculpted way—not quite model- or actress-beautiful, a little too harsh—and unusual bright leaf-green eyes; her bronze-gold hair was drawn back in a bun, and she wore a headband as well as fingerless leather exercise gloves that had seen enough use to be a little ragged.

And in years, about twenty-six, maybe a bit older. Hard to tell, with that tan. Not exactly slender, not with those measurements, but long-limbed and moving very well.

Altogether too polished for this place, usually—that total-health sheen wasn't uncommon in California, but usually in circles much higher than the secretaries, state government employees and dental hygienists who frequented Grayson's.

"Hi," she said, coming over to him. "You using this bench?"

"Just finished," he said, thinking mock-mournfully, *Ah, she only wanted me for my bench space.*

He looked at her left hand anyway as he replied. It was encouragingly ringless, and the mark of his own wedding band had had years to fade. There *was* a ring on her thumb, a distinctive circle of braided gold and platinum.

"Thanks!" she said pleasantly.

She had an accent, though not the flat Californian one with the perky rising inflection on the end of sentences, which he'd always found rather grating. This was more like a very faint Southern tinge underlying General American, a pleasant softening; there was something else too, a lilt and roll he couldn't place at all. Possibly European of some sort. At a guess, she was Bay Area, or possibly points a bit north. The long-fingered hand in his as they shook was pleasantly solid and strong; she looked like a human being, not a Dresden figurine. Petite women made him nervous, which was a handicap even when it wasn't mutual. His wife had been a cheerleader when he met her; football was where he got the slight kink in his nose, although the wedding had been long after high school.

"I'm Adrienne Rolfe," she went on, holding out a hand. "Just got into town to do some lobbying."

Oh-ho! he thought. *The game commences, Watson!*

Her eyes narrowed.

Damn! My poker face isn't quite as good as I thought.

"Yes," she said. "I'm one of *those* Rolfes—and I did hear about that embarrassing little episode in Los Angeles. As a matter of fact, I was investigating it myself—for the family."

He nodded noncommittally. Although it was hard to be entirely detached . . .

"Tom Christiansen," he replied. "Department of Fish and Game. Warden." That was reflex; in the state capital you established your tribe. She probably knew already.

"Ah!" she said, her eyes widening in an interest that looked sincere. That *was* unusual. "I love the outdoors. I fish and hunt myself, whenever I get the time."

Better and better, he thought.

To a lot of people here in California, hunting anything but the wild tofu-lope was equivalent to sacrificing babies to Satan. It was amazing how little contact with real nature a lot of people who thought of themselves as environmentalists had; if there was one thing that was completely natural, it was killing your food.

"Me too," he said. "Though not so much recently."

She nodded and went on: "I don't know anyone here. Would you mind spotting for me, if you have the time?"

"Sure," he said, grinning; she matched the expression. "What weight?"

"One-sixty," she said. "Three sets of twelve reps; just a maintenance program while I'm away from home."

He blinked as they rearranged the weights, the cast-iron disks of his program clanking as they unclipped them from the bar and dropped them onto the appropriate pegs and replaced them with hers. One-sixty was awfully heavy; it must be a good twenty over her own body weight, maybe more. She didn't look like a bodybuilder, though she wasn't skinny, and the definition on the long straplike muscles of her arms and shoulders was excellent.

More likely dance training, maybe acrobatics, or just a fitness freak like me, he thought.

They both looked like human beings, not anatomical diagrams; the "ripped" look required special diets and programs to get rid of the normal thin coating of subcutaneous fat; it was also violently bad for you, not to mention the hormones those idiots stuffed into themselves. Not to also mention that when a woman drove her body-fat content down that far her breasts disappeared, which with Ms. Rolfe was obviously not the case.

She lay on the bench, breathed in and out sharply three times, and put her gloved hands on the checked grip section of the bar. Tom stood at her head and kept his hands between hers, palm-up but not quite touching the metal rod, ready to grab it if she lost control. She didn't; instead she lifted the weight smoothly out of the rests, paused for a moment, then lowered it slowly until the bar almost touched her chest. A quicker lift, and then again the slow descent as the breath went out. Tom admired the technique, and admired what the effort did to the woman's flat stomach and extremely unflat bosom as the pectoral muscles pushed her breasts against the thin sweat-wet fabric. He was careful to keep his face to a neutral alertness; that was polite, which he'd been raised to be, and besides which you didn't take any chances when people were using free weights. Far too easy to break a bone or rip a tendon if something went wrong.

When she was finished they went outside, walking around the brick patio-garden behind that linked the buildings to the outdoor handball courts. It was late afternoon, bright and dry and hot, but only in the mid-eighties, not bad for a Sacramento summer, and the breathing was a lot better than it had been in LA.

"I'm going to run for a few miles," she said. "Care to join me? Good to have someone around who knows the place."

"Delighted," he said. *The pool can wait; and we can have our little talk. Damn, but I'll be disappointed if this turns out to be all business.* "I'd suggest heading for the State Capitol."

"I like the park there," she agreed.

They turned onto the street in front of Grayson's, crossed H Street, and went down Ninth past his HQ at the Fish and Game Department headquarters. Traffic was light, and there weren't many pedestrians to annoy, or too much in the way of detectable pollution to suck into their lungs; one of the most startling things he remembered about his trips to LA was driving in from the airport and seeing someone jogging *beside the freeway.* With the air dense enough to mine for building blocks, if you had a ripsaw handy.

He let her set the pace, which was as fast as he'd have chosen, and must be a little more intense for her—she was around five-nine, six inches shorter than he, and while they were both long-legged in proportion to their torsos, there was a good deal more of him to be in proportion to. She ran well, too: lightly, with the weight coming down on the ball of the foot and pushing smoothly off bent knees in a way that made no jarring thuds and put minimal stress on the joints. After a few minutes he found himself breathing a little harder than he'd intended. That, and dodging people, limited the conversation until they reached the capitol; he learned that she "lived in Berkeley, or the family place up near Rutherford," that her grandfather had come from a small town near Williamsburg, Virginia, that she'd gone to Stanford and that she'd never been married. That gave him a moment's worry, until he recalled the unmistakable glance he'd gotten in the gym; he wasn't what they used to call a lady-killer, but he knew what the female version of the oh-that's-nice once-over look felt like on the receiving end.

It didn't always come to much, women being less enslaved to their eyeballs than men, but you couldn't mistake it.

They halted for a moment to catch their breath before the huge wedding-cake pile of the State Capitol, gleaming with white stone. The arched entranceways supported an upper platform fronted by six great Corinthian columns; the architrave above was decorated with a central Athena, flanked by allegorical figures of Justice, Agriculture, Industry and Education. One level up to either side were mounted Indians fighting a grizzly bear on the left and a wild bull on the right; to his eye, the Indians always looked as if they were about to lose. A drum-shaped segment rose above that, with more columns all around, and then a circular wall pierced by tall arched windows and engaged false columns supporting a golden dome. He liked it; it looked just the way a state capitol building erected in the exuberantly self-confident 1870s should.

"If that had been built anytime recently, it would be a glass shoebox," she said.

"Ah, a fellow provincial reactionary with no taste." He chuckled. "Of course, it *could* have looked like a collection of frozen intestines or a chemical plant instead, in this progressive age."

They turned left; the park around the capitol building covered forty acres. It was more crowded than the streets had been, with in-line skaters, brown-bag picnics, children chasing dogs and the odd derelict; but there was also a welcome shade from an assortment of trees brought from all over the world, and green lawns. They stretched themselves a little more, and he lost himself in the simple enjoyment of breath and muscle, feeling his body like an engine of living springs and rubber. They stopped halfway around to buy bottled water from a vendor. Tom was surprised to see her grimace a little at the first drink; it was perfectly ordinary plastic-bottle stuff, probably exactly the same as the variety

that came out of taps, but not bad. He drank down his half in
five long swallows. They stood under a tree whose foliage
involved long tendrils hanging down with seedpods on the
end, and now they were really sweating. He could feel his
skin shedding heat as the dry air sucked at the wetness running on it, and was acutely conscious of the clean female
smell of hers.

"So, who *are* you lobbying for, Ms. Rolfe?" he asked.
"And how does it tie into what happened in LA?"

"Adrienne, or Adri. The Pacific Open Landscapes
League," she said.

"Call me Tom, Adri. . . ." *Pacific Open Landscapes
League?* "Ah," he said, snapping his fingers as it rang a bell.
"Agricultural land easements?"

Some conservation groups bought up development easements on open land or farmland threatened by urban sprawl;
the owner sold the right to subdivide the land, while keeping
title and possession. Subsequent heirs or buyers were under
the same restrictions. It had become quite popular lately,
mainly because it was completely voluntary and more effec-
tive than zoning or land-use controls. A few thousand well-
placed acres of easements could stop a tendril of sprawl
cold, protecting far larger areas beyond.

"We do a lot of that," she said. "God knows, with nearly
fifty million people in California, it's needed."

He winced inwardly at that, the way he did whenever the
figure came up. *Ouch.* That was the basic fact that made so
much of his work like trying to sweep back the ocean with a
broom. The number of people got bigger every year; the
state didn't.

"And we're pushing for more habitat protection, and trying for some stricter laws on trafficking in endangered
species," she said.

"God speed your work," he said. "But LA?"

She leaned back against a concrete planter and crossed
her arms, which did interesting things to her cleavage.
"Well, if you've been investigating what happened there,

Mr. . . . Tom . . . you'll know there was some possibility of a link to one of our subsidiaries."

"Our?" he said, lifting a brow.

"The league is the outfit I work for," she said. "But it's pretty well one of the Rolfe family's good works. We're all, mmmm, not exactly Greens . . . conservationists. Have been for a long, long while, since my grandfather's time. He joined the Sierra Club in the 1940s; he was a country boy, and a hunter. The suggestion that some of our companies have been used to smuggle endangered-animal products . . . well, it has my father and grandfather both absolutely livid, let me tell you. But it's also unfortunately *possible,* since we do so much import-export work; a big organization, thousands of employees. They have the usual corporate security at work on it, but they asked me to look into it as well, as someone they can trust absolutely. I've done investigative work before—a lobbyist is uniquely well placed to find out who's leaning on who to get environmental set-asides and exemptions."

Tom nodded again. "Looks like we're on the same side," he said cautiously. *Or you're trying to scam me; but it* fits *better than a megacorp risking bad PR on penny-ante smuggling.*

"When did you get into town?" he went on.

"Late yesterday," she said. Then she smiled at him, the green eyes narrowing. "And by the way, no, I didn't have any plans for dinner tonight. Which is what you were about to ask, right?"

"Right." He felt his face flush even more, but laughed good-naturedly. "Mind-reader. Ahem. Adrienne, would you like to have dinner tonight?"

"I'd love to, Tom. Say about seven-thirty?"

"Right."

Now was the awkward question of where. She was undoubtedly the sort who simply went where they liked and didn't have to worry about prices. Wardens at his level made a decent middle-class income, but he *did* have to think about where he went and how often. Otherwise he could come up empty at the end of the month.

"How about something Oriental?" Adrienne said, looking around and tossing the empty water container into a trash basket. "I always . . . that is, I really like that."

Tom nodded. Inwardly he was blinking in bemusement; coming from the Bay Area to Sacramento and going out to eat Chinese or Japanese or Thai was like . . . well, as his grandmother had been fond of saying, that was like taking herring to Bergen, only in reverse. Even now Sacramento was basically a glorified Valley cow-town.

Still, I'd cheerfully eat gray toadburgers at McDonald's with you, Ms. Rolfe. "Let's see . . . Does that include In dian?"

"East Indian, you mean? Love it."

Hmm, he thought. *Doesn't* everyone *mean East Indian nowadays?* You could get a serious rebuke at his job for not using "Native American" for what people used to call Indians, and what Tully privately referred to as "Premature Siberian-Americans." *Probably you don't have to be as cautious when your family owns the business.*

"How about the Maharani, then?" he said aloud.

Her smile went wider. "I bow to the superior experience of my native guide," she said. "And now . . . back to Grayson's."

Tom found his second wind remarkably easily. He whistled in the shower, and felt even better when Adrienne was waiting to exchange addresses and phone numbers. She was staying at a B-and-B spot, Amber House; the sort of place that had about twelve rooms, each with a name, a private two-person-size Jacuzzi and an Italian marble bathroom. That was only eight blocks east of the capitol, within walking distance of downtown, and it explained what she'd been doing at a private health club—unlike similarly priced hotels, it wouldn't include exercise facilities.

Down, boy, he thought. *Just because you've met a beautiful woman who shares your hobbies, seems to think like you, and seems to be interested in* you, *doesn't mean the millen-*

nium has arrived. For one thing, she's seriously rich. That can create problems. For another, there's something slightly funny about her. I can't put my finger on it, but it's there. Maybe RM&M is legitimate. On the other hand, maybe not, and she's their Mata Hari.

That nagged him all the way back to his modest apartment. He could have afforded a house, but he thought of the one-bedroom as his contribution to slowing down the paving of California, and besides that, he was saving for a small place up in the Sierras. The comfortable bachelor shabbiness suddenly looked a little different as he walked in, although it had contented him since the divorce.

The "shabby" suddenly overwhelms the "comfortable," he thought.

He phoned in the reservations, then flipped on the computer. He *had* indulged in a good optical cable-modem connection; it saved a lot of time. Whistling between his teeth, he leaned forward with his strong fingers moving over the keyboard and mousepad.

Yes, the Pacific Open Landscapes League was a legit operation, headquartered in Berkeley, which was no surprise—the People's Republic was exactly the place for this sort of endeavor. Donors were listed, and included the usual assortment of individuals and companies who wanted to show concern, a desire to buy respectability, a lust for good PR, or all of the above. Amounts weren't specified, but a Google search had turned up evidence that this was a seriously well-heeled outfit, with annual expenditures well up into seven figures, although they didn't have a mass membership like the Sierra Club et al. And Adrienne Rolfe was right there on their Web site, under "Investigation and Appraisals Division."

So she was a troubleshooter and fixer; awfully young for it, and he would have expected someone with a law degree. Hers was in history, with some wildlife-centered biology courses.

Aha! he thought; Charles Rolfe was there on the board of directors. Nepotism raising its—in this case—very attractive head. Nothing inherently wrong with that, of course. It looked as if the Rolfes had been spending a lot of money on a cause he thoroughly approved of, for generations.

Hmmm. Let's see: small permanent staff, about twenty; headquarters in a converted Victorian; doesn't go for headlines. Genteel as hell, all very well-bred. OK, looks good . . . let's try cross-checking.

The founder of the league was still alive and on the board but retired; he must be pushing ninety by now; that would be the grandfather she mentioned.

Tom winced slightly. He'd be delighted if the evening ended in Ms. Rolfe's bed, but . . .

But, dammit, I really like her. She seems . . . real. And if she's that rich, it could be a serious, serious barrier to anything serious. I'm tired of one-month girlfriends and relationships that go nowhere. A man wasn't meant to live alone.

He shook himself, noted the time and scrambled to dress. The first rule of a first date was simply to relax, enjoy yourself and not think too much about what *might* happen down the road—that was the surest way to start giving off "needy" vibrations, which women detected and shunned the way submarines did the sound of a destroyer's propellers.

Time to go.

❋ ❋ ❋

"*You're* indecently cheerful today," a voice said as Tom Christiansen hung up his jacket and flipped on the computer in his cubicle. "You get lucky, or what?"

Tom laughed. Roy Tully was a good sort, even if he had a fair bit of little-guy complex. He might feel a need to prove himself, but as far as Tom was concerned he already had. The short man in the high-waisted pants stood in the entrance of the cubicle, his tie a particularly vile yellow-and-green checked number, grinning and holding a Styrofoam cup of the usual execrable coffee in each hand.

The office was coming to its usual institutional-bland life, a structured world where status was marked by the size of your cubicle or—for the very successful—a corner office with a view and a real desk. Tom had never wanted one of those; the money was nice, but if you got to that level, you had to *stay* in the office most of the time. He sipped at the coffee, made a face at it and said, "No, actually, I didn't get lucky. But I don't give a damn. I did have a very nice evening with a very pleasant young woman I met at the gym."

His mind went back to the parking lot of Maharani's. Adrienne had been stunning in gym clothes; the effect in a short black dress gathered with a gold-link belt, a little simple makeup and a silver-and-turquoise pin holding one fall of her bronze-colored hair over the left ear had reduced him to stuttering idiocy for an instant. Luckily it had passed. . . .

"So, what's the broad like?"

"*Broad?* Roy, nobody says 'broad' anymore. You spend too many nights watching old movies on your DVD player."

"Okay, what's the *young woman* like?"

Tom gave a brief description. Roy groaned theatrically.

"What I wouldn't give to be built like a Greek god chick magnet, and get all the goddamned action—"

"Like a Norski god, not one of those Greek swishes; Baldur, I think—Asa-Thor was a redhead, and Tyr had a hand missing. When I get back to Aasgard, you can be one of the dwarf thralls. And get your mind out of the gutter, lest I smite thee with a lawsuit alleging the creation of a hostile work environment."

Tully leered. Tom went on: "And her name is Adrienne . . . Adrienne Rolfe."

With perfect timing, he'd caught his partner in the middle of a sip. Tully choked, staggering about the cubicle; Tom thumped him helpfully on the back.

"You're not serious!" Tully managed at last.

"Eminently serious," Tom said. "Yes, she knew who I was—it's not really a secret, after the way the fire got into the papers. She's working for the Pacific Open Landscapes League—"

"I know the outfit," Tully said, his voice serious and his eyes level. "Didn't know they were tied in with the Rolfes."

"I looked that up myself, just before we had dinner. They're good guys."

"The league is, yeah," Tully conceded. "That doesn't mean the Rolfes are, necessarily."

"Not necessarily," Tom said. "But it's the way to bet. You were going to tell me about their setup in Oakland?"

"Yeah," Tully replied. "Let me call up my notes on your screen, and a skyview . . . OK, it's here." His finger traced an area of several blocks. "Used to be a run-down residential neighborhood in West Oakland not too far from the docks. A lot of what's around it still is—they say crime's down, but Kemosabe, I felt plenty nervous around there! Anyway, it was rezoned after 1946, and now it's a big warehouse complex—they've got their own sidings to their own docks. Pretty massive, and their rent-a-cops are on the job, let me tell you. No in or out without clearance; but there's a lot of traffic. Cargo containers, mostly, but trucks with loose cargo too. Anything could get lost in that shuffle."

"There you are," Tom said. "You said it could be an inside job—some ring or group inside using the company for smuggling. That's what Adrienne thinks, too, and she wants the perps as bad as we do. God knows that sort of thing happens all the time with drugs . . . which, incidentally, we should check on too, you betcha."

"I did," Tully said. "Guy I know on the Oakland PD—don't worry, strictly unofficial."

"What did he say?" Tom asked.

"That RM and M is so clean it squeaks," Tully said. "Pays all its city taxes, even ones it could get out of. Contributes to all the right charities, and has since the late 1940s. Gives the city libraries and fire engines. Does everything but help little old ladies across the street. Makes big donations to local politicians, but spreads them around so it doesn't look funny if they get favors; mostly they insist on being left strictly alone."

Tom remembered an elegant drawing room on Nob Hill,

and a bewildered bitterness hiding behind good breeding. He pushed it aside, summoned logic and went on: "That fits with Adrienne being on the side of the angels," he said. "Granted, she probably wants information from us, too, but that's natural."

Tully nodded, seeming oddly reluctant. "We don't want a civilian getting under our feet," he said. "Far be it from me to ruin your pickup line, Kemosabe—"

Tom snorted. "We *do* want access," he pointed out. "We do *not* want RM and M pulling strings here in Sacramento to get us told to do something else. We—"

"OK, OK," Tully said, grinning. "Guess it's been a long time, huh?"

"I had a nice dinner with a nice young lady. Not impossibly younger. We talked about our families and our lives. . . ."

❋ ❋ ❋

". . . and I do envy you that," she'd said at one point in the evening, after he'd described a winter hunting trip he'd taken with his father and brother just before he joined the army back in the nineties.

"Envy me what?" Tom replied. "Growing up on our farm, or getting away to the Upper Peninsula?"

"Neither. I spent a lot of my childhood in the country too. And I'm California born and bred; I don't like snow unless it stays on ski slopes where it belongs—my ancestors were all either Southerners or Italians. What I envy you is being so close to your father."

"You weren't?"

Adrienne propped her chin on a palm and looked past him. "I'm afraid not. My family was . . . is . . . sort of conservative. And I was a tomboy to start with, then a wild handful as a teenager, always in and out of trouble, and all my brothers and sisters—"

"How many?" Tom asked curiously.

"I'm the youngest of six: John, Robert, Lamar, Charles,

Cynthia, and me. John—John Rolfe the Seventh—is forty-three."

Tom nodded, hiding his surprise; with a brother and a sister, he'd had more siblings than most even in a deep-rural part of the northern plains.

She must have been born in the eighties, he thought. *She's definitely younger than me, and I'd say at least four, five years younger, Gen-Y. Well, statistically there have to have been some upper-crust Bay Area WASPs who had families that size in the post-baby-boom era, but it's certainly unusual.*

It wasn't as if they were some variety of weird fundamentalist; she'd also mentioned that her family were Episcopalians.

She went on: "As I said, I was the youngest, and the rest were always much more . . . dutiful. My father's no fool, but he's, mmmmm, shockable, let's say; and I just couldn't resist shocking him and Mother, and everyone else who looked so smug—nobody's more judgmental than a fifteen-year-old full of herself. Things went from bad to worse."

"I know what you mean," he said. "I was lucky; Lars and I had the usual head-butting you do with your father, but it was mostly good-natured. I've seen how things can get out of hand."

"And Mother was worse than Dad, if anything; she kept trying to be so *understanding,* when she was obviously yearning to throttle me. If it weren't for Grandmother—my mother's mother—and Great-aunt Chloe, I think I'd have gone nuts."

"What's your grandmother like?" he asked.

"Was, I'm afraid. She was Italian—a contessa, no less, a war bride—although she always insisted on being called a Tuscan and claimed that everything south of Sienna was 'baptized Arabs.' Her family lived up in the hills east of Florence, because they'd lost their *palazzo* in town and pretty well everything else but a couple of olive groves and heirlooms; she met Rob Fitzmorton—he was my paternal grandfather's cousin—when Uncle Rob drove a tank-destroyer into their courtyard."

"That's romantic enough," Tom said.

"Well, Uncle Rob always thought so. I suspect the K-rations may have had something to do with it. They were probably literally starving then, what with the war. Living on olives and bread and what rabbits they could shoot, at least; and serving them on Renaissance silverware."

Tom chuckled. "Sounds like an interesting old lady."

She smiled fondly. "She was absolutely dreadful, a monster, a snob to the core, and callous as a cat to anyone she didn't like. She could flay the skin off you with an arched eyebrow and four words. And the way she treated anyone who worked for her was a scandal. People were even more frightened of her than of the Old Man, because he was hard but fair. The Contessa Francesca Cammachia di Montevarchi; she usually didn't bother adding the 'Fitzmorton' unless she was signing a check. Everyone called her Contessa Perdita, or the Diamond Contessa."

His brows rose. "You liked her, though?"

"I adored her; she made me feel like a fairy changeling. She told me once that all my brothers and sisters were tainted by bourgeois respectability, but that she saw from an early age that I had inherited something of her soul and could be productively corrupted by spoiling and indulgence. Even when she was old—in my first memories of her she must have been about sixty—she always wore these lovely clothes, appropriate but so chic and soigné, drove Italian sports cars on our dirt roads . . . I remember her perfume, and those stunning diamonds came out at the slightest excuse. She saw it as her mission to civilize a bunch of Saxon barbarians—meaning the Fitzmortons, her husband's family, and us Rolfes—who had all sorts of boring virtues like industry and determination but lacked the aristocratic ones like savoir faire, style and ruthless selfishness."

"So she accepted you the way you were? That must have been a relief."

"Lord, no! But she didn't disapprove of the same things

my parents did. Looking back, a few people did accept me as I was—Ralph, for example. . . ."

"Ralph?" he asked. *A boyfriend?* He tried to keep a quick flush of hostile interest out of his voice, and by the slight quirk of one elegant red-blond eyebrow, didn't quite manage it.

"Ralph was one of Aunt Chloe's odd friends; he ran— runs—a burger joint near, ah, near Martinez." That was a town west of the Delta, on the Carquinez Strait. "Sort of a sixties type, you might say."

"I wouldn't think your grandmother would approve of him, then," Tom said with a grin.

"And you'd be *soooo* right," Adrienne said. "'A sweaty, shaggy peasant,' and I quote."

"Your grandmother had a rough edge to her tongue," Tom observed.

"More like an edge lined with razors. She told *me* I had no dress sense and was far too fond of things like riding horses; a little was good for the posture, but too much was rustic, and shooting animals was just too, too boring. But she'd sweep me off when things got too impossible at home, off through . . . off to San Francisco, which she reluctantly granted was a real city, if provincial compared to Florence."

"Took you to the zoo and suchlike?" Tom prompted. *She can't have been all bad, if she took that much trouble for a grandchild.*

"Usually she'd take me to the ballet and the galleries and the best theater and restaurants, and sit up talking with me till all hours while we ate these amazing chocolates, and let me sleep till noon, and then take me to have my hair and nails done. Mind you, I knew from the time I was eight that she'd drop me in an instant if I started being more boring than amusing. She found my mother terminally dull—over-shadowed her completely from infancy; it must have been like growing up as a minor moon attendant on a star—and she detested my father as a prig . . . well, Dad *is* a prig, I grant, or at least very stuffy."

"And your great-aunt Chloe?" Tom said, watching the

play of emotion on the sculpted face, trying to imagine her as a sullen rebellious teenager.

The warm affection that showed when she spoke of her grandmother made her face more human; there was often a slight edge of coldness to her expression, something that you didn't notice until it melted away. His own grandmother had been as different from this exotic contessa creature as it was possible to imagine, a Norski farm wife as tough as an old root, short-spoken and direct. He could remember her birch syrup, though. . . .

"Oh, Aunt Chloe was completely different. Everybody loved her, and she took in strays of the oddest sorts. She took *me* in, and put up with me when I was a perfect little beast. And she was the best listener I ever met—although you're not bad in that respect yourself, Tom."

He blushed. "Well, I try not to do the stereotypical thing; you know, the man who natters on about himself whenever he meets a woman, as if his life was necessarily interesting just because it's his."

"I think yours *is* interesting," she said. "Not to mention your work."

"Nine-tenths paperwork, I'm afraid," he said. "Wait a minute—your aunt took you in, you said?"

"Great-aunt. Took me in informally; I more or less ran away from home for a while. Things got extremely messy. My parents wanted me put in therapy; committed and tranked out, in other words. Chloe wouldn't hear of it, and the Old Man—her brother, my father's father—backed her up, and of course what he said went. Looking back on it, I blush with shame at the way I treated her and everyone else at Seven Oaks—that was her place in the country—but I was monstrously preoccupied with my own grievances, real and imagined. At that point my parents pretty well washed their hands of me; the consensus was that I was either a psychopath, a dangerous juvenile delinquent—I got caught smoking weed at a wild party with people making out in the darker corners—or a lesbian degenerate—possibly all three, though not necessarily at the same time. I *am* crazy, of

course, and you can outgrow juvenile delinquency like
spots. . . ."

"Two out of three isn't bad." Tom grinned. "Tried to get
me worrying there for a moment, didn't you?"

Her gaze came back to his, and a mischievous twinkle lit
the green eyes. She ate a forkful of the curried lamb, made an
appreciative noise, took a sip of her red zinfandel, then
chuckled and went on: "And alas, I turned out to be incorri-
gibly straight. I mean, have you ever tried to have a romantic relationship with a girl?"

This time his shout of laughter turned heads. He turned it
down, and saw that she was chuckling helplessly too; it was
a husky, wholehearted sound, with nothing of a giggle in it,
and he liked that. His ex-wife had had an unfortunate tendency to giggle, and what could be charming at eighteen
turned into a fingernails-on-slate torment later.

"Well, yah, you betcha, I *have* tried that, repeatedly,"
Tom said. "Not always successfully, but I keep at it. A dirty
job that somebody has to do."

"Ms. Malaprop strikes again; but seriously, from my
viewpoint it was like attempting a nice hot shower in lukewarm chicken soup. While trying to live on nothing but
chocolate éclairs. God have mercy." She sighed. "It would
have been so *convenient*, though. Women don't *always* think
you've invited them to run your life just because you sleep
with them."

"Neither do all men, not these days," Tom said, a little defensively. Silently: *I guess I don't know the Bay Area as well
as I thought. Sensitive Guys in Touch with Their Feelings
Who Understand Her Need for Personal Space are a dime a
dozen there, aren't they? And the family in a tizzy in the
nineties because she smoked a joint, or there were kids neck-
ing at a party? This whole saga—the big, sprawling, inter-
married families and crazy rich grandmothers and country
houses with names and fathers obsessed with proper behav-
ior and such . . . sounds sort of Southern Gothic, or even European, and Old European at that, Faulkner or Chekhov
with a few Californian touches. Maybe things get really dif-*

ferent up beyond the last thin layers of the middle classes? Because I'd swear she's telling the truth.

Perhaps Adrienne saw something in his face. "Let's say the, ah, families in our crowd were sort of behind the times," she said. "Still are . . ."

This wasn't a conversation he could imagine having in, say, Ironwood, the small town where his high school had been located; too much Lutheran primness lingered there. Nothing out of the ordinary for California, though, and it was enjoyable to be doing the mutual-exploration thing again. Particularly when you liked the personality revealed, and thought it was true in reverse too.

"Sorry about you and your parents, though," he said sincerely. *You appreciate having a solid family in childhood more when you get to know people who didn't.*

"Oh, we get along well enough now. When Aunt Chloe died—"

"I *am* sorry," he said, and meant it. Impulsively, he put his hand on hers.

She returned the grip for an instant; he felt the touch of her fingers for minutes after their hands parted.

"—she died, and she left me Seven Oaks, asking me to take care of the estate. *That* shocked me silly. I'd taken her for granted, and assumed that she'd just go on and on like the mountains and the seasons and the Old Man. You know how it is, the first time you realize death is *real,* that someone you loved is *gone,* you'll never get the chance to say the things you were planning on . . . and you realize that you're going to die someday too?"

"Yes," he said somberly. "I remember it when my mother died. As if you're hatching from an egg, and you don't much like what you've found outside."

"Exactly. There I was, eighteen—it was nine years ago next May twenty-first—and I suddenly realized that the people I'd spent all my adolescence rebelling against would be *gone* someday. So I decided to buckle down and make some use of the circumstances I'd been handed."

"Like your work with the Pacific Open Landscapes League?" he said.

She smiled. "Yes, that and other things to do with the family business. Here I had an opportunity not one in a hundred million of the human race had, to do something *significant* for my family and my . . . country, my people, and why was I wasting time—time that I suddenly realized I'd never get back? Aunt Chloe thought I was competent to look after her things, and the contessa had told me someone of good blood shouldn't care what the smelly peasants thought. I decided to go out and do something with the talents and the chances I'd been handed."

"Bravo," Tom said softly.

"I even manage to get on well with my parents now, except that they keep nagging me to get married and produce grandchildren; at least, Mother does."

"Don't your brothers and sisters have any?"

"Every one, three or more each," Adrienne said. "But evidently there's never enough."

Tom shook his head. "My family sounds a lot duller than yours," he said.

She cocked her head to one side. "Restful, not dull. Incidentally, fair warning: What I've told you is all true, but it's incomplete. But as we native-born Californios say, enough about me. Let's talk about you. How do *you* feel about me?"

She laughed at his sudden alarm, and went on: "No, really, what I'd like to know is why you went into the Fish and Game Department after you left the army."

"Well, I'd gotten to like California while I was stationed here. Yes, it's been mucked up beyond belief, but even what's left of it is the most beautiful place I've ever seen. So . . ."

✷ ✷ ✷

And the whole rest of the evening we talked about my *family and* my *work,* he realized, coming back to himself and the present with a slight wince. She'd been very interested in the details of this bizarre poaching-smuggling case and the disaster in LA; he hadn't mentioned anything about the SOU's sources, or the Bureau's, of course. RM&M wouldn't need that to do their own internal housekeeping.

He hoped he hadn't been the stereotypical male after all.

Roy was grinning sardonically, and Tom realized that he'd drifted off into a reminiscent daydream for a good minute by the clock.

"So, you talked family?" Roy asked. "*That* gave you the dazed look and the sappy grin? Or the sheer careerist joy of finding a good source for this little investigation of ours?"

Well, the fact that the evening ended with one short kiss, one long passionate kiss, and a murmured "I like you a lot, but we should get to know each other better," and a date to go running together may have something to do with that.

"And we talked about things we've done or would like to do," he went on aloud. "She says she makes a good venison ragout—and she actually likes hunting."

"Bambi? She shot *Bambi?*" Roy said. "And *ate* the poor little fucker?"

"I didn't notice you turning down those venison chops last Christmas."

"It doesn't count if it comes in boxes. Everyone born in civilized urban surroundings knows that there are magical warehouses where neatly wrapped steaks and chops and roasts appear, probably through some miracle of superscience. Better watch it; remarriage is the triumph of hope over experience."

Tom shrugged. "Maybe I need to work on my divorce technique. I haven't had as much practice at them as you," he said, with malice aforethought.

Roy winced. He was currently in the middle of his very messy second.

"Anyway, we're scarcely engaged yet. A date to go running is not part of the wedding ceremony. She's on the side of the angels. RM and M has put a lot of money into conservation. She's just a nice, smart"—very rich, very sophisticated, very beautiful—"girl, Roy."

Hmmm. Although she seemed entranced with the food at the Maharani's. I wonder why? If there's one place in the world you can get good East Indian food, it's Berkeley— probably better there than in Bombay. Maharani's is nice, but it isn't world-class.

"OK, I'll leave your love life out of things . . . for now. Anything on the LA bust from the city cops or Fart, Barf and Itch? I want to hear how the forensics turned out."

"I'm expecting something from the San Diego Zoo—"

The phone rang, and Roy left for his own cubicle with a wave. Whistling quietly under his breath, Tom reached for the telephone.

"Yes, this is Mr. Christiansen . . . Hi, Manuel? Anything yet on the bird?"

There was a long silence, which wasn't like Manuel Carminez; he loved explaining things about his specialty. With a lurch of fear, Tom went on: "Look, it didn't *die* or anything, did it? Not smoke inhalation, or stress shock?"

"No," the voice on the other end said; it belonged to a biologist at the San Diego Zoo's captive-breeding program. "The problem is that bird is *too* healthy. Among other things."

"How so?" Tom said, pulling a pad towards him and poising a pen.

"To begin with, it isn't a condor from California."

The pen hung fire. "I could have sworn—"

"Oh, it's a *Gymnogyps californianus,* all right—young adult male. The thing is, Tom . . . you know how you find a California condor in the wild?"

"I'll bite."

"It's the bird with the four ornithologists standing around it in a circle. We captured the last wild one for the breeding program back in 'eighty-seven, at which point there were exactly twenty-seven in the entire world. There are barely two hundred twenty total today, with eighty in the wild. Not only is every single one accounted for, but we have tissue samples and DNA of every single one alive and every single one that's died in the last thirty years."

"So how did the poachers get one without the four ornithologists noticing?" Tom asked. "It's not as if they were ripping off abalone—the seabed is a lot less closely watched."

"They *didn't* get one of ours. They're all accounted for—I checked. And that's where things get *really* interesting. All the California condors alive today are descended from the same twenty-seven individuals. That makes them all pretty closely related; it's what we call a 'near-extinction event' or a 'genetic bottleneck'—"

"Manuel, you *do* remember who I work for, don't you?" Tom said gently.

"Oh, sorry. Anyway, they're all pretty closely related. We can trace their relationships easily. So we did; took a sample, put it through one of those handy-dandy new gene-fingerprint machines, the one with the nanoscale gold electrodes, to see which pair of wild birds had a chick we somehow didn't notice."

"Wait a minute," Tom whispered. "You mean it's *not* related to the known condors?"

"Not even remotely. It's as unrelated to them as it can be and still be a member of the same species. There's more genetic variation between that bird's DNA and the others than there is among all the other condors left. Which will make it tremendously useful to the breeding program, *amigo*. But it still leaves the question of where the son of a whore *came* from."

"You mean it's as if it came from an entirely different population?"

"Right in one. And there is one, repeat one, breeding population of Californian condors."

Now I wish I'd gotten more samples from that chamber of horrors at the warehouse, Tom thought. *Oh, how I wish I'd gotten more samples!*

"Anything else?"

"Yes. We also did every other test we could on the damn overgrown vulture. You know the main cause of death for wild condors?"

"Lead poisoning, from shot."

"Right in one again. Hunter shoots something, something runs away and dies, condor eats thing, condor also eats buckshot, and then it's 'Go walk with God, condor.' Well, *this* condor never met a lead buckshot pellet. There's no lead in its feathers or tissues *at all,* much less dangerous amounts. But wait, there's more. This condor never ingested any pesticides, or herbicides—none, not even trace amounts—or any of a dozen other things that a bird in the modern world eats . . . *por Dios,* things that we all *breathe* every day."

Manuel paused. "If you can find out the valley this condor lived in, I would like to move there! Because that place . . . it is like nowhere on earth for this hundred years and more."

"Where could it have come from, then?"

"Well . . . possibly . . . a very isolated group somewhere up in the Sierras? I don't see how the hell we could have not found them, given their flying range, but it's the only thing that occurs to me, frankly. And it's a pretty lame explanation; there aren't any places in California that pristine, and condors scavenge open lowland areas by choice. It would take a whole series of fantastically unlikely coincidences for the past hundred years. Or some mad scientist has been cloning them, using frozen tissue that's been around for sixty, seventy years, to get any possibility of an unrelated bird . . . take your pick."

"Thanks, Manuel."

"Thank *you, amigo.* This bird improves our chances of succeeding with this program by more than a bit. I just can't figure out where in the name of *todos santos* it comes from. But if you find any more—send them along!"

"Yah, you betcha I will," Tom said.

He paused and looked thoughtfully down at his notes. *Well, here's a pretty how-de-doo,* he mused. *Apparently we not only have poachers who are ruthless enough to trade in a species on the brink of extinction, but smart enough to find members of it where the California DFG and all the biologists in the state can't.*

"Thanks, and— Wait a minute," Tom said. He didn't

know precisely why he asked, but extra information never hurt. "To change the subject, do you know anything about the Pacific Open Landscapes League?"

Manuel was silent for a moment. "That rings a faint bell . . . could you hold?"

Tom made affirmative noises, and waited while a faint clicking of keys came over the line.

God, but computers make it hard to hide anything, he thought. *Nothing ever goes away, if you know where to look.*

"I'd heard of them vaguely myself," Manuel said a moment later, in the peculiar half-strangled tones of a man who is holding a telephone between his jaw and shoulder while working at a computer.

"*Sí,* got it. They're a contributor to the zoo's fund; an annual hundred and fifty thousand. But they've been dealing with us for quite a while—since the late 1940s—only then they had a different name. Let's see . . . Zoological Studies and Research. They had an arrangement with us on captured animals—they'd fund the expedition, and we'd split the beasts with them. They wanted the animals for experimentation, I'd guess, from the name. Mostly standard African animals: rhino, giraffe, lions, cheetahs; some Asian varieties as well—tigers, Siberians and Bengals. That sort of thing was more common then; we had exchange operations with zoos and even circuses all over the world—we got our first stock from a circus, you know, back a century ago. The arrangement seems to run for about six years, 1949 to 1955; then they shifted over to a straight donation and doing research through us and people we recommended, a lot of projects on historical ecology—how the early colonization affected California by bringing in new grasses and so forth—and then in 1970 they changed the name. Odd, eh? Why do you ask?"

"Just a feeling I should," Tom said, uncertain himself. "Talk to you later."

He hung up the phone and stared down at his notes again. They were clearly organized; the only problem was that they were nonsense. His father had once told him that if you couldn't solve a problem at one end, the trick was to start at the other.

"All right, let's move on," he murmured, and reached for the telephone again; the number he wanted was on the frequently-used list. "One ringie dingie . . . two ringie dingie . . . This is Warden Thomas Christiansen from the DFG . . . that's the Department of Fish and Game . . . Special Agent Perkins, please . . . Hi, Sarah. Any news for me?"

"Hi, Tom. We have gotten some new leads." His pen poised again. She went on: "It turns out the buyers for that stuff were . . . upset . . . when it all got burned up. They'd already paid for a good bit of it. They think—"

"*They* being?"

"A Vietnamese group, we're pretty sure. Not as good citizens as most of their community, to put it mildly. They'd have the Asian connections for marketing."

Tom nodded, then remembered to produce an audible "uh-huh. Yes, DFG has been having plenty of problems with that. Now that the war's over and the Asian part of the Pacific Rim is booming harder than ever, the market for animal parts has heated up again. Bear paws, rhino horns, tiger glands, exotic furs, ivory, you name it, and the prices make cocaine look like bottled water."

And that would fit in with RM&M's Pacific Rim operations, if it's a rogue group within the company the way Adrienne suspects, he added silently to himself, before going on: "Who were the ones selling it in the first place?"

"A group of Russian 'entrepreneurs.' Based out of the Balkans or possibly Turkey, we think; things aren't quite so wild and hairy in Russia proper these days, not like it was in the nineties, and the 'Stans are getting downright respectable."

"Amazing how much respect GPS-guided weapons can instill," Tom said. "Not to mention the nasty example of what happened to Iraq. How did you find out?"

"Well, the Vietnamese gentlemen seemed to be under the impression that the Russians were having some sort of internal power struggle, which resulted in their customers getting ripped off. We got an anonymous-concerned-citizen tip by a very excited young man, fingering them. Voice analysis pegged him as born here but brought up in a Vietnamese-speaking household, and we're working that angle."

"Wonderful!" Tom enthused. "And the Russians?"

"Them we can move on faster; we know where they live. You doing anything later this week? Like to take a trip to beautiful San Francisco?"

He felt a sudden twinge. *Adrienne will probably be leaving town next week.* Duty was going to get in the way of his social life again; that had been the proximate cause of his divorce, too.

"Can do," he said. "You've got my cell-phone number."

And as compensation, he might well be on the track of the people responsible for the condor, along with a good deal else.

And I want to meet them, he thought, as he scooped up the file and set out for his supervisor's office. *I want that very much indeed.*

✸ ✸ ✸

Colletta Hall
June 2009

The Commonwealth of New Virginia

Giovanni Colletta turned the swivel chair and looked up at his father's picture, where it hung behind his desk. It showed him in this very chair and room, seated with chin propped on thumb and forefinger.

The portrait had been painted in late middle age, which was how he himself best remembered Salvatore Colletta: streaks of gray through the sleek, slicked-back raven hair, lines grooved from the hooded eyes to the corners of an unsmiling mouth, the somber elegance of dark suit and cream silk tie, ruby stickpin, discreetly gleaming gold cuff links, snowy linen, on a body that stayed slender and tough into his sixties. Until the cancer racked him to a shadow and he lost his last battle, murmuring a final confession to a priest who turned pasty-pale as he bent his ear to the wrinkled mouth.

Hard to believe that I'm getting to be that old myself, the Prime of the Collettas—*the* Colletta—thought. He'd been the third child but the first son, born in the Commonwealth in the 1950s. Minchia! *I'm a grandfather and fifty-nine this September.*

The painter had been very good, and fearless. The eyes of Salvatore Colletta reminded his son of Byzantine mosaics he'd seen on trips FirstSide, in the ancient churches of Ravenna—the eyes of the empress Theodora the Great. Dark, fathomless, knowing, somber with unacknowledged sins—although he could hear the wolf-yelp of laughter the first Colletta would have given, and the playful-serious cuff across the side of the head.

Hey, I got eyes on me like a Greek buttana, *eh? Show your father some respect, kid!*

Giovanni's mouth quirked. Salvatore Colletta had insisted that his son study the arts and graces and learning of a *galantuomo,* a gentleman, a real *civile*—despite the fact that he'd been the scion of a long line of laborers and sardine fishermen in a grim little village near Messina, and had himself grown up catch-as-catch-can on the shrill crowded streets of Manhattan's Little Italy in the twenties and thirties. That education had given Giovanni Colletta a vocabulary and perspective his father could never have imagined, but he'd never been absolutely sure that he'd kept the razor-keen aggression and cold realism that had made the Collettas second only to the Rolfes here in this new land. He could only hope he had, for on that the survival of his blood depended.

"But I certainly inherited the ambition," he murmured to the terrible old man whom he'd loved and feared and hated every day of his life, long after he became a man himself. "And everything we do is for the Family, Poppa."

As if to underscore the fact, his youngest daughter burst into the office, throwing a laughing word over her shoulder to the friends who giggled and chattered without. His smile grew broader, half from delight at seeing her, free-striding and tanned and beautiful in her tennis whites, sky-colored eyes sparkling as she twirled her racket, hair the color of dark amber honey held back by a silken headband. The other half was from the amusement. . . .

Well, Poppa, you wanted me to be a civile, *and you wanted a tall, slim, blond wife who was a "real lady."*

The woman Salvatore Colletta married had been a junker's daughter from east of the Elbe, whose surviving family had had very good reasons for jumping at a one-way passage through the Gate in 1946—reasons beyond the Russians overrunning their ancestral estates, and having to do with certain political decisions they'd made in the 1930s. The von Traupitz family soon discovered equally good reasons for a matrimonial alliance with one of the founders and overlords of New Virginia.

Between your social ambitions and your taste in women, Poppa, you certainly made something different out of the legitimate line of the Collettas! Of course, Giovanni had helped the process along. Marianne's mother had been a yellow-haired daughter of the Fitzmortons.

"Daddy!" she said, giving him an enthusiastic hug as he came around the broad desk to greet her.

"Picciridda mia," he replied fondly.

"Oh, Daddy, I'm too old to be called 'little one' anymore," she said, holding him at arm's length, and tactfully not mentioning that she was his height to an inch. "I'm a grown-up young lady now. Which you'd know if you would only get out of this office more, instead of sitting here all the time playing spider-in-the-web. I hardly see you at all, even when I'm at home!"

"I'd just cast a damper on that great drooling tribe of wellborn young men who follow you around," he said, smiling at her fondly. "You should pick one to be your prince, little heartbreaker, and give me more grandchildren."

"I would, if only I could find one like you, Daddy," she said, smiling at him.

His heart melted with love—and not a little with admiration for the skill she used to manipulate him.

"And what is it you want to wheedle out of your father this time?" he said.

At nineteen, Marianne Colletta had the family's diamond-hard concentration on getting what she wanted, but was still working on the subtlety that often went with it, and the knowledge of *what* she wanted above all. She wrinkled her small straight nose at him.

"Well, can't I come to see my own father just for the fun of it? There's nothing right now . . . it's not important, I suppose . . . but I *could* use another maid. . . ."

He sighed and shook a finger. "Young lady, you've got a perfectly good maid, what's her name, Toto, *and* a secretary, not to mention all the staff running 'round to your whim here, or at the town house when you're living in Rolfeston—"

"Well, yes, but it's a lot of work, and Totochin's going back to that horrible place with all the X's in the name when her contract's up next year, I just *couldn't* persuade her to stay. I *really* need one who can learn enough to be useful before Totochin goes home, and it looks so silly to have only one to run errands and carry things and everything when I'm in town, and a Settler maid is just horribly unfashionable. I'm going to be working at the Gate computer center after the spring semester, too, so I'll be so *busy* with that, and then there's all the parties and—"

He sighed. *More of the damned Rolfes.* It was their policies that made it at least a little difficult for him to get a new *nahua* maid for his favorite daughter—he, Prime of the whole Colletta Family, its collaterals and its affiliation! And it was their law that required every young member of the Thirty Families to contribute time to the Commission's needs. Although to be fair, he could see a good deal of sense in *that*.

"I'll see what I can do," he grumbled, and accepted her hug and kiss on the forehead.

He looked at his watch when she left: eleven-fifteen, which gave him a few minutes before Anthony arrived, and an hour before the business lunch with Dimitri Batyushkov. That was going to be embarrassing. Anthony was at least partly responsible, for all that his claim of bad luck and foul-ups by the FirstSider element had some merit. He'd been in charge. Excuses didn't matter. Results did.

He had the report on his desk memorized; he picked it up and threw it in the discreet disposal slot. Equipment hummed, and then there was nothing left but powdered paper with traces of ink, sitting in the hidden waste receptacle and waiting for the cleaning woman to dump into her bin. Giovanni Colletta looked around the big office; it was a square room mostly lined in polished light-gold beewood paneling, and bookcases filled with volumes bound in tooled leather. There was space here and there for a painting or a vase. The porcelain was his own selection, Selang-Arsi ware in subtly mottled eggshell colors, brought from New Virginia's version of Manchuria. He'd led a trading-and-exploration expedition there, as a young man.

The paintings were his father's, some excellent Old Masters, some garish as only a Sicilian peasant's idea of beauty could be, but both were reminders of the founder—good and bad the old man's own choices, not bought taste. The floor was marble squares separated by thin strips of lapis, with glowing Eastern rugs beneath the leather-upholstered chairs and settees and tables of rare tropical woods.

Behind the desk was a solid section of wall bearing Salvatore Colletta's portrait, flanked on either side by tall glass doors. Outside was a broad terrace, with a balustrade at its outer rim and man-high stone vases spaced along the inner, tumbling sprays of blossom in hot gold and white and purple down their pale sides; hummingbirds like living jewels of malachite and crimson hovered around them in a blur of wings. He went past the sweet-scented glory and leaned his palms against the stone of the balustrade to look northeastward; he often used this sight to hearten himself.

It was a prideful thing, the view down from where Colletta Hall stood in the first upthrust of the Santa Cruz range's eastern foothills, over the broad lands that acknowledged him lord.

"Vallo du Beddu Cuore," he said softly. It was a fitting name for the Colletta domain. *Valley of Heart's Delight.*

They had called it so on FirstSide, until urban sprawl had eaten the orchards with microchip factories sheathed in black glass and hideously priced little houses, with shopping malls and freeways—he'd seen that on his last trip, and still had nightmares about it.

Here the lower Santa Clara valley stretched off northeastward to San Francisco Bay; the hall's gardens with their tall trees and green lawns, pools and fountains and the cool fire of flowers falling from terrace to terrace; the red roofs of the little town that served Colletta Hall below and the farmsteads of the Settler families beyond. Blocks of plum and almond and apricot trees stood green and regular; in springtime they became a riot of pink and white blossoms that scented the air for miles. Vineyards had turned to rows of shaggy green; grain bowed to the breeze in rippling sheets of gold cut by the dark green of trees planted in lines as windbreaks, ready for next week's harvest; corn stood tall and beginning to tassel; ant-tiny cattle and sheep moved through pastures dotted with wide-spreading oaks; tractors crawled, leaving swaths of rich dark soil upturned, followed by the wheeling flocks of gulls.

The distant ticking of their engines, or the occasional car or truck drawing a white plume along a dirt road, were the only mechanical noises that intruded among the slow sough of the warm June wind through tall trees. Other sounds melted into that music: an ax splitting wood, human voices in speech or song, the buzzing whirr of hummingbird wings from flower to flower. Behind him were the steep low mountains, rolling toward the Pacific and turning green with redwood groves.

"And it's all part of old John Rolfe's fantasy of a Virginia that never really was," he murmured. "A pretty fiction of foxhunting squires and sturdy yeomen. A pleasant dream, and a good place to start. But not to *stop.*"

The true power of the Collettas was in their share of the New Virginia gold and silver and mercury mines, the oil wells and factories and power stations, the Settlers who were affiliates of the Colletta family, the weight he and his allies could pull on the Central Committee . . . and above all, the Colletta share of the Gate revenues and the vast corporate holdings FirstSide. But the Rolfes and their allies dominated the committee and the Commission through it, and imposed a policy of caution that irked him more with every passing year, playing at rustic lordship and keeping the Commonwealth of New Virginia inside its kernel. His hand clenched into a fist on the volcanic stone.

"We must learn to dream more grandly. There is a *world* awaiting us—two!"

A discreet cough brought him round. His personal executive assistant stood there: Angelica McAdams, a plain middle-aged woman of formidable efficiency, whose family had been Colletta affiliates since the 1950s. He was easy enough with her that it didn't embarrass him to be caught talking to himself—making a political speech to himself, in fact.

Probably because it's one I want *to make before the committee, but don't quite dare,* he thought as he nodded to her.

"Mr. Anthony Bosco is here for his appointment, sir."

"Thank you, Angelica. Hold any incoming calls."

Anthony Bosco was third-generation; the Boscos were members of the Thirty Families but only as collaterals, relatives Salvatore Colletta had brought in a few years after the opening of the Gate; and Anthony's mother had been of the Filmer Family. He was an unremarkable young man in his late twenties in a neat brown-silk suit, with carefully combed dark-russet hair, a faint trace of acne scars across his cheekbones and currently a hangdog air.

That broke into a painful smile as he advanced to bow deeply and kiss the Colletta Prime's hand with a murmur of *"Bacciamo le mani";* that was a custom of the Collettas that had spread widely among the Families, like the Rolfes' riding to hounds or the von Traupitzes' student saber duels or the Fitzmorton boar hunts with spears.

"Sir—" he began.

Crack.

"Idiota!" Giovanni snapped, as his hand slapped the young man's face to one side. *"Ricchiune scimunito!"*

Anthony's face paled, save where the fingers had left red prints. Normally Giovanni Colletta spoke English, like everyone else except recent immigrants. It was a sign of extreme danger when he started cursing in the Sicilian dialect picked up from his father in infancy. From outside the charmed circle, being a member of the Families looked more important than being one of a collateral line. From the inside, particularly if you were a *Colletta* collateral, getting the Prime this angry with you could make life intolerable. And when the business you managed for the Prime was a capital crime by Commonwealth law . . .

"Sir, we delivered the materials *exactly* as per the plans. It's—"

"You should have overseen the final distribution, so that news of it did not leak to the American police, and from them to Gate Security. As it was, we have only Gate Security to thank that the American authorities didn't find the goods intact! And only blind luck to thank that Gate Security did not grab *you.*"

"Sir, those people *don't* appreciate having a seller look over their shoulders while they make their own deals. If you want me to oversee them more closely, then you must assign me more shooters. Otherwise they will kill me, and you will have to assign someone else to deal with the matter."

Good, the Colletta thought. *He is no coward. And he dares to remind me that I* cannot *give him more gunmen.*

The Commission controlled Gate transit too closely; only adults of the Thirty Families could travel freely back and forth between the worlds, and even their travel was carefully watched. There were only a limited number of Family members with Gate access he could bring into this . . .

Call it by its right name, he told himself. *It is a conspiracy.*

"That was the last large shipment, in any case," the Colletta said gracefully. "Perhaps the next meetings will be more carefully managed. You may stay; it is possible you may contribute. Say nothing unless I tell you."

Giovanni seated himself behind his desk, pressing a discreet control. A screen slid upward, and he pulled out a drawer and tapped at the controls as it lit. A surveillance camera at the main eastward gate of the hall's gardens showed a convoy of vehicles approaching from the south, the long plume of their dust behind them. The Batyushkov home estate was much farther south, over the Santa Cruz Mountains and down into the northern edge of Monterey Bay. The earlier distributions nearer the Gate had gone to the American majority among the Thirty or to the English, German-Balt, Franco-Algerian and British-African creations. There had been quite a gap between the last of those and the time the Russian Batyushkovs and Afrikaner Versfelds were granted committee status in the 1990s. That meant that they were farther out, in the Parajo Valley and the Los Angeles basin respectively. That seemed to bother the Batyushkovs more than it did the Versfelds; they were also the only two Families whose Primes were still FirstSide born.

Except for the Old Man, of course. Even he had been handing over more and more of his duties to his son Charles in the last two decades, although he seemed determined to make the century mark.

Dimitri Batyushkov came in a small convoy, his own hard-topped six-wheeled Land Rover preceded and followed by open Hummers mounting machine guns. All of them had the double-headed eagle on their doors; the New Virginia Russians had adopted Czarist symbolism, Orthodox piety and Cossack customs with ostentatious zeal, for all that many of them had been KGB and presumably at least nominal Marxists before they met Commission recruiters looking for desperate men. There was a black-robed bearded priest in the Batyushkov's car, for that matter.

Perhaps there is something in the air of the Commonwealth of New Virginia which inclines us to pageantry, Giovanni Colletta thought, and smiled slightly as he spoke to the air.

"Angelica, the refreshments."

It wouldn't do to go down to the door and greet the Batyushkov; he wasn't ready to imply that much equality of status, not quite yet. Nor would it do to insult him by showing himself less than prompt in offering hospitality.

Besides, Russians don't consider any business serious unless it's accompanied by a drink, he thought.

He watched his eldest son walk out the tall carved doors of the hall to greet the Batyushkov; Salvatore Colletta II was *not* in his father's inner circle on this matter; the third-generation scion of the Collettas was too cautious to endorse a plan such as that his father had devised, preferring a quiet life. Giovanni was confident he'd go along when confronted with a fait accompli, and in the meantime greeting a distinguished guest with proper protocol was part of his duties as heir apparent.

The cars came to a halt at the foot of the long stairway, and a servant sprang to open the main car's door. A squad of troopers in sharp-pressed gray Commission Militia uniforms—their Family affiliation marked by Colletta shoulder flashes—brought rifles to present arms. The Batyushkov reviewed them gravely; when he had passed, their commander saluted his opposite number from the Russian's escort and led them and the drivers off to appropriate entertainment. Father Sarducci greeted his Orthodox opposite number with the strained politeness of a cat forced to put up with a strange feline on its territory; doubtless they'd either exchange limping chitchat or end up pulling each other's hair over the *filioque* clause to the Creed, the one Catholics and Orthodox had split on in 1054 amid a flurry of mutual anathemas and excommunications.

Giovanni's smile grew to a shark's grin for an instant at that. His son conducted the Batyushkov and his immediate retainers—two bodyguards in black leather jackets and a technician with a briefcase—to the elevators.

Meanwhile the Hall staff had bustled in, spreading linen

tablecloths and laying out a buffet lunch around the long rosewood meeting table. There was thin-sliced cured wild-boar ham wrapped around ripe figs and melon, caviar in glistening mounds surrounded by artfully arranged sprays of crisp rye toast, prawns grilled with garlic and chili beside equally dainty skewers of spring lamb, colorful salads, oysters fresh in the shells or wrapped in strips of bacon and fried, sliced roast loin of pork stuffed with figs, almonds and olives, breads and cheeses and glistening pastries of kiwi and cream, fruits in glowing piles, wine bottles resting in silver coolers on gleaming shaved ice. It was a meal that could be eaten without servants present; his retired discreetly before the guests arrived.

Another surveillance camera showed them walking up the curving staircase and into the long carpeted hallway outside the master's office, with the Russian's bodyguards and his circling each other like stiff-legged dogs. They settled down to mutual watchfulness, and the Batyushkov and his attendant came through the doors of ebony and silver.

"Dimitri Ivanovich!" Giovanni cried, springing to his feet and walking forward with outstretched hand. "Welcome to my home, my friend. It has been far too long since we met."

The Batyushkov's firm stride missed a half step as he raised his eyes and met those of the portrait behind Giovanni's desk. Behind his affable mask, the Colletta bared his teeth again at the picture's effect; even from his grave, Salvatore Colletta was still fighting for his blood. The two Family Primes shook hands, and kissed each other on the cheek.

The Russian was a thickset man, a few inches shorter than Giovanni but broader, with a wide snub-nosed face and pale blue eyes and an air of straightforward bluntness that was a lie in itself.

"Giovanni Salvatorovich, it has indeed been too long," he said; his English was excellent, though thickly accented. "May I present my nephew, my brother's son, Sergei Ilyanovich? He has met your young collateral, I believe, here and FirstSide."

Not just a technician, then. A tall, slender, sharp-featured man in his early thirties, dark of hair and eye. *I've heard the name.* Sergei was a real scientist, a rarity in the Commonwealth, orphaned when his father was killed fighting in Afghanistan, and raised by Dimitri and his wife.

The younger Russian bowed deeply and kissed the Colletta's hand; Anthony Bosco followed suit with the Batyushkov, and then the juniors shook in the gesture of equals.

"But come," Giovanni said, indicating the table. "Drink; eat; honor my house by using it as your own."

The men seated themselves. Giovanni lifted a small frosted glass of chilled vodka, looked the Batyushkov straight in the eye and said: *"Za nas!"*

He breathed out through his mouth and tossed the cold spirits back, a streak of chill fire down his gullet.

The Russian drank his in the same manner and replied: *"Za nas*—to us, indeed!" Then, with an unfeigned smile: *"Khorosha chertovka.* Damned good drink!"

"From FirstSide," Giovanni said. "Stolichnaya—Dovgan."

"You were well-advised: an excellent brand."

The two men smiled at each other, neither under any illusions that they were bosom friends, but more relaxed; young Sergei opened his leather-covered instrument case and did a quick, discreet check of the office while the Primes conferred.

All in the game, Giovanni thought, putting down the vodka glass and using chased-silver tongs to transfer some of the ham to his plate while the Russian scooped caviar onto rye toast.

Batyushkov showed deference by coming to Colletta Hall and Giovanni's office; Giovanni showed respect by closeting himself with the Batyushkov on equal terms, and taking the effort to learn Russian drinking rituals.

Who knows, they may spread! If there is one thing in which Russians excel, it is drinking, after all.

For that matter, making the Batyushkovs one of the

Thirty Families, with a seat on the committee and a share in the Commission's revenues, was itself a gesture by the established Family lines. Batyushkov had been helpful in recruitment, and in establishing contacts with post-Soviet Russia's burgeoning commercial demimonde; that eased the perennial problem of laundering the Commonwealth's minerals and gems on FirstSide. It had enabled the Commission to step up shipments quite substantially, more than compensating for one more minimum Family share of the take.

Still, there had been no absolute necessity to put him on the committee.

Yet there were several thousand Russians in the Commonwealth now, and they had been very useful in this land-rich, labor-starved economy. Inevitably they were still mostly at the bottom of the occupational pyramid, working in factories, mines, fishing boats, farms. Knowing that one of their own had been raised to the highest circles of power was likely to ease their adjustment to New Virginia's unfamiliar society; and a Russian member in the Thirty Families could jump-start several hundred of his compatriots up the ladder of preferment and patronage.

Or so the Rolfes and their allies thought, Giovanni mused. It *had* worked, all the other times the method was used. *But this time, they have elevated a Prime with wider ambitions.*

Batyushkov glanced at his nephew; the young man nodded. That meant the Colletta's office was clear of bugs planted by the Commission's police, or any of the other Families, as far as he could tell.

"So, Giovanni Salvatorovich, I find that I must apologize," Dimitri said.

He knocked back another glass of the icy vodka; strictly speaking, Giovanni should have matched him drink for drink, but he knew his capacity and the Russian's, and contented himself with a sip of white wine instead. A minor breach of Slavic drinking etiquette and loss of face was preferable to losing his wits.

"A blunder occurred," Giovanni agreed tactfully. "There

is blame enough to go around. As we grow closer to the time of action, the risks increase; they are proportionate to the stakes for which we play."

Dimitri nodded. "You understand, these people we deal with FirstSide may be my compatriots—my former countrymen—but they are not my subordinates. I—we—must persuade and convince them." He sighed, and chewed meditatively for a moment. "That is not merely a matter of money. Money is very persuasive, but for hardheaded, realistic men—"

Translation: a bunch of paranoid a' pinna, Giovanni added to himself.

"—to be persuaded of the reality of a Gate to another world, this is difficult." A rumbling chuckle. "I did not believe it myself, until I stepped through. I thought that the wealthy *Amis* were, how do you say, putting one over on me."

The Russian spread his hands in a deprecatory gesture: "And we cannot, of course, show them directly—anyone who sees the Gate is stuck here in the Commonwealth. It is a system with a built-in fail-safe; Sergei here has been instrumental in convincing them. As of course have your animal specimens, even more than the pictures and videos. Videos can be faked; living animals which are extinct cannot. And, after all, they *have* sent us those personnel we requested. That is the key to our plan."

"If there are no more desertions from the Strike Force," the Colletta said dryly. "If any of *those,* and the weapons they have stolen, are discovered . . ."

The Russian winced slightly. "Yes, well, the *speznatz* discipline is hard for primitives. It will be better after Operation Downfall is complete and we need no longer rely upon them."

"If we get that far," Giovanni Colletta said.

If we can assemble a force strong enough to take the Gate by surprise. And if we can make it stick afterward . . . then we will be the rulers of the Commonwealth. Then there will be changes.

He went on with a smile: "Which of course we will. The time to strike is near. We have only to get through these few months, and it will all be over."

Sergei leaned forward. "With your permission, Uncle Dimitri." The Batyushkov nodded, and the young man went on: "Our . . . associates on FirstSide do, however, have one request. One additional request."

Giovanni smiled behind gritted teeth. If they wanted more money, he would simply tell them that that well was dry.

"They wish to send through several scientists, suitably disguised. To study the Gate."

At that, the Colletta laughed and waved a hand. "By all means," he said. "Let them study to their heart's content."

The Gate was incomprehensible. That was well established.

INTERLUDE
July 15, 1971
Rolfeston
The Commonwealth of New Virginia

"I think you know my associates," John Rolfe said, his voice smooth and friendly. He raised a hand to right and left, toward the men who sat on either side of him behind the long polished table. "Solomon Pearlmutter and Salvatore Colletta."

Think of them as my good and bad angels, he didn't say aloud; his mind threw up a vision of a miniature Sol in a white robe and a tiny red-suited Salvo with a pitchfork, standing on his shoulders and whispering into his ears.

"Yes," said Ralph Barnes, sometime professor of physics. "I think I met your kid at Stanford." He nodded to Pearlmutter, and then turned to Colletta. "And your goons doped my drink and dragged me here."

He was a burly man in a tie-dyed shirt, jeans and moccasins, with long brown hair falling to his shoulders and a trimmed beard. Rolfe thought the whole ensemble looked ridiculous—something like a flaming pansy crossed with a Viking warrior—but apparently it was the fashion among the younger set back on FirstSide these days, and Barnes was in his mid-twenties.

Young to be on the verge of fame, he thought. *In any profession but physics.* From what Sol had told him, most great physicists did their best groundbreaking work between twenty and thirty. *And I suppose it doesn't look much more ridiculous than what some of my Cavalier ancestors affected at court.* The haircut was about what Charles I's courtiers had worn, beard ditto, and at least Barnes wasn't sporting high heels, lace and beauty patches.

"Yes, I think I could come up with something to explain the phenomenon," Barnes went on. "Now that I've had some time and equipment to study the Gate. Outta sight."

He closed his eyes, obviously deep in thought. Then he opened them again, staring across the room at John Rolfe. The master of the Commonwealth forced himself to relax.

By God, to control *the Gate! To know what it is, and how to make more!* Vistas of fire and glory opened beyond the eyes of his mind, worlds for the taking—

"Nice place you've got here," the scientist went on. "Too bad I won't see much of it."

Rolfe's eyes narrowed, and he felt a stirring of unease; he hadn't commanded men for thirty years without learning how to read them. The beard and hair emphasized the man's massive foursquare build, the thick forearms, and the hands like a builder's or farmer's, spadelike and callused. Not at all what he'd thought of when the word "professor" came to mind, but Sol's agents had been extremely careful. It wasn't easy to find a young, brilliant researcher who wouldn't be too badly missed, but Barnes had a reputation for eccentricity, as well as genius. For it wouldn't be utterly out of character for him to . . . what was the phrase FirstSide? *Drop out?*

"Real nice," Barnes went on, nodding to the tall windows that let in a scent of sea and flowers on the warm summer air. "Pity I'm not going to see much of it. It'd be interesting."

"And why aren't you going to be seeing more of it, Dr. Barnes?" Rolfe said in a soft, chill tone, leaning forward with hand over hand and his elbows braced on the polished rosewood of his desk.

Without false modesty he knew that he was a strong-willed man, and a frightening one when he chose to be. He'd daunted brave men before this. Now his eyes found the younger man's brown gaze, and saw no fear there at all, and a stubbornness to match his own. Pearlmutter sighed and put a hand to his forehead, muttering something like *gevalt* under his breath.

"Because I'm not going to give a fascist bastard like you that sort of power, which means you'll probably kill me," Barnes said cheerfully. "Maybe I can't do anything about you getting *this* world in your clutches, but I'm not going to give you an infinite series of them to play with."

"Infinite?" Rolfe said, raising a brow.

"Of course. Now that I've seen the Gate, the only thing that makes sense is that the Big Bang was really a quantum fluctuation, the beginning of a universe in a series; in fact that explains the dark matter problem. A standing waveform drawing on zero energy to— Oh, you're a *tricky* fascist bastard, aren't you? Nearly got me going there."

Rolfe smiled thinly. "More tricky than you know, Dr. Barnes. I know you feel an understandable resentment at being, ah, shanghaied here"—a blaze of pure rage confronted him, all the stronger for being wordless. He'd counted on the man's curiosity overcoming anything else, combined with promises of rewards. Now he'd have to fall back on threats, and he didn't think those would work very well. He went on, his voice suave—"and normally we don't do that, unless someone stumbles across the secret of the Gate and it's the only alternative to killing him. But we've never been able to get many first-rate scientists here. You'll understand we're anxious to develop some control, some knowledge, of the

Gate. After all, our lives and fortunes depend on its functioning." He turned the smile charming. "And I assure you I know better than to deny an able man his share."

Barnes snorted and crossed his arms. "No dice. Hey, asshole, a question for you: Did you ever take lessons from Nixon?"

Rolfe blinked his eyes closed for a second, controlling his temper. "No, in fact, Dr. Barnes, I did not. For one thing I'm not a Quaker, and neither were any of my ancestors. And I wasn't in the navy."

"Naw, your folks were slave traders, right?" Barnes said. "I said it once: No dice." After a moment that stretched: "And yeah, you can call in those goons outside to kill me, or work me over. That won't get you much physics done, man. And beating me up won't, either. It ain't like digging a ditch or picking cotton on your fucking plantation."

"Tobacco," Rolfe corrected absently. "My family grew tobacco and raised horses. Well, that raises the question of why I *should* bother to keep you around, Dr. Barnes . . . if you're not useful as a physicist. Or perhaps you could be useful in another career . . . gold mining, perhaps?"

"Yeah, send me to the mines. Lot of good *that* will do you."

A quiet chuckle came from the corner. "I think I better get involved here, Cap'n."

Barnes's eyes swiveled around to the small, dark, graying man sitting in the corner. The scientist still didn't look frightened, but he did look wary—the way a man might, confronted with a small, swift, poisonous snake.

"Thing is, Professor," Salvatore Colletta said, "the cap'n, he's a *civile*—a gentleman; and Sol here, he's the kind who'll pick a bug up and throw it out the window insteada swattin' it. I ain't, you know? That's got its drawbacks, which surprised me when I found out, but it sort of gives me advantages too. Like maybe, yeah, a working-over with the rubber hoses wouldn't get you doing this physics stuff right; you could go through the motions and say nothin' was working.

On the other hand . . . maybe there's organs you're fond of? Or people? Your mother still alive, *dottore?*"

Barnes began to come out of the chair and froze as Colletta's hand moved with the speed of a striking mantis. An automatic pistol appeared in it, the muzzle gaping like a cavern and pitted with use; the rest of his short, slight body stayed relaxed, lounging at ease. Rolfe gave a small quiet snort. Sometimes in the midst of the inter-Family maneuvering, you forgot just how deadly the little man could be in person. That would be a mistake.

"He's no use to us dead, Salvo," Rolfe said. To Pearlmutter, in a soothing tone: "Don't worry, Sol. Relax."

Rolfe sighed, resting his chin on his thumbs and thinking. *Let's see . . .* "The problem is, I think the good doctor here would call my bluff," he said at last.

Colletta shot him a resentful black-eyed glance. "I ain't bluffin', Cap'n."

"Yes, but I would be," Rolfe replied.

Salvatore Colletta gave a sour grunt, holstered the gun and stood, adjusting his suit jacket and brushing lint off one sleeve, and taking a cigarette out of a gold case. He shrugged and lit it, puffing and going on: "Then I've got things to do. See ya, Cap'n. That soft heart of yours is gonna kill you someday."

Colletta left; Pearlmutter followed, shrugging and spreading his hands as he passed in a well-I-did-my-best gesture. Rolfe turned to Barnes, his mouth quirking slightly.

"I'm a ruthless man, Dr. Barnes," he said. "And if I thought it expedient, I would have you killed without hesitation; by the time I was your age, I'd seen and inflicted enough death that it became fairly trivial to me. There are, however, limits . . . at least for me. I've never found Salvo to have any."

"I can believe it," Barnes said. He cocked his head. "Why didn't you try bluffing me?"

Rolfe made a single spare, elegant gesture. "Respect."

"Respect?"

"I knew that you wouldn't cave in to a simple threat, and

there would be no point in it if I wasn't prepared to follow through." He cocked his head and examined Barnes again, openly this time. "Experience does confer some benefits—the ability to tell the difference between bluster and the real thing among them."

Barnes looked at him for a moment, then nodded grudgingly. "Well, you're a fascist bastard, but I suppose you draw the line at torture."

Rolfe smiled, and Barnes blinked in startled alarm. "Oh, not at all. I've had men tortured—during the war, for example. If it was a choice between my men's lives and the Geneva Convention . . . well, there's a time an officer should walk around the hill and let someone like Salvo handle things. But I don't inflict pain for amusement, or to settle a grudge. Or just to get something I'd like, but can do without."

"You *are* a bastard," Barnes said.

"Yes, Dr. Barnes, I am. But you'd better hope that I'm a long-lived one. Salvo doesn't like being balked, and unlike me he *does* hold grudges."

He chuckled a little at the brief look of alarm that passed over the young physicist's face. *And good-cop bad-cop may be a cliché, but it works.* "And what will you do here, if I let you live? Please abandon any thoughts of teaching at *our* university, if you won't cooperate over the Gate."

"Oh," Barnes said. "I think I might like to open a burger joint. I figure you owe me the seed money."

CHAPTER FOUR

Sacramento, California
June 2009

FirstSide

The park along the American River was one of Sacramento's better spots. It stretched along both sides for twenty-four miles from the junction with the Sacramento River, and it was big enough to form a fairly considerable corridor for wildlife and birds. Tom parked his battered compact, paid the admission fee and looked around for the sleek little two-seater Italian job Adrienne Rolfe had driven to meet him at Maharani's. It wasn't there, and his chest gave an abrupt lurch; then he saw her stretching on the grass beyond the pavement, under the shade of a big willow tree. She was doing splits, then curling over to each side with her chin pressed to her knee and fingers touching around the sole of that foot. A water bottle and fanny pack lay against the base of the tree.

Ballet training for sure, he thought, watching her for a moment with sheer pleasure, then walking forward past a Ford Windstar.

Discovery Park was the western end of the riverside trail, at the mouth of the American River where it joined the Sacramento, and just north of downtown. It was flat—this was a spillover zone during the late winter when the river crested—but pleasantly landscaped, with open grassy fields, a band of alder and willow along the riverbank proper where it swelled out into a small lake, and some impressive valley oaks. A double-crested cormorant was sunning itself on a stump in the hot brightness beside the lake, with its black double-V wings spread and its snaky neck curved in an S, altogether looking rather like an organic Stealth Fighter. Pelicans and gulls rested out on the surface of the water; the sun was still high at five-thirty on a summer's day, and the bands of strollers, kids Rollerblading and happy dogs leaping after Frisbees added to the pleasure of the scene. Still too urban for his taste, but a lot better than concrete and steel, and it smelled of water and fresh greenery.

The background faded as Adrienne looked up at him and smiled. *Lot of megawattage there,* he thought, smiling back. *If they could hook that up to the grid, California's energy problems would be solved.*

"Hi," he said. "Didn't spot your car."

"Oh, I walked," she said. "Thought you might give me a lift back to Amber House afterward, and perhaps we could catch something to eat."

"I'd be delighted," he said sincerely, and began his own stretching.

"Want some help on that?" she asked, when he was seated and bending forward.

"Thanks," he replied.

Adrienne went down on one knee behind him, pushing properly—a forearm just below the point between his shoulder blades, and a hand just above the small of his back. You were supposed to bend at the waist with your spine nearly straight, and try to lay chest and chin on the ground before you. He gave a grunt when the tightness in his back and hamstrings told him to stop, and held it while he controlled his breathing.

"That must have been alarming," Adrienne said.

He could feel her breath on the skin of his neck, and the pressure of her hand and arm on the knotted scar tissue where three 7.62mm rounds had punched through his body armor. *In-*

teresting that she knows what a bullet scar feels like, he thought.

Fortunately they hadn't penetrated very deeply, and God bless Kevlar and ceramic inserts for that. It *had* been alarming, afterward; at the time his first thought had been worry for the mission. The Rangers didn't leave anyone behind, and humping *his* carcass out would be a genuine burden. Luckily they'd pretty quickly won the firefight that followed the ambush, and then had called for a dustoff. For an instant he was out of the hot Californian sunshine; the wind was bitter and cold and intensely dry, flicking grit and thin dirty snow into his eyes as he lay and let the medic cut the harness off. Explosions and the rattle of gunfire echoed off the great gaunt slopes of the bare mountains. . . .

"Up," he said, and shook his head as he eased back and got his feet under him. "Nothing too dramatic," he went on as he rose. "We here heading up a gully, a dry wash. Had to be done, but the enemy were *real* good at hiding, even from our sensors; the recon drone said the way was clear. I was on point, and *I* didn't see 'em either."

"You remind me of Granddad," she said. "He doesn't talk much about Okinawa, either. Let's go!"

They set out, running along the edge of the bicycle path to let the odd cyclist or Segway rider go by.

Now, that's weird, he thought. *Why on earth ride one of those things* here, *when you could walk?*

The little two-wheel computerized electric scooters were fine for getting around cities, for distances where a car was too much and shank's mare too little; he wished there were more of them, and fewer lawsuits and regulations to keep them out of towns, to cut down on smog and congestion. But what earthly purpose was served by standing on a platform and letting gyros and computers and electric motors do half the fun part *here?*

"Strange," he said, indicating one of them with his chin.

There was an art to talking while running; you couldn't do too much of it, and you had to synchronize your breathing.

"Yes," she replied. "That's like using a machine to live and hanging yourself in the closet."

Hmmm, he thought. *I approve the sentiment . . . but why doesn't she ever use certain contractions? The next "yeah" I hear from her will be the first.*

Aloud he went on: "And that's a lazuli bunting, I think."

The bird gave a *pit . . . pit . . . pit* as they went by, followed by a series of rising and falling warbles. It was a male, the head and upper parts a pale powdery blue with an iridescent sheen, very much like lapis lazuli, the wings blue until a white bar crossed them, and the chest orange fading to pale cream on the belly. Tom thought they were nearly as pretty as hummingbirds, and it was a pity they were so rare. It was a little odd that Adrienne gave it only a casual glance; it wasn't that she didn't know her birds. In the next mile she picked out as many as he; one was a black-headed grosbeak, a spectacular little black-and-orange bird with a fast, sweet warble.

"So," she said after a few minutes of companionable silence broken only by the *plop* of a fish in the river and the sound of their feet. "What do you read? I'll give odds you do."

"Ah . . ." He did; the problem was his tastes were a little plebian. "A lot of wildlife and biology . . . some history now and then . . . If you mean fiction, mostly SF and mysteries."

"Me too!" she said. "I was mad for Tolkein as a teenager, of course. Nowadays De Lint, Martin—and Turtledove and Williams, too; it's not all Big Fat Fantasies."

"Anderson?" he said, and she nodded. "Bujold? Baxter?"

She countered: "Dick Francis?"

"James Lee Burke?"

"Ford Maddox Roberts?"

"And the classics—Christie . . ."

They laughed and continued the game—she called it name-dropping in a good cause—until they reached a bridge that spanned the river across a little islet. They stopped there to catch their breath, and to lean on the railing and watch the water flow past, green and cool-looking below. Daddy longlegs skimmed over the surface, and there was the odd predatory glitter of dragonflies.

"Too bad we can't just dive in," she said, wiping her face with a wristband.

"Inviting, but I wouldn't advise it," he replied, with a wordless gesture eastward.

There was a lot of Central Valley in that direction, and that was the birthplace of industrialized agriculture. God alone knew the full list of things that were sprayed or pumped onto the fields, and then drained into this water; the ones Tom knew about were bad enough. He'd met farmers who kept special gardens for their own use, upwind of the fields where they grew vegetables for sale. Things were better than they had been, and there were more fish below than there would have been in the year of his birth. He still wouldn't eat anything that came out of this river, though.

She shook her head angrily as they started back. "That's one thing I hate about this . . . about the modern world. The feeling that I'm taking in all those chemicals every moment, and there's nothing I can do about it." She gave a shudder that seemed only half-assumed.

"Nothing much we *can* do about it," he said, a little surprised. *Bit vehement, surely?* "Although we're both trying, in our way."

"Still . . . have you ever thought what California might be . . . have been . . . like? One city, and a few towns, a scattering of farms and ranches in places that don't need massive engineering to function. All the power from small-scale hydro and geothermal . . ."

He laughed. "It's an appealing fantasy, but if I let myself dwell on it, it would drive me completely crazy," he said. "One of those 'if I were king' things."

She smiled. "We all do our bit, though. I think I'm making progress convincing a couple of key legislators that something has to be done about the illegal animal trade. It's coming back, and strongly; one of the unfortunate by-products of prosperity."

"Damned right," he said. "Any progress on the LA thing from your side?"

"Nothing so far," she said. "We're combing through the transit records at our Oakland facility, cargo manifests and so forth, but of course it would have been covered by fake documentation."

"Bet the publicity doesn't help," he said. "There was more coverage of the LA thing than I'd have wanted."

"Yes, and the TV people did their usual distort-and-get-wrong," she said. "Bizarre indeed. There was even something about extinct animals! Did you turn up any dinosaurs or saber-tooths?"

"No, just rare ones—and a live California condor, believe it or not."

"A genuine California condor is impressive enough. Quite a nice bit of knight-errantry, rescuing a *Gymnogyps californianus,* no less. To hell with beautiful princesses."

He chuckled; the run was starting to make his lungs burn a bit, but it was a good feeling. He paced the words to the rise and fall of his barrel chest: "Not exactly extinct," he said. "Not that that was any credit to the poachers; they were trying hard enough."

She managed to glow at him while running, and he smiled to himself at his instinctive urge to preen. *I'm no more immune than the next man to showing off before a pretty girl,* he thought, and went on: "Yeah, and a damned strange bird it was; too *clean.*"

"Clean?" she said, frowning.

"No lead, no pesticides—and strange. The San Diego Zoo people had its DNA tested. It wasn't related to any of the other condors, which . . ."

It was a relief to talk to somebody about the aspects that had been teasing at his mind. When he was finished they ran in silence for ten minutes or so; he glanced aside from time to time, watching her frown in concentration.

"I think your friend Martinez's explanation is the most likely one," she said after a long moment. "Excluding time travel, that is! But if there is *one* condor from an unknown breeding population, it's nearly certain that there are more. And the poachers know where they are, and might well kill some while they're trying to capture them. They're not likely to be experts, or very careful."

Despite the heat of the day and the sweat that was running down his body and plastering the T-shirt to his muscular torso, Tom felt his blood run cold.

"Yeah," he said. "I was afraid of that."

"Best bet would be to have people out looking, and beat the poachers to it," she said thoughtfully. "I can pass the word to HQ and have our contacts in the Sierra Club and some of the birding clubs keep an eye out. If they knew there actually might be unexpected condors, they'd be a lot more likely to find them, right?"

"Good idea!" he enthused. *Lord, tell me I haven't become a* complete *bureaucrat, and started discounting whatever nonofficials can do.* "Hey, we're back!"

"How time flies when you're having fun!" Adrienne said. "Just a second—I have to make a phone call."

Tom walked up and down while he waited, cooling gradually—or cooling as much as you could on a Sacramento afternoon in June; it had the great merit of being better than July or August, but that was about it. He caught a few words of what Adrienne was saying, particularly toward the end of it, when she raised her voice.

"... cuz ... condors! ... need to know ... plenty, and ASAP. Hand-carry ... the Old Man ... Nostradamus ... I said hand-carry and I meant it, Filmer! Just do it!"

Evidently the Pacific Open Landscapes League ran a tight ship; the tone in her voice took him back to his time in the Rangers, especially the last snap. She was scowling slightly as she walked toward him.

"The good thing about a family business is that it's full of people you've known all your life," she said, a waspish note in her voice. "And the *bad* thing about a family business is that it's full of people you've known all your life."

Tom chuckled. *I'd find that command voice fairly persuasive even if you* were *a kid sister,* he thought silently. Aloud he went on: "Well, if we're going to get something to eat, I need to get home and shower first. Otherwise I'm afraid I'd put everyone else off their feed, unless it's a restaurant for plow-mules."

"Hmmm," she said, and came closer, looking up into his face and sliding an arm around his neck. "You wouldn't happen to have a change in your car, would you?"

This time he managed to avoid flushing. In fact, he grinned; and a kiss seemed quite natural. It *did* emphasize their mutual stickiness.

"As a matter of fact . . ." he said, looking down into the leaf-green eyes, "I do."

"Well, there's self-confidence. And this *is* a town where you can get good take-out pizza, so . . ."

❋ ❋ ❋

The outside of Amber House was pleasant, a big white-painted home built back in the expansive years just before 1914, linked to two others like it. That was on Twenty-second Street, only eight blocks from the Capitol, but in a neighborhood of quiet streets overshadowed with huge trees. Adrienne went ahead of him, opening the door of the suite. He followed, the pizza box in one hand, his bag in the other, and looked around. It was elegant, in a carefully old-fashioned way: big iron-framed four-poster bed, king-sized and draped in sheer curtains; sofa, dressing table, lots of burgundy and gold—and with a name of its own.

The Renoir Room, if you please, Tom thought. *I suppose one could get used to this.*

He could see through into a marble-tiled bathroom with a separate shower stall and two-person Jacuzzi. There was a slight scent of wax polish and an herbal sachet. It wasn't exactly what he'd have picked, even if he could afford to drop two c-notes a day for bed-and-breakfast and the fresh chocolate-chip cookie on a little plate by the turned-down sheets of the bed.

But it'll certainly do, he thought. "Not bad," he went on

aloud, conscious of a slight tightness in his throat. *Hell, you're not a teenager on his first heavy date, for God's sake!* he told himself sternly.

A bottle of wine was resting in a silver cooler on the table by the sofa, with two glasses. He looked at her and quirked a brow slightly as he set the pizza box down beside it.

"You're not the only one capable of foresight," Adrienne said gaily, tossing her key on an antique armoire and walking toward the bathroom, peeling off her T-shirt as she went. "And now, desmellification. I'll go first, since you'll be quicker."

He fought down an impulse to suggest that taking a shower together was even more economical of time; that would be a bit premature and presumptuous. *Do not spoil things now!* he told the part of himself that was still governed exclusively by hormones and instinct. It was a slightly smaller part of his psyche overall than when he was twenty-six, or sixteen, but not all *that* much smaller; and it had been quite a while.

And you've never, not even as an impossibly horny teenager, had a woman hit you this way. So you will *remain in control. I don't think there's much doubt about where this evening's going to end up, either.*

Besides, he was enjoying himself hugely, more than he could remember doing for years. *Roy was right; I've been hit hard and bad.* Raw physical attraction was there in plenty, but he genuinely enjoyed her company. . . . *And her sense of humor, and her attitudes, and her taste in books, and even the weird stuff about her relatives,* he thought. *I can compromise on the music.* She was evidently a classics-and-folk enthusiast, sixties revival stuff, to his old-time country and alternative rock. They had some overlap; she loved the Dixie Chicks too, particularly "Goodbye Earl," and the Poyns, and Enya, and WaterBird, and Pint & Dale.

The water hissed on; his imagination filled in pictures. For that matter, since she'd left the door open, he didn't have to rely completely on that. He poured glasses of the wine; if he remembered correctly, it was supposed to "breathe" awhile before you drank it. Tom himself had been brought

up a beer man, when he drank; years in California had taught
him to enjoy wine, but he didn't pretend to be a connoisseur
or an expert. In fact, he found the more pretentious type of
wine enthusiast a bore—

"Penny for them," Adrienne said.

She was wearing a cloth bathrobe, and drying her hair as
she spoke. The robe stuck to her in interesting parts, and
when she lowered the towel the loose-curled bronze hair
fanned out around her face like an umber cloud, slightly
darkened by its dampness.

"Woof," Tom said. "Woof, woof, *woof.* Thoughts? You
need to *ask?*" Then he grinned. "I was thinking about the
wine breathing. But isn't red supposed to be at room temperature?"

"*European* room temperature: fifty-five degrees Fahren-
heit," she said, taking a glass from his hand and sipping.
"That rule was made by Frenchmen—and northern Frenchmen at that, who lived in stone barns where you had to stand
in the fireplace to get over sixty degrees. Provençals and Italians always put the bottle in a bucket of water to cool a little.
Speaking of water . . ."

He went into the bathroom and under the rush of hot water. It felt good to get the stickiness off his skin. Looking
down as he soaped himself, he thought seriously for a second of turning the water on cold.

But then, it probably wouldn't do any good, anyway, he
thought. *Let's go, boy!*

One of the advantages of a Ranger-style crop haircut was
that it dried easily.

When he sat down beside her on the couch, Adrienne fed
him a bite of the slice of pizza she was holding in one hand.
He scooped up one himself and returned the favor; it was an
extremely good thin-crust, done in a brick oven, and he was
hungry. That was a pity, since he hardly tasted it at all, or the
wine. They smiled into each other's eyes, and then hers took
on a hint of sadness for an instant.

"There's only one problem," she said. His eyes flickered
toward his carrying bag, and she laughed a little. "No, that's

all taken care of. The problem is I really like you. As a person."

"That's a problem?" he said.

"It could be, later," she said somberly.

"To hell with later, then," he replied, and gathered her to him.

* * *

"Rosy-fingered dawn calls," a voice breathed in his ear.

"Hnnnn!" he grunted, and sat upright.

For a long moment he didn't know where he was. Then memory rushed in. A long slow smile lit his face, and he ran a hand up under Adrienne's chin. Evidently she'd been up for a while, since her hair had been washed and dried, and she was already dressed in an expensively conservative jacket-and-skirt outfit with a cream silk shirt. She took his hand, kissed the palm, and slid down toward him.

"Breakfast," she said, a few breathless moments later.

He grinned, and continued. She made a wordless sound, half passion and half exasperation. "Dammit, I have to run! They want me back in Berkeley by nine-thirty."

"Duty calls in its shrill unpleasant voice," he agreed, looking at the clock; six A.M., and dawn *was* just stealing through the east-facing windows with rosy fingers. "You must move like a cat, Adri. I'm usually not a light sleeper."

"Cat yourself," she said, wiggling her eyebrows. "Tom the tomcat."

"That makes you my queen," he said, standing and sweeping a bow, then striking a pose and flexing when she ran her eyes up and down him again.

"I'd say you were boasting, but it's all true," she said, as he picked a robe up off the floor and donned it. Then: "God, but I wish we could stay together all day."

They looked at each other, the laughter dying.

"Me too," he said, and then forced his voice back to lightness. "Breakfast."

It went far too quickly, even while they made arrangements to meet again on the weekend. When she left, the electricity that had been keeping him running went too, and he realized that he'd had only three hours' sleep that night. He poured another cup of coffee and took it into the bathroom, looking at himself in the tall mirror. There were circles under his eyes, and he probably smelled disgusting. His teeth could stand brushing, too, and she'd still kissed him good-bye. . . .

"This," he said to his image, "has all been absolutely incredible. And you want to see her again, very badly. Very, very badly."

Which meant that Roy probably had it right: He'd been hit hard and bad. When you'd just gone to bed with a woman and she seemed *more* interesting, there was definitely a lot more involved than the libido. When you couldn't think of anything else but her . . .

He grinned whitely at his reflection and gave a double thumbs-up. A shower shocked him back toward normal wakefulness, although it did sting slightly on the scratches on his shoulder blades. That prompted a memory of her fingers there, and her heels stroking down from the small of his back. . . .

"And it's not often that guys my size get a murmured 'you're so sweet,'" he told himself aloud. "Pure discrimination, but we don't. Only this time I did."

He was still whistling when he came out of the elevator at headquarters. Roy Tully was there, with a Styrofoam cup of coffee in each hand—not likely to be anything as good as the fresh-brewed in the carafe at the Amber House, though.

Tom extended a finger that looked as if it could punch through sheet metal. "Don't ask, Roy. Not a word. Or I turn your head around until you're looking at the part of your anatomy you keep your brains and morals in. *Capisce?*"

"Capisce, amigo," Tully said, with a lewd grin and a wink that left Tom torn between carrying out his threat and laughing. "The bossman wants to see us."

Their supervisor occupied one of the corner offices. Henry Yasujiru was in his late fifties, blocky and impassive, with gray streaks on the sides of his raven-black hair; a neat man, formal and precise. Tom disliked him, without being entirely sure why. The office was as spare and unadorned as its occupant, with only three pictures: one of Yasujiru's father in Italy, wearing the badge of the 442nd—a Japanese-American outfit that had collected more medals per man than any other Allied unit; one of Yosemite; and one of his mother as a young woman in front of a big Carpenter Gothic house somewhere in the Bay Area.

He began abruptly. "The affair in Los Angeles was less than satisfactory."

Tully nodded. "Yessir, no doubt about that. Except for the condor Tom managed to get out."

Tom nodded gravely himself, carefully not smiling. Roy wasn't brown-nosing, but the carefully calculated razor edge of sarcasm in his voice would sail past Yasujiru like a beam of invisible energy.

"The condor is irregular," Yasujiru said. "Most irregular. I do not see that we have achieved anything by becoming involved, Warden Christiansen. The source of the material remains elusive."

The supervisor was holding a transcript of the San Diego Zoo's report, as well as the one he'd turned in himself after he got back to Sacramento; Tom could see that the odd digital fantasy photograph from the warehouse was there as well.

The older man went on: "Our jurisdiction only extends to material from endangered species secured within California."

Tom and Roy exchanged the briefest of glances out of the corner of their eyes. They both knew the bureaucratic impulse to avoid getting involved in anything unusual; here it was clashing with the equally powerful urge to get involved in anything remotely related to the organization's mandate.

The mighty demon Cover Your Ass makes war with the evil spirit known as Build Your Empire, Tom thought.

"The condor is definitely of the Californian type," Tom said. "And the sea-otter pelts probably came from this state."

Yasujiru nodded reluctantly. "But what use is our participation if we cannot offer any information of our own?"

"We'll have to find the poachers, after the middlemen are closed down," Tom said. "And if we aren't engaged with the operations, they may be able to scatter and avoid us—any delay in getting full information would be fatal."

Another long silence. "Very well, then."

"Thanks, Chief!" Tom said enthusiastically.

"I'd like to see this again, if I could, Mr. Yasujiru," Roy added, snaffling the copy of the Aztec Grateful Dead off his senior's desk.

"I hope there will be more . . . substantial results from the San Francisco operation," Yasujiru said dubiously.

"You can count on us, Chief," Tully said before the older man could object, shepherding Tom out like a corgi with a mastiff. "The whole thing will be resolved."

"Phew!" he went on, as they made their exit. "Resolved and tied up with a pretty red-tape bow. Something has put fear in the heart of Fearless Leader."

"I think he's getting weirded out," Tom said, as they checked their Berrettas and made sure their SOU identification was at hand. For this trip they were dressed to look nondescript, jeans and T-shirts and loose shirts over that to hide the holsters. Tully's shirt was lime green with little dancing orange sea otters dressed in top hats and bow ties and brandishing walking sticks, Tom's a plaid check worn soft with use.

"He likes everything aboveboard and respectable," Roy said, and handed Tom the photograph. "This is turning out to be a seriously *un*respectable investigation. Come have a look at this bit of historical reconstruction when you're through with Fart, Barf and Itch."

Tom looked it over while he phoned Sarah Perkins and finalized the meet with the FBI agent. There was a puzzled frown on his face when he put down the receiver.

"You know, this smells, Kemosabe. I looked it over yesterday and it's just as fucking odd today," Roy said.

"I know it is; and who are you calling asshole, Tonto?" Which was what *Kemosabe* meant.

"I'll stop when you stop calling me *idiot*," Tully replied—which was what *tonto* actually meant. "But seriously, asshole, this thing is *strange*. Weirder than you described it in the report."

"Obviously, idiot."

"No, in *non*obvious ways," Tully said. "Here, take a look." He pulled out a magnifying glass. "Look at Mr. Cardiodectomy Is Part of My Cultural Identity there."

Tom did; he hadn't looked all that closely before, and Roy had an eye for detail work, as well as a mind that worked slantwise at things where Tom often just bulled ahead.

"Hmmm. Looks pretty ordinary, Mexican guy, middle-aged, except that he had a *really* bad case of acne once."

"Not acne. You don't get acne on your arms or gut like that. Look closer."

Hmmm, Tom thought.

There *was* a scattering of pits across the arms and stomach below the T-shirt, and on the man's muscular, scarred hands as well as on his face, or what you could see of it behind the mask. Which meant . . .

"Smallpox," he said quietly.

"Yeah. Which has been extinct for what? Thirty years, most places? I saw a couple of old guys with scars like that in Somalia during my spell of humanitarian intervention and Skinny-slaughtering. Wait a minute . . ."

Tully looked at his watch to check that they had the time, then did a quick search—all their computers had the latest Britannica installed. The "Images" section of the article showed several photographs of smallpox scarring; the resemblance was unmistakable.

"Yeah," Tully said. "Last known active case, Somalia, 1977. Thirty years and change. So what's it doing in this picture? And take a look at the blood pooling on the floor there."

"Looks like a pretty good imitation. It even has flies."

"Exactly. Not many get *that* careful, even in these days of universal CGI. And look at the *shit* all over that altar, and around the bodies. Nobody puts that in, even when they're going all hyperrealistic."

Tom felt a crawling at the back of his head and down between his shoulder blades. He'd seen enough dead bodies to know that was one of the things you remembered, and which didn't get into movies.

"Hell, you're not saying this sacrifice is *real?*"

"I'm not saying a goddamned thing, except that *he*"—Tully stabbed a finger at the high priest holding up knife and heart— "had smallpox, and *they*" —he moved it to the tumbled bodies—"look like the real thing, dead-and-disenhearted-wise."

Tom laid down the magnifying glass. "Poachers I can believe. Poachers with time travel I don't."

"You're the one who reads that sci-fi stuff," Tully said. "I'm just pointing out the facts."

Which would account for the ivory and pelts and the excessively clean condor and— No, stop it, Christiansen! Time travel is scientific nonsense, self-contradictory. And time travelers would have better things to do with their time than smuggle endangered-species products into twenty-first-century California!

"It's definitely more weird shit, though," Tom said aloud, thoughtfully. "In a case that's full of it."

"Like those investigating. Let's get on our way. Got an appointment with F, B and I and hopefully we're going to make arrests this time. Nothing like sweating a suspect to get some real facts."

INTERLUDE
October 29, 1962
Rolfe Manor
The Commonwealth of New Virginia

I wonder why people have taken to calling them the Thirty Families? John Rolfe thought. *Only twenty-eight, so far.*

The first meeting of the Rolfe Hunt every year had become a central part of the Commonwealth's social calendar, and all its brand-new ruling class attended, unless caught beyond the Gate by press of business. This autumn very few had missed the occasion here, not while the empires back on FirstSide snarled at each other in the Caribbean and the city-smashing weapons waited on a hair trigger.

At least "The Commonwealth of New Virginia" took, he thought with a wry smile as he took a glass of white wine from a tray and murmured thanks to the girl who carried it. Her father farmed part of this land for the Rolfes, and he made a point of being punctiliously polite to the Settlers affiliated with his family. Apart from being the right thing to do—his father had gotten the importance of manners into him early, with a belt when necessary—in this labor-short economy it was also common sense. Not to mention the political benefits.

The first foxhunt came in late October, after the majority of the grape harvest was in, but before you got much really chilly-wet weather. Rain wouldn't stop the hunt later in the year, but better weather made the social aspects easier. The tables had been set out on the lawns of Rolfe Hall, where it stood looking southward down the Napa Valley; the hills showed to either side, and Mount Saint Helena loomed green with oak and Douglas fir and redwood behind the big Georgian manor house. It was just getting on to three o'clock and the sky was blue after yesterday's rain, with a mild pleasant warmth; the hills to either side were turning green, which was a relief after the brown-gold of the Californian summer. Southward past the edge of the ha-ha—a hidden brick-lined dropoff that served to keep livestock off the lawns without a fence to break the view—the leaves in the vineyards were putting on their autumn clothes in fields edged with Lombardy poplar and Italian cypress.

They glowed in every color from pale gold to deep wine red, turning the fields to a dimpled Persian carpet. The Eastern and Rocky Mountain maples he'd planted here back in '47—several years before the house was started—were tall enough now to add to the symphony of color, scarlet and orange and yellow. Beyond that stretched the yellow of harvested grain fields, and pasture studded with great spreading oaks.

Everyone was here, even ones like Sol Pearlmutter and Andy O'Brien who rode like sacks of potatoes and hated the whole business. The whole pink-coated crowd was circulating as the late posthunt luncheon got under way, socializing and deal making and what Sol called schmoozing; Pearlmutter and his affiliation carefully avoiding von Traupitz and his, and vice versa. Servants were bustling up with trays of appetizers and drinks, and the long table glowed with centerpieces of roses and petunias and rhododendrons. The cheeks of the guests were flushed with country air and exercise, and there was a faint but unmistakable smell of horses among the cut grass and flowers, though all the mounts had been led away to the stables tucked out of sight to the west.

His eldest son Charles came toward him, leading a certain guest. John Rolfe hid his smile of pride behind a grave nod. The fifteen-year-old was nearly his father's height, already five-foot-nine. He would be taller when he had his full growth, and a bit broader; his hair was darker, a brown touched with russet, and his eyes hazel. Right now his face was a little stiff with the responsibility—Charles was a good lad, intelligent and hardworking, if anything a little too conscious of his duties as a Rolfe and the eldest son.

A bit shy, I think, his father thought. *And more serious than I was at his age. Less of a wild streak.*

"Thank you for showing Lord Chumley around, Charles," he said aloud.

"My pleasure, sir," Charles said.

"And now you're free to seek company younger and prettier," Rolfe replied with a smile, letting it grow a little at the boy's blush.

"My apologies for not showing you around personally," he said to the older man when young Charles was lost amid the crowd. "The news about the Cuban crisis has been rather disturbing and I've been keeping close tabs through our contacts on FirstSide. None of the missiles there could reach California . . . but there might be a Soviet submarine off the coast. Or even inside the bay."

"Too right," the other man said. "Still, we're safe enough here."

"Yes. But it's been difficult, keeping our FirstSide operations going while evacuating everyone from the Families here to the Commonwealth. I trust you've not been unduly inconvenienced."

"It's been interesting. Damnation, it's been fascinating, Mr. Rolfe."

"John, I think?"

Lord Chumley was a little shorter and plumper than his host. His hair—and a mustache worn in the bushy style the RAF had favored during the Battle of Britain—had turned white, where gray had only begun to streak the temples of the Virginian. His eyes were blue and very direct, and more intelligent than his bluff manner might suggest; his upper-class British speech had a hint of something harder and more nasal beneath it. By hereditary right he was *Baron* Chumley, and could claim a seat in the House of Lords, but his father had come to the equatorial uplands west of Mount Kenya in 1905, and he had been born and reared there. He'd also spent much of the 1950s leading a countergang against the Mau Mau in the forests of the Aberdares mountains.

"And Cecil, by all means. But returning to business, John," Chumley said. "I'm certainly going to accept your offer. My oath, I'd be a bloody fool not to!"

Rolfe nodded. Chumley had been offered a seat on the Central Committee; it would be the *twenty-nine* families then; thirty in truth when Auguste Devereaux arrived, if he managed to dodge both de Gaulle's "bearded ones" and his ex-friends from the OAS. With a committee appointment came a share of the Gate Control Commission's revenues, and a portion of its political power in the Commonwealth.

The Kenyan went on: "It'll make me a very wealthy man, and I've fallen in love with the climate and the game here; it's like Kenya in my father's time, only better. Completely different from FirstSide California, of course: I wouldn't live *there* for all the oil in Arabia. Odd, to think that one man living or dying could make so much difference."

Rolfe nodded. "Although when that one man is Alexander the Great . . ." He shrugged and smiled.

Here Alexander the Great hadn't died in Babylon in 323 B.C. Instead he'd lived to a ripe old three score and ten, and handed an undivided inheritance to his son by Roxanne. At its peak a century later, the empire he founded stretched from Spain to Bengal, before sheer size and entropy and Greek fractiousness broke it asunder in civil war and barbarian invasion. From what the Commonwealth's explorers could tell, most of that area still worshiped Zeus-Alexander, and spoke languages descended from ancient Greek—in much the same way as Italian and Romanian and the other Romance tongues came from the Latin spread by Imperial Rome. There hadn't been time or resources to do much more exploration yet, but they *had* found none of the city-states or kingdoms or tribes in the Old World to be much beyond a late medieval level of technology.

"Evidently science and machinery are unlikely accidents," Rolfe went on. "Fortunately for us!"

"Fortunately indeed!" Chumley said, returning to their business. "Which gives us this wonderful opportunity. But how many of my compatriots I can bring with me, that's another matter. Living here would be . . . well, very different. Not many natives, for one thing; not much labor available."

"That's true of Western Australia on FirstSide as well," Rolfe said. "And a number of them are relocating *there*. The Commonwealth will be a lot better than going back to England and the crowds and the drizzle."

"But more are heading for Rhodesia and South Africa on, ah, FirstSide," Chumley said.

Rolfe gave a wry smile. "And in anything from five to forty years, we'll be recruiting there," he said. "Hate to say it, but that's the way I read events; it's not going to stop at the Zambezi. That's one reason I've restricted the import of native labor here; we *could* get any number of workers from the kings and warlords down in Mexico, but we're keeping our *bracero* program strictly limited. Inconvenient in the short run, I grant you—but I don't want my grandchildren to be facing a mass of half-assimilated Aztecs who've been reading Locke and Tom Paine, not to mention Marx. Even without foreign countries to stick their oars in, it would be too likely to end badly. Unless we went right back to ox-plows and handicrafts, and while I'm full of reverence for the good qualities of the past, that's more filial piety than I'm willing to invest."

"A point, old boy, a most cogent point. I *will* certainly be able to get several hundred new settlers, possibly a thousand. And as you say, Rhodesia may provide more fairly soon, and I have contacts there—relatives and friends. They won't all be farmers and planters, of course. Small businessmen, skilled workmen, civil servants. A few white hunters, too—they'd *kill* for a chance to move here."

"All useful," Rolfe said. "Good pioneer stock, like my own English ancestors. And—"

A man in the black uniform of Gate Security came up. He held a sealed message, and his face was pale beyond the degree natural to one with his ash-blond Baltic complexion.

"Thank you, Otto," Rolfe said, and tore it open, his face an unreadable mask as Lieutenant von Traupitz stood at stiff attention.

That changed to a sigh of relief. Conscious of the glances on him—Salvatore Colletta had noticed something, and so had Louisa Rolfe—he spoke loudly enough that those nearby could hear: "The Russians have backed down. They've accepted Kennedy's terms without qualification. It looks as if there won't be war on FirstSide after all."

Chumley nodded and ran a hand over his thick white hair as a murmur spread through the crowd, and the laughter of relief from unacknowledged tension.

"That was too close for bloody comfort," he said. "I've been glad the family was here already."

"Yes," Rolfe said. "Although who can tell how the next crisis will go? War now would have destroyed Europe and

Russia and hurt America badly. Twenty years from now, with more bombs and missiles to carry them, it could end civilization FirstSide. Or even the human race."

"That's something that will get you a few more men willing to move," Chumley said shrewdly. "This is the ultimate in fallout shelters, old chap. Although . . . how well would we do here if the Gate were lost for good?"

"There are contingency plans," Rolfe said, carefully noting the "we." "Once the formalities are done, you'll have access to the secret files."

They'd brought over a vast hoard of technical books and drawings and microfilms, for starters; stockpiles of machine tools and gauges and metals, of crucial parts and materials; and it was all constantly updated. The Commonwealth's own workshops and skilled men could keep civilization going here, after a fashion, at need. Still, a few score thousand people were not enough to keep up the full panoply of twentieth-century industrial technology. They would have to gear down and give up much of the more complex equipment until population built up. Of course, there would be advantages to that, as well. He hadn't founded this nation to have it follow exactly in First-Side's footsteps.

"Still, I'd prefer it came much later, if ever," he said. "Much, much later."

CHAPTER FIVE

San Joaquin Valley—Lake Tulare
June 2009

The Commonwealth of New Virginia
I feel good, Adrienne thought, as the descent began.
*Wired, though. It's been a long time since anyone affected me
the way Tom does. God, but he's cute. Sweet, too.*

Her skin tingled, and all her senses seemed preternaturally sharp, so that even the flat neutral oil-ozone-metal odor
of the helicopter seemed as deep and subtle as fine wine. She
felt nimble and quick and clever, as if she could dance between the whirring blades of a harvester unharmed and handle this damned smuggling case with the flick of a finger.

*Be careful, woman. This is exactly the way people feel
when they're about to screw the pooch. You've had a good
idea about fixing a horrifying oversight. That doesn't mean
you're omniscient. Besides which, when and if Tom learns
the full truth . . .*

The rolling foothills of the Coast Range were behind
them, and the southern San Joaquin Valley spread beneath,
turning from the thin green of spring to the dun-colored
wasteland of summer drought. At two thousand feet she
could see southward to where bare brown mountains and the
Tehachapi Pass closed the southern end of the great north-south lowland; a little higher, and she could have looked
north to see the San Joaquin join the Sacramento and flow

into the delta before emptying into San Francisco Bay. A haze of heat lay over the land beneath her, though it was only an hour past dawn, and most of the game that hadn't moved up into higher country had retreated to the odd stream that drew a line of trees across the plain, or simply lain down to wait for nightfall.

A herd of mustangs drew a plume of dust across the barren land, spooked by the Black Hawk's shadow, and pronghorns scattered like drops of mercury on a block of ice. Ahead was a vivid, livid green, where the tule swamps spread around the great shallow lakes that occupied much of this end of the valley even in summer. Looking east she could see the harsh glitter of sunlight on water through the rippling sea of reeds twice the height of a man. Beyond them lay open blue, and beyond that rose the source of the life-giving flow—the snowpeaks of the Sierras. They floated salt white and ethereally lovely in the distance, turned to an eye-hurting brilliance by the morning sun, a wall between her homeland and the deserts and plains of the far interior.

A smoke flare cast a long streak of orange-red across the yellow-brown steppe not far away from the edge of the marsh. Nearby was the camp she'd come to find, vehicles parked in a square laager, a dozen hobbled horses in a swale that still kept a little green and had a single scraggly valley oak, and a set of tents grouped around campfires. The pilot nodded when she leaned forward into the crew section and pointed, his bulbous helmet and face shield making him insectile as he swung the helicopter sharply in a banking turn and cut toward the flare. It was suitably distant from the tents and the long row of wire cages covered by an awning; it would be just what she needed to send the birds into cataleptic shock. Suddenly the ground was closer; a falling-elevator sensation pressed her into the web seat, and hot dusty air flicked grit into her face as the side doors were opened and swung alongside the fuselage.

Adrienne hopped down with one hand holding the floppy-brimmed canvas hat on her head against the blast of the helicopter's slowing rotors; she could feel sweat starting out under the thin, tough cotton fabric of her bush jacket, and dry instantly in the blade-wash as the turbine howl of the engines died.

Schalk and Piet followed her toward the camp. Closer, she could see eight big Land Rovers, the Aussie SAS six-wheeled model designed FirstSide for long-range desert patrols, plus two Hummers and a Cheetah light armored car with paired machine guns in its little octagonal turret. A heavy-duty field radio sat on a table under a large tent with its sides rolled up; the other tents were rigged as shade-only as well, with bedrolls resting beneath them. Most of the thirty or so men there were in wolf-gray militia uniforms, wearing peaked caps with neck flaps and the von Traupitz double-lightning-bolt-and-eagle Family badge on their shoulders; there were three men in Frontier Scout khaki as well. The Scouts were the Commonwealth's wilderness and frontier experts. As a sideline, they handled relations with Indian remnants who'd survived the plagues.

She recognized both the commanders; the militia platoon was led by Heinrich von Traupitz, scion of a younger-son branch of that Family, and the Frontier Scout was a Settler by the name of Jim Simmons. Both were her contemporaries, in their twenties and of the third generation born in the Commonwealth; she'd met Heinrich socially any number of times since her sixth birthday party, and had worked with Simmons before. The troops were all young men doing their national service except for a grizzled sergeant; probably all from farming and ranching households affiliated with the von Traupitzes, too, and experienced hunters. That Family had their main holding southeast of the Rolfe domain in the Napa watershed, over the Vaca hills and out on the edge of settlement in the Suisun Valley, deeply rural even by her people's standards; they and their Settlers raised a fifth of New Virginia's wheat crop.

"Jim, good to see you," she said, shaking their hands. "Hi, Heinrich. How's Caitlin, Cuz?"

"Last time we talked, she said, 'I'm feeling well, though enormous.'"

Members of the Thirty in the same generation usually called each other Cuz—Cousin—but Caitlin was one in the literal sense, daughter of one of Adrienne's paternal uncles. She'd always been fond of the girl in an elder-sister fashion, and Heinrich was a nice enough sort. For a von Traupitz.

Unlike the older generation, she thought with slight distaste.

Their founder had been a colonel—in *Das Reich,* a Waffen-SS division with an unsavory reputation, if that wasn't redundant, and a nasty piece of work personally. The third generation were quite human, most of them. Of course, Heinrich's mother had been an O'Brien.

Heinrich smiled back; he was a black-haired man with amber-colored eyes and pale skin that glistened with sunblock.

"I *would* like to be back for the birth; it's our first, you know," he went on. "I suspect my men wouldn't turn down a cold beer at the Mermaid Café, either."

He looked over her shoulder. The Black Hawks were Commission property, usually used as air ambulances to bring in patients from outlying settlements. This one had been fitted out in "militarized" mode, with stub wings bearing a six-barreled Gatling minigun on the left side and rocket pods on the right.

"Fancy carriage there, Cuz," he said, raising an eyebrow. "Is there something I should know about, or is this the Old Man's usual overkill?"

"The 'copter is staying to take me back once we've got the cargo," she replied, jerking her thumb over her shoulder. "It's just what was available."

The pilot and his assistant were out, doing a maintenance check on the engines and weapons systems, something of which she heartily approved. Her years as a Gate Security agent had taught her that if you didn't take care of equipment, it wouldn't take care of you when you needed it. And while you might not need any particular item often, when you did you'd need it *very* badly.

"Can't be over too soon for me, Adri," Heinrich said. "If

I owned this place and hell, I'd live in hell and rent it out. They say *our* area is hot and flat!" He slapped at a mosquito and cursed as it squashed against his neck in a smear of blood and sweat. "Jim and his boys did all the work. All *we've* done is sit and stare at dust-devils and the occasional pronghorn and listen to our frying skin crackle and pop."

"You might as well get packed, then. Sorry I don't have time for the social amenities, Heinrich, but this is Gate Security business, and I have to wrap it up fast. Then you can get your men back to civilization and cold beer."

The soldier nodded, shrugged, slapped another mosquito and walked off toward his troops, calling orders. There was a chorus of cheers, and they began striking camp with commendable enthusiasm.

The Frontier Scout laughed as they walked toward the cages; he was about her height, with sun-streaked brown hair, a close-cropped gingery beard and blue eyes startling in his tanned countenance. His broad-brimmed hat had a leopard-skin band, and old sweat had left rings of salt stain on his jacket, still visible beneath the new ones despite multiple washings; a leather thong around his neck bore grizzly-bear teeth and lion claws.

"What were they thinking of, sending that bunch of farm boys and clerks' sons?" Simmons said. "We don't need soldiers, and I doubt many of them have been twenty miles east of the Coast Range before. My oath! Half of them aren't old enough to shave. A couple of Frontier Scouts are all that's necessary for a job like this; the condors don't have artillery, after all."

"The Old Man is fond of saying that few operations fail because too much force is used. The troops are just for insurance; and they're not from Rolfeston, you'll note."

"Operation? What operation?" Simmons said, taking off his hat and waving it at the flat, heat-shimmering circle of the horizon while he wiped a sleeve across his forehead. "This isn't the 1980s, for sweet suffering Jesus' sake. This valley's nearly as pacified as the good lieutenant von Traupitz's ancestral acres back northside of the delta. Most of the natives died off in the first epidemics in the forties and the smallpox got the rest—the nearest wild tribe of any size is up in the Sierras."

"There *are* still some renegades and hostiles in the lakes and swamps," Adrienne pointed out. "At least a hundred, worst case a thousand—there are lots of little islands in there, and plenty of fish and game. A few of them have stolen guns, too. They'd like to get their hands on our weapons and gear. Very, very much. Plus they're not really fond of New Virginians, which is understandable from their point of view."

"Oh, I wouldn't want to camp out alone around here, or set up house, or try to graze stock," Simmons agreed. "But they've learned better than to come out in the daytime, or in any numbers. I doubt they're going to attack a party of mounted Scouts, either."

"They're even less likely to attack a platoon and an armored car," Adrienne said. "Trust the Old Man's judgment. He knew you're someone who could be trusted to produce twenty closely related condors on short notice without shooting them, for example."

"Wasn't hard," Jim said. "The Valley isn't half as challenging as things were *when we* were back in Kenya during the Mau Mau."

The remark was made with malice aforethought; the British-African immigrants were popularly and unflatteringly known as *when-wes*. He dropped into a semi-British clipped accent as he spoke. Normally apart from an occasional turn of phrase his voice had the same slight New Virginian drawl as hers or Heinrich's, the legacy of many languages and generations of linguistic drift in relative isolation.

Adrienne snorted. "Jim, you were born in the Commonwealth and you've never been back. Your *father* was born in New Virginia and never went FirstSide in his life either. Your *grandparents* came from Kenya in 'sixty-three."

"That skipped my mind," he teased, grinning.

The other two Frontier Scouts waited by the cages; they

were cut from much the same cloth as Simmons—in fact, one was his younger brother and one his maternal aunt's son; New Virginia ran on nepotism, and not only in the Thirty Families. The wire containers were in a double row, eighteen of them, with an awning rigged above. Inside the cages huge vulturelike birds perched and stank and brooded, their naked yellow heads twisting on the ends of long scabby necks to cast a baleful eye on the movements of their captors. With their wings folded, the distinguishing white patches underneath were invisible, and they looked like huge ill-tempered bundles of feathers with claws. A condor high above was a sight of heart-catching grace and beauty, but close quarters were something else again. Occasionally one would utter a disconsolate, croaking squawk or engage in a feather-ruffling, beak-stabbing dispute with its neighbors.

"Well, there the bloody things are," Simmons replied. "Bugger-all explanation *I* got; just a message from your father to go get them, countersigned by the Old Man no less, at which I genuflected, salaamed, saluted and got on my way . . . and I was *due* to go up to Fort Tahoe Station, which I will remind you has a much better climate than this. What's going on—is there a barbecue planned at Rolfe Manor?"

Adrienne grinned at his plaintive expression. "Well, they *do* weigh in about the same as a turkey, and I suppose with some chipotle rub and a sage-and-herb stuffing, maybe a little garlic . . ."

The birds all looked healthy, and they all had a dish of water and a gobbet of fly-swarming meat that stank even worse than they did, a gourmet meal for what the biologists called an obligate scavenger, which meant carrion eater in plain English. She nodded in satisfaction, and sipped from a tin cup of strong camp coffee someone put in her hand.

"Good work, though, and quick," she said. There were thousands of condors in the Commonwealth, but that didn't mean you could walk around scooping them up with a butterfly net, particularly when they had to be unharmed. "I'm impressed; I'll tell my father and the Old Man so, too."

Simmons swept off his hat and gave her a mock-courtly

bow. "That gladdens the cockles of my heart." His expression was sly. "Is the lady impressed enough to sweep me off my feet, take me away from this piece of refried hell, make an honest man of me and elevate my lowly but roguishly charming Settler self to the demiparadise of collateral Family status among the august Rolfes?"

Adrienne punched his shoulder; it felt like striking a board. "You'd go toes-up in a month, living in Rolfeston, or even on an estate in Napa," she said. "And working a regular job inside the frontier would drive you to suicide. You're a wilderness man through and through."

"True . . . true . . . how about a brief, meaningless affair, then?"

"You're incorrigible!"

"No, the name's Simmons. . . . Right then; how about charming you into telling me what this is about?"

"Sorry. Gate Security business."

His eyebrows went up. "Gate Security requires twenty condors? Half of which have to be fed one lead shotgun pellet, and the rest a package of mysterious powders flown out at vast expense?"

"Yes," she said, and laughed with good-natured schadenfreude at his frustration.

"Adrienne, do you have any idea of what it's like making a condor eat something? They have projectile vomiting down to a science. I deserve to know!"

"Really, I can't tell you; not only that, you're supposed to keep quiet about it too. Any prospect of getting the last two soon?"

"We shot bait all along a front north and south of here," Simmons said. "Mostly wild cattle, some antelope, and a few feral camels. The cars would spook the birds, so we ride out when— Ah, here he is."

A lone figure came trotting out of the northeast, where the marsh made a green line on the horizon, which meant a considerable distance hereabouts. There was an old joke that when your dog ran away in this part of the Commonwealth, you could stand on a chair and watch it going for three days.

Adrienne wore a monocular in a case on her belt; she snapped it open and put it to her right eye. A man was approaching, barefoot and clad only in a deer-hide breechclout. His long black hair hung to his shoulders beneath a head-band, and his body seemed to be comprised exclusively of bone, gristle, jerky and sinew sheathed in dark brown hide. He moved at an effortless smooth trot through the calf-high plain of yellow-white dried grass, the short bow in his left hand pumping as he ran. A quiver was slung across his back; his belt bore a steel knife, hatchet, militia-issue canteen, and a bag that probably contained most of his other possessions. His broad high-cheeked face was flatly impassive, and he was hardly even sweating in the vicious heat.

"Ah, that's one of your tame Yokut trackers, right?" Adrienne said.

"Kolomusnim, or Kolo for short. He's not particularly tame, but he's a bloody good tracker. Good man, when he can keep away from the booze."

"Most can't, judging by the specimens I've seen around your Frontier Scout stations," Adrienne said.

"I'd be tempted to drown my sorrows myself, in their position," Simmons said, surprising her. "Let's to business, then."

Kolomusnim came up at the same swinging trot, stopping and sinking to his heels in front of the Frontier Scout, who squatted likewise to watch as the Indian drew in the white dust and spoke in a mixture of his native tongue and garbled English; after a moment she could follow the latter, at least.

"Three?" Simmons said.

"Three *something-something*," Kolomusnim replied, holding up that many fingers. The unintelligible word had far too many consonants, and probably meant *condor*. "And man-sign. Mebbe two days, mebbe right after shoot. Belly cut, liver, kidney, tongue, haunches gone, loin—good meat. No man-sign after that."

"Hmmm." Simmons thought, elbows on his knees; the squatting posture looked nearly as natural to him as to the Indian. "Probably some little band of holdouts scavenging the edge of the marsh."

He rose. "There are three condors feeding on some camels we shot. You can wait here, Adrienne. I'll have the birds netted inside a couple of hours, and then you can come in with the cars."

She had been looking over his horse lines; there were twelve mounts, not counting two pack-mules. Sensibly, he'd been using the Land Rovers as a base to carry fodder and water, and then ranging out to check his baits with the less noisy horses. That would minimize the chances of scaring off any feeding condors.

"To hell with that, Jim," she said. "I'm the Bad Girl of the Rolfes, remember? I'll ride in with you, and we can have the chopper pick the birds up, bring them back here, load the rest and be back at the Gate before sunset."

He hesitated for a moment, and then nodded. "All right," he said. "Never could stand to be left out of the boys' games, eh?"

She shrugged. "I'm not Little Miss Cindy Lou Magnolia-blossom," she said dryly, patting the FN FiveseveN automatic holstered high on her right hip.

There are some *advantages to FirstSide,* she thought. *The extinctions there fortunately include a lot of Cindy Lou-ism.*

"I noticed; Alf, saddle an extra horse."

Until then Schalk and Piet had been silent as boulders. Now Piet stirred.

"*Nie, nie,* miss," he said. "We go too." At her frown, he raised a massive hand and went on. "Miss, if something happened to you and we weren't there, your *oupa* would have our bliddy ba . . . our bliddy heads."

His face had taken on a mulish look she recognized; she shrugged and said, "The more the merrier. It's only a couple of miles, right?"

"About ten," Simmons said in a resigned voice. "Alf, saddle *three* extras; you'll be staying with the birds here. Jake, run over to the lieutenant and borrow three spare rifles." He turned to the Afrikaners. "You *do* know how to handle a standard O'Brien rifle, I suppose?"

"It's a bliddy *gun,* isn't it?" Schalk said, taking the semi-auto weapon and checking the action with businesslike competence before slapping in a twenty-round magazine. "Your bushman any good?"

Kolomusnim looked up. "Better than lard-ass white man needs horse go ten milcs," he said, and grinned as Schalk's complexion turned mottled with fury.

Then the tracker looked at Adrienne, glanced over to Simmons and spoke in his own language.

"He says what do we need a woman along for? If we're not hunting for game that has to be skinned and cooked," Simmons said, suppressing a smile.

"Ha. Ha. Ha," Adrienne said, pronouncing each syllable separately, as if she were reading it from a page.

The horses were good mixed hunter blood; the Commission had never imported anything but the best, and she trusted Jim Simmons to choose his working stock carefully. Schalk and Piet Botha picked two bays of about seventeen hands that looked capable of handling their weight; they rode reasonably well, although she knew they'd both been city born and raised, Johannesburg and Cape Town respectively. Either they'd picked it up here, or had been well taught FirstSide; she seemed to remember reading somewhere that the old South African government had used mounted infantry for patrol work, and Botha had a farm down in the south country. She chose a fifteen-hand dappled-gray mare that had a good deal of Arab in its bloodlines, to judge from the rather small and elegantly wedge-shaped head, and the arch of neck and tail. It snorted slightly as she checked the girths, slid her own rifle into the scabbard that slanted back under the flap on the right side, put her foot in the stirrup and swung into the saddle. That was the lightened Western type the Frontier Scouts used; there was a machete and a canvas chuggle of water strapped to the left side, with jerky and biscuit and raisins in the saddlebags, plus the various items regulations required.

Kolomusnim turned without another word and began trotting back the way he'd come. They fell naturally into a column behind him; she rode beside Simmons, with the two Gate Security operatives behind her and the other Scout bringing up the rear, leading two pack-mules; one carried an empty condor cage on either side of its panniers, the other a large folded net and a spare field radio.

Adrienne took a deep breath of the hot air, full of the dusty scent of the dry grasslands, horse sweat, and a hint of the marshes. There were insects aplenty in the air, and the horse twitched its ears and various parts of its skin as she squeezed her calves against its barrel and brought it up to a round trot. She realized that, for some reason, she was intensely happy.

And I'd really like to be able to show all this to Tom, she thought wistfully. *Not likely. If he ever gets to our beloved Commonwealth of New Virginia, he's not likely to be feeling very good about me.* Since that would happen only if he stumbled on the Gate secret, in which case he'd be shanghaied here as an Involuntary Settler and could never go back.

"Can't your Yokut learn to ride?" she asked Simmons.

The Indian had been dropping back occasionally to run gripping the Scout's stirrup with his right hand, then loping ahead again.

Simmons chuckled. "Kolo rides quite well. He also thinks horses are for girly-boys and white men, if there's a difference. We could beat him to the bait if we galloped, but the horses would be blown and he'd be ready to go on running all day. He covered fifty miles in twenty hours once, on a bet, when we were shepherding a bunch of Collettas and Morrisons on safari east of the Sierras."

They rode quickly, alternating between a trot and a quick walk. The reeds grew nearer, and the mosquitoes more persistent, along with buzzing horseflies and half a dozen other types of noisy insects. In the abstract, Adrienne knew that marshes were vital to the food chain, nurseries for fish and wildfowl and any number of other good things. In the concrete here-and-now, she found this one seriously interfering with her good mood.

Simmons reined in well away from the edge of the marsh, throwing up a hand to halt the others. The verge was scalloped here, a tongue of very slightly higher land running inward to make an egg-shaped embayment of dry ground about a thousand yards deep and half that across at the mouth, with the fat end toward the swamp. Two dead camels lay near the bottom of the egg, and the stink was formidable even at this distance; they must have been caught coming back from grazing on the reeds at the edge. The three condors crawled over the carrion like greater versions of the insects that swarmed about the feast in a glittering cloud.

"Dropped both camels with head shots from right here," Simmons confirmed; he was a little vain of his marksmanship, and the rifle in his saddle scabbard had a telescopic sight attached. "The condors'll be heavy and sleepy, ought to be slow to take off—not that they're hummingbirds at the best of times."

The big birds were feeding; one had its head deep in the feral camel's body cavity. It pulled it out, looking curiously around, and returned to its meal. Adrienne didn't consider herself squeamish; she'd been reared in the country, had watched livestock slaughtered since she was barely six, and had gutted and skinned plenty of game herself, starting not much later. She still had to swallow slightly as she surveyed the scene with her monocular.

Condors were *spectacularly* messy feeders, and the camels were extremely ripe after days in this heat.

"Keep it quiet," Simmons said—quietly. "Dismount, spread out, and don't get too close. Jake, get the net. Kolo, you're our backup."

Condors had never been hunted in New Virginia; they were a protected species, which could be taken only with an authorization from the Central Committee or the Chairman. They wouldn't be very wary of human beings, but their dim little instinct-machine minds would associate anything large and alive with danger if it was close enough.

The party all swung down from the saddle, drew their rifles from the saddle scabbards and slung them over their backs, moving cautiously and with minimal noise; it was very quiet, nothing louder than the sough of wind through the tule reeds and the buzz of insects, punctuated by an occasional clatter of harness and clop of hooves as the horses shifted position. Simmons's cousin Jake drove in a tethering stake and tied the pack-mule's leading reins to it before he unlimbered the net and hurried up to join his relative at the front of the party. Adrienne and her two assistant-bodyguards followed on foot as well, leading their mounts; she admired the smooth way Simmons and his cousin deployed the net between them, stooping carefully to reduce their height and visual signal to their prey. Kolomusnim waited farther back, the cages at his feet and the reins of the two white men's horses draped over his arm.

The Scouts came closer and closer to the carcasses, moving more and more slowly, until there was a pause of several seconds between steps and a freeze every time the condors seemed to pay attention. The birds looked, ruffled their feathers and then quieted again, looked and ruffled. . . .

"Go!" she heard Simmons whisper, when the condors didn't seem to quiet down at all after the last advance.

He and the other Scout sprinted forward at a dead run. The birds croak-squawked their alarm, turning and running awkwardly away with their wings spread out to their full ten-foot span, trying to build up enough momentum to take a leap into the air and thrash themselves upward—condors spent most of their time soaring on thermals, and they weren't very efficient at getting off flat ground quickly. That let the men get within casting distance; Jake let go the net at another command, and Simmons whirled it in a circle over his head before he let fly.

It glinted in the harsh sunlight as the lead weights along the edge spun it open into a perfect circle, pausing for a moment at the top of its trajectory and then dropping like a swift-stooping eagle. One of the panic-stricken condors made its escape, hoisting itself into the air with desperate strokes of its great wings and banking out over the swamp, turning and circling to gain altitude and escape. Its cries drifted down through the hot still air. The others were a heaving, squawking chaos under the net, their flapping terror serving only to tangle them more securely. Simmons and his assistant waded in, cautious of the beaks and strong snaky necks. They used the net to throw the birds down; then Jake immobilized each in turn while Simmons slid a loose sock over its head. That quieted the big scavengers enough for a swift but gentle trussing.

Adrienne smiled to herself; it was always enjoyable to watch experts at work, and Jim Simmons's boyish pride in his skills was entertaining in its own right. She watched Kolomusnim bend to pick up the two wire cages . . . and then freeze and come erect slowly, his head swiveling back and forth toward the walls of tule reeds on either hand. Then everything seemed to happen at once, yet in slow motion.

An instant before the Yokut called out a warning, Simmons came erect as well, reaching for the rifle slung over his back. Jake looked at him, puzzled, and then the expression went blank. The crack of a rifle followed instantly; she could distinctly see his body jerk, then a spot on the front of his khaki jacket blow out in a shower of red.

Another rifle spoke as the Scout fell, and a horse screamed; her head whipped around to see Schalk's mount collapsing, thrashing with a broken foreleg. Then more shots, a fast rapid *crack-crack-crack:* two rifles at least, and used with more skill than Indians could generally achieve with pilfered ammunition and stolen weapons they didn't know how to maintain. Of course, the shooters could be renegades; occasionally criminals or malcontents from New Virginian settlements ran off to live with any tribe that would take them in. They usually ran farther than this, though. . . .

The thought ran through her head as she tried to get her horse under control and the rifle off her back. Then there was a sudden *shhhhhwhup—shhhhhwhup—shhhhhwhup* sound, and the saddle sprouted an arrow. The head made an ugly whacking sound as it stuck in the leather and wood, standing there with the shaft humming like an angry bee. Two more went into the animal's rump with wet, meaty sounds, and the horse went wild—screaming and squealing as it reared and then went into a twisting buck.

"That's torn it," she said in a snarl, then took a step back, drew her FiveseveN automatic and shot the horse three times, the last one striking right behind an ear, not without a slight wince; the poor beast hadn't done anything but what she asked of it. It hadn't asked to be born in the Commonwealth, either; this wasn't its fight.

The horse fell with a limp thud and she cast herself down behind it; the little 5.7mm bullets were high-velocity and armor piercing, but composed of some dense plastic that deformed and gave up all its kinetic energy when it struck soft tissue. This one had drilled through the horse's skull and turned its brain into jelly; she had the pistol back in its holster before her mount's final reflex kick, and the rifle out across the flank she huddled behind for cover. The smell of blood and offal from the horses was added to the stink of the rotting camels, and the ground was turning to mud underneath her as the animal bled out, but the knot of tension under her breastbone made all those things details she could ignore easily enough.

This isn't the first time I've been shot at, exactly, but it's certainly the most serious, she thought grimly. The other occasions had all been short, for starters. *This one looks like it could spoil my entire day.*

Simmons was down on the ground, leopard-crawling toward Jake with his rifle across the crook of his elbows. Three Indians were out of the reeds, their bodies striped in horizontal bands of white, black and ochre; they were howling like wolves and loosing arrows as they ran toward Kolomusnim. The Yokut shot one in the chest with the arrow on his bow; Adrienne carefully led the last and dropped him at a hundred and twenty paces. The militia battle rifle kicked against her shoulder, a quick hard punch, and the brass of the empty .30-06 round spun off to the right, glinting in the sun and then tinkling on some metal part of the horse's bridle. More arrows came *whupp-whupp-whupp* out of the reeds and she had to duck, curling under the barrel of the horse as they plunged down at her from out of the sky, dropping like mortar rounds. From that angle and past the head of her former mount she could see the third Indian and Kolomusnim go over in a tangle of brown limbs. Then the tracker rose on top, his hatchet in his hand, smashing it downward over and over again in a quick hard flurry of blows accompanied by sickening cleaving thuds.

A quick glance behind her. Schalk and Piet were alive, but their horses weren't; one of the mules was down too, and the other had pulled the tethering stake loose and was dragging it behind as it fled westward, braying hysterically. The two Afrikaners and she formed a rough triangle about a hundred feet on a side, each crouched down behind the carcass of a dead horse.

The ambushers must have shot to kill the mounts first, which showed lamentably good tactical sense. Horses were free to whoever could catch them—there were uncounted thousands in the feral herds in the Central Valley and the foothills, and more swarmed all the way to the Mississippi these days—but saddle tack was something they'd have trouble getting their hands on, and rifles and ammunition were beyond price. Not to mention the opportunity to kill a few of the hated New Virginians, the evil wizards whose touch was death, the destroyers of worlds.

Another arrow went *thunk* into the body of her ex-mount. She looked around; Kolomusnim had finished off his opponent, then leaped to the back of one of the horses he'd been holding for Simmons; the other was down. He pulled its head around and raced for the open mouth of the pocket of dry land; arrows went after him, and bullets—she thought something struck him, but he might have been hugging the horse's neck to present a smaller target. The hooves of the galloping horse went past her, throwing up clods of earth, a thudding she could feel through her belly as she lay on the hard clay ground.

"So much for the bliddy tame bushman!" Schalk yelled, and turned the muzzle of his rifle after the fleeing tracker. *"Jou hol bobbejan!"*

"Schalk! Eyes on the swamp!" Adrienne shouted, and the Afrikaner reluctantly obeyed.

They wouldn't be missed for hours. The radio would have brought support in a few minutes, but it was quite thoroughly crushed under the side of Simmons's horse that had hit the ground—even good solid-state milspec field electronics rarely survived eleven hundred pounds of horse landing on it. There were two spares, of course: one with the horse Kolomusnim had ridden out, and the third in the pack-saddle of the mule that had fled westward and was probably at the Coast Range by now. . . .

Simmons had reached his cousin. "He's a goner!" he called, as he drew his knife and cut the sling of the dead man's rifle so that he could drag it away.

"Covering fire!" Adrienne called.

The Scout began to crawl rapidly toward the dead horse that marked the spot where Kolomusnim had stood; there was a dead Indian beside it, his face chopped into red ruin by the tracker's hatchet, and another lying where her bullet had punched through his body just above the hipbones; he was still twitching a little, but effectively dead for all that. The hollow-point rounds would have plowed a hole about the size of a child's fist right through and out the other side.

The problem with giving Simmons covering fire was that there wasn't much to see or shoot at. And the Indians could fire their arrows upward, from several yards within the tule reeds; they'd know the safe paths through them. She took out the monocular and scanned along the edge nearest Simmons's crawling passage.

The rifleman in there was firing slowly; every ten seconds or so a puff of dust would pock the surface of the clay where Simmons was crawling toward cover. *That* shooter would have to come close to the edge of the reeds, so . . . a glimpse of brown skin . . .

"Standing figure, my left, two-fifty yards," she called;

probably the two men had seen the same thing, but someone had to coordinate for best effect. "Jim, get ready to run for it."

All three rifles shifted; there was a moment's hesitation as the men picked out the target, or what they thought might be it. Adrienne breathed out slowly, letting her finger tighten gradually on the trigger in a gentle stroking motion, the way Uncle Andy had taught her. . . .

Crack, and another *ting* of cartridge on metal. The shadowy glimpse of the target vanished, if it had been anything more than a trick of the light in the reeds. She squeezed off half a dozen rounds into the same patch of reeds, and the two men did the same.

"Run for it, Jim!" Adrienne shouted.

The Scout didn't need any prompting. At the first shot he was up and dashing toward the horse. Reckless of the other rifleman hidden in the reeds, she came up on one knee and fired off the rest of the magazine. A bullet made an ugly *wiizzztft!* sound past her ear, and more arrows came arching out of the reeds, seeming to start slowly and then accelerate as they slid down the arch toward her—no less disconcerting for being an optical illusion. She dropped flat again to eject the empty magazine and slap in another; there were ten in the bandolier across the dead horse's neck, and another two hundred rounds boxed in the saddlebags, and she spared some brief flicker of consciousness to thank the God of Regulations for that.

Jim Simmons staggered and cried out as he ran for the scant cover of the fallen horse. An arrow had gone through his leg above the knee, and it buckled under him as he moved. That sent him to his hands and knees. Another shaft plunged down and took him in the back below the left shoulder, and he collapsed flat with another cry.

"Oh, *hell*," Adrienne said in a snarl, profoundly unhappy at what happened next. "Give me a hand!" she shouted, and came up from behind the body of the horse, running forward crab-wise and shooting at the reeds as she went, trying to find the bowmen by backtracking the shafts.

Behind her, Schalk van der Merwe gave an inarticulate cry of rage and ran forward as well, bellowing his anger at what the crazy Rolfe woman had gotten him into now. They ran zigzag, with arrows and an occasional bullet whipping past them. Simmons was alive; she could tell by the trembling jerks that ran through the shaft sticking up out of his back—it must have stuck in the shoulder blade, though only time would tell whether it had penetrated past that shield of bone into the lung.

"Take him!" Adrienne said.

Schalk fired off the rest of his magazine at the reeds and the half-seen figures dodging about in the fringe of the swamp, then gripped the back of Simmons's jacket in his left hand and hauled him up like a suitcase before he slung him over his shoulder, ignoring the hundred and seventy solid pounds the smaller man weighed. His sprint back toward cover showed no effect from the weight, either; van der Merwe was nearly as tough as he thought he was. He dropped the Scout behind Adrienne's barricade of horseflesh, then did another jinking dash back to his own.

Adrienne slung her rifle and scooped up Simmons's weapon. It had a cut-down forestock, a glass-bedded barrel, an adjustable cheekpiece and a sniper's telescopic sight. Her run back to the shelter of her dead mare turned into an undignified tumble as an arrow plowed a shallow furrow across the outside of her right buttock, the sharp steel head slicing the fabric of her trousers like a pair of scissors in the hands of a tailor.

"Goddamned ass cutters!" she shouted in frustration.

Simmons was conscious, but sweating with pain and shock; he couldn't move his left arm, and cried out through clenched teeth when it was bumped. His skin wasn't gray, and his pulse was thready but regular; the arrow wounds were bleeding, but not in pulsing jets; and there was no blood on his lips—hopefully the point in the back hadn't penetrated the lung. The Lord alone knew what was going on inside, but for the present it was better to leave the natural tourniquets of the wooden shafts in place. Blessing the God of Regulations once more, she got the medical kit out of its boiled-leather case on the saddle, pulled out a hypo of morphine, stripped off the cover on the needle with her teeth and stuck it into the back of his thigh, pressing the plunger with her thumb. After a moment he sighed and closed his eyes.

"Lucky bastard," she mumbled, and stole a glance at her watch. *Ten minutes?* Nine and a half, to be strict. *That's ridiculous; it must have been longer.* A glance at the sun told her that it was correct: still not quite noon.

"This is bad. This is very bad," she mumbled as she checked over the Scout's rifle and adjusted the cheekpiece and shoulder buffer for her size. "This is very, very goddamned bad."

From the volume of fire, there must be at least two rifles and maybe twenty bows among the Indians, and they'd killed only three or four of them all told. There *could* be a hundred of them waiting to attack.

"I'd better use this fine product of O'Brien engineering to buy us some time," she muttered. "All right . . ."

The sight had adjustments for ranges from x3 to x10. You could estimate the range yourself, or just point it at a target and look. The scope showed crosshairs, and upper and lower stadia on the vertical line. Turning the adjusting knob so that they rested on the head and belt of a man moved a cam to zero the crosshairs for that range.

She wrapped a turn of the sling around her left hand, rested the stock on the barrel of her dead horse, and brought the scope to her eye. The edge of the reeds leaped to arm's length through the scope, and she gave a hiss of satisfaction as she saw an archer a yard inside the tules drawing a shaft, his teeth bared in effort as he bent the short thick bow staff— she could see sweat glisten, and the whites of his eyes against the band of black paint over his upper face. The stadia marks fitted neatly over his head and belt, which put the crosshairs precisely on his breastbone. . . .

Crack.

The archer fell backward, chest-punched by the bullet. A spray of bone and blood and shreds of flesh erupted from his back where the mushrooming hollow-point round blasted out a hole the size of a small plate. The arrow wobbled up and fell to stand in the ground thirty yards beyond the edge of the marsh.

Ouch. Unfortunately, the scope also let you see the expression on the man's face when the bullet hit. *Granted he was trying to kill* me, *that's still something I would rather not have seen.*

She panned the scope down the edge of the tule reeds closest to the New Virginians' position, methodically shooting as targets presented themselves. Barring rescue, their only real chance of survival was to kill so many Indians that the rest were sickened with the business and ran.

Silence fell, save for the buzzing of the insects, something of which she was suddenly conscious again. An occasional arrow came out of the swamp, but the Indians had backed farther in and were shooting more or less blind.

"Good shooting, miss!" Piet Botha called. "They may give up."

Cautiously, Adrienne raised her head. A bullet cracked by overhead, another kicked up a puff of dust fifty yards to her front, and a third struck the horse.

"Shit!" she said with quiet viciousness, dropping down behind the protective barrier of flesh. Then louder: "I don't think so, Piet. I don't think they *like* us, somehow."

"Ja," the Afrikaner said ruefully. "They have us pinned down." A hesitation. "If we kept *them* pinned down with some rapid fire, miss, you might be able to get out into the open and make it back to camp, get a rescue party here."

Adrienne turned on her back, thinking carefully as she scanned the way they'd come. There was no point in heroic gestures. If running gave them all a chance, then she'd run; Adrienne didn't have testosterone poisoning to cloud her mind. She *would* be the logical choice; all three of them were in top condition, but while the men could lift a lot more weight, she could run faster than either of them over any distance longer than a sprint. And she could keep going a lot longer, too; she had ten years on Schalk, and fifteen on Piet.

On the other hand, they were about halfway into the embayment in the swamp, a little closer to the north edge than the south. The entrance narrowed several hundred yards behind them, and anyone running out would have to pass through a bottleneck between two and three hundred yards across. *After* running a five-hundred-yard gauntlet . . . with only two shooters to suppress the hostiles . . .

"I don't think so," she called back to Piet. "Neither of those two riflemen are very good shots, and I think they're short of ammo, but they'd get anyone who tried to run. And there are probably somewhere between twenty and a hundred bowmen, too. Tell me you don't think they've got some of them back there where the swamp edges pinch in toward each other at the edge, waiting to rush anyone who tries to get out. If either of you want to try it, I'll give a written authorization."

A pause. "You're probably right, miss," Piet said; there was a sigh in his shout. "Bliddy hell."

The Indians didn't want to pay the butcher's bill that rushing three rifles firing from behind cover would exact, but it was going to get dark eventually, and then . . . On the third hand . . .

"There's a good chance Heinrich will get suspicious and come investigate before sundown," she said. "If he's not here by seven, we'll reconsider."

"*Ja,* that's our best chance," Piet said. *"Alles in sy maai."* Which meant, roughly, that everything was *really* screwed up. Adrienne wished she didn't agree.

She took a swig from the canvas waterbag, then ate a handful of raisins and chewed on a strip of jerky. Now and then she took a cautious peek over her dead-horse sangar, careful not to do it twice in the same place. One of the Indian riflemen shot at her about every second time, usually not coming very close, but if she didn't pop up occasionally the bowmen would creep right to the edge of the reeds and start dropping arrows accurately again. The horse was beginning to bloat and stink even worse in the clammy heat, adding postmortem flatulence to the general unpleasantness; it struck her that this would be a very bad place to die.

Of course, is there a good place? Well, in bed, asleep, at 101 years of age, surrounded by great-grandchildren, maybe . . .

"Water," Jim Simmons whispered.

She put the nozzle of the waterbag to his mouth; it took considerable squirming around to do it without exposing herself to fire from the reed beds, and most of it dribbled down his chin—it wasn't easy to drink lying flat on your stomach and unable to move without pain.

"Hope this was worth it," he said, a little stronger.

"I *still* can't tell you, Jim, but yes, this is really important. Sorry about your cousin."

The man sighed and closed his eyes again.

I am going to find out who was responsible for all this, Adrienne thought with cold rage. She didn't believe this ambush was a coincidence. Someone was violating the Gate Control Commission's edicts, either for profit or for power, and using murder to cover things up. *And I am going to see them die.*

A sound caught at the edge of her consciousness, far and faint, but growing louder. A knot between her shoulder blades loosened. That was a helicopter, and it was coming her way. Which meant that Simmons's tracker hadn't just lit out for home; it also meant—

"Look sharp!" she called. "They may try to—"

The sound was louder now, unmistakable even to ears that didn't have much experience with aircraft; the *thupa-thupa-thupa* of a helicopter. Craning her neck around she could see the Black Hawk coming, like a deadly raven-colored wasp sliding through the blue heat-shimmer of the cloudless summer sky.

"—rush us," she went on.

Less than three seconds later, fifty Indians left the shelter of the reeds and charged, screaming. Adrienne fought an almost irresistible impulse to curl up behind the dead horse and hope none of the sudden storm of arrows hit her. Instead she made herself switch from one target to another, squeezing steadily and unhurriedly. As she fired the last round and let the scope-sighted rifle drop—a hell of a way to treat a precision instrument, but needs must—the helicopter arrived overhead. Most of the Indians still on their feet fled. They were still screaming, but with despair now.

One paused a few feet away from her, and this one had a militia rifle. He squeezed the trigger . . . and the pin clicked on an empty chamber.

The Indian shrieked with frustration and sprang at her, the rifle reversed and swinging in a wide circle; the man was two inches shorter than the New Virginian, but he had shoulders like a bull, and the butt would smash any bone it struck. Adrienne did the only thing possible; she threw herself to the rear and down, landing on her back with stunning force. The hostile recovered from his swing and brought the rifle up over his head, his face a contorted mass of teeth and eyes and paint. Her hand scrabbled at the holster of her FiveseveN automatic, fighting the winded paralysis of the fall, and managed to get the weapon free. It snapped once, and the bullet smashed her enemy's knee by sheer blind chance, the heavy plastic sawing through tendon and cartilage like an edged steel blade. She forced herself back to her feet, skipped nimbly forward while he thrashed and ululated his pain and kicked him in the head—not too hard, so that he could answer questions later. He didn't look quite like a typical Indian from this area; for one thing he was too well fed, and for another his hair was short on top and very short on the sides, like a FirstSider military cut.

Then she stood erect, her rifle held up horizontally over her head; Schalk and Piet were doing likewise, driven by a similar desire to make absolutely certain that there were no mistakes about who should be shot from the air.

The Black Hawk sat five hundred feet above their heads, raising dust with the prop wash. The pilot aimed by a method that was simplicity itself; he pointed the prow of the helicopter down at the fleeing Indians and the edge of the swamp, jammed his thumb on the firing button of the minigun and swiveled the aircraft in place through a hundred-degree arc. The long roaring *braaaapppppppp* of the weapon's six thousand rounds per minute overrode even the shriek of the turbines, and Adrienne had to lean over Simmons to protect him from the sparkling shower of empty brass cartridges that poured down from above. They were hot, too, painfully so.

The fleeing mob disappeared in a cloud of dust as the hail of bullets chewed at the surface of the ground; clods of earth, bits of cut reed and body parts spurted up out of it. The dust was less as the finger of red fire speared into the edge of the swamp, but the fourteen-foot-high wall of reeds shook and toppled as if God were running a Weedwacker across them. When the gun fell silent her eyes were ringing, and a huge, shallow, irregular bite had been taken out of the tule swamp. It was covered with a thick mat of bullet-cut reeds, with here and there an arm or torso or head protruding.

Adrienne prudently went down on one knee as the helicopter slowly moved out over the swamp, the reeds bowing away from its prop wash in rippling waves. It was moving slowly for an aircraft, but faster than a man could run. *Much* faster than a man could run on foot along narrow paths through a bog. Occasionally it would stop to fire the minigun, or let the door gunners lash the swamp with the .50-caliber Brownings mounted on each side; once it made a curving run at almost reed-top level and ripple-fired the rocket pods, probably at some clump of hostiles, or an island with the round huts of a *ranchería*. Flame bellowed skyward, crimson and orange against black smoke; that spread as the reeds themselves caught fire. Their roots were in the damp mud, but the stems and feathery tops were dry with summer, and the flames danced through them.

She sighed, and let the tension drain out of her. *And to think this morning I was in a good mood,* she thought sourly; even the smell of the place came back, when mortal fear left.

She propped her rifle and Simmons's against the dead horse, checked the semiconscious man once more—no change that she could see—and looked out toward the mouth of the clearing. Plumes of dust were approaching across the flat valley floor, Land Rovers and the armored car; they rolled into the pocket with a whine of heavy tires on clay. Soldiers jumped down, and others manned the pintle-mounted heavy machine guns and belt-fed grenade launchers, scanning the reeds. A medic and stretcher party ran over to her; a man with a red cross on his arm bent to check Simmons while others hurried past to collect the other Scout's body, zipping it into a plastic body bag.

"He's stable," the medic said after a moment; he quickly rigged a plasma drip and hung the bag up on a collapsible stand to let gravity take the liquid into the wounded man's veins. "How much morphine did you give him, Miss Rolfe?"

"One full shot from the field kit, Corporal."

"That ought to hold him; I wouldn't like to use too much when there's danger of shock. Better leave this one in the leg for them to deal with at Rolfeston Hospital, but this . . ."

He took an odd-looking instrument out of his satchel, something between a pair of scissors and a narrow spoon, stripped the covering off it, and slipped it down the shaft of the arrow to the tear in the victim's flesh. Then a quick push . . .

Jim Simmons quivered back to full consciousness, his eyes opening wide. "Bloody hell!" He gasped, straining rigid.

The medic plucked the arrow free, looked at the head—it was stamped out of cheap sheet metal, of the type used for trade across the frontier—and flipped it away; the wound bled freely until he swabbed it clean with something that stung, from Simmons's quiet swearing, and bandaged it.

"They'll stitch that in the hospital, sir," he said cheerfully. "And get the other one out. I've given you a broad-spectrum. . . . You've had your tetanus boosters? Good, good; this one just nicked the shoulder blade, and with any luck you'll be walking again in a couple of months."

"Kolo," Simmons said. "My tracker?"

"Oh, the Indian?" the medic said. "No problem. An in-

and-out bullet hole; I sewed it up and put him out. He'll be fine. And *you* have to rest, sir."

Simmons managed a slight smile as the stretcher bearers lifted him. "Now *you'll* have to cage those condors, Adri," he said.

Heinrich von Traupitz was riding in a Hummer in the lead of the convoy; he leaped down almost before it stopped, snapped a few orders to his sergeant, and then strode over to her. He was livid with anger as he watched the body bag and the injured man pass by. Literally livid, his pale face splotched with patches of red on the cheeks. He tore his militia cap off, crumpling it in his hand.

"Bastard acorn eaters," he swore softly. "We'll show these filth the price of a white man's head! Clean them out once and for all! The Old Man has ordered all the Bay Area Families to call up a militia platoon from their affiliates, and three more from Rolfeston; and there are aircraft coming, and a recon drone—the biggest mobilization in ten years."

A sharp cry brought her head around. Schalk had locked the head of the Indian she'd shot in the crook of his elbow, and another hand clamped on the back of his head. As she opened her mouth to snap an order he made a quick wrenching motion, and there was a snap like a green branch breaking. The Indian's body jerked once and went limp. As if prompted, the militia soldiers began finishing off the other wounded Indians with bayonets or shots to the head, and von Traupitz nodded approval.

Adrienne opened her mouth in sheer inertia, closed it, and shrugged, coughing in the bitter reek of the burning reeds. Schalk simply liked killing people—black people by preference, but anyone would do at a pinch—and the young militia officer wasn't in a taking-prisoners state of mind. He'd probably ignore her if she tried to interfere in his chain of command, too. The last thing they needed now was another inter-Family head-butting match.

Well, may God have mercy on any redskin you catch, Heinrich, because I don't think you're *in the mood for it.*

The officer was probably thinking about his children-to-come; it *was* a bit shocking to have an incident like this happen so close to the settled zone. Silently, she picked up the rifle the dead Indian had been using and pulled back the bolt, holding the weapon up so that light ran down the barrel. It wasn't new, but it was well cared for, the metal bright and gleaming. She ran a finger over the inside of the action and brought it to her nose; the unmistakable nutty odor of fresh Break Free gun oil. She worked the operating rod again, very slowly; the resistance was smooth and easy, without any feeling of grit from dirt or sand, and no loose parts rattled when she shook it. And the woodwork of butt and forestock had been lovingly cared for as well, buffed and polished and oiled.

Hmmmm, she thought, noting a filed patch where the serial number should be on the receiver. *I'll have to check with Nostradamus about any missing weapons. If nothing was stolen in the past day or two, then whoever this Indian was, somebody taught him how to shoot and how to maintain a weapon.*

That was very, very, *very* illegal—hanging illegal.

"I need some help and transport, Heinrich," she said pointedly to the militia officer. "I still have my mission to complete. It would be pretty silly to let the hostiles interfere with that."

"Oh! Oh, sorry, Adri. Yes, of course, Cuz. There's another helicopter coming to our campsite to lift you and those damned vultures out, along with one for the wounded; no expense spared."

Getting the condors into the cages proved to be even more unpleasant than she had anticipated; Jim hadn't been exaggerating about their using projectile vomiting as a defense mechanism, and these had been very well fed on rancid camel, now half-digested. With malice aforethought, she called Schalk van der Merwe in to help her; if he was going to let his bloodlust cost her a potential lead on this ratfuck, he could at least suffer a bit for the error. It meant she had to smell him as they sat in the Hummer on the way back to the campsite, but at least it was mutual.

As they rolled and jounced over the plain of dried grass, four aircraft passed by in the other direction, swooping down from above the Coast Range and passing at barely a thousand feet, close enough to see the grinning shark-mouth markings. They were twin-engine prop planes, sleek Mosquito fighter-bombers built new locally to a classic World War II design and modernized with fancy electronics. Each mounted eight .50-caliber machine guns in the nose and rockets beneath the wings, and the internal weapons bay carried a ton of cluster bombs and napalm.

These hostiles are going to learn there's something much *worse than being chased into a swamp and ignored,* she thought.

INTERLUDE
Rolfeston
September 30, 1968
The Commonwealth of New Virginia

Salvatore Colletta smiled and spread his hands. "Hey, Cap'n," he said. "It's just a bit of an accident, eh?"

John Rolfe reined in his temper. That shouldn't have been particularly difficult; he'd been brought up with the belief that self-control was the first mark of a gentleman. There were several open scowls down the long table, and some of the fine china coffee cups clanked back into their saucers with dangerous force. The heads of all the Families were here, and many of them had their heirs by their sides as Rolfe did, acting as assistants or simply to learn the procedure. It struck him with a sudden shock that four of the Primes were the sons of the men he'd brought in at the founding of New Virginia.

I'm forty-six. Charles is twenty-one, and a father himself. Christ, where did the years go?

"So, no need to get upset," the Colletta said, still imperturbable.

Although if self-control makes a gentleman, that would mean Salvo was one, too. I doubt he ever says or does anything without thinking twice. He was like that even as a young man, and he's gotten colder as he gets older. Right now, I feel like pounding the table and yelling.

Rolfe looked out the tall windows and over the green tree-lined streets of the young city named for him, and calmed himself for a moment by watching the distant whitecaps on the indigo waters. Unfortunately, that also reminded him of the reason for this meeting of the committee. When he turned back, his face was a polite mask.

"Mr. Colletta, introducing smallpox to the Hawaiian islands is not a minor matter," he said, his voice deceptively mild.

The Colletta's eyes narrowed thoughtfully as they met the deceptive calmness of Rolfe's leaf-green gaze. There was not the slightest trace of fear in them; Rolfe knew from half a lifetime's experience that there was nothing on earth that could terrify Salvo, from land mines to a political dogfight. There was plenty of respect there, though. Salvatore Colletta fought to win, not to make points.

"Hey, it's not like I did it deliberately," he said, spreading his hands. "Giovanni, tell the Old Man."

Rolfe's eyes turned to the Colletta's eldest son, hiding a trace of sympathy behind a quirked eyebrow. Growing up with Salvo as your father would be enough to drive anyone crazy. Young Giovanni—equivalent to John, and John Rolfe was the boy's godfather—was taller and fairer than his father, a legacy of his Prussian mother. He spoke with stolid earnestness that could have concealed anything.

"Sir, we loaded a full cargo of Selang-Arsi wares in Toushan."

That was this world's equivalent of northeast China, near FirstSide's Yingkou, inhabited by a weird mixed people the scholars said spoke Tocharian, whatever that was.

He'd never found the time to look into it further; the

trans-Pacific trade had never been very important, until now, and he'd let the Collettas handle it. He'd been prepared to let them have Hawaii, too—if it proved possible to take it over without much effort. He'd made it clear that he would not approve annexation if it took a big garrison to hold the place; the Commonwealth still had less than sixty thousand people. Australia had seemed more important in the long run, thinly inhabited and rich in gold.

Giovanni went on: "The cargo included several hundred tons of assorted textiles—silks, cotton, wool and wool-and-silk rugs. We used some as presents with the Hawaiian chiefs. I'm told that's probably how the disease spread."

Rolfe nodded noncommittally and looked over at Solomon Pearlmutter. The Pearlmutter looked in turn at his son, who'd studied medicine on FirstSide and worked with the University of New Virginia's medical department.

"Abraham?" the Pearlmutter said.

"Sir," the younger man replied. He leaned forward to look at Rolfe. "Yes, that's probably what happened. I've examined the cloth. There are scab fragments containing live virus in some of the wool blankets and rugs. Unless it's exposed to bright sunlight, high heat or extreme cold, the smallpox virus can last indefinitely on something like that. The moderate temperatures and high humidity in a ship's hold would be ideal."

The Colletta shrugged again. "Hey, we didn't cry when all the local Injuns dropped dead of flu and measles and menin-whatsis, did we? This is just another accident, only from China instead of FirstSide."

Rolfe bit back, *No, we didn't cry. And we didn't infect them deliberately, either.* Back in the 1940s he'd been vaguely aware from high school history classes that European diseases had wrought havoc in the New World, but nobody had suspected just how *much* havoc.

I don't pretend to be a humanitarian, but there are limits, he thought. *I'm perfectly prepared to take advantage of the plagues, but not to start them with intent. I don't think there's anything that Salvatore wouldn't do, just for the sake of convenience.*

Saying that aloud would mean an irreparable break between the two Families, which would endanger the stability of the whole Commonwealth. He'd need solid evidence to challenge the Colletta or impose any sanctions on the Family. As Chairman, he *could* order an investigation . . . on the other hand, there would also be hell to pay politically if he put Gate Security onto the matter, unless he came up with damned solid proof. There was always a little murmuring among the other Families about the Rolfes' dominant position.

And if I know anything about Salvatore Colletta, I know he wouldn't leave evidence lying around. Salvo isn't the only one who knows how to pick his fights.

He looked at young Abraham Pearlmutter. "What are the effects in Hawaii likely to be?"

The young man spread his hands. "From what I've read of similar virgin-field outbreaks in FirstSide history, and from the photographs and notes from Hawaii, we can expect at least a fifty percent die-off there. Probably more; this is hemorrhagic smallpox, the type with the highest mortality. It seems there was a simultaneous outbreak of chicken pox spread by contact with some crewman with shingles, and if so then the die-off in Hawaii could be as high as ninety percent. That's including the usual secondary effects, lack of nursing because so many are sick, unburied bodies producing other diseases, disruption of the food supply, and so forth."

"Unfortunate," Rolfe murmured, then went on: "And here?"

"Well, sir, there's one hundred percent smallpox vaccination among the New Virginian population, of course. We managed to contain the spread among the *nahua* workers here by quarantine, and my people are vaccinating them all right now. A few hundred are dead or dying. But some of them managed to steal horses and run before we could identify all the infected individuals, and if any of the wild tribes take them in"—another shrug—"it could run all the way from the Pacific to the Atlantic and bounce back from the Arctic down to South America, the way the earlier plagues did. The native population is very much thinner on the ground now than it was back in the forties, of course, which might interrupt transmission. But this is a very nasty and persistent pathogen; it can sit for years on a blanket or piece of leather. And these days a lot of the inland Indians have horses, which lets them move around faster, and trade blankets, so infected individuals and things they've touched spread the virus further before they die. It'll probably kill at least half of any previously unexposed population, and more likely up to nine-tenths. Small groups might be wiped out altogether as they fall below the minimum numbers for viability."

His father winced visibly. The best estimates were that the native populations of the Americas had already gone down by more than three quarters in the twenty-odd years since the Gate opened; by over ninety percent here on the West Coast, where fresh pathogens kept seeping through the Gate despite decontamination. There had been epidemics of everything from measles to malaria to viral meningitis, and a fresh variety of flu every couple of years. Old World childhood diseases and minor maladies were mass killers here in the Americas and the isolated Pacific islands, just as they had been in FirstSide history after Columbus. The Pearlmutter Family had pushed for medical missions, once the scale of the thing became obvious, but that had been a drop in a bucket. You couldn't vaccinate a thousand tiny bands of nomads, most of whom ran at the first sight of a New Virginian.

Rolfe tapped his VMI class ring against the smooth mahogany of the table, a habit of his when he'd made up his mind.

"Very well," he said. "No use crying over spilt milk. That leaves the question of Hawaii. The probable depopulation does make annexation a simple matter, since we don't have to consider a policy change. As the Colletta has pointed out, the islands would be useful as a base for trade in the Pacific, and to produce tropical staples like coffee and sugar we're currently using valuable Gate transit to import."

Salvatore Colletta's eyes narrowed again. He might not have much formal education, but Rolfe had found he had an instinctive grasp of small-group conspiratorial politics— particularly when someone was about to put the shaft in.

"But," the head of the committee went on, "since we're all anxious to avoid any appearance of impropriety, and in recognition of the burden the Collettas have borne so far, I think we should declare the Hawaiian islands to be Commission properties, governed directly as common land, like Rolfeston and the gold-mining districts. Subsidiary landed properties and development franchises on the islands to be granted on the usual investment and lottery basis for those Families who wish to apply; and with reservation of some choice areas to the Collettas, as recompense for their patriotic willingness to open up this new territory. And we should certainly look favorably on the Colletta's request for a grant in the Owens Valley by way of compensation."

"I second the Rolfe's motion," the Pearlmutter said quickly.

The Colletta opened his mouth. Rolfe cut in smoothly, "Of course, if the committee doesn't have a consensus, we could refer the matter to the House of Burgesses."

Salvo looked as if he'd just swallowed a green persimmon, rather than been reminded of a mistake. He had been loudly against establishing a representative body at all, however limited its powers, and that had cost him badly in the elections. His own affiliates had voted for his candidates, of course, but few others. The Rolfes had a bigger affiliation and had done much better among the unaffiliated free-agent Settlers, which in turn gave them more clout on the committee. And it was highly unlikely that Salvo would want to set a precedent for giving the Burgesses more authority. He subsided, visibly relaxing back into his chair.

"Motion has been seconded," the clerk droned—he was a young scion of the Kimmels; nobody but members of the Thirty Families attended Central Committee meetings. "All in favor? Carried by acclamation. Let the will of the Commission be recorded as . . ."

Salvatore Colletta lingered after the other Family heads and their scions had left; John gave his son an imperceptible nod, and the younger Rolfe followed Colletta's heir out the door. The two older men looked at each other for a moment, and then Rolfe shrugged.

"Fine boy . . . young man . . . you have there, Salvo."

The Colletta was wearing one of his Milanese silk suits today, and Rolfe had to admit that he carried it off well; he'd gained a good deal of smoothness over the years that had put a sprinkling of gray in his raven-black hair

"And the same for yours, Cap'n," he said.

Their eyes met, and said much more than either of them intended to lay out in words. *But then, we always understood each other well, even back in Baker Company,* Rolfe thought. *We haven't necessarily* liked *each other, but we certainly knew how the other man's mind worked. Which is a commentary on one or the other of us, or possibly both.* Aloud, he went on: "They do seem a bit . . . quieter than we were at their ages."

"Hey, Cap'n, we was *condotierri,* at their ages," Salvo said, with that charming grin he'd always had at hand when he needed it. "Running mule-trains upcountry and fighting off wild Injuns an' icing big shots and bosses on FirstSide who tried to muscle in on our action. These boys, they're studying to step into our shoes. They're *civile,* not wild men like us."

CHAPTER SIX

San Francisco
June 2009

FirstSide

"Well, at least this isn't as ugly as that asshole-of-the-universe part of LA," Tom Christiansen muttered, looking at the shuttered windows and locked doors of the building across the street. "Crowded, but the crowds are friendlier. And it isn't so hot."

Mark Twain had once said that the coldest winter he ever lived through was a summer in San Francisco. This June day was a little on the cool side of warm, with the sun high and bright in a sky that was clear but slightly hazy. It might have been March or November just as easily as June. There was a strong wind from the Pacific, too.

"Yeah, and we fit in so fucking well," Roy Tully replied. "Or at least you do, Kemosabe."

Not here in the Mission District, I don't, Tom thought.

Of course, six-foot-three blonds with shoulders a yard across weren't exactly inconspicuous most other places, unless he wanted to confine his career to the upper Midwest and/or Scandinavia. They stood out even more in the heart of San Francisco's traditional Latino district. It could have been worse, though. The action could have been in China-town.

Tully's shorter and dark, but he's not stylish enough to be a real San Franciscan, I suppose.

They weren't really on a stakeout; they were just checking that nobody was at the other location owned by the people who were supposed to be at the first location . . . and he felt even more useless than that suggested. This operation was FBI, with the SFPD handling backup and supplying manpower. The Fish and Game men were embarrassingly superfluous. If Special Operations had gotten any sort of a handle on where the local varieties of contraband were coming from, they might be contributing something valuable to the investigation. As it was they were tagalongs, and if this went on they were also going to look like completely incompetent tagalongs.

And I know things about RM&M and the Oakland angle, the problem is, so far they've been completely useless.

"Well, let's be *good* little tagalongs," he said. "Obviously, nobody's here. Plan B—we go play with the big boys and girls."

He pulled out his phone and keyed Sarah Perkins's number. "Yo," he said. "Minding the store? This one's definitely not open for business."

"This one is. We're going shopping in twenty minutes," she replied. "You're welcome to come along. This time it's tasteful merchandise, not that garish LA stuff."

"Wouldn't miss it for the world," Tom replied. To his partner, he went on: "They're going in—discreetly, not with a SWAT team."

Tully nodded. "Well, this is the town of refinement, not LA Brutal. I'm surprised they don't send a scented notification card, so nobody's feelings will be hurt when they bust 'em."

They turned up Twenty-fourth and onto a side street near Balmy Alley, past bakeries with mouthwatering scents, little produce stores spilling over with vegetables and fruits—some of them he couldn't recognize—and butcher shops and thrift stores. . . . Salsa poured out of music stores and slow-moving cars, and the crowds surged around him, past an amazing variety of colorful murals and more *taquerías* than he could count.

It occurred to him that if he'd really been sight-seeing here, it would be quite enjoyable—for a day or two. If he had to live here, he'd soon run screaming for Golden Gate Park and dash around waving his arms in the air and babbling for a while before he went over a cliff and into the ocean. Where the waves would burst into steam as they touched his brain. It was just too completely, classically *urban* for him to tolerate for long.

The *taquerías* prompted a thought: "Let's at least look like tourists and not cops trying to blend in and failing," he said, looking at his watch. It was 10:10 exactly, and time to be moving.

Plus the Mission District has the best burritos in the world, he added to himself. *All others are a pale imitation. And one of their burritos makes a pretty good lunch.*

They stopped and bought two: rice, beans, strips of grilled beef, salsa, guacamole and sour cream wrapped in a flour tortilla, and that in aluminum foil, which kept it warm and less messy. He chatted with the server in Spanish— although the *Tejano* accent he'd picked up from a girlfriend during his first year in the army struck the Guatemalan lady serving the takeout as hilarious—and then they strolled along taking in the sights as they ate. Two friends eating burritos were a lot less suspicious than two empty-handed Fish and Game agents. He took his first bite with real enjoyment; the rice was flavorful and not mushy, the beans had a hint of a tang to them, and the salsa was appropriately nuclear, soothed by the richness of the meat and the soft coolness of the sour cream. There was nothing like the competition in the burrito capital of the world to keep the vendors honest.

"Who do you figure blew up the warehouse in LA?" Tully said around a mouthful of his own.

"I think the Viets had it right," Tom replied after a swallow. "Some sort of internal power struggle going on in the Russian Mafia. Maybe a policy disagreement; say some of them want to get into the endangered-animal smuggling, and some think it's too dangerous and want to stick with nose candy, horse, selling girls and generalized racketeering . . . or even going respectable, the way the Italians eventually did. That's pretty standard gang stuff; you always get a conservative faction squabbling with a fangs-out-and-hair-on-fire bunch. The wild men are the ones who probably linked up with the dirty group among RM and M's employees."

"Pretty skanky that their 'conservative' bunch got to the warehouse just when we did," Tully observed. "Of course, once is coincidence."

"Twice is happenstance, and the third time proves it was enemy action all along and you were a dummy for not seeing it the first time," Tom said. "Yup, there's a leak somewhere from police sources. Probably more than one. There's serious money involved."

"The sort that could get Spider-man to smuggle shit across the border," Roy said as they wadded up the foil wrappers of the burritos and threw them into a waste container along with the napkins they used to wipe their mouths. "And here we are."

Indrasul Pan-Pacific Exports occupied a tiny storefront in a twenties-vintage three-story building, flanked on one side by a recycled-clothing store and on the other by a dusty-looking shop window filled with an amazing mixture of junky used furniture and real curios—everything from glass net-floaters to flamboyantly colored Balinese dancers' masks. If he'd been on his own time, he could have spent a couple of enjoyable hours there, and he made a note to come back.

Hell, I could come here with Adrienne, he thought, and then shoved it aside—a nice notion, but too distracting right now.

Sarah Perkins was across the street from it, leaning her butt against a car and reading a paper with her face away from the target; she was also wearing glasses to conceal an ear mike for feed from various surveillance cameras.

Tom and his partner walked across the street and looked in the shopfront.

"We're go at eleven P.M. exactly," she said casually, shaking the paper flat and turning a page. "Targets went in at nine this morning and haven't come out; one visitor, unidentified Caucasian male, mid-twenties, left about half an hour ago. We've had full surveillance since a little after that. Everything looks exactly the way the anonymous Vietnamese-American good citizen said it would. Any news on your weird condor?"

"Nada," Tom said. "He still sits in solitary glory in San Diego, being prepared for life as stud of the captive flock."

He turned and leaned his own shoulder against the building; from that position he could look across the street without appearing to stare. Sure enough, he could see a man's head and shoulders over the back of an office chair.

"Uh-oh," Roy said. "Awful crick in the neck there for Mr. Stationary."

"Oh, yeah," Tom said under his breath. That position would be extremely painful if you kept it for more than a few seconds. "Sarah?"

"Shit!" she said crisply, throwing down the paper and turning to stare at the window. "Give me a magnification on the subject . . . switch to thermal . . . shit, he's room-temperature. Go!"

All three of them were sprinting across the street with their guns out before Sarah's paper finished hitting the ground. Tom had been a running back in high school—and attracted the notice of several football talent scouts before he decided to join the army; he was halfway across the street and dodging a car that came to a screeching, cursing halt just short of his hips as he twisted aside like a matador. Tully and Perkins were six very long strides behind, and they had to scramble around the automobile. That might have saved them injury when the windows of the second-story office blew out in a spectacular flash of light, blue-white and then orange.

Tom caught the first flicker with a subliminal alertness common to those who'd survived being shelled. He dove forward onto the sidewalk, thankful for the body armor under his T-shirt; an elbow abraded painfully, but the sensation was distant. A quick look over his shoulder showed half a dozen people injured, but none of the wounds looked serious; a lot more were screaming and running—the war had been over for a while, but after those years people in the United States took bombs extremely seriously. Flames were shooting out of the shattered windows above his head, hot enough to instantly darken the stucco around them and with only a little smoke. That meant a fairly small explosive charge—Semtex to kill, and incendiaries to cover up the evidence with a fire hot enough to make steel burn.

He shoved himself off the ground and catapulted forward, through the open door and up the flight of stairs that ran up from it—the ground-floor shop was already empty and the door at its rear still swung. Halfway up the stairs he could feel the heat blasting out through the half-open doors, and he stripped off his shirt as he ran, winding it around his left arm. Tom sheltered his face with that as he kicked the door open, holding a fold of cloth across his mouth with his teeth as he peered squint-eyed into the offices—an outer receptionists', and the inner sanctum whose window he'd seen from the street. They were already an inferno, fire running in sheets up the walls and flaring out along the ceiling and spreading among a chaos of shattered desks and doors, tumbled filing cabinets and their contents and scattered computer components. The paper was smoking, nearing its ignition heat, and so was every piece of wood not actually on fire. Squinting, he could make out a body lying on the floor with its feet still up on the toppled swivel chair; the once-white shirt showed where four bullets had been pumped into the man's chest, grouped rather neatly around the middle of the breastbone.

Nothing to be done about him, Tom thought, slightly relieved.

The fallen man was probably a poacher and smuggler—almost certainly was. The warden would still have tried to rescue him if he'd been alive, but he was glad that he wasn't; the heat was savage even here at the door and getting worse by the second, with a dull pulsing roar that gathered force like the lungs of some huge angry beast. He stooped to make sure, and snatched up a small silvery recording disk lying on the floor that fell under his hand. Then he froze, even as flaming bits and pieces began to fall from the ceiling.

It wasn't that he didn't recognize the bird in its cage, thrown into a corner by the blast and very dead, its feathers blackening.

The problem was that he *did* recognize it.

It was an ugly roly-poly bird, about the size of a large turkey, with a huge, bulbous, hooked orange beak looking like a swollen excrescence on its bare gray head—it had feathers only on the part above and behind the little yellow eyes, rather like a late-period Elvis haircut. The body was gray-brown with hints of gold as well, apart from the thick bright-yellow feet and white plumes at the ends of the absurd stumpy little wings that gave a final dying quiver as he watched.

It was an ugly, cartoonish creature. And very familiar, although he'd never seen one alive. Nobody had, not since a Dutchman chased down and killed the last one around A.D. 1680, on the island of Mauritius in the Indian Ocean. There were plenty of artists' reproductions in books; it was far more famous than many living creatures.

"It's a goddamned dodo, for Christ's sake!" he screamed, and lunged toward it, into a wave of heat like a solid wall.

✸ ✸ ✸

He didn't hurt much.

That was the first thing he checked on, as the blackness in his head became the blackness behind closed but waking eyes; the first thing, before thinking about where he was. No pain was a good thing; and you usually hurt pretty badly when waking up from a serious concussion. Which he'd done six or seven times in his life, depending on your definition of serious. Not much pain, which meant he could probably count on skipping the blurred vision, nausea, and recurrent headaches that could plague you for months after getting a solid sock to the head that sent your brain surging back and forth like a walnut in a loose shell.

Either he'd slept for a good long while, or he'd gotten off lightly, or both.

The smell told him it was a hospital before he opened his eyes: disinfectant, linoleum, ozone, a faint underlay of something unpleasant, and the odor of utterly inedible food. Memory struggled for a moment, and he thought it was the MASH unit in Tashkent. Then he knew better. That wakening had been far from painless.

His eyes opened. He was in a hospital bed and wearing one of those humiliating gowns that fastened up the back; a privacy screen stood around the enclosure, and there was a scanner hood clipped on the bedstead over his head—the medics had been monitoring his brain activity, then.

Yup, I did get a conk on the head, he thought. *They wouldn't waste one of those on me if I didn't.*

A variant of the same electronic process could produce an artificial analogue of natural sleep to hasten healing these days, and he had a bandage taped over the skin of one elbow, where a drip needle had kept him hydrated and nourished.

An amber light was flashing on the machinery now, so he could expect company. A cautious inventory showed him that there weren't any casts, splints or broken bones either, and everything moved the way it should. He was a little sore and stiff when he tried to move, but it was all functional.

The nurse's aide who came at the machine's call was a heavyset black woman, looking tired with a tiredness that had probably set in for good about fifteen years ago when she turned thirty. She brought him water, which took some of the mummy dust and sourness out of his mouth and throat, and then a doctor—a thin, harried-looking Chinese-American. The name tag on his white coat read *Edgar Chen,* and he looked as if he'd given up luxuries like sleep. Probably a public hospital, then. San Francisco General, which was on Potrero Avenue near the Mission district.

"Good afternoon, Mr. Christiansen. You're quite lucky," he said. "The falling joist wasn't burning, and your friends got you out quickly. No more than a few scorches and very minor smoke inhalation; you can thank heaven for all that muscle protecting your bones. We kept you under to make sure there was no brain trauma. Breathe deeply, please."

Tom did, and coughed, as always—there was something about the feel of a stethoscope on the skin of his chest or back that *made* him cough, had since he was a kid. His lungs did have a faint soreness, the way they felt after a cold or a bout of the flu.

"Excellent. OK, let's see if the machinery was telling the truth. Look at this light. Then at my finger. Follow the finger. . . ."

The examination was brisk but thorough; he supposed they'd done the EMR and the rest of the sophisticated stuff while he was unconscious.

"Well, you need more rehydration, and there was a mild concussion, but apart from that you're fine. You can be discharged in a few hours. Take it easy for the next week and drink plenty of water, bouillon or fruit juices. Avoid caffeine or alcohol."

"Ah . . . how long was I out, Doctor?"

"It's shortly after ten A.M., Sunday."

Whoa! I lost nearly forty-eight hours!

The doctor smiled. "We let you get some rest. Believe me, sleep induction is a wonderful tool. Your friends have been in to see you."

"Friends?" Tom asked.

"A Mr. Tully, and a young lady—"

"Late twenties, gorgeous?" Tom asked with a grin, and grinned wider at the doctor's nod. *Well, well,* he thought. *It wasn't kiss-and-run.*

He basked in the glow of that for a second, then let the two help him up and through a small ward—four beds—to a washroom. He felt a little weak, and stiffer than a board, but that faded as he moved. A hot shower made him feel even better, as if the hurt were washing off with the sluicing water and swirling away down the drain in the middle of the little

tile floor; he didn't even much mind the crowded feeling that
the hospital shower stall gave him—he was used to that.

Roy Tully showed up first, and laughed outright at Tom's
poorly concealed disappointment. There was a bandage on
his right hand, smelling of some sort of burn lotion. Tom
made a note of it—as a sort of mental game, he liked to keep
track of the people who'd saved his life, and vice versa. This
time put Roy up two to one.

"I ran into your Ms. Rolfe in the lobby yesterday," the little man said. "Oh, sweet Lord Jesus—"

"I can fill in the details," Tom said dryly, then coughed
and took another drink of water. "Nope, nothing serious," he
went on at his partner's look of concern. "Just need a day or
two to get the pipes back in order. What's up?"

"Wait a second," Tully said, ducking out of the privacy
curtain.

The other beds in this room were vacant at the moment.
He dropped a rubber wedge under the door and heeled it
home, then brought out his PDA and jacked in a set of display glasses that looked like old-fashioned Ray-Bans. Tom
cocked an eyebrow at the precautions but put them on and
slid the little mikes on the sides into his ears. The world disappeared; he slitted his eyes against the light that would
come when the tiny mirrors and lasers began to shine images
onto his retinas.

"This is the disk you had in your hip pocket when we
dragged you out. I've looked it over, and now you should.
It's . . . sort of remarkable, Tom. I haven't let anyone else
look at it. Palmed it so Fart, Barf and Itch wouldn't notice."

"You haven't shown it to the boss?" Tom asked, puzzled.
Cutting out the competition was fair enough, though he liked
Perkins, but the usefulness of data tended to degrade rapidly.
"If there's important information, we should—"

"Shut up and watch."

The disk was obviously homemade. A professional job
would have given a seamless wraparound 3-D effect, with
only the fact that you couldn't alter the viewpoint by turning
your head to tell it from the real thing. Here he could see the

black-line limits of the visual world at the edges of his vision; the first shots were people at a barbecue or outdoor party: well dressed, wealthy, and at a guess somewhere in the northern Bay Area—*Adrienne's stomping grounds,* he thought whimsically.

Then he looked again. There were a couple dozen people visible, and all of them were white; that was *not* something you'd expect in the Bay Area these days. People moved in and out of the view; an unstaged setting was always less orderly than Hollywood. A flash of bright hair brought him bolt upright—it was exactly the shade of Adrienne's. Then the woman turned around, and the face wasn't hers; a strong family resemblance, but a good decade older, and not beautiful—merely good-looking in a horsey way that went with the tweeds, riding boots and breeches she was wearing. Children ran by, chased by a nanny who looked Guatemalan or Mayan.

The icon in the lower left-hand corner showed a date: May 17, 2009.

The view panned up past a big Georgian-style country mansion, and then to a mountain behind it. He blinked, racking his memory. . . .

Looks like Mount Saint Helena, north of Callistoga, Tom thought. *But it can't really be.*

For one thing, he'd be *in* Calistoga if it were Mount Saint Helena, and for another this mountain was a lot shaggier, thickly forested with oak and Douglas fir and even redwoods.

The viewpoint changed. The date was the same, but the camera pickup was on an open hillside, looking out over a smallish city or big town on the flats below, and beyond that a huge bay. Something nagged at him as the view swiveled south and then panned slowly north again.

"Holy *shit,*" he whispered. "That's the bay—San Francisco Bay, from the hills above Berkeley!"

Only it wasn't. It had taken him a full minute to recognize it, because so much was different. *His* San Francisco Bay was half the size of this—the legacy of a century and a half of silting and draining and reclamation. This one was huge, and it still had its broad skirt of marsh and swamp and tidal flat; through the sound pickup he could hear the thunder of millionfold wings arriving and departing across miles, streams of birds rising like skeins of black smoke from reed swamp and cordgrass salt marsh and open water. The land around the bay was mostly open as well, a checkerboard of farmland south where Oakland should be, marsh and slough and oak-studded savanna elsewhere, and directly below him . . .

"That should be the campus of UC Berkeley," he whispered.

There was nothing there but forest and flower-studded openings, and then a road and a complex of what looked like neoclassical public buildings where the city proper should start. The town beyond was a small fraction of Berkeley's size, and its skyline was utterly without steel and glass.

About twenty, thirty thousand people max, he thought. *Same as Fargo, North Dakota.*

It was mostly low houses, one or two stories with red-tile roofs, and embowered in trees that made it look more like a forest; there was a port toward the southern edge of the built-up area where the marina should be, a modest factory zone, and then a grid of squares, residential alternating with small parks, rather like the older part of Savannah in Georgia. The bayside freeways just weren't there.

The Golden Gate and Bay bridges weren't there either, and neither were the container ships and tankers that should have thronged the surface. Instead only a scattering of vessels could be seen on the cobalt-blue water streaked with whitecaps, and none of them were very large. Some were sail-powered, or at least had masts—big schooners and a couple of ship-rigged three-masters. Across the water . . . the peninsula that should be covered in white tiers by the buildings and towers of San Francisco was mostly sandhills and scrub, with another biggish town along the water's edge.

Maybe ten thousand or a few more there, Tom's mind stuttered. Aloud: "Is this some sort of historical reconstruction? It could be . . . well, maybe CGI of the Gold Rush period."

"Kemosabe, I don't think they had quite as much air transport then."

There was an airport about where Alameda should be, on an island just off the shore. He recognized a pair of C-130 Hercules transports lumbering into the air, and there was a small control tower and a medley of smaller aircraft, including some amphibians. No jets, but a fair assortment of helicopters, Chinooks and Black Hawks and smaller jobs. And there were cars on the roads, and some of the ships and fishing boats out on the water were definitely motor-powered: diesels, from the lack of smoke. The camera swung down to where four saddled horses waited, and a fifth with a gutted mule deer slung over its back. Evidently the camera was a miniaturized cyberstabilized model on a shoulder mount; he could see hands come into the field of view as the bearer put a booted foot into the stirrup and swung into the saddle. The other men in the party—it was all men—were in denim pants and leather jackets, with automatics at their waists and rifles of a model he didn't recognize in saddle scabbards. The jackets had a blazon on the shoulder, a stylized tommy gun.

Tough-looking bastards, he thought. They rode through a patch of tall grass, high enough to brush the horses' breasts—

"That's native bunchgrass," Tom said softly. "About half of it, anyway. As if it hadn't been replaced by wild oats and the other intrusive stuff yet, not all of it."

"Yeah, and that happened . . . when? The first generation or two after the Spanish arrived in California?" Tully said. "In the bay, that should have been finished by the 1820s or a little after."

Tom nodded; the native grasses hadn't been able to compete with the hardy Mediterranean annuals, especially not when cattle and sheep started grazing on them, and the seeds had arrived in hay and bedding when the first European colonists shipped in their foundation stock. In the field he was looking at, that process was still going on.

The horsemen rode down through a forested gully. It was definitely the Berkeley hills—he recognized the lay of the land and the general shape—but more empty of man than Glacier National Park—only the trail, and that might have been made by game. As if to underline that they broke out into another sunlit meadow, starred with orange California poppy, yellow goldfields, purple lupine and dense mats of cream-white yarrow thick among the tall grass. A herd of Roosevelt elk raised their muzzles to watch, then turned and trotted off without overmuch concern; the bull elk's antlers showed against the morning sun for a moment, broader than Tom could have spanned with both arms. He couldn't keep track of the smaller game and birds; everything was in bewildering profusion, and once the horses shied at the passage of what had to be a grizzly, although he caught only a fleeting glimpse of silver-tipped brown fur. The trees overhead included huge redwoods, nearly as big as those in Muir Woods; black oak mixed in on the upper slopes, trees giving way to open grassland on the ridges.

All the redwood in the East Bay was logged off in the 1850s, 1860s, he thought. *Those trees aren't second growth, though. That one there must be three hundred feet high! It was growing there when Columbus went looking for Japan and ran the* Santa Maria *onto Haiti.*

The viewpoint changed again, and again Tom had to grope for the location. It went faster this time; he anticipated it, and the camera swung back and forth.

"That's Mount Diablo over on the right," he said. "The Carquinez Strait." That was where the combined waters of the Sacramento and San Joaquin ran out of the delta into San Francisco Bay. Except that the great oil refineries were missing, and the bridge that spanned the strait. Grizzly bears thronged the shore, hundreds of them. They were wading out into the waters, scooping migrating salmon from throngs that whipped the water into froth. Farther out a half dozen big wooden fishing boats were doing the same, swinging in bulging netfulls. Pelicans and cormorants and ospreys stooped and struck, and golden or bald eagles hijacked their catch in a swarm of wings and a chorus of raucous cries. The camera zoomed in, and he could see that many of the salmon were enormous, fifty or sixty pounds each.

Another jump, and this time the landscape wasn't Californian at all; it looked like somewhere on the High Plains, rising into mountains to the west; the date icon switched to fall. The camera was in an aircraft now, but flying at less than a thousand feet—a small two-engine job, by the shadow. Below stretched a herd of bison moving south, great shaggy brown-black beasts, half-hidden by the cloud of dust they raised from the dry shortgrass prairie. The mass of animals stretched out of sight in both directions, and you could see an awfully long way from eight hundred feet in flat country; not quite a solid carpet, but more buffalo than open space. He'd long ago learned to estimate numbers and distances quickly, skills valuable to a hunter and a soldier both, and essential in wildlife management. Which meant—

"There have to be better than three *million* buffalo in that one herd!" he blurted.

"Spot on," Tully said, his voice coming from another world. "I ran a count. That's north-central Montana, incidentally. At least, the mountains and those buttes over there say it should be, according to the geolocation program."

Three million buffalo were more than five times the total number in the whole of North America in 2009, and most of *those* were on ranches, behind barbed wire. These were running free over a plain that showed nothing of modern man— no roads, no fences, no power lines, not so much as a distant ranch house. But the estimates said there had been somewhere between twenty-five and fifty million, back a few centuries ago. . . .

The shadow of the aircraft swooped downward, the ground swelling until they were flying nape-of-the-earth, above a section of the herd that had decided to bolt cross-country at a dead run. He could see the reason, a band of men on horseback clinging to the edge of the great mass of buffalo, galloping along beside them. The picture leaped closer as the camera's operator dialed up his magnification, and the Indians jumped to arm's length; the picture jiggled a little, as the close-up and the plane's motion stressed the limits of the camera rig's stabilizer.

There were two dozen of the Indians, wild-looking men in breechclouts and leggings with braided hair and bars of paint across their faces and naked chests; here a spray of feathers tucked into the raven hair, there a necklace of wolf teeth. Their mounts were not Indian ponies, though; they were big long-legged horses, and the hunters rode saddles rather than bareback. They were using short thick bows and long lances with steel or obsidian heads, riding in recklessly close to send shafts slamming into the ton-weight bodies, or thrusting the spears behind a shoulder. Maddened dying buffalo ran with blood frothing from their nostrils, and then collapsed in tumbling chaos as others behind with no room to swerve tripped in multibeast pileups.

The men left off their hunting as the plane approached, shaking their fists or lances at it, or launching futile arrows into the sky. A hand extended into the camera's view, giving the hunters below the finger, and he heard laughter over the engine roar. Then the aircraft swept on, over another group of Indians; these were families on the march, probably the home base of the hunting party, with more horses and—he blinked—spoke-wheeled carts. Women had stopped in small groups to skin and butcher the slain animals, with children and dogs running around; the adults stood and shaded their eyes as the aircraft circled above. They weren't as openly hostile as the hunters, but he saw fists raised, and a man in a weirdly complex costume of bison horns and plumes shook a feathered stick at the camera.

Indians who hunt buffalo on horseback—but know what airplanes are.

Scavengers followed the bison herd, as the plane flew along the broad trampled path of its passage, coyotes and turkey buzzards and condors. Scavengers and predators: grizzly bears, a pack of big pale-coated lobos, the white Plains wolf that had been extinct since the 1920s . . .

And resting around a partly eaten bison carcass, a pride of lion: half a dozen females, cubs, and a black-maned male who put his paws on it and roared as the aircraft's shadow swept by.

"*Shit!*" Tom said, ripped off the viewer goggles. He and Tully stared at each other, and the silence stretched. "*Lions?* Indians hunting three million buffalo? *Lions?* How the *hell* am I going to explain this to Yasujiru?"

"You don't have to," Tully said, the usual edge of humor absent from his voice for once. "I tried imagining it myself, and it's unimaginable. In fact, I'd strongly advise you not to. If you have to show it to him, just hand it over and let *him* think up an explanation."

Tom stared at him again. "You're not serious?" he said.

"I'm dead serious, partner. That thing is seriously weird. Weirdness is contagious, and Yasujiru hates the least little hint of anything that's outside regular channels. He doesn't like either of us as it is, despite the fact that we've got the best records in Special Operations."

Tom took a deep breath. "Roy . . . I haven't told you why I tried to get into that office you pulled me out of."

The smaller man's face cocked to one side. "I guessed there was someone alive in there, and you were trying to get them out. SFPD forensics say there was bone mixed with the ashes, but that's about all they could tell; it was a pretty damned hot fire. No salvageable DNA."

"Some*thing* was in there." He paused again. "This is going to sound crazy."

"So? Isn't everything in this ratfuck? It started weird in LA and it's been getting worse."

"Roy, there was a bird in a cage in that office. Dead, I think, but only just—still twitching. It wasn't fifteen feet away from my face, and I got a good long look at it."

"Another condor? Hell, Tom, I know they're rare, but *you'd* have been well-done if we hadn't dragged you out pronto. The stairs collapsed behind us the second we stepped out into the street."

"Not a condor. A dodo."

Tully began a laugh, then sobered at the flat seriousness of his partner's expression. "A *dodo?*"

"Yeah. *Raphus cucullatus*. And yeah, I know it's extinct and has been for centuries. So either I'm lying, or I'm nuts, or *there was a fucking dodo in that office*. You're going to have to take your pick, Roy, because I swear I'm not lying and I don't think I'm crazy."

Tully's hands twitched in a way that showed he'd been a two-pack-a-day man until a few years ago. He looked over at the PDA and the viewing goggles, and slowly nodded.

"OK, Kemosabe," he said. "There's a third alternative—you could be having a false memory, on account of your head getting whacked and roasted like a chestnut, but I'm not buying that. *Losing* some recent memory, yup, that happens fairly often with a concussion, but detailed hallucinations? Only on TV."

Tom exhaled with relief. "I did have nightmares about having to tell Yasujiru this alone," he said.

"If you tell him, you'll be completely alone—and *I* tell *you* for a third time, don't do it."

Tom jerked his head around. "You're kidding!"

"Nope," Tully said, shaking his head slowly. "Tom, OK, you saw what you saw. Someone can get dodos. And condors that never met birdshot. And great big loads of sea-otter skins. And yeah, it's probably from that place on the disk, wherever or whenever or what the fuck it is. But if I didn't know you pretty damned well, if I hadn't known you for years, I wouldn't believe a word of it. I'd say you were subbing for an anal probe from the saucer people. There's no *proof,* man. Maybe if you had the dodo in your hands, but you *don't.* The disk? CGI can do anything these days; hell, you've seen orcs and elves and dragons on screen, haven't you?"

"What about the condor?" Tom said. "There's no way to explain that otherwise."

"Oh?" Tully said. "And yesterday, who was laughing off time travel as an explanation?" He went on gently: "Tom, I may be a hick from Arkansas instead of the big cities of North Dakota, but I know about Occam's razor. What's the simplest explanation—that a Fish and Game warden has gone bugfuck, or that there are . . . hell, aliens, time travelers, whatever, among us?"

"Jesus Christ," Tom whispered. "But think about it, Roy. We have to get after these people, whoever they are. We *have* to."

Roy Tully looked him bleakly in the eye. "And getting fired and possibly sent to the place where the nice man in the white coat has a pill to help you is going to do that exactly how?"

Tom opened his mouth and then closed it. "Roy, think a little more. We have time travelers . . . dimensional travelers . . . in touch with . . ." The words came with difficulty; his mind kept trying to slide away into denial. *I saw what I saw,* he thought stubbornly.

Tully's eyes opened a little wider. "In touch with the Russian Mafia," he went on. "Oh, man, that is *not good*. It shows distinctly skanky motivation and mucho power. Not a good combination."

"Doubleplus ungood," Tom said grimly. "But there's more to it than that."

"More to it than them maybe going back in time and rearranging things to suit their preferences?" Tully said; he was pale now, and sweating a little. "More than the *Russian Mafia* rearranging history?"

"I don't think we have to worry about that," Tom said. "Once you accept that the clues are real, they don't point to, ah, time travel."

"Why the fuck not?"

"Well"—he pointed to the PDA—"Think about it. That looks like the past, right? Only it isn't; there's planes and cars and a couple of small cities . . . and the lion. There haven't been lions in North America for, hell, something like twelve thousand years—the big extinctions after the Paleo-Indians arrived. That was before the end of the last Ice Age, and the disk definitely isn't showing us glacial-era San Francisco Bay: wrong size, wrong vegetation, wrong sea level. It looked like the bay before or right after Europeans arrived.

You know the alternate-worlds theory? It was in that comic book you were reading—"

"It was a graphic novel, not a comic book!" Tully said, with a hint of his usual goblin grin. "Yeah, I know the concept. South wins the Civil War, Hitler wins World War Two, that sort of thing. Been some pretty good movies that used it."

"So that place on the disk, it looks like an alternate history—one where Europeans never got here, ah, there—hell, you know what I mean."

"Didn't get there until recently," Tully corrected.

He looked calmer, and his eyes shone with a hunter's instinct. "That town, those guys with the planes and choppers and ships. We're talking thousands of people. That would take a while, if you were doing it in secret."

"Yah, you betcha," Tom said, feeling his way along the implications of what he'd seen. "And that's more evidence it's not time travelers or aliens from another dimension—or even humans from an alternate history themselves."

"How so?"

"They wouldn't be talking English, or having garden parties, or using Black Hawks or any of that stuff. Well," he conceded, "they might if they came from a history a *lot* like ours, branching off fairly recently—but if they have, ah, hell, call it cross-time-line travel, then they should have a technology a lot more advanced than ours, because there's nothing in our science that more than hints at it. From the evidence, I'd say it's some bunch of people from *here,* here and now, who learned how to get over *there* a while ago. Learned how to do it once, with only one . . . machine or passageway or whatever."

Tully snapped his fingers. "Gold," he said. Tom looked at him. "Brother, you *are* a pure-minded soul. What's the first thing you think of when the words *California* and *history* come together?"

"The Gold Rush, by Jesus," Tom said. "The days of old, the days of gold, the days of 'forty-nine."

Tully nodded, smiling a smug smile; evidently his natural spirits were returning. "Hell, half the towns in the Mother

Lode country get more gold out of the rootin'-tootin' 'forty-niner tourist stuff than they ever got out of the ground," he said. "So say you're Mr. X—must have been a long time ago to build up all that stuff we saw on the disk—and you find out, somehow, that you can nip from here over to a California where 'wealth' means 'acorns.' What do you do? Call in our beloved Feds and have them take it all? *You* might, because you're such a goddamned Boy Scout. Hell, *I* might, after wrestling with my conscience and wiping my sweaty palms. But how many would just get themselves a pan and a pick and a mule and head for the goldfields?"

Tom nodded, rubbing a big hand over his face. "And you'd want to recruit some help, too—you'd need a base over there, and support, logistics. Christ, though, what a racket, if you could keep it secret!"

Tully snapped his fingers again. "*Two* sets of 'em," he said. "Not one bunch using this other universe, two—one working against the other. That's why our busts keep getting bombed and the people we want to arrest turn up dead. What would be your priority, if you were Mr. X?"

"Keeping it secret," Tom said. "That is, assuming I was the Mr. X sort of perp."

"Yeah, but this operation's big and it's been going on for a while. At a guess, at least twenty, thirty years, maybe more. By now there's thousands and thousands involved. From the look of it, there are tens of thousands of people *living* over there—you could see farming country off to the south of what should be Berkeley, and there were those fishing boats, and a couple of good-sized towns. So what happens when there are thousands involved in something like that?"

"Someone gets greedy," Tom whispered. "Someone wants to knock over the apple cart so he can get a bigger share than the big bosses are giving him."

"Right, partner. So we've got this bunch peddling stuff to the Russians, and we've got some sort of cleanup squad going around shooting and burning the evidence and trying to shut the whole thing down before it blows up. I'd guess the ones dealing with the Russians are doing it on the quiet, that they're smugglers—maybe with a bigger agenda, but not out in the open over there, not now."

"Yah," Tom said slowly, nodding. "But there's one thing that bothers me. The lion."

"There *were* lions around here once," Tully said. He had a fair grasp on wildlife biology and ecology, but he wasn't as well-read in the subject as Christiansen.

"Right, but it was *Felix atrox,* the Plains lion—bigger than African lions, nearly as big as a horse. And those were modern bison—they evolved from a much bigger breed after the Indians got here and killed off the megafauna, the giant sloths and antelope and suchlike. And the dire wolves and saber-tooths and lions that ate 'em died off when their prey species went. Back before humans arrived, the Americas were more like Africa: lions, saber-toothed tigers, cheetahs—which is the reason pronghorn antelope are so fast; the slow ones ended up as cheetah food—and there were mammoths and mastodons in place of elephants, dozens of types of big grazing animals, you name it. That's what condors evolved to scavenge. There was a bit of an overlap between Paleo-Indians and lions and horses, but they weren't *riding* the horses or using bows or wheeled carts. They went through two continents with javelins and throwing sticks."

Tully looked interested. "Hey, then how come we human types wiped out all that stuff here, and not in Africa?"

"Because African animals had two million years to learn how to deal with us—the usual evolutionary arms race. Places like the Americas, or Australia, got fully modern humans unleashed on animals with no genetic preparation, and back around the end of the Ice Age the humans were specialist big-game hunters. The big, tasty, easy-to-catch beasts got wiped out in a blitzkrieg of barbecues. Back to the topic, Roy."

"OK," Tully said, shaking his head. "So the, ummm, Mr. X gang, they must have *introduced* lions."

"Probably a lot of other stuff, too, God damn them. They don't seem to have much compunction about letting exotic species loose."

Tully nodded. "OK, and probably they did that from somewhere around here—I mean around *their* Bay Area. From the look of things, that's where this Mr. X got started, and where his operation's still centered."

"We can't be sure of that—let's not get too in love with our assumptions. But it does look that way—"

He stopped, appalled, grunting as a sudden pain twisted his gut. Tully reached out, alarmed; Tom ground his right fist into his left hand, the skin around his lips going white with the force of his anger.

"Jesus Christ, I've been played for a sucker. *Adrienne*."

"How do you figure that?" Tully said.

"The bunch she works for, Pacific Open Landscapes League. Son of a *bitch*. Back in the fifties—they had a different name then—they had an arrangement for importing animals with the San Diego Zoo. Lions, tigers, elephants, rhinos, the whole menagerie. Why? Who the hell knows? Maybe Mr. X likes big-game hunting. And both those groups were—are—tied really tight with Rolfe Mining and Minerals, run by—guess who?—Adrienne Rolfe's father and grandfather. A company that got its start in the later forties, developing gold mines in the Far East and the Congo."

"Gold mines," Tully said, shaking his head with the reluctant admiration a policeman develops for a really good scam. "You just mix the gold you're bringing in from a goddamned *alternate world* together with what you're getting out of the real mines here and now, in countries where you can fake invoices easily by greasing a few palms. Who's going to notice? You're paying your taxes on the full amount—the only thing our cops and IRS and customs inspectors look for is people reporting *less* than what they're actually bringing in."

"And with the gold you buy guns and trucks and planes—"

"And anything else you want," Tully finished for him. "Dredges. Lions so you can go on safari . . . hey, that means they probably can't get around all that much over there, or they'd just go to Africa for their big cats."

"And that's why the sailing ships," Tom said. Tully

looked at him, and Tom continued: "Those were too big for yachts, some of them. They must have fuel sources near the Bay Area, but not some of the places they're sending ships to."

"Slick." Tully nodded. "San Francisco, you can sail anywhere in the Pacific Basin from there . . . anywhere in the world, I suppose, eventually."

"And Adrienne must be a . . . hell, maybe they think of it as cops," Tom said bitterly. "Or spooks. Company security, just like she told me. Trying to plug this leak, this group who're scamming the bosses . . . her family. She needed to get information out of *me,* so they could get to the smugglers before we did. And I fell for it hook, line and sinker!"

Roy Tully sent him a look of sympathy that stung like acid. "Wait a minute," he said, pulling a chair close. "Look, could you give me the details? Everything she said and did, and the order she did it in?"

The big man did, forcing his voice to steadiness; he knew the value of a second viewpoint, one more objective—free of infatuation, or the rage of betrayal. When he was finished Tully was sitting back in his chair, looking up at the ceiling with his hands linked behind his head.

"Look, Kemosabe, for what it's worth, I don't think she was *just* playing you for a sucker," he said gently.

"How do you figure that?" Tom replied roughly.

"Because she got all the information she needed *before* you did the wild thing with her. And let's be honest, Kemosabe: She could have gotten everything she needed to know with a little cock-teasing, right? No need to go all the way."

Tom flushed. "Right," he admitted. "I sang like a canary."

"And all that stuff she told you . . . hell, she even said it herself, right?"

"'Everything I've told you is true,'" Tom said, quoting. "'But it isn't *complete.*'" He snarled. "I'll say it wasn't fucking complete! She didn't mention knocking people off, for starters."

"Hey, hey, Kemosabe, control the emotions, right? Easy

for me to say, but we need your head working now, not other parts of your anatomy. You're not the first man to find a woman had some ulterior motives, my friend, or the first one to fall for a honey trap."

"OK," Tom said, filing it for future reference.

"Now fit that stuff she told you about her family and her relations in with what we know now."

"Right," Tom said, nodding decisively. "That was a run-down on the setup they have over there. It must have seemed like a real side-splitter of a joke for her to tell me all about it."

He frowned. "You know, from what she let slip, they've got a whole *country* over there, pretty well. All run by her family and their friends and relations. I *thought* it sounded a bit screwy, the whole landed-gentry thing. I know a lot of wine-country types like to play those games, but this was *very* old-fashioned."

"Not a surprise," Tully said. "Hey, didn't you tell me that this John Rolfe was one of those old-money, big-brick-mansion types in Virginia?"

"His grandfather, not him. The family lost their money in the Civil War."

"All the more reason he'd go for that sort of thing if he had the chance. Anyway, we need to get some research done," Tully said. "Going to be tough, doing this and our regular jobs. I hope I've talked you out of going to the boss with this."

"You're right; we can't take this to Yasujiru or anyone else without a lot more proof. I doubt Special Agent Perkins would believe me, even."

"That's not the only thing. Yasujiru might be one of the leaks."

Tom grunted. "Hope not. I always thought he was an *honest* pain in the ass. OK . . . how much vacation time do you have coming?"

"Two weeks," Roy said. He smiled, and then let it grow into a broad white grin. "Yeah, now you're talking. Christ, can you imagine what it'll be like if we *can* prove this? Hell, imagine if we can find whatever the hell it is that lets Mr. X . . . this Rolfe bastard . . . pull his magic trick? We could write our own tickets."

A fresh thought swept some of the intent anger out of Tom. "Jesus Christ, Roy, think about being able to *go* there! Go to that place on the disk."

He reached out and rapped his knuckles on the PDA. They looked at each other again, a simultaneous wild longing in their eyes. Nobody went into Fish and Game without loving the wilderness; it wasn't an easy job, you never got rich, and much of the work was frustrating beyond belief That millions-strong herd of bison, that vision of Carquinez Strait nearly solid with salmon . . .

"I'd give a lot to see that, ah, that *world* with my own eyes," Tom said.

"Yeah! Especially before Exxon and Archer Daniels Midland get their mitts on it," Tully enthused. "If we pull this off, I figure we can get some sort of deal on that."

A slight chill ran up Tom's back; he shook it off, and concentrated on what needed to be done. "Come on. We need to tell Yasujiru we're on vacation."

"How are we going to do that?" Tully said.

"Well, I'm recovering from a brush with death," Tom said, a fierce hunter's grin lighting his normally calm square features. "And as for you . . . the honorable Yasujiru never wanted in on this investigation anyway, for one reason or another. Tell him we haven't spotted any more probably-Californian animal stuff, which is true. That'll put you at loose ends as well. He'll reassign you after you get back from your vacation time. We'll say we're going on a hiking trip together—we've done it before, *amigo*."

Tully slapped him on the shoulder. "And afterward, nobody can say we didn't turn in all the evidence. That is *classic* cover-your-ass, my friend. You're developing a bureaucrat's reflexes after all!"

"Now you're getting nasty." Tom laughed. "But I have been a civil servant for a while." He stood. A slight dizziness passed almost immediately. "Let's go grab a steak and start making some notes."

INTERLUDE
September 15, 2001
Rolfe Manor
The Commonwealth of New Virginia

"How was the safari?" John Rolfe asked his favorite grand-daughter.

"Fun," she said with a laugh, wrinkling her nose as he lit his pipe. "It was fun."

Looks a bit like her grandmother, he thought, with a twinge of well-worn grief; Louisa had been dead thirty years now, and he still missed her despite a happy second marriage. *And she looks even more like me.* The torrent of bronze-colored hair was the exact shade his had been, and the leaf-green eyes, and the cast of the long regular face. She was five-nine now that she'd gotten her full growth, though: taller for a woman than he'd been for a man, and fuller-figured. *Athletic with it, though.*

One of the housemaids set a pitcher of lemonade between them, with a tinkle of ice; they were seated in loungers on either side of a table beneath a pergola covered in climbing roses, part of a patio in the gardens behind the manor. Those were more informal than the ones the great house presented to the outside world, and this stretch looked over a swimming pool edged in marble, with a bronze Triton statue spouting water in its center and a view of the forested slopes of Mount Saint Helena to the north. A round dozen youngsters—his great-grandchildren and their friends and children of the house staff—were shouting and splashing and swimming, apparently doing their prepubescent best to drown each other. John Rolfe smiled at the sight, then winced slightly as he reached for the handle of the blown-glass vessel. The elderly mastiff lying beside his lounger on the sun-warmed pavement raised its gray-flecked muzzle in concern.

"Are you all right, Granddad?" Adrienne Rolfe said.

"I'm nearly eighty years old; of course I'm not all right," her elder said, mock grumbling. "All right, you do it."

She tilted the frosted pitcher, pouring for him first, and offered him the plate of pastries.

Girl has good manners, when she's not being deliberately provocative, he thought. *And even at her worst, she usually doesn't do that to me.*

That was one of the advantages of being a grandparent as opposed to fatherhood. *Although . . . come to think of it, my kids didn't sass me much either. Possibly I was too hard on them?*

The tart-sweet taste of the fresh-squeezed lemons went well with the strong scent of the roses that hung in tight red clusters above, and he sipped again as he looked at the statue of Diana and her hunting dogs that stood on a plinth between him and the water. It was ancient, a little time-blurred, but the bronze was whole—a bright graceful thing of elongated limbs and prancing greyhounds and a lovely face whose smile was utterly enigmatic. New Virginian ships had brought it back from an Athens where the Parthenon was still whole and whose temples still saw sacrifices to the Olympian gods—albeit they included the deified Alexander, identified with Zeus. He'd never been able to get away long enough to visit himself, but he'd seen photographs and films and digital video.

And if I keep rationing myself, the scrolls will last my life-time. Classical literature survived here intact, not the few shards and fragments that FirstSide history had. Cities had burned here in this world's history as states rose and fell, but never to the point of a real dark age.

For one thing, the Hellenes just got too big for every copy of anything important to vanish. For another, they did invent printing and paper, at least, if not gunpowder or positional arithmetic. It had been worth the effort of relearning a command of ancient Greek worn to rusty fragments, worth it a thousand times over.

"Thank you," he said to the young woman. "Now some details on the trip, if you please, miss."

"Well, the trip from Virginia City to Fort Chumley was pretty routine," she said.

That was the easternmost outpost of New Virginia, roughly on the site of Denver. It was still a tiny struggling thing, useful mostly as a trading post with the Indians and for hunting trips of the type his granddaughter had just taken. Eventually much more: It would be the jumping-off point for Breckenridge and Victor, Cripple Creek and Leadville. In time a city and the center of a new zone of settlement along the Front Range and eastward along the rivers; but that was for his grandchildren's children.

He bent his attention back to the girl's account, enjoying her bubbling good spirits.

"Spectacular scenery along the way, of course; we stopped at the Great Salt Lake, and I bagged a near-record bighorn head in the mountains. We went south along the foothills from there, and I got a really nice lion in the San Luis valley—ten feet if it was an inch. They're thick as fleas there by now—that book was right; there *was* an open ecological niche for something big enough to tackle an adult bison. Then we spent some time around the Pueblo country. They weren't what you'd call very friendly, but it was fascinating, and they wanted our trade goods very badly. We saw some of the dances, and I collected some interesting handicraft work. No problem getting more horses there, either. Jim Simmons did an excellent job of ramrodding the outfit, too, even if you did think he was young for it."

"Ah." He nodded in satisfaction. "I knew his grandfather and father, and the lad shapes well."

"Cute, too," Adrienne said.

"I wouldn't notice," her grandfather said dryly, then went on seriously: "Good to see the Scouts keeping up their standards. They're a big reason the wild tribes usually know better than to attack New Virginians passing through, even that far east. Then?"

"Then we moved on down the Rio Grande. The farming villages there collapsed after the plagues, just a scattering of wild hunters left, and they are *really* wild—we didn't see much of them, though, just a couple of tries at our horse lines. What we did see was nearly a dozen rhino."

They're spreading fast, he thought. *Well, my hobby is going to affect this world for a long time to come.*

"Wish I could go on a safari of my own, but there's nothing more ridiculous than an old man playing youngster."

"You'll last forever," she said, and sounded as if she meant it.

Rolfe harrumphed. *Flattering, my dear, but not likely.* The old wound in his leg ached more every year, along with everything else. His hair was still thick, but snow white now; he had the same belt measurement that he'd had the first time through the Gate, and thank God his mind was clear as ever, but he could feel the teeth gnawing in every joint pain and his shortness of breath and the way he tired so quickly, and in the way his early memories seemed more solid and real than yesterday. Another decade at most, if he was *very* lucky.

"Or maybe not forever," she went on, her leaf-green eyes innocent. "Which is why I'm going to nag you about getting into Gate Security again, so Dad can't tell me it's unsuitable and make it stick. I owe the Commonwealth two years, and that's where I think I could do the most good, not doing data entry for the Commission."

"And Gate Security would mean you could spend more time FirstSide, and take university courses there—"

"Stanford. UNV just doesn't have all the facilities that the best FirstSide schools do yet."

"—and avoid your mother's nagging you to get married right away. After that embarrassing little incident particularly."

"She can relax. I want children eventually," she said defensively. "I just don't want to settle down and start making babies right away. I want to *see* things and do something *important.*"

"Reproduction is generally considered of some significance," he said dryly, and then raised a hand. "I see your point, my dear. It's scarcely women's work, though."

"FirstSide—"

"This isn't FirstSide, thank God," he said, and waited out her expostulations. An evil grin split his seamed, ancient-eagle countenance. "But on the other hand, what's the point of setting up a system of hereditary privilege if you can't get special favors for your grandchildren? All right."

She leaped up and hugged him enthusiastically.

"Spare my antique bones!" he said. "I'll tell Colonel Throckham tomorrow. But"—he extended a finger—"you get a *chance* at field operative work. *If* you can handle the training and the discipline; I know you're smart enough, I think you're strong enough, and you're not squeamish, but I have my doubts about your ability to take orders. I'm not going to put a finger on the scales where it'll get you killed, or endanger other Gate Security personnel. *Dulce et decorum est, pro patria mora,* but not *pro* wellborn idiot *mora.* Not while I'm in charge. Understand?"

"Of course, Granddad." She glowed at him. "And I'll make you proud of me. I swear I will."

"I don't doubt you will, my dear," he said. "We Rolfes get things done."

He glanced back at the great house, obviously lost in his memories. Adrienne smiled indulgently; it was only natural in a man of his years, to live as much in the past as the present day.

And what he has to remember! she thought.

CHAPTER SEVEN

High Sierras
June 2009

FirstSide

Adrienne Rolfe pulled the knit woolen cap off and rubbed at her face with one hand as she drove. She was tired to the marrow of her bones, after the nightmare of getting the condors through the Gate and out of Oakland. She'd dozed a little as they drove across the Valley and into the mountains, but once off the Interstate and onto the little country roads she took the wheel herself. You couldn't get lost here anyway, with a GPS unit tied into a map screen on the dashboard. They didn't have that in the Commonwealth; the cost of bringing in equipment to put satellites in orbit would have been too much, even for the Commission. Night pressed against the windscreen behind the cones of the lights, moonless-dark, and she drove carefully, feeling the bump and rumble of the van's wheels on the rough dirt of the roadway—just two lines of dirt across pasture and around sagebrush, bitterbush, scattered pinion pine, and twisted juniper. The roadway curved and jinked to avoid the bigger rocks and trees, the ruts worn only by infrequent use.

The windows were open to cut the thick stink of the birds in the back of the van, and the air that came through was thin but clean, cutting like crystal knives. At last she saw the lights of the waiting cars and pulled up, turning off the engine. Deep silence fell, broken only by the ticking of cooling metal and the birds shifting in their cages; it was something she always missed on FirstSide. Most places were never free of the drone of machines in the background, even those FirstSiders thought of as rural.

The vehicles waiting were Jeep Cherokees, with a small roadster in attendance. The men who waited were dark-clad like her, black jeans and boots and jackets and gloves. One of them thumbed on a lantern, and she put up a hand to shield her eyes from the light.

"Put that out, you idiot," she said—quietly, but not whispering.

As far as they knew, there was nobody within miles, but far to the east and below this mountain meadow she could see the occasional set of headlights crawling through the benighted vastness. Light traveled far in this thin clear air, across these distances.

"Hey, Cuz—"

"Don't 'Cuz' me, you brainless pudding, *turn it off.*"

Joseph Filmer probably flushed—she couldn't see his face much, since he also obeyed, and the lamp had turned off her night sight for a while. She knew he was a slightly plump brown-haired man of twenty-one, and more dangerous than he looked.

There was anger in his voice as he replied: "You don't take that tone with me, Rolfe," he said. "I've been doing my end—"

"And a piss-poor job of it," she said, her voice low but cutting like a whip. "I'll take any tone I please, fool; I'm your superior officer and you've been screwing up—badly. If we weren't so shorthanded I'd have you broken and denied Gate privileges right now! You had a simple in-and-out, and you ended up with FirstSider police right on your flabby butt; they may have made your face, God damn it, in which case there'll be a warrant out on you for murder—you'll never be any use on this side of the Gate again."

"I made the hit," he said huffily. "In, killed him, planted the incendiaries, and out in less than ten minutes."

"And the FirstSider police went in *exactly* at the end of the very *long* period you set the timers for."

"You didn't do any better in LA," he said sullenly.

"*I* didn't have two days' warning, which *you* did because *I* got the information out of the FirstSiders."

"Well," he said maliciously, "*I* don't have all your . . . talents."

The silence seemed to come closer. Adrienne stepped closer to the young man herself, until their faces were nearly touching, and spoke very quietly: "Well, if you want to make it a personal matter, Filmer, there are several ways we could discuss it, once we're back in the Commonwealth."

Dueling among the Thirty was legal in New Virginia, but very rare; the Old Man could resurrect laws a hundred years dead, but even he couldn't erase what that century had done to the minds and ways of men. Not all at once, at least. It did happen every now and then—her grandfather said that there should be an ultimate restraint on discourtesy, a limit past which you could go only at risk of life and limb. Filmer would never have been able to challenge her himself—he'd be a hissing and a byword for calling out a woman, given the Commonwealth's mores, even a woman with her rather anomalous standing. For variations on the same factors, he couldn't possibly refuse a challenge from *her,* which was an advantage to throw in with all the trouble her gender had caused her over the years—the *tsouris,* as Uncle Sol had put it.

And he knew full well that if he did accept the challenge, she'd kill him before his pistol was halfway to its aiming point.

He stepped back, and she was in the near-silent night again, cold air against the rough cloth she wore, and somewhere the doglike barking *hooo-hooo-hooo-hoooah!* of a spotted owl.

"Sorry. No offense meant," he said, his voice rusty. "There . . . the target wasn't alone until just then."

"All right," she said. "Let's get on with the mission, and pray God it's sufficient to throw the hounds off the scent.

This smuggling ring is the worst danger to Gate Security since the founding."

He nodded. "Damned right," he said.

She could feel the indignation in it. Endangering the Gate's secret was the worst sort of treason, and there was the shame of knowing that the betrayers were of the Thirty, the lords of the Commonwealth.

"Damned right," she agreed. "And if I never see another condor, it'll be too soon," she added lightly; he chuckled, accepting the peace offering.

They released the last of them at dawn, on a little slope that ran down to the edge of a cliff, above a steep valley carved into a deep U-shape by glaciers gone ten thousand years ago. It waddled out of its cage, striking at the stick that prodded it, looking about suspiciously. Then it turned into the wind and waddle-hopped forward. . . .

And then it flew, catching the winds of the upper air with the great ten-foot spread of its wings, the long feathers of their tips splaying out like a wizard's hands to caress and master the breeze. Then for a moment, as it soared and the rising sun across the gorge caught and gilded those wings, she forgot the nightmare dangers of catching the condors, terror and grief, even the disgust at their stink.

"Ahhh," she said, watching it rise. "I take it back. It'll be too soon if I ever have to *smell* a condor again. Seeing them I can take."

"I know what you mean," Filmer said. "I just feel guilty for trapping the poor bastard birds here on FirstSide."

* * *

"Got the Chinese," Roy Tully said, jiggling the tray of cardboard containers. "And a newspaper."

Despite himself, Tom felt his stomach grumble at the smell of shrimp wontons and mushu; he'd been too busy to eat much for most of the past couple of days, and his stomach too tight with anger. He scooped the newspaper off as Tully pushed piles of documents aside to make room on the low table in front of his living room couch, and snagged a container of hot-and-sour soup, stripping the lid off with his teeth and sipping as he read.

The headline screamed: LOST BREEDING POPULATION OF CALIFORNIA CONDORS FOUND!

Tom swore softly and skimmed the article before he tossed the paper onto the table. It was *USA Today,* which meant everything was aimed at an eighth-grade level of comprehension; that also meant it was fairly succinct.

"North of Death Valley," he said. "Just over the state line in Nevada, not far from Beatty. Jesus Christ, *ten* of them identified!"

Tully took the paper out of his hands. "Yeah, the Rolfes don't do things by halves, eh?"

"Bet this was Adrienne in person," Tom said, an edge of bitterness in his voice—bitterness tinged with respect. "Smart, quick and decisive. And I'll bet you these are genetically related to the one I got in LA. And that they show *some* signs of modern life, like a lead pellet or two in the gizzard, but not much and not all of them. What an *amazing* coincidence."

"Yeah, and the fact that they're all adults will be put down to a lack of breeding success," Tully said. "What else could it be?"

"That's what we're supposed to prove," Tom said grimly. "Let's get back to work."

Every flat surface in his apartment—including the kitchen table and the counters—was piled thick with hardcopy; the walls of the living room were covered in printouts from the disk and from files they'd accessed via his computer. Most police work was done this way, in offices—it was only when you had the framework that you could use shoe leather and start talking to people.

"OK, Kemosabe, we've got another problem," Tully said an hour later, speaking around the pencil gripped in his teeth.

Tom sipped lukewarm weak coffee—he still brewed it the way they did in North Dakota, made so you could drink endless cups through a winter's night—and looked up from an article on the history of Rolfe Mining and Minerals.

"Great. Another problem. That'll make six hundred and thirty-two," he said. "Lay on."

"The more we keep looking, the more money we find," his partner said. "It's not just gold; it's everything else they've been shipping out: silver, diamonds, you name it— there's that seagoing diamond-dredging stuff and marine diesels they bought back in the sixties; give you odds they've been working coastal deposits all over the world, picking the richest pockets, laundering through those mines in Africa they own here and now. And all the proceeds out at compound interest. We've got better than sixty years of compound interest working here, and it looks like they invested it carefully, good solid annual profits on all the holdings they bought. Something like"—he paused to consult a list— "thirty to forty *billion* in assets, all up. Assuming we're estimating the stuff held offshore accurately. It could be twice that, easy, or maybe more."

"Yah, you betcha, they're filthy rich," Tom said, moodily scraping the last of the fried rice out of a carton with a spoon.

"You're doing that aw-shucks farm-boy thing again, Tom," Tully said wearily. "Money that big gets cozy with politicians. It has to. Which means—"

"Which means any case against them has to be solid-gold plated," Tom said.

"It means we have to get a signed confession *and* solid evidence, and even that may not get us a warrant to look at their facilities," Tully said. "They can laugh any accusation of crazy stuff off—and even if it were conventional crime, no *way* any state agency would touch this, not with the contributions these guys have been making to both parties—and to half a dozen good causes, too. That'll bring all of them down on anyone who tries to upset the applecart. Did you see how much they spent on that new library and the hospital in Oakland?"

"Yeah, I did," Tom admitted. "But that tells me something too." His long thick fingers—strangler's hands, his ex-wife had said during a quarrel—sorted papers. "Look at the patterns. Lots of good-cause PR greasing all over, but these guys have been subsidizing Oakland pretty heavy since the early fifties. Donations elsewhere, yeah, but an early and heavy concentration there."

"And there's that big warehouse complex," Tully said, closing his eyes and chewing on the pencil. "I think I see the drift of your thoughts, Kemosabe."

"Let's not get ahead of ourselves. I've got a hunch. Let's hit those land-registry files, if they ever came up. Damn the registry for still using dial up modems, anyway—why not runners with letters in cleft sticks?"

The files had finally come up. What followed was work, eye straining and mind numbing. *Not to mention butt numbing,* he thought. *But there it is at last.*

"All right," he said under his breath. "Get the old map."

Tully handed him the map of Oakland, this one dated from the late 1940s. "All right. There's the house; run-down neighborhood then, but residential. Owner . . ." Tom blinked in astonishment. "Samuel Yasujiru?"

"Our esteemed boss's grandfather," Tully pointed out. "His until they got sent to the camps—most of those people sold up for cents on the dollar. The compensation later was money, not restitution of title. OK, let's take it from there. Sold to one George McSwain, resident in San Jose. Let's look him up. . . . Yeah, primary residence stays San Jose until he sells this Oakland house in May of 1946 to—aha!— one John Rolfe."

"Must have been a rental property during the war and right afterward," Tom said, riffling through more maps of Oakland through the next decade. "License to print money, from what I've heard, especially when rent control came off. Right, sale in May of 'forty-six—that's a very good price, in 'forty-six dollars. Cash, too, no rollover on the mortgage. Then over the next year, every other property in the area changes hands. Some to Rolfe; some to these other names— Colletta, O'Brien, Pearlmutter, Fitzmorton, Filmer, La- timer—then they all transfer to Rolfe Mining and Minerals.

All outright buys, all cash transactions. Then it gets rezoned in 'forty-eight, and they put up the warehouses over the next couple of years . . . railway siding . . . that's it!"

They looked at the irregular-edged green lozenge in west Oakland, not too far from the water. On an impulse, he checked the original shoreline before reclamation; the complex would be closer to the shore there, with a thick fringe of tule swamp and mudflats.

"That's where this all started," Tom said, sitting back. "Sometime in 1946."

"And by the money and attention they've spent on it, it's where it's going on to this day," Tully said with satisfaction. "Nothing else they've got looks like this; the rest is all paper and data and financial apart from the mining operations offshore. I'd lay five-to-one odds this is their sole and solitary way of getting"—he made a waving gesture—"over there."

The little man was chewing a toothpick, a habit he'd picked up when he quit smoking, along with chewing gum. Now he went over to the keyboard of Tom's computer, tapped in a series of rapid commands, then prodded the frayed end at the screen.

"And ain't it another amazing coincidence that there aren't any Web cams there, or pictures of it on any of the Oakland sites?" he said. "And none of the local police surveillance cams are close. Despite Oakland having a net thick as anywhere outside New York and DC."

"Just some warehouses," Tom said with a gaunt smile. "Why bother?"

Especially if strong hints get dropped from very civic-minded businesses that the city really had better places to spend redevelopment money, he thought.

It was late, and warm and still in the apartment's three rooms. His eyes felt sandy and gritty, and there was a sour taste at the back of his mouth. *Haven't done anything but sit on my ass and look at a screen for two days,* he realized.

"OK, I think we know as much about Rolfe Mining and Minerals as we're going to from public sources," he said. "And as much about their *real* operations as we can figure out from the information. What we need now is a link to this internal struggle they're having. It's the weak spot, the only weak spot this operation has."

Tully looked at him with sympathy in his eyes, then away—which was consideration too.

"I'll have to give Adrienne—*Ms. Rolfe*—some more bait," Tom went on. "And it'll have to be good. Then we move in on her. And then, by Jesus, she'll start telling us the truth."

"One thing we should keep in mind, though," Tully said thoughtfully. At Tom's curious look he went on: "These people . . . if we want to predict the way they're going to react when we poke 'em, we should remember that we're not dealing with an American gang."

"Not?" Tom said. "Rolfe—"

"John Rolfe came from a different country, Kemosabe. Put it down to my love of old movies. You soak up enough stuff from the 1930s, 1940s, you realize that that *was* a different country—forget the hambone plots about Maltese falcons; look at the people in 'em, and the background stuff nobody thought about because it was like water to fish, ways of doing things and looking at things and such everyone accepted as natural. They thought different, they acted different, hell, they even *moved* different. You can see it in the way they held a cigarette or got into a car. And—"

Tom snapped his fingers. "Yes. They've got to have kept two-way traffic through the Gate tightly controlled. So things would have changed less on the other side."

"Yeah. Like my hillbilly ancestors, keeping the old ways goin' up in the hollers, only more so. Thing is . . . remember all the crap we went through in the war, keeping civilian casualties down? Even when it meant taking losses ourselves?"

Tom nodded, and his partner went on: "Well, in the war John Rolfe fought, they burned whole enemy cities to cinders and never thought twice about it; carpet-bombed targets in France, too, and if French civilians got caught in the middle—hard cheese, there's a war on. And they stuck the honorable Yasujiru's folks behind wire without a moment's hesitation."

"I see what you're driving at," Tom said. "They made people harder-grained back then; respectable people, not just lowlife types. Whole different attitude toward risk, too; they built their first experimental nuclear pile under a football stadium in the middle of Chicago. And remember how for a while they thought there was a chance the first nuke would set the whole atmosphere on fire and burn the planet bare? They just went on ahead anyway."

Tully nodded. "And I don't think, from the way this little caper has been going, that they'll have ripened into a nice soft banana over there in Frontierland."

INTERLUDE
July 17, 1954
Rolfeston
The Commonwealth of New Virginia

"I don't get it, Sol," O'Brien said. "You just said that it wouldn't pay; then you say it will."

"It wouldn't pay *now*," Solomon Pearlmutter said; he restrained himself visibly from adding, *you big dumb mick.* "But using the Gate's going to get more and more expensive every year."

O'Brien's thick red brows knitted over blue eyes. "How can it?" he said. "The Gate . . . all it costs is keeping that radio set of the Old Man's working. It's free as air, or nearly."

"Wait," John Rolfe said, lifting a hand; Salvo looked about to speak, and that might cause a quarrel. Andy O'Brien had gotten on better with Sol over the years, but worse with Salvo. "You're thinking about relative volumes, right, Pearlmutter?"

"Yes, sir," the Jew said, nodding.

Silence fell down the long table; there were a dozen men

around it, all of his first partners who could be in Rolfeston today. The big second-story meeting room looked out on an arched colonnade, and that in turn looked over what Rolfe had christened Stonewall Square.

After the general who got my grandfather's leg shot off, Rolfe thought with a hint of wry self-mockery. *While winning a lot of battles and losing the war. But a man's entitled to his nostalgia, when he's making dreams real.*

Beyond the square was a scatter of dirt streets, trucks bumping along in clouds of dust, houses and buildings of brick and adobe fading off into Quonset huts and tents, swarms of men working at everything from laying sewer pipe to planting roadside trees. Beyond that San Francisco Bay reached, whitecaps across deep-purple waves, lovely under a sky of aching blue thick with wings.

"You explain it, then, Sol," Rolfe said. "You'll do it better than I could."

Sol Pearlmutter grinned at him, and ran a hand over brown hair already going a little thin in front, although he was still only a few years past thirty. He was a thin, sharp-featured, big-nosed man an inch or two below medium height, no longer quite the deadly weasel-quick young soldier he'd been in the Pacific; prosperity and years had put a slight pot on his skinny frame. His hazel-flecked brown eyes were still disconcertingly sharp.

"It's like this," he said, holding up his thumb and index finger in a ring and then pushing a pen through it. "And shut up with the laugh, Andy, you dirty-minded *gonef.* OK. That's the Gate. It's only twenty-eight feet, six inches by nine feet, two inches, and it's never getting any bigger. No matter how well we organize the way we push stuff through, only a certain amount *can* go through in a day. There are, what . . . nearly twenty thousand people altogether here in the Commonwealth? It's not just a combination mining camp and weekend country club anymore; it's turning into a real . . . well, a place where people live, kids get born, the whole *schmear.* Including *our* kids. Someday not too long from now there'll be fifty, sixty thousand people here, then more—and every new head means more supplies through the Gate. In the long run, we need to keep the Gate for things we *can't* get here; like we're already growing our food, for example, and cutting our own timber and manufacturing cement. Shipping through bulk commodities is dumb."

"Yeah, I think I see your point, Solly," O'Brien said. "If we keep on bringing our fuel through, we'll need more Gate time every month, until we'll have no space for anything else."

"Right," Pearlmutter said. "And besides—everyone here will still have to buy the oil from *our* wells and *our* refinery. Long-term, we've got to keep thinking about our economic position here, too. People resent taxes they don't get anything for. Buying stuff's different."

Salvatore Colletta nodded. "When you've got control over what people really got to have, you got a little gold mine." He snickered. "Every bit as good as a real gold mine, eh?"

Pearlmutter sighed. "If only we could get some really first-class physicists . . . can you imagine what Einstein or Oppenheimer would make of the Gate? And what we could do if we could make more Gates—to FirstSide, or to other, hunh, other New Virginias?"

Rolfe nodded impatiently. "If ifs and buts were candied nuts, the world would be fat," he said. "I'm keeping an eye open for scientists. The problem is that finding physicists good enough to be worthwhile, inconspicuous enough not to be missed, and willing to work for us—particularly the latter—is . . ." He shrugged. "But you made a good point there, Sol, about planning for the future. I've been thinking about that. Things are sort of . . . fluid here now. It's easy to make decisions; but further down the road what we do now will be set in stone. I think we should set up a subcommittee for things like that. First and foremost, we need a legal system; it's getting just too time-consuming to have everything referred to the committee when some Nazi bashes a good ol' boy over the head or a Lithuanian knifes a Pole. . . ."

"Over who should own Vilnus, of all things completely

meaningless here," Pearlmutter said; the case had been a ten-days' wonder in Rolfeston. "With Poland *and* Lithuania occupied by the Russians, too. *Meshuggeneh!*"

Rolfe nodded. Shipping people to another dimension didn't necessarily make them forget the feuds they'd left behind, not at first and sometimes not ever. Hopefully their children would. He went on: "For the legal subcommittee I propose . . . let's see. You'll head it up, Sol; under you, hmmm, Dave Howden, Harry Throckham, and Andy O'Brien."

"Captain!" the big redhead yelped. "I'm working my ass off getting the machine shop back in shape after the fire! And I'm no shyster, by God."

Rolfe grinned; Pearlmutter had given a stifled groan of resignation and an appealing glance. *He'd* figured out what the head of the committee had in mind immediately, and wasn't looking forward to paring things down enough that O'Brien didn't object. Andy wasn't stupid by any means, but he wasn't an intellectual either.

"That's the reason, Andy," he said. "Sol's smart as a whip, but he does love splitting a split hair until the remnant violates the laws of physics. You don't have fifteen generations of Talmudic scholars in your blood. I want something straightforward."

"I make sure what Sol produces is simple enough for a dumb mick to understand, eh, Captain?" O'Brien said, laughing. "Well, when you put it like that . . ."

"Any objections?" Rolfe said, looking down the table at the twelve men who sat on the Central Committee of the Gate Control Commission. "All right, both measures passed by acclamation. Next item . . ."

When the meeting broke up, Pearlmutter lingered for a moment. Rolfe gave the window a longing look—he had a sweet little ketch docked, just begging for singlehanding on a day like this—but business was business. A leader's business was mostly managing his subordinates and knowing how to delegate and how to keep them working together;

that was turning out as true here as it had been running Baker company.

"What's bothering you, Sol?"

"Captain . . . you mentioned it." The Jew's face took on a twist of distaste. "Did you have to recruit those fucking Nazi *mamzers?* Please, no more of them!"

Rolfe sighed. "Sol, we've been over this ground before. We needed skilled labor—and best of all, they really, really wanted, *needed,* to jump into a hole and pull it in after them. They're not going to complain about staying in New Virginia, not if they were too hot for Brazil or Paraguay to hold. The supply of Americans who fit the ticket is limited."

"Yeah, I recognize the logic. I still want to puke every time I see one of those SS fucks. Puke on his dead body after I shove my bayonet into his guts and twist it."

"Well, look at it this way, Sol. *They're* taking orders from *you.* Can you imagine how happy that makes them?"

That brought a snort of unwilling laughter. "There is that; if they weren't here, I'd never get to kick a Nazi's *tokhus,* would I? Which, I grant you, is some satisfaction; so is the way they have to smile and pretend they like it. A *kholereye* on them all anyway. But they could be dangerous, Captain. Don't think they've given up dreaming of a little Aryan kingdom all their own."

Rolfe grinned. "Sol, do you think I'm idiot enough to trust them?"

The smaller man blushed. "Sorry, Captain."

"Sane, sensible people aren't likely to be desperate enough to want to come here—not to live, at least. Sane, sensible people stay home in their stalls and chew their cuds; what we get, are going to get, are desperate broken men, mad dreamers, or both. I'm not going to let enough of any one kind in to have any chance of taking over, and I'm not going to let too many of them settle in a group. Spread around, von Traupitz and his cohorts'll eventually vanish into the New Virginian majority, the good old melting pot. Besides, that well's about dry. The ones left FirstSide have either found good hiding places or been caught."

"Where do we go next for manpower?" Pearlmutter said. "Labor's our big bottleneck, now that we have enough First-Side mining properties to cover our output. We're too big to get all our supplies through the Gate, which means as we expand, a higher share of each new input of labor has to go to support functions here, everything from schools to power plants. Now, if you'd let us use hydraulic mining—*that's* a labor-saving method."

"And it chews up the landscape even worse than dredging," Rolfe said. "What's that saying you told me? 'We don't crap where we eat'? From now on, I'm only going back FirstSide for business and visits to a gallery or two. Let *them* dine in the latrine."

"Then we need more workers," Pearlmutter said.

"I made some contacts in Africa FirstSide last year. They may be very useful; it wasn't just a safari. That area could be valuable for recruiting settlers as well as covering our gold output."

Pearlmutter's eyes went up. "I didn't think you were that keen on the *schwartzers,* Captain."

Rolfe made a dismissive gesture. "I've no problems with well-behaved Negroes, in their place; I've known plenty who were better citizens than a lot of poor whites—it's just simpler not to bring them here. I meant colonists of various sorts, like those Dutchmen we got from the East Indies. We're already getting a few French from North Africa, and that's going to be a major source. From what I saw and heard and what I've read since, the African pot is starting to boil and it'll get hotter fast. A pity; I enjoyed Kenya, but it'll give us opportunities. And I think we may be able to get more people from the U.S. over the next decade; from the South, particularly, for much the same reasons. The war—both the world wars—cracked the foundations of the white man's empires, and the dust will be a long time settling."

Pearlmutter rolled his eyes. "Oh, wonderful. The KKK, yet," he muttered.

"Not very likely," Rolfe said, his lip curling in a slight sneer. "The scum who call themselves the KKK in modern times are nothing but dim-witted sadists and white-trash Negro haters, led by confidence men out to make a buck. I wouldn't hire them to shovel out a stable, not least because they'd be too drunk to do a good job."

He relaxed. "Sorry. The original Klan after the Civil War was a gentleman's outfit, Confederate officers fighting against Northern occupation—Forrest himself disbanded it when things got out of hand. What I mean is that there will be a fair number of respectable people unhappy that their right of community self-government's being trampled, and ready to move."

"Well, you'd know, Captain. Until I joined the army, I'd never been farther from New York than the Catskills," Pearlmutter said.

"Rebecca and you on for dinner Sunday? She and Louisa can talk about that Schools Council business afterward, and we can play chess."

"I don't know, Captain," the Jew said mock dubiously. "You're learning too quickly."

Rolfe laughed and clapped the other man on the shoulder. He enjoyed Sol's company, in reasonable doses; he played a wickedly challenging game of chess, and he shared some of the Virginian's taste in books, and he really knew classical music with a passionate zeal, enough to work hard at getting a chamber group started. Andy was more fun for a drink and a night out on the town, Salvo had taken to yachting with surprising enthusiasm, and his own relatives were the men for a horse-and-hounds meeting or a hunting safari.

All in all, the Commonwealth of New Virginia was shaping up to be a very pleasant place to live, as well as to make money.

I've just got to see that it develops in the right way, he thought. *Having children changes a man's perspective; I've got my sons' legacies to think about now.*

CHAPTER EIGHT

Sacramento, California
June 2009

FirstSide

"You were holding out on us," Sarah Perkins said.

"Yeah," Tom answered, looking her straight in the eye. "And on our own chain of command as well. After you've listened to what we have to tell, so will you. Or," he went on with a wry smile, "you'll talk soothingly as you steer us to the rubber room."

Tom watched the black woman's thin eyebrows go up a little, then further as she looked about her at the documents and printouts heaped around the apartment. They'd cleaned out the empty Chinese food cartons and pizza boxes, and made a quick-and-dirty attempt to get things into order. It still looked pretty messy.

"This had better be good," she warned. "I don't get enough weekends at home with my family as it is."

Tully snorted. "This is better than good. This is *X-Files* come true."

Bad move, Tully. Bad move, Tom thought, watching her face.

"Let's start with that condor," he said hurriedly.

Four hours later she sat back; for the first time in the months he'd known her, Special Agent Perkins's face looked slightly slack.

"You have *got* to be shitting me," she said slowly. Then she looked from one man to the other. "No, Tully could do it, but you're too much of an Eagle Scout. You really believe this, don't you?"

Tom nodded. "It's not that I want to believe it," he said and held up his hand with two fingers upraised and the thumb crossed over the others. "I actually *was* an Eagle Scout. So . . . Scout's honor."

The FBI agent looked at him for half a minute by the clock, steady and silent, a slight frown bending her thin brows. At last she sighed, a half-angry sound.

"All right," she said. "I'm not going to call for the rubber-room division just yet. This is the craziest story I've heard since I started with the Bureau, and we hear some fine varieties of paranoia. I don't—didn't—peg you two for woo-woos, though."

"I admit it sounds crazy," Tom said earnestly, leaning forward with his elbows on his knees and his big hands knotted together. "And a lot of it depends on evidence we're asking you to take on faith. So what we want you to do is check yourself, in a way only the Bureau can do. Check Adrienne's . . . Adrienne Rolfe's movements. Look for patterns. If we're right, there'll be some unmistakable evidence."

Perkins looked at them. The FBI system could do that: another legacy of the war. It wasn't supposed to be used for domestic surveillance except in situations where terrorists were involved, or an extremely unambiguous threat to innocent life. Even then, under very careful safeguards. Doing so without authorization would be a career-wrecking move, and could possibly put Perkins in jail, unless they were retroactively blessed by success.

Then she sighed again. "You two boys go for a walk and come back in fifteen minutes—I'll be in enough trouble without letting anyone outside the Bureau see exactly how I'm going to do this. Congress would shut the whole system down in a minute if there was a *hint* of outsiders getting their hands on it. The ACLU is raising its head again, you know."

Tom nodded, carefully not smiling—the last thing he

wanted to do was disturb a fragile equilibrium of belief. Outside the door, Tully extended a palm and they gave a silent high five, the smaller man grinning like a shark.

"You nearly queered the pitch with that *X-Files* remark," Tom said, turning down a stick of Tully's gum. "God damn you *and* your hobby."

"Sorry," Tully said. "Couldn't resist. My sense of humor's gonna be the death of me, someday."

* * *

"All right, you sons of bitches," Perkins said in a growl as she opened the door and beckoned them back inside. "You know what you've gone and done now?"

They looked a question at her, and she went on: "You've put me in the same goddamned position you were in—believing something I can't prove. What the hell are we supposed to do, convince the world one friend at a time?"

Tully shrugged. "Sort of slow," he agreed. "Even for those of you who do *have* friends."

"*You* I wouldn't have believed if you told me shit stinks," she said. "I've got enough to convince *me,* now, but—"

"What did you get?" Tom asked eagerly.

"I used the identification net," Perkins said.

She nodded toward her PDA. The FBI had set up the system during the war; computers collating input from retina scanners, fingerprint and voiceprint scanners, and public surveillance cameras running face recognition software and reading things like license plate numbers. It had been extremely useful, but it had also never been popular—there were already calls for dismantling the whole system.

I've wished that myself, Tom thought. *But it is so damn useful.*

"I turned the information into hardcopy and then erased everything I could," she said. "I've got clearance for remote-accessing it, although they're probably going to restrict that soon. I will catch hell in a month or so, when they review requests and ask for a justification report."

Her PDA was securely fastened; the printout had been routed through Tom's machine. *And I'm willing to bet several of my favorite organs there's no data trace back,* he thought. *Perkins's name will be recorded at Bureau HQ, but she's kept us out of it.*

"This is recorded movements of your Ms. Rolfe," the black woman said. "Back as far as we go—some of the early data predates the system; it was collated later."

"Aha!"

"The early stuff might just be an artifact," Perkins said, pointing and flipping. "Back then our surveillance net was skimpy—there weren't nearly so many biometric ID scanners, or face-recognition systems, and they weren't tied into the national grid the way we set it up in the last part of the war. But the stuff for the later period is good; we've had the Bay Area tied up tight as a drum for a while now. Here's the pattern."

The dots showed unmistakable clusters. There was a tight grouping around the HQ of the Pacific Open Landscapes League in Berkeley . . . but only a few near Adrienne Rolfe's putative address in that city. A massive cluster, dots blurring into black blobs, near the RM&M warehouse complex in south Oakland.

"But now, look at them sorted for time."

Tom's breath hissed out between his teeth. *Yeah.*

Perkins went on: "Ms. Rolfe evidently goes into that warehouse area and *stays* there. For months at a time. Then she comes out of the warehouses, spends time at the POLL HQ and the Rolfe corporation in San Francisco, travels around the Bay Area—and beyond, of course—stays an occasional night at what's supposed to be her main address, and then goes back to the warehouses. In fact, she spends considerably more than half her time inside that complex."

Slender black fingers flipped at the printout. "OK, here's a specific instance, the day of the LA bust. She comes out of the warehouses, after a two-month stay, and scoots her pink ass over to San Francisco, picks up two guys, and drives a rented van—registered to RM and M—to LA. Gets there three hours before we go in."

This time the printout map was a long strip, showing the California coast and then Los Angeles.

"She blitzes down 101 to LA, gets into the area—no scans for a while, probably off the area under surveillance—and then, here! On a couple of the pickups on the LAPD and our vehicles, right after the explosion. Leaves LA, goes back in the warehouse for a couple of days . . ."

She produced a final, less detailed schematic. "Now this is something that occurred to me . . . does anyone else fit this pattern? Spending long periods of time in these warehouses, that is. According to this and the Bureau's brand-spanking-new computers, which were one good thing we got out of the war, plenty of people do. Couple of hundred people. Most of them spend a lot *more* time in the warehouses. A lot of them appear outside only every couple of years. And some people who should show up—this mysterious grandfather, for example—don't register at all. What we have here is a secret society of extremely rich people who like to live in an industrial storage area."

"Or an industrial storage area that's a gateway to another world," Tom said.

Perkins winced, touching her fingertips to either side of her head. "Please," she said. "Let me get used to the idea. My mind accepts it, but my gut hurts every time the mind says yes."

She showed out two last printouts. "Incidentally, these are the badasses Ms. Rolfe drove down to LA with. They show up fairly frequently, same pattern, and often with her over the past six months."

Tom took the pictures; they were black-and-white, evidently reproductions of passport photographs; those were all stored digitally these days. One man in his thirties and lean, with a washed-out fairness, and a dark one in his forties with a square, scarred, brutal face and an expression like a clenched fist. Serious badasses, or he missed his bet; he knew the look. And . . .

Yes, I saw them. That day in LA. Just a glimpse, but it was them. Which means it must have been Adrienne too. Of course, she told me she'd been in LA. . . .

"Schalk van der Merwe and Piet Botha," she said. "South Africans, and not the most savory types, both with early ties to the AWB—extremist group over there, sort of like the Aryan Brotherhood but for real. Employees of Central African Minerals since 1996; CAM is, surprise, an RM and M subsidiary. Legal residents here, with green cards. And *they* spend a lot of time in the warehouses as well. Oddly enough, Botha's family came through San Jose airport in 1996 . . . and there's no record of them anywhere ever again."

"Yah, you betcha, it's a pattern," Tom said. "The question is, what can we do with it?"

"Well, we can't go to management with it," Perkins said decisively. "So far all we've got is screwy travel and residence patterns. In these days of peace and freedom, all we'd get for reporting them is trouble."

Tom nodded somberly. "We need real proof," he said.

"A smoking gun," Tully said meditatively.

Perkins smiled. "Well, in for a penny . . . there was something I was going to tell you. We know about another meeting of the perps we've been tracking in this animal-products smuggling ring. It's not due for a bust, because we're hoping to plant a bug on one of the Vietnamese; I don't think that'll work, myself. The other side's electronic security has been very good in this whole investigation. But we also know that the Russians and the Vietnamese aren't going to be the only people there; someone else, the ultimate suppliers, the moneymen, are going to be attending as well. Trying to patch things up after the recent misunderstandings."

Tully grinned and let his toothpick roll to the other side of his mouth. "The mystery men. Who are probably the ones the beauteous Ms. Rolfe and her Boer Banditos are trying to suppress. She'd be *very* interested in trying to get her hands on them. The way they led us right to their precious secret, she and her pa and grandpa are probably *very* unhappy with them."

"Aha," Tom said. "Not a bad idea, Sarah. You want to poison the well."

That was a standard covert-ops trick. If you found out someone had a double agent in your operation, you could use the fink to feed the enemy disinformation, making him an unwitting triple agent. In this case, Tom had been the leak; and now he could give Adrienne Rolfe information she'd probably take at face value.

Making me a very witting triple agent, Tom thought. He still felt a hot flush of anger every time he remembered how she'd played him for a fool.

"There's only one problem," Tully said. "Well, a lot of problems, but they all start at the same place. If we try to catch her red-handed—not to mention the mysterious dissident from RM and M—we'll have to do it by ourselves. Just the three of us. No backup. Luckily, Ms. Rolfe and her opponents both seem to prefer to work quiet, but this time we'll be on the same scale. If we screw the pooch, we're rogues and we all get cashiered and probably do time. Anyone want to bet RM and M hasn't got enough political pull to see that done?"

"Unless we can blow this open and bring them down." Tom shrugged. "We'll just have to be very careful."

✵ ✵ ✵

"Sorry," Tom Christiansen said into the phone. "But I can't make it tonight."

"Is something wrong, Tom?" Adrienne's voice said. "You sound odd."

Because I'm trying not to scream and jump around, he thought tightly. *Undercover work is not my thing. And I really liked you, God damn it.*

"Work," he said. "Another bust, believe it or not."

"Ah," she replied—and was it his imagination that heard a sharper interest? "You're really making progress! Where would that be?"

When he'd finished sweat beaded his brow, and he could

feel it cold and clammy in his armpits. *She* had *to suspect something fishy. God, that was lame!*

To his surprise, Tully gave him a grin and a thumbs-up. He looked at Perkins and raised his brows.

"Not bad," she said—which was her equivalent of Tully's gestures. "That should have worked. After all, the last time you told her we were going on a bust it worked like clockwork for her."

"Yeah," Tully said, spitting his gum into a wastebasket and crackling his knuckles with glee. "Only this time, we're going to be there first."

✴ ✴ ✴

"I wish we had more backup," Tully said.

"Then we'd have to convince 'em we weren't crazy," Perkins pointed out.

Maybe we are *crazy,* Tom thought.

The three of them pulled the dark knit hoods down from their foreheads to cover their faces; the night-sight glasses were a lot less conspicuous that way, too. Perkins had gotten them Bureau-issue, better than the SOU could afford, and better than the military ones he'd used in the Rangers—of course, that was years ago now, too. These were the latest model, not much bulkier than sunglasses, and there was less of the green glow he remembered unfondly from the 'Stans and Iraqi Kurdistan. He took a last look at the copy of the building diagram before stuffing it back into his pocket; in, upper left-hand gallery, fourth entrance from the far end.

The glasses revealed the deserted nighttime street in all its seediness, down to the piece of newspaper blowing along the sidewalk with a tiny *scritch . . . scritch . . . scritch* of crumpled newsprint on concrete. They said Oakland had boomed since the nineties, but you couldn't tell that from this neighborhood; the only other car in sight was resting on flat rims and probably hadn't moved in years. A couple of failed attempts at renovation punctuated the decay of the buildings.

Even the air seemed to have a stale smell, far from the living stinks of the bay.

"All right," Tom said quietly, racking a round of double-aught into his shotgun; he'd have preferred a machine pistol or an automatic carbine, but they couldn't go to the armory and draw as needed in this operation. "Everyone receiving clearly?"

The other's murmurs came through the button microphone in his left ear. "We go in, collar the perps and then wait until Ms. Rolfe and/or minions arrive, at the time I gave her." Λ grin. "I do hope *your* information was good, Sarah."

She shrugged. "The Russians are bringing their Viet contacts to meet their source, so they can all kiss and make up," she said. "Or at least that's what our source said. Knowing what we know, that means at least two people from . . . ah . . . you-know-where." Perkins had been avoiding the phrase "alternate universe." "We grab everyone, call in the good guys, and break the news on an unsuspecting world. . . . Let's go."

They did, walking across the street with their weapons down by their sides, unnoticeable to a casual passerby in case one came through this run-down part of West Oakland. A few of the buildings were sealed, windows shuttered and marked with FOR RENT signs; not far away traffic hummed along the Nelson Mandela Parkway, and nearer the water to their south a diesel locomotive blatted mournfully as it drew a load of containers up from the docks. Tom checked the street number twice, because the building looked as shuttered and deserted as anything here. He was surprised at how nervous he felt, until he realized it was mostly a peculiar form of institutional loneliness.

I've been a team player too long, he thought. *First in the army, then with Fish and Game.*

It wasn't just a matter of having backup in the physical sense; operating on his own was nothing new. But he was used to being on the side of the angels, or at least on the side of the duly authorized, licensed and officially approved. If things went messily wrong here he'd be filed under *rogue cop,* and so would his friends. The sensation made him a little queasy, and it was unfamiliar. Somehow the thought of being killed wasn't nearly as nerve-racking as the thought of being classified with the villains afterward.

I may be nervous, he thought, suppressing the sensation with an effort of will. *But I'll be goddamned if I'll be scared.*

He drew his foot back for a boot-heel entry—the door was sheet metal around the lock, and didn't look especially strong.

"Let me," Perkins said, touching him on the sleeve.

She pulled out what looked like a blank Yale with a miniature doorknob on the handle. It hummed a little as she inserted the key end, then went through a series of barely audible clicks before turning inert.

"Sensors on the key," she said softly, twisting the knob. "Adjusts it automatically . . . there! Standard-issue these days."

"Fart, Barf and Itch get all the cool toys," Tully said, his jaws working on a wad of gum.

The front doors led into a long two-story hall, part of an old converted warehouse that someone had hoped would become a nest of boutiques, upscale shops and eateries. Spiral staircases on either side led up to two galleries, giving access to shops and offices mostly vacant, like the ones on the ground floor. Most of those that were occupied had signs in various Asian scripts.

Tom brought the shotgun up, eyes flickering back and forth. "Go," he whispered, hearing his voice in an eerie echo from the ear mike, ready to suppress anyone who shot at them. Hopefully the villains wouldn't know they were coming, but nobody ever got killed by being too ready for trouble.

Unfortunately, very few operations have ever failed for using too many troops, either.

Tully and Perkins went up the left-hand staircase in a rush, their soft boot soles making quiet rutching noises on the perforated-steel treads. Roy dropped prone, covering the long gallery while Perkins ran halfway down it. Tom kept his stance until she was ready, down on one knee and weapon in firing position; then he went up the stairs himself, no louder than the others despite his greater size, moving like a great dark cat. It was a pleasure to work with people who knew what they were doing, and that was a fact.

He felt the same thing, in a distant abstract way, when an amplified voice bellowed: "Freeze! You're covered!"

Both his companions did what he did: froze, with their eyes active. Jumping up and shooting at nothing would be highly unprofessional, also fatal.

Then the voice went on in a more conversational tone: "Look at the pretty red dots, motherfuckcrs."

He did roll his eyes down. The glasses showed the laser aim point clearly, right on the upper part of his breastbone, right in the "sniper's triangle." And whoever was doing the talking had an accent like Adrienne's, only stronger.

Urk, he thought.

"Throw down!"

"Do it," Tom said, bending and slowly setting down his shotgun and pulling his Glock out to join it with two fingers.

If they wanted us dead, we'd be dead, he thought.

That was slightly reassuring; criminals rarely killed police officers except in the heat of the moment. Cop killers were unlucky—they tended to be shot while resisting arrest or while attempting to escape, or to commit suicide by throwing themselves downstairs in stir. The mystery men from the other dimension might not think like that, but most of the people here were good, honest terrestrial scumbags.

Men came out of the door that had been their destination, with pistols in their hands. They didn't make any attempt to cover their faces; that *wasn't* reassuring, even slightly, because it meant all three of them could make the perpetrators. Which meant they didn't care . . .

A gun tapped him on the back of the head, then withdrew—reminding him it was there, then withdrawing out of range of a sweep if he tried to turn.

"Forward march, asshole," the voice with the not-quite-Southern accent said. "Hands on your head."

* * *

Their captors were arguing, out in the waiting room beyond this office; all except for one Vietnamese gunsel who was standing with a machine pistol trained on them.

"Just kill them," someone said; someone with a thick Slavic tinge to his vowels. "Not to get fancy, not to fall on ass."

"We need to ask them questions," the voice with the accent like Adrienne's said. "*Then* we can kill them."

"Our money!" said a third party to the dispute. "You give us our money!"

Oh, that is all soooo not *good,* Tom thought.

The hood and night-sight glasses were gone; he was sitting in a metal-frame chair, with his hands tied behind his back and behind the backrest; his feet were lashed to the legs. Tully and Perkins were to his left and right, along one wall of an industrial-décor office, bare brick and metal strut ceiling, and a discouraged-looking potted plant in one corner. They all exchanged glances.

Well, we knew it was a risk, he thought, swallowing the fear that made sweat trickle like cold grease down his flanks. *Sometimes the cat's alive when you open the box; sometimes it's dead.*

There was a big desk at the other end of the room near the door, and through it came a group of men; they were arguing, with a lot of hand action. Six of them: two East Asians, two white men who looked enough alike to be brothers, squat and broad-faced, and three who looked like something from a *Sopranos* rerun—right down to the expensive bad taste of their aggressively cut business suits and the bulges under their left armpits.

A youngish man seemed to be the leader of the suits; he was talking, and with that same impossible-to-place, not-quite-Southern accent that Adrienne had, but much stronger: "I told you that we had our own channels into the police," Young Suit said. "And it worked out, didn't it?"

He gestured toward the desk. It carried their weapons and ID; the folders open to show their pictures. Young Suit walked over to the prisoners and grinned at them; then he went on: "Your boss, the slope," he said. "You found out about his father's house, hey? Didn't know that the Yasujirus got a big payment from RM and M right after the war . . . and a nice note saying how sorry the company was to be buying the property they'd been cheated out of, and would they please accept the very generous purchase price . . . and the help later, the scholarship and suchlike. Always pays to have friends. Friends who can plant a bug on someone's car, so you know when they're coming, for example. Easy as salmon in spring."

Even then, Tom felt a slight surprise at the odd turn of phrase. Then a prickle ran up his back, remembering the videodisk and the enormous, unbelievable weight of fish thrashing their way through Carquinez Strait.

He's one of them. One of the people from the other side. Also . . . he couldn't have gotten a warning about this operation from Yasujiru, or a bug on the car—not unless he was monitoring that continuously. It must have leaked from Adrienne . . . but how? She's been chasing this guy.

"Mr. Bosco, the question is what to do with them now," one of the squat men said. He had an accent as well.

Russian, Tom thought; he recognized it from his years in Central Asia. Then: *Aha! Bosco, as in Bosco Holdings. Another piece of the puzzle.*

Young Suit—young Mr. Bosco—smiled. "Toni, please, Alexi. I said, we'll take care of it. Rest assured, no bodies will ever be found."

The Russian scowled. "Better to make sure of them now—after we find out what they know."

Toni Bosco spread his hands soothingly. "That's what we had in mind. But carefully, carefully. The FBI would get *very* upset if they found one of their special agents in, ah, bad condition. It'll be a while before we can deal with them."

Alexi jerked his head westward. "The ocean hides many sins."

Bosco's grin was broad, but it reminded Tom of a circus magician's professional grimace; if he'd been in the Russian's position, he wouldn't have trusted it an inch.

"We know a better trick than that, Alexi," Bosco said.

His words were mild, but the men behind him were stone-faced and alert, their gun hands ready to move. Tom silently willed the others to accept the proposition; whatever Mr. Bosco had in mind, it had to be better than immediate torture and death. Not to mention the prospects of being tied to a chair in the middle of a firefight, if a disagreement broke out among the business associates here. Bosco reached inside his coat—carefully, carefully—and brought out a thick envelope, which he handed to the hitherto-silent Asians.

"Mr. Nguyen," he said. "I believe this will be full compensation."

The Vietnamese-American opened the envelope, riffled through the bills, and raised a brow. "More than sufficient," he said. "However, we are no longer prepared to engage in this animal-products venture. The . . . difficulties . . . are more than the profits. Your friends will have to find someone else to market your goods in the East. Good-bye."

He and his companion turned and walked out the door. Bosco shrugged and turned to the Russians, opening his mouth to speak—

And there was a sound from the gallery outside, muffled through the intervening room but unmistakable to an experienced ear; a sound like a series of large books being slapped closed, very quickly.

Submachine gun, Tom thought. *With a sound suppressor. Someone just took out the Viets.*

Silencers didn't silence. A gun going off was going to make a loud noise, whatever you did. The baffles that slowed the muzzle gases down to subsonic speeds did reduce the sound a lot, though; enough that it didn't carry very far, especially indoors. There were very few neighbors here, and probably none of them would report a firefight.

The Russians went for their pistols. Toni Bosco's men dove for their attaché cases, which probably held something heavier. Even as they moved, an also-familiar hollow *schoonk . . . schoonk . . . schoonk* rang out.

Grenade launcher. Tom took a deep breath and screwed his eyes shut. That wouldn't do any good at all if the grenades were loaded with high exposive, but . . .

Bitter, itching, burning gas exploded up from the shells that went spinning on the hard tile floor of the office. Tom heard screams from his captors, followed closely by retching; that meant military-strength puke gas. He held his breath as long as he could, and then forced himself to breathe shallowly instead of gasping as his lungs craved. The air seemed to be burning lava, an overwhelming itching all down his throat and into his lungs, and tears streamed down his cheeks. After a moment the nausea grew too intense to resist; sour bile filled his mouth, then spilled down the front of his jacket in an uncontrollable racking cough. In the middle of that he could hear similar sounds from Perkins and Tully, and a cold stab of fear shot through his own agony; vomiting was no joke when you were tied up and couldn't move. You could choke to death on your own puke if you sucked it in.

There was another burst of fire—pistols this time, sharp yapping barks, and more screams, of pain instead of rage. Then someone fired four times, slow-paced shots.

Into the backs of heads, Tom thought queasily. *Finishing them off. Well, that rules out an official rescue party.*

The gas was mostly out of the air now. He blinked and shook his head, coughing and spitting to clear his mouth. When he could see again, vision blurred but workable, both the Russians and Bosco's two goons were down, and very dead. His nose twitched at the stink. Bosco himself was standing very still except for retching and smothered coughs, hands on top of his head, and a huge thickset man was patting him down; his face was covered by a pig-snouted breathing mask with a sensor shield over the eyes. Another man was checking the bodies, even taller than the first but lanky, with hair the color of old sun-faded straw spiking up around the straps of the mask. Both wore thin-film gloves on their hands.

Schalk van der Merwe and Piet Botha, Tom thought.

And Adrienne Rolfe, also masked and gloved. She came through the office door, tucking away a pistol—he recognized the make, a Belgian 5.7mm job, expensive, lethal and in theory for police use only. Her face was neutral as she pulled off the mask, took an experimental breath, and coughed.

"Clear," she said. "More or"—another cough—"less."

The other two men took off their masks as well, folding them and tucking them into pockets in their dark Banana Republic–style jackets.

She tossed them canvas bags, and they began stuffing things into them—wallets, weapons, the IDs of the three tied to chairs.

The blond man looked over and spoke: "Need someone to finish off the *kaffir?*"

"Schalk, shut up," Adrienne said, her face thoughtful as her eyes went back and forth between Bosco and Tom.

"What's going on?" Tom asked hoarsely.

"Well," Adrienne said, "you *did* sound odd. I suspected you were being naughty. So we paid a visit to your place first. Tsk, tsk. All that research! Why did you leave it in place?"

"Too much to move quickly, and we were in a hurry," he said. "But there are backup duplicates, and it'll all be—"

Adrienne laughed a little, shaking her head. "Going down swinging, eh, Tom? I'd expect nothing less. But you know as well as I do nobody would believe a word of it without more proof—that's why you're here, to *get* the proof. Lucky you didn't give me an even later false time, though, or I'm afraid Toni here would have done something really unpleasant to y'all before I arrived."

Her leaf-green eyes turned to Perkins. "I presume the FBI agent is in it with you—this must be unofficial, or there would have been more of you. From the date on that movement survey on me, you only told her today. . . ." Her tone altered, losing the bantering note. "I'm trying to come up with reasons not to kill anyone, Tom. I really am. So tell me the truth."

"Yes," he said bitterly, and spat—clearing his mouth and expressing his opinion at the same time.

Perkins spoke for the first time: "Fuck you!" she snapped with a flat murderous glare. "You've killed plenty, and you'll get the needle for it."

Adrienne inclined her head. "I don't think so, Special Agent Perkins. Schalk, one dose of neurotone."

The man began to complain, and she made a chopping gesture. "Schalk, for the last time, shut up and do as you're told!"

"What is that stuff?" Tom asked.

He tried to keep the fear out of his voice as she pulled a disposable hypodermic needle out of a case the Afrikaner handed her. Perkins simply glared silently as the injector approached.

"Think of it as a chemical equivalent of electroshock, which mimics the effects of a moderately severe concussion very closely," Adrienne said, working the plunger with her thumb until a bead of clear liquid appeared on the tip. "Developed for the GSF—the Gate Security Force—here on FirstSide; not that the developer knew who we were or what we wanted it for. Usually the subject wakes up with a splitting headache and no memory of the recent past. The past day or two."

"Usually?"

"Sometimes the effects are . . . more drastic." She looked up at him as she pulled back Perkins's sleeve. "Good, the bruise here will hide the needle mark. . . ."

The black woman didn't flinch when the thin steel pierced her skin. A few seconds later she yawned uncontrollably; then her eyes rolled up and her head slumped. Adrienne waited a moment more, then peeled back an eyelid with her thumb and studied the reaction of the pupil.

"Looks good," she said. "No adverse reaction." At his glare, she went on: "Tom, the alternative is letting them find her body and making it look like you killed her. We can't just disappear an FBI agent, not these days; they would keep looking until they found something. They know she's been working with you, and the cover story we're using with you wouldn't wash."

"Cover story?" he croaked. *Damn, I'm turning into the straight man here!*

"Well, when they search your hurriedly abandoned apartment, I'm afraid they're going to find very convincing evidence that you and your short friend here were involved up to your necks in the endangered-species racket. Not to mention a forgotten stash of twenty thousand dollars in cash, and clues that with some work will lead them to offshore accounts with over a million. That will be *extremely* convincing, since we've also removed all trace of what you found. It'll be assumed you got out of the country and are living in affluent retirement somewhere else."

She smiled—a little sadly—at his fury. "It was necessary. That dodo, and you clicked faster than I thought you could . . . none of it will matter where you're going, Tom."

"Through your dimensional portal," he said. "That's how you dispose of the inconvenient, isn't it?"

"We usually call it the Gate," she replied. Her smile grew broader for an instant. "Think of the other side as bizzarro Sunnydale. Or another dimension of time and space."

She hummed under her breath: *du-du-du, du-du-du.* Even then, Tully couldn't control a strangled grunt of laughter as he recognized the theme song. It was his partner's reaction that prompted Tom's memory.

And Perkins was still alive, unconscious but twitching. Adrienne's attention had turned to Anthony Bosco. With the adrenaline of rage still running through his brain, Tom was still grateful that the look wasn't directed at him. It was an expression he'd never seen on her face before, calm and implacable and colder than the moon.

She tossed a comment over her shoulder, not taking her eyes from Bosco's face. "This is the man responsible for the warehouse full of skins and the condor," she said. "And the dodo." She leaned forward slightly. "Why, Toni?"

Bosco licked his lips, but spoke calmly enough. "Money. I've got expensive tastes I can't satisfy back in New Virginia. All right, you got me; now take me back to the Commonwealth and we'll have the fucking trial."

Commonwealth? Tom thought. *Not the Commonwealth of Letters, I think. Well, it beats "Hole in the Wall."*

"Toni, don't insult me," Adrienne said. "I get very upset when people insult me. You can draw on the Colletta accounts FirstSide and live like a pasha without going to all this trouble and risk. That's what put me onto this in the first place. And the dodo wasn't just a risk; it was insane. Unless you weren't really trying to cream off some extra FirstSide currency. If you were trying to convince some FirstSiders that the Gate was real, seeing as how you can't actually *show* it to them . . . now, *then* the dodo would make sense."

Bosco went silent, shaking his head.

"Come on, Toni. We both know that Giovanni Colletta's behind this somehow. You're one of his hatchet men and you've been carrying water for him for years. What does your Prime get out of this? And don't say money. This is political."

Another head shake, but Bosco's eyes were flicking back and forth in an instinctive search for escape.

"Hold him," she said.

Piet Botha grinned like a gorilla and seized the smaller man by the back of the neck with a shovel-sized hand.

Bosco gave a grunt of pain and glared at her. "Tell this Settler bastard to get his hands off me, Adrienne," he said. "You know the law—he can't touch one of the Thirty!"

Adrienne walked over and stood close to the young man, wrinkling her nose slightly at the smell of vomit from his jacket. She reached out and pulled a ring off his left thumb— Tom could see that it was like hers, gold and platinum braided together.

"I do know the law," she said. "Since they're Gate Security operatives, they *can* touch you, over here on FirstSide.

In fact, if I tell them to, they can kill you. Habeas corpus doesn't apply this side of the Gate. You know that part of the law, don't you? And the provisions about treason?"

She flipped the ring into the air. "Now talk, Bosco. This isn't a scam you were running on your own. Your Family Prime is involved. You needed access to Nostradamus' classified channels to read the message I sent about there being a bust here tonight—that's *why* I used Nostradamus this afternoon, instead of a courier. You couldn't have trapped these FirstSiders otherwise. Give me the details: who, where, when, why. I don't have time to waste."

He snarled. "Take me back to the Commonwealth and put me on trial before the committee," he said. "They'll have that Gate Security commission off you so fast— *Shit!*"

At her nod, Botha relaxed his mechanical-grab grip enough that Bosco could take a shuddering breath. She reached into her jacket and took out a small steel rod; at a flick of her wrist it extended into a short truncheon with a knob at the end. Bosco's eyes went wide, and he began to struggle as Botha grabbed one of his hands, forced it down on the desk and then thrust a painful thumb on its back, making his fingers splay out in uncontrollable reflex.

Adrienne sighed again. "This is going to hurt you a lot more than me, but I'd really rather not have this sort of memory in my head," she said. "So why don't you spare us both and talk?"

He shook his head again. She flicked the truncheon up, then down again in a short whipping arc. Bosco screamed and convulsed as the knob smashed down on the little finger of his right hand; there was a distinct crack under the louder, mushier sound of steel hammering flesh against unyielding hardwood.

Jesus, Tom thought, his mouth going dry. He'd done as bad in the field: When you needed information desperately, lives were at stake and some *shaheed* wasn't talking, the type who really believed in the seventy-two virgins . . . those were times when the officer walked around the hill so he didn't have to officially see what went on and you did what you had to. Watching brought back memories he'd . . .

Rather not have in my head, just as she said, he thought unwillingly.

When Bosco had drawn himself together somewhat, shuddering, she leaned forward and pushed the knob on the steel whip against his nose.

"Now listen carefully, Bosco," she said. "There are two hundred and sixteen bones in the human body. That was *one.*"

She paused for a second, then went on, her face like something carved from ivory, and her voice flat and cool, the tone neutral: "I'm going to break one bone every thirty seconds until you tell me what I want to know. After half an hour, you'll be like a rag doll. Except that rag dolls don't feel pain. And you *will.*"

The knob descended on the broken finger; Botha clamped a hand across the smaller man's mouth to muffle the scream.

"Now, you're a scion of the Thirty—you're a brave man—we can take that for granted. But everybody talks in the end. So why don't we just skip to the confession? Why take the fall for the Colletta? Twenty-nine. Twenty-eight. Twenty-seven."

Bosco's sweat-slick face worked, as if he were chewing something unpalatable. Tom looked away; he didn't have to watch, at least.

That meant he saw the tall pale Afrikaner draw his pistol, moving smooth and fast. The American responded without time for thought, some distant-observer part of himself blinking in surprise at what his subconscious had decided to do.

"*Look out!*" he screamed, and threw himself forward.

That was hard when you were tied arms-and-ankles to a chair. The weight of heavy muscle on his shoulders made it a bit easier, by raising his center of gravity. The chair tipped forward; he caromed off the shooter's knees and then bounced painfully to the floor. Lying there he could hear the sharp crack of the little weapon, and see the red bloom of an entry wound appear on Bosco's chest. He could see Adrienne turning as well; he'd never seen anyone move quite as fast. Her hand dropped the metal baton and knocked it out of the way as it swept inside her jacket, up and out and level.

Not Adrienne, he thought, dazed. *The guy was shooting for Bosco first.* And then: *Remind me never to get into a quick-draw contest with her.*

Two other pistols barked then; there was a shatter of glass breaking, and a soft heavy grunt from above him. The long form of the Afrikaner gunman dropped over his body, hiding the light and dripping a disgusting salt-and-iron wetness on his face. He spat aside when it was lifted away, knowing his face must be a glistening mask of red.

"Thanks," Adrienne said, looking down at him. "He would have got me too. . . ." She looked up. "But *why?*"

Then she turned to the big dark man, who was staring down at his ex-partner with an almost childlike confusion.

"Botha, snap out of it. We need the cleanup team here *now.*"

INTERLUDE
March 16, 1997
Commonwealth of New Virginia

"Like the country around Stellenbosch, east of Cape Town," Piet Botha said to the friend beside him.

Winds and shadows fell toward the west, and the mountains stretching toward the Pacific went from purple-green to a dark sawtooth against the northern horizon.

"Like it, but better," Schalk van der Merwe said grudgingly. "It's good land; I grant you that."

The Cape Dutch–style farmhouse behind them was rawly new, a long single-story rectangle with a *stoep* in front where they sat, two short wings on the back, and a tall gable over the teak doors; it was whitewashed in the traditional style, but the roof was tile rather than black thatch. Ten acres of young orange trees to either side of the house scented the night with their perfume as the western light cast long shadows across the empty vastness to the south. The day had been sunny and mildly warm. That lingered in the stones of the wall behind them, making the veranda pleasant despite a cooling wind from the sea that picked up smells of manzanita and sage.

He'd picked a spot where the land began its climb toward the Santa Monica Mountains, although there was already a request in to the Commission to rename them the Krugerberg. His grant was part of the new home estate of the Commonwealth's latest addition to the Thirty Families—the Versfelds, who now had their seat at what another world called Santa Monica, and which this one named Hendriksdorp. The location gave Botha's new home a view across the land that stretched away across the foothills and down to the flat plain of the Los Angeles basin. It was green with the winter rains, flower-starred tall grass with groves of willow and oak, cottonwood and sycamore along the streamsides and about the surprisingly numerous sloughs and swamps. He'd ridden over the countryside enough to get a feel for it: the open land where the soil rose a little higher, and the lower stretches often impassable with clumps of alder, hackberry and shrubs woven together with California rose and wild grapevines, blackberries and brambles.

The big Afrikaner had been surprised at how wet this area seemed, after having seen the same places FirstSide; swamps covered a third of it even in the dry summer, not counting salt marsh along the coastline, and vast fields of wild mustard rose higher than a rider's head, thick with game. It didn't rain that much on the low country in either universe, but here all the runoff from the mountains seeped into the great underground reservoirs, and welled to the surface in innumerable springs and damp spots where the lay of the land forced it to the surface. Nobody had pumped the aquifers dry here, or logged off the mountains, or crammed twenty-five million thirsty human beings onto the land.

Piet Botha's wife came out onto the *stoep* and set a tray

with coffee and *koeksisters* on the table between the two men. She was a short, slight woman in contrast to her hulking husband, with curling brown hair and blue eyes.

"Dinner will be ready soon," she said, turning and finishing over her shoulder as she walked back into the house, wiping her hands on her apron, "if I can keep that *nahua* girl from ruining it—she throws chilies into *everything* if you don't watch her like a hawk. Lamb *sosaties* and rice today."

Piet smacked his lips; that meant cubes of lamb marinated in wine and vinegar, spiced with coriander, pepper, turmeric and tamarind, strung on skewers with apricots and peppers, and grilled over a clear wood fire—chaparral scrub oak did wonders.

He and his companion sipped their coffee, ate the dough-nutlike sweet pastries and watched the Botha children playing in the garden; the plantings were three years old and it was already well along, trees sprouting amid the flowers with Californian speed, some of the blue gum eucalyptus already thirty feet high. A grove of native oaks gave an illusion of age offset by the half-built buildings in a clump to the east; storage sheds, stables, barn, garage, all in a litter of beams and planks and stacks of adobe brick. A pump chugged in the background, pulling water from a reservoir fed by mountain springs for the house and the automated-drip irrigation system.

"Much better," Botha said, after a spell of companionable silence. "Man, talk about luck! I'm glad I listened to *Oom* Versfeld, I'll tell you that! They don't call him *Slim* Hendrik, Clever Hendrik, for nothing."

Schalk van der Merwe scowled. "He should have held out for the *real* Cape," he said. "Not just land here. If not for our own land, what were we fighting for?"

"We fought for South Africa," Botha said, his slow deep voice giving an extra gravity to the guttural sounds of Afrikaans. "We lost. What do Boers do when we lose? We *trek,* man, we go somewhere else."

The moaning rhythmic grunt of a lion's roar sounded in the distance, as the first stars appeared overhead. A loose scattering of house lights stood miles apart along the foot of the mountains, and a few headlights crawled along the north-south road that ended at San Diego.

Botha chuckled. "This is about as *else* as you can get. Being beaten once was bad enough. I don't want to start the same fight over again right away."

"Hell," Schalk said, waving his doughnut; a little syrup dropped onto his khaki shirt. "The bushmen and the blacks in South Africa—on this side of the Gate—they're bare-arsed savages. Just like the ones our ancestors beat at Blood River; and we'd have machine guns and armor and aircraft, not ox-wagons and flintlock *roers*."

"And just where would we get the armored cars, and the ammunition, and the fuel, if we were on the other side of the world from here?" Botha said.

He pointed southwest, toward Long Beach. "*Kerel,* eighty kilometers that way is the only oil well in the world. And the only refinery." He pointed over his shoulder, northward toward Rolfeston and the Gate. "And up there's the only place with access to modern weapons or anything else. We'd be back to ox-wagons and flintlocks bliddy soon, if we tried leaving for Africa! Even if the Commission would allow it—which they won't."

"We could set up our own factories, in time," Schalk said stubbornly. "We'd have our own country with our own language and customs, where we wouldn't be scattered among damned foreigners the way we are here. A *Boerstaat* for *ons volk*."

"Oh, all three thousand of us could man the factories, while we were conquering and settling the country?" Botha said. "Or the Commission would allow a mass migration from FirstSide—and explain to the world why all the Boers were leaving, and where they were going?"

He paused, stroked his jaw as if in thought, then spoke: "I have it, man! Even if there are only a few thousand of us, we could use the *kaffirs* in our factories. Of course, we'd have to teach them to read, wouldn't we, to make them useful? Hand out Bibles, hey? And we'd give them modern medicine so all their children survived. . . ."

Botha spoke with heavy sarcasm: "Haven't I seen this film before, someplace, *jong?* You know, it started well, but I didn't like the ending!"

Schalk flushed. "It would be different this time. We could keep the *kaffirs* in order without any outsiders telling us—"

"*Ja,* it would be different—for a while. Maybe a long while. Maybe not. Schalk, if you really want to do something for the *volk,* you should find a girl, get married and have a dozen children. *That* would help."

The door behind them opened.

"It's ready; come in to dinner," Botha's wife said, and then called to the children. When they had been sent off to wash their hands, she went on: "And stop talking foolishness about going back, on *either* side of the Gate, Schalk. If I never see one of *them* again, it'll be too soon."

CHAPTER NINE

Oakland Gate Complex, California
June 2009

FirstSide/Commonwealth of New Virginia

Perkins went out on a stretcher; the bodies of the dead were dumped unceremoniously into a big metal crate. Men were scrubbing at red stains on the gallery floor outside, presumably where the departing Vietnamese had departed much more permanently than they anticipated. Industrial-strength cleaning machines foamed and whirred—and their users wore overalls with the name of a well-known janitorial company. Others moved about scanning with eyes and instruments for any sign of the firefight. He saw one group extract a bullet from the plaster of a wall and begin repairs immediately, grouting and plaster and quick-drying paint. The heavy smell of the cleansing chemicals overrode the feces-and-blood stinks of violent death; in half an hour, even a forensics team would have trouble proving anything untoward had happened here.

"That's the cleanup squad, I presume?" Tully said. "Impressive."

Adrienne started slightly, brought out of a brown study. "Yes. We've managed to keep one of the biggest secrets in human history for sixty-three years now. We didn't do it by being incompetent."

"Impressive," Tully said again, his voice full of enthusiasm. "Say, you don't really need to keep the cuffs on us—"

Adrienne looked at him, snorted, and walked faster.

Tom whispered to his partner: "Brilliant. Short, but brilliant."

An ambulance was parked outside, and a Ford Windstar van, as well as a truck with the logo of the cleaning company supposedly at work within—or for all he knew, RM&M actually *did* own the firm. It would certainly be a good way to hide a cleanup squad. As he watched, two men got into Christiansen's own vehicle across the street and drove away. The pseudo-paramedics loaded Perkins into the ambulance and did likewise. The big metal box with the bodies came down on a dolly and went up on a hydraulic lift into the truck with the company name.

Bet all the other evidence goes the same way, he thought. Then, with a hint of eeriness: *And it'll all also go where we're going—somewhere literally out of this world. Maybe it isn't quite so crazy that they've been able to keep the secret. When you can throw evidence away and know it'll never come back . . .*

Adrienne stopped at the rear of the Windstar. "Are you up to handling them, Botha?" she asked sharply.

"Ja," he said, and shook himself like a bear. "Yes, miss. It's . . . I didn't think anyone could buy Schalk. He was a good man, not *slim,* not clever, but a good soldier."

"I don't think anyone could buy him either," Adrienne said, and put a hand on his shoulder in a moment's odd gentleness. She looked about to make sure that nobody was within earshot. "Not with money. This is political; that's why you've got to keep quiet about how it happened. As far as the official debrief is concerned, he was killed in the firefight. Now let's get going."

With their hands cuffed behind their backs, Tom and Tully needed help as they climbed awkwardly into the back of the van; the big Afrikaner's hand had the impersonal strength of a mechanical grab. Tom evaluated him objectively as they passed close.

I could take him, he decided. *He's about my weight and*

plenty strong, experienced too, or I miss my guess, but I'm a decade younger at least and I'm not carrying any fat.

Of course, that was in anything like a fair fight. Being woozy from a dose of tear-and-puke gas, and having your hands fastened behind your back, did *not* count as "fair" under reasonable definition. As it was, Botha could crush his skull with a couple of blows of his massive fist.

The van had seats around the interior, with storage bins beneath them. It also had two wheelchairs fastened to the floor, facing backward and equipped with restraints on the legs and arms, the sort they used for violent patients in mental hospitals. Adrienne stayed on the road between the doors until they were secured, one hand under her suit jacket. Not many people could draw and shoot accurately in conditions like these; he was willing to bet she was one. Botha put Tully in his chair first, then Tom, working from behind the wheelchair, then took up a position behind them as the doors slammed shut and locked.

"There's redundancy for you," Tully said, and Tom snorted a bitter chuckle.

Yes; four-point tie-down on these chairs, a human-gorilla hybrid behind with a gun on us, and all of it all inside a locked vehicle.

"Shut up," Botha said, and prodded him painfully in the back of the head with the muzzle of his pistol.

There was a spell of mixed boredom and rising tension; they couldn't see much through the small dark-tinted windows in the back of the van. Roads, then alleyways between tall buildings, occasional halts. Then brilliant light. The doors were thrown open and the wheelchairs unfastened and rolled down a ramp by silent armed guards in standard rent-a-cop outfits. They were inside a building's loading dock; then they were pushed down corridors of blank pastel, lit by overhead fluorescents. The place had the cold, deserted, silent feel of a facility where only the night shift was on duty.

Well, it is three-fifteen in the morning, Tom thought.

They stopped in a set of rooms that had the unmistakable

cold, astringent smell of a hospital or clinic. A check-in desk was labeled DECON AND CONTAINMENT.

Tom's ears perked up when a nurse in a white coat looked up from the desk and spoke; she had the same accent as Bosco and Adrienne. Rather stronger, if anything, as if she wasn't trying to tone it down. She did not, he was interested to notice, have one of the platinum-and-gold thumb rings on her left hand.

"This clinic is under continual surveillance," she said, indicating the cameras in the corners. "If you cause any trouble, the guards will be back here in seconds. The exterior doors are locked, and won't open for anyone without the right retina and palmprint. Are you going to make trouble?"

"Ma'am, we wouldn't dream of it," Tom said.

"Good," she said, getting up and undoing their restraints. "This is FirstSide Decon. You'll be checked here, and then given sleeping space until the next available transit, which is scheduled for"—she glanced at a computer screen on her desk—"seven tomorrow."

A shower followed, in hot water that contained some sharp-smelling antiseptic, and a few minutes in a chamber with UV lamps all around. The medical exam was thorough, and used all the latest equipment. They were shown to a small cubicle with a thick locked door, a single toilet and sink, and two bunks; he took the lower and sank into unconsciousness with a swiftness the thin lumpy pallet didn't deserve.

❋ ❋ ❋

"Kemosabe." Tully's voice brought him awake and sitting upright on the bunk. "Thought you'd want to cut the beauty sleep short."

Tom shook his head and stretched. They'd lost their watches along with everything else, but his internal clock, not to mention his stomach, said he'd slept at least twelve hours. After the stress of the past twenty-four, that was only to be expected. Possibly shoving them in here buck naked was supposed to keep them subdued, which might have worked with ordinary civilians.

Not that the state of our morale makes much difference in a bare concrete cubicle with a steel door, he thought. *And doubtless under constant remote surveillance.*

"Anything in the way of food show up?" he said carefully.

"Couple of ration bars, sort of like pressed granola," Tully said, and threw him one. "Being the sweet guy I am, I didn't eat both. Also some munificent toiletries and fancy duds via the dumbwaiter there." He jerked a thumb at the swivel-box arrangement in the plain steel door.

There were plain dark sweat suits, underwear, socks and sneakers, all smelling both new and cheap. Disposable razors, soap, toothpaste and brushes came with them, along with one plastic comb. After he cleaned up as best he could there was nothing to do but sit on the bunks and make desultory conversation, of the type you didn't mind being overheard. Doubtless the boredom, without even a variation in the light or a distracting sound, was also intended to shake inmates. Neither of them had a problem with it; both police work and military service were good training for waiting. In the long spells of silence, he found his thoughts returning to Adrienne—humiliation at the thought of how he'd been duped, and an obsessive replay of each word and action since the fiasco at the meet.

Could I have played it better? he thought. Dozens of methods occurred to him, each crazier than the last; when he found himself doing the if-only-things-had-been-different daydream game and imagining she'd really been the dewy innocent he'd first assumed, he wrenched his mind away with a concentrated effort of will and did calisthenics instead, mostly isometric types, the sort you could do lying down on a narrow bunk.

When the guards came with the wheelchairs, it was almost a relief. Another stretch of corridor led to an echoing metal-box building with the look of a warehouse—most of the floor was great stacks of boxed goods on pallets, with forklifts whining about and the prickly ozone smell of heavy-duty electric motors. A people mover stood waiting, and Adrienne and Piet Botha stood beside it.

He looked as before, save for a rumpled and red-eyed look that argued sleeplessness. She was wearing a tight black uniform, cloth and gleaming leather, pistol and dagger at belt, and the stylized letters GSF on the shoulder. Despite himself, he looked her up and down and quirked an eyebrow.

"Don't blame me," she said with a shrug. "*Sturmbanführer* Otto von Traupitz had a big hand in designing the uniform—nobody else paid attention until it was too late to change things without offending him, and he *had* done a lot of the gruntwork setting up Gate Security."

Then she turned one leg. "You'll have to admit we have really, really spiffy boots, though."

Tully chuckled openly. Tom gave a snort and looked away. His stomach was beginning to clench; he knew what was coming, and it was starting to feel real. The people mover slid forward, to where tall metal doors gave on to another warehouselike building. Armed guards waited at the junction; one covered them while another shone a handheld retina scanner into their eyes.

"What have we here?" the guard with the machine carbine said, looking at the men in the restraints.

"Couple of IS," Adrienne said. "Off to help build our beloved Commonwealth."

"Haven't seen any Involuntaries in a while, Miss Rolfe," the man said.

"Do you have much longer on your tour?" she said.

"A month, miss. I will be *so* glad to get back to the real world. I understand why furloughs home aren't practical, but it gets pretty boring never leaving these buildings . . . pass, then."

Tom looked up; the metal-stringer ceiling above was frosted with lights, surveillance cameras and an occasional guard platform. Below was an expanse of concrete, bare except for notional roadways outlined in yellow paint; everything converged at the far wall, where a big glass-walled control room hung from the ceiling, and below it a long paved ramp. Trains of flatbed trolleys drawn by electric carts waited or moved to the promptings of the control room, loaded with boxed computers, digitally controlled machine tools, diesel engines, knocked-down cars and trucks, tires, ball bearings, tractors, carboys of industrial chemicals, flats of designer clothing and French perfume, DVDs, MRI scanners. . . .

Everything necessary to keep a civilization going, he thought, fascinated despite himself. Imperious beeps brought trains forward, down the ramp and out of sight—and then others emerged upward, loaded with gleaming stacks of gold and silver ingots, small steel boxes of diamonds or emeralds or tanzanite, rare earths. . . .

"At least we smell better than we did before the shower," Tully muttered.

It sounded as if the situation was getting to him, at least a little. Tom felt alert enough; very thirsty, and his bladder was painfully full again, but he could take in his surroundings.

"That's us," Adrienne said, as a green light flashed and a *beep-beep-beep* sounded from the dashboard of the electric cart.

He licked dry lips as it whined into motion. It was one thing to read about a gate between worlds, or talk about it, or even reluctantly believe in one. Seeing one was something else. And this . . .

As they came to the bottom of the ramp it looked like a basement, of all things. There was steel tracking laid down over synthetic sheeting over flagstones, running straight to—

"What's *that?*" he burst out involuntarily, at the sight of the rectangle of silvery light.

Adrienne grinned. "That, my friends, is nothing less than the *Gate.*" Her voice put the italics in the word; she added quotation marks with her fingers. "The Gate to the Commonwealth of New Virginia." The capitals came across well too.

The big dark Afrikaner gunsel smiled unpleasantly. "Take

a good look at the Gate Chamber, *jong,* because this is the last time you see it."

He ignored the possible threat and did as he was told; he intended to see it again, in his official capacity, and the information might be valuable in getting that done. The wall opposite the . . . Gate . . . was solid and smooth; sandwich armor lifted from a M1 tank, from the look of it. Blisters mounted heavy machine guns and a flamethrower, and compact unmanned armored turrets with video pickups and more machine guns peered in from four spots around the ceiling. A clear plastic enclosure in one corner held a wooden table, with some archaic-looking electronic equipment on it.

Adrienne saw where his eyes fell. "That's what started it all," she said. "As of April 17, 1946. It's just what it looks like; a modified forties shortwave set. How does it do what it does? We have thousands of guesses—some by physicists—and not one goddamned shred of proof. All we know is that if everything connected to the circuit is kept connected and in roughly the same relative and absolute positions, it goes on happening. The Commission bought up the factories that made all the components, just so we could get identical replacement parts. Interrupt the circuit or move things more than a couple of inches, and the Gate closes . . . and someday I'll tell you about the panic *that's* caused, the times it's happened. For a week once, after the 'eighty-nine quake. Ah, here we go. Don't worry—you won't feel a thing. I've done the trip to the Commonwealth and back hundreds of times."

The people mover jerked forward. Tom's mind accepted the reassurance, but his gut lurched involuntarily. Passage through the sheet of rippling silver turned out to be exactly as advertised. One instant he was *here;* the next he was *there,* wherever the Commonwealth was. The first glimpse turned out to be fairly boring; it was pretty much like the place he'd just come from, although he didn't think it was underground. A glance upward showed frosted-glass skylights. Another showed that the four corners of the huge room were armor-and-concrete pillboxes mounting General Electric six-barreled Gatling miniguns, and that the overhead gridwork included a complete net of surveillance equipment.

The people mover scooted off to the side, out of the path of the two-way traffic; it stopped before something like an airport security setup crossed with a pillbox—except for the squad in black uniforms that looked as if they covered spider-silk-soft body armor, armed with assault rifles—slab-sided German G36 models, with laser sights plugged into Land Warrior–style helmet computers with VR-display optics over the left eye. You didn't have to aim with that gear; you just moved the muzzle until the crosshairs in the optic rested on what you wanted to hit.

Somebody's been selling Uncle Sam's latest toys, Tom thought.

There were a few more of the black uniforms sitting at desks, and those included two women and a stout man in his forties, with a graying mustache. The troopers were all male, all young, all fit, with an arrogance he recognized from his time in the Rangers, that of men who thought themselves the best.

The sign above their station read:

INSPECTION AND IDENTIFICATION STATION
COMMONWEALTH OF NEW VIRGINIA
BY ORDER OF THE CENTRAL COMMITTEE—GATE
    CONTROL COMMISSION
ALL THROUGH-GATE PERSONNEL MUST USE THIS
    STATION
ALL NEW IMMIGRANTS MUST USE THIS STATION
HALT FOR IDENTIFICATION OR BE SHOT
ATTEMPTED UNAUTHORIZED GATE TRANSIT IS A
    CAPITAL CRIME
EXECUTION IS SUMMARY AND WITHOUT TRIAL
NO EXCEPTIONS
THIS MEANS YOU

"Friendly bunch," he murmured.

"All sarcasm and most bullets just bounce off Gate Security," Adrienne said cheerfully. She hopped down as the people mover slowed, undid the restraints on the two Americans, then spoke to the man behind the first desk. "Gate Security Agent Adrienne Rolfe. GS Operative Piet Botha. We've been cleared through FirstSide decon. Thomas Christiansen and Roy Tully, Invol-fours, and they should be in the databank. You can skip sending them to the familiarization hostel; I'm taking custody."

Tom, Roy and the silent Afrikaner came down from the little vehicle, and it scooted away. All of them had to pass through the scanner arch, and then put a palm on a plate and look into a fitted eyepiece; it was all familiar enough biometric ID machinery, retina scan, DNA print and fingerprint. It even had the Hitachi logo. The big Afrikaner walked off after exchanging polite good-byes with Adrienne, ignoring the two Americans as if they didn't exist.

I love you too, Piet, he thought.

He steadied Tully; Roy still looked a little woozy, but he was coming to fast. A machine on a bench whirred and hummed, and extruded ID cards. The technician extended them between finger and thumb. Tom took his; it had his face, name, a number, and coded machine-readable data. At a guess, his data was burned into a file with some sort of read-only central databank; people had talked about that for years during the war, especially after the Charleston disaster, but the ACLU had always killed it. Evidently they thought differently here.

"These are your probationary Settler's ID cards," the tech said, in a bored bureaucratic singsong. "It's your driver's license, your Social Security card, your debit and credit card, and all your other ID rolled into one. Don't lose it. There's a heavy fine for replacement. Carry it on your person at all times. There's a heavy fine for not producing it when requested by a law-enforcement officer. Don't try to tamper with it. That never works—the scanners check it against Nostradamus' central files and your biometric data every time you use it—and it gets you five years at hard labor in the mines. Here is your wallet. It contains one hundred dollars in local currency; remember that prices here are much lower than on FirstSide. Here's your brochure. Welcome to the Commonwealth of New Virginia, and may you have many productive years as law-abiding citizens."

"New Virginia?" Tom asked, stuffing the wallet and card into the pocket of his sweatpants.

His voice was calm, but tension sent a slight sour taste into the back of his mouth as they went out into a corridor in institutional beige, with overhead fluorescent lights. Waiting rooms stretched off to either side, very much like an airport, and were full of people in overalls or business suits or family groups—those last looking very much like first-class passengers, and sitting in bubbles of social space. The surveillance cameras were airport-like too, except that no attempt had been made to disguise them.

"Formally, the Commonwealth of New Virginia is what this country—the Pacific coast of North America and inland for a ways, plus Hawaii and a few other bits—is called," Adrienne said. "Wait a minute and it'll start to become clear."

She looked up at the cameras, checked her angles and then winked at him, holding a finger to her lips in the *shhhhh!* gesture for a moment.

He grunted and swung his head toward the men's room sign. She nodded and leaned against the back of a row of chairs to wait, elegantly hipshot in the sleek black uniform.

Tully paused to splash water on his face before joining him at the row of urinals. "So, looks like we're in the hands of the Bad Guys, who rescued us from the Even Badder Guys?"

"Looks like," Tom said.

Then he raised his eyes to the ceiling. Tully's face changed; Tom felt a moment's warm comfort. *At least I have some backup. And Roy doesn't need me to dot all the I's; this place is probably sewn up tighter than the Gaza Strip.*

Adrienne was similarly quiet when they returned. They swung through a pair of automatic doors, and out into a sidewalk fronting on a road; he was reminded again of a medium-sized airport. It was evening, the sun sinking toward the west; big rectangular sheet-metal buildings painted green stretched off to the right; ahead of them was a parking lot, with many SUVs and four-by-fours; to the left was some rather nice landscaping, flower beds and trees, including a couple of fine valley oaks, a two-lane blacktop road, and then—

He choked, gasping for breath; knowing was one thing, seeing another. Adrienne supported him with a hand under his left arm, guiding him to lean against a six-foot ceramic planter full of impatiens. Tully was staring and whistling. Tom shook his head, conscious that his mouth was hanging open, something that he'd always thought was a figure of speech before, and not caring a damn. Beyond the road and stretching northward and west was classic California lowland savanna, more big oaks and tall grass turning from green to gold, starred with yellow poppies and blue lupine and camas lily. Beyond that . . .

. . . was San Francisco Bay, with the sun casting a glittering path across the azure surface. Only there was no San Francisco; the day was brilliantly clear, some low whitecaps on water intensely indigo, and he could see the outlines of the peninsula past Alameda—which had a small airport where the Naval Air Station had been once, and was otherwise bare of human works.

Yah. It's just West Oakland, if you subtract the city, and all the landfill on the shore. Subtract the—

A little farther up the coast long piers had been built out into the bay, with fishing trawlers and a couple of smallish wooden ships tied up next to them; cranes swung cargo nets ashore to a clutch of sheds and warehouses, and trucks carried cargo out onto the highway.

Across the water there were no buildings on the hills where San Francisco should be, only a town along the waterfront. No East Bay bridges either, no Golden Gate, and Alcatraz was white with seabird droppings and swarming with the pelicans that had given it its name. The ships on the water were fewer by an order of magnitude, and small— schooners, a couple of them six-masters, barges and tugs, a clutch of sailboats and some fishing boats under a white-winged storm of gulls. He looked up and saw strings of pelicans and cormorants, golden eagles, and—he counted frantically—half a dozen condors. The sky was alive with wings, and it wasn't even the season for migratory birds. Out on the bay a whale spouted, then submerged in a smooth black curve. Sea lions hauled themselves out along the shores of Alameda, and he could just make out a sea otter on the nearby shore.

I'm where that video was taken. It's as if I'm standing in Oakland before Columbus, he thought. *But it can't be. And there are paved roads and Ford SUVs and Hummers and a great big building with a* Gate *in it, and that little port and—*

His vision faded. He felt something pushed between his lips and sucked reflexively; it was brandy, potent and smooth, in a silver flask. That brought on a fit of coughing, blessed pain that called his spirit back into his body. Tully was hovering nearby with a frown of concern on his face; evidently the smaller man was more mentally flexible.

"Takes a lot of FirstSiders hard the first time," Adrienne said. "And yes, it's exactly what it looks like, only it's not the same San Francisco Bay you grew up with. Different . . . time line. A different history, two different universes existing in the same space and joined only by the Gate. You know the concept?"

"Yeah," he said hoarsely. "Yeah, you know I read science fiction. You saw my research on you. What the hell . . . ?"

"Showing is faster than telling, but it's stressful," she said. "You feeling better?"

"Yeah. Thanks a lot."

She chuckled. "Why do I hear a lack of enthusiasm? But come on; I'll buy you two dinner and fill you in. It's the least I can do, after getting you into this mess."

They passed over into the parking lot; it was unbearably prosaic to slide into the front passenger seat of a Hummer and pull out onto the road, heading northward and tending away from the water. His head tried to swivel all possible ways at once; he felt a little undignified, but it was a whole new world—literally.

After a few hundred yards, Adrienne pulled the Humvee over to the graveled side of the road. Tom waited, distantly noting the incredible, intense freshness of the air, even with the mudflat smell that came fairly strong now and then. She took a small black box out of her jacket and went over the vehicle and all three of the humans in it, before shrugging.

"OK, that's about as secure as I can get, this side of the Sierras. Now we can talk."

"Someone listening in?" Tully asked. "Mind if I have a swig of whatever it was, by the way?"

Adrienne raised an eyebrow, but handed over her flask. "It's Seven Oaks brandy—from my own land," she said. "And as to listening . . . I think that Nostradamus has been compromised."

"Nostradamus?" Tom said.

"Formally, the Commonwealth Information and Communications System," she said. "Nobody calls it anything but Nostradamus except in official documents."

Tully handed back the silver flask. "Pretty good brandy, by the way. Sort of cognac style, hey? And Nostradamus is your Internet?"

She nodded. "Sort of cognac; Ugni Blanc grapes, at least, and the same style of distilling; this batch was laid down when I was six. Nostradamus is . . . Imagine . . ." She paused for thought.

". . . imagine that the U.S. government ruled the whole civilized world, that it owned AOL, and AOL was the whole Internet, everywhere. That it owned and operated every ISP, and there was only one type of modem and one set of software for it, and the super-AOL owned all the cables and servers and the whole communications industry and the telephone net and all the TV stations and on-line databanks and the public library as well. It's an intranet, a closed system. No computer-to-computer contact outside it at all, unless you use floppies, and those can be read anytime you upload to a computer in touch with the system. And you have to use your ID card and get a scan anytime you log on, even from a public terminal."

Tully snapped his fingers. "Hey! Al Stewart! It's named after the song, right?" He hummed, and then sang in a half chant:

Mortal man, your time is sand—Your years are leaves
    upon the sea
I am the eyes of Nostradamus—All your ways are
    known to me!

"Yes, that one was popular about the time the system was first put together," she said, and nodded with a tinge of surprised respect. "It's been updated frequently since—all high-broadband fiber now."

She turned to Tom and looked him in the eye: "All right; Bosco was the man behind that endangered-animal smuggling. He couldn't have been doing it for the money; that doesn't really make sense. And somebody got to Schalk—thanks, by the way—and if I wasn't the nasty suspicious sort who never tells anyone anything until they need to know, he'd have screwed my investigation worse than he undoubtedly did. Schalk was willing to court almost certain death to shut Bosco up when it looked like he'd talk. You were a police officer—"

"Am," Tom corrected.

She shrugged. "All right, are a police officer. What does that suggest to you?"

"What would Bosco have gotten if he confessed? In the way of punishment." *Because if you burn 'em alive, it would be perfectly natural. And how do I know you* don't *burn people alive here?* "He put up a lot of resistance, as if the stakes were extremely high."

"Punishment for smuggling? As long as there wasn't any question of revealing the Gate secret . . . ten or fifteen years 'assisting in the dynamic growth of the mining industry so important to our beloved Commonwealth.'"

"Sent to the mines, hey?" Tom said. "I presume that isn't a death sentence?"

"Of course not. Gray jumpsuit, monotonous but adequate diet, hard bunk, hard work, unsympathetic guards. Maybe half that time, if the Prime of his Family was willing to pay heavily and twist arms for him. He might get a trusty's job in a year or two; after all, he *was* one of the Thirty Families. A pretty poor specimen of the breed, but the principle counts. Do you think he was just unable to bear the thought of a few years turning ore into ingots?"

Tom thought, then shook his head. "Hell no. He was hiding something big, very big. Something that would have gotten him killed if he confessed. Something that *did* get him killed because it just *looked* like he might confess."

Adrienne's lips skinned back in a notional smile. "Yes. I think he was a small part of a very big conspiracy; a conspiracy against the Gate Control Commission and the Gate secret. One of which Schalk was a tool."

The big man nodded again. "Now," he said coldly, crossing his arms, "tell me why we should care."

For a moment she looked shocked, then shook her head. "All right, it's natural you should still be thinking like First-Siders. Reasons? Three reasons you should care."

She held up three fingers, and turned them down one by one: "First, Bosco was a collateral . . . sort of a fictive-kinship thing . . . of the Collettas. If the Colletta Prime, the head of the Family, is involved in this . . . well, the Collettas have long memories, and they carry grudges. You were partly responsible for their boy's death. If they were to take over here, your lives wouldn't be worth squat. Second, even if they were willing to let you live, you'd still have to live *here* after they took over, and I doubt you'd like it—you'll know what I mean when you've seen more of how things work here."

"And third?" Tom said, expressionless.

"Third, if the conspiracy takes over, think about who they were operating with back on FirstSide, and how. The Commission—which we Rolfes and our friends run, more or less—believes in leaving a minimal footprint back there and limited expansion here; that's why our faction is called the Conservatives. The Collettas are more ambitious. . . . Oh, hell, it's complicated, sixty years of politics. The Collettas are the head of the Imperialist party here. They want to conquer this world, more or less, and rule all the natives as slaves, more or less. They don't put it quite that way, and don't mention that they'd also like to be kings, emperors, themselves. They're buddy-buddy with the Batyushkovs, who I think still have political ambitions back FirstSide, not just here, ambitions in Russia. Think about the sort of mayhem someone in control of the Gate's resources and the Commission's wealth could create here *and* back FirstSide, if they got their hands on it."

Tom exchanged a glance with his partner. They both nodded slightly, and he replied, "We don't have enough information to decide on that . . . Ms. Rolfe."

He thought she winced slightly, but she went on coolly enough: "That's fair. Look, if you want me to do it, I'll just drop you off in Rolfeston. That hundred dollars you each got will keep you for a month, two if you're very careful, and there's plenty of work here for men with your skills. *Or,* you can let me show you around, and try to convince you that you should help me."

"Why do you need help, if you're in the all-powerful Gate Security?" Tom asked.

Adrienne laughed bitterly. "Oh, if only you knew! I can just imagine going over to Colletta Hall"—she pointed in the direction of what should be San Jose—"and waving my little pistol at Giovanni Colletta and telling him he's under arrest. For that matter, if Bosco had been caught here in the Commonwealth . . . Let's say this isn't the most centralized country in human history. And I've got to assume that Gate Security is compromised as well, after what happened with Schalk; there are Collettas and Batyushkovs and their affiliates all through it, of course. I need some help I can trust."

He looked at her. She flushed, but continued to meet his eyes.

"This *is* my country, and I'll do whatever it takes to protect it," she said. "Including kill, lie and deceive. You never have?"

Tom nodded in grudging acknowledgment. "I'm an American," he said. "And I'll do all that for *my* country. Possibly we can work together."

"Possibly," Tully said. "Depends on how much of what you're telling is the truth, and how we assemble the facts once we know 'em."

"Fair enough," she said.

Then she smiled, and despite himself he felt his lips curve up in response. "First, I get to show you my home country."

Tom straightened up and looked around. Anew, the knowledge that he was really here struck him.

"Dodos?" he murmured. "And tigers and bears, oh my!" *Christ, the things we could see here!* he thought. Tully gave a sudden strangled whoop; the same thought must have struck him.

"Dodos? Only in the zoo, this side of Mauritius," she replied, chuckling. "They swarm like vermin there. As for the tigers and bears, the hills here are lousy with 'em."

✳ ✳ ✳

"It's not far to Rolfeston, which is roughly where the People's Republic of Berkeley is located FirstSide," she said. "Which is a deep irony, once you know Rolfeston a little."

They stopped for another checkpoint a thousand yards from the Gate complex parking lot; this one had those perforated plates that hid tire-ripping spikes ready to spring up at the push of a button, and two more strongpoints on either side of the road. This time the weapons peering out of the slits included 25mm chain guns, and guided antitank rockets mounted on a rotating cupola on the roof. Another of the black-uniformed soldiers in high-tech gear brought out a mobile reader to scan Adrienne's fingerprints and retinas, and those of her passengers.

"GSF," Adrienne said as they accelerated again. "Gate Security Force—reports directly to the Commission. The next layer of security is militia. Right around here is farming country, except for the Gate complex—we keep that closely guarded, as you can imagine. Minefields, dogs, electrified wire, and robot guns included, by the way, so don't get any funny ideas about sneaking back FirstSide and calling in the marines. This isn't the United States. *Our* guard details don't have lawyers paralyzing their trigger fingers. They spot you off the road within the prohibited area, they kill you dead and investigate later."

He nodded; there were still more pillboxes at strategic points, sensor towers, a six-wheeled armored car mounting a 40mm automatic cannon in its turret, and more troops—these in gray uniforms, and equipped with what looked like M-14s but weren't. Occasional aircraft went by overhead, including a big blimp and a tilt-rotor, but one of them was a Black Hawk helicopter with door gunners, flying a patrol pattern.

The vacant countryside around the Gate complex was tawny-green grass and bush studded with enormous live oaks with their characteristic thick, gnarled limbs like the hands of arthritic giants. They passed cars and trucks headed both ways on the north-south bayside road, none very large, but the air held virtually nothing of the hydrocarbon stink you'd get in this area on . . .

FirstSide, he thought. *Get used to the terminology.*

Beyond the checkpoints the land was wild, like something out of an old book about the California lowlands, grassland and trees shading into a fringe of bird-swarming salt marsh; he saw a herd of small tule elk trotting off as the Hummer went by. Some of the valley oaks were over a hundred feet high and stretched out to shade circles nearly twice that diameter.

"What, no bears and wolves?" he said feebly.

Adrienne waved a hand toward the blue-and-green line of the Oakland-Berkeley hills that fringed the plain to their right.

"Plenty up there, and mountain lions. We don't let 'em too close to town, of course."

He twisted around. Tully had found a pair of binoculars kept cased in a holder attached to the back of the driver's seat. Tom grabbed them, seeking detail, but the landscape was too alien and too large. He did see the waters of Lake Merritt behind them, and beyond that a glimpse of a house that must be huge to show at this distance. Farming country filled the coastal flats beyond that, a softly colored checkerboard of fields rimmed with the tall shapes of poplars and cypress.

"Why's all this land here empty?" he asked.

"Partly parks, partly reserve for the expansion of Rolfeston . . . and we're here."

The town had a perfectly ordinary sign: ROLFESTON, POP: 29,855. It started more abruptly than a typical American settlement of its size, though, without the untidy fringe of derelict land awaiting development. There was a modest-sized industrial park of low-slung buildings on both sides of the road. Plantings and trees hid most of the factory-warehouse-whatevers; he could see that many were tile-roofed and stuccoed in various pastel colors, although others had sawtooth skylights and tangles of piping. A line of power cables looped in from the hills to the east on tall wooden poles that looked like whole Douglas fir trunks, before descending to a transformer station; the distribution lines must be underground, and the phone lines if there were any. Trucks pulled in or out, and buses, and lines of workers on foot or on bicycles or Segways: Evidently people were knocking off for the day.

Adrienne swung the Hummer into a parking lot, edged by more greenbelt—this laid out as a park separating the workshops from the residential part of the town. It had the flamboyant loveliness you could get in lowland California with plenty of water: rhododendrons, tree-roses, hollyhocks and gardenias and sheets of lavender Chinese ground-lilies in shady spots. Plus copses of trees, pools, fountains surrounded by tiled plazas, streams, a bandstand, benches and brick walks, street lamps on ornate cast-iron stands. A row of bicycles stood at the junction of asphalt and greenery, and Segways—two-wheeled platforms with a vertical handle and crossbar arrangement. A sign over the rack prompted users to remember to plug in the recharger when they dropped one off.

"These're free?" Tom said.

"Municipal service, like the bikes and the buses," Adrienne said.

"I remember a couple of places tried that with bicycles," Tully said. "Seattle, or somewhere else up in the Pacific Northwest. Didn't work. Somebody always ripped 'em off."

Adrienne waved around them. "Petty crime isn't really practical here. For a bunch of reasons, startin' with the fact that there's nowhere to run and nowhere to hide, unless you want to go renegade and live up in the hills with the bears."

Tom shrugged; there must be some way to beat the system here; he could think of several, offhand. It would have to be small-scale, though. Shock was receding, and his mind was starting to function clearly again. The Gate was the key to New Virginia; whoever held it had the place in a vise that needn't even be very obvious elsewhere.

They stepped onto the little two-wheeled platforms; he hadn't used one in a while, and that only as a curiosity, but the gyro-sensor computer system made operation instinctive, and you couldn't fall off. They took off at a little better than a fast walk. There were a fair number of people about, getting out of work or school; his eyes sharpened as he took in the passersby and the scene. It had the same old-fashioned look as the farmland, with an overtone of *Leave It to Beaver* and the *Partridge Family*.

Asians were rare enough to be conspicuous; there were no blacks, no obvious Hispanics. There *were* a fair number of young men and women who looked like Mexican or Guatemalan Indians, unmistakable with their brown skin and Amerindian features, dressed in baggy white pants and shirts, or blouses and skirts, and sandals—and *only* adults, he realized; no children of that race, or old people; most in their late teens or early twenties, a few as old as Tom himself.

Their body language and gestures were wholly alien, and he overheard snatches of languages that weren't Spanish, or anything he recognized, full of hissing, guttural sounds—his mind heard them as impossible combinations of letters, *tz* and *zl* and *rr*.

Hmmm. Can't place them, but otherwise it looks a little like a crowd back in North Dakota, he thought. Then: *A crowd in Fargo a long time ago.*

He studied the rest of the townspeople. Half the men in the crowd sported hats, and most of the adult women wore skirts, with only a few in slacks or jeans; there wasn't a single tattoo or body piercing to be seen on the numerous teenagers, many of them in uniforms that looked like they were modeled on a Catholic school's.

Hell of a lot of teenagers, too . . . wait a minute . . .

There were a lot of baby carriages and toddlers and kids running and playing with barking dogs, too, enough to make him look twice and deliberately count.

Adrienne saw the direction of his glance. "The baby boom never stopped, here; it always hits me when I go back First-Side, how few children there are. Our average family is about four kids—I've got four older brothers and a sister myself, and twelve nieces and nephews with more on the way—and the average age of the population is twenty-five years younger than FirstSide America."

"No kids yourself?" he asked. *You said not, but God knows you told me enough howlers . . . though I remember how odd a family that size seemed. . . .*

She laughed and shook her head. "Oh, I'm a freak of nature—ask anyone."

They wheeled on through a pleasant residential district of winding streets and single-family homes set in modest-sized lawns and very pretty gardens; most of the houses were built in a Mediterranean Revival style that reminded him of Santa Barbara. American elms arched over the streets and brick sidewalks, looking to have been planted about the time he was being born back in 1976; obviously they hadn't let Dutch elm disease through the Gate. Vehicular traffic was light, mainly small hybrid gas-electric runabouts and a fair smattering of silent fuel-cell buses, but with swarms of bicycles as well, plenty of Segways, and the odd horse-cart. The houses were medium-sized, all single-story; some of the older ones looked like they were made of adobe, many others of plastered brick; there were no frame homes, and all the roofs were tile.

The intersections often had a clutch of shops—none with familiar chain names, none large, but selling ordinary groceries and hardware, computers and personal electronics. There were small parks and churches every now and then—mostly Episcopal, he noted, with a scattering of Baptist and Methodist and Catholic, a Lutheran, a few onion-domed Orthodox and a couple of synagogues; and a fairly big school, two stories, set amid a couple of acres of garden and trees, built in California-Spanish style with its walls overgrown with climbing rose.

"This is the blue-collar section of town, more or less," Adrienne said. She waved to her right, toward the blue-and-gold patchwork of forest and grassland on the hills. "Then there's the town hall and the public buildings, and the main business district, and then more expensive housing, well-to-do Settlers, and the town houses of the Families. The steep part's all Commission reserve, parkland."

They went past a giant farmer's market, stalls and stands under a huge truss-timbered roof and enormous redwood pillars stretching upward like the legs of dinosaurs. A cleared laneway wide enough for delivery trucks cut through it lengthwise; she led them into that, slowing down to walking speed perforce among the crush of pedestrians and handcarts.

Well, that's a switch, Tom thought. *A farmer's market where most of the people selling things look like actual farmers.*

Which was a change from FirstSide's California. That wasn't the only difference, either; the fruits and vegetables and flowers were in the expected gorgeous Californian abundance, but there were live chickens and other poultry in cages, and rows of butcher's stalls like a carnivore's dream, with stout pink-faced men and women in white aprons and square hats beside glass-fronted compartments holding piles of steaks, chops, roasts, garlic-smelling sausages, pâtés and terrines, whole elk and deer and bison carcasses—

"For some reason, most of our butchers are Balts and Germans," Adrienne said. "We got a bunch of 'em in the forties and the businesses stayed in the same families. Most businesses do, here."

The fish section opened his eyes and made him lean back unconsciously, bringing the Segway to a slower pace. It was a pungent mass of vats and piles of shaved ice topped with sixty-pound yellowtails and huge albacores, barrels of writhing crabs the size of dinner plates, mounds of three-inch prawns, rock lobsters, abalone by the gross, oysters bigger than his fist, ling and flounder, cauldrons of shrimp. . . . Knives flashed and paper-wrapped parcels were handed out to shoppers; the prices looked absurdly low.

"Wait a minute," Tully said shrewdly. "What's a day's pay here? Entry-level, grunt work."

"Two dollars and all found," she said. "Three-fifty if you're finding your own eats and bunk. That's for a day laborer, a deckhand on a fishing boat, that sort of thing. The deckhand might get paid in a share of the profits plus fish."

Nickel a pound for filet mignon and three cents for shrimp still sounds pretty cheap, Tom thought.

"Where's the catch?" he said aloud. "Taxes? Housing?"

"You can get a two-bedroom house around here for two thousand," she replied. "And taxes are low; mostly local school taxes, that sort of thing. No more than a tenth of your income, less for the bottom of the pyramid."

"Where's the catch?" he asked again.

She grinned. "Tom, the Families own the Gate. Also the gold mines, the silver mines, the power company, the oil wells down in Long Beach, the refinery, the public utilities, a lot of the factories, and pretty well all the land. Taxes? We don't need no steeenkin' taxes!"

Tully snorted. "There's got to be a catch somewhere."

"Well, food and housing *are* cheap," she said. "So are clothes and shoes—most things made here in the Commonwealth are low-cost—except gas, which is kept expensive deliberately, ten cents a gallon. Stuff from FirstSide can get pricey, especially if it's big and bulky. Cars are a luxury—ordinary people in Rolfeston usually rent one if they want to get out of town, and use public transport or bicycles inside. The Old Man—ah, my grandfather, John Rolfe the Sixth—doesn't like sprawl. A town should be a town, and the country should be the countryside, he says."

"Not an obvious horror show, I'll admit," Tom said.

Be honest, he told himself. *It actually looks pretty good. But I'm seeing what she wants me to see, so far. Remember what happened to those poor dopes the Russians used to show around, back during the Cold War. A lot of them came back singing hosannas.*

"See why we're not so hot to have everyone and his cousins from FirstSide pouring in?" Adrienne asked sardonically, as they came out onto the street again and leaned forward to pick up speed.

Tom nodded grudgingly. "You've got a sweet racket going," he acknowledged. "The authorities—"

"The U.S. authorities would somehow find it in the interests of the United States and universal truth and justice to confiscate everything we own and ram forty million people through the Gate," Adrienne said. "Not to mention taking away our national independence and probably throwing half of us in jail."

"Well, you've got a point there. . . ." Tully began, before Tom glared him into silence.

Beyond the open-air market was a commercial section of two-story buildings, shops with apartments for the owners above, and in their windows what he suddenly realized were the first advertisements he'd seen in New Virginia. A few posters at newsstands urged him to vote yes for Bond Issue

34, proclaimed the urgency of electing Michael Taconi to the school board and lauded George McCarthy's merits for city council.

That makes sense, he thought. *Whatever these Thirty Families are, I don't suppose they want to handle the drudgery of day-to-day administration themselves.*

Adrienne pulled up before a high white wall topped with brick and overgrown with climbing roses, splashes of crimson against green leaves and whitewash beneath. It enclosed the end of a U-shaped building, forming the courtyard of a restaurant that proudly announced in tiles set over the arched gateway:

CHANTAL'S.
FINE PROVENCAL AND FRENCH CUISINE SINCE 1961.
SE SIAN PAS ME—SIEGUEN PAS MEN

That building was adobe, the genuine article; he recognized the thick-bottomed tapered walls with a slightly melted look; the roof was curved red Roman-style tile. The cooking smells seized him, garlic and fried onions, roasting meat over wood coals, good coffee brewing and the maddeningly delicious scent of baking bread, making him swallow involuntarily as his body remembered that it had been a very long day on one granola bar and that he'd upchucked yesterday's dinner. They left their Segways at a rack and went through a wrought-iron gate, past a fountain and into a tiled patio shaded by spectacular wisterias growing over trellises, purple and white flowers hanging in clusters like grapes and trunks thicker than peach trees; galleries ran around the court on three sides, supported by wooden pillars made from whole tree trunks. The outdoor patio was scattered with tables that were—

Jesus! Carved out of slabs of redwood six inches thick, he thought.

Some of them were fifteen feet long and six across, too, varnished and polished to show the grain and the deep sienna-red color of the wood. Tile or stone set into the wood showed in the middle of the place settings.

It was busy, with a dozen would-be patrons waiting on padded benches along the inside of the walls, or at a cheerfully noisy bar that could be seen through the open doors of the main building; somewhere a piano was tinkling and an accordion playing. A plump middle-aged woman with black hair and an olive complexion came bustling up and whisked them past the crowd to a table set for four—a waiter scooped up the extra set, and Adrienne ordered for all of them.

In a corner a huge, ancient and somewhat scruffy parrot slumbered on a perch, occasionally waking to cry raucously: *"A bas De Gaulle! Salaud, salaud, salaud!"*

He eyed her narrowly. "Rank hath its privileges?" he asked.

"I *am* one of the Thirty Families," she said. She held up her left hand, showing the braided gold-and-platinum ring on her thumb. "Incidentally, this is something all the members of the Thirty Families wear. We get them at a ceremony in our early teens—sort of a bar mitzvah thing."

"Mr. Bosco had one of those," Tom said ironically.

"Well, I'm also a Rolfe, not to mention a granddaughter of the Old Man himself." Then she grinned. "And you look like a man recovered enough to eat and ask questions."

A bouillabaisse came, rich with prawns, clams, crab, rock-cod, eel and whiting; with a flourish the waiter mixed in the rouille, a paste of garlic, fish stock, crumbs and red pepper, and laid down a platter of bread fresh enough to steam gently when it was broken, and olive oil for dipping. A carafe of chilled white wine accompanied it. That was followed by grilled potatoes with herbs, green salad, and a beef-and-olive daube, which came with another carafe of red; evidently standard procedure if you didn't order a specific vintage. Even then, he was hungry enough to do the meal justice between sharp questions and digesting the answers; the cooking was superb even by Californian standards, and the materials better still. Sun faded from the sky; lights came on, candles on the tables and frosted globes in curlicued wrought-iron brackets along the walls. Moths and assorted bugs immolated themselves in both.

Over coffee she concluded: "—near as we can tell, the difference starts in 323 B.C. Alexander the Great didn't die on schedule. *Here* he lived another forty years, and he's still worshiped as a son of Zeus. The Jews got assimilated by the Greeks, so no Christianity; Zoastrianism died out. . . . The details don't matter. What's important is that nobody from the Old World discovered the Americas, here, apart from some Scandinavians on flying visits to Labrador and Maine. But no sustained contact; the European and Asian parts of this world are sort of . . . oh, equivalent to the Middle Ages, technology-wise. In terms of countries and suchlike . . ."

She looked around, then pointed for a second. "See those two?"

The two men followed her eyes. Two obvious foreigners were sitting not far away, dressed in long-skirted silk coats lavishly embroidered in writhing animal shapes, baggy pantaloons and curl-toed boots. They were tall, broad-shouldered men with hair worn shoulder-length, youngish but weathered, with a half-Asian look; high cheekbones and slanted eyes contrasted with prominent noses and dense close-cropped beards. One . . .

"Dude's a dead ringer for Keanu Reaves," Tully commented.

The other was similar, save that his hair was a sandy color. Both of them were handling their forks with the slow care of those used to eating with their fingers, and they had sword belts looped over the back of their chairs. The weapons were straight double-edged broadswords with cruciform hilts and dragons curling in gold and crimson along the black leather of the scabbards.

"Those are Selang-Arsi nobles," Adrienne said. "From kingdoms in Manchuria and Korea and northeast China, in FirstSider terms. The Macedonian Greeks took over Central Asia—the 'Stans, Tom; they call it Bactria here—and stayed strong there. They bounced the north Iranian nomad peoples eastward, the Alans and Saka and Sarmatians and Ye-Tai and whatnot. Back FirstSide, those tribes kept going west and south, as far as India and eastern Europe, with the Asian nomads from east of the Tien Shan, the Huns and their successors, pushing them on and following them. It went the other way here, and the Huns and Turks and Mongols and Manchus disappeared in the ruck."

"So those guys are basically sort of Persians?" Tully asked, interested.

"No, they're Tocharians mixed with north Chinese and Tungus peoples; the Tocharians were from Sinkiang and Shansi, originally. Sort of like Celts; they were the easternmost of the Indo-European peoples. In our history the Uighurs, Turks, conquered and absorbed them about seven hundred years after Christ. Here the Iranian-speakers pushed the Tocharians directly east, then went past them south into China in waves, mixing with the locals. The Han only kept their identity in Indo-China. . . . It's a long story; two and a half thousand years of different history, all over the world. We trade with the Selang-Arsi a fair bit; they've got some gorgeous artwork, and they've picked up a lot of simple technology from us. The important point is that nobody here ever developed a real science; our best guess is that the Industrial Revolution needed the equivalent of a toss coming up heads a thousand times in a row."

"Wait a minute," Tom said, cudgeling his brain for remnants of high school history. "That means . . . well, if Europe stayed backward—"

"Did it ever!" Adrienne said. "Outside Spain and Italy, they're still painting themselves blue and hunting heads."

"—how did that affect the Indians?" he continued doggedly. "A lot less than the Old World, I'd guess."

"Hole in one," Adrienne said. "When the Old Man stumbled through the Gate in 1946, he found things here in the Americas pretty much the way they were when Columbus arrived, barring details."

"Details?" he asked.

She waved a hand. "You can look 'em up at the library. The Aztecs are gone; it's a mess of little city-states down

Mexico way, and they've all learned how to make bronze tools and weapons . . . that sort of thing. Less obvious differences up here in hunter-gatherer territory. My grandfather thought this was the past, FirstSide's past, until he was able to check."

"And the Old Man decided to make a good thing of it," Tom said.

Adrienne leaned back in her chair; the waiter brought desserts concocted of fruit and cream, and more strong coffee in a silver pot.

"Well, wouldn't you have?" she said. "Granddad told me he took about five minutes to decide that he'd given Uncle Sam everything he owed on Okinawa—remember, when and where he was a boy some people still stood up for 'Dixie' and sat down for 'The Star-Spangled Banner.' Besides, you two, you're supposed to be environmentalists. What do you think would have happened if the U.S. government had gotten the Gate in 1946? With a whole preindustrial planet to plunder?"

"So he's still dictator here?" Tom said, deliberately needling. *I can get really angry later,* he thought to himself. *Right now it wouldn't be tactful . . . or prudent.*

Adrienne shrugged, unaffected.

"He's certainly still big alpha-male bull gorilla and Chairman-Emeritus of the committee," she said. "My father's his number two, and Dad'll succeed him when Granddad finally decides to go do a hostile takeover on the afterlife. Succeed to his offices, at least. Nobody will ever have quite the Old Man's position here."

"Committee?"

"Central Committee of the Gate Control Commission, representing the Thirty Families—Thirty-two, strictly speaking—some of them men who served with him in the Pacific, the rest relatives from back in ol' Virginny, then a few more with each wave of immigrants. The Rolfes, the Fitzmortons, the O'Briens, the Collettas, the Hugheses, the Ludwins, the Carons, the Pearlmutters, the von Traupitzes, the Chumleys, the Versfelds—well, you'll pick up the names fast enough."

She waved a hand around. "To simplify, they've been running things ever since, pretty well. This doesn't look so bad, does it?"

"Not bad, for a pirate kingdom," Tom said.

Adrienne laughed, the warm chuckle he'd grown to like—and now couldn't trust.

"What's that old saying?" she said. "'The first king was a lucky soldier.' Or a fortunate pirate. The Old Man's a rascal and the Thirty are a gang of bandits, but he's a likable old rascal, and we're pretty enlightened bandits . . . most of us, most of the time."

Tom looked around. "That's one thing we'll have to look into. Your Old Man doesn't seem to have been much of an equal-opportunity employer, for starters," he said.

She spread her hands. "Ah, you noticed 'diversity' wasn't a priority in recruitment? Yeah, it's white-boy heaven here." A wry smile accompanied that. "Emphasis on the *boy,* by the way . . . Anyway, Granddad always said he believed in learning from experience, that importing Africans into old Virginia hadn't turned out all that well for either party, and that if anyone objected to his priorities, they could go find their own alternate universe and run it any way they pleased."

Tom snorted. "So it's the WASP promised land?" he said sardonically.

"Not exactly. We've got the Blackfeet, the when-wes—"

"Whoa!" Tully held up a hand.

Tom's head felt heavy, as if the flow of information were clogging the veins there. He went on: "You're losing me again. Blackfeet? Indians? What's a when-we?"

"Oh, sorry. Blackfoot is a translation of *pied noir.* North African French, like the folks who own this restaurant. When-wes are"—she nodded toward another party at a nearby table, three generations in khaki shorts and bush jackets, from a white-haired elder down to a clutch of tow-thatched children—"that comes from 'when we were in . . .'

Kenya or Rhodesia, usually, which they're always going on about. You've met some of our Afrikaners, quite a few of those over the last fifteen years, and Russians and some Balkan Slavs—all of 'em with reasons to find a bolthole, the biggest groups of immigrants we've had in my lifetime. It was the same back in the forties, Granddad got Germans and Balts with, ummmm, a strong incentive to go somewhere they'd never be found; a fair number of Italians; east Europeans running from Stalin; and Brits tired of rationing and things going downhill. Plus we've always had a steady trickle of Americans; they're about half the total, and much the largest single group."

"Plus people who stumble on the Gate," Tom said sardonically.

She spread her hands, acknowledging the hit. "There haven't been more than a few hundred Involuntaries all up, and most of them settle in well enough. Meanwhile, all the original groups have been intermarrying enthusiastically, the melting pot in action. The ones in the first twenty years were the most numerous; by now three-quarters of the Settlers were born here, and nine-tenths of the Thirty. I was, and my father was too, and my nieces and nephews, and some of *them* have kids already. With our rate of natural increase we double every generation even without immigrants. And of course, nobody leaves."

"Ah," Tom nodded. *So there* is *an element here against its will. That has possibilities.*

She paused. "I don't want to tell you any more lies, Tom. You two are Involuntary Settlers. That means you can do anything here . . . except go near the Gate. That will never be allowed, ever, under any circumstances whatsoever; and trying means dying. It wouldn't matter if you had the Old Man himself as a hostage; they'd shoot you both down. Ordinary Settlers only get near it if they're on official business, like Piet. Members of the Thirty Families can visit FirstSide, but they need clearance—and if they endanger the Gate secret, the Commission sends someone like me after them and they never, ever do it again.

"But all that's rare," she went on more cheerfully. "Not many stumble on the secret anymore."

Tully broke in: "OK, if this was a California, an America, that didn't get discovered by Europeans . . . what happened to the California Indians? I suppose they were the people we saw on the way, the ones in the *Viva Zapata* campesino costumes?

Adrienne pursed her lips and examined the play of light on her wineglass as she turned it between long slender fingers.

"No, those arc the *nahua*."

"Nahua . . . Nahuatl, the Aztec language? Mexicans?" Tom said.

She nodded. "*Gastarbeiter.* Contract workers, *braceros,* mostly from Mexico; we call them *nahua* from the main language down there. About a third of the population, half the labor force."

"What about them?" Tom asked. "I can't see your Old Man welcoming them with open arms. Or is this more like the Old South than you were letting on? Contented darkies . . . brownies . . . singing in the quarters, stealing chickens and cating watermelon?"

Adrienne grinned. "Now, give credit where it's due. The Old Man *could* have done just that, bought slaves to do the dirty work here, you know. The warlords and priest-kings down Mexico way would have sold us any number. They'll do anything for steel tools and muskets, not to mention brandy and aspirin and plastic beads. They have swarms of slaves of their own, and given the national obsession with chopping out hearts, those are the lucky ones. Lots of wars."

She frowned, obviously thinking hard. "As I said, the Old Man likes to learn from other people's mistakes—says it's less costly than making your own. So we recruit on five-year contracts, and in limited numbers—there are fifteen or twenty applicants for every slot. They don't settle here—the wages are enormous by their standards, and they go back with nest eggs and a lot of new skills. We've had sons of princes volunteer to dig ditches."

"Oh, sure, and none of them stay on regardless—and what about their kids?"

"Norplant for all the female new arrivals," Adrienne said. "Or more modern long-term contraceptive implants. And this isn't FirstSide, Tom. Remember Nostradamus and those ID cards you got issued? It's impossible to live here without valid ID, not for more than a couple of weeks. Unless you want a long-term career in the borax mines of the Mojave."

"They're all happy to go back to Aztec land, when they've had five years of flush toilets and modern medicine?" Tom asked skeptically.

"Oh, any who want to stay after their contracts expire can, on certain conditions."

"Conditions?"

"Well, only one major condition. An injection of P-63."

Ouch, Tom thought.

That was an immunosterilizant the Chinese had developed back around the turn of the century. It made the body's immune system sensitive to some of the proteins on the surface of sperm, programming it to treat them as foreign tissue. It was quite popular back on the other side of the Gate because it didn't have any other symptoms; in fact it mimicked a common natural cause of infertility that had been a complete mystery until the 1990s.

By God, her grandpa certainly does think ahead. I suppose they used tube-tying and vasectomies before that.

Back home, the Germans and French and a lot of other Europeans had found that "guest workers" tended to become very long-term guests, and a lot of them weren't at all happy with it. Old Man Rolfe seemed to have found a way to have a foreign underclass that was guaranteed not to start families or become a permanent part of the social landscape—without even provoking mass discontent, since they were all volunteers. In fact, the more he thought about it, the more diabolically clever it was.

Because there's no new generation raised here, none of the nahua *will ever really understand how Westerners think, and none of them will ever really learn our way of looking at things—or read Jefferson, or Marx—and they'll never have the second-generation immigrant's hopes for full equality, or their frustrations. They're all perpetually fresh off the boat.*

He gave a slight mental wince. *The "Old Man" seems a lot more interested in getting the result he wants than in the "how" part, though. Christ, but that man must give new shadings to the word "ruthless."*

He and Tully exchanged a quick glance, and the smaller man nodded. When he spoke, it was to Adrienne: "What happened to the real natives, though? Plenty of them, if I remember the history."

"Nobody was counting, but the Old Man recorded in his journal that he was surprised at how dense the population was, even though the California natives weren't farmers. Most estimates of precontact Indian populations back in his day were way too low, of course."

She sighed and went on after a moment's pause: "What happened to them? Well, influenza in 1946. That took off about half of them, we think; Uncle Andy—Andy O'Brien, one of the founders—was coming down with it on his first visit and it spread like fire in dry grass; the Ohlone, the local tribe, treated the sick by putting them in the village sweathouse and everyone crowded in with them to keep them company. Then when it got bad, the survivors of each little band ran off to the neighbors, and then they ran to *their* neighbors, and so on. Like dropping a stone into a pond, with the ripples bouncing back and forth from the Pacific to the Atlantic."

"Ouch," Tom said, and added to himself: *Again.* "Didn't it occur—"

Adrienne poured herself more coffee. "Why should it have occurred to anyone? The Old Man was a soldier—and in 1946, historical epidemiology was something most *historians* didn't know much about. I *was* a history student, at the University of New Virginia and then at Stanford. The first serious research wasn't until the sixties, seventies—*Plagues and Peoples, Ecological Imperialism,* the groundbreakers. Until then most people, most historians, just assumed a pre-

Columbian population too small by a factor of ten or fifteen."

Tully cocked his head. "Bet that flu epidemic wasn't the last one, either. With the Gate setup, you'd get a unified disease environment on both sides, unless you used air locks and a whole lot of other stuff, including a long quarantine period. That decontamination procedure you put us through wouldn't catch everything."

She nodded. "In 1947, some Latvian refugees recruited as Settlers brought over viral hepatitis and typhus both. They got flown in and shoved through the Gate quick to avoid trouble about visas."

"Ouch." Tom winced.

"They threw out the clothes of the sick; some of the local Indians picked them up, and there were lice in the seams—amazing how hard it is to kill all the nits—and all of *them* had lice. . . . Then measles, mumps, polio, chicken pox from FirstSide; and smallpox from our Selang-Arsi trading partners in the sixties; and influenza every couple of years. Virgin-field epidemics. Plus some of the Asian kingdoms have taken to trading across the Pacific on their own—they're very quick to imitate things they can understand and apply, like better sailing ships—so smallpox and the other big killers hit again and again."

"Jesus Christ," Tom whispered; the meal turned into a rancid lump under his ribs. "At least they'll be building up immunities."

"'Fraid not," Adrienne said. "Or not much. There are a couple of hundred million people in East Asia on this side of the Gate. Some of the Selang-Arsi and Dahaean cities like Changdan or Hagamantash have hundreds of thousands each, enough to keep the big killer plagues going as standard childhood diseases. But even Mexico and Peru don't have that sort of density here, not anymore they don't. The plagues burn themselves out and vanish, and a while goes by before another ship happens to have an infectious crewman. The next generation grows up without being exposed, so they're just as vulnerable as their parents were, and the *next* plague hits just as hard. When that happens three times with something like hemorrhagic smallpox or pneumonic plague or chicken pox . . . well, there's not much left. The few who don't die of the fever are likely to starve or go mad. Then there are chronics like syphilis and gonorrhea. They spread widely and reduce fertility. We *did* manage to keep AIDS from getting through the Gate though, thank God."

"So you don't have to fight for the territory," Tully said thoughtfully.

"Not much, usually. We just move into vacant land, or give the survivors some horses and beads and knives, and point them east. Sometimes a little skirmishing."

Tom made a choked sound. "That's . . . pretty ghastly," he said.

She snorted, but he thought there was a slightly defensive note in her voice as she continued.

"Exactly the same thing happened after Columbus on FirstSide, Tom. Ninety percent die-off within a hundred years. Here, it's been about the same in sixty-two, because we have much better transport and maps."

"Moving in on their territory before they could recover, though . . ."

Her shrug was expressive. "Oh, don't be a hypocrite, Tom. What do you think happened with the Sioux in North Dakota, when your great-grandparents arrived from Norway all eager to sink a plow in the sod? I'll tell you what *didn't* happen."

She placed her palms together in an attitude of prayer, rolled her eyes skyward and intoned in a voice dripping with mock compassion: "'Oh, look at these poor Norski immigrants,' said the noble, selfless Lakota. 'Let us spontaneously give them the rich prairies swarming with game on which we currently dwell, and then we'll move west to the dry badlands of our own free will so our descendants can enjoy malnutrition, TB, diabetes, despair and alcoholism on a miserable reservation for the next hundred and fifty years.'"

After a pause: "Not."

"Well, granted," Tom said, flushing. "But that was a long time ago—"

"This is 2009. *Nineteen forty-six* is a long time ago. Why should I get upset over what happened before I was born any more than you do, just because it was three rather than six generations before? Sooner or later someone from Asia or Africa or Europe was going to learn how to sail here, and then it would have happened anyway. For all the breast-beating idiots back FirstSide, I don't see anyone packing up to leave the continent to the Indians. What nation isn't built on someone else's bones? That's how human beings operate."

"I suppose it could have been worse," he said. To himself: *That's even true. Though it's not saying much.*

Adrienne smiled and patted his hand. "I knew you'd be sensible," she said. "The Old Man's no ogre, no Pol Pot or Omar. He does have his preferences and crotchets, of course. He likes things clean and tidy and orderly. He likes useful gadgets, but he doesn't like big cities, or big industries, or agribusiness, or the Internet, or shopping malls or fast food, or modern architecture or freeways, or traffic jams, or . . . Well, as I said, you can guess the outline. Have either of you heard of the Southern Agrarians?"

"Don't have that file on my hard drive," Tom said. "All I know about the South is what I saw in the commercial strips outside places I was stationed."

"The Agrarians are a big part of the school curriculum here, as far as history and civics go," Adrienne said. "You should read *I'll Take My Stand*. It'll help you understand the Commonwealth a lot better."

Tully frowned, evidently searching his memory; he was a Southerner himself, of course. "Yeah, I remember something about them. Big back in the thirties of the last century, weren't they? Objected to progress and such. Didn't like 'damn Yankee' notions."

Adrienne chuckled. "The Agrarians thought laissez-faire capitalism was a dastardly subversive plot, and that Adam Smith and Karl Marx were six of one and half a dozen of the other. Things were different back then—real conservatives like the Agrarians worried about pollution and thought factory smokestacks were ugly and wanted people to be in touch with the land and nature. Commies and leftists and liberals loved steel mills and coal mines and wrote folk songs about building dams and bridges."

"That's a switch," Tom admitted, a little startled. His brows knitted in thought. "That explains a bit of what I've seen here."

"It does. Just don't think the Old Man's a Green. Some of the results are the same, but the attitude's completely different. Anyway, Granddad was quite taken with the Agrarians back at VMI. Considering that for us Rolfes everything had been going to hell since 1783 or so—we were the ones who wanted to keep the Articles of Confederation and reject that newfangled Constitution—it's not surprising. Most of the people the Thirty Families brought in here agree with him, roughly. So do most of their children, and the grandchildren, my generation. They came here to get *away* from modern life, remember, and they raised us here with not much of an outside world to offset their influence. Even the Thirty Families don't live FirstSide anymore. We visit, we shop, we do business there, but this is our home."

Tom gave her a considering look. "You didn't come across as . . . different," he said. "I'd think that being raised here would be harder to hide. At first I just thought you were a bit weird because your family was rich."

"Well, thanks," she said dryly, and then shrugged. "I visited FirstSide a lot, and spent a couple of years at Stanford. And I had special training in blending in over there; I can understand how modern America operates. The Old Man doesn't give a damn what FirstSiders think, though, and neither do most people in the Commonwealth. This is another country, and we do things differently here."

"Not to mention that here, you Rolfes are kings and your word is law."

"There's that. This isn't a dictatorship, but it isn't a democracy either. Sort of like a reasonably law-abiding and benevolent feudal oligarchy." Her glance sharpened. "And we—myself included—intend to keep it that way, against *all* threats."

❋ ❋ ❋

Adrienne's apartment building was off the main square, halfway along the length of Lee Street's passage at the lower edge of the Berkeley hills, and nestled in the first rolling upswell; it was a two-story block built around a courtyard with a small swimming pool and a fountain, the whole thing rather like the French Quarter in New Orleans. Tom felt himself stumbling with fatigue as they climbed to the bedrooms. It wasn't even any particular effort to decline an unspoken invitation and fall into one of the beds in the guest room. He woke for a moment then, just on the verge of sleep, to hear Tully say: "You know, Kemosabe, sometimes you're too stubborn for—"

"Shut the fuck up, Tonto."

INTERLUDE
May 21, 1996
The Commonwealth of New Virginia

The Mermaid Café had been busy all day, and Ralph Barnes was mildly contented with the take once he'd added the cash to the amounts paid by direct debit—he'd make payroll and expenses and a bit over, so far this year. He dropped the last of the bundled bills into the strongbox, followed by coins that he poured into the appropriate tray by denomination. A few were gold ten-dollar pieces, about the size of a dime; at this time of year, he got a lot of boat crews from the fishing craft working the salmon run up Carquinez Strait. Twenty hungry men per boat could work up quite a tab, even at the extremely reasonable prices he charged for steaks, chops, lavish salads, first-rate burgers and pretty damned good home-brewed beer.

He flicked a gold coin up toward the ceiling, watched it

spin in the lamplight, and then snatched it out of the air with one thick-fingered, hairy-backed hand. He might be pushing fifty, he might be putting on weight despite the hard work—*hell,* he thought, looking down at his belly, *face it, I'm getting fat*—but his reflexes were still pretty good. The coin bore a California condor in flight on one side, with John Rolfe's straight-nosed profile on the other and the Latin motto he'd given the country he founded: *Carpe diem et omnia mundi.*

"Seize the day. And everything else you can lay your hands on, you fascist bastard," he said in a growl. "It's no wonder you made a giant vulture the national bird. Why not the skull and crossbones for the flag?"

A knock came on the door, followed by: "Hey, Dad?"

He looked up. His eldest son was in his twenties, a close match to his father's blunt-featured stockiness; the black hair and hazel eyes were his mother's coloring.

"We've got a customer, Dad," Sam Barnes said nervously.

"So?" Ralph said.

So why aren't you taking care of it? he didn't say. That would reduce the boy—young man—to stuttering.

Sam was a good kid, but he was a lot more respectful of authority and his elders than his father had been at that age; Ralph wasted a moment on a mental sigh for the Bay Area in the sixties. If what he heard on the news was true, the current generation FirstSide didn't care about anything but money. Certainly the music they were making over there was pretty well crap these days; disco had been bad, and it was all downhill since then except for Al Stewart and that Enya chick. Of course, what you heard on the news wasn't necessarily true, and that was truer here than on FirstSide.

The really disappointing thing was that the Stones were still touring, when they'd promised not to.

"Ah . . . it's someone from the Thirty Families, Dad: I saw her ring. A girl, seventeen or so—a real pretty girl. She's, ummm, upset. I think I've seen her here before, but not since I came back from the militia. She said she wanted to talk to you."

Fucking draft, Ralph thought, but absently.

His eldest had been away for most of the past two years, doing his national service—with fairly frequent visits back home, since the Commonwealth wasn't that big. You were more likely to end up doing construction work than fighting, anyway.

"Yeah, I'll take care of it, Sam," he said. *Can't be anyone else.* There weren't many teenagers from the Families who knew him well; he was a suspicious character, after all.

The office was an adobe cubicle with a sloped tile roof supported on Douglas fir beams; it had been the bedroom–living room–storage back when he started building the place. You went out the back door to a covered porch and across the courtyard to the long low block that held the kitchens. He did, slapped some sandwiches together, and drew two mugs of beer before he went out onto the front-side patio with its trestle tables and benches and umbrellas—all furled now. The patio had been laid out around a coastal live oak with a trunk four men couldn't have joined hands around. Leaves rustled in the great gnarled limbs above, and in the eucalyptus grove that he'd planted between the patio and the road; they had a spicy, medicinal scent that mixed well with the remnants of cooking. It was dimly lit and slightly chilly, and the stars overhead were very bright; a new moon rode like a silver ship toward the west.

Ralph deliberately let the screen door clatter a little as it shut. That gave the girl at the far table time to scrub an arm across her face and get composed.

"Hey, princess," he said softly. "Sorta late, ain't it? Been a long while since you dropped by."

Adrienne Rolfe looked at him and smiled. Her shoulders slumped a little in relief, although her face was still streaked by tears. They'd been friends for quite a while; he'd always had a sympathetic spot for a teenage rebel, and she was smart to boot; he'd tutored her a little in physics.

"Not many places a girl can go to get a drink and a sandwich at night around here," she said.

Ralph laughed as he set the tray down and swung onto the bench across the table from her. That was an understatement. There were a couple of lights in the hills behind him, farmers in the valleys leading southward from the strait, and the ferryman's house down by its pier on the water, and that was pretty well it, short of the radio beacon on Mount Diablo. The ferry didn't run all night, either—either Adrienne had come down from Napa by the last run, or up from Rolfeston.

He took a sip of the beer and waited, his fingers idly tracing the initials someone had—probably with immense effort—carved into the tough canyon oak of the table's surface. Adrienne ate a bite of the sandwich in a halfhcarted fashion, then set it down and blurted: "Aunt Chloe's dead."

He reached out awkwardly and patted her hand. "Bummer," he said. "Total bummer. She was a good sort."

Getting her as an occasional customer certainly helped me get the café off to a good start, he thought. *For someone in the Families, she* was *a good sort.*

In a noblesse-oblige sort of way. She'd certainly helped save Adrienne from her parents, which counted as a good deed any way you looked at it. He listened, making occasional sympathetic noises as the girl talked about the swift illness—some form of rapid-spreading marrow cancer. Apparently there hadn't been much pain, which was proof of some substantially good karma on Chloe's part; he'd had relatives go from cancer in ways that a benevolent God wouldn't have inflicted on Nixon.

Well, maybe on Hitler, he thought.

"And she left it to me," Adrienne said, choking back a sob.

"Left what, princess?" he asked.

He hadn't known Chloe well—nodding-acquaintance level; she *was* one of the Thirty Families, and a Rolfe collateral, at that—but everyone knew *about* her. Her habit of taking in strays, in particular; he'd have been surprised if she *hadn't* left the girl something. Enough to be independent of her parents; her father, Charles Rolfe, in particular was up-tight beyond belief, a serious pickle-up-the-ass type of es-tablishment authoritarian. Chloe hadn't liked him either; their feuding was legendary, and he thought it was partly to twist his scrotum that she'd let Adrienne take lessons with the disreputable and borderline-subversive Ralph Barnes. And Chloe hadn't had any kids of her own.

"Left me Seven Oaks," she said. "*Everything,* her share of the Family trust money as well as the land. Not even when I'm of age, but right *now.* There's some lawyers, but they've only got a—what do they call it—a watching brief." She raised her tear-streaked face. "What . . . what the hell am I going to *do* with it, Ralph? I never imagined—"

"Whoa!" he said in surprise. Then, more slowly: "Do you want it?"

"Yeah," she said frankly. "I mean, Seven Oaks is where I've spent most of my time since the blowup with Dad; it's more home than Rolfe Manor. The folks there are my friends. But how'm I supposed to handle all the, oh, the de-cisions, and keeping things going—"

"Hey!" he said sharply. "What did I tell you?"

"Ah . . . 'You can try and maybe fail, or not try and *al-ways* fail,' " she said, and managed a grin. "Yeah. You know, you and Granddad think a lot alike about some things."

"Now you're getting *nasty,*" he mock-growled. "And re-member, you don't have to do everything yourself," he said. "Listen . . ."

When they'd finished talking he got her another beer, which made her sleepy. "Sam!" he yelled over his shoulder as she yawned and stretched.

The young man stuck his head out of the kitchen en-tranceway, with a crock of olives still balanced on one shoul-der. He *was* a good kid—no head for math or the sciences, but smart and steady. And polite, although he couldn't hide a certain gleam at the sight—Adrienne was wearing a pretty tight sweater. His own approval was purely avuncular, or so he told himself.

"Tell Jeanne to get one of the rooms made up, would you, Sam?" he said.

It wouldn't be the first time he'd put Adrienne up—first time in a while, though, since she left home for good and Chloe took her in. *Christ, she was carrying a doll first time I saw her. Where do the years go?* He shook his head at the thought and went back to his office. Not quite his bedtime, and his mind was too wired for sleep anyway; he poured himself a quick bourbon and water to help himself unwind— at times like this he still missed pot—and sat down with a scientific journal from FirstSide to pass the time, and a CD starting with "Spanish Train" in the background.

There was a very interesting article on superstring theory by a Russian named Sergi Lermontov. After a few minutes, Ralph put down his drink, turned off the music and began to take notes. They were in his personal code, and they'd have to go into the concealed file, but it was just the sort of mental effort he needed to work off some tension.

CHAPTER TEN

Rolfeston
June 2009

Commonwealth of New Virginia

The smell of coffee brewing woke Tom Christiansen, and the sound of voices. This time there was no bewilderment; he remembered exactly where he was. It was the day after their arrival; he and Tully had been laid out most of Saturday with shock and leftover symptoms from the puke gas. Adrienne had tactfully found business elsewhere until the evening, returning with an excellent pizza and retiring early.

He lay for a while, savoring the sensation of physical well-being and of waking up without a chemical hangover, and with a lot less of that glassy sense of dislocation. He put his hands behind his head and grinned at the plaster.

Here I am, on a whole new world, he thought. *A whole, fresh, non-mucked-up new world to see. Hell with a vacation in Yosemite or even Glacier National Park!*

Well, it was probably *relatively* non-mucked-up. Socrates had complained that Attica was eroded and barren due to overuse back in . . . well, it had been a couple of hundred years B.C., at least. *I should have studied more history; I only know that bit about Socrates because it was in a textbook on environmental studies.*

"Of course, Ms. Rolfe thinks I'm here for good. We may have to agree to differ on that," he continued out loud.

She'd used a fairly cunning dirty trick to cover her tracks, but if he got out of here he could probably get enough proof to expose the disinformation. And in the meantime, he *was* here.

"Christ, what an . . . hell, an adventure!"

Adventure usually meant someone else, in deep shit, very far away. This could turn out like that, but the scenery would be some compensation.

Suitcases stood at the foot of his bed. He looked at them, blinked, looked again. They were *his* suitcases—and his old army duffel bag, as well. He heaved one up on the bed and snapped open the catches; it was filled with his clothes, as well.

"Well, that settles the question of what to wear," he said, caught between fury and amusement. "Ever thoughtful, our hostess."

The bathroom was a little daunting; it gave out on a veranda that looked downslope. Objectively he knew it was perfectly private—the closest thing in sight was another small block of flats, a hundred yards downslope. Then he forgot everything for a moment as his eyes lifted to the fog-streaked grandeur of the bay, lit by the morning sun. Right below him roofs were emerging as the silver-white vapor retreated, and the tops of trees. . . .

And for the first time in my life, I don't have to mentally edit out the works of humankind, he thought after a moment.

By the time he'd showered and shaved, the scent of the coffee had driven even that sight from his mind. The kitchen and bedrooms were on the same level; he walked in to find Adrienne at the stove, dressed in a thigh-length bathrobe with her hair hanging in a loose, damp fall down her back. The urge to run his fingers through it was almost irresistible.

But will be firmly resisted, he thought. *Once burned, twice vulnerable—and there's business to attend to.*

Tully was sprawled at his ease, the remains of his breakfast before him on a table of some satiny reddish-brown wood. He was in one of his Banana Republic safari suits, a mug of coffee in his hand, grinning ear to ear as Adrienne threw some remark over her shoulder. The kitchen was a rectangle set along the same veranda that fronted the bathroom; the floor was tile, the countertops smooth granite, and the appliances upscale-familiar, with a flat-surface cooker.

"Coffee's fresh," Adrienne said, nodding to him. "There's scrambled eggs, bacon, flapjacks, fruit and cream."

"You don't have a cook?" Tom asked.

"Not here," she replied, turning back to the stove and flipping a pancake. "This is just where I hang my hat in town, when I've got business and don't have time to go back home to Seven Oaks. I could stay at the Rolfe townhouse, but Dad and I get along a lot better when we're not at close quarters outside business hours."

"You can cook for me anytime," Tully said enthusiastically, mopping his plate with a piece of toast.

Tom frowned at him behind her back. His partner scowled back, briefly extending the middle finger of his free hand and mouthing a word.

The taller man cleared his throat. "I'll have the eggs and bacon, and some of the pancakes, thank you," he said coolly, and poured himself a cup of the coffee. The milk came in a glass bottle, which was something he'd heard about but never seen; the cream on top had separated.

Well, he thought, *they would have checked all the cattle they imported for infection. No need to be as finicky as we are.*

His first sip of coffee brought his brows up. "Where do you *get* this stuff?" he said, despite himself. Rich, nutty, mellow, strong but not a trace of bitterness . . .

"Hawaii," Adrienne said. "The Big Island, to be precise—it's Kona Gold. One of the few forms of farming in the Commonwealth that actually makes money. The sugar comes from the islands as well."

He nodded noncommittally and tucked into the breakfast.

"Roy was right," he said after a moment. "You *can* cook. Let me guess: all organic ingredients?"

The eggs were done with cream and diced scallions and a little tangy paprika, and they had a smooth intensity of flavor that perfectly complemented the smoky richness of Canadian-style bacon smoked with apple wood.

"Not exactly," she said. "But it all comes fresh from close-by Rolfeston. Farming's an artisan-scale industry here. There's no point in anything capital-intensive, and we don't have to squeeze out the last bushel. The Old Man likes it that way; he also likes 'food that tastes like food,' as he puts it."

"Mmmph," he said, mouth full of the boysenberry pancakes. "I'll have to find a gym," he said, when he could. *If I'm here any length of time,* he did not continue aloud.

The orange juice had tiny bits of pulp floating in it, and a wild, sweet flavor he'd never met before. He suppressed an appreciative noise and went on: "Otherwise your Gate will be absolutely safe—I wouldn't *fit* through after a couple of months."

"Well," she said, chuckling as she brought her own plate to the table, "Roy and I were talking about something related to that."

Tom gave his partner a brief glance that he meant to be quelling; apparently he was getting entirely too friendly with her. She *was* the opposition; at best, an ally against someone worse, and that wasn't proven yet.

The way Adrienne was sitting and Tully was leaning back from the table, she couldn't see his face. That let Tully mouth words; long practice made them easily comprehensible: *Fuck you, Kemosabe.*

"You said you needed to see the Commonwealth," Adrienne said. "Roy suggested that he take a look around Rolfeston, use the archives and library and meet people. You could come up to Seven Oaks with me, and get a feel for how the countryside functions. Rolfeston's the only city here; most people live in smaller settlements or on farms or the estates of Family members."

Roy Tully was nodding his head vigorously behind her back and mouthing: *Yes! yes!*

Tom rubbed his jaw. "What's your total population?"

"About two hundred thousand, according to Nostradamus," she said. "Just over three thousand in the Thirty Families, a hundred and fifty thousand Settlers, and fifty thousand *nahua;* there may be ten thousand or so wild Indians left in what you'd call California, say thirty or forty thousand between the Rockies and the sea from Baja to Alaska, but we don't have much contact with them. More than half of us live around the bay; there are pockets of settlement down the coast to San Diego—we get our oil from the Long Beach field—and another outpost up around the site of Portland in Oregon. A few thousand in Hawaii and the Australian colony near Adelaide. And a chain through the Sierras to Nevada, with some small outposts further east; that's the hardest to keep up, so far from the sea."

"Then why—" He stopped and thumped himself on the forehead with the palm of his hand. "Oh, right. The Comstock Lode."

"Not to mention Tonopah and Alder Gulch and Cerro Gordo and other places," she said.

"Yah," Tom said, nodding slowly. "That sounds reasonable. Sure, I'll drive north with you. But . . . what's that got to do with a gym?"

She grinned, and despite himself he felt his mouth quirking up in response for an instant before he forced his face back into an expressionless mask.

"Well, the reason I want to get back to Seven Oaks today is that my *mayordomo*"—she pronounced it Spanish-fashion—"my manager, that is . . . says that we have to begin on the wheat tomorrow. And rest assured, that'll work off a lot more breakfasts than one."

"You always put your guests to work?" he said. *Or just lowly peasants from FirstSide?*

"At harvesttime? Damned right I do," she said. "Since I intend to be out there helping too. You have no idea how hungry a landholder here can get for men when something gets ripe. Ogres ain't in it by comparison; everyone pitches in. And it'll give you a chance to see the Commonwealth from the bottom up, as it were."

She paused for a moment. "Also, I've spoken with my grandfather, and he'd like to meet you too. Seven Oaks is close to Rolfe Manor."

And I'd like to meet him, he thought, a hunter's eagerness behind the expressionless mask of his face.

✦ ✦ ✦

"Look, Tom, you've got to be professional about this," Tully said, as Adrienne left to dress.

"I'm *trying* to be," Tom said. "You're the one who's acting like she's your long-lost sister."

"No, you're *not* being professional," Tully said, his face serious. "I *am* being professional; I'm doing my Roy the Friendly Goblin shtick."

"You think she's falling for it?"

"No, but she thinks I'm funny—and knows it's an exaggeration, not just an act. *You* are pouting, except when you forget and it slips. You're letting your resentment at being led around by the dick and made a fool of risk alienating our only source of information here."

"Not to mention she made everyone back home think we're dirty," Tom said grimly.

Tully shrugged. "Hey, Kemosabe, there are two possibilities with that. First, we never get back. In which case, who gives a flying F-word what people on the other side of the Gate think? It just plain doesn't affect us here. Second, we *do* get back—and chances are our names are cleared. Hell, we'll be heroes, famous, and rich after the interviews and quickie book deals!"

"It still grates."

"Without her, we've got zero chance of finding out what's going on here—not to mention of ever doing anything about it. We'd have to give up and start looking around for jobs, because we'd be citizens of the great and wonderful Commonwealth for the rest of our lives whether we liked it or not. That still may happen, but do you want to make it a sure thing?"

Tom opened his mouth, flushed, and closed it again. After a moment he replied: "OK, Roy, you've got me. I *am* being resentful. But Christ, I'm not an actor or an undercover type. She *did* lie to me and I *do* resent it."

"Yeah, but you don't have to keep hugging it tight, do you? Flashing between warm and chilly according to whether you're remembering to be mad that moment? Jesus, Tom, the woman really does like you, you know."

"And . . ." Tom hesitated, but if you couldn't talk to your best friend, you were limited to conversations with your mirror. "And she didn't just lie about what she did. She lied about what she *is*. She's a killer."

Tully let the chair he was leaning back in fall forward onto all four legs with a thump. He stabbed a finger at his partner.

"Hey, Kemosabe, I've got news for you! I don't see nooobody but *killers* in this room! *I* killed a fair number of people 'cause Uncle Sam said they deserved to die, and sometimes I killed people who happened to be standing too close to Those Officially Classified as Evil when I set off the area-effect munitions. So did you, not to trade war stories. You think it's worse because she's got different plumbing? And she did what she did in the line of duty; she could have offed Perkins, but she didn't. Have you never done something that stuck in your craw because it was the only way to get the job done?"

"Not quite on that level, but I see what you're driving at. OK, OK."

"She's got her job to do," Tully said, driving home the point with his customary subtlety. "We've got ours."

Tom grunted in reply and picked up a newspaper from the table, looking for refuge from the embarrassment that made him squirm slightly. Instead he half choked on a sip of coffee as he read the headline: TWO FISH AND GAME WARDENS FROM FIRSTSIDE TO COMMONWEALTH!

His picture was there next to Roy's; neither of them were looking at their best, and the prints must have come from the ID machine at Gate Security. No matter how high the tech became, official photographs always made you look like a criminal degenerate, a moron, or someone who'd been dead for several days. Often all of those at once. Apparently that was true in all possible universes.

The story below listed their CVs, right down to their military service in the Rangers and Tenth Mountain Division, respectively, and had the chutzpah to wish them well, and recommend applying for jobs with the Frontier Scouts, whatever the hell those were.

"Gate Security don't miss a trick, do they?" Tully said. "This place is a small town—hell, this whole *country's* a small town. Now everyone will know our faces."

Tom gave the rest of the paper a quick scan. The focus was strictly local, with virtually nothing about events back on the other side of the Gate. The politics made no sense to him except for picayune stuff, school board and road improvements. Foreign affairs were *really* incomprehensible, stories about events abroad, in the Mexican city-states or East Asia. He simply lacked the background information the writers assumed in their audience; it was like a man from Mars trying to understand why the secessionist movement in Iraqi Kurdistan was important to Turkey. Who, what or where the hell was Changdan? And why was it interesting that someone named Lord Seven Flower in a place called Zaachila was buying more horses via San Diego? The back pages were full of amateur theatricals, sports and reviews. Movies, he noted, were often from FirstSide; books seemed to be largely local, and so did TV shows apart from very old reruns.

There *was* one domestic item that drew his eye.

"Well, lookie here," he said. "Ahem. 'Hostile Indian remnants skulking in the Tulare marshes have been taught a stinging lesson for their unprovoked attack on a party of Frontier Scouts accompanied by the adventurous granddaughter of our Founder. Lieutenant von Traupitz reports that even though Miss Adrienne Rolfe, daughter of Chairman Charles Rolfe and granddaughter of the Founder, was temporarily in some danger, timely intervention by his force of Commission Militia—'"

Adrienne came back wearing laced hiking boots, loose brown cords and a black polo shirt. She looked over his shoulder; he was acutely conscious of the slight warmth, a scent of laundry-fresh clothes mingled with shampoo and *her*.

"That's where those extra condors came from," she said. "And Karl von Traupitz has an inflated sense of his own place in the world. The whole Family is like that. If they decide to build a new bacon-curing plant they boast about it beforehand, they tell you how world-historically important it is while they're doing it, and then they write a seven-volume epic complete with footnotes about it afterward. Maybe it's genetic—although you'd think all the intermarriage would have diluted it by now."

She had a floppy broad-brimmed canvas jungle hat on her head, with the cord under her chin; she also had two holstered pistols in her hands, and a rifle across her back.

"Here," she said, sliding the pistols across the table.

Tom caught his automatically; it was his Fish and Game–issue 9mm Glock. "Ah . . . I presume carrying a gun's legal here?" he said.

"For Settlers, carrying anything short of mortars and heavy machine guns is legal," Adrienne said cheerfully. "But be cautious. Dueling is legal here too, with single-shot pistols, usually."

Both men looked at her in disbelief. A little defensively, she went on: "Well, it's not *common*. Maybe once a year. But it is legal—and when a man in town carries a gun openly, he's saying he's ready to fight. Sort of like the Code of the West. I'd advise concealed carry, which is also legal here. I wouldn't put it past the Collettas to set someone on to pick a fight with you two, if my dark suspicions are correct. I'd have canned that story in the *Commonwealth Courier and Herald* if I could. That would have caused a fuss, though, and they'd probably be fully informed anyway."

"Do you really need the artillery for a trip into the country?" he said, his eyes sharpening on her rifle.

"No, but it's sort of customary to have a rifle in the rack beyond city limits," she said. "We'll be going through a couple of reserves where big predators are common and big, irritable herbivores are *very* common."

"That's not a Garand, is it?" Tully asked curiously, as she laid the weapon and a rucksack down on the table and turned to a wall-mounted screen.

"No," she said over her shoulder, as she pressed her hand to the plate beside the screen and looked into the scanner. "It's an O'Brien-Garand; a modification that Uncle Andy— Andy O'Brien, the first O'Brien Prime—made back in 1949. He was the Old Man's top sergeant in Baker company, in the Pacific, and he thought the Garand was the perfect battle rifle except for two things."

A slight sadness touched her face. "He taught me rifles; and he used to play grizzly bears with me when he came visiting, back when I was a little girl, and give me sips out of his wineglass."

Tom examined the rifle; it was the classic WWII semiauto, but with the gas port moved back four inches from the muzzle and a twenty-round detachable box magazine instead of the awkward eight-round integral clip you loaded from the top in the GI version. The Pentagon, in its infinite multilayered bureaucratic wisdom, had taken until 1959 to make similar changes—Tom's grandfather had soldiered through Korea with the original model. The only other difference he could see was a slotted flash suppressor–cum–grenade launcher attachment on the end of the muzzle.

He removed the magazine and looked at the cartridges; they were the old full-power .30-06, but these were hollow points, like a game-hunting round, designed to mushroom inside a wound. Pulling back the operating rod, he saw that the chamber and barrel were chrome-lined; the construction was excellent but in an old-fashioned way, everything beautifully machined from solid metal forms, rather than assembled from stampings and synthetics and powder forgings.

And the stock was some close-grained hardwood, polished silky-smooth save for the checker work on the grip and fore-stock.

"I notice your Gate Security Force has assault rifles," Tom said, laying the weapon down again. "G-thirty-sixes, weren't they? Good gun."

"Just a second." The screen had come alive, and was showing a logo with a central CICN. "This is Adrienne Rolfe," she went on to the machine.

"Confirmed: voice, retina, palm."

"Ronald Tully and Thomas Christiansen, ident numbers as follows, to have access to these premises. Transfer one thousand dollars to each account."

"Confirmed."

"Wait a minute—" Tom began.

"You wanted to investigate this place. Having money of your own will help."

He couldn't say anything to that. *Because it's so self-evidently true, idiot,* he thought, and went on aloud: "Thanks. That *will* help."

"Good, because I don't think we have all that much time to get started." She tossed a house key to each of the men. "I like to have old-fashioned backup locks. Try not to run wild in the fleshpots of Rolfeston with the thousand while we're gone, Roy."

Roy frowned, and spoke with grim seriousness: "It'll be a tough battle, but a twelve-step program will see me through the temptation."

She went on to Tom: "You're right about the assault rifles, but the Gate Security Force might have to fight FirstSiders. The militia's probable opposition uses bows and arrows. And it doesn't hurt to have the GSF stronger than any equivalent number of Family militia."

Tom pocketed the key. "Isn't it a danger to your reputation, giving dubious characters like us door keys?"

"Oh, my reputation can't be damaged; it got wrecked back in my teens," she said with a chuckle. "Popular perceptions of my standards of *taste,* now . . ."

INTERLUDE
April 17, 2003
The Commonwealth of New Virginia

"Good day, Dimitri Ivanovich," the young scientist said.

He looked uncertain, a slight dark fellow who still blinked as if he had thick glasses on his face, despite the expensive corneal surgery Batyushkov had financed.

"Uncle Dimitri, please, Sergei," the Prime said, and the two Russians smiled at each other. "Sit, sit—refresh yourself."

The Batyushkov country seat was only recently completed; it was not far from FirstSide's town of Aptos, with the sea breaking at its feet and the Santa Cruz Mountains to the north, stretching eastward along the valley of the Pajaro River and south nearly to the site of Castroville. He'd been offered a selection of coastal properties, all the way from Oregon to San Diego—he supposed he could have picked something in Australia, for that matter—but this had been his choice. It was close enough to Rolfeston to be convenient, but not close enough that the Commission was looking over his shoulder every moment of the day; and it was even closer to Colletta Hall, over the hills in the lower Santa Clara. He sensed opportunity there; the Prime of the Collettas was a discontented man.

"It reminds me of the Crimea," the young scientist said. "Mountains, the sea, fertile land between, and the climate of heaven."

Batyushkov nodded. That was true, and as a bonus the land was spectacularly beautiful. Greener than much of New Virginia, which soothed his Leningrad-born eyes. At this time of year, the young apple and apricot orchards of his Settlers left patches of fragrant pink mist strewn along the valley, and the colts kicked up their heels in the green pastures thick with golden poppies. The mansion's design was based on that of a nobleman's manse from the old days before the Revolution; one he'd seen on the shores of the Black Sea, converted to a sanitarium and resort. Waves crashed on the cliffs not far away.

Many of those Settlers were Russian too. Most were not, which Batyushkov grudgingly admitted was a wise precaution from the Commission's point of view. They would let him flavor this part of the stew, but not make a separate pot of his own.

"Yes, the Crimea is a little like this," the Batyushkov said. "Many have said so." He scowled. "That is as well, since the real Crimea is lost to the *rodina,* the motherland. Part of that absurd Ukraine, like amputating a man's leg and calling it a brother . . . and probably those Ukrainian peasant bumpkins will let the Tatars take it over sooner or later. Stalin was a fool to kill only half of the Tatars when he deported them, and Khrushchev was a worse fool ever to let a single one return from Kazakhstan."

The younger man nodded. "Uncle Dimitri . . . I thank you for bringing me here. Science no longer prospers in Russia; things are not as bad as they were even five years ago, but they are not good. And the Gate!"

His face took on a transfigured look, one Batyushkov had seen on mujahideen in Afghanistan, as they called on their stupid Allah just before they were crushed under a tank's treads from the feet up to encourage them to talk.

"The Gate . . . our theories have only the merest hints of the possibility of such a phenomenon. Many would call it impossible; until this month, *I* would have called it impossible!"

"I would have as well, until I saw it," Batyushkov said. "The question is, though, can you understand it? Can you *duplicate* it?"

Sergei Lermontov spread his hands. "I do not know," he said. "If I *can* understand it, it will take much time—much effort—many facilities, supercomputers, experimentation. Eventually, I must bring colleagues to join me."

Batyushkov smiled, a smug expression. "And the *ami,* they have no hint of what it is?"

"Very little," Lermontov said. "I have studied the papers

of the physicists at the University of New Virginia. They are
not particularly capable men."

"They are what the Commission could get," Batyushkov
said. "Men embittered by failure in their original homes.
And they are not allowed free transit, so they have no access
to the laboratories or talent of FirstSide." The satisfied smile
grew broader. "And you, my *nephew,* will be. Thus you may
study the phenomenon, have access to the facilities of First-
Side, and travel freely."

Lermontov nodded. "This will be helpful. I cannot, however, guarantee results. Certainly not at anytime within the
next two years."

"Nichevo," Batyushkov said: *It cannot be helped.* His hand
closed into a fist on the table as he went on: "Understand, you
must take no chances. Playing at *boyar* here, that is acceptable; certainly better than living in today's Russia and looking
always over my shoulder. The wealth I gain as a member of
the committee, that is more than acceptable, and I can keep it
and hand it down to my children, which would probably not
be the case in Russia. But control of the Gate—knowledge of
how to make more—that is *power.* Imagine whole new
worlds . . . better still, imagine being able to establish more
such gates to *our* world. To be able to come and go anywhere,
at any time; the storage facilities of a nuclear facility, the inner chambers of any headquarters or fortress . . . given that,
much that we have had to accept as inevitable becomes much
less so!"

"Za nas!" Sergei Lermontov said, springing to his feet
and raising the glass.

"Za nas!" Dimitri Batyushkov replied. "To us, indeed!"

CHAPTER ELEVEN

Mermaid Café
June 2009

Commonwealth of New Virginia

> MERMAID CAFÉ
> RALPH BARNES, PROPRIETOR AND FREEHOLDER
> BEST BURGERS IN NEW VIRGINIA
> GASOLINE AND DIESEL SOLD, ENGINES SERVICED
> ALL STANDARD FIREARMS AND PARTS
> BEST CHANCE FOR FUEL AND AMMUNITION THIS SIDE
>   OF TAHOE
> BEDS BY THE NIGHT
> ALL WELCOME, EVEN YOU FASCIST BASTARDS FROM
>   THE FAMILIES
> AS LONG AS YOU MIND YOUR MANNERS
> THIS MEANS YOU

Tom grinned at the big billboard—it was the first one he'd seen this side of the Gate—and put the binoculars back into the case between the front seats. The wind from the water ahead dried the sweat on his face. For the moment they were stopped at the crest of a low hill, where two live oaks overhung the road in a patch of grateful shade, to enjoy that and the silence. Ahead the land fell away to a flat valley that ran down to the strait.

"No respecter of persons, eh?" he said, before he pressed the starter button. "I like Ralph Barnes already."

"Ralph's a law unto himself. He's not lying about the burgers, either."

The Mermaid Café was roughly where the downtown section of the city of Martinez would have been, although differences in the details of the shoreline made it hard to be certain. A thousand yards farther north there was a long wooden pier out into the blue water of the Carquinez Strait, with a second cluster of buildings at its base. The road was graveled dirt, as it had been since they left the northern outskirts of Rolfeston, which ended in a Tivoli-style amusement park. After that the bayside road had run through man-empty country nearly to the site of Richmond—the sheer absence of the great oil refineries and chemical plants had left him speechless—and then they'd doglegged back down the Briones Creek and along Vaca Canyon, much of the trip through hills he remembered as the upscale suburb of Orinda.

Here . . . the hills dreamed under the early-summer sun, grass turning the color of champagne colored by late wildflowers, oaks and firs green and cool by contrast, and redwoods in the sheltered bay-facing canyons. He'd seen two grizzlies, including one that stood in the road until they were within rock-throwing distance; other game too often to count; and once he'd heard the unmistakable rebel-yell squall of a catamount. They'd stopped often, to ramble or just sit and listen to the wind soughing through the grass. He kept noticing the taste of the air, as well.

Now that they were over the hills another dusty-white road wound southward from here, through farming country in the valley lowlands between the Berkeley hills and the Diablo range—lightly settled, mostly tawny pasture, but with the evidence of man in fields of grain, the regularity of orchards, planted windbreaks around tile-roofed farmsteads. This country was solid suburb on FirstSide, of course, built up in the fifties and sixties of the last century. Here it looked as if the first settlers had moved in about then and not many since.

Right, Tom thought. *Let's not get euphoric; yeah, all that wilderness along the bay looks wonderful, but that's Mother Nature, not the Thirty Families and their Commission. Let's get some input on how the* people *do here. The present population, that is; we already know what happened to the original one.*

Tom waved a hand toward the farms. "This belongs to . . . ?"

"The Filmers, from Ralph's land back a ways; their Prime's seat is where Concord's located FirstSide. Then the Tuke and the Hammon domains, down through Amador and Livermore valleys. The uplands on both sides are permanent Commission reserve; so's Mount Diablo."

"Yah, but how do the farmers fit in, if your friends and relatives own all the land?"

The houses scattered across the flat-to-rolling valley land were at roughly half-mile intervals, and the fields were modest-sized. It didn't have the look of ranching country or large landholdings worked as single units. The Christiansen home place in North Dakota was a lot farther from the nearest neighbor.

"The farmers are tenants, allod tenants. The way it usually works is that the head of the Family, the Prime, keeps a seat—a home place—from his domain, and hands out the rest in estates of a few thousand acres to his kids and collaterals—everybody but the Prime and the eldest of the firstborn's line are collaterals; I am, for example, but my eldest brother and father and grandfather aren't. I hold Seven Oaks, and I can farm it, hand it down to my children when and if I have any, and sell or will it to another Family member. I'd need the Prime's approval to sell. I can't subdivide it or alienate it outside the Family. The landholders rent to farmers on shares; they provide the land and fixed assets, buildings and fences and irrigation and so forth, pay any taxes, and get three-tenths of the crop. The farmer finds the labor and working capital, the machinery and livestock, and keeps the other seventy percent."

Tom grunted, and thought back to the prices he'd seen in

that farmer's market. "I don't see how that makes the land-lord any money," he said.

"It's hobby farming as far as the landholders are concerned, so far," Adrienne said with a laugh. "Our country estates are how we *spend* our money, and where most of us live—the money comes out of the Gate and the mines."

"And what does the 'allod' part mean?"

"Allod? It means 'inalienable'; I think it's a German word originally. As long as the tenant keeps the land in good heart and pays his share, he can't be turned out, nor his heirs; the landholder only gets a say and part of the price if the tenant wants to sell it outside the farmer's bloodline. Not that anyone would lean on his tenants anyway—good ones are too hard to find! Most landholders rent their land except for a home ranch around their country house, but I keep Seven Oaks in hand and work it directly myself, the way Aunt Chloe did. It takes more of my time, but I've got a good manager and usually I manage to keep in the black . . . a little, at least."

She nodded down into the valley. "Ralph's a special case. Granddad got him three hundred and sixty acres of Commission land here, rent-free. Long story."

Tom grunted again, and put the Hummer in gear. The Mermaid Café sprawled parallel to the road but a hundred yards back and to the west of it; beyond was a stretch of lawn, then outbuildings, paddocks and a small reservoir that did double duty as a swimming hole, to judge by the kids swarming around it. One swung out over the water whooping as Tom watched, on a rope suspended from the branch of an overhanging tree, let go, and landed in the middle with a heroic splash.

The inn itself was an I-shape of single-story whitewashed adobe, with the inevitable red-tiled roofs, but the blocks were of slightly different sizes and the alignments were all a bit off—it gave the structure a funky look, something of a relief after the manicured neatness of Rolfeston, and so did the blocks of colorful tilework here and there on the walls. A line of big eucalyptus separated the parking lot from the roadway, their scent familiar and faintly medicinal. The dirt and gravel lot was dotted with the same great valley oaks that surrounded the rest of the inn, each on an island of long tawny grass extending out halfway to the drip line of the branches. There were a dozen cars in the parking lot, and another dozen pickup trucks—working vehicles, to judge from the dust and dings. They swung in and parked, the tires crunching on the crushed rock surface. Adrienne pulled her rifle out of the rack behind the front seat as they stepped down from the Hummer, carrying it casually in the crook of her left arm.

"Doesn't all this adobe give a lot of trouble?" Tom asked, following her toward the café. "It isn't *southern* California, after all."

"Not with a powdered waterproofing compound in the stucco," Adrienne said. "With that, as long as you keep the foundation dry and the roof tight it lasts like iron, it's fireproof, and it's good insulation. Dirt cheap, too."

"Ouch," he said, missing a stride, and found himself grinning for an instant.

More trees and a flower bed separated the cars from the outdoor patio with its picnic-style tables. Off to one side was a row of brick firepits; smoke and an intoxicating smell of grilling meat came from there, and several cooks wielded tongs and spatulas. Others, mostly teenagers, bustled in and out through the doors of a long adobe kitchen. A girl came and took the rifle, unloading it, working the action to make sure there wasn't a round in the chamber, and then stashing it in another rack by the main doorway with matter-of-fact competence. About half the tables were occupied, mostly with family parties, and there were a few kids running from one to the next; a pleasant burr of conversation and well-wielded cutlery filled the air. An oak cast fifty feet of shade in the center; farther out there were striped umbrellas above the tables; chalkboards with the menu stood at several places.

A big man came out from the main house as they entered the patio, a little under six feet but bear-wide, the kettle belly straining at his tie-dyed T-shirt simply adding to his impression of burly strength. He had a grizzled brown beard, and his graying shoulder-length hair was held back by a beaded headband; the shoes on his splayed feet were beaded as well, moccasin-style.

Leftover hippie, Tom thought automatically—California was still lousy with them, particularly in the backcountry, and would be until the last of the boomers went to their reward. Then: *But a smart one,* as he met the small shrewd eyes in the hairy face.

"Ralph Barnes," Adrienne said in an aside to Tom. Then, louder: "Ralph! How's my favorite subversive seditionist?"

"Hey, princess!" the thickset man said, in a happy bull bellow. "How's it hanging in the Gestapo?"

"A continuous merry festival of arbitrary torture and death, Ralph," she replied, and they exchanged bear hugs.

After a moment she turned. "This is Tom Christiansen—you'll have seen his picture in the paper this morning. Tom, Ralph Barnes—one of the few people willing to talk to a wastrel like myself, back when I was doing the pimples and rebellion thing. You wondered where I picked up the taste for classic rock and folk songs?"

"Pleased to meet you," Barnes said, looking him up and down and extending a hand. "Christ, it's the Swedish Superman. You're the game warden, right? Don't let any of the von Traupitzes see you. Those Nazi shits'll shanghai you off for breeding stock."

"My family were Norwegian, actually," Tom said as he took the hand and shook it; it was as strong as he'd expected, and callused with work. "Pleased to meet you," he went on. "I presume you're not as hostile to the Thirty Families as your sign suggests?"

"I hate their guts," Barnes said with a broad white snaggletoothed smile, shepherding them to a vacant table. "I just make a few individual exceptions, like for the princess here. So sue me. I am vast"—he slapped his belly and misquoted—"I contain multitudes."

"Could you get Henry over here?" Adrienne said. "I think Tom would like to meet him."

"Aha," Barnes said. "You want to get the Bitch-and-Moan squad together, hey? Show him the revolutionary element—right on! Sure, we ain't too busy right now." He turned and shouted: "Hey, Henry! Over here—two of the usual, and some beer!"

The man who came bearing the tray was younger than the innkeeper; in his late thirties, of medium height, lean and fit. He was also the first black Tom had seen this side of the Gate—light brown in fact, but unmistakably of that mixed breed miscalled African-American, with regular blunt features and inch-long, wiry, tight-kinked hair.

"You the one who bellowed like an ox with a hernia, beloved ol' massa?" he said, setting the tray down. It held four pint steins of beer, moisture beading on the thick glass, two hamburgers and a basket of chunky-looking French fries.

"Show some respect for your father-in-law and set your worthless cop ass down on the bench," Ralph replied genially.

Tom coughed and took a drink of his beer; then he stopped and savored it as it deserved while Henry joined the party, sitting beside the older man across from Tom and Adrienne.

"Not bad," Tom said, putting his mug down. "Well hopped, and a nice sharp taste . . . some local microbrewery?"

"We brew it ourselves," Ralph said.

"*I* brew it ourselves," Henry said, and offered his hand. "Henry Villers. Ex–Oakland PD. Welcome, fellow Involuntary. I'm the Black Settler of this little transdimensional Rhodesia." He jerked a thumb at Ralph. "He's Zorro, but don't tell anyone; if they found out, they might stop him branding big Z's on the Thirty's asses with a red-hot iron."

"It's a sword, man—how many times do I have to tell you? Zorro uses a *sword*."

"I sell them the hops," Adrienne cut in. "Also the meat for these hamburgers."

Tom shook the black man's hand, smiling. "How'd you end up here?" he said.

The other three burst into laughter, and he looked at them curiously.

"That's not . . . usually considered a tactful question here, Tom," Adrienne said gently. "Commonwealth etiquette. A lot of people are sort of, ah, sensitive about what they or their ancestors did back FirstSide. The way some Aussies don't like the word 'convict,' only it's a lot fresher here."

"No problcmo," the black man said. "Mc, I got here 'cause I was *smart*. I cunningly went undercover as an RM and M warehouse employee. In the outer circle, of course, the ones they keep as camouflage. Everyone in Oakland said that RM and M was the greatest thing since grits, but in my prodigious wisdom, I knew they were a bunch of evil honky despots down deep. I could tell from the way the company executives *looked* at me, on their rare visits—which somehow always included the same secluded set of warehouses in the old section. And wasn't I right?"

Tom looked at Adrienne. "What happened to your Old Man's indifference to FirstSider sensibilities?"

She shrugged: "Well, we'd look pretty conspicuous with an all-pink-faces workforce in twenty-first century *Oakland,* wouldn't we, Tom? Lawsuits would be the least of it. A lot of genuine traffic goes through that complex—which means we can divert a certain amount without suspicion. We keep shuffling the deck so that nobody notices the kernel at the center of the peanut, to mix a metaphor. That means the outside has to look as genuine as possible."

Henry Villers nodded vigorously. "RM and M is Oakland's mostest equal-opportunity false-front scam. So, patiently and slowly I accumulated clues that something funny was going on there. All the while neglecting the really funny thing."

He paused, and Tom took up the obvious straight line. "Which was?"

"Which was that RM and M had the Oakland police in their pockets, starting about thirty years ago. If I hadn't been quick and pigheaded, they'd have steered me away from investigating, the way they did with most others who smelled a rat."

"Make it forty-odd years," Adrienne said. "You got caught in 1998, right? According to the GSA records, we've had our nominees running the Oakland police department continuously from about 1956. Not that they actually know *who* they're working for."

"That would take a lot of . . . Sorry," Tom said.

Henry Villers grinned whitely. "Brother, with the sort of money RM and M had to throw around, you could bribe Superman." He adopted a man-of-steel pose: "'Ten million dollars,' the Man says. 'No, no, I am Superman!' Then it's thirty million. 'No, no, I stand for Truth, Justice and the American Way!' So then it's fifty million, and Superman comes back: 'I'll kill anyone you want! I'll fly shit across the border! Up, up and away! Whoooosh!'"

Villers took a pull at his beer. "Ahhh . . . So my reports got a lot of attention. Right from the top. Oh, gosh-wow-goody-gumdrops, says I, visions of promotions dancing in my head. Then one night I get called to a private, off-the-reservation meeting with the chief, no less . . . and wake up here," Henry finished sourly.

"Have you had . . . a rough time here?" Tom asked.

"What, you mean apart from better than half the people thinking I'm a rape-crazed subhuman just-down-from-the-trees dope fiend nigger barbarian and locking up their daughters and sidling away with their hands on their wallets at the first sight of me?" Henry said with a twisted smile. "Apart from *that,* not much. It beats getting dropped into the bay in concrete overshoes."

He laughed bitterly. "It's funny, in a way. This place is full of the worst sort of rednecks—"

"Oh, come now, Henry," Adrienne said. "Not the very *worst* sort."

"OK, I grant you, your grandpa didn't like the one-gallus,

white-sheet, burning-cross, three-hundred-pounds-and-pimples-and-that's-just-the-women set," Henry conceded. "But that was because he despised them for being no-'count white trash, not because of they way they felt about black folk. He's just so fucking genteel about it his ass bleeds, like Robert E. Lee or something. Anyway, the odd thing is that there's no *official* discrimination here. Unless you're a *nahua*, of course, and most of them aren't in our beloved Commonwealth long enough to stop being glad they're not starving or getting their hearts chopped out to juice up Monster of the Week. They don't have time to realize the way they get fucked over *here*."

Tom thought rapidly. "Ah, there's no official discrimination because there aren't enough African-Americans here to count?"

Henry drank some of his beer and thumped the tankard down, extending a pointing finger at Tom.

"Give the game warden a chocolate spotted owl!" he said. "I mean, man, all twenty-seven of us—not counting my two kids with Susie, Ralph's daughter—are not exactly going to start sitting down in many lunch counters. That's twenty-seven out of a hundred and fifty thousand, with no more coming. None since me, nearly ten years ago, and mostly we live over in New Brooklyn, so people in the other Family domains don't see much of us."

"New Brooklyn?" Tom asked.

"Uncle Sol—Solomon Pearlmutter—called his domain's main town that," Adrienne said. "He wanted to call it the New Lower East Side, but got talked out of it. It's over where San Francisco got started FirstSide; the Pearlmutter domain runs from the Golden Gate down to a little beyond San Mateo. Everyone thought he was crazy for claiming it, since there's not much good farmland or timber there."

She grinned, and the two men chuckled.

"After the Old Man, Uncle Sol was the smartest man I ever met," she said. "And Granddad always said Uncle Sol had more sheer wattage, he was just less practical. When they played chess, it was like mountains colliding. New

Brooklyn is the second-largest town in the Commonwealth now, a big seaport and manufacturing center with fifteen thousand people, and it all belongs to the Pearlmutters and their affiliates. They make almost as much off it as they do off their cut from the Gate and the Commission's properties. Not to mention they donated the land for the University of New Virginia, which is about where Stanford sits FirstSide. Uncle Sol always said knowledge isn't just power; it's also wealth."

Henry Villers nodded. "No flies on that dude; I met him once just before he died, old but still sharp as a razor. He also said only dumb krauts like the von Traupitzes would think you could get rich here growing wheat. Anyway, nobody's afraid of us; most people don't even see any of us more than once a year, which means only a few get upset about us. I think our Supreme Honky is content to let us vanish like a handful of soot in a snowstorm and pat himself on the back about what a goddam humanitarian realist he is. Motherfucker. If there were twenty-seven *thousand* black folk here, or even twenty-seven *hundred,* it'd be a different story."

You betcha, Tom thought. *Point scored. You can't have much racism when there aren't any other races to practice it on, so to speak.*

"Adrienne," Henry went on, "put me in touch with Ralph when I got shanghaied here." He raised his stein to her. "For which I thank you."

"De nada," she said. "Now, Ralph's story . . ."

The older man told it, then concluded: "So the bastard gave me this land and a loan to get started, yeah. And I love my wife and my kids and grandkids, and I've had a pretty good life here. But it ain't the life I'd have chosen, and if he thinks all this charity-from-on-high makes up for that, he's got another think coming."

Tom finished his hamburger. It had been about as he'd expected: delicious, the meat leanly flavorful but juicy and basted with just a touch of fiery sauce; tangy onions and tomatoes tasting of the earth; homemade garlic mayonnaise; all on a kaiser-style bun warm from the beehive-shaped earth oven on the other side of the patio with bits of caramelized onion in the crust, and a spear of pickle on the side that crunched nicely. Quite possibly the best hamburger he'd ever tasted, even including the ones his own father used to make at Fourth of July barbecues. The fries had been done in olive oil, and they weren't formed from extruded powdered potato painted with beef fat.

"OK," Tom said. "Now"—he looked questioningly at Adrienne, who was wiping her fingers on a checked cloth napkin. She nodded—"if you wouldn't mind a hypothetical question, would this Commonwealth be better or worse if the Collettas were running it? Instead of the Rolfes and their supporters."

Ralph Barnes choked on his last swallow of beer. Henry Villers thumped him on the back, but there was a gray anxiety in the glance he shot Adrienne. She made a soothing gesture.

"Let's consider that a hypothetical hypothetical, for now," she said.

Ralph nodded vigorously. "Oh, hell, that's no contest. Yeah, the Old Man's a throat-cutting pirate," he said. "And unlike a lotta people here, I don't use 'pirate' as a compliment. Sorry, princess, but I'm not going to start shading it at this late date. Yeah, he's a nasty piece of work. But he's smart, and he's consistent, and he was willing to stop when he got what he wanted. He makes the rules to suit himself, but then he keeps 'em, usually. And you can trust his promises. The Collettas . . . old man Salvatore had about as much of the milk of human kindness as a lizard does; he and Otto von Traupitz were neck and neck in the Sheer Absolute Fucking Evil sweepstakes, in their different ways. Giovanni tries to live up to the old bastard. Neither of them ever heard of the concept 'where to stop.' And they'd *change* the rules whenever it gave 'em a moment's advantage. Plus, personally, I'd be a dead man if they took over. I dissed his dad to his face. Giovanni don't forget."

"Ditto, ditto," Henry said. "Those Collettas would have had me on an auction block. Not that they're prejudiced.

They'd do it to anybody they could. Not to mention their friends the Batyushkovs, who *are* prejudiced 'gainst us black-asses, as they so charmingly put it, and the von Traupitzes, who'd probably render me down for soap. Me for starters."

Barnes frowned and thought for a moment. "Don't get me wrong, Warden Tom. If there was a chance for a revolution here, I'd be out on the barricades in a minute, and I'd dance around the guillotine when they chopped the heads off the whole rotten gang—present company excepted."

"God, that's big of you, Ralph," Adrienne said, chuckling.

Barnes scowled and waved the interjection aside. "There's a lot here I don't like. But it could get a hell of a lot worse. And I've got my kids and grandkids to think about. They were born here and it's their home."

He looked at Adrienne. "This hypothetical . . . it ain't *totally* hypothetical?" She nodded. "Then anything I can do, princess, you just ask."

She put her hand on his and squeezed; he returned the pressure.

"And say . . ." He frowned. "One thing. The Collettas're close with the Batyushkovs these days, right? Well, there's something I ran across a while ago. You know Sergei Ilyanovich Batyushkov?"

"The geneticist?" Adrienne asked. "The Batyushkov Prime's nephew?"

"Well, for starters, he ain't a geneticist. He's a theoretical physicist," Barnes said. "I read some articles by him a while ago. And yeah, he was called Sergei . . . but the last name wasn't Batyushkov. Sergei Lermontov, Ph.D."

* * *

"I'm definitely going to be less conspicuous without Tom along," Roy Tully said to himself as he finished washing the breakfast dishes. "I love the big guy like a brother, but . . ."

What had Anna Russell said about Siegfried, the hero of

the Ring Cycle? He murmured it, trying to match Russell's upper-class British drawl: "He's very *young,* and he's very *tall,* and he's very *strong,* and he's very *handsome,* and he's very *stupid.*"

That was unjust; he knew his partner had plenty upstairs. He was just very . . .

Straightforward, that's it, Tully thought. *Straightforward. And he certainly stands out in a crowd.*

Before he left he spent some time with Adrienne's computer; she had it set up in the living room, which gave him a lovely view of the morning fog and then the town as he sat sipping coffee and tapping his way through some public files, sampling a few chat rooms and getting a feel for how to shift data around. He had to admit Nostradamus was organized with systematic clarity: research, TV, e-mail, auctions, catalog buying, music and everything else in one neat package. It still felt odd, compared to surfing the Net: as if you'd moved from Castle Gormenghast to a utility apartment—no matter how tidy and well laid out it was, you were still going to be disappointed at the lack of crannies and dungeons and attics full of junk and sheer size. After half an hour or so he printed up some maps, stuck them into the pocket of his jeans, fastened the holster of the Glock to the small of his back under a light jacket—it was yellow, with green suede elbow patches; he was very fond of it and glad Adrienne's cleanup squad had brought it along—then went outside. The East Bay wasn't as chilly in summertime as San Francisco, but a jacket wouldn't be completely out of place.

"Time to soak up some atmosphere," he said to himself, and patted the gun for reassurance.

Not that he anticipated any firefights; but the weapon itself was a sign he had the trust of some powerful people here in this miniature pirate kingdom. *Everything in miniature except the planet,* he thought. *Well, that ought to make things easier.* There couldn't be more than a few dozen decision-making individuals involved in whatever machinations were going on. *Have to watch my step, though,* he reminded himself. *Remember that these people aren't mine, even though they speak the same language and wear the same clothes.*

He left the Segway in its rack; a town of thirty thousand couldn't be too hard to see on foot, and you got a better grip on a place that way. It was a little eerie though, looking out and seeing nothing of the ten-million-strong megalopolis he remembered. He had to keep reminding himself that he was living this, not watching it on a screen.

Adrienne's flat was on a low foothill rise; the ground grew steeper and trackless directly behind it. He turned northward, along a broad avenue that ran along the inner edge of the flatlands. It was about as wide as one of the major arteries in DC and had the same slightly artificial feel; he'd noticed the same thing in St. Petersburg, which he'd visited, and in pictures of Brasilia and Canberra, which he hadn't.

Planned city, he thought. *Planned from scratch. Pretty, though.*

The median strip was also broad, and a mass of flower beds: roses, hollyhocks, rhododendrons, penstemon and more, in patterns of purple, pink, white and yellow and green, with a shade tree every so often and a brick pathway down its center. The sidewalks on either side of the road—it was called Lee Avenue—were wide as well, brick-surfaced, with trees in circles of wrought-iron fence surrounded by stone benches. They were also fairly crowded, mostly with families heading northward on foot, all dressed to the nines and this time all wearing hats, down to the little girls in frilly pink dresses and their resentful brothers in ties.

Oh, Tully thought. *Right. Sunday morning.* He could hear bells ringing, too. *Everyone heading for church.*

The heights to landward were much more densely forested than the Berkeley hills he remembered, green and shaggy and marked by the distinctive spikes of old-growth redwoods in the west-facing canyons. Save for bridle paths, they were also empty of the marks of man. Between there and the roadside were what his map called the Golden Mile, evidently the high-rent district. He couldn't see much of it, because the inner side of the sidewalk was paralleled by high brick walls, usually topped by iron spikes. The gates showed a little more, being mostly wrought-iron openwork themselves: curving driveways, lawns and sprinklers shedding silver mist on them, tall old trees, and half-hidden houses. Those continued the Spanish-revival motif he'd noticed, although many were too hidden by greenery and distance for him to tell for sure.

The other side of the avenue was commercial, two-story buildings enclosing small courtyards surrounded by shops or restaurants; those alternated with theaters, live and movie, nightclubs, and a couple of art galleries. The streets westward of that seemed to be residential, with houses and lots getting smaller as they declined toward the bay. Looking downslope, what you mostly saw was trees, with the red of roofs peeking out from among them.

Feels odd to be in a city with no really tall buildings, he thought.

This wasn't much of a city, as far as size went; less than half the size of his California's Napa; about the same size as Paso Robles minus suburbs. But there were no skyscrapers at all; not a hint of anything Bahaus, in fact, not even the low-rise version.

Big Tom's gonna love it. He always did have a major hate-on for modern architecture.

That didn't mean there weren't any *big* buildings. Just short of Jackson Square both sides of the street were lined with three- or four-story office blocks, set back behind narrow strips of garden. Small discreet signs labeled them Commission offices charged with various functions—one was Gate Security Force HQ and at least partially open on a Sunday; it had black-uniformed guards standing before the doors.

Jackson Square was a rectangle with its longest axis parallel to Lee Avenue; bigger than its namesake in New Orleans, and named for Stonewall instead of Andy; about the size of the park around the State Capitol building in Sacramento. The perimeter was a broad avenue, of the same sort as Lee; another took off from the middle of the western edge and ran down to the water. The parkland in the center held a tall white stone basin and fountain, throwing its plume high in the air and falling into a large oval reflecting pond marked with water lilies, the big showy flowers dotting the blue surface with blossoms of copper, red, blue, white and purple. A marble-paved circle surrounded it, set with planters full of impatiens and flowering vines and with more stone benches; paths radiated out to each corner, separated by flower beds, trees—mostly wide-spreading native oaks—and greensward.

Public buildings rimmed the square. The westernmost corners each held a big church, one vaguely Italianate in style and the other a spare white-steepled structure—the Roman Catholic and Episcopal, respectively. Most of the crowds were hurrying in their direction. Between them along the western edge were a couple of other churches, somewhat smaller, and with their own crowds. The other buildings were official-looking; this time the architecture was neo-Classical, rather than Santa Barbara's 1920s riff on Spanish Renaissance and Baroque.

He grinned at the big Commission headquarters that stood in the middle of the square's long eastern side, standing and staring at the structures that rose at the top of a long ceremonial marble staircase until he was certain. "That's not just *like* the rotunda of the Palace of Fine Arts building in San Francisco. It *is* the rotunda of the Palace of Fine Arts building."

That made him laugh out loud. *Built in lath and plaster for the 1915 Panama-Pacific Exposition,* he thought. *Restored in reinforced concrete when that started to wash away. And copied here in the real-McCoy stone!*

"Or possibly reinforced concrete with stone cladding," he added to himself—this was earthquake country, after all.

The great central rotunda was a duplicate as far as dimensions went, an octagon over a hundred and thirty feet across, supported on pillars over a hundred feet high and topped with a low dome—here, though, sheathed in genuine polished gold leaf, not gray concrete, sending out blinding flashes in the bright midmorning sun. Behind that was something different—a long rectangular structure, with arcades and a second-story balcony on either side; it was set into the hillside, which gave it a view out over the dome. He walked closer to the rotunda; the eight panels in low bas-relief around the exterior were different too, allegorical sculpture showing scenes he didn't recognize.

The floor of the rotunda held another piece of marble statuary. First and foremost was John Rolfe, Adrienne's grandfather, dressed in rough hiking clothes with a forties look, a rifle leaning against the rock at his back, and a map in his hands. Others—he presumed they were the Founders of the Thirty Families, or some of them at least—were doing various pioneerish things behind them; mostly involving digging, plowing, pounding on a presumably symbolic anvil, piling up bricks, using surveying instruments or standing and peering at the horizon with weapons ready. The murals around the interior of the dome had the same themes, and a similarity that nagged at him before he identified it.

"Nineteen-thirties WPA style," he said, attracting an odd look from a woman passing by. "New Deal Socialist Realism."

He whistled cheerfully and cracked his knuckles. There was more of the same inside the big building at the rear—evidently known as Commission House—murals in paint and mosaic; the public areas were open, though nearly deserted. There were also a couple of exhibitions set up in the big lobby, with pictures and artifacts, evidently for visiting school classes and Scout troops and suchlike.

Hmmm, he thought, scanning one such, "The Heroes Who Built Our Country." *Must be interesting, the records of a country founded after people had cameras and the habit of recording everything possible.* The faces glared out at him, grim, stiffly self-conscious, with an archaic toughness.

Apparently Mr. John Rolfe had brought a camera with him starting with his second trip, and plenty of others had followed suit. Besides the group photos, there were shots of

Indian *rancherías,* dome-shaped reed huts, and of dancers in costume. More of boats and horses and construction machinery; pictures of gold operations in the Mother Lode country, starting with washing pans and working up through diesel-powered rockers and dredgers to hard-rock mining.

One wing of the government building was a library-cum-archive, all pale wood and flooded with light from tall windows; there was an excellent digital filing system as well as a librarian, and he collected a round dozen introductory texts—mostly those aimed at the junior-high level in history and civics; the science was imported from FirstSide. He read partly for the information, and partly for information on how information was presented to kids; that would be a pretty good way to find the official line. He somehow doubted that an academic Mafia would be able to take over the textbook market here and cock its snoot at the powers that were.

OK, the Founders were heroic adventurers, he thought, leafing through *A History of New Virginia. Don't make much of a muchness about taking this place over. "Freebooter" and "buccaneer" are complimentary terms, here.*

That was no surprise: He didn't think conquering pirates would have a self-esteem problem. The book made a lot of comparisons to the founding of the original thirteen colonies, to early Texas and to the Bear Flag Revolt in California. The tone was completely different from recent history books back FirstSide: self-confident arrogant swagger versus agonized sensitivity. Tully grinned, imagining the authors of this one meeting the people who'd written the books he'd studied in high school, back in the late eighties. Cries of "wimp" and "wussy-boy" would meet anguished howls of "Chauvinist! Imperialist!" with a good deal of truth on both sides.

Then he dove back into the narrative. The Indians got a few cursory paragraphs; they were backward and unprogressive, at best picturesque though doomed, and they all died when the newcomers sneezed on them. It wasn't actually stated, but the implication was strong that this was just what they deserved, mainly for being no-account losers who couldn't even develop basics of civilization like farming or a working machine gun. Those who resisted the New Virginians' turfing the few plague survivors out of their homes were wretched, treacherous, vicious savages.

Yup, I guessed right, he thought. *Injuns still the Bad Guys here.*

That was no surprise either. Usually you didn't start beating your breast and feeling guilty about overrunning someone and taking their stuff until they'd been reduced from "threat" to "pathetic remnant," the way Australian aborigines had FirstSide. His collection of old movies had let him see the process in American popular culture, with Indians going from a faceless mob of scalping, raping, torturing two-legged wolves in *Drums along the Mohawk* to noble natural-ecologist victims of the Bad White Man in *Dances with German Shepherds.*

For that matter, the same thing had happened to public perception of wolves, and for about the same reasons—it was a lot easier to love thoroughly disarmed Indians who didn't have anything left worth stealing except casino receipts, and a lot easier to coo about wolves when you weren't trying to raise sheep next to them.

Speaking of Bad Guys, let's see what the party line is on us FirstSiders. . . .

FirstSide was evidently a sink of degeneracy and crime, where all the "wrong people" had taken over; plenty of pictures of slums, riots, shots of LA freeways at rush hour, New York and Tokyo subways, terrorist attacks during the war, eroded hillsides, industrial wastelands, mosh pits, homeless addicts slumped against Dumpsters, AIDS victims in Africa, RuPaul, Marilyn Manson wanna-bes and chemical waste dumps. A hell on Earth, from which the heroic Founding Families had led the chosen seed into the wilderness to build a New Jerusalem, and incidentally get rich and make themselves overlords.

From this, you'd think FirstSide was All Blade Runner, *All the Time,* he thought, with an amused chuckle. *Of course, to someone raised here, it might really look that way.*

"And let's check on that, shall we?" he said, stacking the books and dropping them in the return carousel. "Now I've seen things from the top down, let's go look at things from the bottom up and see what the sweaty masses think."

Whistling, he strolled out past the impressive rotunda, down the marble steps, and across the square.

He walked past the churches, where the morning service was over and people were milling around, strolling, chewing the fat and dishing the dirt and admiring one another's infants, and vendors were selling ice cream from little push-pedal carts.

"Pistachio and cherry, two scoops in a bowl," he said—he'd always hated the way cones dripped on your hand.

Then he paid, raising his brows and thinking, *My, my, a place where pennies are actually some use.*

It was a nice day for strolling, and the ice cream was good; the last of the fog was gone save for some wisps over where San Francisco wasn't; it was sunny and bright and the temperature was up to the mid-seventies, about as high as the East Bay got unless there was a heat wave. The long street that stretched down to the water was named Longstreet; evidently John Rolfe had a sense of humor, as well as a Civil War fixation. It was mostly commercial two-story buildings of whitewash and tile, mostly open-plan, varied with an occasional small park. He walked along under the shade trees, and conscientiously dropped his empty cardboard ice-cream dish into a trash container, along with the little wooden spoon. That was a datum too.

"No plastics," he muttered. "Not where anything else will do."

He kept going until he was west of the big produce market they'd come through on Friday, then turned south. That was the area closest to the docks and the factories, and as he'd expected, it didn't have quite the burnished look the rest of the town did; not a slum by any means, or even really run-down, but the houses were smaller and older and all made of adobe, looking much alike. He estimated they'd be about fifteen hundred square feet each, with a small open front yard and fences out back, set on a plain gridiron of streets; the arch of tall shade trees over the pavement was still agreeable, though. Men in undershirts and women in print dresses sat on their verandas, drinking lemonade or beer or sodas and smoking; children and dogs ran around playing; music blared now and then from open windows, or the sound of TVs. He dodged a young man on a bicycle, wobbling along with a girl sitting on the handlebars; others were shooting hoops, mostly fastened to roadside trees. Now and then he smelled a barbecue grill in operation.

Hmmm. Biggest difference is there aren't any garages, he thought. There *were* some cars, but they were parked by the side of the road, and there weren't very many of them. *And no mobile homes, of course.*

He paused to talk with a few of the children. Nobody snatched the kids away from conversation with a stranger, and he discovered another difference from the lands he knew: He hadn't heard so many "sirs" since he'd mustered out of the Tenth Mountain after Iraq. What he sought stood within smelling distance of the mudflats, and a stone's throw from the first factories of the industrial district.

The neighborhood watering hole was called Bobcat Bites; he looked at it for a minute before he realized what the main structure must be. Then he laughed out loud; somebody had taken a medium-sized Quonset hut and stuccoed the outside and whitewashed it—probably, given the degree of uniformity elsewhere, to coincide with the letter if not the spirit of some town-wide building code. Crossing that like the bar of a T was a two-story boxy adobe structure with racks for bicycles and Segways outside, a parking lot to the side with a scattering of cars and pickups, and a sign that gave the tavern's name and encouraged all passersby to sample the free lunch until two-thirty, three P.M. on weekends.

Tully looked at his watch: Twelve P.M. *Why not?* he thought.

There was a long bar on either side of the entrance to the Quonset, complete with mirror, brass footrail and polished bar. "What's the deal on the free lunch?" he asked the woman behind it.

The woman paused in her slow shoving of a rag over the oak. *Now there,* Tully thought, *is someone even Warden Christiansen would admit is a "broad."* She was around forty, with yellow hair that had rather obviously come out of a bottle. A few years older than him, and she looked it, but in a nice way, wearing a long apron over a red dress, and smoking a cigarette. *Christ, it's going to be hard to keep on the wagon here. The secondary smoke stokes the old craving something fierce.*

She looked him up and down; he could tell she was amused, in a friendly sort of way. *And Christ, it's a good thing women don't go as much by looks as we uncouth males do, or after a few generations everyone would look like Tom. Turn on the charm, Roy.*

"It means what it says, stranger," she said. "You buy a drink or a beer, you get all you can eat—ain't that the way it usually is?" Then a pause, and: "Say, aren't you the guy in the paper this morning? From FirstSide?"

"Yeah, the famous Roy Tully," he said, smiling back at her with his best leering-imp impersonation and sliding a New Virginian dime across the counter. "Make it a beer. Whatever you've got on tap."

"Bayside Steam," she said, getting out a frosted glass mug and drawing it full, with the foam edging slightly down the sides. "Enjoy."

He snagged it, then went down to the spread. There were deviled hard-boiled eggs, half a dozen varieties of bread, sliced meats, soups over heating elements, butter and cheese and olive oil, oysters, smoked salmon, shrimp salad, potato salad, raw vegetables and guacamole, and most of the rest of the makings of a good smorgasbord, plus cakes and muffins under glass.

He loaded a plate, snickering slightly when he thought about the look of resentment he'd get from Tom if he were here. The big guy wasn't exactly a chow-hound, but he liked his food and hated the fact that he had to work hard to burn it off. Tully liked to eat too, but knew from family example and his own experience that he'd be able to stuff himself his life long and stay slim . . . or scrawny, as some unkind souls had called it . . . without bothering to work out unless he wanted to. His father had never lifted anything heavier than a briefcase full of legal papers, and still had the same belt measurement he'd graduated from high school with.

"So, what's a nice girl like you doing in a place like this?" he asked, sitting on a stool, taking a drink of the beer—quite good—and a bite of pumpernickel loaded with shrimp—excellent.

"The name's Maud, I'm not a girl, and I own the place, mister," she replied. "Have since that worthless bastard I married drowned hisself."

"He probably deserved it," Tully said.

"He certainly did, not knowing better than taking a boat out while he was drunk," she replied equably. "Second beer's a nickel."

Tully sat, ate, and talked with Maud when she wasn't busy with other customers. That was less often as the lunch crowd thickened, and then the families started coming in for a Sunday-afternoon outing. He'd judged right about the location; it was all working stiffs, a cut below the lower-middle-class and skilled-labor area nearer the farmer's market.

They were ready enough to talk to a newcomer, as well: small-town friendly, but with little of the underlying standoffishness you often found in little out-of-the-way places.

Probably because it's new and growing, instead of a place where you're born and people are more likely to move out than in, he thought.

Gentle prodding was more than enough to set people talking about themselves. Most of the women were housewives; the rest were in the service trades, or were things like elementary school teachers, with a few nurses. The men worked in the factories—consumer goods, boatbuilding, an electric-arc foundry owned by the O'Briens, small machine shops that made a surprisingly broad range of spare parts—or in construction, or drove forklifts at the Gate complex, or crewed fishing boats and coastal ships, or did things like sewer maintenance. A large majority had been born in the Commonwealth, and many were second or third generation; a majority of their grandparents had come from America, with a bias toward the upper South, and the rest had ancestors who were German, French, and Italian, with a scattering from all over Eastern Europe. The immigrant minority included Russians, Afrikaners, and a few Croats and Serbs.

The talk wasn't all that different from a bar-cum-restaurant in a small deep-rural Arkansas town somewhere in the Ozarks: sports, weather, gossip, fishing and hunting, how the farmers were doing that year—the main difference was the absence of national media and their stories. He heard a fair amount of grousing about the Thirty, mostly straightforward envy, and a fair amount of gossip about them as well, mostly of the sort you heard about the upper crust back home, but with more personal knowledge, and a bit less lurid. The main buzz was an elopement between the children of two Family heads, Primes.

People he spoke to often congratulated him on getting out of FirstSide; they generally thought it was pretty bad, even if they also discounted some of the Commission's propaganda.

A little later he overheard a political conversation.

". . . doesn't sound too bad to me," one man said. "Couple of *nahua* girls to peel grapes and drop 'em in my mouth while their brothers do all the work and I kick their asses now and then."

The other man snorted; his English had a thick South African accent, clipped and guttural, like the late, unlamented Schalk van der Merwe. "Man, where exactly are they going to work for *you?* On the big farm you don't have? The factory you don't own? Down the mine you'll never get?"

The Afrikaner held up his hands. "All you've got is your house and these, just like me, you bliddy fool. If we get a lot more *nahua* in here working for fifty cents a day, and staying around long enough to learn skilled trades, what's to stop your boss paying *you* fifty cents, and telling you he'll put one of them in your place if you complain, and then you can live on nothing? Bliddy poor whites, that's what *we'd* be."

"Ah, hell, Rhodevik, it ain't gonna happen anyway." The other man shrugged. "So who do you like—San Diego or Rolfeston?"

"None of you *soutpens* can play rugby anyway," the immigrant said with a friendly sneer. "Now . . ."

And on that note, Roy thought, rising and dropping a nickel tip. *Tomorrow I'll take a look across the bay.*

INTERLUDE
August 21, 2007
Zaachila, southern Mexico
Commonwealth of New Virginia time line

Lord Seven Flower held the meeting in the ruins of Zaachila, for the sacredness that dwelt in the stones of the lost city. No living men had made their homes here for a long time; what the plagues that swept through in his grandfather's day had begun, the wars and chaos that followed in their wake had finished. He kept his own seat of power in the great city of Tututepec, much closer to the coast and the foreign trade that had helped make him overlord of half the Zapotec peoples. Yet once this had been the place of the *Vuijato,* the Great Seer, the Speaker to the Gods—he whose hand conferred sovereignty on kings.

That would help to overawe turbulent nobles, and even his closest advisers could turn back into such, if his grip wavered. The setting was the more numinous because it was night, and because of the day—Eight Deer—in the holy calendar. The trees had gone far in their reconquest of the sacred city and loomed about like living green walls, but he had had this courtyard kept clear of the encroaching bush and vines. Except where staircases ascended at the four corners, the great courtyard was flanked by walls higher than a man, carved in bas-relief from hard limestone and still vividly colored despite years of weathering. They showed the story of the first Eight Deer, the great leader who seized power in the War of Heaven—showed it in long pictures, and word-glyphs. The rise of the rival cities of Tilantongo and Red-White Bundle, the feuds and marriages of their lords, the suicide of one such forced by the machinations of Lady Six Monkey, the blood sacrifice of the defeated king of Red-White Bundle by the victorious warlord whose naming day this was . . .

Eight Deer had no royal ancestors, Lord Seven Flower thought. *Like me, he was the son of a priest, and a great warrior. Like me, he seized power in a time of chaos. Like his, my name will live forever, and my dynasty rule for a thousand years!*

Torches burned at the staircases, torches of aromatic wood that added a heavy, spicy scent to the odors of damp and growth and ancient stone, heavier than the mouthwatering scents of roasting dog and brewing cacao from the cooking-fires nearby. Around the courtyard shone the kerosene lanterns he gained in trade, brighter than any torch. The guards at the staircases bore bronze-headed spears and wooden swords set with bronze shark-tooth edges on both sides, the weapons of his grandfather's day, before the Deathwalkers came from the northern sea.

The guards who stood about the walls in the courtyard below bore modern steel machetes and flintlock muskets. The lesson was one he wanted driven home frequently and hard.

Lord Seven Flower himself was in the traditional costume: silver armbands and greaves, a loincloth intricately folded so that a long flap of snowy cotton edged with embroidery hung to his knees before and behind, gold chains and a gold pectoral across his chest, and a headdress made in the form of a snarling silver jaguar's head with golden spots, eyes of turquoise and ivory teeth, sporting a huge torrent of colored plumes from its rear in gaudy crimson and green and mauve.

The face that looked out between the jaguar's jaws was

square and hard, dark brown save where white scars seamed it, his narrow eyes a black so deep the pupil merged with the iris. It was pitted with the marks of the Great Sickness—as were those of most men and women of his generation.

Those who lived, he thought mordantly.

The priests and generals and high nobles who sat on cushions before him numbered twelve, dressed only slightly less gorgeously than himself. They also looked a little surprised that the feast had not begun; in the holy city one ate to bursting, drank to drunkenness, ate of certain mushrooms, and then the idols of the gods would speak—or the mummified bodies of one's ancestors, in the old days. Like him, few of the men before him came from families of sufficient ancient rank to have their forefathers preserved. The idols were present—great Bezelao with his cup of wisdom, Xochipilli with his crest of macaw feathers, and many more.

Also present were twenty men tied to upright wooden posts: common men, naked, slaves or peasants—men of no account, unlikely to be missed, as he had specified to the officials in charge of such matters.

Lord Seven Flower raised the ceremonial sword he bore in his hand; it was so old and holy that the blades were edged with bits of obsidian instead of bronze, like a priest's sacrificial knife.

"Stand forth, Five Deer," he called.

A man stepped forward, plainly dressed in cotton loincloth and sandals, but bearing himself proudly. He carried a weapon. There were gasps as the grandees recognized it; not an ordinary musket, although shaped much like it—this one had a projecting box in front of the trigger guard, and no hammer at all, but a complex of metal shapes in roughly the same position.

"These men offend me. Slay them," he went on, pointing to the stakes with his stone-edged sword.

The strange musket leaped to Five Deer's shoulder. *Crack!*

The sound was not like the boom of a musket: harder, sharper, quicker, the flash a brief jet of hot flame in the darkness. A brass cartridge jumped out of the odd metal shapes, and the leftmost of the captives jerked and then slumped, a red spot appearing on his breast.

Crack!

Again, and again: twenty times, as fast as Five Deer could shift his aim and pull the trigger. Lord Seven Flower's generals and priests were watching with fullest attention, swearing and pounding their fists on the mats that covered the stone pavement, some giving high yelping cries of excitement. There were screams from some of the captives, too; not every shot killed at once, though some did so dramatically—one took the whole top off a captive's head, and spattered his brains across a mural of human sacrifice. At Lord Seven Flower's nod, one of the guards stepped forward and silenced the wounded with a knife across the throat. Thick straw mats kept the blood from flowing too far and inconveniencing the great men.

"A rifle of the Deathwalkers!" a general said. "But Lord Seven Flower, always they have refused to trade such with us. Not for silver, or gold, or turquoise, or cacao or hummingbird feathers will they trade such!"

"A rifle of the Deathwalkers," Lord Seven Flower agreed. "And for one thing will they trade such—some of them, at least. Fighting men. They too have their factions."

"Ahhhh!"

All of his chief followers were survivors of the long struggles between the Zapotec cities, and within them. The land had heaved and shifted like bubbling cornmeal in a pot for three generations now, brought to a boil by the plagues and the new weapons and goods. Intrigue and assassination, war and battle and sudden revolt were in their blood. None of them had to be told how useful foreign mercenaries could be in a faction fight. All of them bowed their heads to the ground in a wave of colorful feathers and fur, silver and jade and gold. Several were smiling as they rose to a sitting position again; they also knew how *useful* foreign mercenaries could make themselves useful in ways not intended by their employers.

The general who'd spoken before added: "How difficult are these weapons to learn to use, o man made in the image of the gods?"

"Easier than a musket," Lord Seven Deer replied. "As a musket is easier than a bow. In any case, the lords of the Deathwalkers will provide instruction; when the instruction is complete, the men will be used for their purposes, then returned to us for ours. Ammunition and spare parts will also be sold, though not cheaply." His gaze sharpened on his supporters. "Each of you will find fifty warriors. Tried and tested men, but young. Cunning, but obedient and loyal. And none of such note or name that they will be missed. This must remain a secret of secrets."

He rose and clapped his hands. The slaves filed in, bearing trays of carved wood heaped high with steaming food; others carried golden vessels of cacao and fermented fruits and northern brandy.

Only the king and the nobles, priests and the most trusted guards would return from this meeting, of course. The others would serve to buy the favor of the gods.

CHAPTER TWELVE

"Africa"/Rolfe Domain
June 2009

Commonwealth of New Virginia

The ferry that ran across the Carquinez Strait was a big wooden rectangle with movable ramps at both ends, diesel-powered; when the wind blew back toward them for an instant the smell reminded him suddenly of FirstSide, and the way he'd hated the big-city stink of exhausts. That prompted another train of thought; he looked at the power lines that ran down to the northern edge, borne on wooden tripods and crossbeams made of whole Douglas fir trunks a hundred feet long with their feet braced in cast-concrete drums. The cable looped down to a ground station on the northern bank—there was a small hamlet there, where the city of Benicia stood in *his* California—and then reappeared on the southern shore, striding down the valleys, and he supposed over the hills to Rolfeston and the other Bay Area settlements.

"Where's the generating station?" he asked curiously. "What's the energy source?"

Adrienne looked over at him and winked, laying a finger along her nose. "Geothermal," she said. "And on Rolfe land. Up north of Calistoga—in the geyser country—the Rolfe domain holds everything from Napa Town up through Clear Lake, and over to the Berryessa Valley. You might say we understand the power of power!"

"Ah." He nodded. That was the world's biggest geothermal-power area FirstSide, and the geography was the same here. "That the only power station?"

"The only one between Mendocino and Monterey, apart from some very small-scale hydro, and emergency generators at hospitals an' suchlike," she said. "The settlement up in Oregon uses hydropower, and down around San Diego they've got a turbine setup running on natural gas."

Her accent's gotten a little stronger since we came through the Gate, he noted silently. *Not acting as much, I suppose.* Aloud, he went on: "I suppose Sierra Consultants did the design work?"

"Yes, as a matter of fact," she said, looking at him with surprise and respect. "One of their last studies for us, in the late fifties. We've got about a hundred and fifty megawatts capacity installed as of now, and since *we* weren't dumb enough to neglect pumping the condensed steam back down the holes, the Commission thinks that we can eventually pull out ten times as much or more on a sustained-yield basis. That'll be enough; we aren't going to let the population here grow indefinitely."

There were stairs to a walkway that ran along each side of the ferry. Tom took the ones on the left—*port,* he thought—and they stood on the gallery there, looking about and at the water that foamed by below. It wasn't much disturbed; the blunt bow of the ferry threw its wave in a correspondingly wide arc, and only smooth surging ripples ran along the hull amidships. The water was blue but clear, amazingly free of silt despite being downstream of the Central Valley and the marshes; he could look straight down and see a pair of fifteen-foot sturgeon swimming slowly downstream, and then a school of eight-inch threadfin shad so thick that they made the water boil, leaving him staring into an infinite blue-tinted chamber of mirrors full of flickering silver.

There was a thick fringe of marsh along the strait's northern edge; it suddenly occurred to him that upstream the delta country would be eight million acres of nothing *but* marsh. He looked around again, eyes on the blue cloud-flecked sky.

This was a little past the main spring migration season and a month early for the start of the autumn one, but the flocks made those he remembered from his own Red River country in the fall season seem like a tattered remnant. In one casual glance he saw curlews, pelicans numerous as snowflakes slanting down to the surface of the water, ospreys falling like miniature thunderbolts and thrashing back into the air with silver fish writhing in their claws, red-throated loons diving from the surface, three types of grebe, great blue herons striding along the edge of the water, and on and on.

"This area really swarms with life, doesn't it?" he said.

Adrienne nodded. "Even more than when Granddad arrived," she said softly; he turned his head and surprised an expression of soft pleasure on her face as she watched the pageant. "God, I love this."

That surprised him a little, both the expression and the words.

"*More* than when your grandfather came?" he said. "I know he's a conservationist of sorts, but—"

She put a hand on his shoulder for a moment; it felt good. *And hell, I'm just being professional.*

"It makes sense when you think about it," she said. "After the Gate opened, three hundred thousand top predators who hunted every day for food got replaced by two hundred thousand—mostly concentrated here around the bay—who hunt occasionally for fun. And the Indians used a lot of the wild plant life, too; acorn mush was their staple, plus they burned off millions of acres every year to keep the countryside open. Ecologically speaking, we New Virginians are grass eaters who get most of our food from restricted areas in a few valleys."

Tom nodded. "So the Indians were the keystone species here; humans generally are. I imagine you've had some pretty wild ecological swings since then."

Like an engine without a governor, racing and stalling, he thought; and tried not to think of the bands and villages struck down by bacteria and viruses from—literally—beyond their world, most likely the last survivors dying from sheer thirst or hunger as they lay tossing with none but the stinking corpses of the dead for company.

My ancestors may not have cared much, any more than these people do—but I'm not my ancestors.

"Right. I can remember the forest and bush getting thicker and encroaching on open country in my own lifetime— though we're trying to use controlled burns to slow that down." She glanced sideways at him as they leaned on the railings. "And speaking of wild ecological swings, we're nearly in Africa."

"Africa?" he said.

"Formally it's the North Bay Permanent Wilderness Reserve and Acclimatization Area, but nobody's called it anything except Africa since 1950."

She pointed and moved her arm from west to east against the low hills that rimmed the horizon.

"From Miller Creek to about there, and from tidewater inland through the Carneros hills. The whole north shore of San Pablo and Suisun bays, all the wetlands and a rim of dry country too. Easier to show you why it's called 'Africa' than tell you. It's the reason Ralph called his place the Mermaid Café, though."

At his curious glance she went on: "You know, Joni Mitchell? 'Carey'?" A sigh: "I forgot, you didn't have Ralph shaping your musical tastes as a teenager." She began to sing in a husky soprano:

> The wind is in from Africa
> Last night, I couldn't sleep

"All right, all right," he said. "Yeah, I *have* heard that golden oldie." He gave a snort of laughter. "I like that man's sense of humor."

"Rock music's still faintly scandalous in the Commonwealth," she said. "So there! You thought I was a fuddy-duddy for liking the classics."

There was a rush of feet and blasphemous cursing from the crew as they came into the U-shaped pier on the north bank, thick ropes were made fast, and the ramp at the front of the vessel was let down with a clattering thud.

Their Hummer was first on and first off; several two-and-a-half-ton trucks loaded with boxed cargo followed, and another with a huge coil of cable. Adrienne took the wheel, letting the other vehicles pass her as she drove through a pleasant, sleepy-looking village nestled among trees and then past a formidable turf-covered earthwork and ditch. The road forked there, one branch heading northeast, the other more sharply west of north, where it cut like a winding ribbon through the rolling hills and crossed their creeks on trestle bridges. Those looked odd, until he realized the huge size of the interlocked timbers.

There was no fringe of cultivation beyond the town's gardens; a mile later she turned off the road, downshifted and splashed through a small stream, and then tackled the side of a thirty-degree hill's slope. The Hummer took the uneven steepness with ease; he'd always liked the way the power-shifting system to the four wheels made them grip like giant fingers. Coming upslope they startled a flock of ostriches into explosive flight, and halted beneath a single small oak near the crest of a hill.

The cooling engine ticked; the cries of birds and the endless sough of the wind were louder. The smell of hot metal was quickly lost beneath the aromas of laurel, ceanothus and minty yerba santa crushed beneath the wheels. Long champagne-pale grass rippled in the cool wind off the water, thickly sown with late California poppies in drifts of small golden coins; nearer the water's edge, vast fields of tule rushes tossed like a rolling poplin-green sea. Freshwater marsh lined every stream among the many that meandered southward toward the bay. There were trees on their edges, and clumps elsewhere, but everywhere the land stretched immense to the blue horizon.

She handed him the binoculars, and he silently looked about, restraining an impulse to swear and exclaim alternately. A group of brown-and-cream eland wandered along the edge of a patch of blue oak in a swale between two hills, big antelope the size of an ox but with longer legs, dewlaps and spiral horns. A herd of about two hundred elk were scattered in fawn dots up a farther hill; scattered among them were pronghorns, wildebeest, mule deer, and what he thought might be Thomson's gazelle. A distant drumming of hooves heralded a group of wild horses, flowing over a rise like a wave and then down into a vale; water and birds splashed up as they breasted the damp ground there and vanished over the next hillcrest. Scattered bison grazed, and a grizzly rested under the shade of a blue oak, while two yearling cubs wrestled and fell around her.

"Is there anything that maniac of a grandfather of yours *didn't* turn loose here?" Tom asked.

"Well, chimps didn't do so well in California; they didn't like the winters. But see that edge of swamp over there? Those knobs and twitchy things are the nostrils and eyes and ears of a bunch of hippos. They're finally adjusting well. The chimps and the gorillas are doing fine down in Central America. We didn't introduce just African animals, of course: tigers from China, snow leopards and the ordinary variety, European wild boar—"

"Arrrgghh!" he said, a cry from the heart. "Feral swine are organic bulldozers! They —"

"Don't worry; the wild pigs aren't as much of a pest as they are FirstSide. The cougars and wolves and lions and tigers and leopards keep 'em down. And it turns out golden eagles *love* raw suckling pig. Tom, there are a lot more predators large enough to tackle a boar here than there are FirstSide. Not to mention we hunt them."

"I certainly hope so," he mumbled.

"This acclimatization was a really big thing with the Old Man; he spent a pile of his own money on it, and a fair bit of the Commission's, as soon as the first mines were going. We used this reserve to establish breeding stock, then spread them around—by riverboat, truck, overland drives, sometimes by air. On the east coast and down in South America by ship too, a little later. You should see what the pampas are getting to be like in Argentina; it makes the Serengeti on FirstSide look like a paved-over parking lot."

"Arrrghh!" Tom said again. He clutched his head in his hands, and Adrienne laughed in a clear peal of mirth.

"You remember that book, *Ecological Imperialism?*" Tom nodded. "Well, it looks like Crosby's thesis about the pre-Columbian Americas having a lot of vacant ecological niches after the Pleistocene extinctions was right. At least, nearly everything we introduced spread like dandelions—including dandelions, by the way. The total biomass is up, and the variety of large mammals is *way* up. Plus the introduced Old World beasties coevolved with human beings. They aren't helpless like the ground sloths."

"That's the reason your grandfather did this, Crosby's book?"

"Oh, no, he just thought all the new animals looked cool and improved the hunting," she said, turning the engine back on. "Read too much Tarzan when he was a kid, I suppose. But he felt *very* vindicated when I pointed the book out to him!"

On the one hand, releasing exotic species like that is insanely risky, he thought. *On the other hand, it* does *look cool. Hunting here would be a bit too much like shooting a dairy herd, though.*

He turned his head to say so, and yelped. A twelve-foot-long, five-ton mass tipped with a massive curved horn on its snout and another, shorter one above that had risen from a muddy wallow. It looked at them with little piggy eyes, twitching its ears in bad temper. Tom's mind gibbered for a second, but his voice was calm as he said, "Adrienne, I think there's one enormous rhinoceros looking us over about fifty yards thataway. And your grandfather is fucking *insane*."

Long bronze-colored hair whipped across his face as she turned her head to look. She also hit the gas hard enough to send a spray of gravel shooting rearward. That decided the beast; it put its head down and began churning the tree-trunk pillars of its legs. Gravel spurted from under *its* feet as it hit the roadway, and Tom thought he could feel the ground shaking under the massive thudding impact of those broad three-toed feet.

Hummers had excellent acceleration, for a diesel-engined vehicle. Experiment showed that for a while a rhinoceros could do even better. The thick dust spewing out from behind the little truck partially hid the giant beast, but the continuous rain of stones thrown up by the rear wheels enraged it further; he could hear its hoarse squeal and the great bellows panting of its breath. That was the problem with animals too big and tough to have natural enemies—their impulse was to charge anything that annoyed them. Charge it and gore it with that huge horn and stomp it under those pile-driving feet . . .

"That's a white rhino!" Adrienne shouted over the rushing air and the engine's growl. "I thought all the ones in this reserve had been trapped and relocated!"

"Looks sort of reddish gray to me!"

"No, it's from *wit*—the Afrikaans word for wide—the square lip. It's a grazer, not a browser like the black rhino."

"Could you just drive, please?" he shouted, and grinned back at her; it was an odd combination of fright and exhilaration, a little like hitting the white water in a canoe.

"Drive, woman! Right now its wide square upper lip is too close for comfort. There's a goddamn big horn just above it."

For an instant he thought the beast would reach them, to flip over the Hummer and send them flying in bone-breaking arcs to the ground—the wide, squat vehicles didn't tip easily, but he'd seen what happened when they did. Then it began to drop behind; he glanced over at the speedometer and saw they were doing forty miles an hour, about as much as was safe on this winding dirt road in hilly country, or a bit more. The rhino slowed, lumbered to a stop, turned three-quarters on to the Hummer he hadn't been able to catch and stood in a slowly dispersing cloud of dust, jerking his horn through short savage arcs to left and right as if to show what he'd planned to do when he caught them.

"By Jesus, that was a little too close," he said, as Adrienne slowed down. "Adrienne, please tell me there aren't any elephants around here."

"Not anymore," she said cheerfully. "There's a whole swarm of them down in the southern basins, though—the LA area, you'd say. They've spread from there into Sonora and west to the upper Rio Grande, too; they can take a frosty winter, but not hard blizzards."

"I repeat my remark about your grandfather," Tom said.

"Then there's elephants and tigers we dropped off in the Galveston–to–New Orleans area—"

"I don't want to know!" he cried half seriously.

They drove in silence for a while; the countryside about was too beautiful and too weirdly alien not to keep his eyes busy. Occasionally a car or truck would pass them—the cars usually four-by-fours of one sort or another, the trucks pick-ups or, fairly often, army-style deuce-and-a-halfs. The dust would have been worse if they were more frequent; it was often enough for Tom to be thankful for a spare bandanna Adrienne lent him.

"I thought the area north of here was fairly well settled," he said after a few minutes. "Shouldn't there be more traf-fic?"

"It is well settled, by our standards," she said. "But we use the rivers and bay for transporting freight." Pointing from east to west: "There's the von Traupitz domain, and the Chumleys up around Yolo; they ship their produce out through Suisun Bay; Napa's the riverport for the R-Fitzmortons in Sonoma, the Hugheses around where Healdsburg is FirstSide, the Throckhams the same around Santa Rosa."

Another ditch marked the northern border of "Africa"—this one extending east and west out of sight, steep-sided enough to make a rhino cautious, if not an antelope or lion. Just past it they came across a road gang of men in gray overalls doing repairs on the dirt highway's surface, filling in potholes and spreading crushed rock, with a mechanical roller to pack it down. Overseeing them was a stringy, lean thirty-something man on a big glossy horse, a classic Southern-sheriff type down to the sunglasses, Smokey the

Bear-style hat, cigar clamped between his teeth and the shotgun whose butt rested on his hip.

Tom thought he would have suspected the workers were convicts, even *without* the word "Convict" printed on chest and back in large red letters. They weren't fettered—very little point in that amidst swarming wildlife eager to convert them into either food or irritating leftover bits stuck between the toes—and didn't look beaten or starved. They did look hangdog, and they worked with steady effort.

"Can we stop here and ask a few questions?" he asked Adrienne, a note of challenge hovering around the edges of the words.

"Yah, you betcha," she said with an impish grin, gently mocking his Red River accent, and pulled the Hummer over to the side of the road. "Hi, there, Deputy Gleason!"

The man looked and did a double take as the Hummer crunched to a halt on the roadside verge. Then he spat the cigar butt out of his mouth, raising his shotgun in an informal salute. He turned his head toward the crew as they paused to look, and shouted, "You boys keep workin'!" Then, to Adrienne, and with respectful politeness: "Afternoon, Miz Rolfe, an' you, sir. Any way I can help y'all?"

He had Adrienne's accent, but stronger still, pronouncing the words "I can help" as *Ah kin hep*. It was impossible to see his eyes clearly behind the sunglasses, but Tom felt himself quickly scanned, summed up, and to judge from the instinctive slight shift in the man's seat in the saddle, found formidable. Tom nodded politely himself.

"I was wondering if you could tell me a bit about your working party," Adrienne said. "My friend Mr. Christiansen here would like to know. If it's not too much trouble, Deputy Gleason."

"No trouble t'all, Miz Rolfe, Mr. Christiansen," he said, smiling. That turned into a bark: "Front and center, y'all! Line up and sound off—name, crime and sentence!"

The half-dozen convicts downed tools and came at the run, lining up along the verge of the road and bracing to attention with their straw hats held in both hands across their chests and eyes to the front.

"Montgomery, John, drunk and disorderly, unable to pay fine, six months!"

The sheriff chuckled. "That ol' boy, he drove a car into the bar when they wouldn't sell him no more cheap brandy. Lucky he didn't hurt nobody."

"Leclerc, Martin! Domestic violence, one year!"

"Slapped his missus, and gave her a black eye. She wouldn't press charges, or he'd be workin' in the mines, and for a lot more than a year."

The tally continued—minor crimes of violence or semiminor ones against property. Adrienne cocked an ironic eyebrow at him as they drove on northwest.

"Well, let me guess: The Commonwealth isn't big into rehabilitation," he said.

"Criminals aren't sick people who need therapy," she said. "They're bad people who need a whack upside the head to get their attention. We put them in stir to suffer, not to heal. It seems to work rather better than the I-feel-your-pain approach."

Tom chuckled; that was one sentiment he couldn't really find fault with. Few people who'd spent much time in law enforcement would have, in his experience.

The town of Napa announced itself with a sign stating that its population was 4,562, and that it was the "Gem of the Valley" and "Gateway to the North"; the Kiwanis, Elks and Masons added their pitches. He had an excellent view as they left the rolling hills and coasted toward the river that gleamed like a twisting silver snake in the afternoon sun, throwing glitters back through the leaves of the trees that fringed it. The eastern shore held little but a golf course, a racetrack with wooden stands, and a fenced-in parklike expanse with a shut-down Ferris wheel and roller coaster. A sign outside bore the Rolfe lion, red rampant on black, and announced that the domain fair would open on August 15, sponsored by the Family.

"Domain fair?" he asked.

"County fair, more or less—livestock shows, bake sales and prizes for flowers and jams, big dance, floats, bit of a carnival. The domains of each Family do pretty well the same things a county does in the U.S. back FirstSide. The fair comes between wheat harvest and the beginning of the crush. There's a big polo match, too."

The bridge over the river was yet another web of huge timbers fastened together with arm-thick steel bolts and set in stone piers; the surface was asphalt, and the road on the other side was paved likewise. Tom looked up and down the Napa River as they crossed, estimating how far back from the water most of the west-bank town stood, and the width of wild dense riparian forest that stretched north like a lumpy green quilt on either side of the stream.

"Let me guess," he said. "You don't have much trouble with flooding."

"Yah, you betcha," she said again. "Because we don't build on flood plains much. There's no need to when you've got plenty of elbow room."

Napa town was at roughly the same spot on the river as the settlement FirstSide, and for the same reason; this was the head of navigation for shallow-draft vessels, particularly in the dry season. Dozens of barges lined the wharves, mainly on the west bank of the river; tugs brought more, or towed them away in strings; both types were smallish by the standards he was used to, and wooden-built. A slipway on the water's side held several more under construction. There were more cars and trucks on the roads than he'd seen in Rolfeston, although the traffic was still light by any standards he'd known before, including those of the little North Dakota town of Ironwood.

Back from the docks and warehouses on the southern side of town were workshops and factories; the residential part of town was north of that, a little more spread out than Rolfeston had been, equally hidden in trees—some the tall oaks and sycamores that had once occupied the site, more planted since its founding. Between those houses and the vacant lowland along the river was the business district, small shops and offices along streets with timber-pillared or stone-built arcades, and a broad square with central gardens, benches, brick paths and bandstand.

The riverside itself north of the wharves was a semiwild park, the bigger trees left standing, undergrowth cleared back and some plantings made. It was full of picnickers, people taking advantage of a big municipal swimming pool, impromptu volleyball and touch football or soccer games, people tossing Frisbees to each other or leaping dogs, and plain strollers; it took him a moment to remember this was Sunday afternoon.

"My alma mater," Adrienne said, pointing to a big two-story stone building overgrown with climbing rose and surrounded by playing fields. A baseball game was going on in one, and the people in the bleachers let out a shout as they drove by. He could see flickers of it between the tall Lombardy poplars that fringed the way.

"You went to the public high school?" Tom asked curiously.

"Everyone does," she said, sounding surprised. "Why not? Getting a high school diploma *means* something here, about equivalent to a FirstSide BA. I did very well, when I wasn't on suspension or waiting to get paddled by the principal. I grant you that was far too often, and if I hadn't been a Rolfe, I might have got expelled for good."

"How did you produce grades for Stanford?" he said.

"Oh, we fake 'em," she said. "Phony private school FirstSide . . . well, it's actually a real one, but we slip an extra notional student in now and then for when someone goes to a university there. We endowed it and pick the headmasters, of course. Paying full tuition at the university also helps; they don't check as hard."

"Why *did* you go to Stanford?" he asked. "Why not, ah, University of New Virginia?"

"I started there, but UNV's still small," she said. "Particularly the humanities departments, and I wanted to study history." A wry laugh. "Not that that's the only difference;

you're *not* going to find many postmodernist professors of postcolonial studies at UNV, thank God."

He digested that while they cruised past the town hall. The white walls, square tower and big arched courtyard entrance reminded him strongly of Santa Barbara's post office; then they turned down a street with palms on both sides and two-story adobe buildings behind a continuous arcade roof supported on columns made from varnished black-walnut trunks. The streetlights were black cast-iron pillars with fanciful detailing, and the sidewalks colored brick in geometric patterns.

"I've got to do some business here," she said, taking an empty parking place; there were, he noted, no meters. "Care to come along?"

He nodded. One of the buildings had rounded corners and tall glass windows along both street-side walls, now swung wide under the arcade overhang. A tilework sign over the open doors read FOUQUET'S. Adrienne walked into the entranceway and halted.

The interior was a single great room, with a roof spanned by exposed wooden beams; one end held a pool table, and there was a flat-film TV screen over the big counter with its top of polished stone and revolving seats on stainless-steel pillars. Elsewhere there were long tables, made of the inevitable giant slabs of redwood, here topped with harder varieties in a sort of parquet arrangement, plus booths along the walls. People bustled about, coming and going; the air was full of the smell of frying food and some sort of plangent country-style music and chattering voices. The waiters behind the counter or circulating with trays were dressed in white, with white fore-and-aft caps and aprons.

Tom blinked. *It's the half-familiar that gets you,* he thought. *This is the closest thing I've ever seen to a real old-style soda joint, the kind in Roy's movies. It's not a revival or deliberately retro, either. It's just . . . what it is.*

The crowd within must have numbered a hundred or so, none of them over twenty or younger than early adolescence. Some of the girls were wearing those Catholic-school-uniform arrangements he'd seen in Rolfeston, with white shirts and ties (often loosened), pleated knee-length skirts, and knee socks. Most of the rest were in summery cotton dresses, with a minority in slacks or jeans; none of the girls had short hair, or the boys long, and there were a fair number of pigtails tied with ribbon. The boys were more varied; fewer of them were dressed in their version of the school uniform, which included khaki shorts, and some wore suits. It took him a moment to realize something about the ones in overalls.

That isn't a fashion statement, he thought. *Those are their* clothes.

A giggling clutch of sixteen-year-old females in a booth near the door were looking at Tom out of the corners of their eyes; in the next a boy and girl were actually sipping from the same malt with two straws, something he'd never seen outside a book of Norman Rockwell prints. A dozen or more of the older boys and a couple of girls were smoking, but casually, not as if it was an act of defiance; another clutch argued amiably around the jukebox—which was the latest digital model with flash memory storage.

It took him a moment to estimate the ages of individuals accurately, too; after a second look he realized his first estimates for most were at least a year too high.

Not that they're baby-faced. In fact, they look pretty fit, he thought. *There's a couple of lard-butts and some pimple-faces, but not many for the size of the group.*

It was something indefinable about the eyes. . . .

"I thought I'd find a good big crowd," Adrienne said to him as they stood in the doorway. "When I was a teenager, townie kids always used to hang out here after church in summertime. School year ends on June fifteenth, by the way—the day you got here."

Then she put two fingers in her mouth and whistled piercingly, followed by a shout: "Hey, kids!"

Silence fell raggedly, and someone turned the music down in the ensuing quiet. Then there were exclamations; it reminded Tom a little of the way a rave crowd responded to a popular deejay, but not quite so open.

"Hi!" he heard over and over. Variations on "It's Miss Rolfe—Adrienne!"

A pair of boys in their late teens with platinum-and-gold thumb rings waved in a more casual manner from a corner where they held court with their girlfriends and a gaggle of hangers-on, and Adrienne nodded back to them.

"How was the prom?" she said to the room at large.

More enthusiasm, and she lifted hands for quiet. Into it, she said: "OK, I'm back. Look, I need a dozen or so people for the Seven Oaks harvest. Five days, twenty bucks, and the usual trimmings on Saturday. Who's interested?"

The ensuing babble took some time to quiet down. After it had, she went on: "Nobody under fourteen, nobody without the letter from the parents—and it had better be dated, kids; I remember all the tricks—and bring a sleeping bag, swimsuit and enough working clothes. And a good pair of gloves. Don't waste my time if you don't qualify, OK? Truck'll be at the school gate tomorrow morning at six sharp."

Eager hands shot up; Adrienne pointed at one after the other, until she reached the number she needed. "Oh, all right—you too, Eddie and Sally. But that's it. No! It's a business proposition, not a public holiday—I'm asking for work, not your votes. 'Bye!"

"That seemed popular," Tom said as they turned away.

Adrienne chuckled. "Farm work's high-status here."

"*That's* a switch."

High-status, instead of being the only occupation in which specialists with degrees and hundreds of thousands of dollars' worth of equipment are considered ignorant yokels, he thought. That had been one reason he didn't envy his elder brother Lars too bitterly. Plus he'd been able to understand what getting caught in a cost-price scissors meant even when he was eighteen.

She went on: "Also, four dollars a day is top-notch summer job money for kids; wages double in harvesttime—it'll keep them in sodas and pretzels and beer and movies for quite a while. And I've got a reputation as being less of a, ummm, nosy-parker chaperon than most at the party afterward," she said. "Of course, I've got to watch that things don't go too far, or the parents wouldn't sign off."

They walked half a block southward in the pleasant shade of the streetside arcade; that covered half the herringbone-brick sidewalk, and the roadside maples and oaks and elms the rest. People drove by, or walked, or rode bicycles and a few Segways; a lot of the latter three types stopped to exchange a word or two.

"Our next stop likes to work Sundays," Adrienne said. "An anticlerical."

Then the covered arcade ended, and the shops and eateries; they were into the fringe of the factory area. Gates of some pale-colored varnished wood split a high blank wall, stucco over stone. Sounds of hammering and clattering came from within, and occasionally the whir of a power tool. Adrienne pressed the button. Someone opened a small eye-level slot with a clack before the main doors swung wide.

The man inside was in his early seventies but still tough and lean, only a little stooped; the hand he extended to Adrienne was strong but gnarled, callused and scarred with the marks of a carpenter or metalworker. He had a floppy black beret on his head, bushy white eyebrows over bright blue eyes, a cigarette hanging out of one corner of his mouth, and rough baggy overalls below; the *bleu de travail* Tom had seen in old movies. Like the overalled boys in the soda parlor, he wore it without self-consciousness.

Of course, Tom thought with a prickle of eeriness. *He's not just capital-F French; he left before looking like this died out. And on* this *side of the Gate, he'd have no reason to change. Nobody to mock or nag him into it.* The trickle of books and movies wouldn't be enough, particularly if certain people took care to see it wasn't.

"Ah, Mademoiselle Rolfe," the Frenchman said. "Bonjour; it is a pleasure to see you safe home once more."

"Pour moi aussi, Marcelle," she said in reply. *"Ça va?"*

The old man waggled a hand. *"Comme ci, comme ca,"* he said, and went on in accented English: "My liver is not a young man's, but then what can one do? The rest of me is not a young man's, either. But come in, come in."

"*Je vous presente mon ami,* M Thomas Christiansen," Adrienne said as they walked into an open concrete-floored courtyard. "Tom, M Marcelle Boissinot; proprietor of the best *tonnellerie,* cooperage, in the Rolfe Domain. Christiansen is newly arrived in the Commonwealth; perhaps you saw the article in the newspaper this morning?"

Tom could follow basic French, if not speak it beyond things like *defilade fire* or *mines;* he'd done a little work with the Legion, but he was glad that the conversation had shifted to his mother tongue. The old man gave him a hard, dry handshake.

"An infinite pleasure, but I had no time for papers," he said. Then, shrewdly: "Monsieur is a hunter, but once also a hunter of men, *n'est pas?*"

"U.S. Army Rangers," he said. *Here's* one *person at least who didn't read my biography, by Jesus.* "Up until a couple of years ago."

"Ah!" The pale eyes glittered, and Tom felt a sudden unease. "Then monsieur has also been a slayer of *les salarabes. Bon!*"

He turned and shouted over his shoulder, speaking rapidly in a quacking guttural-nasal dialect Tom couldn't begin to identify except that it was French of a sort.

Open-sided workshops and storerooms surrounded the courtyard, with ten or so men working. A couple of them looked like sons and grandsons of Marcelle; the rest could have been anybody, and their chatter was mostly in English, with a word or phrase of French here or there. There was a strong smell of seasoned timber in the air, and of sawdust and fire and hot wood. Long planks of blond oak were stacked crisscross up to the high rafters along the inside walls of the workshops, and a businesslike clutter of barrel staves and blanks, iron hoops and tools stood against walls and on workbenches. Several younger men were assembling chest-high wine barrels on the open courtyard, each splayed cylinder of smooth curve-sided oak boards resting open-side-down over a low hot fire of scraps. Tom watched with interest as one man bent the heat-softened wood to shape with a rope and winch, while another slipped an iron hoop over the top and drove it down to its place with quick, skilled strokes of mallet and wedge.

"Always a pleasure to watch men work who know what they're doing," Tom said sincerely.

As he spoke, a youngster came out with a tray and three glasses of white wine. The old man lifted his. "Death to *les salarabes!*" he said.

Tom touched his lips to the wine but didn't drink; the word meant *wog filth,* roughly, and he'd worked with plenty of good-guy Arabs—and Kurds and Afghans and Kazakhs—during the war, ones who hated the loony killers as much as he did. Or more, having a more immediate grudge.

Marcelle Boissinot's eyes were fixed on something in the distant past, and he was smiling, a remarkably cruel expression. He took another sip of his wine, and murmured under his breath, *"Vive la vin, vive la guerre, vive le sacre legionnaire . . ."*

Then he shook himself slightly, and turned politely to his guest, looking up the tall blond length of him. "Monsieur is perhaps of German extraction? In Algeria, I served with some Germans in the First REP—I enlisted claiming to be a Walloon, of course—and they were formidable fighting men."

"I'm Norwegian-American," he said. "But I agree; we operated with some German special-forces units."

"But this reminds me," Marcelle said to Adrienne. "Of a certainty, you have heard the scandal?"

"Scandal?" she said, arching her brows.

"On the afternoon news; the elopement."

"Who?" she asked curiously.

"Siegfried von Traupitz," he said. "A sudden marriage before a magistrate. In Santa Barbara, most naturally."

Adrienne whistled. "The von Traupitz heir?"

In an aside to Tom: "Santa Barbara is Commission territory, like Rolfeston—common ground, not part of any domain. The justices of the peace there are elected neutrals who have to take anyone who comes; and it's a holiday resort, a lot of honeymooners go there."

To the cooper, she went on: "Who with? Tell me instantly, Marcelle!"

The ex-Frenchman's grin turned enormous, and the cigarette worked at the corner of his mouth.

"With the child of another Prime," he said, stretching out the delicious tension as she considered and rejected the limited pool of young women it could be. "With . . . Rebecca Pearlmutter!"

"With *Rebecca*?" Adrienne gasped. Then she gave a peal of laughter that set all the men within earshot grinning in sympathy—and stealing glances at her face, which lit with an inner glow. At rest, her face was beautiful; when she laughed, it went several notches up from there. Tom wrenched his attention away from her to her words.

"I don't *believe* it."

"But I assure you." The old man cackled triumphantly. "What a scandal!"

"Romeo and Juliet," she said, shaking her head. "I knew they got on fairly well at UNV—they were both in one of the post-Alexandrian history courses I took, and neither of them had much time for the old feuds   but . . . old Otto will *plotz!* He'll have an apoplexy. He'll melt down into a steaming *puddle* thinking about Rebecca's children being his heirs! Abe Pearlmutter won't exactly be happy, either."

"And your grandfather will laugh *comme un loup* until *he* has an apoplexy," Boissinot replied happily.

Adrienne shook her head. "Ah, that will be a year's sensation," she said. "But unfortunately, time presses, Marcelle, and I must get down to business."

"Bon," the old man said briskly. "You wish?"

"I need one hundred and fifty new, standard-size aging barrels this fall before the crush," she said. "And fifty reconditioned. First quality, Oregon oak, and from north of Puget Sound."

Tom made a curious noise, and she turned her head. "California oaks don't make good cooperage. Too porous and splintery. French oak staves are impossible to get here, but Oregon oak—that's *Quercus garryana*—is just as good. Particularly if you can get slow-grown wood from northern stands."

"Oregon oak is *nearly* as good as French," Marcelle replied pedantically. "*Bien,* I can have those for you by September. Twenty-five dollars a barrel for the new, eight for the reconditioned."

Adrienne threw up her hands. "Twenty-five dollars! Extortionist! Assassin!"

Boissinot's face was calm as he lit another cigarette and made an expansive gesture with it. "Mademoiselle, as a young man in the OAS I *was* an assassin, and a very good one, even if we unfortunately didn't get that overgrown Alsatian pimp. Now I am a old man, head of a family, with expenses and a payroll to meet."

"Fifteen for the new. Four for the old," she said.

He made a contemptuous sound deep in his throat. "Fifteen? I am offering finished work, not raw logs off the dock. Is mademoiselle's name Rolfe, or Pearlmutter?"

"If I were a Pearlmutter, you old fraud, I'd be off to Cressaut in Tara as easy as salmon in spring," she said. "I wouldn't let sentiment make me pay a ridiculous price to you just because you've been a Rolfe affiliate forever."

"Mademoiselle is a wealthy aristocrat. She can afford sentiment. I, however, am a man of business; and I need at least nineteen dollars for each new cask. Possibly I might concede six dollars seventy-five apiece for the reconditioned barrels. Transport costs on a special shipment would make up any difference on a quote you could get in Tara, and while Cressaut's barrels are good enough in their way, mine are better."

"Nineteen is only slightly less ridiculous than twenty-five," Adrienne said with passionate sincerity. "And the best is the enemy of good enough. You try this with me every summer, Marcelle, and it never works."

Tom sipped his wine while the haggle went on; personally he detested bargaining, but he had to admit both parties here were skillful, and thoroughly enjoying themselves. This Marcelle Boissinot seemed like a nice enough old duffer, undoubtedly a fine craftsman, beloved by his grandkids and a pillar of the local church and boule club . . . except for that one disquieting glimpse of something else.

Sort of like the Commonwealth of New Virginia, he thought.

* * *

June 2009
Louisa Rolfe Memorial Hospital, Rolfeston

Commonwealth of New Virginia

"Ai!"

Jim Simmons swore quietly under his breath as the doctor probed the healing wound in his back.

"Not bad," the physician said.

"Not bad for *you,*" the Frontier Scout replied.

"Healing well, considering it's been only two weeks since you were hurt," the doctor said.

"You try lying on your stomach for two weeks," Simmons said.

There were only two beds in this hospital room: his and Kolomusnim's. The Yokut looked even more absurd in a patient's gown than the Frontier Scout, but he lay with an infinite hunter's patience, eyes fixed on the window and the glimpse of blue sky beyond; both of them were here under the Scout medical insurance program. Kolo's arm was healing well, but he'd lost more weight than Simmons despite the latter's more severe injury; probably because he couldn't adjust to the hospital's idea of "food" as easily, possibly because the environment was just too weirdly alien for him.

"Well, here's some reading material, then," the doctor said.

Simmons brightened; he already had a stack of books on

the adjustable bedside table, and a computer with access to Nostradamus, but a fresh one would be welcome. One of the advantages of having lots of relatives was that there were plenty of people who felt obliged to send you stuff. Of course, they also felt obliged to *visit*, but you couldn't have everything, could you?

It wasn't a book, though: It was a letter, a single cream-colored envelope. Without, he saw, a postage stamp.

"I wonder who couldn't just send an e-mail?" he said to himself, as the doctor finished with his poking and prodding and left the room. "Ah, Adrienne! What a woman!"

He read the letter once, and whistled softly. Then he read it again and again, to make sure the elliptical wording meant what he thought it meant. When he'd finished, he called out to the other man—in his own language.

Simmons wasn't really fluent in Yokut; no more than a hundred or so souls still spoke it, and more than half of those could get along in pidgin English. Still, he'd learned enough to carry on an elementary conversation; Kolo and he had worked together for years, and Simmons had been raised on the frontier, at Scout outposts and stations. It was an interesting tongue; there were things you could say in it with a word or two that required paragraphs in English, and there were English concepts that you couldn't put into Yokut at all.

Some things, however, worked quite well in both their mother tongues. Kolomusnim's face lost its blank look of endurance and came alive as the Scout spoke.

Revenge was a concept that translated quite easily.

CHAPTER THIRTEEN

Rolfe Domain: Napa   Seven Oaks
June 2009

Commonwealth of New Virginia

Napa town ended with the abruptness Tom had become used to in this weird through-the-looking-glass place, with a belt of wild country that marked the future limits of the built-up area. Evidently it was never going to be more than about half the size of its FirstSide analogue, at least according to the plan.

The road up the valley was two-lane blacktop flanked on either side by broad grass verges and by rows of Italian cypress trees, a little west of the streamside forest. The trees beside the road were giants forty feet tall and more, standing like dark green candles casting endless flickering bars of shade across the road as they drove north; more were growing as field-edge windbreaks among the cultivated land. Their shadows lengthened as the sun dipped westward toward the rough sawtooth ridge of the forest-shaggy Mayacamas; eastward the lower, drier Vaca hills were distant shapes colored in olive-green chaparral and golden grassland; the flat valley floor was never more than five miles from edge to edge, nowhere out of sight of the mountains.

Much of the land was in pasture the color of old honey tinged with green, enclosed with chest-high redwood fences weathered nearly black. The fields were starred with violet

camass, blue-flag and golden mariposa lily, and still dotted
with a thinned-out scattering of huge oaks that gave the
whole valley the look of a great park. Herds of glossy black
Angus or white-faced Herefords ambled through grass to
their knees and rested in the shade; so did sheep with the
rather silly naked look the beasts always had after shearing,
and sounders of black-and-tan pigs rooting for last season's
acorns. Horses drowsed, or looked over the fences at the vehicles passing by. Every fifth or sixth field was in wheat or
barley, ripe now and the same bronze-gold color as Adrienne's hair, almost glittering as it swayed in the long shadows of the evening sun, and so thickly splashed with
crimson poppies that he knew without asking they didn't use
herbicides here.

Occasional modest vineyards stood green and shaggy
with their summer foliage, the earth between the rows disked
clean and showing through the leaves in tones of cinnabar or
pale gray or brown. The grapevines were well west of the
road, close to the foot of the mountains; he blinked again,
seeing in his mind's eye the endless monoculture of grapes
that was the Napa in the California he knew. Here they were
a minor element in the landscape's symphony, and small orchards of other fruit seemed as numerous: cherry and apricot, pear and plum, pomegranate and almond and walnut,
gray-green olive and bushy fig. Close to the road an occasional strip of land lay under the whirling spray of irrigation
sprinklers, watering crops of vegetables and soft fruit; a
crew handpicking tomatoes into boxes waved as they
passed.

"Pretty," he said after a moment. *Actually, it's fucking
beautiful, but let's not get overenthusiastic.* "And it looks a
lot more . . . mmm . . . established than I'd have expected,
considering how recent it all is."

Adrienne nodded. "The climate helps," she said. "Things
grow fast here; we started settling the Napa in the late forties. And the Old Man is fond of saying that one of the merits of aristocracy is that it encourages the people in charge to
think about long-term consequences. If your descendants are

going to be living on the same piece of land, you're careful how you treat it. 'Specially if you think in terms of blood-lines and families, and we New Virginians most emphatically *do* think that way."

"I can see aristocracy might look nearly perfect, if you're on the top of the heap," Tom said dryly. "Or one of the kids of the people on top."

"Oh, Granddad also says the drawbacks include continual feuding and faction fights," Adrienne said. "We've managed to keep those political rather than shootin' affairs. So far."

They drove slowly, not because the traffic was thick, but because much of it was tractors towing flatbeds loaded with hay or other cargo. One was filled with a pungent material Adrienne identified as Peruvian guano. It made the freshness more of a contrast once they'd pulled by; the air was warmer here than it had been near the strait, in the high seventies, and it had an intense scent that held sun-cured grass, wild-flowers, turned earth, a breath of coolness from the jungle-like riverside forest to the east.

That was a thick mass of jade green, deep green, brown-green; tall valley oaks with interlaced crowns; beneath them sycamores, black walnut, Oregon ash and box elder, laced together with a thick mass of California blackberry, poison oak and willow, interwoven still tighter with wild grapevine and blossoming Castilian rose. Birdsong was loud even over the engine noise, and the buzz of insect life nearly as intense; they had to stop a time or two for explosions of monarch but-terflies, drifting across the road in orange-white clouds dense enough to hinder vision. Now and then a gap showed a small sunlit meadow or the glitter of the river's flow, or a bend opened up into a little marsh. A half hour north of Napa town they saw a swath cleared for a long timber bridge to the eastern shore, and beneath it a trio of boys on an improvised raft valiantly trying to pole their ungainly craft off a gravel bank in the bright shallow water.

"Probably convinced they're on the Mississippi, if I re-member my brothers," Adrienne said.

Tom had to grin; there were a lot worse ways to spend a

summer afternoon stolen from chores than imagining you were adrift with Jim and Huck and the Professor. *He* certainly had, and it took a lot more imagination when you were using the Red River of the North with its bare banks running through endless fields of flax and sunflowers. The two Irish setters splashing around the raft seemed to think it was great sport too.

Boys and dogs probably came from one of the steadings he saw now and then at the end of a tree-lined dirt side road heading westward; farmhouses low-slung and roofed in Roman tile, built of whitewashed adobe or pale cut stone, and all set well back from the river. They were surrounded by gardens, often with some of the huge coast live oaks and valley oaks left standing near them. Big red-painted hip-roofed wooden barns loomed behind the dwellings.

Nobody builds that type anymore except for tourists, he thought.

But these were real barns, holding fodder and livestock and equipment; and none of the other outbuildings were the simple utilitarian sheet-metal shapes of modern working agriculture either. Even the silos were plank bound with steel hoops, like giant cylindrical barrels.

He turned a farm boy's eye on the tilled fields; harvested flax, some potatoes already lifted and others still roughly green, and the yellow-gold grain.

"Winter wheat, I suppose?" Tom asked.

"Plant in late November or early December, harvest in June," she confirmed. "Barley and oats too, of course."

"Wait a minute," he said, thinking back.

Wait a minute, squared. At the rate I've seen, there can't be more than a few thousand acres of grain in this whole valley, much less this "estate" of hers. It's three-quarters pasture or grass leys. Why all the labor?

The tractors he'd seen on the road or working in the fields were little red fifty-horsepower models with open cabs and small front wheels. That was the obsolete image most city folk had when the word "tractor" went through their minds, the sort of thing his grandfather had used when he got back from Korea.

I wonder just how old-fashioned they are here? Tom thought. *They could import anything they wanted, after all.* He went on aloud: "How exactly do you harvest your wheat?"

"Tractor-drawn reaper-binder," she said. "Then we pitchfork the sheaves onto a flatbed wagon, tow it back to the barnyard, and build big grain ricks. Blessing of a dry summer—we've got until October to get it threshed. Why did you think I needed all those extra hands?"

"Why not combines?" he said.

"Those million-dollar air-conditioned monsters twenty feet high you use FirstSide?" she said, and snorted. "Aesthetics aside, they wouldn't pay."

"Harvest's risky enough without borrowing trouble by dragging it out," he said. "A modern John Deere can do better than three hundred acres a day, with one driver and some trucks to unload into."

"Not here it wouldn't," she said. "Seven Oaks and Rolfe Manor are the only estates in this domain that have three hundred acres in small grains anything like close together. Big combines would have to spend half their time on the road between tenant farms with maybe thirty acres of wheat each, tops—and this is pretty well the only paved rural road in New Virginia, and that's because of the power projects up north and the quicksilver mines. We'd need a couple of combines for every pocket of settlement from San Diego to the Willamette, because there aren't any roads to speak of between a lot of them—and shipping them up and down the coast by sea would be ridiculous. Say three to each area, so there'd be one working, one traveling between jobs, and a spare in case one of the others broke down unfixably in the middle of the harvest. Call it eighty acres a day, maximum, in actual output and counting all three machines. It'd be a waste of capital."

"I see your point," he said, doing a little arithmetic in his head. "You'd be paying a lot more than twice as much for a machine that only doubled the acreage per day."

"Right," she said. "Plus it would spend the rest of the year sitting in a shed depreciating, while a good Fordson-type tractor with a power takeoff can be out doing other work all year 'round."

He grinned, shaking his head. After a moment she added: "Penny for them."

Tom shrugged and spread his hands. *Actually, I was thinking that it was a long time since I'd met a woman I could talk farm machinery and costs with,* he thought. *But I'm not sure I want to get* that *friendly again just yet.*

"That makes sense," he said instead. "I warn you, though—I've never pitched a sheaf of wheat with a fork in my life. Maybe my grandfather did when he was a kid." *Mixed farming with a vengeance,* he thought. "I can learn, I suppose. . . ."

The road swung west around a series of low hills that reared up out of the flat land, then back east toward the river as the valley broadened out again. They'd been passing tall stone gateways every few miles, the entrances to the estates of the Rolfe domain's landholders. Another gateway appeared: stone pillars, joined by an arch of wrought iron that spelled out "Seven Oaks." Underneath it the same metal curlicues showed the outlines of seven great trees.

"Home," Adrienne said, and sighed.

Odd, Tom thought. *Been a long time since I had a place I could call home.* His apartment in Sacramento had just been the place he lived; so had a long succession of billets and married quarters and barracks before that, ever since he left the house his great-grandfather had built.

The estate road ran west and a little north, toward a deep V-shaped notch in the low mountains that rimmed the valley. Tall palms lined it on either side, their tips catching the sun's gilding as it dropped ahead of them. He could see white buildings in the west now, flickering glimpses through the trees. The road ran on to a creek lined by a narrow strip of forest, crossing it on a wooden bridge. He looked down into the little stream as the Hummer's wheels did a rhythmic thutter across the thick planks; a school of steelhead trout lingered around the pilings, gleaming metallic blue-gray like streamlined river wolves.

"Does it rain more here?" he asked Adrienne.

Usually creeks this size would be drying up by now. And steelhead didn't run anymore even in the main stream of the Napa River back where he came from, much less the tributaries.

"Oh, no, it just looks like it. Higher water table, less silting and erosion, more forest on the hills. You get more dry-season flow that way; more springs and sloughs, too." She pointed toward the dense forest and brush that clad the mountain slopes and gullies. "Those were never logged off or grazed; they hold the water and release it gradually all through the summer. There's a little check-dam and a reservoir up there to collect springwater for the houses and the winery and barns."

Over the creek the road turned left and ran more directly west; he could see a large stone-built house set in lawns and landscaping ahead; there were seven large oaks grouped on the long sweep of bright-green grass. To the right of the house grounds was a stretch of vineyard, the goblet-trained vines rising from the earth like arthritic fingers covered in green, and beyond that an orchard of smallish trees with gray-green leaves—olive groves. Off to the left were other dwellings—a two-story adobe, with the beams of its vigas protruding through the thick sun-dried brick, and several smaller houses, with a long structure that looked like a ranch bunkhouse as well. Beyond and behind those were barns, stables, corrals, equipment and storage sheds, and one odd structure that looked like the front of a stone building with double-car-garage-sized doors and a central gable pasted into the face of a steep hillside.

The great house itself seemed naggingly familiar: a big red-tiled foursquare Italianate building of two tall stories, with wings set back on either side and quoining work at the corners. Seven tall windows spanned the second story of the main block; a wrought-iron balcony fronted the one over the heavy carved wooden doors. In fact, if you subtracted the ebony of the doors and the silver lions' heads that adorned it, and the climbing passionvine that covered a lot of the building's stone with white flowers shaded in pink and lavender . . .

"I'd swear I've seen this before," he said.

"You may have," Adrienne said with a chuckle. "It's, ah, inspired by—read 'stolen'—from a design Julia Morgan did in Berkeley back in the 1920s. On Claremont Avenue, to be precise; the residence of the vice president of the University of California. Aunt Chloe's husband picked it, shortly before he drank himself to death in 1952."

"Any particular reason?" Tom asked, looking around at the great estate, tinted gold by the evening sun. "For his crawling into a bottle, that is, not for picking the design—steal from the best, I say."

She shrugged, keeping her hands on the wheel and her gaze straight ahead; from her carefully neutral tone he suspected some lurid family stories about the late unlamented great-uncle.

"Aunt Chloe was the Old Man's sister, but nobody much liked her husband; one of her less successful strays. He never really adjusted to life here in New Virginia, especially after he lost his Gate privileges—he couldn't keep his mouth shut back FirstSide when he'd had a few. He broke his neck taking a horse over a fence when he was so pie-faced he couldn't have walked to his bedroom without an assistant and a map."

A pair of girls working in a field full of vegetables flagged the Hummer down and tumbled into the back, along with big round baskets full of baby lettuce and peppers and green onions. He missed their names in the hasty introduction; one was brunette and bashful, the other an enormously freckled redhead and outgoing, and they both made him feel ancient with their sheer burbling energy.

"That's the *mayordomo*'s house," Adrienne said, her voice eager with homecoming, pointing to the big adobe, mostly hidden now behind hedge and trees. "Cindy and Anne-Marie here are his eldest granddaughters. That false-front thing is the entrance to the wine caves—cut into the rock; that's where the stone for the big house came from."

A crowd stood waiting to greet them at the entrance to the inner garden around the main house. In fact . . .

"Sort of a village, judging by the numbers," he said.

"Seems that way sometimes," Adrienne said. "We New Virginians do go in for big families. It mounts up. Four generations now: two, four, sixteen, thirty-two."

The Hummer came to a halt and the passengers alighted. Most of the people waved; a line of ten young *nahua* bowed with their straw hats in their hands; the senior adults came forward to shake hands; large dogs with a good deal of Alsatian and mastiff in their ancestry came leaping around, adding an element of chaotic enthusiasm to the whole proceedings. Particularly as several of them were dedicated crotch sniffers determined to make the tall newcomer's olfactory acquaintance. Adrienne made introductions:

"This is Vance Henning, my *mayordomo,* and his wife, Jenine; his sons, Robert, Sam, Eddie . . . Mitchell Desjardins, crop boss and winemaker . . ."

The names and handshakes turned into a blur. *Christ, there must be thirty people here, not counting the* braceros, *and the little kids,* Tom thought.

The last to be named were a couple of single men and women who cheerfully classified themselves as "corks" who turned their hands to anything; he got the unspoken impression they were temporary, and they were all quite young as well.

"Got the hands we need, Vic," Adrienne said at last to the *mayordomo;* he was a lean, weathered-looking man with sun-streaked brown hair going gray. "Twelve—or possibly fourteen."

He nodded. "Thanks, Miz Rolfe," he said. "That does relieve my mind. We'd be right pressed for time if we waited any longer."

Tom recognized his reflexive look upward; it was the glance of a farmer worrying about weather and time.

Who ever got the idea that the countryside has less in the way of anxiety? he wondered. *There's nobody more dependent on things going right, things they can't control at all.*

Henning looked around. "Miz Rolfe will be wantin' to settle in, everyone," he said, and the crowd dispersed.

A murmured question to Adrienne revealed that everyone except the *nahua* and the corks had been born here, and there were half a dozen retirement-age parents as well. When the others had left, a final figure tottered forward—a thickset Indian woman in a Mother Hubbard who looked older than God, with wrinkled brown skin, tattooed lines from lower lip to chin, and sparse silvery hair. She had a stick clasped in one knotted hand to help her hobbling walk; when they came close Tom realized that she wouldn't have stood over five feet even when her back was straight. The younger woman who helped her forward might have been her granddaughter, if her other three grandparents were Caucasians in that particular woodpile; she had straight raven-black hair and a hint of ruddiness to her complexion. She was also extremely good-looking—in a buxom, full-breasted and wide-hipped way. He suspected that a lot of outdoor work had contained a natural tendency to a brick-outhouse build; she was in her late twenties, possibly a year or two younger than the owner of Seven Oaks.

Adrienne sighed as the crone poured out a torrent of some language that definitely wasn't English and hugged her around the waist. She patted her on the head and replied in the same tongue—haltingly—and waited patiently. At last the Indian woman dropped into English; she was still speaking earnestly, reaching up to grab Adrienne by the lapel with one hand while the other held her stick.

"'. . . but listen to me now,' Coyote said. 'I am going away. My grandson doesn't like it here, so I am going away. I am going away. We are going away.'"

Adrienne nodded. "Yes, good mother, I know. I remember the story. And then he said to his wife, Frog Old Woman:

'Come on, old lady, gather your beads and your baskets; let's go.'"

The old woman nodded eagerly, and took up the tale: "Then he spoke again to the human people: 'When you die, you are to come to my land. Not living people. Dead people only. After four days they are to come to my land, the dead people.' Then he went away with Frog Old Woman, Hawk Chief, and all his people."

Over the bent head Adrienne mouthed something silently to the young companion. That one urged the old woman away; the wrinkled apple face was smiling as she hobbled off.

"What was that in aid of?" Tom asked, pulling their luggage out of the Hummer.

"That's poor old Karkin," Adrienne said. "Ah . . . long story. Karkin was a chief's daughter of the Ohlone tribe around the Gate in 'forty-six. She had a child with Salvo Colletta . . . that sort of thing happened fairly often back then in the very early years, when there were only a few people here in the Commonwealth and not many families. It went badly, of course, and then all her people died, and . . . well, Aunt Chloe took her in, and her daughter—she died in childbirth—and granddaughter. That's the granddaughter, Sandra Margolin. I met Karkin when I was a little girl, and I thought she was a witch. Quite a nice old lady; completely mad, of course."

"What's with the story?" he said. "That's what she was doing, wasn't she? Repeating some sort of legend?"

"Oh, she's always going on with these old stories of hers. She used to tell them to me over and over, and I picked up a little of the language; as much because Mother hated me hanging around her as anything. I think Aunt Chloe wrote them all down somewhere."

* * *

Adrienne had turned in fairly early. *Without* the unspoken invitation, this time, something that left him relieved and disappointed both. The *mayordomo* had dined with them, and Tom mostly observed the conversation—apart from the upcoming harvest, it centered on thinning the leaves of the grapevines, which was apparently important and delicate, and on the state of the livestock. Neither was something he was very familiar with: Grapes weren't a North Dakota crop, and few of the Red River farmers kept much in the way of stock anymore; between high land values and long winters, cash crops paid much better.

He felt a little too restless to turn in early himself, his mind battered by a rush of strangeness and things half-familiar and half-alien that were harder yet. Instead he prowled about a bit. The house was just that, a big and quietly sumptuous country house, rather than a palace. He'd been surprised at that, and had gotten a laugh out of Adrienne when he mentioned it.

"Rolfe Manor's a bit more grand," she'd said. Then, in a sardonic tone: "And Colletta Hall is what San Simeon might have been, if William Randolph Hearst hadn't been crippled by a limited budget and aesthetic restraint."

Coming down the stairs to the front hall put a great window to his left—glass and Venetian Gothic stone tracery, looking out on a courtyard garden; the panes had been turned out, letting in night-scent of cool air, greenery and flowers to add to the wax and herbal smell of the house. The hall went up two stories; looking from here to the carved ebony of the front doors in the dimness he saw the subdued lights gleaming off wood floors, and from heavy silk carpets that looked Oriental but weren't, quite; at least not the Orient he'd grown up with. A long tapestry hanging on one wall was woven of hummingbird feathers, lustrous and shining in greens and blues and crimsons almost metallic; beside it was a paddle-shaped weapon of some tropical wood, edged with bronze wedges in the shape of shark's teeth. The opposite wall held a portrait of an imperious-looking matron in a black dress with a long string of pearls, evidently the famed Aunt Chloe. A wrought-iron gallery ran along the landing above the front entranceway; each side of the hall had one large arched opening.

He took the one that led into the library-study. A black cat with a white bib of fur on its chest jumped down from an armchair as he entered, came over inquiringly, and then stalked on by when he tried to make friends.

The library lights came on as he touched the plaque inside the door. It was exactly what a house library should be: big windows on the courtyard side, with more Venetian tracery, wood-lined elsewhere, with some tables, desks and plenty of bookshelf space. There was even one of those sliding ladders, so you didn't have to strain or stand on a chair to reach the top shelves. Most of the books looked like they'd been used, particularly those toward a working desk that sported a big thin-film display screen, with an office chair and a lounger nearby.

He went to a glass-fronted liquor cabinet and poured himself a brandy, then looked at the shelves nearest the desk. Nonfiction on one side, reference works on forensics and intelligence techniques, computer security, personal combat methodology, farming, biology and ecology, with an accent on California and the West—naturally!—plus some titles published here in New Virginia: *Post-Discovery Ecological Transitions* and the like.

The history shelves were well stocked and extremely varied—he didn't even know what half the titles were about—but slanted towards the pre-Columbian western hemisphere, the Hellenistic world, and the Colonial period in America.

A few were histories of *this* world; *The Rise and Fall of the Alexandrian Empire, The Post-Alexandrian World, Folk Migrations in Early Historic East Asia, The Selang-Arsi Kingdoms, The Eastern Iranians* and *Post-Celtic Europe*.

His fingers itched to take them up, but there would be time later. Ditto for the translations from the Greek, and from languages that had never existed in his history.

He recognized the authors and titles of a lot of the nearby fiction section, and a few piled on a table beside the lounger, but not the editions—these were leather-bound with stamped gilt lettering on the spines. Unless he was much mistaken, this was Adrienne's personal corner.

Some children's books sat on the top shelves, preserved for affection's sake—*The Jungle Book, Little Women, Treasure Island,* the complete *Tarzan,* other Edgar Rice Burroughs, a well-thumbed set of the *Narnia* books of C. S. Lewis. Then poets; he recognized Poe and Frost, Dickinson and the Brownings, then Kipling and Tennyson; he wondered who Betjeman was, but not enough to take down, and *Hassan* by Flecker looked intriguing—there were some lovely twenties Art Deco Oriental illustrations. Two shelves held authors like Sabatini, Farnol and Richard Davies Hanson from the early twentieth century—*Captain Blood, Martin Coninsby's Vengeance, The Sea Hawk, Ransom's Folly* and many more. They were all bound in the same patterned black leather with gilt-stamped spines; he examined the title pages and found that they were the Commonwealth standard editions provided to schools and public libraries—highly approved reading, evidently. A few of the novels were completely unfamiliar, by New Virginian authors.

The rest were eclectic: *The Dream of the Red Chamber* and *Genji Monogatori* next to Proust, Mary Renault and Updike. And there was a good deal of mystery and science fiction, as he'd expected; evidently Adrienne had been honest when she said her personal revelations were authentic as far as they went. It was even good tradecraft to be as honest as you could, he supposed; the fewer lies you told, the less you had to remember when you opened your mouth.

One whole shelf made him grin: *Into the Alternate Universe, A World Unknown, The Gates of Creation, Lord Kalvan of Otherwhen, The Complete Paratime, Three Hearts and Three Lions, A Midsummer Tempest, Chase the Morning, The Key to Irunium, Worlds of If, Sideways in Time, Lest Darkness Fall, Guns of the South . . .* He could see why an imaginative youngster in *this* neck of the dimensional woods would pick them up.

He settled down in the lounger; it creaked a little under his solid weight, but was remarkably comfortable. He pulled out the keyboard and swung it into a comfortable position, then signed on to Nostradamus.

"Just as a theoretical exercise, what would be the Colletta assets, if they want to take this place over?" he asked himself. "Purely theoretical. Assume that what Adrienne shows me is going to convince me to help her and her extremely successful pirate-clan family. . . ."

The cat returned, jumped up on the side table, sniffed at the brandy with a slight whisker flick of distaste, then rearranged the folds of Tom's bathrobe and settled down on his lap.

CHAPTER FOURTEEN

Rolfe Domain: Seven Oaks, Rolfe Manor
June–July 2009

Commonwealth of New Virginia

A soft three-note tone woke Tom Christiansen the next morning. He blinked himself awake and turned; the screen on a table not far from his bed had lit, and he belted on the bathrobe and walked over to it. It was early; the light through the east-facing window showed only a shimmer of red across the mountains to the east through a curtain of fog, and there was a cool, damp smell in the air.

Adrienne's face was in the screen. "I just got a call that you might want to share," she said.

Tom had never had a problem coming to full consciousness when he had to. The screen split; the other face was Piet Botha's; the square, brutal countenance was frowning as he spoke.

". . . Schalk," he finished. "I've been asking around about him, and—"

"Ah, yes," Adrienne cut in. "I remember you mentioned that you were *concerned about his wife and children.* That's something *nobody but we* should discuss. We were there, after all; I'm sure you *remember it as well as I do.*"

Tom saw the eyes in the jowly pug face widen and then narrow as the Afrikaner caught the slightly off-key stress she put on certain words.

"*Ja,* Miss Rolfe," he said. "Well, I'll be coming north on that business I mentioned, hey? We could talk about it then."

"That would be fine, Piet," she said. "You're calling from Rolfeston, right? Looking forward to it. We can't start our harvest here until the fog lifts and everything dries out, anyway."

"*Tot siens.*"

Tom sat silently for a moment, until she came into his room; she was in a bathrobe, with her hair still tousled from sleep. She crouched down and pulled the jack that tied his machine into Nostradamus before she spoke.

"Uh-oh," Tom said. *So you're worried someone might be tapping your phone, and Schalk had friends in on whatever he was in on.*

"Uh-oh," she replied. "Look, Tom, things are moving a little faster than I'd have liked. According to Botha, there are a lot of Versfeld affiliates in on this thing too; or at least that's the way I'm reading what he carefully didn't say. Have you seen enough of the Commonwealth to decide whether you're going to help me or not?"

He rubbed at his chin. "Enough to make a preliminary judgment," he said. "I'll have to talk to Roy. I have some points I could go over with you."

"We can get him up here quick," she replied. "And then I think it's time to talk to Granddad."

※ ※ ※

Jesus, I'm nervous, Tom thought. *You betcha I am.*

Meeting Adrienne had been a complex thing, with a lot of highs and lows—more highs than lows right now, but the lows had been doozies. Meeting her grandfather . . .

Rolfe Manor stood near the head of the Napa Valley, not far from where Calistoga was FirstSide, and the scale was quite different from Seven Oaks. There was a pleasant-looking leafy little town of about a thousand people to serve the Prime's residence, and beyond it a mile-long paved lane through pasture and vineyards and olive groves—the pavement itself being a sign of something unusual, by Commonwealth standards. It was flanked on either side by a double avenue of redwoods. The king trees didn't start naturally on the valley floor here, but they grew fast if you watered them well and the soil suited—three to five feet a year, once they were established. These must have been transplanted as saplings about the time Tom's grandfather got back from Korea, and they towered a hundred and fifty feet into the air, each at least six feet around at head height. The branches just met overhead, and the cool, resin-fragrant shade gave a cathedral feeling to the drive despite the hot morning sun, a tinge of awe and stillness under the hum of the tires.

Which is probably just what was intended, Tom thought, looking aside at Adrienne for a moment.

They'd been together long enough for him to get a handle on her expressions. The careful casualness he saw now hid a tension that probably wasn't entirely due to the real reason for this meeting: Rolfe Manor was where she'd been born and had grown up to a notably stormy adolescence. Seven Oaks was her home; this was the place she'd escaped from.

The avenue of redwoods ended at an open space with a large fountain at its center; the roadway divided around it. At the other end was a brick wall stretching far on either side, broken by a tall wrought-iron gate. The gate showed the Rolfe lion outlined in iron facing its mirror image; flagpoles bore the domain emblem on one side and the crossed bars of the Commonwealth on the other. There was a small guard detachment there: gray-uniformed, helmeted household troopers with the same lion in red on black on their shoulder flashes. The men reminded Tom of himself, minus a decade and change: big, tough-looking plowboys with serious, solemn faces; their sergeant was older, obviously professional cadre recruited FirstSide, with a scar on his left cheek that was probably from a shell fragment.

From the look of his squad they were disciplined and at least knew which end of the rifles a bullet came out of, and he didn't doubt they were brave. The skill level of the Commonwealth's miniature military remained to be seen, though, especially the way they were split up.

The sergeant saluted Adrienne, and matched faces to ID cards for Tom, and for Tully and Piet—who were sitting as far apart as they could in the backseat of the Hummer.

"Pass, Miz Rolfe," he said.

He signaled for the gates to open. They did, smooth and silent; Tom noticed a pair of discreet surveillance cameras on either side. There were probably a lot of other ones he hadn't seen; the Commonwealth was a fairly peaceful place, but its lords didn't take that for granted.

Or maybe it's peaceful because *they don't take it for granted,* he thought mordantly.

Inside the gate was parkland. The road was white crushed rock, and flanked on either side by big glossy-leafed evergreen magnolias; their plate-sized white flowers lent a heavy scent to the warm still air. The avenue curved in a graceful S shape, first through a pretty amendment of nature, with fallow deer grazing under ancient valley oaks and an occasional stream or pond that looked original but probably wasn't; then as it straightened and turned toward the great house there were flower beds, lawns, a hedge maze, an increasing formality. The house itself was Regency Georgian, redbrick, built in the form of an H with an elongated central bar two stories high. A long walkway of russet tile led up to the main entrance; that was surrounded by eighteen-foot marble pillars with gilded—literally—Corinthian capitals, supporting a second-story balcony; identical columns soared up from that to support the pediment roof.

The doors opened . . . and a torrent of children poured out, kids just short of adolescence mostly, dressed in riding clothes. They stopped at the sight of the Hummer, then crowded around with cries of "Aunt Adrienne!" and stayed for a few moments of hugs and kisses on the cheek and hair ruffling.

When they'd been shepherded on by a governess—herself in jodhpurs—he turned to Adrienne as they climbed out.

"*Aunt* Adrienne?" he said with a smile. "Hard to think of you as an aunt, somehow."

"Hard to think of *them* as that big," she replied, shaking her head. "Time's getting away from me . . . those were my eldest brother's larvae, mostly, and some of my sister's; she's staying here last I heard while her husband's on a trade mission in Hagamantash. Nice kids, but it's a good thing this place has room."

It did. A secretary—male, middle-aged and taciturn—showed them in. Tom blinked at the entrance hall, with its sweeping staircases on either side and squares of green malachite on the floor, inlaid in larger squares of white marble; they went on from there, down groin-arched corridors where niches held things bizarre or beautiful—one held a shallow twin-handled painted cup whose lines were so numinously perfect he nearly stopped right there—and up another long staircase. The second-story hallway there was the full width of the building, tall windows on either side alternating with paintings that had Tully's eyes popping—his partner had some nodding acquaintance with art history.

"Kemosabe," he murmured, "either those are some very good fakes, or a couple of museums back FirstSide are showing some extremely good fakes . . . and I suspect it's option number two."

Adrienne chuckled softly at that. "This is the public wing," she said. "The business section. One thing I'll say about growing up here—there was always somewhere you could get away from your folks."

The secretary frowned but stayed silent, until he led them through an outer office and to the doors of another.

"Sir, Miss Rolfe and party," he said.

OK, now I'm really *nervous,* Tom thought.

The inner sanctum was oval, flooded by light from the windows around most of its circumference. There was a fireplace on one side, and an eighteenth-century iron-and-bronze chandelier overhead; a large desk; and settees and chairs around a low table of some rose-colored wood, polished to a high sheen. A maid laid out coffee and biscotti, and the man who'd been leaning on a walking stick before one of the windows that looked out over gardens and the side of Mount Saint Helena turned.

"Thank you, Margaret," John Rolfe said, with a gracious nod as the servant left.

He was shorter than Tom's subconscious had expected— an inch or so taller than Adrienne's five-nine—and gaunt with age, but still ramrod straight. His hair was silver-white, receding only a little from brow and temples; the eyes were pouched and sunk into an ancient eagle's face, but the same leaf green as his granddaughter's, and very keen; you could see where she'd gotten the cheekbones, too. He walked forward slowly but firmly, leaning into the walking stick to spare a lame leg—acquired on Okinawa in 1944, Tom remembered—and halted close to them; he was wearing a lightweight linen suit of subdued elegance.

Adrienne stepped forward first, bowing low, taking his outstretched left hand in hers, and kissing it.

"*Baciamo le mani,*" she said, then stood and kissed him on the cheek. "Hello, Grandfather."

"And it's always a pleasure to see you, child," he replied—the voice was raspy, but clear and accented with a purring drawl.

Piet Botha repeated the ritual. Tully looked at Tom, shrugged almost invisibly, and followed suit.

I also feel like a damned fool doing this, Tom thought.

Nevertheless, he bowed and kissed the hand of the master of New Virginia with a murmur of *baciamo le mani* of his own; the fact that everyone else in their party had done the same thing before him made him feel a little less conspicuous.

"Sit, by all means, all of you," John Rolfe VI said, letting smoke trickle out of his nostrils. "Make yourselves comfortable."

He seemed to sense Tom's discomfort as he walked slowly to the spindly curved-legged settee, leaning on his stick, and sat with careful dignity. The upholstery sighed beneath him, but the lined, scored face remained impassive as he pulled a narrow cigarillo from a humidor and lit it.

"Think of it as a salute, Mr. Christiansen," he said softly. "In any organized society there must be forms, gestures of respect. I am founder and master of this nation. My fellow Virginian Washington followed a similar policy of emphasizing formal etiquette during his presidency, for much the same reason; I've often found his solutions useful when an analogous problem came up."

The green gaze was sardonic as he took in the two Americans' stifled reaction to the implicit comparison. "By the way, do you know what the Iroquois call my distant cousin? George Washington, that is."

"Ah . . . no, sir," Tom replied.

"It translates roughly as the Burner of Towns, which is a fairly accurate description of what his forces did to them during the War of Independence. 'The immediate objects are the total devastation and destruction of their settlements,' to quote the precise words of his written orders on the subject. Houses burned, food stores stolen or spoiled, civilians driven out into the winter cold without sustenance or shelter, and exile and starvation for the survivors."

"Ah . . . I hadn't known that, sir," Tom replied. *Hmmm. Have to look it up, but I'd bet that's substantially accurate. Well, live and learn.*

"And the Indians here called me—may still, for all I know—Johnny Deathwalker," Rolfe said. "My own people refer to me as the Founder, or the Old Man—which latter, nowadays, is literally true. It's all a matter of perspective."

A smile. "Although that particular hand-kissing ritual was Salvo's idea. I went along with it . . . not least because custom and tradition add color and meaning to life; a new country needs to establish traditions not less than it needs guns or plows. Perhaps I've been too much enamored of the picturesque; the product of a romantic boyhood, perhaps. Now, to business. Adrienne?"

"Yes, sir," she said in turn. "I presume you've read my report?"

John Rolfe nodded. "I have. I've also discussed it with Charles."

Must mean her father, Tom thought. He hadn't met the man yet, and wasn't looking forward to it, particularly. Meeting the father of someone you'd been dating was always a bit fraught, and probably more so here in fifties-never-ended land. *Fortunate—or well planned—that he isn't here right now. That would be awkward.*

She poured her grandfather coffee and added cream; he sank back with the cup in one hand and the cigarillo in the other, and went on: "What I'd like to have is a firsthand redaction from all of you. This place is as secure as any in the inhabited parts of the Commonwealth, I assure you."

Adrienne cleared her throat and started. It was soothing, in a way—doing reports was something that had occupied a good deal of Tom's adult life, one way and another. Everyone here seemed to know the drill: facts and interpretations clearly separated, concise and short as possible. The old man's questions were sharp and to the point as well. Tom kept his account unemotional when his turn came around; that would be best, considering the rather awkward fact that he'd been on the other side—or *an* other side—when all this began.

John Rolfe sighed. "It seems definite, then, that there is a conspiracy." He shook his head. "A pity that Salvo died so young. He would have known better than this. . . . Ah, well, forgive an old man's tendency to dwell upon the past. What we must know now is, first, who is involved in this conspiracy, second, what are their goals, and third, what do they hope to accomplish."

Tom cleared his throat; John Rolfe raised one snowy eyebrow. The younger man went on: "Sir, I don't think that there's much doubt as to the aim. The aim is to seize power here, and I'd give any odds that the means is through seizure of the Gate itself. It's the point failure source . . ."

"I'm familiar with the term," the Commonwealth's ruler said.

". . . of your whole setup here."

Adrienne nodded. "It's the Collettas, too, sir," she said. "Almost certainly with the help of the Batyushkovs. And as Operative Botha has made plain, with at least some elements among the affiliates of the Versfelds."

John Rolfe nodded, blew another plume of smoke and thought in silence for a long moment.

"I should have anticipated this," he mused at last. "The first generation of Primes were mostly personally loyal to me—even Salvo, in his way. Those who weren't were mostly too grateful to be here to cause much trouble. That isn't quite the case with the Batyushkovs, obviously; and many of the second generation of Family heads know me only as the irritating elder statesman who keeps them in a permanent political minority. . . . I suspect Karl von Traupitz is numbered among those."

"I don't think *Oom* Versfeld would support such madness, sir," Piet Botha said, with an edge of diffidence to his tone. "But some of our people . . . well, they dream of a new South Africa, *in* this world's South Africa. I can understand it. I do not think it would be a wise thing; nor does *Oom* Versfeld. But I understand."

"Which leaves the question of *how* they plan to take the Gate," Tom said.

Adrienne nodded. "They've obviously done something nasty and clandestine to Nostradamus," she said. "Still, they can't really *control* the system, not overtly. And they couldn't have subverted anything like enough of the Gate Security Force to take over the gate complex . . . and how could they hold it against the forces of the Commission and the loyal Families? Not even all the Imperialist faction would all go along with something as raw as a coup d'état."

"Coup de main," her grandfather murmured. "If I were organizing such a thing . . ."

"Yes, sir," Tom said. "A sudden blow in overwhelming force to take the Gate."

"On both sides," the ruler said. "You'd have to take the FirstSide facility. It's that—my old shortwave set—which really gives the holder control. Anyone who smashes it smashes the Gate; and the power to destroy a thing, combined with the will to do so, gives you the power to control it absolutely."

Listening to that voice, and those words, gave Tom a slight cold prickle down the spine. Tully exchanged an imperceptible flicker of eye contact with his partner. Tom could hear the thought: *One seriously scary dude.*

Adrienne leaned forward. "That's probably what the contact with the Batyushkovs' Russian friends on FirstSide was about," she said. "But there's also the possibility that they're planning something . . . outside the box. The fake nephew who's actually a physicist."

John Rolfe chuckled and stroked his jaw. "I *knew* that keeping Ralph around would be useful someday," he said with satisfaction. "It's surprising how often mercy has practical utility. Hmmm . . . that would be a backup plan, unless I miss my guess—and one quite secret from the Collettas, as well. That's the problem with organizing a treasonous conspiracy: The other parties aren't likely to be the most honorable of men either."

"Unless they're secessionists, of course," Tully said, exaggerating his Arkansas accent a little. "Sir."

John Rolfe shot him a sharp glance, then smiled wryly. "That isn't the most tactful possible remark in this house, Mr. Tully," he said dryly. "Still testing, eh? No, I won't send for the headsman. Let me rephrase my remark: a treasonous conspiracy in the sort of society we've established here. Aristocratic polities are prone to faction, but the factions tend to be personal, rather than dividing on matters of principle. That . . . *simplifies* things, shall we say. Unless the system has broken down completely, it also makes bloodbaths like the War of Southern Independence unlikely; there isn't enough at stake for ordinary folk to make mass mobilization possible."

"There's a great deal at stake here, sir," Adrienne said.

"In the long run, my dear. In the long run. In the short run, which is where most human beings live most of the time, it would be only a change of personnel at the top—I doubt

Giovanni would go in for a widespread purge, and he cannot afford to fatally alienate all the Families, even if his coup were to succeed. That's why a civil war would be inadvisable, as well as disastrous—too few would stay willing to fight when the damage grew great enough."

A long silence fell; Tom began to wonder whether the elderly Rolfe had fallen asleep. Then the older man's eyes snapped open again.

"There are two ways to approach this. I can use the means at *my* disposal, and Charles's, but we will have to be extremely cautious. If we alert the Collettas, they might try to strike at once out of desperation—possibly succeeding, possibly bringing on a real civil war here."

"If we're too cautious, they may strike while we're still dithering, sir," Adrienne said.

"Only too true, my dear. Although we are somewhat forewarned, which means they cannot achieve complete surprise."

He brooded for a moment. "The Collettas can't possibly think to raise the necessary force from their affiliation. For one thing, it would be too conspicuous; for another, they're not popular enough with their clients to be able to call on them to fight the Commission. Not all of them, and not quickly."

Adrienne nodded. "We've done some research, sir. Tom and his friend have identified a crucial factor, we think."

The pouched, faded green eyes turned on him. Military habit stiffened Tom's spine. "It's Colletta Air, sir," he said. "They're a wholly owned Family company; they use modified C-130s, mostly. The records on your computer system—Nostradamus—look clean, but I think that over the past decade they could have, ah, *lost* a number of them. That would be enough to bring in a battalion, and from a considerable distance. There's a lot of wilderness out there."

Adrienne nodded. "And I think that the only way to get enough men would be to recruit locally. Well, locally as in this side of the Gate. From somewhere in Mexico or points south."

The elder Rolfe nodded. "Perhaps; it's a solid line of reasoning, at least. In theory, with the ability to fiddle with Nostradamus, you could slip recruits in as ordinary *nahua* contract workers . . . use some outlying property of the Collettas as a base. I suppose the Batyushkovs could provide cadre and training, and some Versfeld dissidents; they'd have a lot more recent combat veterans than the clients of any other Families, and they could bring them across as Settlers . . . quietly divert arms from militia requirements over a number of years . . . hmmm."

"Is that enough for you to launch a question before the committee, sir?" she asked eagerly.

Rolfe sighed. "No," he said. "For the same reason—unless we know they're not ready, it might provoke an immediate strike. Charles must have hard evidence, and then we can ram through a suspension of the guilty Families' powers immediately, paralyze them . . . most of their affiliations would sit on their hands in that event, and we could be certain of a quick, relatively bloodless end to this monstrosity."

He stubbed out the cigarillo. "We have moral certainty. We need proof and details. As I said, Charles and I will have to move *very* cautiously, and also cautiously begin some other precautions in case things go badly wrong."

Adrienne wet her lips. "Sir . . . perhaps I could investigate as well. I'd certainly be less conspicuous than any direct agents of the Rolfe Family's security force or household troops, and since the GSF is compromised . . ."

"Yes," her grandfather said. "I'm afraid you're right, my dear."

"I'd appreciate authorization," she said frankly. "I may have to use . . . questionable . . . quasi-legal . . . methods."

"By all means," he said. Then one corner of his mouth quirked up. "By all means."

He opened the drawer of the table and drew out a sheet of heavy cream paper and a circle of sealing wax. Then he took a fountain pen from the breast pocket of his jacket and spoke the words in a murmur as he wrote in an elegant copperplate: "June sixteenth, 2009: The bearer . . . has done what has been done . . . by my authority . . . and for the good of the State."

He signed it with a quick, powerful scrawl—*John Rolfe, Chairman Emeritus*—then peeled the protective paper disks off the sealing wax, attached it by the signature and stamped it with a signet ring he wore on the third finger of his right hand—a VMI class ring, Tom realized. He folded it, tucked it into an envelope, sealed that likewise and handed it to Adrienne. Tully and Adrienne were smiling; Tom exchanged a look of bafflement with Piet Botha, and then they both shrugged.

"Do be careful, milady," the head of the Rolfes said dryly. "I've just given you a blank check. I suggest you be extremely cautious in attracting the attention of the Collettas or Batyushkovs. The death of Anthony Bosco is going to raise enough of a fuss as it is. Move slowly, when you're where they can see you."

❋ ❋ ❋

"Phew," Tom said when they were back in the Hummer.

Adrienne chuckled as the tires crunched on the white rock of the roadway. "It can be a bit overwhelming, meeting the Old Man for the first time. I'm afraid we're going to have to do as he suggested: move slowly, when every instinct I've got screams at me to hit them high and low right away. It'd be a dead giveaway I had emergency business if I ran off somewhere else in the middle of the harvest."

She shook her head and sighed. "Well, there's one cure for the jitters, and it's one we've got available, thank God."

"Which is?" Tom said.

"Physical labor," she said cheerfully.

Tully groaned.

❋ ❋ ❋

Giovanni Colletta had visited the Owens Valley many times before, beginning as a young boy with his father; it was an outlier of the Family domain, and the hunting was excellent. Theoretically, that was why he and the Batyushkov were here now.

"An excellent choice of location, Dimitri," he said. "Not only of a convenient layout and size, but isolated—without a land-link connection to Nostradamus, for instance, and not on any regular flyway."

"*Khorosho,*" the Russian agreed. *Excellent.*

He'd had several vodkas; he wasn't drunk, but his cheeks were a little flushed. The Colletta wished he could drink; he'd never liked flying, but he maintained an iron self-control. And if you had to fly, a customized C-130 was about as comfortable as you could possibly want. His technicians simply loaded a giant container through the big rear ramp of the transport aircraft and into the square hold. He had a suite of rooms that could be transported anywhere in the Commonwealth he needed to go; when he didn't need them, the whole mass could be extracted and the aircraft returned to regular service. Best of all, there were no windows unless you went forward and up a staircase to the control deck, and you could pretend you were on the ground.

The vibration of the four big turboprop engines still came through the walls, paneled though they were in padded bison leather. This was a man's room: dark furniture, racked guns, a bar, books on hunting and wildlife, large comfortable chairs, bear and tiger pelts on the floor.

"We have seen no sign of the Rolfes or the Commission moving against us," the Batyushkov said. "Hopefully that means that your unfortunate young collateral died without revealing anything of our plans. If the Rolfes knew how close those plans were to implementation, they would certainly attempt something."

"That's the best-case analysis." Giovanni Colletta nodded, suppressing a surge of fury. *And that unnatural wolf-bitch of the Rolfe's will pay,* he thought. *You will be avenged, Anthony.*

"Alternatively, they are preparing a trap for us," the Russian said meditatively. "Yet unless they act soon, we will be able to kick open any trap from the inside. Our plan is robust and does not depend upon all things going as we hope."

"Adrienne Rolfe is being carefully watched," the Colletta assured him. "So far she has done nothing out of the ordinary. If she does, we will be immediately informed."

The commander of his household troops came through and saluted, a slim man of medium height with a thin black mustache, a sallow complexion and a strong hooked nose. He was a Colletta collateral himself, sent through the American military academy at West Point and several years of active service in the Eighty-second Airborne. That had been done at vast trouble and expense—establishing the identity and faking his later "death" convincingly had been a nightmare, in these days when DNA tests were routinely done as part of a coroner's examination. It was an investment that would pay off handsomely in times to come, when the Commonwealth came under the rule of the Collettas and went conquering worldwide.

"Sir," he said. "We are approaching the landing strip at Lake Salvatore."

"Thank you, Major Mattei," Giovanni said.

The note of the engines changed, a lower growl as they crossed the Sierra heights and began their drop toward the landing strip. Giovanni made conversation, nearly certain the Russian knew nothing of his nervousness—it would not do to lose face.

There was a jolt as the plane's wheels touched down, and a juddering rumble as it slowed, then a jerk as the parachute brake deployed. The aircraft slowed to a halt, then taxied for a few minutes on the long dirt strip. There was a whine as the rear ramp descended; then hot, dry air cataracted in as the rear doors of the lounge were opened. Giovanni walked forward, squinting a little against the harsh bright desert sunlight; his cotton bush jacket stuck to his skin for an instant as the heat set sweat flowing, then sucked it up.

A Hummer was waiting beside the ramp, and beside it a tall blond man in uniform. He saluted and kissed the hands of the Primes.

Batyushkov embraced him. "Yuri Alexeievich!" he said. "It is good to see you once more."

"Colonel Garshin," Giovanni said more coolly, nodding politely but maintaining a proper distance.

They climbed into the hardtopped Hummer; two more of the open topped model preceded and followed them, with machine guns at the ready. The lodge stood a few miles north of the shore of Lake Salvatore, a long, low ranch-style dwelling of adobe, with wooden galleries on both sides. North of that was something new: several hundred acres of tilled land, tall green corn and potato vines and wheat stubble, fed by furrows diverted from the river that ran down from the High Sierras to the west. Those stood along the horizon like teeth reaching for heaven, towering fourteen thousand feet above the flat sagebrush-covered valley floor; scattered near the lake and the settlement were herds of cattle tended by mounted cowboys. From the buildings a new road drove south and east, into the Inyo range, more barren and bitter than the Sierras, the outliers of deserts as stark as any on Earth.

Dimitri Batyushkov waved his hand at the mountains on both sides as they drove past the lodge and turned southeast, along the lakeshore and toward the lower peaks that separated the Owens from Death Valley.

"An excellent protective barrier, and an even better location for surveillance radar," he said jovially.

Giovanni nodded; that emphasized the primacy of the Colletta contribution to the enterprise.

"How does the training progress?" he asked Colonel Garshin.

"Fairly well, sir," the man replied; his English was thickly accented but fluent enough. "The men are of fairly high quality for black-arsed savages; the main problem apart from teaching them a civilized language is that they are wholly illiterate and unfamiliar with the simplest machines—with wheelbarrows, even. You will understand that this renders the most elementary training more difficult and time-consuming. Certainly they are ferocious enough. Their main complaint is the lack of liquor and women."

"I trust you can maintain discipline," Giovanni said.

The Russian officer smiled thinly; he had a broad, high-cheeked face with slightly slanted eyes of cool blue, below cropped hair the color of birch wood.

"Oh, we maintain a fine discipline, you will find, sir," he said. "Basic infantry training is complete, and we have moved on to the specialized segments. Within broad limits, the more time we have for those, the higher our chances of swift success when we strike."

It was only twenty miles to the site of the mine, but that meant climbing nearly eight thousand feet in the last eight miles; they began by bumping and jouncing up a wash, and then up a poor excuse for a road that wove drunkenly along the mountainside. The air felt chilly and thin by the time they reached their destination nearly three hours later. Dun wilderness stretched away to the west and north and south; they were nearly at the crestline, on a gently sloping plateau below a much steeper section of the mountainside. As they turned, the road seemed to disappear; the blue surface of Lake Salvatore glinted like a great turquoise jewel set amid the dun-green sage; the lodge was barely visible, the runway a brown thread drawn with a ruler, and the cultivation a postage stamp on a land that extended for infinite blue distance.

Barracks built of fieldstone mortared with mud sprawled about the camp; the entrance to the false mine hid the main armory, and the crisp new lines of a great square building were supposed to contain crushing mills and smelters. Smoke did pour out of a stack; what the Russians called *maskirovka*—not just camouflage, but concealment that actively misled.

And at the edge of the camp, on an X of great timbers, a naked brown man hung in chains spiked to the wood.

"As you can see, we take energetic measures to maintain good order," Garshin said. "This man attempted to desert."

"Well, that ought to teach them the consequences of failing to make a clean break," Major Mattei said, his voice and face carefully neutral.

"Indeed," the Batyushkov agreed happily. "Now, you are proceeding to more specialized training?"

"Yes, sir," Garshin said. He pointed to the larger, newer building. "That is our duplicate of the Gate complex. All units have been through the assault training at least once, and we are stepping up the pace. Things go faster, since the unteachables have been eliminated. I anticipate little further attrition; no more than one or two percent."

CHAPTER FIFTEEN

Seven Oaks Manor, Rolfe Domain
June 2009

The Commonwealth of New Virginia

Roy Tully nodded warily to the big Afrikaner as he walked through the gardens at the rear of the Seven Oaks manor house. Piet Botha returned the gesture with a control that showed he returned the same cautious respect, untinged with anything so sentimental as liking. That told Tully something in itself: The bigger man was smart enough not to let the contrast in their sizes fool him into underestimating a possible opponent.

That is one serious badass, Roy thought. *If the time ever comes, there won't be any "Freeze" or "You're under arrest" bullshit. I'll just put a clip right through the center of mass—and then a couple of rounds into the head to be really sure.*

Adrienne had "suggested" that he report to the stable boss, since he'd been emphatically uninterested in helping took the shocks, or whatever you called throwing parcels of wheat around. That was one advantage of *not* being a big muscular slab of beef like Tom: People didn't automatically look at you and think of all the work you could accomplish. He managed to find the laneway to the stables, a strip of hoof-marked dirt under the cool shade of an avenue of pepper trees. But it was blocked by people and two horses bearing pack saddles, each carrying a pair of wooden barrels; the crowd included several kids of around ten or so and one extremely good-looking young woman in jeans and checked shirt and Western hat. She was black-haired and full-figured, and leading the animals with easy competence.

"Hi!" Tully said brightly. "Looking for the stable boss."

"You're looking at her," the young woman said. She transferred both leading reins to one hand and shook with the other. "Sandra Margolin."

"Roy Tully," he replied. "I'm supposed to report to you."

"Thank God," she said. "Henning's taken all my people for the harvest and I'm trying to do six men's work with myself and a bunch of kids. You know anything about horses?"

"They're big and they've got four legs and they eat grass," Tully said helpfully, grinning. Sandra smiled broadly herself. "Well, hell, that's honest," she said. "You're the other FirstSider, right? Here. You lead one of these. We're taking some water out to the harvest gangs, me and these imps of Satan here."

He took one of the leading reins, holding it the way she did—the slack in the left hand, and the right close to the horse's chin, ignoring the way it slobbered slightly. The powerful earthy, grassy smell of the animal filled his nostrils as they took a right turn onto a graveled lane that fronted the houses that stood south of the manor.

"So, Sandra," he said, "how did you get to be stable boss?"

Yelling and spreading your tail feathers worked wonders for peacocks, but it had limitations for humans; a lot of guys didn't realize how much women liked it when a man *listened* to them. He suspected that that went double for New Virginia.

✱ ✱ ✱

Well, this is a new experience, Tom thought, leaning on his fork and watching the tractors pull away from the group of workers.

The fork was a shaft of polished ash nearly six feet long, topped by two thin, elegantly curved steel tines—the original style of pitchfork, nothing like the digging implement. The overnight fog had lifted since they returned from Rolfe Manor, except for banks that hung like drifting mystery among the thick riverside forest—perhaps the fervent prayers he'd heard, interlarded with equally heartfelt curses, had something to do with it. The sun was clear of the Vaca hills to the east and gave promise of a long, hot, cloudless day; he was grateful for the big-brimmed straw hat he'd been given. Everyone was wearing one, or a cloth equivalent; most of the women had bandannas tied around their heads beneath.

Four tractors were pulling their side-mounted reaper-binders through the ripe wheat, the first vehicle's wheels running along a grass verge that lined the inside of the fence. The others were in a staggered line, each ten yards back from the one in front, with the tractor moving through the stubble left by the machine in front, its reaper out in the grain. The long creels turned, pushing a swath of grain backward over the cutting bar; the tying mechanism bound the straw into sheaves and dropped them in a neat, closely spaced row. The noise of the tractor's diesel and the clattering rattle and buzz of the reaper made him suddenly conscious again of how quiet it was here—no background hum of machinery and traffic and aircraft and voices, so the sound of the harvester echoed distinct and solitary.

"Wait a minute," he said as another tractor came up pulling a flatbed trailer with an outward-slanting frame fastened to the front and rear, ten feet high; several more followed it. "Why do you have to get all these sheaves up right away? It's not as if you've got to worry about summer rains here!"

Adrienne looked up from where she was conferring with Henning. "Well, you may have noticed that we have a lot of birds here," she said, nodding upward.

Tom looked up. There *were* a lot of them there, even by local standards. More waited in chattering flocks in the cypress trees that ran into the distance along the side of the wheat field, or in the boughs of the occasional valley oak left amid the cultivation: rock doves, band-tailed pigeons . . . Even more birds were scrambling or flying out of the path of the reapers—great explosions of ring-necked pheasant going *kaw-kwak!,* and even larger coveys of brown California quail, chicken-sized birds looking a little as if they'd been squeezed between the leaves of a book, the males with an absurd little feather plume dangling over their noses, and all of them going *chi-CAH-go* at the tops of their voices.

"And deer," Henning added. "Nocturnal, but they can clear these fences easily enough. Ditto mule deer, elk, and a couple of those new types of antelope. There's one not much bigger than a rabbit that's a bigger *pest* than the rabbits."

"Dik-diks, that's what they're called," Adrienne said. "Not to mention bear, black and grizzly. And rabbits . . . The only ones that don't like wheat are the cougars and leopards and wolves. Even the coyotes will eat grain. Not to mention grapes, but that's another story—everything loves grapes."

Henning nodded. "If we let the sheaves lie out more than a couple of days, we'd lose half the yield," he said. "No way we could stand guard on three hundred acres for months."

"Just asking," Tom said. *Seems there's a downside to the abundant wildlife.* "I suppose the ones that won't eat grain like sheep," he said.

"Tell me about it," Adrienne said, rolling her eyes, and Henning grunted agreement. "And they like veal and pork, too. And when a grizzly decides that the walnuts or the cherries or the figs belong on the ground, where he can eat 'em, not on the tree . . ."

Then she looked over at the progress the reapers were making, nodded and waved the first tractor pulling a flatbed forward. It came up between the two rows of sheaves and geared down to a slow walk, then stopped.

Adrienne whistled. "All you first-timers, over here!" she called. "Gather 'round!"

Tom obediently gathered 'round with a bunch of fourteen-year-olds who came up to his breastbone, and several of the younger *nahua,* who were about the same height. An older *nahua* gave a running translation for the Mesoamericans.

"All right," Adrienne said. "There are going to be six tractors pulling flatbeds—four loading, one on its way back to the rickyard or unloading there, and one on its way back here—three people on both sides of each flatbed; you load for forty-five minutes and rest for fifteen while your flatbed is away. You'll be tossing the sheaves to the spreaders."

She pointed to the flatbed. Two workers were standing on each of the flat trailers, wearing canvas bib aprons over their working clothes, and gloves with elbow-length sleeves attached. Adrienne went on: "Don't toss too hard. You'll wear yourselves out if you do, and waste grain, not to mention stabbing people with the pointy end. Just put the fork into the sheaf a little behind the binding . . ."

She walked up to the trail of grain and suited action to words. The tines slid into the bundled grain with a slight *shink* sound; her gloved right hand moved backward.

". . . slide your hand back on the handle . . ."

She lifted, turned, pivoted, movements as smooth and graceful as a seal sliding off a rock, and the effort was just enough to present the sheaf at the right height.

". . . and swing it up."

The worker on the flatbed was one of the teenagers they'd picked up on the way to the house yesterday, the bashful dark-haired one. The youngster took the sheaf off the tines with the same deceptively easy-looking skill, bending to place it horizontally against the frame at the front of the trailer, and tamping it down with a kick of her boot heel.

"Don't try to rush," Adrienne said, moving on to the next. "Everyone's got to be synchronized. You're all partnered up with an experienced hand; listen to them. OK, people, let's go!"

She walked over to Tom; evidently she was the one "partnered up" with him; a big dog ambled at her heels, occasionally wagging its tail and then flopping down to watch the people work, with the air of someone humoring lunatics. The flatbeds moved off at the pace of a leisurely stroll, arrayed in a staggered line like the harvesting machines. That was the only leisurely thing about the proceedings; when you had to keep up *and* keep the wheat flowing smoothly, your movements tended to the brisk. Yet the sheaves weren't heavy at all, and Tom was hugely strong, and in first-class condition. The first half hour was just enough to bring out a sweat.

"You're going to regret that," Adrienne said, swinging up another sheaf with an easy, smooth motion, timing each word to her breath.

"Regret what?" Tom said, following suit.

His pitch wasn't as practiced, but it got the sheaf where it was supposed to be, and the stacker didn't have to dance back from the points of the tines the way she'd had to do a couple of times with the other greenhorns.

"You're muscling the sheaf up," Adrienne said. Her breathing was slow, even, controlled to a perfect match with her movements. "You're lifting it."

"That's bad?"

"It will be in four hours, or six," she said. "Use your left hand as a fulcrum and the shaft of the fork as a lever. Pivot the sheaf up. Like this."

He tried it for a while, but the effort of moving his hands on the ash wood seemed more than it was worth, particularly since he was wearing rather stiff work gloves. He was also going to get blisters eventually; they were task-specific. It got a little harder as they went on; the stackers were standing on layer after layer of sheaves, and he had to lift a lot more to get each sheaf to them. After three quarters of an hour, the flatbed carried a huge mass of yellow grain on paler white-blond straw, piled up like a giant blunt wedge between the frames at each end.

"That's it!" the brunette girl—*Anne-Marie, that's her name,* Tom reminded himself—cried out from the top of the stack. "Full up!"

The tractor backed and turned carefully, then drove off across the reaped stubble with the great stack bouncing and swaying behind it. Tom and Adrienne and the rest of their group walked over to the section next to the unreaped grain, leaning on their forks and waiting for the flatbed to return; Adrienne's dog followed, shifting into a patch of shade cast by the standing crop. The wheat whispered with a dry rustling voice; it was a lot taller than the short stiff-stalk hybrids his family had raised, waist-high on him instead of knee-high-and-a-bit, but it had a familiar smell—dusty and mealy at the same time. The itchiness of culms stuck in his sweat was familiar too, and not nearly as bad as after the days he'd spent in the bed of a truck shoveling the loose grain pouring out of a combine's spout.

A kid came up to him holding out a big mug of water; it had a slight mineral tang, product of the volcanic mountains to the west, and tasted wonderful. He nodded thanks, and the boy—he was about eleven, wearing a baseball cap and shorts—dashed off; Tom looked around and saw two horses loaded with barrels of water, and a bucket brigade of kids a bit too young for the work he was doing trotting around handing people cupfuls.

And Roy, talking to . . . Say, that's the old Indian woman's granddaughter. Sandra Margolin, he thought. She threw back her head and laughed, a caroling sound that carried across the hundred feet between them.

He nodded toward them. "Looks like Roy's made a friend," he said.

Adrienne looked and nodded. "I'm not surprised," she said. "With his line of patter, that is. He makes you laugh." She frowned in thought, then spoke quietly after checking that nobody else was likely to overhear. "I think we need to bring Sandra in on this."

Tom blinked in surprise. "I thought we were supposed to keep things confidential."

"Sandy knows how to keep her mouth shut; I've known her all my life, and we can trust her. She's my stable boss here; her father was before her. What she doesn't know about horses isn't worth knowing, and she's done a lot of rough-country work; I suspect that we're going to be needing that skill set before this is over. . . . I've had a few thoughts on what the Collettas are up to. Specifically, on where."

* * *

Jim Simmons extended his hand. "Botha," he said.

The Afrikaner took it, a firm shake without any squeezing nonsense. "Simmons," he replied.

His gaze probed the stiff way the younger man sank into a lounger on the terraced pavement behind the manor. "How are you doing, man?"

"I'm mobile," Simmons said. "The doctors say I'll be fit for duty in two weeks or so; it's healing fast—neither of the arrows went very deep. Kolo's ahead of me."

The Indian was sitting on his heels with his back against a planter and his face unreadable. Simmons lay for a moment, soaking up the morning sunlight and the smell of flowers and water and the wild forests on the mountains rearing to the westward.

God, but I'm glad to be out of that hospital, he thought. *And glad to be out of the city. All those people and buildings in one place always give me hives.* The trip up from Rolfeston had been a bit rough, but . . .

"Sorry to hear about your partner, old boy," he went on. "He saved my arse from those hostiles."

Botha nodded. "Miss Rolfe said I should fill you in," he said.

Simmons felt his lips curl back and show teeth; it wasn't a friendly expression, but Botha echoed it—they were on the scent of the same game this time. They'd also both been hunters their entire adult lives. Hunters, and hunters of men not least.

"Bit of a bliddy coincidence, those bushmen having rifles and knowing how to use them, wasn't it?" the Afrikaner said. "Here's what I heard among my own folk, when I went back to my farm after we got back from FirstSide. I should have suspected it; hell, Schalk was always trying to get me interested. . . ."

* * *

Tom pitched another sheaf. This was the first time he'd ever gotten a producer's-eye look at a California farming landscape, in contrast to the view from a car, or backpacking through the wilderness.

Of course, this isn't much like anything in my *world's California,* he thought dutifully. *Except in the basic geography.* And this wasn't the view from the cab of an eight-wheel modern tractor either, high off the ground and enclosed.

On his own feet, it looked . . . *larger,* he thought. *Quite a bit larger.*

He would have expected the valley to feel narrow, but instead it simply seemed directed, oriented by the mountains looming to his right as he looked south and the more distant ones to his left. The flat fifty-acre field of wheat was big when you were attacking it this way, a rustling mystery as the tractors chewed their four staggered swaths through it. The redwood fences and rows of cypress windbreaks alternated, closing in the view either way; he knew consciously that this trough in the earth was only an hour or so drive from top to bottom even on the local gravel roads, but emotionally it seemed to stretch for days both ways, as if his mind were putting it on a foot-travel scale.

A rabbit came out of the wheat and looked at the humans. Adrienne's dog pointed an alert muzzle its way, and the rabbit obviously decided that discretion was the better part of valor, by the way it turned and dashed back into the standing grain.

The stubble was also taller than a combine would have left, which made the boots and gaiters a good idea—cut wheat stems had sharp ends. He looked down and kicked the stubble tentatively; there were thick green shoots wound into the straw, some just tall enough to be lopped off by the reaper's cutter bar. Far too uniform for weeds, probably some sort of fodder crop undersown into the grain in the spring.

"Grass ley?" he asked her, half grunting as he lifted another sheaf.

"Legume-grass mixture," she replied. "Two years in grain, four in grass, then back."

The tractor came back, pulling the empty flatbed. Adrienne whistled cheerfully, and twirled her fork around her body for a moment like a martial-arts staff.

"Do many of your, ah, landholders pitch in like this?" he asked as they resumed work. "I would have thought horse-backing around and directing the peasants with a riding crop would be more appropriate."

"I don't have any tenants here, which means there's a lot more to do than most landholders have with just their home ranches, and I always did like to lend a hand—Dad thought it was an affectation, 'playing at peasants,' as he called it."

"Which was why you kept doing it?"

Adrienne shrugged ruefully. "Well, at that time, if Dad had said sleeping with grizzly bears was a bad idea, I'd probably have decided that they were really sort of cute. . . . Anyway, different domains, different Family traditions. The von Traupitzes like to do the blood-and-soil Germanic chief-tain thing; I doubt any of the Collettas or their collaterals get closer to harvest than eating the results, or watching. The Contessa approved of that, though she despised old Salvo—and it was mutual, believe me. Not that it makes much difference; allod farms work this way too, just on a much smaller scale, the tenant's family and a couple of extras."

The sheaves got a little heavier as the day wore on, the sun went higher in the cloudless blue sky and the tempera-ture went up to the low eighties, although it was a dry heat that sucked the sweat off his skin. There was less chattering, as most of the workers fell into a steady rhythm that didn't call for thought. He did himself; it had been a while since he'd worked on a farm, and never like this, but it wasn't as bad as humping the boonies in body armor and full pack with an M240 machine gun in his arms.

Much better, in fact; more like backpacking. He wasn't fighting to keep alert all the time so some *shaheed*—or just plain "shithead," as the army slang put it—the sensors missed couldn't shoot him, or wondering if he was about to step on a mine.

The sound of a long spoon beating on an iron triangle jarred him out of his trancelike state. His back twinged just

slightly as he stood erect and peered from under the brim of
his hat; that happened when you repeated the same sequence
of motions over and over, and especially if they weren't motions you were used to. A tractor and flatbed loaded with
wicker boxes were parked under one of the oak trees.

"Lunchtime!" someone shouted, which raised a ragged
cheer; he looked upward, and then confirmed it by a glance
at his wrist—one o'clock in the afternoon.

Everyone stacked their forks and headed toward the valley oak near the edge of the harvested zone; he'd asked
someone why any of the big trees were left in the fields, and
the reply had been, "For nice." The dappled shade felt very
nice indeed; the native turf had been left out to the drip line
of the tree, in a smooth oval eighty feet long. The long grass
was getting dry and prickly with the season, and the asterlike
blue flowers that looked pretty from a distance had fanged
stems, but the flatbed's cargo included blankets. Those gave
evidence that horses could sweat, but he was fairly pungent
himself by now. Adrienne settled down not far away, stretching like a cat.

"Stiff?" she asked.

"Well . . . a little," he said. "Maybe I should have listened
more carefully."

The flatbed also held two large oak casks, used ones that
had once held wine for aging; from what he'd heard, you
could do that only once or twice before switching to new.
Now one held ice-cold water, and the other fresh-squeezed
lemonade, equally icy. He sluiced the dust out of his throat
with a mug of the lemonade, downed three of the water to replace what had left rimes of salt on his T-shirt, then took another of the lemonade, savoring the cool tart-sweet taste.
Eager hands helped to unpack the wicker baskets. They held
wrapped piles of sandwiches made by splitting long loaves
of crusty bread in half—bread so fresh-baked that the butter
had half melted into the inner surfaces. The filling was
shaved honey-cured ham, slathered with homemade mayonnaise, onions, pungent cheese and garlicky mustard. There

were also crocks of potato salad speckled with bits of pickled red pepper and laced with boiled shrimp, and . . .

"Roast quail?" he said dubiously. "Bit fancy for lunch in the field, isn't it?"

Someone laughed, picked up a rock from the dusty soil and shied it at a section of bound sheaves not far away. A dozen quail who'd been pecking at grain on the ground—and still in the ear—ran or flapped away.

"Watch out for the birdshot," the wag said, and got a round of laughter.

"Point taken," he said, loading his plate; saliva was flooding into his mouth at the smell. "No objections."

He began stoking himself, then stopped for a moment to spit out a piece of the predicted birdshot and chuckled. At Adrienne's lifted brow he went on: "I was remembering times I was so hungry even MREs tasted good," he said. "I'm not quite that hungry now . . . but this is a lot better than MREs."

"Mmmphf," she said, taking the meat off a quail's drumstick, then waving the bone around. "Not quite the gulag-style horror you were expecting, hey?" she added with an ironic tilt of an eyebrow.

"Well, not so far," he said grudgingly. "Pass the salt, please."

She did so with a shrug, still smiling slightly. The whole party had been working since dawn, and working hard. When the chatter began after the first wolfish assault on the food he listened and then joined in cautiously; he *was* here to gather information, after all. Most of it was nostalgically familiar from his own boyhood in the upper Midwest: crops, weather and gossip. A few of the older teenagers were going steady and sat together; the rest tended to clump by boys and girls, with a lot of mutual teasing; the older residents of Seven Oaks made a clump of their own, and the *nahua* sat off to one side. A few of the youngest of the contract workers were picking dubiously at food strange to them, but the rest were tucking in enthusiastically. Nearly everyone was ready enough to chat to the newcomer; they assumed he was a friend of Adrienne's, which gave him massive status.

The kids from town were having a reasonably good time; this was harder work than other summer jobs, but paid a lot better too. They and the estate-born seemed to have similar plans, for the most part: finish high school and do their two years of national service. That would be nominally military for the boys, but he got the impression that it involved more time laboring on public works; they did get basic infantry training, and every adult male had to keep his militia weapons at home. Girls did their service as teaching assistants in elementary schools, helpers in hospitals and nursing homes, or various types of government jobs. Both regarded the service with a mixture of resignation, excitement at getting away from home, and a straightforward corn-fed patriotism that indicated that ironic cynicism wasn't well regarded here.

A few were going to try for the University of New Virginia afterward; evidently you did that only if you were extremely bright, or wanted to be a doctor or high school teacher or something of that order, or had parents who could afford to pay a stiff price for putting on a little polish. The domain—the Rolfes—would pay the fees for a student who did well enough on the entrance exams. The majority said they'd just look for jobs, which none of them were very worried about, and get married. A few wanted to be policemen or sailors exploring worldwide, or Frontier Scouts or troopers in the Gate Security Force; most of the Seven Oaks youngsters planned to work here, or on other estates, or to become farmers on their own eventually.

"Ever wanted to set up for yourself?" Tom asked Henning.

The *mayordomo* shrugged and ate a fig—they were finishing off with those, and cherries, and watermelons. He was a middling-tall man in his forties, with graying brown hair and a slender, wiry build. Tom ate some of the cherries; he'd always liked them, and these were right off the tree, with a dark, intense sweetness better than anything he'd tasted before.

"Couple of my brothers did take up allod farms here in the domain," he said. "Mrs. Durrant—Miz Rolfe's great-aunt—loaned 'em what they needed to get started and said a good word for 'em with her kinfolk. I like it better working here at Seven Oaks. Money's about the same, year over year, and it's steadier—I don't have to worry so much about prices and such."

He waved around at the estate. "Managing a bigger operation's more fun, too, plus it's less grunt labor. A lot of what you're seeing is my work, and my father's and grandfather's—our sweat, and our brains too."

"I meant own land, not rent it," Tom said.

Henning laughed. "Like my grandfather?" he said. "*He* came through the Gate as a man grown, and *he* owned land in Oklahoma. Leastways, he thought he did—until the bank taught him different."

He shook his head. "Heard enough about it from him! He was a good farmer and a hard worker; just not someone to be always figuring how to swallow up the neighbors. So one of his neighbors ended up swallowing *him*. No, thanks. I'd rather answer to a real human being I can talk to, not some set of flesh-and-blood computers who chew you up and spit you out whenever the numbers say they should."

Tom winced slightly. *Well, yeah,* he thought.

Unless you were doing something like growing individually manicured organic zucchini for a high-powered gourmet restaurant, American agriculture meant getting bigger every year or going broke and getting sold up—that was what rising costs and falling prices in a static market meant. As far as he could tell, an allod tenant's rent here in New Virginia was considerably less than most on the other side of the Gate paid in mortgage and taxes. The tenant here lived better on the whole, and wasn't under anything like the sort of relentless competitive pressure his American equivalent was. Landholders competed to get tenants instead; it certainly sounded a lot easier for a young man to get started—there were reasons the average farmer back home was in his fifties.

Of course, here you have to defer to a patron from the Thirty Families, Tom thought. *Of course number two, they don't seem to be as nasty as the Internal Revenue Service, most of the time.*

"What's Ms. Rolfe like to work for?" he went on.

"Not bad," Henning said. "Bit wild as a kid, but that was in Mrs. Durrant's day. Settled down good after that. She knows she's boss, but doesn't think she's great God almighty, if you know what I mean, or that she knows everything." The older man got up and dusted crumbs off his shirt. "No rest for the wicked—I don't like the sound of the engine on Maconi's rig. Better have a look at it before we start up again."

Tom rejoined Adrienne; something she'd said back in Napa had come back to him. "What was that bit you said to the kids at that soda joint in town? That you weren't asking for their votes? What votes?"

"For the House of Burgesses." At his quirked eyebrow she went on: "The name's from Old Virginia's history. Sort of a House of Commons to the committee's House of Lords; it votes on taxes and suchlike. Of course . . ."

". . . we don't need no steenkin' taxes," Tom said. "And I'll give you any odds you want the Families put up most of the candidates, right? Competing by proxy in this burgesses thing."

"The Old Man set it up that way," she said; they were a little apart from the others, a social space she seemed to get automatically when she wanted it. "He's not what you'd call a fervent advocate of democracy, but he does believe in checks and balances. People need the Families, but every member of the Families needs the support of his Settlers, his affiliation. If he tries riding roughshod over them, they'll go find someone else."

Everyone dozed for an hour after lunch. The rest of the day was harder; he was thinking too hard, and couldn't get his mind back into an easy working rhythm. The working day in harvesttime continued until sundown, too, which was around eight—longer, for those whose turn it was to take shotguns or rifles and night-sight goggles and try to keep the wildlife out of the cut grain. There would probably be more quail for lunch tomorrow. By the time he'd ridden a flatbed back to the manor, showered, and wolfed down an enormous portion of stew and bread and steamed vegetables, he was also feeling the truth of what Adrienne had said—muscling the sheaves high all day had been a bad idea. Individually their weight was trivial, but doing some quick mental arithmetic showed how many tons of the stuff he'd been heaving, mostly to a height well above his head.

I'll feel worse in the morning, he thought.

He did.

CHAPTER SIXTEEN

Seven Oaks, Rolfe Domain
June 2009

The Commonwealth of New Virginia

"I always find a map helps me think," Tom said, looking up at the one he had pinned to the corkboard, as the people summoned to the meeting trickled casually in.

At least I'm not too tired to think, he mused. After four days of the harvest his body was adjusting nicely; he had plenty of energy for the after-dinner planning session. *I think I'm even losing a little weight—and I didn't think I had any surplus.*

"Feeling better?" Adrienne asked, bending to thump the ribs of one of the big dogs that hung around her. The white-bibbed cat looked down disapprovingly from the top of a big globe mounted in a wheeled frame of oak and polished brass.

"Somewhat," Tom replied.

In fact he was feeling excellent, better than he'd felt since his last long hiking trip, up in Glacier National Park. The aches had gone; he was in fundamentally good condition, after all. He also felt loose-limbed and strong and quick, as if a spring in muscle and bone that had been fading for the last few years without his being quite conscious of it had come back sometime in the past week.

"I always get the sensation my body's flushing out poisons after a spell FirstSide," Adrienne went on. "Whether or not it's true."

"Ah . . ." Tom said. "That's interesting."

Because I feel just like that now, and don't want to admit it, he thought, and then shrugged hopelessly as he saw her sly grin and knew she'd followed the thought. *Let's face it, for someone of my tastes, this place has a lot of the features I'd pick for Wish Fulfillment Land. Of course, in other ways . . .*

The map room at Seven Oaks was an annex off the library; there were big tables and slanted desks, atlases, rackboxes to hold maps and graphics, and a smell of paper and book dust and leather, mixed with greenery from the open windows giving on a courtyard garden. There was also a big thin-film screen for calling up data, and a printer that could handle large maps at need.

There were seven people in the room: Tom and Adrienne, Tully, Piet Botha and Sandra Margolin, plus a brown-haired young man named Jim Simmons, and a silent Indian called Kolo in a breechclout who crouched in a corner, his black eyes intent. They were Frontier Scouts, evidently something like his job with Fish and Game mixed with the sort of thing he'd done in the army Rangers.

The stock of paper maps included an excellent series for the western part of North America; they were marked in the lower left-hand corner with the words *Commission Cartographic Authority.* He supposed that the basic geography would be the same as FirstSide, minus the draining and damming and clearing of the past three hundred years—there might be differences in the details, the course of rivers and so forth. Evidently the Commission had spent a good deal of effort over the past sixty years to keep theirs current.

The land was familiar, but man's borders were utterly strange. The map showed the outlines of the domains: a thick clump around the Bay Area, an outlier around Puget Sound, and another series down the coast of Southern California culminating in a big blotch in the lowlands between Santa Monica and San Diego. A trail of dots ran from Sacramento to the Mother Lode mines, then up through the Lake Tahoe area and from there into Nevada; they faded off to a last tiny outpost on the site of Denver.

"All right," he said, moving his hand from Oregon to Baja. "It's unlikely in the extreme that the enemy would be trying to train their clandestine force anywhere close to the coast. Too many people, too many aircraft."

Though that's an irony, he thought as the others nodded. *Two hundred thousand all the way from Portland to San Diego! And a couple of hundred planes all up, including little puddle-jumpers.*

"At the same time, they have to be close enough to Rolfeston to strike at the Gate. Unfortunately, with a C-130, that means anywhere within two thousand miles—two thousand with a full load, more if you trade off cargo for fuel."

"Good plane, the Herky Bird," Tully added. "I spent a lot of time aboard them myself—and they're still making them, which is not bad considering the design was finalized in 1951."

"We've been using them since 1958," Adrienne said. "They're our standard heavy transport and passenger aircraft . . ."

"And Colletta Air owns dozens," Piet Botha said. "Sorry, has owned dozens—every once in a while one is lost or wears out. Or so the reports they file on Nostradamus say."

"Or they could just divert some at the last moment," Adrienne said. "Most of the pilots would do whatever Giovanni Colletta tells them unless they had very good reasons not to; they're part of his affiliation, after all. Telling them to go to point X would be simple enough, and once the troops were on board they'd be committed."

The Indian said nothing. *But I suspect he's following the conversation much better than he lets on,* Tom thought. There was a disturbing, feral quality to the man's gaze, and the way he squatted and held himself was subtly different from anything he'd seen before. *Of course, I've never seen an Indian whose people haven't been in contact with us for a century at least.*

"Ten Hercules would be enough to carry a thousand infantry and their equipment, which is more than they'd need," Tom pointed out. "Cruising at just under four hundred miles an hour. At full range, that means anywhere within *this* radius."

He picked up a compass, set it to the right distance, and scribed a three-quarter circle with the center on the Gate. "Everything within this line. That's half the continent. Let's start eliminating what we can."

"They wouldn't want to be farther away than they must," Simmons said. "To hit fast when they go for it, and to cut down on the number of trips they'd have to make to bring in supplies while they're getting ready."

"Yeah, the usual logistics problems," Tully said. "Five hundred men minimum, plus some support personnel . . . who also eat their heads off and need bunks . . . say seven hundred to twelve hundred all up, even with a real high teeth-to-tail ratio, and more if they've got more than five hundred troops. That's a couple of tons of food a day, plus water, housing, uniforms, stores, spare parts, medical supplies, barracks or tents, fuel. . . ."

"Cover," Adrienne said thoughtfully; she was sitting with a pad of paper in front of her, tapping her chin with a pen. "It would be somewhere remote, but with something going on to cover a lot of transport. *And* somewhere they could produce some of the supplies themselves, to keep the transport needs to a minimum."

Tom looked at the map again. All the mountainous parts of California and the Pacific Northwest, not to mention the deserts, were marked in green as *Permanent Commission Reserve*. That meant they were national parks, near enough; shades of the color indicated whether they were slated for sustained-yield timbering, hunting preserve attached to one of the Families, or absolute wilderness. The coastal valleys like the Napa or the Salinas or the Santa Ynez were settled, or parts of them were. Sections of the southern basins around the site of LA and San Diego were too; the rest, and the Central Valley, were part reserve, part unallocated land waiting to be handed out as the population grew.

"I don't think there's much doubt as to the where, when you take all that into account," Adrienne said.

She pulled a thick reference work down from a shelf and began to thumb through it: *Territorial Domains and Possessions of the Thirty Families, 2007 Edition.*

"'Chapter Seven: The Colletta Family. Primary domain . . . estates in Hawaii . . .' Aha!" she said, and Tom felt a hunter's grin appear on his face. She went on: "'Owens Valley: Colletta outlying possession, granted in 1962 . . .' right, the Old Man told me about that once—something to do with keeping old Salvo Colletta sweet after taking Hawaii away from him. Hunting lodge and small airstrip until 2005; then the Collettas petitioned the committee and were granted permission to open the Cerro Gordo silver mines; construction work began the following spring. Hmmm. Quote: 'Doubts were expressed as to the profitability of the venture,' end quote."

Tom ran one thick finger down the Sierra Nevada until he came to its southeastern edge. It ended in some of highest peaks in the continental United States; Mount Whitney was over fourteen thousand feet. The less lofty Inyo Range paralleled that north-south scarp to the east; between them was a long, flat trough, with a river running down it to a sizable lake—the Owens Valley, and Owens Lake. On FirstSide the river was the source of a lot of LA's water, brought down from the snowmelt of the Sierras' peaks and glaciers and then over the deserts and mountains via aqueduct and siphon and canal. The valley floor was high semidesert; right across the Inyos was Death Valley, much lower and hotter—a desert, plain and simple, with no "semi" about it.

Southward was the Mohave; not as bad as Death Valley, but pretty damned bleak, as he knew by experience.

"Bingo," he said softly. "Just far enough away to be remote—"

"There isn't anywhere within the zone we control that's *more* remote," Simmons said. "No overland traffic at all—

everything goes in and out by air. It might as well be an island."

"*Yes!*" Adrienne said, hissing the word. "The Collettas operate the mines there under license from the Commission—nobody would ask any questions, as long as the silver output was consistent with the ore body and the labor they were putting into it."

Tom peered more closely at the map, then got out a smaller-scale one that covered the southern Sierras. "I've been through there FirstSide," he said. "The old Cerro Gordo mines are up this side canyon, just east of Owens Lake, or what used to be Owens Lake."

"This isn't FirstSide, thank God," Simmons said, leaning forward and then wincing slightly. "Owens Lake is very much there, a hundred and twenty square miles of it. It's officially called Lake Salvatore, of course."

Tom frowned. "But if the Collettas are supposed to be operating a silver mine here and they aren't really pulling out silver . . ."

". . . then they could slip the silver in from their share of other mines," Adrienne said. "The committee checks pretty carefully to see that none of the Families running the smaller mines shorts the Commission. They aren't going to look further if the amount *is* right—it's the same trick we use First-Side, with the mining properties we own there. If the Collettas want to waste money on a marginal operation, who cares? Most of the production comes from the big digs that the Commission runs directly, anyway."

He whistled. "Perfect, then. Hmmm . . . an aerial recon run? Visit by an inspector?"

He looked around; Adrienne, Simmons and Botha were all shaking their heads.

The woman explained: "First, there probably wouldn't be much to see from the air; not if they've kept it quiet this long. Second, that would let them know what *we* know, or expect—which might trigger off the coup we're trying to prevent. And yes, they'd know the minute the plane lifted off. There aren't enough airports in the Commonwealth to keep that secret, and you'd have to use military aircraft, either the committee's or requisitioned from one of the Families. Not to mention that if *I* were running this, I'd have radar surveillance running from Mount Whitney, and maybe some light ground-to-air missiles, if I could manage to smuggle 'em in from FirstSide."

"Hercs would be perfect for this," Tully said. "They're made to lift from grass and dirt strips. Anything hard and level would do."

"And the Owens would be a good place to grow supplies, too," Tom added. "Plenty of water, this side of the Gate. That means we can't judge their maximum numbers by the amount of supplies they ship in."

They sat and looked at each other, thinking. Sandra went out and came back with a tray of sandwiches and soda; Tom munched at his—excellent thin-cut roast beef with horseradish—and went right on thinking. The soda was a copy of Dr Pepper, the old-fashioned kind.

"The only way I can see to settle this is to go in on the ground," he said at last. "A small party, overland, could get definite well-documented proof and then get it out again. I take it your grandfather could move once he got that?"

Adrienne nodded. "Not a problem. The committee would suspend the Collettas and the Batyushkovs and any other Family involved—raising private forces beyond their quotas, a no-no, arming natives with modern weapons, a really *serious* no-no, and attempted overthrow of the state, pretty well the ultimate no-no. They'd be far too outnumbered, without surprise, and with all the other Families prepared and united against them."

"Well, let's get in on the ground, then," Tom said.

Again, he was conscious of the way the others looked at him—the ones who'd spent a long time here in the Commonwealth, or who'd been born here.

"Easier said than done," Adrienne said. She stood and traced her own lines on the map. "You could try to get a small party in through the San Joaquin, south to Lake Tulare and then over the Sierras. Trouble is, you'd be like a bug on a plate coming in that way, not to mention everyone seeing you as you went through the Carquinez."

"Well, you could come straight up from LA and through the eastern Mohave," Tom said, drawing the pathway. "It's only a couple of hundred . . . ah."

Botha and Simmons nodded, and began to speak at the same time. They exchanged glances, and the big Afrikaner spoke: "Man, there aren't any roads across the desert, except for the one to the borax mines—I live just south of there, on the sea side of the mountains. You might get a caravan of good four-wheel-drive bakkies through, but then again you might not. You'd have to take all your fuel . . . and you'd be bliddy conspicuous dragging a plume of dust, eh?"

Simmons nodded. "The only way to do it without hanging up a HURRAH, WE'RE HERE! sign would be to go on horseback. Over the Krugersberg—the Santa Monicas— through the San Fernando Valley, over the San Gabriels, then north to the Tehachapi and up the eastern front of the Sierras—"

"*Nie, nie,*" Botha said. "Too bliddy obvious, *kerel*. That's the easiest way across the Mohave. We must swing further east, through the springs at Atolia."

Simmons winced slightly. "Love punishment, do you, Piet? You'd have to travel mostly by night . . . but you'd do that anyway, in the Mohave."

Unexpectedly, the Indian spoke, mixing weirdly accented English with his native tongue. Simmons looked at him and replied in the same, then addressed the rest.

"Then there's the Mohave nomads, the"—he spoke something unpronounceable.

The Indian spoke up again: "*Kinun'ya'tuk.* Means 'mixed-up,' or 'many tongues.' People from all peoples."

"They're hostile?" Tom said.

"Very, some of them." Adrienne sighed. "When we cleared out coastal southern California a couple of generations ago, we gave the surviving natives some presents and horses and pointed them east. Some of them kept going— some of them crossed the Mississippi! But a lot didn't; they joined up with the tribes who were already in the Mohave. A fair number of white renegades ended up there, too—deserters, criminals, escaped convicts. A mixed bunch, very tough, and more of them than you might think. There's enough continuous contact across the mountains with the New Virginian settlements that they don't get hit by once-in-a-generation plagues. Plus there are a couple of missionary groups there who do vaccination programs against smallpox and measles and so forth for children brought into their stations."

Tom rubbed at his chin. "Can't see the Mohave desert supporting many people, though."

"Some of them farm part-time along the Mohave valley and the middle Colorado," Simmons put in. "The acclimatization program really changed the ecology in that region, too. Lot of introduced plants—spinifex, saltbush, smooth-skin cactus—and animals. Camels, and things like oryx that metabolize their own water from their feed and don't need to drink. Plus they learned a lot of tricks from us, well-drilling, herding and suchlike."

Botha nodded. "They've been more active the last few years. The occasional hunter or trader in the desert gets chopped, even a few raids over the mountains to steal livestock—"

Tom held up a hand. "How *extremely* convenient for the Collettas," he said dryly. "If they're trying to hide something on the other side of the Mohave Desert."

There were a few heartfelt curses at that; evidently paying Indians to attack your fellow New Virginians was something that made the general treason more emotionally immediate and intolerable.

"A small party will be easier to hide," Adrienne said. "But not too small, or we'd have real problems getting across the desert and past the tribesmen. Everybody here's in, I presume?"

Nods, and a grunt from Botha. "That makes seven," Adrienne said. Botha and Simmons both turned to look at Sandra, who glared back.

"She's good with horses, she can shoot, and I can trust her

not to talk. We need a couple more. Who can we trust, who's got the experience we need?"

Botha rumbled, "My eldest boy, Jan. He's twenty—lived on my *plaas* there more than half his life, and he's been over the mountains before, chasing stock thieves and hunting. Guided *Oom* Versfeld's son on a trip last year; wants to be a white hunter. No nonsense in the boy; I'll vouch for him."

Adrienne nodded, her eyes lost in thought. "That gives us eight guns. I'd be easier with a dozen, but . . . wait. Ralph's too old and he was never a boots-and-saddles type, but Henry Villers would probably be up for it. And I *know* I can trust him."

"Wait a bliddy minute, miss, not a kaffir—"

Adrienne's finger stabbed out at him. "Botha, don't be more of an idiot than God compels you to be. And *don't* try any of those boys'-school pissing-match tricks with me, either. I don't have time for them and I'm not equipped to enjoy them."

They locked eyes for a moment, and then he nodded. "You're in charge, miss."

"I am. While we're getting things settled, let's clarify things. I'm in overall command. Tom here is number two. Sandra will be horse wrangler; Jim will be trail boss. Everyone else is a 'cork.' Jim, what'll we need?"

"Two horses each," the man with the sunstreaked brown hair said. "Three would be better except for the lousy grazing . . . and six mules. Taking it slow and holing up most of the day—which we'd have to do anyway in high summer—two hundred and fifty miles as the crow flies, call it three-fifty our way, and allowing for accidents and a fair share of bad luck . . . we're talking a month to get to Lake Salvatore. Ten, fifteen miles a day at most, and we'll have to stop and rest the beasts when we hit water. Have to carry some barley for them; the grazing will be sparse."

"Make it ten," she said. "I want to talk to Tom about some special gear that might be useful. He was a Ranger, after all. Do up a list of equipment, and we'll see about getting it together without leaving traces on Nostradamus."

She smiled at them, or at least showed her teeth. *Quite the human whirlwind, you betcha,* he thought, amused and bemused at the same time.

"That leaves the question of when," Simmons said. "I'm not fit for action right now; a week, maybe two, the quacks say."

She sighed with exasperation. "I begrudge every minute . . . but we can't charge right in, not just after an interview with the Old Man. I've got to make it look as if I really think we wound everything up FirstSide. So do the rest of you . . . I've applied for long leave from the GSF; I'm overdue on it, anyway. Once the harvest's in, it'll be natural for me to go on holiday. And it'll be natural for you all to stay on until the harvest supper's over, at least—Jim, you and your tracker can use the rest, too. We can finish our planning, do some quiet training, get the gear together, then split up and make our separate ways to a rendezvous point."

Botha shook his head. "High summer in the Mohave! God be with us."

"I hope He is," Adrienne said soberly. "I surely do."

* * *

The harvest ended on Friday, with the last sheaves twisted into a rough human form and everyone following the flatbed into the long strip behind the barns where the wheat ricks were—like thatched huts for giants, each formed around a long pole set in the earth. The local Episcopalian priest blessed the sheaf, and then everyone went off to shower and sleep.

Saturday was a holiday for everyone except the cooks to rest up for the evening's banquet and dance; the smell of baking bread and cooking came in a faint mouthwatering waft from the kitchen wing, along with the woodsmoke smell of oak-fired ovens.

They stood in the gardens behind the manor house. A stone reservoir stood at the hillside end, and from twenty feet up its vine-covered side water poured from the mouth of a cast-bronze lion's head to fall in a shallow pool and then flow into the main basin. The young harvest hands Adrienne had hired were playing around it now, pushing each other under the flow of water and tobogganing down into the swimming pool; it was one of the perks the youngsters had signed up for.

"Up for a ride?" she said, nodding toward the mountains. "Things are going to get serious soon enough."

"Why not?" he said.

"Good thing you were raised in the country," Adrienne said as they walked through the lawns and groves toward the hedge that marked off the service sector of the house grounds. "It's a little rough up there for someone who's never ridden before."

Tom grinned, and felt himself relaxing completely into the smile for the first time since the Gate.

"Hell," he said, "I didn't learn to ride back in North Dakota. Nobody kept horses around our neck of the woods; that would have been a luxury. We used pickups. I learned to ride in Central Asia. Lot of rough unroaded country there, and sometimes we had to move over it in small teams."

They walked through the hedges, down a dirt lane lined with pepper trees, fantastically gnarled light brown trunks and spreading branches that met thirty feet overhead in a tangle of light-flecked green, full of pendulous six-inch clusters of yellow-white flowers. The two dogs who'd followed them were tearing back and forth along the lane, wagging frantically and jumping, with a general air of *Going for a ride, great idea!*

Board fences surrounded grassy paddocks; the stables themselves were a series of low buildings along brick-paved walkways, with adobe to five feet and wood-framed wire grates above. There was an air of neatness, in a stable-esque sort of way; wheelbarrows leaned against buildings, tools racked inside doorways.

The old Indian woman he'd seen on the first day here was sitting in a patch of sun with her back against a stable wall and her feet outstretched, crooning to herself as she wove a basket of willow shoots, sedge, and fern roots; feathers and pieces of abalone shell added to the strange beauty of the pattern. The senile haze cleared for an instant as she saw the two of them walking by and she grinned, exposing a few brown snaggles of tooth and calling out in her own language. Adrienne tossed a reply in the same tongue over her shoulder and the crone cackled louder.

"What was that in aid of?" he asked.

"A speculation about your, ah, height," Adrienne said, glancing at him out of the corners of her eyes. "The Ohlone weren't shy, let's say."

"What did you tell her?"

"Do you really want to know? It had to do with comparing the dimensions of a baby's head and those of—"

"No, not really," Tom said hastily.

Am I blushing? he thought. *Well, let's be honest. I am horny. Very.* It was hard not to be, next to a woman this good-looking, and one you'd made love with, one you liked as well as resented. Some of his mind was still angry; other parts of him had different imperatives.

"Need a horse, Adri?" Sandra Margolin said, setting aside a shovel. "Need an ox, Tom?" she went on with a good-natured smile, as she looked Tom over from head to toe.

"I'll have Ahmed, Sandy. Tom'll take . . . oh, Gustav, I think."

"Oh, you *do* want an ox for him," the part-Indian woman replied, then went on more seriously, "Good idea. We've been skipping things for the harvest, and they could both use some exercise."

She leaned the shovel against a wall and whistled sharply for her assistants, then relayed the order. They led two horses up. He could guess which one was Gustav without much trouble; it was a gelding and stood a bit over seventeen hands, black and glossy and muscular.

He ran a hand down its neck and over the legs. "Sturdy," he said. "I don't recognize the breed." *Not that I'm an expert on horses.* "Reminds me a little of some I saw in the 'Stans. A lot bigger, though."

"Gustav's a crossbreed," Adrienne said. "Hanoverian

warmblood on a Kabardin mare—you know, those north Caucasus mountain horses. Gustav here's certainly plenty agile for his size, and he has extremely tough feet."

Her mount was more lightly built, an Irish hunter, dapple-coated and two inches over fifteen hands. Sandra Margolin and a *nahua* stable hand came out with the blankets and saddles; they were a modified Western type, with several rings in the frame for ropes or gear, and machetes strapped to the left side beneath a coiled lariat; the horses champed a little with eagerness to get going. The young woman came back with the rifles, and they slid them into the molded-leather scabbards that rested at each rider's right knee.

The lane ran through the stables, then out into a big grass paddock right at the foot of the hills, and then through a gate in a deer-high fence and into rougher country, grassland scattered with blue oak. Beyond, it turned into a track up alongside a rivulet that was probably small in spring and had shrunk back to about half that size now. The tinkling of the water over rock made a pleasant counterpoint to the clop of hooves, the occasional jingle of harness and creak of leather, the happy panting of the dogs as they cast back and forth and charged up the steep slopes to either hand, covering four or five times the ground the mounted humans did.

The track showed more deer and elk sign than horse hooves; the north-facing side of the V-shaped notch they were riding in was covered in big timber. Sparse-needled digger pine on the higher rocky slopes gave way to good-sized madrone and blue oak, goldcup oak, with Douglas fir and the odd redwood near the trickle of water—none of the king trees was a real giant like the ones up on the north coast, but they still towered over everything else, rising from forest shadow into the sunlight like great straight-shafted spears. The wildflowers were dying down as June wore on, but there were still clumps of ocean spray with drooping sprays of tiny creamy-white flowers, thickets of bitter cherry with silvery-bronze bark and sweet-smelling snowy clusters of blossom, thimbleberry and trailing blackberry beside the creek, blue chicory beside the trail. Silver-blue and long-tailed coppery butterflies started up from the horses' hooves, though fortunately there weren't many mosquitoes.

The air grew cooler as they angled up the ravine. After an hour or so he noticed something odd—a silence. The dogs stopped running through the underbrush and came back to stand by the horses; the mounts themselves tossed their heads a moment later. They both reined in and scanned the trees as their horses stamped and tossed and shifted their weight from foot to foot as a way of indicating they thought it was a bad idea to stop just then. One of the dogs gave a low growl and pointed, its nose locked on a big canyon oak about a hundred yards away. Tom peered closely, pushing back the brim of his hat with one big hand; dapples of sun and shade moved on the scaly gray bark of the trunk and thick limbs, but he thought that about thirty feet up . . .

"There," Adrienne said, leaning close. He was pleasantly conscious of her breath on his ear and the contact of their knees. "That branch . . ."

". . . there," he said. "That isn't a cougar, is it?"

"No," she said softly. *"Chui."* At his incomprehension, she went on: "We got that word from our when-wes. Leopard. A male, very large."

There was something else jammed into the crutch of a branch higher on the tree: a mule-deer carcass, he thought. And the branch the big cat was lying on looked to be just perfect for dropping on anything that came by on the game trail beneath. He didn't feel particularly alarmed; even big predators avoided people unless you cornered them or did something dumb like running away. Still, he didn't intend to ride under that limb, either.

"Shall we turn back?" he said.

"Not unless you want to," she replied. "There's a very pretty little spot a bit farther on I was planning on showing you. *Le Chui* there's probably been shot at before—they love the taste of dog, not to mention sheep. Pull your rifle out and see what he does."

The cat's head came around sharply as he slowly drew the weapon from the scabbard. It came to its feet as soon as he had the muzzle clear, and growled—a sound with more than a little of a rasping scream in it; then it whirled and went down the trunk of the oak like flowing water, disappearing into the bush so smoothly that scarcely a shrub quivered to the passage of three hundred pounds of carnivore.

"Well, *he* knows what a rifle looks like and what it's for," Tom said. "Doesn't particularly like it, either."

"Neither would I, if I could only bite back," Adrienne said, clicking her white teeth together and laughing. "That was lucky. They tend to be scarce near settled country."

The dogs relaxed, and the horses went forward without objections; he judged that meant the leopard had either gotten downwind or far away, or both. After a half hour of companionable silence they reached the spot she'd spoken of; it bore the first signs of humankind he'd seen amid the mountains.

"Here it is. Quite famous."

"Well, you *could* call it pretty, I suppose," Tom said.

They'd come out of pine-smelling forest onto a jutting triangle that emerged from the canyonside to make a flattish area about a quarter-acre broad, with pockets of growth amid the rocks. A spring bubbled up from the base of the overhanging sheer mountainside to the rear; it had been ringed with stones to collect the flow in a shallow gravel-floored pool, surrounded with a lush growth of star jasmine. That climbed the cliff higher than his head, grew thick around the water, and trailed along the sides of the trickling stream as it wound over the ledge and plunged off the rim. The water disappeared as mist among the trees below, turning to a constant drift of rain. The clustered white blossoms were thick among the vines, and the heady scent mixed with the forest smell and the chill dampness of the springwater. The ledge didn't feel exposed, though; it was as if he'd walked into magic and become part of it, connected with everything he saw yet separate from it, safe and walled away.

Yet it was the view that caught at the throat. They were deep enough into the Mayacamas highlands that the ledge of rock seemed to float disembodied above the steep depths beneath and amid the lower rolling peaks about, gashed with occasional cliffs north to the barely glimpsed cone of Mount Saint Helena. The trees and brush about them merged into a deep green velour in the middle distance, fading to indigo that deepened as the sun declined toward the western crest.

They watered the horses, unsaddled them and tethered them to iron rings set in the living rock where the trail emerged from the mountainside; then they walked forward to the tip of the triangle, where a single small oak cast a patch of grassy shade amid poppies and wild hyacinth; the earth fell away beneath their feet. They could see Seven Oaks below them, toy-tiny yet absurdly close after their hours in the saddle, and the soft-colored palette of the valley beyond: the white steeple of a church in a crossroads village to the north, yellow stubble in blocks amid the green of leys, the tree-studded pasture, the occasional geometrical regularity of a vineyard or olive grove or orchard, and long shadows falling toward the riverbank forest from the lines of Italian cypresses. Light glinted on water, on the windows of the scattered farmsteads, and touched the tops of trees with a moving shimmer as people and animals moved antlike below.

It changed as they watched, tingeing the whole with a yellow haze, turning to burnished gold on the bare tops of the Vacas across the valley floor.

"But it's *not* pretty," he said. His arm went around her waist, and she leaned into his shoulder, a motion that seemed very natural. "Its beautiful . . . like something in a dream, or an old book about stepping through a mirror."

"It's the Land of Lost Content," Adrienne said softly.

The words matched what he saw, but they also had the feel of being part of a larger whole. Adrienne must have felt the question through his arm, for she went on in the same half-dreaming tone:

> Into my heart an air that kills
> From that far country blows:
> What are those blue remembered hills,
> What spires, what farms are those?

That is the land of lost content,
I see it shining plain,
The happy highways where I went
And cannot come again.

"But Granddad found it for us again, just for us, against all hope," she continued, and shivered slightly. "That's what scares me about going through the Gate, Tom, scares me bad every time I leave. What if I can't get back?"

She turned in to his embrace and they kissed. Suddenly their hands were eager on each other, scrambling with belts and fasteners; they rolled on the long silky grass. . . .

Some time later Tom Christiansen laid himself back, sweaty and exhausted—and glad they'd paused for a moment to get a blanket to lie on. *Jesus,* he thought blissfully, staring up at the deepening blue of the sky. *I feel like a teenager again—or did for a couple of hours.* They said a man's stamina peaked at sixteen, and it was all downhill from there. *But maybe not.*

Adrienne propped herself up on an elbow and kissed him. Then she started working her way down his throat; her long, bronze-colored hair tickled, then mingled with the sparse pale blond thatch on his massive chest.

"Adri," he said, "I'm flattered. But I'm also thirty-two, not sixteen—I was just thinking about—*Jesus!*"

He was lost for long moments. When his eyes cleared she was swinging astride him.

"You underestimate yourself, darling," she said, and sank back with a shivering moan. "Turnabout's fair play. . . ."

The smell of star jasmine mingled with sweat and musk; his hands clenched on her hips. Her face was remote, eyes closed behind a mist of swaying hair, until she stiffened and froze, crying out—quivering motionless except for the strong internal clenching. He shouted and heaved convulsively, and heard the sound die in echoes against the rock as she collapsed forward on his chest; his hand slid up the slick skin along her spine to the back of her neck.

"Oh, my." She sighed; he could feel the coolness as her

breath met his damp skin, although her face was hidden. "Oh, *my*." After a moment she went on, obscurely, "Now, *that* was certainly no chocolate éclair."

He lay and enjoyed the sensation of her pressed along him—it was a lot easier for him to bear her weight than the reverse, of course; he had a gentleman's chafe marks on his elbows. That went on for a long lazy time, until the sun struck his eyes and he noticed the time.

"I hate to say it, but oughtn't we be going? People might suspect. . . ."

Adrienne chuckled lazily. "Suspect? They'll do more than suspect, honeypie. Seein' as I brought you up alone to Lover's Leap."

"So *that's* what it's called?" he said, and tweaked her.

She yelped and rolled off him, glaring in an anger only half-assumed; the tweak had been delivered in a highly sensitive spot, and one she couldn't have politely rubbed in public. She could here, and did: even in his exhausted state the sight did remarkable things.

"What was *that* for?"

"For taking me up unto a high place and showing me all the kingdoms of the Earth," he said, wagging a finger at her—and then grabbing her wrist when she tried to retaliate with a tweak of her own. They both laughed.

She went on, "Well, it worked, didn't it? Unless you were planning on resisting temptation?"

"I may have Christ in my surname, but the first one isn't Jesus," Tom said.

* * *

A swing band was tuning up as Tom and Adrienne dismounted at the stables; sunset was about over, leaving only a red glow behind the Mayacamas. He grinned at the sound of the music; he'd been a teenager when the swing-dancing revival was at its height, and the thought of tossing Adrienne around to a brassy big-band sound held no terrors. That and square dancing were the most popular forms here, from what he'd heard.

Then a thought hit him with a sudden chill: It probably wasn't a swing *revival*. For all he knew, it had never gone out of fashion, in this enclave of the dimensionally displaced. The population was too small to generate many fashions of their own, and if they were cut off from the living currents of society on FirstSide by choice or circumstance . . . He remembered his father remarking once that an uncle had gone on a trip to the old country in the 1950s. Modern Norwegians had barely been able to understand the archaic peasant dialect the uncle had picked up from the grandparents who'd made the original westward migration.

Tom and Adrienne helped the stablehands unsaddle their mounts, then walked hand in hand back to the manor. They parted with a kiss at the door to his room on the second floor; he took the time for a quick shower—rubbing down with handfuls of cold springwater wasn't enough, considering the amount of exertion of various sorts he'd gone through today. The Commonwealth equivalent of party clothes for this sort of affair made him feel a little self-conscious at first—there was a definite zoot-suit influence—but they fit well; for a semiformal occasion like this they included a jacket with broad lapels, an open-necked shirt and loose-cut slacks, with two-tone leather shoes. He gave a thumbs-up sign to the mirror and went out to meet Adrienne. She wore a cream silk dress with a pleated skirt, and low-heeled shoes with diamond-studded buckles.

Whoa, he thought, taking her in.

It must have shown, or maybe he simply couldn't contain an inarticulate caveman grunt of admiration, for she curtsied; he offered an arm and she tucked hers through it as they walked down the curving staircase and out the tall doors to the gardens.

"And the same to you, sir," she said. "Ready to eat? And dance?"

"Eating sounds good," he replied. "Dancing sounds great in the conditional future tense."

The rear of the great house was bright, the windows a blaze of lights and Chinese lanterns hanging high in the limbs of the trees, stretching away into dimmer reaches to the west. A set of trestle tables had been set on the velvety lawn, surrounding a white fountain of tapering stone basins; the band was setting up farther away, on a low stone platform nearer the paved area around the pool. A crowd of people awaited them, bowing or curtsying as Tom and Adrienne came out the main doors onto the patio that spanned the rear of the building beyond the enclosed courts. Tom felt hideously self-conscious at that; Adrienne waved with every appearance of calm, and the people went back to milling around and chattering, obviously excited and happy at the special occasion.

They were all in their best, and of all ages from just past toddlerhood to the elderly. The children were surprisingly well behaved. . . .

Or maybe not so surprisingly, he thought.

One started to kick up a ruckus; the five-year-old's mother grabbed him by an ear and administered half a dozen solid whacks to his behind with the other hand, reducing the noise to a teary pout that soon vanished in the general excitement and high spirits.

Guess a swift smack to the fundament hasn't been redefined as assault here, he thought, amused.

Tully stood under a string of Chinese lanterns, talking to Sandra Margolin; she was giggling, and then burst out into wholehearted laughter, which with her figure was enough to make you blink; she was wearing a low-cut blouse and peasant-style skirt.

"Not wasting any time, either," Adrienne said, amusement in her tone.

"He usually doesn't," Tom said—he'd always been a bit baffled by Tully's success with the opposite sex. "He never has any problem finding company. *Keeping* the woman interested is another matter," Tom said. Then: "Hi, Roy. Where in hell did you get *that* oufit?"

Tully's jacket was acid green, his shirt purple, trousers fawn, belt-buckle silver and turquoise, and his shoes brown, white and black; the cut of the clothes also had a much bigger hint of the zoot suit than Tom's.

"Picked it up in Rolfeston. I was assured that it's the height of local fashion," the smaller man replied loftily. "Hello to you too, Kemosabe."

"It's not that people in men's-wear stores keep lying to you, Roy," Tom said. "It's the way that you keep *believing* them that gets me."

"I think he looks fine," Sandra Margolin said, and Tom threw up his hands.

Besides, I'm feeling at one with the world, and everyone's friend, he thought, grinning.

A bell began to ring, summoning them to the harvest supper; people streamed off toward the tables set up on the lawn. Those were in the shape of a large T with a double stem and a small crossbar. From what Adrienne had said, Tom gathered that this was a twice-yearly occasion, after the wheat harvest and then in the fall after the grapes were brought in; the manor's cook—a middle-aged woman of Franco-American-Italian descent and formidable heft—her staff, the housewives of the rest of the estate's households, and the odd man who fancied his hand on a grill had all been working overtime, and with a certain ferocious competitiveness. The food reflected the mix of people who'd gone into founding this strange country: the Southern take on traditional Anglo-Saxon cooking, but with a heavy Latin influence via Italy and southern France, and a dash of German and East European.

He suspected that the mix of plebian and haute cuisine dishes was unique to occasions like this, though. Corn on the cob for starters, with an alternate choice of ranch-cured duck prosciutto and pears, or spicy tuna tartare, tomato fondant and chilled coriander broth . . . No, there was a twenty-first-century Californian influence there, too.

The crowd took their places, waiting expectantly. Adrienne had seated Tom at her right, with Tully and his new friend beyond that; the rest of the top table held the *mayordomo* and his family, and the other senior staff and theirs;

Simmons's tracker and the *nahua* sat at a separate section at the base. There was also a large ceremonial salt shaker, evidently a social marker separating the upper table from the hoi polloi even on a community occasion like this.

Adrienne rose, and took her glass of white wine in hand. Silence fell, after a few shouts of "Speech! Speech!" and "Go for it, Miz Rolfe!"

"Friends," she said, "this is the twelfth harvest supper I've hosted as landholder of Seven Oaks. I'd like to thank everyone for the hard work—"

The speech was mercifully brief, and good-humored. The reactions on all the faces he could see were too. He ate—the corn first; he didn't really like raw fish of any sort—and helped himself to Lucillian salads with scallops and lobster tails, and greens he'd seen being picked that morning, a steak of Angus beef lightly brushed with garlic-steeped olive oil from the grove to the north of the house and grilled over oak coals, cauliflower with mustard and fennel seed, beaten biscuits. . . .

Tully made a production of drinking a glass of wine—an open bottle stood between each two diners, with a simple label reading *Seven Oaks,* which included a silhouetted oak tree beneath. Tom drank some of his and decided it was extremely good. When it came to wine he just knew what he liked without pretending to know anything about it. Roy went in for the full wine-country vocabulary.

"Black cherry fruit . . . soft tannins . . . just a bit of vanilla from the oak . . . very nice," he said to Adrienne, after swirling and tilting a glass, looking through the edge at a candle flame, sniffing and sipping. "Basically a cabernet sauvignon, right? But blended. Is it yours?"

"Well, I'm scarcely going to serve someone else's wine at *my* estate's harvest supper, Roy," Adrienne said, leaning forward to speak to him across Tom. "Yes, it's a blend, eighty-twenty cabernet and merlot; the 'ninety-two vintage. That was a wonderful year at Seven Oaks, and it just keeps getting better in the bottle."

"But there's something . . . I can't quite place it. Not bad, just a little different."

"Probably the fermenting vats," she said. "We've got temperature control, but we use open-topped redwood tanks, not the closed stainless-steel ones they have FirstSide." A quick urchin grin. "Our motto—'Malolactic fermentation is for sissies!'"

Tully nodded. "I noticed driving up that you don't have the piped water system in the vineyards that they use in the Napa on FirstSide either. What do you do when you get a late frost after budbreak?"

"Ahhh . . . hope next year is better?" she said, blinking at him, and then they both laughed.

Tom suppressed a slightly miffed feeling and waited until Adrienne was talking to someone who'd come up to the head table; she stood and walked aside with the questioner for a moment. Things weren't crowded, and he could be quasi-private when he leaned close to Tully and asked, "Look, do you think we're doing the right thing?"

"Well, it ain't the U.S. of A., Kemosabe, and I'm not real comfortable with this patron-client setup they've got either. But on the whole, it's not too bad—Uncle Sugar had us defending Allah allies who were a hell of a lot more skanky. The anti-Rolfe league definitely looks a hell of a lot worse."

"I could have told you all that, Roy," Sandra said, refilling her own wineglass. "How anyone can live FirstSide, from what the video shows, is beyond me."

Tom looked at her. "What if you didn't want to work the horses here at Seven Oaks?"

"Why shouldn't I?" she said, obviously puzzled. "I love horses, and this is my home—I was born here and so was my father."

"But if you didn't?"

"If I didn't like it here, I'd go somewhere else and get a job. We aren't slaves, and I'm good at what I do. A dozen places would be glad to take me on; and I've had more than one guy offer me a ring, you know—men with their own farms, or horse trainers."

"I don't suppose you get invited up *here* for dinner all that often," Tom said. "When it isn't harvest supper, that is."

"Once upon a time—you might be surprised," she said, with a twinkle in her dark eyes. "But anyway, yeah, that's true for most people, but how often did you have dinner with . . . oh . . ." She stopped, obviously searching for a FirstSide equivalent to Adrienne or her grandfather.

"The governor? Bill Gates?" Tully said, grinning. "All the *time,* girl. Why, just the other day I dropped in on Bill at home and went into the kitchen and popped myself a brewski. Then I slapped my ass down on the sofa beside Billy-boy and his old lady and I said, 'Bill, how're they hanging? And dude, you gotta do something about the bugs in the new—' "

Tom waved him quiet. "OK, OK, Tonto, I get the idea. Nice not to have to feel too guilty about my own take on things, you betcha."

Sandra went on, "And can you call up the governor or this Gates guy and get help or backup if you need it?" she said. "Doesn't sound like it; from what I've heard it's sink or swim over there. I can go to Adrienne or her dad if I have to—I'm a Rolfe affiliate and so was my dad. We back them up—they back us up."

Tom nodded; it wasn't what he'd been brought up to think of as the ideal system, but as Tully had said, it didn't seem impossibly bad; he'd been in places—Turkmenistan, for instance—where people literally physically broke out into a cold sweat of fear when someone mentioned the Maximum Leader's name without implying he walked on air, or publicly doubted that he'd earned every one of the votes he needed to come out at ninety-nine percent plus every single election.

Adrienne had turned back and caught the last of that. Her leaf-green eyes were full of an ironic amusement . . . and real fondness. "Satisfied?"

"No," he said. "But I'm not completely repulsed, either." He smiled back at her. "In a manner of speaking . . ."

"Glad to know I'm not completely repulsive," she said.

"Roy and I will help you with this . . . political problem you've got," he went on, and felt an absurd lurch at the brilliance of her smile. "Once the"—*carefully unnamed conspiracy, in this rather public venue*—"problem is solved, all bets are off, of course."

"Of course," Adrienne said gravely. "And now . . . we can dance."

The band pealed out a high sustained brass note, then swung into action. Tom led Adrienne out; Tully was already cutting a jitterbug rug on the way over, with Sandra clapping her hands as she followed. A pair of heels and long slender bare legs suddenly appeared over the head of the crowd, as one girl did a daring handstand on her partner's palms. Tom met Adrienne's eyes, nodded, gripped her hands and swung her over one hip, over the other, down between his legs, up in an overhead twirl. . . .

CHAPTER SEVENTEEN

Seven Oaks/Southern California
July 2009

The Commonwealth of New Virginia
"Now, this is the way I like to go on an op," Tully said.
"Landed gentry of goddamned Little Rock, that's me. Natural affinity for horses. Make way, ye peasants!"

"You're not falling off anymore, at least," Sandra replied.

When I stop feeling vaguely guilty, I'm really going to enjoy this place, Tom thought as he watched. *And when I don't have the prospect of a long deadly hike through deserts and savage hostile nomads toward a fortress stuffed full of heavily armed Aztec mercenaries. Of course, if I get a chance to get back, all bets are off.* He'd made that clear.

He and the object of his thoughts stood watching side by side, each with a foot on the lowest plank of the board fence, leaning on posts with their elbows—his at breastbone level, hers just under her chin. Tully *was* staying on better; he didn't have any particular gift for horses, but he did have good balance, excellent coordination and physical training to draw on. And falls didn't faze him, which had won him a good deal of respect from Sandra, who had evidently been put on her first pony about the time she graduated from diapers.

Tom wasn't surprised in the least; he'd never yet met anything in the way of physical danger that *did* faze Roy. He had the scrappy determination of a terrier.

And if we win, and then there's no way to get out of here . . . I won't die of grief, he thought, breathing in the mixed scent of horses, pepper trees, warm dust and greenery.

He'd miss his brother Lars and his sister-in-law and nieces and nephews, but he didn't see them more than once a year anyway. And he had no other close ties. . . .

"Elbows in, and don't flap them!" Sandra called to her pupil. "You're supposed to hold the reins, not try to fly like a crow!"

Tully grinned and obeyed, turning his mount with leg pressure. It broke into a canter—Sandra called again, telling him to keep his knees bent to absorb the harder gait—then into a gallop, and rose over an obstacle of poles and barrels.

"Not bad," Adrienne said judiciously. "He's really a very quick learner."

"Glad you like him," Tom said, and found that he was. *I keep getting these irrational bursts of benevolence,* he thought. *Must be love.*

"Jim Simmons heard from Frontier Scout HQ this morning," Adrienne said more softly. "He and his tracker will be taking a coastal schooner down to San Diego—he's been assigned to look into the tribal raiding there."

"Convenient," he said, and she grinned back at him.

"And how are we to make our descent on the southland look casual?" he asked.

"By making it casual," she said. "Hmmm. Can you fly a light airplane?"

"Yah, you betcha," Tom said. "Roy too. Fish and Game liked its field people to qualify."

"Then we'll—"

One of the stable hands came up and cleared her throat. "Miz Rolfe," she said. "Fella from the paper wants to talk to you."

Adrienne muttered an impolite word under her breath. "Fetch him, then, Terry."

The reporter was a photographer too, carrying the latest digital model. To Tom's eyes it clashed horribly with the suit and snap-brimmed fedora and pencil-thin trimmed mustache;

it was like a computer terminal in *It Happened One Night*. He looked to be about thirty, with reddish-brown short-cut hair and hazel eyes and a sharp, foxy face.

"Miz Rolfe," the man said, "you may not remember me—"

"How could I forget?" she said with a charming smile, extending a hand. "Charlie Carson, isn't it? Society news column for *City and Domain* magazine? I remember the article you did when I got back from Stanford."

"Yeah," he said, flushing a little with pleasure. "That was the first under my own byline. Nice of you to recall. I was wondering if you could give me a few words on the Toni Bosco matter? And maybe a picture?"

Well, I don't think reporters were ever *that polite, First-Side,* he thought.

Adrienne pursed her lips, seemed lost in thought for a minute, and then answered: "I think I might, Charlie . . . provided you do me a favor and keep quiet about my medium-term plans." She glanced at Tom. "I have . . . well, an announcement I don't want leaking. I promise you'll get it first, when and if, if you'll humor me."

"No problem, Miz Rolfe," he said earnestly. "I appreciate that."

"Ask away."

"The Colletta has asked for a judicial session of the committee to investigate the death of his collateral, Anthony Bosco. Do you have any comment?"

"Just that, with respect, the Colletta should remember that Gate Security has plenary authority when operating FirstSide; that no Commonwealth court has jurisdiction over actions done there; and that that applies to the committee sitting in judicial session as well. I killed Anthony Bosco—and I make no bones about it—while on FirstSide, and while he was resisting arrest by an officer of Gate Security, and while himself shooting at Gate Security operatives. And killing one, in fact: Schalk van der Merwe, who left a widow and three small children. Anthony Bosco endangered the Gate secret and put himself outside the law; he fell on his own deeds. Instead of criticizing the Gate Security Force, the

Colletta should be taking measures to exercise a tighter discipline on his collaterals."

"Can I quote you on that, Miz Rolfe?" the reporter said, nearly slavering.

"You may," she said.

The questions went on for a few more minutes. The reporter finished with, "And what are your immediate plans, Miz Rolfe? The ones you don't mind people knowing, that is," he finished hastily.

"You can say that I'm going on an extended holiday," she said, then smiled. "Just between me and thee, Charlie, and off the record, I'll be flying down the coast, and then looking for a crew to take *Sea-Witch*"—she turned to Tom for an instant—"That's the family sailing yacht—take *Sea-Witch* on a cruise to Hawaii, with some friends."

She made it plain who the friend was in the way she looked at Tom. He felt himself grinning back—this was misdirection, but the look itself was quite genuine.

"Thanks a million, Miz Rolfe!" the reporter said.

"Disinformation?" Tom asked, when the reporter had gone and they were out of earshot of anyone else.

"Precisely." Adrienne grinned and squeezed his arm. "Charlie won't publish anything he says he won't, but he'll stop gossiping when he stops breathing. Giovanni Colletta will find it a lot more believable coming as a rumor than as a magazine story, which he'd assume was planted. With any luck he'll really believe I'm off to the islands with my new boyfriend in tow and nothing on my mind but making out like a mad mink under the coconut trees on Waikiki. He's got that Madonna-whore thing, bad. Give you three guesses which category he puts me in."

Tom gave her a round of applause, grinning. "And you'll have this yacht leave, too, won't you? With arrangements that'll make it look like we're on board."

"Hell, yes," she said. Then she hugged him and sighed. "Do you have any idea how nice it is to find a man who doesn't feel scared of a woman who can think?"

"Ah . . ." *Advantages of a FirstSide upbringing,* he didn't say. "The brains are up to the standards of the rest of the package," he said.

By the light in her leaf-green eyes, it was the right thing to say. She pulled his head down beside hers and whispered, "But while we're here, why *don't* we go make out like mad mink?"

✸ ✸ ✸

"So," Tully said, rubbing his hands and looking around like a ten-year-old in a candy store, "what does Santa have for the good little boys and girls?"

Tom looked around the armory too; everyone in the prospective scouting party was there, except for the Indian tracker, who preferred to stick with his native tools. Hunting weapons were in one section of the long room; military stuff was in another, and in the center were workbenches, a reloading setup and a remarkably complete set of gunsmith's tools. Light came from two small barred windows high up on either wall, and overhead fluorescents. There was a comfortingly familiar scent of Break Free oil, propellant, brass and metal.

"I presume everyone's got their own rifle," Tom said, and they all nodded. "Now, we're going to look, not fight, but it's always nice to have some insurance—you can sing or make love when *you* feel like it, but you fight when the *other* guy feels like it."

"How about this?" Jim Simmons said, taking down a light machine gun from the rack. He looked at the two First-Siders. "It's a Bren, rechambered for the thirty-aught-six round."

Tom had heard of the classic design, but never used one before. It had a bipod at the front, pivoted on the takeoff for the gas cylinder, and a top-mounted thirty-round box. There was an alternative C-mag saddle drum holding seventy-five rounds. Tom hefted it; lighter than the 240s he'd used in the army.

"All right; might be nice to have an authoritative

backup . . . I presume you can use it?" Simmons nodded, and so did Botha and Adrienne. "You can give Roy and me—and Sandra—a quick course on it."

Adrienne pulled out three submachine guns—he recognized the unorthodox shape of a Belgian PN90, its synthetics and molded shapes an odd contrast with the angular wood and metal of the older designs. These had a built-in handgrip near the front, a laser designator and collimating sight, and a fifty-round magazine of transparent plastic that lay along the top of the boxy weapon.

"These might be handy," she said.

"Good," he said. Like any workman, he took a proprietary interest in his tools. They had only a few days to make sure everyone was familiar with all the tools at hand. "If it came to a close-quarter firefight, those *would* be handy. Now . . ."

He lifted down a wooden crate and took out blocks of a rubbery plastic substance, timers, detonators and wireless control units.

"Who knows how to handle Semtex?" he went on cheerfully.

* * *

"That's her: the *No Biscuit.*"

"*No Biscuit?*" Tom asked, walking around the small twin-prop plane and doing a quick check.

"That's what my flight instructor said whenever I did something stupid. 'Bad student! Bad! No biscuit!'"

The little amphibian was parked on a municipal airport just south of Napa town—an X of mown grass strips, a couple of timber-framed hangars, a receiving shed and a rudimentary two-story control tower with a wind sock, all drowsing under a clear blue August sky. The air was warm at noon but still carried a hint of morning's freshness, the green damp smell of the marshes to the south, sun-dried grass and a tang of gasoline, solvents and varnish. The craft had a tricycle undercarriage and a boat-shaped lower body; the wheel struts had sections of shaped board attached, with rubber gaskets to form a tight seal with the rest of the hull when they were retracted. The wing was high-mounted with pontoons at the tips, and there were two modest radial engines in smooth cowlings stained with streaks of black from the exhausts.

Closer inspection confirmed his first impression: The *No Biscuit* was built with stone-ax simplicity. The hull was a monocoque of laminated spruce with spruce springers and frames; so was the wing, apart from the main spar. The controls weren't just nondigital—they were plain old cables, not even any hydraulic assist. There *were* some modern electronics on the control panel, flat-screen displays for radar and such, but they were extras. He looked around and saw several more just like her, and a few others with tubby cylindrical bodies suitable for a land-based aircraft, but the same wings, engines and control surfaces.

"All designed and made here in the Commonwealth," Adrienne confirmed pridefully. "Except for some engine parts and the cockpit electronics. We could make the engine parts and do without the digital stuff, at need, even if we're not up to making a C-130 or Black Hawk from scratch."

Tom looked back at the Hummer parked beside the reception block while Adrienne went through her preflight check. Tom had taken the sensitive and heavy parts of their baggage himself, on the take-no-chances principle, since he was something of a demolitions expert and Roy wasn't. Tully and Sandy were supposed to be bringing along the rest of the bags. Instead they were horsing around, something that suddenly developed into serious lip-locking. He sighed; on the one hand, he'd seen it developing over the past weeks, and he certainly didn't begrudge his friend finding someone. On the other hand, when Roy fell he tended to fall hard.

Adrienne looked up from checking the engines. "Glad of that," she said quietly. "Sandy deserves some happiness, particularly with someone who doesn't care who her maternal grandmother was." A slight snort. "We Rolfes had something similar in our early history, certainly!"

"Ah . . ." Tom hesitated. "Tully's a great guy, you betcha, but he's had . . . problems that way. Two divorces."

"Third time lucky, maybe," Adrienne said. "And it's easier to stay married here. Fewer distractions; people stay put more."

She gave a piercing whistle and the two broke apart; Sandra looked embarrassed and Tully didn't, but then . . . *I could count the number of times I've seen Roy embarrassed without taking off my socks,* Tom thought. *I mean, look at that Hawaiian shirt he's wearing!*

They loaded the luggage into a cargo compartment, through gull-wing doors that opened just behind the six-seat passenger cabin. Tom took particular care with several small brass-bound leather trunks. There was no problem with carrying weapons openly here in the Commonwealth; outside the towns and the more settled farming zones everyone went ironed, and even inside them it didn't raise much of an eyebrow. The explosives and night-sight gear in those, though . . .

The rest of the gear was exactly what they would have packed for the holiday she'd described to Charlie Carson—the best way to look like you were doing something was to actually do it. Then he opened the door at the rear of the passenger compartment—it swung upward too—and handed everyone up. There was a wheeled stairway around somewhere, but boosting people gave him an excuse to grab Adrienne below the hips and lift her effortlessly high over his head.

"Show-off," she said, grinning down at him.

"But you like what I show off," he pointed out.

"Point taken."

"Show-off," Tully said as he settled into the seat behind the copilot's, and Tom edged past him.

"You're just jealous," Tom replied. "But I forgive you. It can't be easy being the world's only hobbit. . . ."

"I'm not jealous," Sandra said, and winked. "I'm too fond of breathing unsquashed."

"Not a problem," Adrienne said, "when dealing with a gentleman."

The four of them laughed easily.

Tom stopped after a second, thinking, *Forgiveness is an odd thing,* as he settled into the copilot's seat and adjusted it—which required putting it nearly back to Tully's knees. Leather sighed under him; the aircraft had an unfamiliar smell, less ozone and synthetics than he was used to, more wood and oil and metal. His mind went on working as he watched Adrienne lean out the window to check the control surfaces, her feet moving on the pedals and yoke. The way her neck curved, and the little wisps that escaped the braid she'd made of her bronze-bright hair . . .

Back right after we got shanghaied through the Gate, I could've sworn I'd hate her guts forever. Either I'm a very weak person, or love conquers all, or maybe it was just a snit. Or maybe I'm starting to like this place a lot and resent being brought here a lot less. I don't like all the methods, but the results certainly aren't bad. I like the way you don't have to wade through layers of bureaucrats to get something done, for example. But is that because of the way John Rolfe built this place, or just the scale? With the population of one medium-small city, could *you have as much paperwork?*

The checklist went quickly. They put on their headsets; she handed ear protectors, the kind you wore on a firing range, to Tully and Sandra before she flipped the ignition switches. It had been a while since he'd flown in anything this small, and he'd forgotten how loud piston engines were, radials particularly, and particularly with the side windows open. The port engine lit with a bang and a burst of black smoke from the exhausts and then settled down into a steady *rumm-rumm-rumm* as the twin-bladed prop spun into a silver disk; then the starboard followed suit. The buzzing roar made speaking futile, although the muffling earphones helped; Adrienne's finger pointed out the essential gauges— oil, manifold pressure, temperature, RPM.

"Ready for takeoff, tower," she said.

"Cleared, *No Biscuit,*" a man's voice returned casually. "San Diego's expecting you sometime late tomorrow. Check in a couple of times, would you?"

"Roger, wilco," she said. "Over and out, Napa control."

Well, there's another pleasant lack of formality.

Adrienne worked the throttles and turned the *No Biscuit* into the wind from the south. Tom felt a small flutter of excitement as the nose came up and the wheels came off the concrete; he always did at the beginning of a trip. With it was a bit of the acid apprehension he'd felt getting into transport planes, with a hostile reception waiting at the other end. It wasn't as bad; they weren't going to be seeing any action soon, but it was there. This wasn't a vacation, after all: It was an op, even if the strangest one in his life.

"Do the landing gear, would you?" Adrienne shouted in his ear. At his questioning look, she pointed to a lever between the seats.

"Well, we are back to basics," he muttered unheard, gripped it, flipped off the restraining strap, and began pumping it up and down. The two wheels under the wings and the nosewheel in front of them came up with a rattle and clank of gears, closing with a sigh of rubber gaskets.

They climbed steadily to five thousand feet; it got chilly enough that he zipped up his jacket. There were patches of fog over the bay, and a dense bank of it veiling the site of San Francisco . . . *or New Brooklyn,* he thought. Most of the rest of the Bay Area was clear; he could see Mount Diablo to their left, and Mount Tamalpais over to the right in Marin, rising out of fog like a peak in a dream, densely green with virgin woodland almost to the peak. He grunted a little then, as if hit in the belly.

At his companion's inquiring look, he shouted: "It keeps hitting me—what *isn't* there."

She nodded. "Same thing in reverse! Only it's worse, FirstSide. Like seeing someone you love horribly disfigured."

The plane kept out over the water, a thick fringe of marsh and tide flat ringing the larger bay, a deep indigo blue broken here and there by the whitecaps or the larger V of a ship's wake. Once they lurched aside to dodge a flock of birds rising from the edges of the bay; dark shapes hurtled past, but nothing crashed into their wings or the props.

"You should see what it's like from September on, when the waterfowl arrive!" Adrienne said. "Have to veer inland then, or out to sea!"

They veered east then, to the inner edge of the Santa Clara valley; even through the engine roar, he could hear Tully's long whistle. Somehow seeing Silicon Valley gone, nothing but tawny ranchland interspersed with checkerboard of fields and a few hamlets, drove things home.

I keep feeling I've adjusted to the reality of this, he thought. *And then something new hits me.*

"I'm avoiding the Colletta domain," Adrienne said. "Not that I think they'd try anything as raw as shooting us down—especially when they think I'm taking myself out of the game. No need to take unnecessary chances. Why don't you try her for a while? Get a feel for how she handles."

She leaned back, taking her hands from the yoke as he took over the copilot's set of controls, glad of a distraction from the momentary sense of being adrift from everything solid and real. The *No Biscuit* rocked a little as his feet settled on the rudders; a simple design didn't necessarily mean one that was simple to fly. Turbulence buffeted the yoke in his hands and vibrated up his feet; he kept one eye on the horizon, and the other on the airspeed and altitude indicators and the compass. The *No Biscuit* was doing a steady 110 mph, on a heading that would take them straight southwest to Monterey.

Nice and level . . . so, not too bad, he decided, trying a gentle climb, an equally cautious dive, and a bank right and left. *No particular vices, but I wouldn't want to try acrobatics in it.*

Soon they were over Monterey Bay. He looked down and grinned; nothing there where the city had been but a small fishing village; there was a line of cultivation along the Pajaro River, reaching inland along the south flank of the hills, and a scattering of farms around the lower Salinas. Away from those the land rolled wild: forested uplands, tawny grass studded with oak trees on the fringes of the rivers, dense marsh and slough where water ran down to the sea, long curves of beach. He took the plane down, leveling off again at about a thousand feet.

"That's the Batyushkov domain, up under the edge of the Santa Cruz," Adrienne said. "Then the Morrisons—from Pennsylvania, originally—around Salinas town, and the Sanderses, farther up the river, and the Bauers in the Carmel Valley."

"I always loved this part of the country," he said. "And the Big Sur, especially."

"Here, you look. I'll fly," Adrienne said indulgently.

He unshipped the binoculars clipped above the windscreen and opened the side window again, peering out—the slipstream wasn't too bad. A pod of humpbacks was moving south along the coast perhaps half a mile out, several score—possibly hundreds, from the way one surfaced and spouted every ten seconds or so, a bit early for the usual migration. They were breaching, too: throwing themselves up out of the water, doing a little twist and dropping back with a huge fountain of spray, probably from sheer exuberance. One of their kind had met some sort of misfortune and lay dead on the beach, swarming with gulls and . . . yes, half a dozen condors! Plus at least three grizzlies, feeding at widely spaced spots along the fifty-foot carcass.

"Where's this spot you wanted to stop overnight?" he said.

"A little farther down the coast," she replied. "About an hour's flight. This—all the uplands south of here, the Big Sur country and the Santa Lucia range—is a Commission reserve. Wildlife and hunting preserve—no settlement at all. But there's a place I'm very fond of, and it would be good tradecraft to stop there." A grin. "And fun, too."

He took the controls again for a while, then switched off with Tully; just watching the surf-washed shore passing by below was endless pleasure. Still, he wasn't unhappy when Adrienne took charge once more and began to circle. For one thing, he'd gotten spoiled in the two months he'd been here, used to quiet all the time.

* * *

"Bloody good to be back on the edge," Jim Simmons said, stretching out in the chair and taking a sip of cold beer, savoring the hundred-degree heat and the empty plains and bare rock hills that lay northward.

The Frontier Scout station in Antelope Valley had been founded in the late 1970s, tucked into the northern slope of the San Gabriel Mountains and near a good pass; it served to protect the growing settlements along the coasts and in the basins north of San Diego. The station had grown a little itself in the years since. The original adobe blockhouse and wall now stood among a cluster of cottages, a barn and stable, fenced paddocks, two battered six-wheel Land Rovers, a few eucalyptus and pepper trees, a small grove of pomegranates and pears. A windmill clanked away beside the storage tank, drawing water for houses and garden plots from a deep well, and pumping some to a solar heater. A thousand yards away the small chapel and grange of a Franciscan missionary settlement stood amid more greenery and the tattered, ratty wickiups of its two dozen converts, many of them mixed-bloods; New Virginia's Catholics included a sprinkling of zealots displeased with the changes in the Church after Vatican II.

A small band of nomads who had come in to barter or see the missionary doctors had camped under the rim of a cliff not far away with their leather tents and horses and light carts.

For the rest the arid wilderness about was much as he remembered it: creosote and sage and the odd Joshua tree, sun baking down out of a sky bleached a faded blue, spicy-sulfury scents of desert herbs. Few New Virginians came this way except eccentrics and hunters and the odd trader interested in the turquoise and aquamarines the natives brought out of the wastelands. The Antelope Valley was fertile enough when you had deep wells and power-driven pumps, but it was ferociously hot in summer, often chilly in winter, and there was still plenty of land lying unclaimed closer to the coast.

Even the San Fernando Valley had only a handful of full-time Settler residents; it would be a long time before that tide flowed over the San Gabriels in strength.

Simmons had been to Antelope Station before, posted here once or twice, and for two years as a child while his father was operating in the region. He still wasn't a specialist in the area or its peoples, and Dirk Brodie was.

"I'm just trying to get a feel for conditions here," Simmons said soothingly. "The committee's sort of worried."

Brodie thumped his hand down on the arm of his chair—not the first time a beer bottle had made that trip enclosed in his fist, from the look of the wood.

"Now they get worried," he growled.

He was a lean, tall man, with rusty black hair cropped short and a leathery face. There were deep wrinkles beside his eyes, despite his being a year short of thirty.

"I've been reporting that the tribes are restless for better than two years now," Brodie said.

"What've you heard?"

"For starters, trade has dropped off. And the deep-desert nomads, they've gotten hold of a lot of muskets. Not too bad in itself—"

Simmons nodded; the official thinking was that an Indian with a flintlock smoothbore was no more dangerous than one with a bow, and once they were used to muskets they'd be dependent on the Commonwealth for ammunition and repairs.

"—but it's damned odd. They're getting other trade goods too, from somewhere—are you people up in the Central Valley letting more through than the records show?" He sighed as Simmons shook his head. "Well, somebody is," he said. "And they've been raiding more than usual, too—I've been thinking of calling for a punitive expedition, and I don't like doing that."

"Which clans?" Simmons asked.

"Akaka, Othi-I and Kapata, mostly," he said. "The Ravens, the Salts, and the Turtles—but there's word of a new war leader, Swift Lance, and that he's been Dreaming. And the clans have been Singing his Dreams."

* * *

The *No Biscuit* sank until it was flying parallel to a series of high east-west ridges and well before their crests. Their feet rose out of the surf to make a series of U-shaped pockets; some of them had small patches of beach between them, and in some water seethed white over rock. Deep forest ran up the canyons, thick with Douglas fir and twisted Monterey pine and redwood. The plane shook, shuddered, buffeted by the updrafts along the steep slopes.

"Great country for hang gliding!" Tully yelled from the rear, and laughed.

"Fasten seat belts, please," Adrienne replied. "We thank you for the pleasure of your company on Packed in Like Sardines Air, and we will overbook your next flight with no apologies, because you're just so much inanimate cargo to us. Your luggage may be found in Tibet. Hope to see you again! Better still, send money and stay home!"

The seaplane banked sharply, sideslipped and dropped, then came in out of the west. The water was fairly calm, rippling like a mirror of green malachite before them; the note of the engines changed as Adrienne throttled back, and there was a moment when Tom felt a little lighter than he should. The hull touched the surface, a *skip . . . skip . . . skip* sensation, the seat slapping him in the butt, with a thrumming underneath it like a powerboat at speed as the plywood vibrated to the touch of the water. Then they were on the surface, tall rooster tails of spray arching up on either side; he pitched forward against the belts, then back as the amphibian slowed and the nose came up. Seawater ran down the windows, clearing to give them a view of the shore. In the first passenger seats Sandra and Tully leaned in toward the center and forward to get a glimpse.

To the east a small U-shaped cove was sheltered between two outthrust ridges that fell steeply to the sea. Along its southern edge a sheer drop of vertical rock ran from pine-forested height to the sand, and a stream had cut a V-shaped notch in it—a plume of water dropped fifty feet, falling on a narrow strip of beach to mingle with the waves rolling at its foot. Between the northern and southern cliffs the beach tapered inland to meet a narrow canyon, leaving a sheltered delta of coarse golden-brown sand edged with rock walls on both sides, lowest at the apex where it rose to the mountain slopes.

Tom rolled down the window; a gust of wind caught the bottom of the threaded waterfall, tossing the droplets out to sea in a broken rainbow and revealing a shallow cave behind. Then it died down, and the water veiled the cleft in the rock again. The seaplane pitched as it came landward, then slowed as it maneuvered around a rock reef in the middle of the cove's entrance, white water creaming off the nearly hidden stone. Adrienne slewed the amphibian back toward the center of the beach and chopped the throttles just before the keel touched bottom. They came to rest with a slow *shhhhusssssh* sound; the plane tilted a little until one of the pontoons touched the surface, and the propellers spun down and stopped.

"Timed it just right," she said with satisfaction in the sudden blessed silence. "High tide—the plane'll be secure overnight once we've tied off, but easy to float tomorrow."

By Jesus, Tom thought as he opened the gull-wing door beside him, the quiet like balm on his abused ears. *Talk about peaceful . . .*

Silence flowed in through the opening, and the salt breath of the ocean, the iodine tint of seaweed, and pine from the mountain forest looming above them. It was about as hot as this section of the coast ever got in late summer—in the high seventies—and the wind caressed his face like a damp scented towel.

He shaded his eyes and peered into the inner point of the beach, where sand gave way to upward-sloping rock.

"Ah . . . on second thought, previous occupant still in the room past the checkout time," he said mildly. "Ah, Adrienne, is that what it looks like?" That part of the sand was shaded by boulders on either side, and an overhanging oak.

"You betcha," she said softly, popping open her own section of door; that let Tully and Sandra crowd close and look.

There was a partially eaten game carcass lying there, a purebred European boar by its looks; no feral pig had those massive bristly shoulders, black hide, and long upcurving tusks. Crouched above it was . . .

"A gen-u-wine tiger," Tully said softly; he had the binoculars, and then passed them forward to his partner. "Big 'un."

"But is it a *Colletta* tiger?" Sandra asked impishly.

The beast crouched above its kill, snarling at the humans a hundred yards away. Tom stood, braced one hand like a clamp on the frame of the *No Biscuit*'s hull and leveled the binoculars with the other. That brought the big cat to within touching range, the fanged mouth close enough to draw a startled oath. Its thick, slightly shaggy fur was a pale gold color marked with black stripes, fading to cream on the belly and throat; the paws looked broad as dinner plates as they worked and slid their claws in and out. From its looks, he judged the weight to be about the same as a small horse.

"Siberian," he said. "Got to be—too big and not brightly colored enough for a Bengal."

"Near enough," Adrienne said. "Manchurian; we got a bunch from the Selang-Arsi for release in this area. Tropical tigers find the winters here a trial, although God knows it's warmer than the Amur valley; the Bengal type breed like flies in the southern jungles. . . . We'd better see him off. Hand me that rifle, Sandy, would you?

"Hey!" she shouted, with the weapon in hand. "You there, yes, you—the member of the Future Pelts, Rugs and Trophies of New Virginia—vamoose! Git!"

She slapped a magazine into the rifle, jacked the slide and squeezed off two rounds, a flat *crack-crack!* It came echoing back from the stony walls of the cliff, and a double spurt of sand erupted not far from the big cat. The shells tinkled down the windscreen and off into the sea foam below the amphibian's nose; the tiger snarled, a ripping sound clearly audible over the shushing hiss of the waves falling back down the beach. Then it bent and gripped the boar by the middle of its back. Raising its head to keep the dangling legs free, it turned and leaped up the slope, disappearing into the thick undergrowth.

"Mmm . . . are you *sure* this is a good place to camp?" Tom said.

He'd never seen a tiger except in a zoo; few had, in a time when more than half the tigers on the planet were captive-bred in the United States. *God, that was beautiful,* he thought. And it had been weirdly appropriate for the setting—as much so as the vanished saber-tooths that had perished with the glyptodonts and mastodons not long after the first humans came through this way.

"Oh, they don't bother people, usually," Adrienne said. "And they avoid the smell of fire—these forests have a natural burn cycle."

They climbed out of the plane onto the beach, with the *No Biscuit* moving slightly as they leaped down; with the tide still high it was just barely aground, and it was comparatively easy to swing it around with the tail pointing at the beach. He stretched, something popping in his back, and looked around. Beneath his feet was sand with an occasional pebble; some of the stones felt greasy and had a deep green sheen. He commented on it as they paid out two heavy ropes and tied the amphibian down to convenient boulders, making it secure from anything but a severe storm. The rock he and Adrienne made fast to was suspiciously polished too, and it had an even more suspiciously convenient groove about halfway down.

"It's nephrite—jade," Adrienne said, as they brought the loop of cable around the boulder and secured it. "So's this big hunk of rock here."

"Yikes," he said, looking at it. *Nine thousand pounds of jade; call it half a million. Oh, well, a glut of caviar is a glut of caviar.* "You know, I've been to this spot before—looked at it, FirstSide, never got down on the beach, of course—but I don't remember the jade boulder."

"Mom had it moved here from a little south along the coast," Adrienne said. "One of her better moves; she loved—loves—this spot too. Hell, you can't quarrel with *everything* your parents like."

Making camp was a work of moments; they set up two collapsible bell tents with titanium frames at a discreet distance apart, unrolled their sleeping bags, and dug a slit-trench behind a boulder near the inland edge of the beach. A circle of fire-blackened stones showed where others had made a hearth, and there was plenty of driftwood and deadfall; he shaved the kindling they needed, using dry branches, a hatchet, and a fallen log half-buried in sand as a cutting block.

The gear they'd brought included masks, snorkels and flippers—they *were* supposed to be on a vacation, without a care in the world, after all.

And, he thought, grinning, *why not act like it right now?*

Adrienne caught his mood. "Decided to put the Lutheran guilt-and-anxiety thing on hold for awhile?"

"It's your corrupting influence," he said. "Episcopalians don't do guilt, I suppose?"

"Of course not. It's grubby, tacky and thoroughly lower-class," she said with that irresistible smile. "Let's swim—and get dinner."

They changed; he noticed with some amusement that the bikinis the women wore were distinctly conservative by FirstSide standards, and that they both undressed in a tent—the body-modesty taboo had stayed stronger here than it had back in the parent society. As for the swimsuits . . .

Tully said it for him: "Hey, it's *Beach Blanket Bingo!*"

"Oh, you liked that one too?" Sandra said artlessly, clapping her hands. The results were spectacular, even with Adrienne standing beside her, long and sleekly curved.

"God, a woman who likes old movies *and* looks like that," Roy replied, eyes bulging. "I'm lost!"

"Well, the FirstSiders stopped making good movies—the new ones are too likely to be just disgusting, or not make any sense—so the Theatre Guild has to reissue the old ones a lot here," Sandra said, handing them nets and short, heavy prying irons with sharpened, flattened ends. "Except for the *Mummy* movies, and the *Harry Potter* and the *Rings* series— those were fine, but that was *years* ago now! We should make more of our own."

"Small population, limited talent pool," Adrienne said. "We can't do everything. Let's go!"

They ran—as much as you could run with flippers on—and threw themselves into the shallow water, stroking out. He exulted in the sudden cold shock of the water, a good twenty degrees lower than the air, and the pull and surge of the ocean like some great beast tugging at him. It was crystal-clear as they sculled out past the little rock reef in the mouth of the cove; the stone was covered in bright-colored coralline algae and sea anemones, and beyond it the sandy bottom held a thick growth of giant kelp. A couple of five-foot giant sea bass flicked by below him, muscular, scaly brutes, then a school of bright orange garibaldi fish, and the bottom held lingcod and kelp bass and others by the dozens. He flipped upright and trod water; not far away a young sea otter floated on its back, wrapped in a strand of giant kelp by its mother to keep it in place while she foraged, staring at him round-eyed with its small paws raised as if in surrender.

It made a sound at him, something between *meeep!* and *keeeek!*

"Sorry, kid, it's not your mother," he said in reply. "On the other hand, I'm not after your fur, either."

Just about then its mother did arrive from below, a handsome silvery-brown creature four feet long, with large eyes and a round, blunt-muzzled face framed by long whiskers on either side of a black button nose. She had a foot-long abalone clutched to her chest with one paw, a rock under the other, and looked suspiciously in his direction before she went to check her cub. It greeted her with happy high-pitched squeaks, grunts and coos as it climbed onto her belly and began to nurse, while she juggled rock and shellfish—evidently the problems of working mothers were a transspecies, trans-dimensional universal.

"Don't worry, lady, the kid's OK," he said, grinning around the mouthpiece of the snorkel.

There were more of the otters scattered through the kelp forest; he could hear the *whackety-whack-whack!* as one of them held a shellfish between her paws and hammered it against the rock on her chest, going at it like a pneumatic pavement breaker.

"Time to dive," Sandra said. "This water's *cold*."

It was, particularly without a wet suit; you were courting hypothermia if you stayed in too long. He took a couple of deep breaths and dove; the bottom was about twenty-five feet down, not very far for an experienced swimmer. The abalone was more abundant than any he'd ever seen, despite all the otters topside—and those critters could gobble down a third of their own considerable weights in seafood every day. Plus you couldn't fault their taste: They'd eat abalone in preference to most other stuff, even sea urchins or crabs. Evidently the absence of millions of humans equally determined to get their hands on the big mollusks was enough to make the difference.

Back FirstSide you had to carry a special measuring stick to make sure none of the ones you took were less than seven inches long, and the meat cost eighty dollars a pound. Here he didn't see many that *weren't* seven inches, and plenty were monsters that would have broken records back FirstSide, a foot long and more.

It wasn't the first time he'd pried abalone off rocks, either—although most of his efforts had gone into stopping poachers from doing it. He thrust the flattened end of the iron under the muscular "foot" of one and levered sharply; it came free after a long moment of effort, and he stuffed the twelve-inch shell into the net at his waist. His lungs were burning by the time he'd gotten three; they all stroked for the shore when he came up, and waded out with their lips blue and teeth on the verge of chattering, or over it in some cases—being big meant you lost heat more slowly. The kindling was ready in the stone circle, neatly piled in a little te-pee; Tom blew on his fingers so that he could work the Zippo and get it going. Flames crackled up through the bone-dry shavings, and then through the larger sticks of driftwood as the four of them stood close around it, each couple pressed together for warmth and wrapped in a blanket.

He could feel Adrienne's chilled flesh gradually thawing against him, and a big blanket could hide a fair degree of movement. *Interesting. Definitely interesting,* he thought, and she whispered through a shiver, "I seem to affect you more than the Pacific Ocean itself."

"I'm not complaining, and neither is he," he murmured into her ear.

After a while they were warm enough to go wash the salt off under the fringes of the waterfall—like God's cold shower, as Roy put it—dry off around the fire some more, and dress. He felt relaxed and supple and strong again after fighting the chilly waters, but it wasn't something you'd choose to do every day—or every week.

"Invigorating, though," he said.

"I agree," she said when he voiced the thought, wringing out the thick fall of her hair and running a comb through it with wincing determination before tying it back. "Too bad we're not really on vacation; the family has a place at La Jolla, just north of San Diego, with a beach that's nearly as pretty as this—and the water's a *lot* warmer."

Tom nodded; he liked "the Jewel," even if he found it expensive and a bit *pwecious;* it was probably something to see, here. Speaking of which . . .

"Anyone up for a walk?"

They staked out the nets full of abalone in a pool to keep them alive and fresh, along with a couple of bottles of white wine. Tully went up the steep rocky slope at the bottom of the U of the beach with a coil of rope over his shoulder; that was the only spot where it wasn't nearly vertical. The other three stood with their rifles in the crooks of their arms, keeping a close eye on the climber and his surroundings.

"Nice technique," Adrienne said, watching Tully.

"Oh, yeah," Sandra said. "Climbs good, too."

Tom felt himself blushing a little as they laughed—who'd ever said women were the bashful sex? Roy did know how to go up steep ground, though; Tom fancied he could do it nearly as well, but one-hundred-sixty pounds could go where two-thirty couldn't. At the crest Tully stopped and rove one end of the rope through a conveniently placed eyebolt sunk into living rock, and let the other end fall down to the sand. All of them could have made it up without, but there was no reason not to take advantage when you could.

Tom went next, walking up the steep slope and hand-over-handing along the rope. He was breathing deeply when he reached the top, and it felt a little strange to be hiking in coastal California with a rifle slung over his back, but . . .

"Lions and tigers and bears, oh, my," Roy said as his partner's cropped white-blond thatch came over the edge.

"Tigers and bears, at least," Tom replied. "I understand the lions are mostly south and west of here. But plenty of cougars and leopards."

They grinned at each other for a moment, and then Adrienne's bandanna-covered head came over the crestline; Tom extended a hand, closing it around her strong slender wrist, and pulled her up. Sandra followed, puffing slightly.

"I ought to get out on my own feet more often," she said after a moment. "It uses different muscles than riding." Then: "Lord, that's pretty, isn't it?"

They stood in silence, looking out over infinite blue, along the steep green coastline, down at the white curl of foam along the sand and the arch of the waterfall. Seabirds scattered as a peregrine thunderbolted out of the sky above; it missed its strike, fluttered to a halt just above the shore and then coasted south, gaining height. Then they turned and walked up the line of the creek; it fell in pools and miniature torrents over a rocky bed, under tall cypress and tanbark oak, and then among redwoods—ancient ones, towering above and shading the floor of the forest to a carpet of soft needles, moss and ferns. Tully looked up into the cathedral silence of it, where light seemed to fall like slow honey from gaps above. Then he frowned.

"You know, I'd swear I'd seen exactly the same redwood here on FirstSide—the one with the kink and the big burl."

"You may have," Adrienne said quietly. "The older sequoias up in the mountains, and the bristlecone pines, are the same on both sides of the Gate. They're older than the divergence between this world and FirstSide, and as far as we can tell everything was exactly the same until that day in 323 B.C."

Tom looked at the redwood. It was big, well over two hundred feet tall, but . . .

"I wouldn't think this one was twenty-three hundred years and change old; that's near the limit for a redwood, and this is the southern margin of their range."

"Wouldn't have to be quite that ancient. It was centuries before the changes in the Old World started affecting things here—quite a few centuries. Eventually it did; butterfly-effect stuff there started making it rain on different days here, and so an elk went left instead of right and ate a seedling that he didn't FirstSide, things like that."

They stared up at the great reddish-brown columns for a while, then turned back toward their campsite. The fire had died down to a bed of coals red-glowing or white-hot; he looked at his watch and found it was well after seven. His stomach told him the same thing, and that it had been a long time since a sandwich lunch.

Nothing like a hike and a swim in cold water to work up an appetite, either.

"Just one thing missing for a campsite," he said as they stacked their rifles.

He squatted beside a section of driftwood log and lifted it free of the sand with a long pull and grunting exhalation, then plumped it down beside the fire and brought another across the firepit from the first.

"Well, you pass the brute-strength test, you big, beautiful brute," Adrienne said, handing him the net bag of abalone. "Let's see how you do on manual dexterity."

Shelling and trimming the abalone was a familiar chore. He cut the muscle free of the iridescent interior of the shell with a small sharp blade; once the head and viscera were off and thrown to the attentive gulls he wrapped each one in a towel for a moment, set it on a log and gave it a couple of solid whacks with the flat of a heavy knife.

"Spare the cutting board?" he said.

She passed it over, and he scored the abalone fillets with a series of cuts about half an inch deep and an inch apart and repeated the process on the other side, running the cuts at right angles to the first set and piling the meat on a plate. Adrienne reclaimed the board and sliced a few cloves of garlic as Sandra and Roy unpacked the picnic basket, opened the coolers that held venison sausage and salad whose greens had been picked fresh at Seven Oaks that morning, cut bread, uncorked the wine. . . .

The picnic hamper also held an iron ring on three short stubby legs; he dropped that into the coals and set the frying pan on top. Adrienne dropped in a healthy dollop of butter and waited until it sizzled, then added the garlic. Saliva flooded Tom's mouth—nothing on earth smelled any better than that, unless you threw some onions into the mix.

"The secret of pan-frying abalone is to do it quick," he said, and plopped the first into the hot, frothing butter-and-garlic mixture.

A few seconds on each side and it was ready; he did enough for everyone, then came to sit beside Adrienne; they ate sitting side by side on the log, with their plates on their knees.

"God, that's good." He sighed. "Particularly considering the fact that it's essentially a giant seagoing snail."

"Nothing wrong with snails, done with some garlic and butter," Adrienne said, mopping her plate with a heel of the crusty bread.

"Big fella doesn't like 'em," Tully said. "Maybe he should get a rubber escargot; he likes the *sauce* well enough, but—"

"Hey, I'm just a Dakota plowboy," Tom said a little defensively. "We don't eat snails."

"Abalone is a big item in North Dakota, then?" Roy jibed, and laughed. "OK, each to their own. Let's have some of that chardonnay."

The white wine was chilled from its immersion in seawater, but the temperature of the air was perfect—low seventies. As the sun sank toward the western horizon the Pacific became a glittering road of eye-hurting brightness. The cliffs turned ruddy with the sunset; he refilled the skillet with sliced potatoes, flipping them a couple of times before sliding out a portion for everyone, then putting one of the sage-and-herb-spiced venison sausages on a stick and propping it up with its butt in the sand and the wood over one of the rocks that ringed the fire.

"It's a good thing life in the field isn't usually like this," Tully said, retrieving his sausage and wrapping a slice of the dense, chewy bread around the sputtering, smoking meat before stripping it off the stick. "War might get too popular. . . . Pass that mustard, would you?"

"Here," Adrienne said, and tossed it over. "I suspect we're all going to suffer enough to satisfy the most exacting conscience before this is over, so let's store up some memories while we can."

The sun vanished in a line of red fire and hot gold among the clouds on the western horizon. Stars began to appear above the low crescent moon, and the air grew chillier; he put a pot of coffee on the ring, and Sandra unwrapped some chocolate-walnut brownies.

"Made these myself," she said. "Seven Oaks walnuts—best in the domain."

Tom sat on the sand and threw a few more sticks of driftwood onto the fire before leaning back against the log. The flotsam burned with a snap and crackle, flames flickering blue and green with the salts dried into the wood. Adrienne curled into his shoulder, and he put an arm around her; he suspected Tully and Sandra were doing the same, but his eyes were a little dazzled by the fire.

"Just my luck," he said lightly.

"Kemosabe?"

"I find the girl of my dreams, and she's a spook from another dimension with a license to kill."

Adrienne chuckled. "Here, *you're* from another dimension. Although I grant you're not a spook—you're a game warden from another dimension. . . ."

Tom sighed, taking a sip of the coffee and another deep breath of the cool, sea-scented air. "Just doesn't get better than this, I suppose."

Adrienne's lips touched his ear just as he was taking a sip of the coffee; he might have managed that, but not the tongue that slid in after them. When he'd finished coughing, she thumped him helpfully on the back.

"I'll have you know that I come second to no meal. Or even a Pacific sunset," she said, grinning wickedly.

"Ah . . . I think it's about time to turn in," Tom said, ignoring laughter from across the fire. "Long day tomorrow."

CHAPTER EIGHTEEN

Southern California
July 2009

The Commonwealth of New Virginia
Piet Botha reined in his horse. He rode in Boer fashion, slumped with his legs nearly straight and slanted forward. His son rode beside him, using the bent-knee New Virginian style. They were alike otherwise, given the twenty-five-year gap in their ages. Schalk Botha was a little lighter in his coloring and had eyes of an unusual tawny shade; besides that he was an inch shorter than his father's six-three, and without any of the older man's extra flesh. He was also grinning with excitement.

"*Hell,* yes, Pa," he said. "Sounds like fun!"

"You're not too old for me to clout across the ear," Piet growled. "This is serious business, boy. We may have to fight some of our relatives, not just the bliddy Indians."

Schalk shrugged his wide shoulders. "Only if they're fools enough to get mixed up in treason."

"Treason is what you do when you lose," Piet said. "I'd be on the other side myself, if I thought it would work. But it wouldn't."

He stopped and leaned down from the saddle to fasten the gate. His cow-beasts were all inside the paddock now, and he looked up the long slope of the land to where his farmhouse glittered white and red among its trees and orange groves, and the mountains reared blue behind it. It was a hot day, but tempered by a breeze from the sea; the air was full of the smell of horse sweat and cattle dung and crushed herbs. Behind them was a dirt road, and beyond that a waste of tall dry grass, dead reeds that had grown in seasonal sloughs earlier in the year, an occasional thicket of oak or sycamore or willow, and patches of the tall stalks of wild mustard.

It's home to young Schalk, he thought. *His homeland. He came here young enough; I'll be an exile all my life.*

He shrugged at the thought; he'd be an exile in the land of his birth, too, even if he could live there unmolested by the new government's police—something unlikely in the extreme. The country that had borne him didn't exist anymore, not really. Instead he spoke of practical things. "We'll be getting the horses. Good ones—no show beasts, mind—ones that'll stay alive over the mountains. And the mules."

* * *

Adrienne Rolfe smiled to herself as they climbed out of the amphibian and onto the floating dock, blinking lazily in the bright San Diegan sunshine. *I'm feeling disgustingly sleek and satisfied,* she thought, as the crewmen took the ropes. *I like Tom. I like him a lot.*

She grew aware of exactly how sleek and satisfied her smile was, and shrugged ruefully at Tom's expression; Tully's was carefully neutral, but the little man was alarmingly perceptive.

San Diego was the third-largest city in the Commonwealth, nearly twenty thousand people and growing fast. She rather liked it, in small doses—except when the Santa Ana was blowing, of course. The town was a decade younger than the ones around the bay, and it had a tarry practicality, a big-shouldered quality that gave piquancy to the sun-washed, mountain-backed setting. It was also a Commission territory, not dominated by any Family the way Napa or New Brooklyn were. It wasn't centered around the Families collectively either, the way the capital was. Settler merchants and manufacturers set the tone here.

The floatplane docks were near the yacht basin, and just over from the main harbor, all facing south toward Coronado Island and within the sheltering hook of land that cut off the harbor from the Pacific. The land airport was on the shore to the west; a Hercules was coming in as she watched, with the winged Thompson gun of the Collettas on its tailfin; her mouth quirked at the irony.

The main harbor was busy too, amid a white storm of gulls: ten big windjammers, a couple of flat-decked wooden tankers and dozens of smaller craft, from tugs down to fishing craft and rowboats, all moving about the dredged channels to the redwood piers. New *nahua* workers filed over the gangplanks of a three-master up from the southern ports; cranes swung ashore its other cargo: baled raw cotton, rare tropical woods, cacao in the bean, leather, featherwork cloaks, chilies and caged macaws. Another fair-sized sailing ship was being towed in; the absence of a diesel auxiliary and some subtle elements in her lines showed she was foreign—Dahaean out of Hagamantash, probably, from what FirstSiders would call Shanghai—laden with silk and cotton fabrics, tea, pepper and cloves, cinnamon and nutmeg and inlaid furniture, jade statues and thousand-knot rugs. A Tahitian schooner looked more exotic, with its twin prows and flamboyantly colorful tiki-mask figurehead.

Most craft were from the Commonwealth, swapping northern timber and manufactures and FirstSide goods for refined petroleum, chocolate, cement, brick, tile, borax. . . .

And there she is, Adrienne thought.

A tall young woman with yellow hair came swinging down the docks; she was dressed in a white linen dress with a thin black belt and a wide-brimmed white hat; a little discreet jewelry, and the Families' gold-and-platinum ring on her left thumb. She took off her sunglasses and waved with a bright artificial smile, and walked more quickly.

"Tom Christiansen, my cousin Heather Fitzmorton,"

Adrienne said formally. *The bitch,* she did not add aloud, as they exchanged a formal kiss on the cheek.

Heather was Adrienne's age to a year. Her eyes flicked across Tully, lingered on Sandra for an instant, then took Tom in from feet to head.

"Well, Cuz," she drawled, "I see your taste has improved—and gotten a lot more conventional."

"Ha," Adrienne said flatly. "Ha. You always were such a kidder, Cuz." Heather's handshake was lingering when she took Tom's hand. "And here are the keys. I presume Irene is around?"

"At the town house," Heather said. "It wouldn't do to have *her* standing next to you where people could see; it might give them ideas."

"Thanks for helping out."

"All a *mispocha-mitzvah,* as the saying goes," Heather said, taking the keys and dropping them into her handbag. "And it's a guilt-free chance to get away from my kids for a while." She wiggled her fingers at the rest of the party. "Ta," she finished, and walked away.

Tom blinked. "I got the impression she doesn't like you?" he said, taking in Sandra's black scowl at the retreating back of the woman of the Families.

"I'm not exactly popular, and Heather's a model of respectability," Adrienne said. "I warned you about that, remember . . . but Heather has a perfectly adequate sense of *responsibility,* fortunately, so I could ask her for a favor."

"Mmmm . . . *mispocha-mitzvah* . . . something 'good deeds'?" Tully said. "If that was Yiddish."

"More or less," Adrienne said. "'Clan duty' might be closer to the actual colloquial meaning."

"I didn't think *mispocha* meant family."

"It doesn't, FirstSide. It sort of came to here; old Sol Pearlmutter used to mutter, 'What a *mispocha!*' about the Families, so . . . Heather's my aunt Jennifer's daughter—her father's a Fitzmorton, of course, a collateral, and they have a place just across the Mayacamas in the Fitzmorton domain—Sonoma Valley, you'd say."

"And Irene?"

"Another cousin; and she looks a *lot* more like me than dear Heather. Blame it on the way the Fitzmortons and Rolfes kept interbreeding back on Firstside. In the meantime, let's get to the hotel."

The San Diego Arms knew they were coming in, and sent transport—a brand-new European fuel-cell van; it was open in back, and Adrienne enjoyed pointing out the sights as they moved inland, through the bustle of the harbor district and into the town proper: the paved highway and pipeline stretching north toward Long Beach, the new movie theater . . .

"And who the hell are *they?*" Tom blurted, pointing to two men.

"Those?" Adrienne said. *Got to remember what looks weird to a FirstSider,* she chided herself.

Those were two big brown-skinned men, with middle-aged fat overlying impressive muscles, swirling tattoos over much of their faces and bodies, wearing what looked like crested Grecian helmets made of orange and green feathers, multicolored cloaks and sarongs. They strode along the sidewalk under the pepper trees, occasionally stopping to look in a shop window. Nobody but a few fascinated small boys noticed them.

"Those are Hawaiian *ali'i*—nobles—from Tahiti."

"Ah . . ." Tully scratched his head. "If they're Hawaiian, how come they're from Tahiti?"

"Long story . . . well, about the time we sent our first ships across the Pacific, the Hawaiian islands got hit with a really bad series of plagues—smallpox from the Selang-Arsi country and chicken pox and measles from who knows where. We bought the islands from the survivors—paid them with vaccination and, umm, a few other things."

"And they moved to Tahiti?" Tom asked, his fair brows knotted in thought. "Because they're closely related cultures, I suppose?"

"Well, it was more on the order of Tahiti being part of the

'few other things' we paid them with. Their ancestors had come from there, and they remembered."

"Wait a minute," Tom said. "What did the *Tahitians* say to all this?"

"The 'few other things' also included ships, a couple of thousand trade muskets, some muzzle-loading brass cannon, and a lot of gunpowder."

"Oh," he said. "Then they conquered Tahiti?"

Adrienne felt like patting him on the cheek. *Tom's so gentle and sweet!* she thought. Aloud, she went on: "Sort of. Actually, they *ate* a lot of the Tahitians, as I understand it: You could consider it a conquest, or a really big hunt for long pig. And sacrificed a lot of them to Kuka'ilimoku—the war god."

Tom and his friend winced. Adrienne went on: "Just because someone gets the dirty end of the stick doesn't mean they're very nice," she pointed out.

＊ ＊ ＊

Tom would have enjoyed the *Sea-Witch* more if he'd been able to relax, if they were really headed west to the islands for nothing more serious than scuba diving and surfing and climbs among the mountain forests.

As it was . . . *I'm enjoying myself anyway,* he thought. *Just not as much.*

He'd done a little boating—canoeing in the North Woods of Minnesota, and a little sailing in California; he'd have done a lot more, but it took money he didn't have.

Right now he was standing at the forepeak, clinging to the foresail shroud where the long bowsprit lanced out from the hull, and looking back at the taut curve of the sails. The two-masted schooner was sailing reach before a following wind, slicing its way northwest and throwing bursts of spray twice the height of his head as it rose to the swells. Land had dropped below the eastern horizon hours ago. The sea was indigo under an azure bowl of sky, cloudless save for a little high haze in the east; the wind was not quite stiff enough to show whitecaps, and the waves were long and smooth. Foam peeled back from the yacht's sharp cutwater, and the bow-wave curled deep along the hull, showing the copper sheathing that protected the wood from teredo-worms. A school of bottlenose dolphins rode the wave, lancing out of the water in smooth curves and spearing back with hardly a splash, dancing with the sea and the ship

Let me sail, let me sail, let the Orinoco flow,
Let me reach, let me beach, on the shores of Tripoli.

The tune ran through his head as he watched, like a lilt of infinite possibilities beyond the horizon.

Adrienne waved from the rear of the yacht near the wheel and aft of the deckhouse, a hundred and forty feet back. That was only a little more than the height of the mainmast—the foremast was a bit shorter—and she carried ten thousand square feet of canvas in her fore-and-aft sails. That was a number; the dazzling mass piled overhead was reality, like clouds brought to earth and imprisoned in a suave geometry of curves and lines. He levered himself up and walked backward—*sternward,* he reminded himself—along the deck; it was relatively narrow, nowhere more than thirty feet across, and uncluttered save for the low shapes of the geared winches that controlled the sails.

The crew nodded as he passed, not pausing in their work, and Tom returned the gesture. There were twelve men aboard, and three women. Captain McKay was a taciturn man whose hair had been lion-colored before it went mostly badger gray, with blue eyes and a kink in his nose that looked as if it had been put there with something sharp, and scar tissue half an inch thick over his knuckles. His accent was an improbable mixture of Scots and Aussie, when he did speak; his wife was purser-cook, his daughter her assistant, and his son first mate. Evidently McKay had been running the *Sea-Witch* since she was built in the Pearlmutter yards in New Brooklyn thirty-five years before. What he'd done before that, FirstSide, was not mentioned. The rest of the crew were New Virginian–born, except for one Dahaean picked up recently in San Diego, a dark Eurasian-looking man with the front of his scalp shaved and the black hair at the rear worked up into braids and looped over his ears.

Tom nodded to him, too: The man was dressed in a pair of tar-stained breeches that ended at the knee, showing a remarkable assortment of scars on his whipcord-lean torso. God alone knew how he'd ended up here.

And according to Adrienne, his language is a creolized form of North Iranian with a heavy Sinic influence. Whatever the hell that means.

Captain MacKay was seated at the table on the fantail, under an awning, along with the rest of their party. A steward was just laying out luncheon: salad, skewers of grilled shrimp the size of Tom's thumb in curry sauce, cold meats, bread, cheese and fruit. The skipper of the *Sea-Witch* had his white peaked cap on the table and was filling a foul old briar pipe; luckily the stiff breeze would snatch away everything but a hint of its reek.

"Aye, we'll cruise a bit off Santa Barbara," he said to Adrienne, giving Tom a courteous nod. "Those are well-traveled waters, s'truth. We'll be seen by ships and aircraft both; then we'll turn and head"—he waved to the southwest. "Off the wind on that heading lie the Marquesas, and we'll be nicely making way. Cruise there, up to the islands, and it'll be a while before it's realized you're no aboard, miss, but the *Sea-Witch* herself, she'll be seen and spoken of at once—on the radio, too, no fear."

Tom seated himself. "I'm a bit noticeable myself," he pointed out.

McKay grinned, a snaggletoothed expression in his bushy beard and mustache, and pointed silently to his son.

The young man was in his twenties, and only a finger under Tom's six-three and a bit, but he was gangly rather than broad-shouldered and deep-chested, and until today his freckled face had been topped by a thatch of stiff gingery curls. Tom's eyebrow went up as he saw that the unruly mop had been cut close in a good imitation of the Ranger crop he wore, and dyed silver-blond as well.

"From a distance . . ." he said.

"Aye," McKay said with satisfaction. He cocked an eye skyward. "This wind'll no hold. I may need the auxiliary if we're to make the coast again by sunset."

Tom had the impression that McKay regarded using the diesel engine as a confession of failure of some sort. *Purist*, he thought.

Adrienne's eyes met his; she was wearing a sarong, a halter, and red hibiscus flowers in her hair; she winked slightly, and he knew she'd read his thoughts.

* * *

Now, this *is more like being on an op,* Tom thought. The *No Biscuit* had made its rendezvous with the yacht neatly enough. *One to pilot, one to come aboard the* Sea-Witch *and impersonate Adrienne . . . complicated!*

The *Sea-Witch* pitched slightly as it lay with its nose into the wind blowing from the shore; the sunset was fading sternward, a smudge of red along a horizon fading from green to deep night blue. He could see the outline of the San Pedro hills to the southwest and the mountains behind Malibu—the place where Malibu was FirstSide—to the north. There was enough light from the stars, a frosted multitude that faded only around the one-quarter moon—more stars than he was used to seeing FirstSide except in the most remote desert wilderness.

The *No Biscuit* floated half a hundred yards away, and the inflatable boat shuttled between them. Adrienne's cousin Irene came over the rail with a grin that was more than a little like hers, ready to take her place in the masquerade.

"This is like the story about the wolf, the sheep and the cabbage," the younger woman said. "Good luck, Cuz."

"Enjoy the islands, Cuz," Adrienne replied. "Try to act like me."

"I don't know if I'm up to that, but I'll do my best—it ought to be fun trying!"

Their gear went over the side in a net, hung from a cable

on the long boom; crewmen held the rubber boat close to the
yacht with boathooks. Tom followed, pulling his night-sight
goggles down; the rope was harsh against his palms as they
went over the side. A low, muted throb came from the
schooner's diesel, enough to cover the muted hum of the
outboard; Tom took charge of that, since he'd had a fair bit
of boat training, and the vibration surged up his hand and
forearm as he opened the throttle wider and twisted the tiller
to bring the inflatable around and away, settling on an eastward course toward the black outline of the land. The *Sea-
Witch* turned westward as soon as they'd cast free, her bow
coming about to the northwest and her sails rising with a rattle of winches and a flapping of sheets that turned taut as
they caught the wind. The schooner heeled over and began
to pick up speed; the seaplane remained quiet, pitching
gently on the waves—it would stay there until the *Sea-Witch*
was well away.

"This heading," Adrienne said, settling in beside him on
the rearmost bench and holding out a digital compass with a
faintly glowing display.

The flat bottom of the inflatable struck the water, slapping
it as they picked up speed. Their destination was a little north
of where the Los Angeles River ran into the sea; here and
now the stream reached salt water well to the north of the Palos Verdes hills, along the course of what he'd known as Bel-
lona Creek. And "course" was a misnomer, since the river
wandered through a broad ill-defined zone of wetlands and
swamps all the way to the ocean; on the coast everything between Santa Monica–that–wasn't and Palos Verdes was sea-
side swamp, saltwater or brackish marsh, miles of it. More
stretched between those hills and the site of Long Beach.
Even in high summer the scent from the land was damp,
smelling of those vast wetlands.

"And on FirstSide it's a dry concrete ditch," Tom murmured, and heard Adrienne chuckle beside him.

Spray struck his face, cool and tasting of iodine and salt;
he wiped his night-vision goggles with his sleeve and peered
ahead. An endlessness of reeds rustled to the southward;

now that the mudflats were covered by the high tide, but this shallow-draft boat could go almost anywhere. Tully called to him a moment before he saw it himself; a blinking light, so faint that it would have been invisible to unaided vision. White sand gleamed nearby, where higher land rose northward.

Tom's teeth showed in a fighting grin. The pretense was over, and the mission was about to begin.

* * *

Tom brought the inflatable in quickly, running the bow up as far as he could on the wet sand. Then he jumped over the side of the rubber boat and held it as the waves thumped it against the ground and small tumbling ripples of foam hissed around his feet. The others followed, and the four of them grabbed the rope loops along its sides and ran it higher, up onto the sloping surface of the beach. He looked around; as best as he could tell, they'd landed right on target—around the southern part of Palisades Beach, near where the Santa Monica Pier was FirstSide, at the westward end of Colorado Avenue. A sandstone cliff stood inland a couple of hundred yards, low here but rising to the north; off that way he could just glimpse a few lights burning in the night, a large sprawling house or small village.

He felt a moment of disorientation; the geography was the same, but he was used to seeing this spot in a blaze of lights—some of the most expensive housing in the United States was within a mile or two, and a few miles north were the condos of Malibu, not to mention the meganecropolis that stretched from here to San Diego and inland to the edges of the Mohave. The smell was entirely different, sea salt and iodine, beach wrack crunching underfoot, the silty mud of the huge marshes to the south.

The feeling of weird dislocation wasn't as bad this time. *I'm getting used to it,* he thought grimly.

"We're right on the place they filmed *Baywatch,*" Tully

said reverently, and Sandra giggled. "And thereabouts is the carousel they used in *The Sting.* . . ."

"Roy," Tom said, with warning in his voice. It was scarcely the time to indulge one's old-movie fixation.

The other man chuckled quietly and subsided, shrugging. They all went down to one knee beside the inflatable, unslinging the rifles they wore across their backs and scanning the darkness through their night-sight goggles. They gave good vision, but it wasn't quite like normal sight—there was a bright, slight flatness to their surroundings that made it harder to judge distances. Adrienne pushed hers up and used a pair of powerful binoculars instead for a moment. He recognized the instrument from the square, molded look and the digital controls on the top; it was a cutting-edge FirstSide military model, with automatic light compensation and a built-in range finder. The GPS system wouldn't work here, of course.

"Right on target," she said quietly. "That's the Versfelds' home place—Hendricksdorp, their equivalent of Rolfe Manor or Colletta Hall." She pointed to the lights, shining from around the curve of the bay and a little inland, just beneath the deeper darkness of the mountains.

"Nobody but Versfeld's people will be wandering around here—and Piet can talk his way past them. Better to keep out of their way, of course."

"Speaking of the devil," Tom said.

The cliff sloped down to ground level nearby. A horse whickered quietly from that direction, and several men came toward them—two tall men, and a slighter one of average height; he could hear the crunch of their boots in the sand. A little closer, and he could recognize the gorilloid shape of Piet Botha. The younger man beside him resembled him enough to be his son, and almost certainly was. And Henry Villers. The black man was standing a bit aside from the Afrikaners, and there was something in their body language that spoke of strained politeness all around.

My sympathy is underwhelming, Piet, Tom thought. *I'll work with you, but I don't have to like you.*

Like the four from the sea, the three men waiting for them were dressed in Commonwealth militia uniform—stone-gray bush jacket and trousers of tough cotton drill with plenty of accordion-pleat pockets and leather patches on elbows and knees, and a floppy-brimmed jungle hat; the outfit faded into the background well. They also wore the webbing harness, which seemed to be based on the Israeli design, one he'd always envied: broad belt with adjustable lacing and many carrying attachments, padded straps over the shoulders, and load-bearing pouches in the small of the back. Tom was willing to bet that the designer had suffered through a couple of campaigns in the sort of stuff rear-echelon types thought up for field men to wear.

"Miss Rolfe," Botha said; she nodded acknowledgment.

Adrienne and Sandra kept watch with rifles ready; the men slung their weapons, bent in unison and lifted the boat, with Botha and Tom opposite each other at the rear, where the boxes were stacked. It wasn't all that heavy itself, but the crates of weapons and gear weighed more than twice what any of them did, even Tom or the still more massively built Piet. The soft sand made for bad footing, and it churned under their feet as they panted upslope; he leaned away from the weight, teeth fixed in a grimace of effort and sweat stinging his eyes. The going went easier as they came to rock and dirt held by coarse dry grass; they were all sweating, but the night was pleasant, no more than sixty degrees and with a fresh breeze off the water that made it seem cooler.

"Here," Botha said, indicating a deep pit about the size of a grave; a pick and shovel leaned against a boulder near it.

Thank you, O taciturn man of the veld, Tom thought sardonically.

They lifted the cargo free and stacked it, then deflated the boat with a hiss and smell of synthetic-tinged air. He and Tully rolled it into a compact bundle, stuffed it into the pre-dug hole, slid the silenced outboard engine into a tough canvas sack and dropped that in as well. A few minutes' work buried the whole under sand and tumbled rock; he stopped and carefully memorized the lay of the land, turning in a complete circle and taking a bearing on conspicuous land-marks as best he could in the dark. He noticed that the others did likewise, in their different ways—it was appallingly easy to lose something completely, in trackless country, even if you knew the general location.

I'm glad everyone seems to know their business, Tom thought, as they carried the boxes up a narrow pathway to the crest of the higher ground inland; he slung two on his shoulders and trotted easily under the hundred and eighty pounds of weight.

This wasn't like an op in the Rangers, where he was working with people he'd spent years beside and whose strengths and weaknesses he knew inside out. He and Roy had been together long enough in the SOU to develop an instinctive rapport too. Depending on so many relative strangers made him a little nervous, but there was nothing he could do about it except hope they'd shake down quickly.

The younger Afrikaner went up the slope and returned with a string of mules. Sandra came forward and the two of them oversaw the loading; Adrienne and Botha cut stalks of brush and went back down the beach, sweeping over their footprints. A normal night's breeze would obliterate most traces that didn't remove, and a few days would take care of the rest. While they were about it Tom went a little into the thick brush and crouched on guard with his back to a small sycamore tree; what he could see of the landscape was a lot more densely grown than he'd expected, the vegetation dry and dusty enough in high summer, but plenty of it, ranging from knee level to more than his six-three of height.

"And it's noisy," he murmured to himself, relaxing into a hunter's absolute stillness that let all sounds in, only his eyes moving, and his chest as he breathed.

He could hear the beat and hiss of the waves as the tide went out, like the heartbeat of the world when you were near the shore. There were plenty of insects, too; not many mosquitoes, thank God, since there wasn't a freshwater swamp close by. But a fair swarm of other types, chirping and rustling and buzzing and shrilling and hopping and flying through the darkness. He moved his head occasionally in a slow arc, because the goggles cut off peripheral vision, and more than once he saw a bat twisting through the air in pursuit of some bug or other. There were birds in plenty—nightjars, and he saw a great horned owl whip by at only twice head-height, swerving and jinking like a fighter plane and intent on something inland; then he heard the harsh scream-click-hiss of a barn owl not too far away. A couple of black-tailed jackrabbits passed him, hopping and then landing and coming erect with their tall ears swiveling like radar dishes; one landed near enough for him to reach out and touch it if he'd wanted to. It gave a bulge-eyed double take and a squeal as it realized there was a human at arm's length, and thumped the earth in alarm before it tore off.

Can't be easy to be small and tasty, he thought.

Something larger went through the brush a hundred feet to his north; he couldn't tell exactly what and didn't care to guess, not in the crazy mixed-up ecology John Rolfe's importations had produced, but whatever it was it snorted as it caught their scent and crashed off. A coyote went yip-yip-yip and howled occasionally, answered by others across the huge stretch of wilderness—but then, song-dogs had survived here even when it was all built solid; they were as adaptable as humans, and nearly as clever.

Farther away something gave a grunting moan in the night, an *ooorrrrghhh . . . ooorrrrghhh . . . ooorrrrghhh . . .* that built up to a throaty roar. He recognized it then, more from the MGM logo at the beginning of movies than anything else—the territorial roar of a lion, announcing its claims to the world and any other male thinking of horning in on its pride of females.

Face it, he thought, grinning silently, and breathing deeply to take in the scents of sea air, dry satchet-smelling herbs and dusty earth, *this is as close to paradise as a man like me is going to get. Lots of space, lots of animals, just enough civilization to visit when you want a book or a good dinner or a movie or a cold beer.*

The thought of going back permanently FirstSide, back to

crowding and itchy madness and a world so empty of life, was getting increasingly repellent.

Plus I think I'm in love, and that it's mutual. If only John Rolfe weren't such a ruthless son of a bitch . . . well, for now he's my son of a bitch. Got to admit he's one gutsy and smart son of a bitch, too. I don't like everything he's done by a long shot, but it's impressive that he's been able to do it. He took that one wild chance and ran with it.

Something crackled behind him and to the right, very faintly. Tom spun before the sound was finished, the weapon in his arms coming up to his shoulder in a perfect three-point aiming position even as he threw himself prone. The leveled rifle probed the darkness as his finger took up the slack on the trigger.

More than one man had died because they assumed someone Tom's size had to be slow. Assumptions were nearly as deadly as bullets, and much more popular.

"You fast, not just big, Tall Man," a thickly accented voice said. "Listen good, too."

"Hello," Tom said dryly as a wiry brown form rose from the brush; the dark skin was about as good at melting into the background as his fatigues.

Kolo nodded wordlessly and slipped the polished shaft of his tomahawk back into a loop at his belt, then turned and trotted away through the darkness—making a lot more noise this time; you could move silently through this wilderness of dried stalks and crunchable vegetation, or quickly, but even someone like the Indian tracker couldn't do both. Behind the spot he'd occupied another figure rose—Jim Simmons, with a scope-sighted rifle cradled in his arms.

"Sorry," the Scout said; they shook hands. "We just got here, and Kolo likes a joke. Also he's annoyed that this trip means he can't get back to visit his wife and family."

Tom looked at the sycamore he'd been squatting under. "Yah, you betcha, life is hard—and he was going to put the tomahawk into that tree just over my head, wasn't he?"

He pushed the night-sight goggles up on his forehead; it

was a strain if you wore them too long. Simmons shrugged ruefully, his teeth white in the darkness.

"You know the really funny thing?"

"No, what?" Tom said.

He'd been around Roy Tully long enough to know an appeal for a straight line when he heard it. He didn't mind; Simmons was the most likable of the men on this trip, after Roy. Just about the only one besides Henry Villers who was simpatico at all, in fact—possibly it was because they were in the same line of work and were both men of the wilderness by choice. The smaller man went on:

"The local Indians didn't use tomahawks before we got here. Some Families idiot back in the early days evidently gave them the idea, probably because he'd read *Last of the Mohicans* too many times and thought that Injuns just weren't proper Injuns unless they chucked hatchets about with bad intent, and took scalps. Incidentally, the local tribes didn't do that either—not this side of the Sierras—until it was suggested to them."

Tom winced. "Jim, did you ever get the feeling that John Rolfe and his friends turned this place into a theme park of perverted romanticism run amok?"

The Scout grinned. "All the time. I like it that way. It may be a playpen, but it's *our* playpen, by God."

They went back to the mules, and Botha and his son Schalk—the name gave Tom a bad feeling, but hell, the two men had been partners for a long time before Schalk van der Merwe went rogue—led them to the rest of the caravan.

If I ever have a son, I'll probably name him Roy, after all.

It was surprising how much space ten mules and fourteen-odd horses took up; quadrupeds were bulky. Sandra introduced him to his horses, two big cobby roans; he fed them lumps of sugar and pieces of dried fruit, and did the appropriate horse-language blowing in the nostrils in greeting. The women and the smaller men were on mounts that looked like they had a good bit of Arab in their bloodlines, which was just what you wanted for a desert expedition . . . except that breed tended to be small, and asking one to carry two hundred and twenty pounds of muscle, bone and gristle was a bit unfair.

To his relief, he wasn't expected to pull the spare horse along on a leading rein, or help with the mules. Those had been trained to follow each other on a long looped arrangement, and Sandra would be chivvying the horse herd along cowboy-style; he noticed the two Boers and Simmons keeping an eye on her as they moved out in a loose column of twos on what was probably more a game trail than a track made by men. It couldn't be easy, even though the horses wanted to stay close to each other and to their human protectors in the predator-smelling darkness. He also noticed the men relax—a little—as it became apparent that she was good at what she did.

Adrienne rode knee to knee with him. He leaned over close enough to murmur, "Lot of boars wandering around here—male chauvinist variety," he said dryly.

"Tell me about it," Adrienne said; he thought he detected a trace of bitterness under the mordant humor. "Do you have any idea of how irritating it is when the best you can get is to be treated like an honorary man? And if you think Jim's bad, you should see what the older generation is like. Fast cars and feminism are the only good points about FirstSide."

The Bothas led, father and son; this land was part of the Versfeld domain, only ten miles or so from their farm, and they'd both hunted through it for years. The party went east for a good long while, then began trending a little south, keeping the mountains parallel to their course on their left; the Dipper blazed above them, and the Pole Star was plain enough. The land was pretty well flat, with an occasional hill rearing out of the plain; for a while the vegetation died down to sagebrush and dry grass with an occasional scrubby tree. He was a little startled when one of the trees raised its head and looked at them. . . .

A dry rustling sound stopped; he hadn't noticed it until then. That had been something huge cropping at the top of an oak, and ripping the leaves loose with a long prehensile tongue. It reared up to its full eighteen feet of height as they approached, its two knobby horns and long camel-like head clear against the stars, then turned and paced away, both long gangly legs on either side moving in unison. It looked slow even after it had broken into a clumsy gallop, but he estimated that it was moving at nearly thirty miles an hour.

Adrienne gave a low gurgling chuckle. "There's something intrinsically funny about a giraffe," she said. "Unless it kicks you. In a way, it's a pity this land isn't slated as Commission reserve."

"I admit, it looks a lot better than FirstSide LA," Tom said. "Smells better, too. It would be a shame to see it go the same way."

"Oh, we're never going to let it get like *that*," she said. "Just farms and ranches and small towns, with a couple of medium-sized cities. No long-distance aqueducts, and strict limits on wells—one thing the domain system was designed to do was make it impossible for cities to reach out and suck other regions dry. But it'll be a lot tamer than it is now."

It couldn't be much wilder, Tom thought. *Christ, what a mix-up—Wild West and wild Serengeti!*

They came to a dirt road a couple of miles inland, rutted clay scattered with gravel on a low embankment, flanked by ditches and tall posts carrying wires.

Adrienne pointed southward along the dirt road. "That's Highway One," she said. "It's paved from San Diego to the oil wells and refinery at Long Beach; then it heads north, inland for a way, up to San Luis Obispo and Paso Robles. In theory you could drive all the way from San Diego to the geyser country north of Napa—but a lot of it's rough, not easily motorable like this."

"It's all what you're used to," Tom said gravely. *And I've seen better roads than this in Afghanistan, for God's sake.*

After that the vegetation grew thicker again; for a couple of miles they traveled single-file through stands of castor-bean plant mixed with wild black mustard in a tangle that that ranged from six feet in height to ten; small yellow flowers were still blooming at the end of the mustard's short branches. After the first few hundred yards it was like riding through neck-deep water that occasionally closed over his head—although water wouldn't make you sneeze, which the pollen from the mustard did—or between rustling walls along a laneway barely wide enough for a horse and rider.

"Careful, big Tom," Simmons said on his way back to check on the mules.

"Here be tigers?" he replied.

Adrienne answered for him: "The place is lousy with them. Also grizzly bears and lions. Cape buffalo and American bison, and the odd rhino too; and up ahead"—she pointed southeast—"is the Winkpar."

"Which means?"

"The Indian word was *pwinukipar,* or something like that. It means 'many waters' or 'big swamp.' Hippos. Elephants. Crocs."

"Right where Las Cienegas was, right?"

Before that became a main Los Angeles highway, it had been what its Spanish name meant—"swamps."

"Right. But it's not just one big block—there are little sloughs and seepage springs all over the country between the river and the Santa Monicas. Excuse me, between the river and the Krugersberg."

"Well, that adds a certain charm to a ride in the night," Tom said, and they smiled at each other in the rustling dimness.

And oddly enough, it's true, he thought, feeling himself warmed. *Although if I'm going to be charged by a rhino, better while riding a Hummer than a horse.*

They moved on through the night, stopping every hour or so for ten minutes' rest and switching horses every two. He used the intervals to stretch, grunting a little as he forced head to knee. Mosquitoes grew more common as they skirted the huge swamp to their south; it made him glad he'd had the malaria cellular vaccine just before he left the army. The marshes covered scores of square miles, even toward the end of the summer drought—and so did groves of trees on their edges, sycamores and big cottonwoods and willows mostly, with oaks and California walnut; the shade grew dense enough that everyone put their night-sight goggles back on. They were riding through an open gallery forest most of the time; the problem was that there were patches and outliers of the marsh, where streams ran downhill from the Santa Monicas or underground rock ledges forced the already-high water table to the surface. Those produced jungle, an impenetrable lacework of creepers and California rose. Sometimes you couldn't go around.

He dismounted at a hand gesture and unlimbered the machete from his saddle. "Now this takes me back," he said, as he took his turn.

The blade was a slightly flared rectangle of good steel, heavy and sharp; he waded in, reminding himself that they needed a path wide enough for horses, not just men. Brushwood and branches and thorny vines fell with a *ssss-chunk!* as he struck with blows that might have been timed by metronome, flicking or kicking the cut stems aside when he had to. The ground turned muddy under his feet, but they didn't come to an actual river, just a laneway of lower growth that carried the overflow of the winter storms down from the mountains. Sweat ran down his face and flanks and back as he breathed deeply with the exertion, an agreeable enough sensation—which wasn't something he'd ever thought he'd say about breathing in the LA basin! Back FirstSide, he'd be choking on the air. . . .

Henry Villers came up to spell him. "Nice job," he said. "I thought you did your fighting in dry places, Warden Tom."

"Mostly—Euphrates to Hindu Kush, with excursions north. But my battalion got sent to the Philippines for a while during the war—Abu Sayyef tried a revival. Jungle work."

"What happened?"

Tom grimaced. "Some of us died. All of them died . . . not a happy time. At least it isn't raining here, and there aren't many civilians to get caught in the cross fire."

"I was a dry-area fighter myself," the black man said; he took over, competently enough, if without the machine accuracy and strength of the ex-Ranger.

"Kuwait?"

"Gulf War One, right," Villers said. "Marines—we did the 'hey diddle diddle, straight up the middle' part while you army pukes played at being Rommel's Desert Rats."

"Ah . . . I think Rommel *was* the Desert Fox and *fought* the Desert Rats," he said, hesitating until Villers turned and grinned at him over his shoulder.

"Man, you fell for that one! I hung out with some Brits during the buildup; they still have that dumb-ass rodent painted on their tanks."

Tom nodded acknowledgment at the hit. "What was your MOS, if you don't mind me asking?"

"Hey, *every* marine's a rifleman—even the women. Seriously, it was infantry—I carried the squad's Minimi," Villers said; that meant he'd been a machine gunner. "Anyway, it wasn't much of a war. Never saw anyone so anxious to surrender as those Homers. Taking care of them slowed us down worse than fighting would have."

"Best kind of war," Tom said sincerely. "Even better if you're piloting a Predator through a satellite uplink from Florida."

"Right on, brother," Villers said, panting, dropping back to let Schalk Botha replace him at the front. "Christ, I'm thirty-eight and I feel every year of it. Should have spent more time in the hills hunting deer this spring."

All the men took turns at the clearing, until they were up and through the slough and into more of the cottonwood forest.

"We'll camp here," Botha said. "We'll need firewood—"

"And I'll help put up the tents," Henry Villers said smoothly, with a toothy smile.

Tom filled in the unspoken codicil and smiled to himself: *Draw your own water, Mr. Boer, and hew your own wood.*

CHAPTER NINETEEN

Southern California
July 2009

The Commonwealth of New Virginia

> My words are tied in one
> With the great mountains,
> With the great rocks,
> With the great trees,
> In one with my body
> And my heart.
> Do you all help me
> With your spirit power,
> And you, day!
> And you, night!
> All of you see me—one with this world!

Kolomusnim finished his chant to the setting sun, low-ered his arms and dropped the tuft of burning grass he'd been holding and ground it out under one callused heel; a waft of acrid smoke drifted past them. Adrienne stopped her running sotto voce translation an instant later, and Kolo trot-ted off toward the Glendale Narrows.

They were camped on the low terrace that had been the original site of El Pueblo de la Reina de Los Angeles, not far from the Los Angeles River itself; there was still water in the

stream even in July this far north. The party had pitched its
tents amid a grove of walnuts and oaks, a place of dappled
shade with plenty of grass for the hobbled animals; it gave
them shelter, but they had only to walk a quarter mile north
to be in open grassland with a view that stretched nearly to
the sea. They'd waited here all day, meaning to make the
passage through the pass and into the San Fernando after
dark, and after the Indian tracker had scouted it. There was a
coffeepot at the edge of the fire, and an iron kettle with a mix
of beans and bits of dried meat bubbling in it.

Good to have him check before we go through, Tom
thought.

Kolo came back to the fire two hours later; they were all
sitting on the ground around it, using their saddles as seats or
backrests, and he could feel the leather pushing into the small
of his back. The expedition's supplies didn't run to camp
chairs; they were mostly food in the form of hardtack, beans,
jerky and dried fruit, three small camouflage-patterned dome
tents with collapsible titanium-strut frames, and their weapons
and other gear.

"Ten men," the Indian said abruptly, spooning food onto
a plate and pouring coffee into a tin cup. "Six who watch,
four who rest."

Kolo ate, then placed the map of the pass through the
Glendale Narrows and into the San Fernando Valley on the
ground, with stones to weight the corners. He drew the big
knife at his belt to use as a pointer. Tom leaned closer, conscious of the hard, dry smell of the man, like an ox that had
been sweating in the sun.

There was a good reason that the region was called *narrow;* the hills pinched close, only a few hundred yards apart
at their narrowest point, and most of the bed was the Los
Angeles River. It was the only eastern exit to the valley; freeways used it back FirstSide, and it was a rough track here.

The Indian went on, with Simmons lending a hand with
vocabulary; sometimes Kolo would drop into his own language, and the Scout translated.

"Ten men. They camp beyond the narrows—a mile—

make like it's a hunting camp, some horses, tents. But always two-threes—"

"That's two groups of three," Simmons said.

"—on hills above narrows. With guns, guns like Long Shot carries—"

"Telescopic sights," Simmons put in, and Kolo grunted affirmatively.

"And they are hidden. Not badly, for white men; well enough to fool other white men. Change one-three every four, five hours."

"What did they look like?" Botha put in.

Kolo described them in exhaustive detail; he couldn't read or write, but he seemed to have what amounted to a photographic memory for plants and animals, including people. Botha listened, then shook his head.

"Andries Rhoodie. *Ach, cis,* Andries, I had hoped you were not such a fool, but I didn't hope too much. The others . . . Konrad de Buys, Wilhelm Gebhard, Benny Lang, and Ernie Graaf; I can't place any more."

"You know them?" Adrienne asked softly.

"They're among those I would have expected to be in on this, miss," Botha said, his square face clenched in anger or pain.

"Do you think your Prime would know?" she said.

"*Nie.* Not officially. He would wait, and listen, and keep silent, and then move only when he saw which way the cat would jump," Botha said, with a shrug of his massive shoulders. "That's Slim Hendrick for you."

Tom spoke: "How many of your, ah, former countrymen would be in on this? In enough to fight, that is."

Botha shrugged again. "Hard to say. It's . . . not easy, losing your country. Knowing you can never go back, never see the place you were born, swallowing defeat."

He rubbed a hand over his face, missing the look Kolomusnim shot him from under lowered brows. The Afrikaner went on:

"And then here, it *looks* like there's a chance to get our

own back. Tempting. More than ten. Less than a hundred, I think."

Tom looked at the map again, and then took out a larger-scale one that showed the whole of the LA basin and its surrounding mountain ranges.

"Offhand, I don't think they're waiting for us, specifically. Just for anyone who might be poking his nose into the Mohave without good reason, probably to report rather than kill."

"Or possibly report most, and kill if they see a couple of specific people—like me," Adrienne said. "Either would be fatal, literally or metaphorically. And it means they must be getting ready to strike. They couldn't keep this up for more than a month or two; people would start asking questions if they neglect their farms and shops for that long."

"Well, we could go back and try one of the other passes," Tom said. "The Sepulveda over the Santa Monicas, or go east and take the Cajon over the San Gabriels."

Adrienne shook her head. "That would cost us days, and anyway, a hundred men are enough to guard most of the easy passes across the mountains. The difficult ones are dangerous themselves, for a party this size with horses and mules—and we need those supplies to get across the Mohave. It's really quite good strategy, as long as they don't have to do it very long."

Botha sighed regretfully. "Then we have to kill them. Quickly, quietly. Even then, when they don't report in, there will be suspicion—the Collettas will know somebody went by, if not who."

Kolo spoke, and grinned; it was a slow, cruel expression, and the cut-a-circle-and-tug gesture he used on the top of his own head was unmistakable.

"Not if it looks like Indians did it," Simmons translated, wincing a bit. "And the Collettas and Batyushkovs *have* been stirring up the Mohave tribes, so it would look natural enough. Alarming, but not pointing to us."

Adrienne looked at Tom. "Suggestions?" she said.

"You're more experienced at this sort of operation than any of us."

Tom let out a long breath and looked at the map, calling up old habits. *This isn't a pleasant hunting trip,* he told himself.

"All right, their main weakness is that they've split up," he said. "Six of them there in the pass, the rest a mile away at their base camp, sleeping or doing chores." He thought a moment in silence. "When do they change their watchers? Do they have someone bring food?"

His questions went on. Kolo answered; there was nearly a mutiny when young Schalk Botha was told to stay and help with the camp along with Sandra Margolin.

He was still sputtering about being treated like a girl when his father's hand cuffed him across the side of the head: "Shut up and do as you're told, boy! Or I send you back to your mother!"

Tom grinned a little. "You're staying here because everything has to be ready to move quickly," he said to the young Afrikaner. "Once we've . . . accomplished the mission"— *Killed ten men and created a lot of widows and orphans,* he added silently to himself—"we'll need to get through the narrows as quickly as possible. There isn't much traffic, I understand, but that isn't the same as none. We'll need the horses and the pack-mules brought up, and fast."

The young man ran a hand over his sparse silky beard. "*Ja.* I understand. I'm to guard the woman."

Tom's grin grew harder to control as he watched Sandra steam; Tully quieted her with a wink behind the young Afrikaner's back. Adrienne rolled her eyes silently; he could hear her thought: *What am I, chopped liver? One of the boys?*

"Everyone understand what they have to do?" he asked when he'd finished laying out the plan; they all nodded. Kolo looked at him with a degree of surprised respect, as if he hadn't expected anything so competent.

"Then let's do it, people. Let's go."

✻ ✻ ✻

Just as described, Tom decided. *Two sniper teams, a spare back in camp, and one extra man . . . Jesus, that must be a brutal schedule.*

Which meant that they were probably doing the same at the other passes, spreading themselves thin and working double shifts to keep the coverage as wide as possible. Two posts was *real* sparse coverage for an area this big.

The pass ran east-west; Tom and the rest were high up on the southern flank. It was full dark, lit only by starlight with the moon not yet up. A breeze from the southwest was flowing up through the pass, drawn by the cooling of the air in the great valley beyond—the San Fernando got hotter in the daytime and more chilly at night than the coast lowlands. The wind smelled of dust, and dried herbs like an old-fashioned kitchen. Rocks ground into his belly as he looked downslope; there were real trees down there, before the river and its border of bulrushes and willows and giant tule reeds. Up here it was dense chaparral brush, cacti—he'd had several of the needles prick him in the dark—and yuccas, including Our Lord's Candle, a ten-foot-tall type tipped by a flower that was probably pretty in daylight.

Starlight glinted on the surface of the water moving through the pass; the river was low, shallow enough to walk across without much trouble, but the sill of rock beneath the narrows forced the vast underground flow to the surface here, even in the dry summers when there wasn't any surface runoff; the valley sat on a huge underground lake.

The watchers had dug in cunningly. The post below him was a shallow bowl; no disturbed earth showed, so they must have shoveled it out onto a canvas sheet to be hauled away and disposed of elsewhere. A framework of thin rods held a low roof of earth-colored cloth over the pit; more earth had been thrown on top of it, plus some rocks and vegetation; it gave an excellent view down over the track that ran along the river and the slopes, and an adequate one all around. Luckily, there probably wouldn't be much in the way of sophisticated scanners, the sort that he'd used during the war to give the *shaheeds* conniption-fits. The Commission kept those under tight control.

And now, right on the schedule Kolo had described, someone was riding a horse down from the western end of the pass. The hollow *clock-clock . . . clock-clock* of hooves came clearly through the cooling night air; the man stopped, dismounted, tied his mount to a sapling and climbed up the slope with what looked like a square bucket or box in each hand. He had a rifle across his back, but he wasn't making any attempt at silence, and he called up to the post. A little closer, and Tom could see he was younger than Schalk Botha—a fresh-faced kid with slightly shaggy, sun-streaked yellow hair, reminding the ex-Ranger of the way his brother Lars had looked as a teenager. He was grinning as he called up to the men above him, and they shouted angrily. Tom couldn't follow it, despite a haunting sense of pseudofamiliarity; English and the simplified form of bastard Dutch spoken in South Africa were close cousins.

Goddamn, but I hate this business, Tom thought. *And I'd hoped I was out of this business.*

He made a quiet chittering noise between his teeth. Kolomusnim replied with the same from his left, eastward, and Tully to his right. They began to move forward. Simmons and Botha and Adrienne would be going for the other position; she and the Afrikaner were used to working together, and so were he and Tully.

The rebel Afrikaners knew their business, but they'd probably been at this watching long enough to lose their edge, boredom and exhaustion taking their toll; Kolo had said the camp looked like it had been there for a week. And they might have been soldiers once, but they'd been farmers and clerks for a decade now.

Tom dropped to his belly a hundred yards from the observation post and began to leopard-crawl. He moved carefully, almost silently; he could barely hear Tully making the same slow approach. Despite the goggles and knowing exactly where he was, he couldn't see Kolo moving at all, and any sounds were lost in the background buzz and chir and chirp of insects and birds and small animals, and the slow chuckle of the river below. Sweat dropped down his face and ran under the edge of the goggles, stinging his eyes, salt on his lips. He kept his breath slow and even, ignoring the occasional mosquitoes and something unnamed but insectile that bit him sharply on the back of the neck.

He had a P90 slung across his back, but he wouldn't be using it unless there was no alternative at all. The wounds were unmistakable; Mohave raiders captured the odd militia rifle, but not cutting-edge Belgian submachine guns limited to Gate Security use.

Damn. Hand-to-hand. I hate *hand-to-hand fighting.*

Closer now. The men in the post weren't arguing loudly anymore, and someone laughed. He caught the scent of meat and some sort of hot sauce, overriding the stale-socks-and-sweat odor of men who'd been in the field for a while; evidently the kid had brought some barbecue. Probably he was here like Schalk Botha, helping out his father or elder brother.

The thought was distant. Tom was acting on reflex now, the time and place lost in a dozen others, only the headgear and accents of the targets different.

One of the men sitting in the shallow depression ripped a mouthful of meat from a rib and then looked up, chewing. Tom was close enough to see him frown, and see the bald pate shining under the floppy hat pushed to the back of his head.

The man swallowed and looked upslope, then flicked the bone aside and reached for his rifle—not moving quickly, more out of a long-set habit of suspicion than any urgency.

"*Wie's daar?*" the man called sharply.

Tom had one knee up under his chest. He was springing off it even as the flat *smack* of a bowstring sounded. A whistling, then a wet slapping sound of metal cleaving flesh, and the man was staggering back with an arrow halfway through his throat, head and fletching jerking as he convulsed and arched backward; blood shot out of his mouth and nose.

"Die bosemen! Skiet hulle dood!" someone else shouted, and fired into the darkness, squeezing off half a magazine.

A couple of the bullets cracked past Tom unpleasantly close as he drove forward, long legs pumping and body almost parallel with the ground—but that was accidental. Firing off blind into the dark like that just destroyed your own night vision, if you weren't wearing goggles, and gave away your position even if you were. They'd be blind; he could see quite well, about like an overcast winter afternoon. The goggles adjusted automatically to keep the muzzle blasts from dazzling his eyes.

Ten long strides put him at the earth berm that ran around the shallow pit. Without pause his hands slapped down on it, and his body pivoted forward around the fulcrum of his palms, one leg drawn back. The shooter saw him out of the corner of his eye and pivoted, fast but not quite fast enough; he triggered off a round into the inside of the observation pit just as Tom's boot smashed into his face like a hydraulic piston—with the full strength of the long muscular leg behind it, and the momentum of better than two hundred pounds of dense bone and muscle.

The impact crunched up through Tom's boot sole and into back and gut, killing his forward motion—and the Afrikaner, who was thrown back with a broken neck and his jaw torn three-quarters off, dangling by a shred of cartilage. Tom jackknifed in midair, coming down in a crouch with his great hands ready to strike or grab.

The third rebel was occupied; he was wrestling with Roy Tully and letting his Uzi submachine gun bounce between them on its sling as he struggled to keep control of Tully's right wrist, the one with the long knife gleaming in it. Even as Tom set himself the man doubled over in uncontrollable reflex; Tully had driven a knee into his crotch. A second later Tom hammered the bladed palm of his right hand into the back of the man's neck; he could feel bone shatter, and there was a sound like a green branch snapping with a crunch, hideously familiar.

"Where's number four?" Tully asked, panting and glaring around, the knife moving in little unconscious circles.

"Running," Tom said, drawing deep shuddering breaths. "But not for long."

The fourth man—the youngster who'd brought his elders their last meal—was halfway down the slope to his horse. Not running in blind panic, either; he was keeping quiet and keeping on his feet, obviously set to ride out for help.

Kolomusnim was behind him, gaining fast, a silent streak of brown motion through the blackness of the night. He leaped with tiger speed; starlight flashed on the steel in his hand as he landed on the yellow-haired youth's back. They rolled downslope, and there was a scream, then a long bubbling shriek of agony, and another.

Tom winced slightly, but there was no time to linger. Not that anyone would want to, among the corpses twitching with the last motions of the dead, the death stink mingling nauseatingly with the smell of blood and food and cordite. He and Tully went out of the observation pit with almost identical vaulting leaps, moving eastward up the pass toward the next position.

He went nearly limp with relief when Adrienne rose short of it. "No problems," she said. "Piet talked to them, and then . . ."

Tom looked past her into the pit. One man had a huge diagonal slash across his neck, from the collarbone on the right side to slightly past the middle on the left, opening the jugular and windpipe. Adrienne was pouring water from her canteen over her right hand, and the sopping cuff of her bush jacket above it. As for the rest . . . one had the side of his skull dished in, and the other looked as if someone very strong had put one hand behind his head, the other on his face, and turned his head around until it looked between his shoulder blades.

Ecch, Tom thought.

He *could* do that himself, but the method said something about the man. The disgust was welcome. A little cold observer at the back of his mind reminded him that he'd just missed getting a hollow-point bullet through the gut. Missed by about six inches of random chance; disliking Botha helped push the knowledge further down.

Jim Simmons was a dozen yards on, covering the entrance to the pass with his scope-sighted rifle. Botha was using a walkie-talkie he'd found in the observation post, his square dark face even more unreadable than ever, between the dimness and the night-sight goggles.

"Told them that young Johannes thought a bear was an Indian and shot it up," he said when he'd clicked off the set. "And to save some dishes ready for him to clean to teach him fire discipline." He nodded toward the man with the slit throat; he'd been big, red-haired where he wasn't grizzled. "Andries there had a voice like mine—we both came from the Cape, too. When we go after the rest of them at the camp we can use our guns; if these had been overrun by Indians, the *boseman* would have taken their guns."

Adrienne nodded, with a slight grimace at the stinking destruction. "We'll have to take everything useful, and the scalps as well," she said. "Make this look like an Indian raid."

Simmons came back. "Kolo will take care of that," he said.

Tom looked at him. "Kolo really doesn't like white men much, does he?" he asked quietly.

Simmons shrugged. "No, with a few individual exceptions," he said. "In his position . . . would you?"

"Why's he working with you New Virginians, then?" Tully said, looking behind them.

The Indian came trotting up; both his arms were red to the elbows, and he was smiling. A string of scalps hung in a dripping bag from his waist.

"Because it's the best way to protect his wife and kids, I suppose," Simmons said. He sighed. "And because it's always better to be on the winning side. Let's get going."

* * *

Henry Villers tied the horses in the mouth of the pass below the second observation post and scrambled up. The others were crouched a few yards below it, except for Kolo still at his grim work. Villers gave it a single glance, then shook his head and joined the others.

"Man, that dude has some *serious* anger-management problems," he observed.

"Yes," Tom said soberly. *The bodies have to be mutilated. The Mohave always do that.* "Try not to let it get to you."

To his surprise, Villers laughed. "It don't bother *me* none," he said. "Warden Tom, you've got to remember what these Boer mo'fo's had in mind, why they're helping this essence-of-putrescence capital-E e-vile plot. And man, it had to start on the top of the evil tree and hit every branch on the way down to get *me* risking my precious one-and-only black ass to pull *John Rolfe's* chestnuts out of the fire! Personal considerations aside—and it's hard to put you and your family getting killed aside—can you imagine what these trek boys would do over in Africa, with the Collettas and Batyushkovs running the Commission and shipping them all the modern conveniences, like for starters napalm and automatic weapons, to use on my alternate-world spear-chuckin' cousins? Maybe the people they conquered would rise up eventually, but that might take centuries, and can you imagine what they'd do till then?"

Tom nodded, feeling his gloom lift. Tully came up with the Bren gun. "Ready to handle this?" he asked Villers.

"*Hell,* yes," Villers said cheerfully. "Good gun. The melancholy Dane's been brooding at me here."

"I know how you feel," Tully said. "Sweet Christ, do I know how you feel."

"He does the Hamlet with you too?" Villers asked.

"Oh, incessantly. Gloom, guilt, silences, despair. Well, you know Danes."

"How do you stand it?"

"I keep refusing to marry him, for starters," Tully said seriously. "You know how it is—you can't really change someone that way, no matter what they promise."

"Sociopaths," Tom said, grinning. "Both of you. And it's Norway my folks came from, not Denmark. Hamlet was probably half Swedish. Danes are too goddamned *hygge* to brood."

"What's *that?*" Villers asked curiously. "Hi-ge? Huggy? Some Scandinavian brand of kink?"

"H-Y-double-G-E. Sort of like 'cute' or 'cozy,' but not so sternly unyielding, and without the harsh overtones. Did you think it was an accident Denmark's greatest contributions to world culture were Tuborg, a sweet fruit pastry and the Little Fucking Mermaid?"

Adrienne was a little way off, sitting behind a bush and looking down into the valley with the high-tech binoculars, her elbows on her knees. Botha sat beside her, making notes on a map. She spoke, raising her voice without taking her eyes from the glasses. "If you three have finished with the male-bonding thing, could you come over here for a moment?" she said dryly.

They did, crouching low. West and north the valley floor opened out, silvery in the moonlight even without their night-sight goggles. Save for the area along the river and some of the washes that came down from the south, there was little of the dense growth that covered much of the coastlands. It was replaced by a savanna of knee-length grass, scattered with big round-topped oaks, sagebrush and cactus on dry sandy spots, and the odd walnut tree. A mile away a campfire flickered in the night—the rebels were keeping up the pretense of being an innocent hunting party.

"Now, one of them was a blond, you say?" she said.

"Yes," Tom replied. "Teenager."

"Johann Lang," Botha confirmed. "Just turned nineteen."

"All right," Adrienne said. "Tom's Ranger stunt went off like clockwork."

Even then he felt a small glow of pride at the pride in her eyes.

"But I think this calls for real sneakiness, which is my specialty," she went on.

✳ ✳ ✳

"Where's Johann?" Frikkie Lang said. "He should be back by now."

"Probably still getting his dues from *Oom* Andries," Dirk van Deventer said, poking at the fire.

He'd built the fire up a bit since they'd finished cooking; you needed a bed of low coals for that. They both kept their voices down; they were about Johann's age, and along on sufferance. Johann's father and Pik van Deventer were not ones to tolerate what they considered idle chatter or disrespect among the younger generation, particularly not on an important mission like this, vital to the future of the *volk*. Pik was sitting in a camp chair near one of the big tents, with a hurricane lantern hanging over him from its frontal awning, reading his Bible.

"Serves him right, and now *we* don't have to do *kaffir* work cleaning up for a week," Frikkie said. "Pretty soon we'll all have *kaffir* to do the *kaffir* work."

Dirk lowered his voice and smiled as he leaned close to his friend—both the older men with them were straitlaced.

"Not to mention *kaffir meids* to work on their backs. I hear they—"

They could have discussed *that* subject for hours, both being teenage males, but the sound of a horse's hooves interrupted them. Both of them were farm-born and -raised; they could tell it was a single mount, ridden at a slow walk. The sound came from the east toward the pass.

"Johann!" the boy's father shouted. "Get your lazy backside over here."

The two young men rose, looking away from the fire and slitting their eyes to get their night vision back with the automatic gesture of those who'd hunted since they were twelve. That let them see what was coming: an Indian with bowed head and hands tied behind his back, walking in front of a lone horseman who held his rifle with the butt resting on his right thigh. It had to be Johann; they recognized his horse, and the bright hair that caught the edge of the firelight.

"Prisoner!" the horseman shouted, his voice high and shrill with excitement. "Prisoner!"

"You *sklem!*" Frikkie shouted joyfully, running out. "It wasn't a bear after all!"

The others were all on their feet as well; Dirk ran after him, and the two older men stood to watch. Frikkie had just enough time to realize that the horseman was a woman when the Indian's arms came out from behind his back. The right hand flashed, and as the young man began to bring up his rifle something struck him a massive blow beneath the chin. He never saw the tomahawk that split his throat, only felt a huge wetness when he tried to draw breath, saw darkness, heard a distant fusillade of shots and the stuttering rattle of a machine gun.

Then nothing, ever again.

✻ ✻ ✻

"Well, that was easy enough," Adrienne said.

"It usually is, when you've got surprise on your side," Tom replied.

The party's own horses and mules had come up; they were some distance from the camp of the dead. Botha had insisted on that; it turned out several of the younger rebels had been friends of his son.

"There are things a man should not see too young," he said.

Adrienne and Tom both looked after the big man as he walked off to help with loading the plunder on the captured horses—all the things Indian raiders would have taken, the cloth and tools and weapons and liquor. Kolomusnim had found some of that, and was now resting with his belly over a horse's saddle.

"I wouldn't have thought Piet had it in him," Adrienne said quietly. "Granted he was never quite as bad as Schalk, but . . ."

"It all depends on who you consider human," Tom said. "I suspect Botha has a fairly narrow definition, but he's quite human himself within those limits."

Their hands intertwined. "And I was scared *spitless* when you went in like that," he said, his voice husky for a moment.

"You didn't say anything," she pointed out.

"Wouldn't have done any good," he said. "Besides, you were right."

That got him a sudden tight squeeze. "God, you're a find!"

"You're another," he said, and released her.

Tully got an all-out hug and kiss of relief from Sandra Margolin.

"Hey, I'm alive," he said, when she let him come back up for air.

"That's why, you idiot!" she said, and kissed him again.

And now to work, Tom thought. *We're just getting started.*

CHAPTER TWENTY

The Commonwealth of New Virginia

The elephant put its forehead against the trunk of an oak and pushed, retreated, pushed again. It was a gray-brown mountain of flesh, the thick skin deeply wrinkled and the great triangular ears ragged; even a hundred yards away they could hear the quick exhaled huff of breath as it backed off. Then it curled its trunk high, trumpeted in anger and shuffled forward, head down and big curved tusks almost touching the dry earth as it charged the thing that had irritated it. Even with better than two hundred yards between them and the great beast, the party's horses shied at the sound, and several of the mules threw their heads up and brayed.

Tom whistled softly, standing in the stirrups and shading his eyes against the setting sun with a hand. "What a monster!"

"I've never seen a bigger," Botha agreed.

"We imported the savanna type from South Africa and Angola," Adrienne said. "Couple of hundred young adults, mostly females, and they bred like bunnies; this could be one of the first generation. Piet, what size would you say he was?"

"Old bull, eleven, twelve feet at the shoulder . . . nine tons, maybe," the Afrikaner said. "Big enough to push that tree over, by thunder."

The big valley oak gave a groaning creak, and the branches at the top shivered; birds swept up from it in a cloud like twisting smoke. The elephant bull rocked backward, then thrust again. Roots broke, first isolated *crack . . . crack . . .* sounds, then a fusillade like the sound of battle. Another long groan, and the tree pitched forward, hesitated for a moment, then toppled over on its side. A big ball of the dry soil came up with it, leaving a pit deeper than a man in the earth, and a cloud of dust drifted away and fell. The elephant moved forward and began ripping off branches and stuffing them in its mouth, making small grunting sounds of contentment as it crunched leaves and acorns and twigs.

Tom pushed back his jungle hat and wiped sweat off his face onto his sleeve. They were in the northern lobe of the San Fernando now, northwest of the Verdugo Hills and not far from where Mission San Fernando Rey de España had stood in the other history. The coastal plain had been warm; the valley was no-doubt-about-it *hot,* nearly a hundred today.

"Maybe we should have started traveling by night before we crossed the San Fernando," he said, uncorking his canteen and taking a long draft of warm water.

The mountains to the north were close, blue in the bright sunlight and rising in height from west to east; columns of smoke stood out in several places, marks of the brushfires to be expected at this season. Luckily they hadn't run into any on the flat floor of the basin, nor into any of the occasional hunting parties who traveled here from the settled zones. They'd made good time across the open prairie with its groves of oaks, and its teeming herds of antelope and ostrich and bison, wild horses and feral cattle and innumerable birds. He could see all those right now, and more: particularly the circling buzzards, and probably condors, not far to the north.

"We'd have lost time, and it's not as hot here as it will be in the Mohave," she said. "Plus there's usually nobody around here except. . ." She paused. "Oooops."

As usual, Jim Simmons and Kolo had been riding point;

they'd pushed on ahead to investigate what had brought so many carrion eaters together. Judging from the dust, they were coming back quickly.

Simmons reined in; his face looked a little strained. "Indians—Nyo-Ilcha," he said. "Sun Clan of the Mohaves. They've all got peace brassards, and a helicopter visited them yesterday to make sure they weren't involved in the attack on our rebel friends—pardon me, on the harmless hunting party with the sniper's posts above the Glendale Narrows."

Adrienne looked at Tom: "They probably won't attack us," she said. "Too many guns with us, and it's too close to civilization. Plus they value permission to come hunt here—a lot of game migrates south over the mountains in summer." She turned back to Simmons. "How many?"

"About thirty warriors, and a dozen women for the skinning and drying. Ah . . . ." He looked embarrassed.

"Yes, I'd better hang back while you talk with them," she said sourly.

He nodded. "And I think I know exactly how to put them into a good mood," he said. "They're here for meat." He unslung his scope-sighted rifle. "My grandfather was always boasting about that record tusker he got back when we were in Kenya. Pity the old bastard's dead."

Tom felt an irrational pang as the Scout rode a hundred yards closer and dismounted. *Hell, it's not an endangered species this side of the Gate*, he thought. *Not in Africa, and not here either.*

It knew what a man with a gun was, too; it turned and trumpeted again as soon as Simmons got close, tossing its head from side to side and flapping its ears. Then its head went down and its tail went up, sure sign of a charge. The flat *crack* of Simmons's rifle sounded at the same instant—aimed at the third corrugation down on the trunk, the precise spot that would send a bullet through the vast spongy bulk of the skull and into the brain.

The elephant took three more steps and then stopped. The bullet hole was invisible at this distance, and the trickle of blood almost so. It swayed and crumpled forward, vast columnar legs buckling at the knee, then slumped to the ground with a thud that shook the earth and made his horse dance sideways.

"You don't need an elephant gun for elephant," Simmons said a bit smugly. "Any mankiller with a full metal jacket will do, if you get a brain shot."

* * *

Tom rode out with Simmons to meet the Nyo-Ilcha warriors—or hunters, he supposed—as they rode up in a cloud of dust colored ruddy by the setting sun.

Damned if I'm going to miss the chance of seeing some really *wild Indians,* he thought. A couple days of travel had put the brief, nasty fight at the pass behind him, mentally as well as physically. *It would be fascinating to get out on the plains and see what's happened there, too.*

There were about thirty of them, as the Scout had said, ranging from teens to wrinkled middle age. All of them looked tough as rawhide as they came closer, tall, leanly muscular men with broad, high-cheeked, narrow-eyed faces; their brown skins were weathered from a lifetime of desert sun and alkali wind. They were healthy-looking despite the horrible smallpox scars some bore and the occasional missing eye or finger, giving off a palpable sense of carnivore vigor.

I suppose any weaklings die pretty quick, out in the deep desert, he thought.

A few were lighter-skinned and narrower-faced than the other tribesmen, and one had brown hair and blue eyes; he remembered what Adrienne had said about white renegades joining them, as well as the remnants of the coastal tribes.

You'd have to be pretty desperate to join this bunch, or crazy, he mused. *It's not like back in colonial times in First-Side America.*

Plenty of white settlers had "gone native" then, but they hadn't been leaving flush toilets and TV—not to mention modern dentistry and medicine. An eighteenth-century Iroquois shaman was probably less of a risk to your health than an eighteenth-century European medico; at least he wouldn't bleed, blister and purge you to death.

All the Nyo-Ilcha wore their long hair twisted into twenty or thirty ropelike braids; ornaments of shell or silver and turquoise hung from their ears, or were stuck through the septum of the nose; many were tattooed in jagged patters of red and white and black. The overall effect reminded him of some old-style shock-rock musicians; or shock-rock musicians crossed with demons, because these guys weren't kidding or playing for effect. This was what they wore every day, and they really *were* this bad.

Some wore helmets as well, made from the tanned head-skins of animals stretched on wicker frames, with the hide trailing down their backs—heads of wolf, bear, bison, leopard, lion . . . and one that had him boggling for a moment until he realized it was a kangaroo, which was a bogglement in itself.

They went bare to the waist otherwise, apart from blankets slung around their shoulders; everyone wore leather pants and moccasins, and from the rank old-sweat-and-leather way they smelled, they didn't waste water on washing much. Their horses were tall, good-looking beasts, rougher-coated than the New Virginians' but of the same breeds, and a herd of remounts was nearby under the guard of several youths. Every man was festooned with weapons: big steel knives, tomahawks, war clubs that looked like giant potato mashers, round shields of painted hide slung at the cruppers of their simple pad saddles. About half had trade muskets resting across their thighs. Those were simple weapons, replica smoothbore flintlocks, but the stocks had been decorated with bits of semiprecious stone or bone or shell. The other half carried bows, and his eyes widened again at their shape— backed with horn and reinforced with sinew, the powerful double-curved Turco-Mongol type he'd seen in museums and sporting events in Central Asia. He whispered a question to Simmons.

"Some demented renegade taught them," the Scout answered, sotto voce. "He belonged to a bunch of burks First-Side who liked to play at Middle Ages; the bloody things are a menace, believe me. Fortunately they're not easy to make or use."

Tom hoped the tufts of hair on the ten-foot lances every third or fourth man carried were from animals, but he didn't think so—any more than the filed-down butcher knives used for points were ornamental. From the looks he was getting, he was pretty sure any of them would make a welcome addition. He'd been on the receiving end of enough silent hatred for Uncle Sam abroad to recognize it here, and the Indians weren't being particularly subtle about it—some were fingering their knife hilts, hopefully an unconscious gesture.

The Nyo-Ilcha leader reined in and raised a hand when his horse's nose was about five feet from that of Simmons's mount; he was a thirtyish man with a rat-trap mouth shadowed by the lion's-head helmet he wore—it was complete with teeth, and with turquoises for eyes—and white bars painted horizontally across his scarred, sinewy arms. Kolo rode right behind the Scout; the Nyo-Ilcha glared at him, and he sneered back. Botha was on the right hand and Tom on the left, picked for their impressive size. They all carried their rifles in the crook of their left arms—not really as a threat, more as a matter of etiquette.

The two leaders began talking in a fast-rising, slow-falling language accompanied by many gestures. The chief's face went slack with surprise for a moment when Simmons made a swooping hand motion in front of his nose—imitating an elephant's trunk, Tom realized—and pointed behind himself to the south, toward the toppled oak tree.

The chief said something in reply and placed both thumbs near his upper lip, drawing them out in a swooping curve.

"Ahi," Simmons replied, throwing his right hand out in an extravagant wave with the palm curved back.

"Kwanaeami!" the chief said, and reined his horse around.

Simmons blew out his cheeks in a relieved gust. "I told him they could have the elephant, and the ivory too," he said.

"It ought to keep them sweet for awhile; that's six thousand pounds of usable meat, as much as they can carry, and the ivory will be worth a fair bit of trade goods. Not to mention all that tough leather, and the fat. They don't hunt elephant much themselves, although there are a few in the desert and a fair number down the Colorado."

"Why not?" Tom asked curiously.

Simmons snorted. "Would you, if all you had was a spear or those single-shot guns made out of pieces of water pipe?

"We're reasonably safe with this bunch now," he went on as they trotted off to join the others. "They accepted our gift—it's bad luck among the Many Tongues to eat your own kill, so swapping is something friends do for each other. Fear of retaliation aside, it's unlikely these will try anything sneaky, at least while we're still on this side of the mountains." He gestured toward the San Gabriels to the north. "Over there, it'd be a different matter."

The dozen women with the Nyo-Ilcha hunting party were all driving carts, two-horse vehicles with a pair of spoked wheels seven feet high, their sides festooned with water bags and nets full of gear, and hoops over the tops covered in hide. They looked at the dead elephant, unharnessed and hobbled their horses, and went to work with knives and hatchets. A few of the younger ones set to putting up stick-and-thong racks to dry the meat, and began to gather wood for smoking fires—the downed oak tree provided plenty of both. The women wore their hair in a simpler fashion than the men, cut square across the eyes and long behind, and they wore nothing but kilts or aprons of rabbit fur or trade cloth; their faces were painted in vertical stripes, and they had lines of tattoos running down from their lower lips over their chins. A few of them spat in the direction of the distant party of New Virginians.

"Good thing you speak their language," Tom observed.

"I don't, really—we were talking trade pidgin, with sign language. From what I've read of FirstSide anthropology, a lot of customs like sign language drifted west in the cen-

turies between the time Columbus *didn't* arrive and the time
we did—more than in FirstSide history."

At Simmons's suggestion, they pitched camp about a
mile away from the nomads—too far for a rush, but close
enough to remind them of the source of their current good
fortune. The routine of setting up the tents and hobbling the
horses went quickly; dinner was antelope, some kind with a
fawn hide, a white belly and horns that curled up in pointed
spirals. Kolo had brought it down with his bow; luckily eight
people were enough to eat most of it at a sitting—fresh meat
didn't keep in this weather.

Tom finished his bowl of stewed antelope with beans and
chilies and dried vegetables; it wasn't bad, for trail food.
He'd just mopped the enameled bowl with a biscuit when
Tully ghosted in out of the night with his goggles pushed up
on his forehead.

"Company, Kemosabe," he said.

They all stood, weapons inconspicuously ready. It was
the leader of the Nyo-Ilcha, alone and holding his open
hands up as a sign that he came in peace. Kolo followed behind him, signaling that nobody was following, then faded
out into the darkness beyond the circle of light to make sure
that nobody did later.

Simmons moved forward, making an open-hand gesture
with his right hand. The Indian extended his, which surprised the Scout, who took it nonetheless.

"Hamose kwa'ahot," the Nyo-Ilcha leader said. "Or, in
English, Good Star."

"Ah . . . you speak English?" Simmons said.

"Heap good English," Good Star said dryly. "Me smart
Injun. I spent three years at the mission school in Antelope
Valley—what you Deathwalkers call Antelope Valley—off
and on, when I was younger. One of Dad's better ideas."

He spoke fluently, though with a thick guttural accent.
"And I trade there now and then. I'm *kohata*—chief—of the
Nyo-Ilcha."

Simmons muttered beneath his breath: Tom thought it

sounded something like, *I'm going to* kill *Dirk Brodie.* Then he went on aloud: "Jim Simmons, Frontier Scout."

Good Star came and squatted by the fire. "I've heard of you," he said. "Spare some of that coffee? And a cigarette would go down nice."

Tom bit down on a bubble of laughter at the expression on the Scout's face and poured the Indian leader a cup from the blue-enameled iron pot sitting on the edge of the fire. Someone else produced a cigarette; he lit it from a splinter, and smoke drifted out from beneath the fangs of his lion-head helmet. As if that had reminded him, Good Star took it off and set it on the dirt beside him, before pouring sugar into the coffee and taking a sip.

"Ahhhh," he said, sighing. "You know, coffee and decent tobacco are about the only good things you Deathwalkers brought here. Well, guns and horses, too. And booze, of course, and chocolate and steel knives."

"And the aqueducts and roads," Tully muttered under his breath; Tom didn't think anyone else heard him. "But besides that, not much."

Simmons produced a bottle of brandy from his saddlebags and added a dollop to their guest's coffee cup. Then he cleared his throat.

"Why didn't you speak English this afternoon? Instead of wasting both our time with trade pidgin and sign language."

Good Star's glittering dark eyes swept around the circle by the fire; Tom thought he caught a sardonic glint under the tattoos and the stink.

"Didn't have any reason to make things easy for you then," he said. "It's always better when the other guy doesn't know how much you know."

His glance lingered on Adrienne's hands, where she sat on her saddle holding another of the tin cups; the firelight flickered on the circlet of gold and platinum on her left thumb.

"For example, that you know what a Thirty Families ring looks like." He took another puff on the cigarette. "Sorta out of place on a humble squaw like you were acting, hey?

Thanks for the elephant, by the way. Especially the ivory. The goddamned Akaka, Othi-I and Kapata are getting too many guns for comfort, and we Nyo-Ilcha need to buy more powder."

Adrienne sipped from her own cup. "We'd heard something about that, Good Star," she said smoothly. "And about a man named Swift Lance."

Good Star spat accurately into the fire. "*That* crazy"—he dropped into his own language, then translated helpfully— "bastard fucker of his own nieces? Yeah, he's the talk of the Mohave. Got a big Dreaming on him, about how we're going to get enough guns to throw all you Deathwalkers into the salt water and take the good lands."

"You don't think that's a good plan?" Adrienne said neutrally.

He grunted and took a swig of the spiked coffee. "I wish. That's not Dreaming; that's . . . what do you call it . . . jerking off. No way. But plenty of people like being told what they want to hear. We Water People got as many fools as anyone else, I reckon."

"Someone's been slipping you . . . them . . . weapons, then?" Adrienne said.

"Hell, yeah—the northern clans, at least. But if *all* of us had *two* of those smoke poles and enough powder and ball to shoot all year, you'd still have the fucking machine guns and helicopters, wouldn't you? Not to mention you outnumber us more every year."

He shrugged and finished the coffee, smacking his lips. Silently Tom poured him more, and Simmons added another dollop of the Seven Oaks brandy.

"Good stuff! Anyway, *my* plan is that we all pick up and move southeast—down Mexico way. Lot of empty land there since the plagues, and what's left of the Ya-ke, Opata, Seri and such don't have any guns at all, or many steel weapons. Then maybe if we were out of the way you fucking Deathwalkers would leave us alone. No offense."

"None taken. So who's giving Swift Lance all these muskets?" Adrienne asked. "That might be . . . valuable information."

Good Star grinned, showing a mouthful of strong yellow teeth. "Wouldn't we both like to know?"

He shook his head. "Before Johnny Deathwalker came from beyond-the-world, all the Mohave clans stuck together, lived all mixed up, didn't fight among themselves, from what the old bastards say. Ain't like that anymore, not with the sickness and then all the outsiders getting adopted, and all the new ways and new critters. These days people are always stealing horses and sheep and cattle and guns from each other. Lot of those Akaka shits, they'd scalp their own cousins for a shot glass of cheap whiskey. Akaka, Othi-I, Kapata, Huk-thar war-parties all over the west and north now. News travels slow."

Adrienne leaned back and whispered to Sandra, then was all attention once more, leaning forward with her elbows on her knees.

Good Star pointed northeast. "That's where we Nyo-Ilcha have our grounds now, just over the mountains. The Akaka and their friends, they're up around Old Woman Mountain, and the Bitter Lake, and west around Black Mountain and Willow Springs; they're part of the *mathal'a'thom*, the northern clans—bunch of half Utes, if you want to know what I think. If you were heading that way—don't. Well, gotta go. Thanks again for the ivory."

"Thank you for the pleasure of your company," Adrienne said with a stately, archaic politeness Tom had noticed before.

She rose and tossed him a bag Sandra had made up—one with a bottle of the brandy, a pack of cigarettes, a bottle of aspirin, a sack of coffee beans, some sugar and a handful of chocolate bars. He caught it, slurped down the dregs from his cup, took a last drag on the cigarette, and rose with pantherish ease and walked off into the darkness.

The party fell silent for a long time after the tall figure vanished into the night; Tom finished his coffee.

"Well, well, well," he said.

* * *

Jesus, it's hot, Tom thought. Then: *Jesus, that's lame.*

He and Adrienne were sprawled under the shade of their bell tent, stripped to their underwear, with the sides drawn up to catch any breeze—but the hot wind dried their sweat almost instantly, with little relief, and on their lips it tasted bitterly of alkali dust. The three tents were strung out in the meager shade of a low steep-sided hill, outlier of a mountain range to the west; it gave a little more protection as the sun declined, and the horses and mules crowded there with listless insistence. To the east stretched a desolation of flat rocky plain, rimmed by more mountains on the edge of sight to the east. It was studded here and there with the low sprawling creosote bush with its yellow-green-gray waxy leaves, a shrub that robbed the soil around it of moisture and nutrients until nothing else could grow; the occasional inch-wide yellow flower didn't seem much compensation. The nearest bush had a diamondback rattler curled around its roots, waiting for sunset like a coil of deadly camouflaged rope. The sight reminded him to check his boots for scorpions when he put his boots back on, but the *thought* of moving was enough to make him tired.

Nothing much moved in the hot, bright stillness, except grains of sand moved along by the oven-mouth wind, and the slow trace of the sun across the aching blue dome of the sky; even the blue was leached out to a tinted white.

Around noon something *had* moved—a bird trying for the shade of the rocks had fallen out of the sky with a thump, struck dead by the heat in midflight. It still lay gape-beaked with its feet in the air fifty yards away, and the ants were beating a trail to it. Once a group of big red kangaroos had bounced by, stopping to munch on some barrel cactus, undeterred by the spines. Tom's eyes tracked them with stuporous indifference; when their long hind feet came down on the creosote bushes a tarry, medicinal scent filled the air.

In the middle distance was a long line of sand dunes. Tom

watched them as his hand groped for the canvas water bag that hung from one of the struts of the tent. A little seeped through the canvas, cooling the contents all the way down to lukewarm by evaporation, and he sucked at the mouth with dogged persistence, ignoring the bitter taste and the rime of soda-rich dust on the outside that stuck to his chest hairs. He hated to think what the minerals were doing to his kidneys— and wondered how *anyone* could live in this desolation year-round—but you could dehydrate very easily here, and it had been a week since they crossed the mountains. Three days since the last spring of bad-smelling water.

"You know the odd thing?" Adrienne said slowly and quietly, timing her words to the natural rhythm of her breath.

"Tell me," Tom said, handing her the water bottle. "Right now, funny would be good."

"This area is a beauty spot in the spring. The flowers are quite lovely."

That *was* funny. It was true, too. This wasn't far from U.S. 40, on FirstSide, and he'd been through in March himself. It was probably even prettier here in the Commonwealth.

"We should come back then, after this is all over," Adrienne said. "It's not so goddamned hot then, either." There was a long pause. "Tom?"

"Yah, Adri?"

"I'm sorry for what I did to you."

He thought for a long moment; his mental processes seemed to be bleached out but had a sharp-edged clarity.

"OK, apology accepted," he said. After a moment: "You want to stay together after this is over?"

"Get married, you mean?" Adrienne said.

He thought again for a long moment. "Yah."

"Done. Provided we survive. There's no giving in marriage in the afterlife, they say."

They shared an exhausted chuckle. "It must be love," Tom said. "I still like being with you when all we can do is lie here and listen to each other sweat."

"It'd be nice to have kids," she said softly. "Not too many.

Four would be about right. Three-year intervals . . . or they can arrange twins, these days."

He opened his mouth to comment on that; he'd been thinking wistfully about children himself for a while, but the thought hadn't been urgent—the world was still too crowded, after all. *Only it isn't,* he thought. *It really isn't.*

Instead he craned his neck up at Roy Tully's voice, from the ledge of rock a hundred feet up where they'd all taken turns on lookout.

"Trouble, three o'clock!"

The smaller man was coming down the cliff at reckless speed. Tom knocked his boots together to evict any poisonous desert dwellers and scrambled into his salt-stiff clothing. That took less than a minute; then he had binoculars out and was looking east—three o'clock, in the conventional rendering that took north as twelve. The sand dunes were too far away to make out individual figures well even with magnification; horses were rice-sized black dots. But he could see a ripple and flash above them.

"Lanceheads," he said.

"To think I was just about to comment on how swinging this far east had avoided trouble with the Indians," Adrienne said. "How many?"

"A lot of them—and if the proportions are like our friends of the Nyo-Ilcha, that's a hell of a lot of other men carrying less conspicuous weapons."

"And I don't suppose they're employees of the Mohave Tourist Agency," Adrienne said grimly; her face was all business once more; even then it had a Valkyrie beauty despite windburn and cracked lips.

"I wonder if Good Star sold us out," Simmons muttered.

"Or one of his followers," Adrienne said crisply. "But it doesn't matter now."

The others were on their feet as quickly, and everyone moved to break camp; they couldn't abandon much equipment, not and survive for long in this desolation. The animals complained and brayed as the blankets and saddles were roughly thrown on their backs; they were used to waiting for the cool of evening, and that was several hours from now.

"We going to have to run?" Sandra said, a little white about the lips but calm.

"Yah, you betcha," Tom said grimly.

"Then we'd better water the animals—give 'em the last of it. They'll go farther and it'll lighten the loads. Give 'em some barley, too."

Adrienne thought for an instant, looked over at Jim Simmons, who jerked his head in agreement, then nodded. "Good idea; do it, Sandy. But leave the mules; they won't be able to keep up. Put the packsaddles on the extra horses." They'd kept the ones they'd taken from the dead rebels after the fight at the pass; turning them loose would raise too many questions . . . "Young Botha, you help her."

They splashed water into folding plastic buckets, and the horses crowded around, shouldering each other and slobbering in their eagerness, the mules braying protest at their exclusion. Sandra took a lariat from her saddle and whirled the end to drive them off, desperate with haste.

Adrienne called the rest of them together for an instant.

"That looks like better than a hundred men," she said. "Good Star's un-friend Swift Lance earning his corn, would be my guess—but that doesn't matter. We can't fort up here; with our firepower we could beat them off, but there's no water and we can't call for help."

"*Ja,*" Piet Botha said. He looked at Simmons. "Afton canyon?"

"Closest place with reliable water," the Scout agreed. He looked at the distant hostiles. "Bugger. They're a bit north of us—they'll cut the angle and gain on us; we have to go two miles to their one. We can't swing west; the hills are in the way. *Bugger.* Let's get going. I wouldn't want to be caught in the open."

Well, this is a switch from thinking about being a daddy, Tom thought as he swung aboard his horse and jammed the floppy hat tighter on his head.

Sandra had a couple of extras saddled as well, with the

stirrups tied up, in case someone had to switch horses in a hurry.

Bless you, my child, Tom thought—the prospect of having a horse go lame or lose a shoe at this particular moment and be stuck trying to transfer his saddle was nightmarish.

Nobody got in anyone's way or wasted effort; the weeks they'd been on the trail paid off: camp was struck in less than five minutes. They turned their animals' noses north and broke into a trot. He kept glancing right despite the kidney-jarring gait. Simmons had called it; with the ridge of broken ground close on their left, the Indians could slant toward them at an angle. Adrienne looked back white-lipped; the herd of spare horses was keeping up well enough, with Sandra and the young Boer chivvying them cowboy-style from the rear. Roy Tully was doing something with one of them, pulling items out of a packsaddle.

The Scout still had his binoculars out. "Dammit, they're pushing their horses!" he said. "We'll have to do it too. Go for it!"

He cased the glasses and leaned forward, flipping the slack of his reins to right and left. His horse rocked into a gallop, and they all followed suit. It *felt* faster than a car—but a horse couldn't keep it up for long, particularly when it had been hard-driven on short rations and bad water for a while. It was hard on the rider's gut and back, too.

"This is going to be close," Adrienne said to him, calling across the rushing space that separated them. "If they get too close, we'll have to circle the horses—use them as barricades—but then they can thirst us out."

In which case we all die, he thought. *On the other hand, this isn't the first time people have tried to kill me, and most of* them *are dead.*

He repeated that aloud, and Adrienne whooped and grinned. Dust billowed up around their hooves; the sound rose to a harsh drumroll thunder that shivered in his bones. Sandra drove the remounts and packhorses ahead and a little to their left, and two streams of dust smoked out behind them, mingling and drifting.

Tully passed him, swerving in a little to shout, "Help! I've fallen into a *Lonesome Dove* rerun and I can't get out!"

The goblin grin was heartening; Roy always got that expression when he was about to pull a nasty on someone. On the other hand . . .

The Indians were much closer now. He could see details; they were equipped much like the Nyo-Ilcha, but the lances had backward-slanting collars of ostrich feathers below the points, and the men all had broad bands of black paint across their faces from the nose up, with yellow circles around the eyes.

"Northern clans, well off their usual stamping grounds," Simmons said. "Akaka, I'd say, from the look and the paint."

"From their looks, either they're all auditioning for a remake of *The Crow,* or it's the clowns from hell!" Tom called, and got another laugh.

The Akaka warriors weren't in the least funny themselves, though. They were men who'd do their best to kill him, and no mistake. Their shrill yelping war cries cut through the hoof thunder, and he could see their open mouths and bared teeth as they crouched low over their horses' necks to urge them on to greater speed. A little closer, and one with a crescent moon of silver through the septum of his nose and elk antlers on a hairy headdress caught his eye and shouted something, gesturing with the long lance he held, and then used the shaft to whack his pinto mare on the rump. It seemed to bound forward, perceptibly faster.

Doubtless he's shouting variants on "Now you die, white-eye!" Tom thought, and gestured broadly with his own right hand—middle finger extended from a big clenched fist.

You know, friend, in the abstract I can feel a certain sympathy for you. In the concrete here and now, I'm going to kill your ass if I can.

The problem was that by slanting in from their quarries' right, the Indians had made it nearly impossible for the New Virginians to shoot; you couldn't use a two-handed weapon on horseback in that direction if you were right-handed, which all of them were. Or you could, but your chances of hitting anything would go down from low to zero.

But . . .

Adrienne whooped again, and Simmons called, "We're going to get ahead of them! Our horses are fresher!"

Tom checked, and the Indians *were* falling behind; their dash along the angle was going to cut through where the quarry had been, not in front of them or in direct collision. In a minute or two they'd have to turn to their right, fall in behind the New Virginians and make it a stern chase.

The Akaka saw it at the same time, and a shout of fury went up from them. One rose in his stirrups and drew his bow to his ear; he was two hundred yards off, but the heavy horn-backed stave of mesquite wood reinforced with sinew sent the shaft flickering past Schalk Botha, the last in their column of twos.

Then the moment of maximum danger was past, and the New Virginians were drawing their O'Brien rifles from the saddle scabbards. Tom followed suit, although he doubted his ability—or anyone else's either—to hit anything at two or three hundred yards from the back of a galloping horse. In combat it was hard enough to score a hit when you were lying prone with good solid earth under both elbows for a brace; thousands of rounds of small-arms fire were popped off for every casualty.

Tully didn't pull his rifle. Instead he dropped a little behind and threw two fist-sized lumps aside. Twisting in the saddle, Tom saw them tumble away . . . and then two quick poplar-shaped columns of smoke with red snaps of fire at their hearts erupted from the dirt as the Indians galloped over the lumps. That had them yelling in panic and reining wide, their horses bugling and rearing and fighting their riders. Tully's grin grew wider.

"Semtex!" he shouted. "With timers!"

It would probably work only once, but it had gained them some time. The pursuers shrank slightly as they dropped behind, and slowed a little more when several riders began firing at them, turning backward in the saddle—what the ancient Greeks had called the Parthian shot, from the trick horse archers used to discourage pursuit. The flat *crack* . . . *crack* . . . cut through the duller rumble of hooves, and the cartridges glittered as they spun away to the ground.

Adrienne drew out of the column, racing along beside it for a moment so that she could look back free of the great cloud of dust twenty-five sets of hooves were kicking up. He could see her mouth work, and read her lips: *Shit.*

"Slow down a bit!" she called as she swerved back into line. "The horses can't take much more of this. The Indians are slackening off."

He suddenly noticed the heat radiating from his mount, and the white streaks of foam along its neck, and the bellows panting through its red-rimmed nostrils. *Can't be easy to carry me at this speed,* he thought, and slowed—more a matter of shifting his balance a bit back than doing anything with the reins. He could feel the animal's relief as its hoof-beat slowed a little.

Good thing too. If we had to stop to change mounts now, they'd be far too close. We could discourage them with aimed fire, but they'd be ready to go. . . .

"What's the bad news?" he called to Adrienne as she rejoined the column.

"They've got a remuda of spare horses following them," she said. "That means they can switch off—it'll be easier for them than us—and a lot of us ride heavier in the saddle than any Indians are likely to do."

"Short form?" he called. *Sorry, not familiar with cavalry logistics,* he added to himself.

"Short form, they'll catch us eventually, if we can't break contact," she said, obviously thinking hard. "Bad if they catch us where there's water. Fatal if it's a dry spot. Or possibly fatal anyway, since the only water near here is at the bottom of a canyon."

"Afton canyon? Just east of Barstow?" he said.

"Right. Give me a minute."

Think hard, think hard, askling, he thought—and even

then was a little startled that he'd mentally used the Norski term for *darling*.

He looked around himself, and was startled at how close the sun was to the horizon. Adrienne rode side by side with Simmons for a moment, then dropped back to each in turn.

"We're going to hit the Afton canyon soon," she said. That was where the intermittent Mohave flowed east before it sank into the desert playas. "We'll turn east, water the horses and fill our bags as fast as we can, then get up one of the low spots on the north face of the wall. If we can get into the Calico range north of there we can lose them and then swing west again."

Tom looked back at the dust cloud their pursuers raised, tinged bloody by the setting sun, estimated times, and then called up his knowledge of the land.

"That'll be shaving it pretty close," he said. "They could cut the angle again, if they figure out what we intend. And that canyon gets pretty damned narrow in places; I've walked it and camped there."

"You're right, but it's our best chance," she said, loud over the drum of hooves and the rattle of iron on rock. Sparks flew up from the feet of her mount as she dropped farther down the column.

Jesus, what a woman! he thought warmly. *Of course, we may die horribly in a couple of hours, but what a rush it's been!*

The pursuit slowed to a canter for a few minutes, and the pursued did as well. Then Tom saw the great clot of horsemen behind them split; sixty or so kept up the chase, and forty angled off to the right, eastward—toward the rim of the canyon through which they'd have to run . . .

This bunch are savages, right enough, he thought. *That doesn't mean they're stupid, especially within their own stamping ground.*

"That's torn it!" he called to Adrienne.

"Going to make it interesting, at least," she said.

"We're going to have to sting them a bit at the crossing!" he shouted back. "Me first."

The land was sloping down before them, sparsely dotted with sage and creosote and clumps of grass dried to blond straw; the plain was interrupted by mesas and buttes, all turning dark purple and gold as the sun sank on their left. It was almost too classically Western; this area had been used for a lot of movies, back FirstSide. Being chased through it by real live Indians intent on killing you gave a whole new perspective to memories of *The Searchers* . . . .

"Yo!"

Adrienne's shout gave them all warning, and they spurred their mounts. The dry bed of the Mohave lay before them— not quite dry here, a muddy trickle in the center, flanked by long grass, reeds, cottonwoods and willows. Water and soupy mud flew up in plumes to either side as the driven horses hit it at a gallop, then jinked hard to the right on the other bank.

Tom pulled in his own mount and let the others pass him; it reared slightly, neighing protest, then stood panting with its body parallel to the river. That put the charging Akaka warriors to his left. The horse was hunt-trained; when he squeezed it with his thighs it stayed motionless save for its rapid breath as he leveled the militia rifle. The Indians were out in the open, still well lit; he breathed out and let the blade of the foresight fall down across the circle of the rear aperture. *Take up the slack and stroke the trigger* . . .

Crack. The .30-06 rounds punched his shoulder harder than the assault rifles he was used to. No use trying for precision, not at two hundred yards in bad light and from an uncertain platform. Move the aiming point and squeeze, squeeze, squeeze. One sharp blast merged into another in a ripple of fire as he emptied the magazine and spent brass spun away to his right; the muzzle blast was a strobing ball of red-yellow, dazzling the eyes.

Horses went down, and men. Some of the screams were of pain—horses sounded like enormous terrified children when they were hurt, an aspect of preindustrial battles he hadn't anticipated and didn't like at all. More were shrieks of rage; other muzzle flashes winked at him, muskets with a duller red than the nitro powder of this weapon, and the near-silent hiss of arrows. He didn't wait to study the results of his fire; he pulled his horse's head around and booted it into motion. The big gelding labored as it cross the riverbed, muck flying from its hooves, and its labored breathing reminding him of how hard it had worked; the smell of the wet earth was heavy in his nostrils after the long dryness of the desert. The Indians were closer, and arrows passed him on either side with hissing *whup* of cloven air; they'd sink to the feathers in him if they hit, or if they struck the horse . . . which would be almost as bad.

Worse, if they took him alive.

Then he was out of the swale and up on the sandy bank on the other side of the nearly dry river. A dark shape loomed there: Henry Villers sitting his horse, with the Bren gun trained on the shallow spot where the pursuers would inevitably bunch as they crossed. His smile was very white in the growing gloom.

"You stung 'em, Warden Tom," he called out. "I'm just going to purely spoil their whole day, then follow right along."

"*Semper Fi,* you betcha!" Tom called to him.

The canyon started as a wedge of flattish sand between two ranges of hills, but it rapidly grew narrower as he pounded east. After a minute he heard a sudden roaring stutter behind him—Villers emptying a thirty-round magazine into a crowd of men and horses; there was a brief pause, and the sound was repeated. Then silence, except for faint screams and shrieks, and the growing drum of a horse's hooves.

Narrower still, rising walls on either side crowded him toward the chain of pools and trickles that made the river; the sun was right behind him, and the fluted stone curtains on either side were striated in red and salmon pink and green and black as the volcanic rock caught the dying beams of sunset.

He caught up with the rest at a broad shallow pool. There was a frenzy of movement around the northern bank, where firm ground ran down to the water under the shade of a stretch of huge cottonwoods. Sandra was trying to keep the desperately thirsty horses from foundering themselves, waving her arms and sometimes slapping noses with her quirt, leading one set in before the others wanted to leave, amid shrill squeals and a snapping, snorting chaos she managed to control—somehow. Jim Simmons was scanning the southern edge of the canyon's cliffs with his scope-sighted rifle; he gave a shout as Tom slugged his horse back on its haunches.

"Company coming!" Simmons shouted, and fired.

"Leave him," Sandra barked as she ran by, leading four more horses by their reins. "He's foundered—just get your gear on this'n."

He snatched at the reins she offered; the horse he'd been riding stood with its head down, wheezing painfully, staggering a little in place. Tom felt a stab of pity; it didn't prevent him from stripping off the saddle and saddlebags and throwing them on the new mount with indecent speed. The saddle blanket was rank and running with sweat, and spattered with foam. The new horse was his original spare—even then he gave a thought of thanks for Sandra, who'd kept track through the confusion. She might well have saved his life; a smaller horse wouldn't go nearly as far or fast under his weight.

His first mount made for the water with trembling legs. Then something went *shwuup!* through the umber-tinted sunset air and hit it with a meaty sound, lost under the huge, piteous scream of surprise and pain from the horse. He saw an arrow quivering in its withers as it collapsed; then more were flying at them from the south rim of the canyon. He could look up from the darkness beneath the cottonwood to see the cliff there ruddy and sunlit, the arrowheads winking as they reached the top of their arcs. The black shafts looked slow then, but that turned to zipping speed as they plunged down. Some went *thunk* into the big trees and quivered like malignant bees; others hit the sand with a *shunk*ing sound. Muskets banged as well; he could see the shooters bobbing up and down from cover, and the puffs of dirty smoke from muzzle and pan.

Simmons's sniper rifle cracked, flashes in the dark and the sharp stink of nitro powder as he tried to keep the enemy suppressed, but there were too many of them—their fire-power was diffuse, but huge. Henry Villers came up on a horse as badly blown as Tom's had been, threw himself out of the saddle and prepared to add the Bren gun to the sup-pressing fire.

"No!" Adrienne shouted. "This place is a deathtrap. Get mounted, everyone; we have to make it past the narrows! *Tully!*"

"Trust me, trust me!" the little man shouted, scrambling components from one of the packsaddles into a canvas bag. "OK! Go for it! Go, go, *go.*"

Villers scrambled aboard one of the presaddled spares. Then they were all splashing through the pond and onto the only clear ground eastward—a strip of wet sand along the southern edge of the stream; elsewhere the floor of the canyon was boulder-strewn and brush-grown. It was also a pit of darkness now; Tom managed to get his night-sight goggles out of their pouch and onto his face, and a new magazine into his rifle, all at a pounding gallop and without losing anything but his hat. That went flying off into the night behind him like a bat as water-worn rock cliffs rushed by, swerving in a crazy snake's passage as they wove among the rocks and fallen trees and ponds. Sand spurted up from the hooves of the horses ahead, flicking him in the face. The Akaka up on top of the canyon wall were pacing them on their right, shooting down into the riverbed—right ahead of him someone's horse went down at the head, its hind legs and hooves flying up almost in his face, and then his horse had hopped over it in a sudden pig-jump that al-most cost him his seat.

He risked a look behind. It was Sandra; she was up and running, and Tully was riding alongside her, bouncing around but staying on. He reached down; she grabbed his hand and stirrup leather and made an astonishing bounding jump, coming down on the horse behind him and clinging tight. His teeth and eyes shone wide, in a face that was all nose and chin and straining effort.

On the cliff face above him something swept through the night amid a circular trail of sparks—and Tom's mind made a leap of its own: It was some sort of primitive grenade, gunpowder stuffed into a clay pot lined with rocks, then a fuse lit and the whole whipped around in a sling for throwing.

It soared down from the cliff, trailing sparks. *Crannggg!* And gravel-shrapnel spurted all around him; his horse missed a step for a heartstopping instant, and then was on its way again. But more circles of sparks flowered on the cliff. . . .

Then they were out into a marginally broader part of the canyon, one where the river ran close under the steep southern cliffs. North of that bend was a broad patch of sand, and north of that a side canyon, a triangular wash that made a path to the northern rim of the canyon, littered with stones from gravel size up to chunks as big as his torso. It was passable . . . just.

"Sandy, young Botha, get the horses up—everyone else, rearguard! Quick, or they'll catch us on two flanks!" Adrienne called.

"No, they won't," Tully said, panting, as Sandra slipped down.

He pulled a controller from a pouch on his harness, extended it westward and mashed his thumb down with vindictive force. A rolling boom shot around the curve of the canyon, with a cloud of dust on its heels.

"Satchel charge under a boulder," he said, and threw back his head for a catamount-in-agony rebel yell that would have done one of his great-grandfathers proud. "That'll hold 'em for a few minutes."

"Good *work!*" Adrienne cried.

Tom slapped him on his shoulder as he passed, then took cover behind a big rock about ten yards up the cut.

"Jim, Henry!" he called. "Fall back by pairs, leapfrog!"

He took two turns of the rifle's sling around his left fist, braced his elbow on the rock—what luxury, after bouncing around on a horse!—and sighted. It was a bit awkward with the goggles, but a lot better than trying to see in the dark like a cat. The range was two hundred yards away and a hundred up; only the height difference had let the arrows reach them. The smoothbores would hit only by accident at that range, but get enough of them going and accidents would happen, and he didn't like the thought of being hit by one of those three-quarter-inch lead balls. They were the size of a kid's biggest conker marble and traveling around eight hundred feet per second.

It's times like this that you miss Uncle Sam's expensive body armor, he thought, and squeezed off a round. Arrows came flickering back at the muzzle flash.

Up on the southern cliff where the sun was dying an Akaka slinger whirled another grenade around his head. Tom brought the blade of his foresight down on the moving blur, squeezed . . .

Crack.

The man lurched backward as a .30-06 hollow-point blasted through his chest and out his back, leaving a small round hole in his stomach and an exit wound the size of a bread plate. The grenade he'd been loading into the soft antelope-leather pocket of his sling fell at his feet, and three seconds later it exploded—right next to the other four in the pouch hung across his chest. A great snap of red fire lit the cliff, and rocks and dust and bits of his body shot out and fell downward over the steep rock.

Just then Henry Villers's machine gun began to stutter, raking rock and water in a flurry of spouts and stone chips and ricochets, driving back the pursuers who'd finally come up along the canyon floor in their quarries' tracks. Simmons's rifle had never stopped. Tom shot his magazine empty, clicked in another one and jacked the operating rod.

"Fall back," he said. "Jim, you and me—Henry, on the word! Watch your flanks, guys."

Because unless the Akaka are conveniently stupid, they're not going to rush a machine gun and two automatic rifles from the front in a narrow slot, he thought. *Of course, a lot depends on how many Tully got with his satchel charge; no way to tell. Maybe we can sicken them of it. Maybe the horse will learn to sing. Fuck it.*

The cut became less well defined as they scrambled up and north. A dead horse lay inconveniently—the stupid beast had slipped and broken its neck and someone had shot it; it said something about the situation that he hadn't noticed. He clambered over the sweat-and-blood-stinking, foam-slick and unpleasantly yielding obstacle and into loose scree that slipped under his feet.

If he hadn't been wearing the goggles, the silent tiger rush from his left would have taken him completely by surprise— the Akaka's soft moccasins made no sound at all as he skipped from rock to rock and flung himself headlong at Tom.

A flicker of motion out of the corner of his eye brought him around and crouching; the duck and lift was purely instinctual. A hard, heavy weight slammed into his shoulders just as he heaved up, and the war shriek turned to a yell of dismay as the warrior flipped up and over. Tom used the same motion to wheel, but even so the Akaka had bounced back to his feet on the rough stone. He was a bundle of sinew and steel-spring muscle no more than arm's length away, and the knife and tomahawk glittered in his hands—they would be in Tom's flesh long before he could bring the rifle up to shoot. Instead he twirled it like a quarterstaff, and the muzzle smashed across the other man's left wrist. The hatchet flew away; Tom's hips swayed aside like a matador's, and he clamped the knife hand between his arm and flank before the razor steel could do more than slice his bush jacket and sting the skin. The rifle clattered away.

The two men strained against each other in the dark for an instant, a private universe of fear-stinking sweat and desperate effort. The Indian's free hand clawed for his eyes and slid off the slick surface of the goggles; Tom's teeth snapped into the wrist, and blood ran sickeningly rank into his mouth. He spat it out and caught his own left wrist in his right hand behind the Indian's back, lifting him off the ground with a surge and wrenching with arms like pythons. The painted gargoyle face inches from his contorted, screaming, and then Tom had to duck his head to save his eyes from the other's teeth; they ground into his scalp, tearing the skin.

That loosed something deep in his gut; the *berserkergang* of his ancestors perhaps—if it was, it was colder than ice, not hot.

"*Yaaaaaah!*" he shouted, a hoarse, guttural sound that echoed through the night.

And his arms ground inward with the inexorable force of glaciers. The tough cotton drill of the bush jacket ripped from the neck halfway to the waist with a crack as his shoulders bunched, and red blood vessels writhed across his vision. The Akaka warrior screamed once more, high and shrill—then flopped limp with blood pouring out of his mouth, spine snapped and ribs driven into his lungs like daggers of bone.

Tom staggered and threw the corpse from him, glaring about. It took an instant for his vision to clear, and for him realize that the others were staring at him. He coughed and shook his head.

"Let's get going," he said, scrubbing his sleeve across the filmed surface of the goggles.

❋ ❋ ❋

"He can't ride with it," Adrienne said. "He'd bleed out inside two miles."

Schalk Botha lay facedown. The wound wasn't one that would be fatal under any circumstances but these—the arrow had gone through the thicker fleshy part of his right buttock, a broad-bladed triangle of metal slicing down out of the night. Adrienne had cut off the shaft at the skin and freed it with a single long pull, then packed the wound with antiseptic pads and strapped them down with strong adhesive.

It would heal in a couple of weeks, without doing anything other than making young Schalk the butt of jokes for the rest of his life. Here and now, it was a sentence of death. The young man knew it, and his face had the strained impassiveness of someone realizing his own mortality and determined to meet it with eyes open.

Tom looked around at the circle of faces, ghostly in the moonlight. Everyone who needed it had been patched up; he had a pad along his forehead over the left eye himself, and another on his side a handspan down from the armpit. A couple of the others looked worse, but there was nothing crippling, nothing that would keep a man—or woman—from riding and fighting.

Piet Botha was crouched on his hams beside his son, both hands—his huge, scarred hands—on the stock of the rifle that rested with its butt between his knees. His brutal face was as impassive as ever; for an instant one hand reached out and touched the younger man's hair.

"*Nie,*" he sighed. "Let there be no foolishness or waste of time."

His chin jerked out toward the darkness. Not far away the Indians were holding some sort of ceremony over *their* dead, doubtless preparatory to coming after revenge. Their howls came out of the star-bright night and echoed up from the canyon, more chilling than wolves because they *weren't* mindless.

"We must have a rearguard," he said. "Or the rest will never break free. Schalk can still fight from cover. I also, of course. And one more fit man able to move about."

The dark somber eyes flicked across their faces. *I can't* believe *what I'm going to say,* Tom thought as he opened his mouth.

"Man, I cannot *believe* that I'm doing this," Henry Villers said, pulling the Bren gun from its carrying rack behind his saddle. "And with these two. OK, you mothers don't give me any shit, now. I'm a machine gunner, and I'm the oldest man here after big brother Boer. So we'll hold them as long as we can, then pull up into those rocks. Tully, my man, you get me some of that Semtex and some detonators, right? And plenty of ammunition. See y'all later."

Meaning in the afterlife, if any, Tom thought.

He shook hands with each of the men and silently walked toward his horse; so did Tully and Simmons. Adrienne paused for a second to speak quietly to each; Henry handed her a sealed letter he'd written days ago. Her face might have been carved from ivory as it passed him; Sandra was weeping quietly, wiping at her eyes with the backs of her hands.

"Hail and farewell," Tom murmured to himself as he swung into the saddle. The desert sky above was an arch of hoarfrost, and the rocks glimmered to the northward.

"Let's go," Adrienne said, reining her mount's head around. "If we push, we can make Jackhammer Gap by dawn."

CHAPTER TWENTY-ONE

Mohave/Owens Valley
July–August 2009

The Commonwealth of New Virginia

"Damn the Akaka for running us so far off course," Adrienne said, looking up from the map. "We've been zigzagging so much we've ridden more miles east and west than south to north."

Westward the peaks of the southern Sierras towered, close now and looking closer in late afternoon; the snow-topped heights farther north were ethereally lovely, but they also made Tom think of iced drinks. The desert had sloped up for a week of hard night travel now, and Tom's inner ear told him they were at well over a thousand feet. It was perceptibly cooler in daytime—just very hot, not a brutal wringing that made your eyes bulge as if someone were tightening a steel cable around your temples. The nights were positively cool, which made traveling a pleasure—particularly since they'd shaken the last of the Akaka warriors in the canyons of the Randburg mountains to the southeast. After that they'd seen an occasional dust plume or the wink of sunlight on steel, but nothing closer.

"The problem is Owens Lake," Jim Simmons said, pointing. "It plugs the base of the valley like a cork. If we want to get to Cerro Gordo in the Inyos, we have to backtrack from here. That's bad country, and we may run into more of Swift Lance's men, too."

"Whatever the Colletta is paying them, it isn't enough," Adrienne said. "Goddamned persistent bunch."

Tom looked at the map, shaking his head. The basic geography of the area they were heading for was the same, a north-south trench between the eastern Sierras and the White-Inyo range. But back FirstSide, the Owens Lake area at its southern end was a waterless expanse of salts, empty since the 1920s. LA's insatiable thirst had sucked the valley dry like a giant mosquito with a proboscis two hundred and fifty miles long.

Here the dry bed he knew was a real lake, over a hundred square miles of it—mostly shallow, salty as the ocean, but indubitably wet.

"Short of going even farther west and then climbing over one of the Sierra passes, I don't think we've got any choice but this," he said, pointing with one long strong finger.

He traced a route up along the flank of the mountains. "Up here, between the Sierras and the Coso mountains— through the Rose Valley. We go around the western shore of the lake, and once we're past the narrows at Little Lake and the Haiwee reservoir—"

"Haiwee Meadows, here," Simmons said. "Flat grassy area, with some marsh."

"Haiwee Meadows, then, we can keep the Alabama Hills between us and Lone Pine."

"The Colletta hunting lodge," Adrienne corrected him absently. "Where the river meets a seasonal creek coming out of the Alabama Hills, just north of the lake. Officially"—she traced a circle on the map—"that and the mine are all there is."

"When we get there, we can take a peek and see what's what," he said. "If they're actually training troops, there'll be indications of where. I suspect up east in the Inyos, the Cerro Gordo site. It's big enough, and out of the way, and they can explain away activity there as mining if anyone notices. We can swing east across the valley floor to the north of the lodge—it's only five miles wide."

"We'd better stick close to the mountains on the way north

and keep an eye on a local canyon," Tully put in. "Because we may need to do the *Run away! Run away!* thing *really* quick. The Owens is long, but it's narrow. And the sides are nearly straight up and down—twelve thousand feet up and down; it's like God's bathtub. If the Bad Guys have somewhere near a battalion training there . . ."

"Yah, you betcha," Tom said. "More crowded, so we're a lot more likely to bump into someone."

They finished their evening meal–cum–breakfast of roast rabbit, hardtack, and dried fruit and got under way; it wasn't dark yet, strictly speaking, but the summer nights were short and they had to take some chances. Simmons and Kolo spread out to the front; the other four rode in a loose line abreast, someone swerving out now and then to keep their little herd of remounts and pack horses from scattering or spending too much time grazing. Tom noticed that he rode with utter naturalness now; his body adjusted to the motions of the horse as easily as it did walking, and controlled it without much more effort. That left his mind and senses free, the swaying and the hollow thudding sound of hooves on dirt like the beat of blood in his ears.

Of course, he thought with an inward chuckle, *I've also learned to ignore the way I smell. Ah, well, that's living in the field for you. At least we don't have cooties. Yet.*

The open land northward narrowed as the sky darkened; off to the right were piles of dark lava, rising into patterned columns farther north in a cliff eerily reminiscent of a giant rattlesnake lying on its side. The canyons to the left were familiar from the times he'd driven up U.S. 395. . . .

No, they're not, he thought suddenly. *They don't have the siphons for the LA Aqueduct crossing them.*

Their path was still through desert except where a seasonal watercourse ran by. This lowland had about the same vegetation as the Mohave proper: creosote, silver-gray sagebrush, screwbean mesquite, clumps of pale yellow grass now and then. There was just a lot more of it for every square foot, and of other life in proportion. The mountains to the west were getting steadily higher and steeper, not the sheer wall they would be farther north around Mount Whitney, but pretty formidable; every couple of miles a canyon slashed back into the granite fortresses, U-shaped if cut by ancient glaciers, V-formed if made by streams that were trickles or dry now, in July.

The wildlife was changing, too. There was game, not an occasional beast but whole herds of browsers heading up into the Sierras for the summer, to feed off the mountain meadows. A mob of impala trotted by; occasionally one would *pronk,* leaping straight up a dozen feet or more as if they were propelled by springs, apparently just for the hell of it; the sight gave him a brief flash of melancholy about Piet Botha, something he'd never have believed when the man was alive. One canyon up—he thought it was Nine-Mile Canyon, which had a road over to the Kern River country on FirstSide—the game was pronghorn, moving along slowly. The pronghorn were nervous, flicking their tails and raising their heads. A forest of funny-looking little horns with backward-sloping tips bobbed as they looked around.

"Hey," Tully said from behind him. "Lookit—they're doing that searchlight-ass thing."

That was an alarm gesture, making the white patch on their rumps bristle, visible for miles. A split second later they were all running westward for their lives—literally, because a golden-brown streak was after them from a jumping-off point behind a mesquite bush.

Cheetah! Tom thought; they all soothed their horses' natural start of alarm at the sight and scent of an attacking carnivore.

Cat and antelope ignored them. The cheetah was accelerating as if it had rocket assist, its great hind paws landing as far forward as its ears, the long slender body flexing in a series of huge bounding leaps. The antelope were a little slower off the mark, but their top speed was a bit better than the cheetah's—about seventy miles per hour as opposed to sixty-five—and they could keep it up a lot longer. One of the rearmost pronghorns nearly ran into the beast ahead of it, dodged to get around it, skidded sideways in a cloud of dust and thrashing of limbs, recovered . . .

. . . but not quite fast enough.

Got him! Tom thought.

The slender-limbed hunting cat rammed into the antelope, knocking it over in another puff of dust, then diving through the murk to clamp its jaws on its prey's throat. Cheetahs killed by bunting their prey off its feet and then choking it; their doglike claws were too blunt to grip the way a lion's did. By the time the riders went by, fifty or sixty yards to the east, the pronghorn's limbs had stopped twitching, and the cheetah was settling in to feed. It raised its head and flattened its ears at the sound of the horses' hooves but didn't stir from its meal. Tom was slightly surprised; in his experience, predators were a lot more nervous around human beings.

"Cheetahs only got taken off the reserved list . . . oh, ten years ago," Adrienne said, giving the little drama a glance. "They don't breed as successfully as the other big cats—frankly, they're too stupid to live. Inbred, and overspecialized."

Tom chuckled. "Still, that one's pretty calm with six people this close."

"I don't think the Collettas came hunting all that often, either, and there haven't been any Indians to speak of around here for a generation or more. The game's not man-wary."

Tom nodded but didn't speak; the sun was just dropping behind the Sierras, leaving the tremendous tawny granite cliff a few miles away in darkening purple, tinged with pink at the saw-edge ridge that topped it; night rolled over the valley floor toward them like a wall of shadow. He'd always found this the most magical time of day, tinged with an inexplicable sadness. It was getting cooler, too. He'd been riding in his T-shirt; now he pulled his bush jacket out of a saddlebag and put it on. That was more complicated than it sounded, since he had to undo his combat harness, adjust it, and put it on again over the heavier garment.

When he looked up he saw Kolo trotting in from the north, on foot. That raised his brows a little . . . and knotted his stomach a trifle, too. The main reason to travel by foot was to avoid kicking up conspicuous dust, which a horse did when you pushed the gait.

The Indian stopped in front of them; that let him address the air between Tom and Adrienne. He knew full well that the woman was in command, but it preserved his self-respect if he could pretend he was reporting to the Strong One, which was how he'd referred to Tom since the canyon fight.

"Camp—old camp, by lake. Many"—he opened and closed his hands several times—"men. On foot."

"Better look into *that*," Adrienne said.

* * *

Little Lake was a sickle-shaped piece of water with the blunt horns pointing westward, about half a mile long and a few hundred yards across; it was full dark by the time they arrived, with starlight glittering on the still surface of the water. Trees and grass surrounded it; water came from seasonal creeks flowing down from what he knew as Sequoia National Park to the west, and from springs that flowed year-round. Those were sweet water, cold and with only a pleasant mineral tang. Eastward were high volcanic hills, columns of black basalt solidified in a devil's-pipe-organ pattern.

If they hadn't found the campfires, Tom would have proposed a swim—the grime and crusted sweat of the Mohave was still thick on his skin. As it was . . .

"The Commonwealth militia use a twelve-man infantry squad, right?" he said.

"Yes," Adrienne said. "Two fire teams of six—four riflemen, a Bren gunner, and his assistant—the assistant totes a machine pistol. Why?"

"This was a military marching camp, about platoon size," Tom said. "Some mules . . ."

"Six," Sandra put in. "And one horse, from the sign."

Simmons nodded. "That's standard, for an infantry platoon in unroaded country. Mules carry the heavy gear, and the horse's for the officer or a messenger."

Tom pointed out where the tents had been. "Those are about the size of your standard militia item, too, aren't they?"

He indicated the other features—the regular spacing of the campfires, the sanitary slit trench filled in not far away. While he spoke, Simmons was quartering the grass, and Kolo crouched by one of the dead fires. They'd been put out with water and buried with a couple of shovelfuls of earth, standard practice. He sniffed, picked up a pinch of the ashes, tasted them.

"Cold for one day," he said. "No more." Then he held up a fragment of bone. "Deer."

Simmons gave a little grunt of satisfaction and picked something up from the dirt. He flicked it up with his thumb like a man tossing a coin as he walked back to join the others, then held it out on an extended palm; an empty brass cartridge case.

"Thirty-aught-six," Tom said.

He handed it to Adrienne. "Rolfeston Armory mark," she said. "Couldn't have been Colletta household troops. Not this many, this far from the lodge. A squad or two around their Prime, just in case—the desert tribes *could* raid here, if they were stupid enough to invite retaliation. But not a third of the whole guard company, fossicking around nowhere in particular . . ."

"It's not legal proof I'm concerned with," Tom said grimly. "Kolo, where did they come from? And where did they go?"

The Indian pointed northwest. "From there. Yesterday, leave this morning." He pointed northeast. "Go that way at sunrise."

"And no sign of them south of here," Tom said. "At a guess, this the southern limit of the area they routinely patrol. Probably for training, mostly."

Just then Tully grunted and straightened up. "Kemosabe," he said, holding out a palm. "Take a look."

Tom did; it was a rind of some kind of flat bread, about as long as his hand. The surface was brown and had bubbles, and it was stiff—not merely stale, but textured rather like a thin cracker. He took it and tasted an edge; the nutty flavor and grainy feel were unmistakable.

Corn tortilla. In fact, it's exactly the sort that Dolorez used to make, back when I was stationed at Fort Hood, he thought—seized for a moment by nostalgia, for a young soldier away from home for the first time, bursting with excitement at the world opening up for him.

Adrienne touched him on the arm. "Tom?" she said.

"Ah," he said, starting. *And this is a* lot *wilder than anything I could imagine* then! "It's a tortilla. Who here eats 'em?"

"None of the local Indians," she said. "Not west of the Pueblo tribes. The *nahua* do, of course—ah."

"Yup, you betcha," he said, tossing it away. "That style of cooking cornmeal is a lot older than Columbus. These soldiers weren't New Virginians; from the look, they were armed and equipped and organized just the way the household troops of your Families are, but they're Mexican. Mesoamerican. *Nahua.* Whatever."

"Thank you," she said, quietly but with a warmth underneath it. From her glance he knew that she'd just quietly thanked God he was there.

Then she went on briskly: "All right, we know where they're going—I'd give odds it'll be up the foot of the hills to the east, then around the east side of Owens Lake." She looked at Tom and the others. "Suggestions?"

Tom tapped thumb and forefinger on his chin. "Well, why don't we follow 'em a while to make sure? They won't be moving at night, probably; too inconvenient when they don't have night-sight equipment. Once we're sure they're going the way we think, then we can cut west like we planned."

"Let's do it," she said, and glanced up. "We've got about another five hours of full dark. We'll have to be careful not to actually run into them."

*   *   *

"Whoa," Tom said softly.

With night goggles, the track of the patrol was plain enough, and he'd been taking it at a slow canter. Now there was something else there. His horse caught the scent a few seconds after he saw the motionless lump, and sunfished; Tom dismounted and walked over to it, leading the beast by the reins.

The lump was a man, spread-eagled, with his arms and legs lashed by rawhide thongs to wooden pegs driven deep into the ground. A short stocky muscular man, naked, and showing the marks of a bad beating—swollen eyes and lips, crusted blood, other bruises on his torso. His black hair was shaven to a bristle-cut of uniform length all over, and his dry tongue showed between his lips. If he'd been left here all day in the summer heat he'd be very thirsty, and very lucky— lucky that some enterprising predator hadn't happened by and started chewing off bits. As it was, the ant bites were like a rash over most of his torso. His glazed eyes cleared a bit as he heard the hooves thudding near him—Tom and the others would be no more than looming shapes in the dark. The teeth that showed in a snarl of terrified defiance were even and white, although a few were missing. He looked more frightened still when Tom was close enough to see more details. Evidently his experiences with big white men in this uniform weren't all that pleasant.

Tom made a warbling sound between his lips, one that carried well in the night without sounding too much like a signal. Then he unhooked the big canteen from his saddlebow, which woke desperate interest and an inarticulate grunt of need. He put his hand behind the bound man's head and raised it so that he could drink without choking, giving the water in sips—after the first gulp the man cooperated, as if he knew that he could not afford to take too much.

"You speak English?" he asked the man.

The Indian shook his head—using the gesture in the manner of Western civilization, Tom noted, and evidently recognizing the name of the language at least.

Adrienne dismounted and went to one knee not far away; she pushed back her goggles and hat, and briefly switched on a flashlight with a cloth across the glass, illuminating her face. The Indian looked at her, said something in a harsh sibilant language, and seemed to relax a little.

Bravo, Adri, Tom thought. *A woman makes it look less like a war party to him . . . hmmm, unless torturing captives is women's work where he comes from. Guess not.*

She said something in another language, and the man answered it in the same, but shook his head.

"He recognizes Nahuatl but it isn't his language," she said thoughtfully. "A lot of our *nahua* are from other language groups, of course; we just use that term because the majority *are* nahuatl speakers. He could be a Zapotec—" The man nodded frantically. "Aha. There's a potentate down that way we've dealt with a bit, named Seven Flower."

"Russki?" the man said. *"Govoroyu russki?"*

That was an extremely ungrammatical way of asking if Tom spoke Russian. He did . . . sort of.

"Da," he said, in that tongue. *"A little. Speak slowly."* In English, to Adrienne Rolfe: "I speak a little Russian, badly, and so does he, even worse. Be prepared for communications problems."

He continued the conversation, then noted out of the corner of his eye Kolo drawing his knife and nearly going for the bound man, until Simmons put an arm in front of him and spoke sharply.

"What's that about?" Tom said.

"When we were ambushed in the Lake Tulare marshes, part of the opposition looked just like Mr. Bondage here," Adrienne said thoughtfully. "Quite different from the swamp hostiles, and they had O'Brien rifles. Well maintained, and they knew how to use them. I'd guess they were deserters from right here; the working conditions don't appear to be too good."

"That fits," Tom said. "So does the way he looks."

He grinned lopsidedly when she raised her brows. "Officers and NCOs beating up and abusing recruits is an old tradition in the Russian armed forces; ditto senior enlisted men picking on younger, stealing their pay and rations. It's really old, goes back to czarist times. They still have a scandal every once and a while, new guys getting killed or having all their food stolen until they collapse, that sort of thing. And if the Batyushkovs are old-fashioned, chances are the military types they recruited for this would be, too."

"Sounds counterproductive," Adrienne said; meanwhile she got the first-aid kit from the pack horse that carried it.

"Oh, it is," Tom said. "But who abandons a tradition just because it's stupid? Also, a lot of Russians have a *really* intense dislike of what they call 'black-asses,' by which they mean anyone brown with slanted eyes; that goes right back to the Mongol Khans. Get a bunch of unreconstructed Red Army men—I'd guess they used veterans of Afghanistan and Chechnya—and give 'em unlimited disciplinary authority and no overview, and this sort of thing is about what I'd expect."

He turned back to the prisoner and spoke in halting Russian, with many pauses to clear up misunderstandings or search for a word.

While he did, the others were studying the prisoner. "Looks like he's seen some action," Tully commented, and Adrienne nodded.

"Lots of scars," Adrienne said. She and Sandra cut the man's feet free and began bandaging and patching from there up. "Old ones."

"Cutting weapons," Simmons said, pointing to the faded dusty-white and purple marks on the brown skin. "I've seen wounds like that, made with an obsidian-edged battle rake. And that one could be a bullet wound—musket ball. A couple of them look like they were infected before they healed."

"Yah, you betcha," Tom said, when the man allowed his head to loll back, too exhausted to speak further. The big man looked up at the others and gave them the gist:

"He's a soldier of some sort back in his home country. His boss is a subordinate of this Seven Flower, and he and a lot of others have been training here for nearly a year." He looked from face to face. "Standard training to start with, and then working over and over again on assaulting a mockup of a big building."

He translated the man's description. Adrienne and Simmons cursed.

"The Gate complex," they said almost in chorus.

Tom smiled wryly, and began cutting the man's hands free with swift jerks of his belt knife.

"And incidentally, he's *real* disillusioned, and willing to cooperate."

Tully nodded. "You know, there are times when being a son of a bitch is its own punishment. What's this guy's name?"

Tom put the question to him; he seemed a little surprised to be asked. "He says the Russians just called everyone by numbers or nicknames. His name . . ." They went back and forth on it for a while.

"It's One Ocelot. That's the name of the day of the month he was born on."

"Maybe it should be One Lucky Cat, instead," Tully said, and grinned. "After all, we got here before the coyotes."

* * *

A day later, Tully took off his hat. "Do you realize where we are?" he said solemnly, pointing to the open country to the north of the creek whose bank they were following.

"No," Tom sighed. "Where are we, exactly, Tonto?"

"This, Kemosabe, is Movie Flats."

He swept a finger around the rolling sage-and-grass-covered circle, taking in the towering peaks of the high Sierras behind them to the west, and the rough upthrust slabs and boulders and wind-worn arches of the Alabama hills ahead. As he spoke the dawn broke over the Inyo Mountains still farther east; they were nearly as high as the Sierra Nevada, towering ten thousand feet above the Owens. The first spears of light hit the snow still lingering on Mount Whitney behind them, then ran down the sheer face of the sawtoothed granite range like a speeded-up film. A few seconds later it struck the tops

of the Alabamas, only five thousand or so feet but still looking formidable in their scarred, tumbled, boulder-strewn
steepness, turning them blood colored for an instant.

Tom felt a prickle of awe at the sheer bleak grandeur of
the view, then thrust it aside. Tully continued:

"They filmed *Gunga Din* here. *Springfield Rifle*. And
How the West Was Won. And *Maverick* . . . And pretty well
all the Hopalong Cassidy, Tom Mix, B-movies, and all the
Lone Ranger episodes . . ."

"You're impossible," Adrienne snorted.

"Naw, just highly improbable," Tully said.

Tom grinned; sometimes Roy's clowning got a little
wearing, but it was also a welcome break in the tension at
moments like this.

After a moment Tully went on more seriously: "It's a lot
prettier in real life, though."

They urged their horses into a canter; they were heading
down Lone Pine Creek, eastward toward the canyon it cut
through the hills. There was no road along it on this side of
the Gate, barely even a trail just north of the water, but there
was plenty of cover—big Freemont cottonwood trees reaching up to nearly a hundred feet, their serrated-edged leaves
clattering overhead; the dark cool damp-smelling air was
thick with their downy seed fluff. Sycamores and willows
formed the understory, hanging over the water; walnuts
showed their furrowed, dark brown trunks. He heard something snort, grunt, and crash aside through the undergrowth
as they passed—wild boar, by the tracks—and there were the
broader cloven marks of feral cattle in the same wet sand,
and the neat prints of deer.

Stone closed around the little stream, but not in unbroken
walls; there were gaps between the tilted rock ledges. Tom
counted them carefully; it was easy to get lost in this tangle,
and easier still when the version he was familiar with was
different in so many details. He'd been through here on Fish
and Game business FirstSide, and on hiking trips, but . . .
There was a lot more vegetation for starters, and no network
of dirt roads, and that didn't complete the list. Hundreds of

years of difference in the details of the weather had made an impression even on the rocks—a boulder falling one way rather than another, or the shape of a wash.

"We turn north here," he said at last.

The open sandy wash was as good as a road for horses; better, since it was easier on their hooves than a hard surface. It was also more open than the growth along the creek, which made him nervous. If *he'd* been in command of the conspirator's forces, he'd have had more Scouts and lookouts combing the area. But there hadn't been any sigh of humans or shod horses, even though the sandy dirt showed tracks well.

Well, that's what you get for using untrustworthy troops, he thought, a little smugly.

Half a mile up the wash a ridge led up to the crest of the hills—and to a weird-looking loop of rock, a natural arch at the crest. They dismounted and handed their reins to One Ocelot; the Zapotec was almost pathetically grateful and eager to please, being even more completely isolated and lost than he'd been as one of the Batyushkov's mercenaries. If he lost their help . . . well, it was a very long walk home. Until they told him, he hadn't ever realized that there *was* an overland connection.

Together the three of them made their way up the steep ridge; Simmons and Kolo were off looking over Cerro Gordo, and Sandra had to stay with their horses at the base camp—you didn't leave a hobbled horse alone in grizzly and leopard country.

The ascent took about ten minutes of hard climbing, enough to have them breathing deeply. They took the last bit before the crest very slowly. He felt the rock harsh and gritty under his hands, the smell dry and dusty in his nostrils; his rifle was across the crook of his elbows. Carefully they raised their heads until their eyes were over the ridge.

"Well, *that's* not just a hunting lodge, by Jesus," Tom said, looking at the settlement several miles away through the clear dry air.

The original building might be—it looked a lot like a

fairly fancy dude ranch, complete with corrals and stables and barns, all in Western form and what looked at this distance to be adobe; the swimming pool added an appropriate touch. . . .

"Marble?" he said.

"There's a quarry of it a couple of miles that way," Adrienne said, pointing southeast. Snidely: "I'm shocked the whole place isn't built out of it."

The patch of cultivated ground northward looked too large, several hundred acres . . . and so did the X-shaped airstrip south of the house and near the edge of the great lake. Each arm of the landing field was fifteen hundred feet at least. A Hercules stood on it, and several smaller two-engined planes he couldn't identify at this range were parked slightly off it in earth revetments. There was an improvised-looking wooden control building with a radar pickup and broadcast antenna on its roof at one end, next to the wind sock. Southward at the edge of the water was a boathouse and a fair-sized sailboat tied up at a long wooden pier.

And east of the house was a tent camp. Several dozen big twelve-man tents were up, with more rising; he could see the unmistakable centipede of a column of marching men there, raising a trail of dust. So did vehicles heading south and east, along a rough dirt track around the lake and back toward the mountains. Guard towers stood at the four corners of the camp, even if it was still mainly empty space; they were tripods of lodgepole pine with a central ladder. The platforms had roofs and walls of thick logs squared and notched, and poking out through the slits were the barrels of heavy machine guns. Searchlights too . . .

"Well, that's proof," he said, softly.

"With a dollop of whipped cream and a maraschino cherry on top," Tully said.

"And you know," Tom said, "those guard towers would be absolutely useless for *defending* that camp. Against anyone with modern weapons, that is; and not even really useful against Indians. Shooting down at a steep angle like that, you don't get a beaten zone. The bullets just hit the dirt and stay there. But they'd be crackerjack for keeping people from getting *out*."

Adrienne hissed softly and began to level her binoculars. "Well, that's of a piece with everything else we've seen."

"Careful," Tom said, adjusting the angle of the glasses with his hand. "Into the sun like that, even with nonglare lenses, you're chancing a reflection."

She nodded thanks, studied the scene, then handed them over to Tom. He used them in turn, noting details. "Those sunken bunkers . . . armory, I'd say; or explosives store; or both. Fuel blisters near the airstrip. HQ tent . . . yah, when they get that setup completed, it'll be tentage for a battalion. Roy?"

He handed the glasses to the smaller man. Roy whistled softly as he worked the area over. "I'd say that bunch . . . looks to be about a company's worth . . . marched in from somewhere about half a day's shank's-mare travel away. Looks like they don't have enough trucks to move the men—I'd guess they were up around Cerro Gordo, like you thought, Kemosabe. Good place to train; you'd build endurance fast at eight thousand feet. *And* it's out of the way. But they must be nearly ready to go."

Tom looked over at Adrienne. She was looking calm enough, but there was a line of white around her tight-held mouth. . . .

Of course, she was born here. It's just an operational problem to me, and a personal risk. To her, it's like me seeing some shaheed *was about to nuke Chicago.*

"What are those smaller aircraft?" he said.

They weren't any type he was familiar with: sleek elongated teardrops with the wing mounted through the middle of the fuselage, bubble canopy forward, and two big piston engines.

"Mosquito fighter-bombers," Adrienne said, her voice tightly controlled. "World War Two design, slightly modified and built here."

"How many would the Collettas have?" Tom said. *And*

this private-armies setup is insane, *whatever your grandfather thinks,* he added to himself.

"Mmmm . . . four. The Commission has a dozen, and about as many more are kept by some of the Families—they maintain them for the Commission's use in lieu of taxes. Those are probably there to escort the transports with the troops. The *swine!*" she added with hissing malevolence. Then, flushing: "Sorry."

"No problem," he said sympathetically. "Well, Simmons and Kolo ought to be on their way back by now."

"Right," she said unemotionally. "Let's get back to camp and settle what we can do."

If anything, hung suspended on the air.

✳ ✳ ✳

"Wait a second," Tully said quietly, and threw up his hand.

They all reined in. Tom looked around; the steep canyon trail up the side of Mount Whitney seemed just the same as when they'd left a couple of hours ago, save for the fact that the sun was near noon and it was warmish rather than chilly. Water chuckled down the center, falling over smooth colored rocks; not far ahead was the little pool and U of meadow where they were camping. The air smelled of warm rock, pines, and water.

"Tonto think it maybe *too* quiet, Kemosabe," Tully said—but his voice was soft and deadly serious; his hand went to the rifle riding in the scabbard by his knee.

A raven launched itself out of a lodgepole pine, giving a harsh *gruk-gruk-gruk* cry. Apart from that, there was nothing. . . .

Sandra walked out from behind a rock; she was carrying her rifle, but she looked white around the mouth.

"It's OK!" she called. "They're friendly! Sort of."

"Who are *they?*" Adrienne said.

"Ah—"

There was a rustling though the woods and canyon sides all around them, and figures were standing—figures whose heads loomed monstrous under headdresses of bear and wolf and tiger. For a heartstopping moment he thought the Akaka had caught up with them. But . . .

One head was topped by a lion with turquoise eyes.

"Hi!" Chief Good Star called. "Surprise!"

The moment stretched. Then another voice called, from upslope:

"Surprise to you too, and don't move!"

Simmons, Tom thought with relief. *Up there with his scope-sighted rifle . . . he got back and didn't walk into a trap.*

The same thought must have struck Good Star; beneath the demon-clown tattoos and paint, his grin went a little sickly.

"No trouble!" he said rapidly. "Hey, Shoots Fast—come out!"

Someone did; it was Henry Villers, unmistakable despite the bandages that covered most of the left side of his face.

"Hello, Warden Tom, boss lady," he said. "What say we all catch up?"

✻ ✻ ✻

". . . so we heard the shooting and hit 'em where they weren't looking," Good Star said, puffing on his cigarette and leaning back against a log. "Some of the Akaka got away, but most didn't."

There were a number of fresh scalps at his belt, and his expression was like a contented cat's as he went on: "Thanks, by the way. Swift Lance and his Dreaming aren't going to look so hot any more, you know what I mean? Especially since one of you Deathwalkers dropped a boulder on his head."

Villers looked at Tully, who was sitting close to Sandra Margolin; the little man had relaxed since she'd convinced him she'd come to no harm except a thorough fright. They were all grouped around a small smokeless fire, not far from the edge of the pond. The meadow was a little crowded, even though the Nyo-Ilcha hadn't brought all their horses here. Adrienne's party and the chieftain shared log seats around the fire, and many of the warriors were crouched outside that circle; others were attending to their animals, or camp chores. Two of them were butchering a brace of mule deer and an elk.

"That was your satchel charge, Tully," the black man put in. "You really pissed them off with that." Then he took up the story: "Yeah, Piet Botha's dead." He shook his head. "Got to hand it to the big Boer, he was one baaad badass. Right at the end, when I was out of it—some Akaka got me with a slingstone"—he touched the bandaged side of his face and winced slightly—"he was standing over his kid in this fold of rock, and man, he used his rifle like a club till it broke and then he picked up two of them by their necks and smashed their heads together. . . . I looked at the body afterwards; must have been like three or four arrows in it, and a couple of knives."

"And then our Nyo-Ilcha friends arrived like . . . if you'll pardon the expression . . . the U.S. cavalry," Tully said. "The kid make it?"

"Yeah, though he's probably going to limp," Villers said. "Over to you, chief."

Good Star chuckled, a harsh sound. "I'd been following you on general principles, and because one of my people finked you out to Swift Lance."

His right index finger traced a shallow crusted cut along his bare ribs. "The stool pigeon tried for me, too, and missed. I didn't. But it peeved me some, I can tell you, my own people getting impressed by Swift Lance's so-called Dreaming. And the chance to take a slap at the Akaka while they were bent over and showing their butts was just too good to pass up. Figured I'd catch up with you and have a talk, but you ran too fast—and we had to take care of a few Akaka on the way, you know?"

Adrienne hissed in vexation. "You mean we were killing ourselves and zigzagging over half the desert running away from *you?*"

"Yup, that's about it, boss lady," Good Star said. "Then I got wind of this setup here—"

Villers looked embarrassed and spread his hands. "Filling him in seemed like a good idea at the time."

"—and decided to come check it out. Guess we Water People aren't the only ones got our feuds within the tribe, hey?"

Adrienne and Tom exchanged a glance. He could see her thought: *It's an advantage, but it's a threat, too. How to make use of it?*

He guessed that she took Good Star's professions of friendship just as seriously as he did; the Indian meant them, in a way . . . and would cheerfully throw them to the wolves, or the Collettas, if he saw an advantage in it for his people.

Which is only fair, Tom thought. *He doesn't owe the Rolfes or their New Virginia anything but a kick in the balls.*

Silence stretched; Good Star poured himself a cup of coffee and waited—grinning, not in the proverbial Indian impassivity. At last Adrienne spoke:

"My name is Rolfe, by the way," she said, holding up her left hand to show the ring. "Granddaughter of the Old Man."

Good Star shaped a silent whistle. *"Masthamo's dick,"* he swore obscurely. Tom winced; if things went wrong, he could see a ransom situation shaping up *real* quick.

"You're Johnny Deathwalker's kin?" he asked, pushing back the lion headdress to look at her more closely. "Yeah, that's what the legends say. Hair like an angry sunset, and eyes green like river rocks and colder than glacier ice."

She sketched out the situation in simple terms. Good Star listened, nodded, and said:

"OK. Now, why should we Water People care which clan of the Deathwalkers runs things down by the sea?"

"The Rolfes have mostly let your tribe alone," she said. "The Collettas are more ambitious."

The chief shrugged; muscle moved under dark brown skin like angular snakes, on a body the Mohave had stripped of everything that wasn't essential to life.

"So you say," he said. "Do you say you won't take the Mohave when you want it?"

"No," she said. "I do say it's a big world. You were thinking of taking your people down south, weren't you? Well, help me and I'll push for the Old Man to give you permission—and help. You know the word of the Rolfes is good, if you know anything about us."

Good Star showed yellow teeth: "Yeah, boss lady. I also know all you're promising is to do your best. You can't pledge Johnny Deathwalker's word, can you?"

"Not absolutely." She hesitated for a moment, then steeled herself and went on: "But I have a lot of influence with him. And he makes a point of always rewarding people who help us and punishing those who hurt. And . . . incidentally, Good Star of the Nyo-Ilcha . . . how would you like to get your hands on hundreds of O'Brien rifles? And machine guns, and mortars . . ."

The Indian froze with the cigarette halfway to his lips. "Son of a bitch," he said after a long moment when their eyes met. "You mean that?"

"Word of a Rolfe," she said. "They're right there"—she pointed eastward towards the Colletta headquarters—"waiting for you."

"Oh, sure, boss lady, all we have to do is to take 'em with our bows and smoke-poles!"

Adrienne smiled like a cat, and looked at Tom. Tom cleared his throat and pushed One Ocelot forward. The Zapotec firmed his shoulders and crossed his arms.

"Turns out," Tom said, "that these particular . . . Death-walkers . . . don't trust their hired soldiers very much." Good Star nodded. Tom went on: "In particular, they don't trust them with any *ammunition* for their weapons, except when they're on the firing range. It's all under lock and key and separate guards—white men—until they launch their attack."

Good Star's smile matched that of the headdress he wore. It was an expression much like the one an antelope would see on the face of the very last lion it ever met.

"Tell me about this," he said.

Overhead, light glinted on metal, and the throbbing roar of turboprop engines came insect-small through the clear sky. A Hercules transport was dropping down over the Sierras; the sound swelled as it approached, then it passed them only a few thousand feet overhead as it stooped for the valley floor. Another followed it, and another.

CHAPTER TWENTY-TWO

Owens Valley
August 2009

The Commonwealth of New Virginia
I don't like the thought of splitting us up, Tom mused,
looking through the light-enhancing binoculars down
toward the Colletta ranch house and the mushroom of military base that had sprung up around it. *The problem is, it's*
the only way I can see us having a chance of pulling this off
at all.

A plan was coming to him, and if he could sell Adrienne
on it . . .

On the other hand, it's a plan that requires a vastly infe-
rior force to divide itself five ways from Sunday. A little . . .
complicated. Too many point failure sources, as they said in
the Rangers. If an officer had come up with something like
this during the war, I'd have considered fragging the crazy
son of a bitch unless he had a real *good track record.*

The binoculars gave the valley floor below an odd flat
look, sharp-edged but carrying less information than his
eyes would have taken in if the real level of light had been
equivalent to what showed. It was oddly disconcerting, because his mind kept telling him the view was blurred, and
objectively it wasn't.

The view was good enough for his purposes; he ignored
the distortion as he did the chill cold seeping through his

jacket and sweater from the rock ridge beneath him. Tom counted the big Hercules transports lined up beside the runways to the south of the ranch house.

"Still eleven," he muttered to himself ironically. "C-130J-30s, the stretched model. Colletta Air has sent its very best."

Then he scanned over to the tented camp. Another company column was marching in to it from Cerro Gordo up in the Inyo mountains; that made six, and according to Simmons that was the full complement from the "mine." Getting in there and getting back with the information had been a damned fine bit of scouting—evidently the Frontier Scouts really meant their title—and he'd done it fast, too, covering forty miles round-trip in a single day.

Six companies, about a hundred and forty men each; call it nine hundred troops, more or less, with the local TOE, and including some of the Collettas we saw down there.

The units were extremely spare even by the austere Ranger standards he was used to; a lot more riflemen, fewer technicians or support spots.

Well, they're intended for one single action. And the armament is a lot simpler, too. Sensor systems are Eyeball Mark One.

"My guess is that they'll load the troops in the morning," he said quietly, glancing at his watch; just after sundown. The military reflexes were back in force . . . *and I'm remembering why I was so glad to get out of the army. Oh, well, the company's prettier this time.*

Adrienne and the others lay on the ridge beside him; so did Good Star. He could barely see the Indian in the darkness, and he moved very quietly. . . . *But the smell gives him away at close range,* he thought. *On the other hand, I wouldn't wash the natural oils out of my skin either, if I had to live in the Mohave year-round.*

The dryness and heat were bad enough, but the alkali dust was full of things that acted like chemical scouring powder—in fact, industrial abrasives and cleaning minerals like borax were the desert's main products, back FirstSide.

"When will they give them their ammunition?" Good Star asked, ruthlessly practical.

"When the aircraft take off, not before," Tom said.

"But first, we have a little problem," Adrienne put in, and pointed. Tiny boxy shapes at this distance; the glasses showed him the angular welded contours of light armor.

The Nyo-Ilcha chief grunted as she handed him the binoculars; he'd picked up on how to use them very quickly.

"Three of them. Killing Turtles. We know them—you Deathwalkers send them against us when you make reprisals. Bad medicine."

Tom wasn't quite sure if that last phrase was a joke, or not: Good Star seemed to have a keen ear for what the local white men expected of Indians, and an ability to play off it. Tom *was* sure that the sight of the armored cars made the Nyo-Ilcha chieftain uneasy. Tom didn't blame him; none of the weapons his people had would make much impression on even thin steel plate, and armored cars were a lot faster than a horse.

Hmmm, he thought, distracted for a fractional instant. *Of course, you could make a Molotov from alcohol and tallow, or lure one into a canyon, or put a lot of musket charges together into a satchel charge and throw it underneath.* Determined men always had *some* chance, even against superior weapons. *But that's all we-regret-to-inform-you and posthumous Medal of Honor stuff.*

"Two Cheetahs and a Catamount," Adrienne went on to Tom. "Two light armored cars with twin Browning fifties, or one and a grenade launcher. And a six-wheel heavy with a Bofors gun in the turret and a coaxial MG. Probably manned by Colletta household troops—there to keep the mercenaries in line until they get on the transports."

"But available for other purposes," Tom said.

Like massacring our Indian allies here. That wouldn't cause Adrienne any grief, I think, but I'm a bit more squeamish. Besides . . . hmmm . . .

Good Star's men were skilled and tough and brave, deadly dangerous killers in their own warrior's life of skirmish and ambush. His own brief experience with their Akaka cousins had vastly increased his respect for the Indian fighters of FirstSide history, who'd broken tribes like this with nothing better than single-shot rifles. But the Nyo-Ilcha war band weren't disciplined soldiers, and they had a well-founded dread of armored vehicles and aircraft and automatic weapons. They weren't going to do a kamikaze for the sake of the House of Rolfe, that was for sure, even if Good Star told them to. Which he wouldn't.

He'd worked with . . . *indigenous forces,* was the polite phrase . . . before, during the war back FirstSide. The trick was to use their strengths, and avoid situations where their weaknesses were important. You couldn't ask them to do too much.

"We'll have to take out the armor ourselves," he said. "And those guard towers will be a problem. If we can do that, and Good Star's men can get stuck into the mercenaries before they're issued a combat load, we can do this."

Tully looked at him, a glimpse of movement in the dark. *Have you been watching too many of my old movies, Kemosabe?* went unspoken between them. Adrienne sighed; he could read that, too.

And I would so *have liked to do that marriage and children thing.* Or another thought as pessimistic.

In fact, he suspected that the only person on the ridge who wasn't thinking something like that was Sandra, and that would be because she didn't have enough experience at this sort of situation to judge the risks properly. He felt bad about her, in an odd way worse than he did about Adrienne. He was worried about Adri, but he also had a lot of confidence in her ability to take care of herself, and she was a professional whose trade involved deadly force, if not on this massive scale. Sandra was just a nice, brave kid who liked horses. He wished intensely that Henry Villers was available, but the head wound had left him with loss of balance and peripheral vision that would probably last for months, if not forever.

He turned his head to Good Star. "The only advantage we

have is that all the enemy's armed troops will be guarding the mercenaries. *That's* where they expect trouble."

Simmons snorted. "I'm surprised they can get their Russian cadre to get on the planes when the men *are* armed," he said. "After the way they've been treating them."

"They'll be in the air, then," Adrienne pointed out. "And the Zapotecs' only hope of ever getting home will be to win and fulfill their king's contract with the Collettas and Batyushkovs. If they did that and got home, they'd be the next thing to kings themselves, or at least rich nobles. His elite strike force. Their time in hell's about over—they just have to get through a battle, and I don't think getting killed in a fight is something any of them desperately dread."

Tom nodded; from what One Ocelot said, they were all veterans—and of a school where combat meant facing edged metal at arm's length.

She turned to him. "Tom, you're the field man here. What's your advice?"

"OK," Tom said easily. "Here's what I think we should do."

She listened, nodding now and then. Tom wished he hadn't been aware of Tully's eyes going wide with horror as he laid out the plan.

* * *

"These are—" Tom stopped and looked at the Nyo-Ilcha warriors as Good Star translated his instructions. "Like gunpowder. Only much stronger."

He held up a one-pound brick of the plastic explosive. Semtex had the consistency of stiff bread dough, and it was about as safe; it could be rolled, pinched or pushed into any shape you wanted. You could set small pieces of it on fire with a match, and it burned very hot—but didn't explode. Ditto hitting it with a hammer. Bury a detonator in it, and it went off like TNT, only better. One version or another was used by every army on FirstSide for demolition and engineering work, and terrorists loved it because it was cheap and hard to detect.

"Take each one and plant it against the legs of the wooden towers. Where the beams come together—in the crutch of the beams. Do that very quickly—you must not stop between here and there. The men in the towers will be looking inward, toward their own soldiers, but you must be quick and very quiet."

He demonstrated with his arms how he wanted the charges placed; if you crammed it into a joint, one charge should be ample to sheer twelve-inch beams and the steel bolts that held them together.

"Then leave them there. We can set them off. You just pull back, and when the towers fall, attack. That will be no later than—"

He gave the time to Good Star; the chief said something in his own language, and all the shadowed heads followed his arm as he pointed to a star, named it, and drew his finger down to the horizon. Not as accurate as a watch, but Tom would be willing to bet that it would work within five minutes or so.

"Everyone understand?" Tom finished.

Oh, Jesus, help us, he thought, as the half-seen ranks of faces nodded eagerly, scars and tattoos and animal-skin headdresses, braided hair and massed stink. *On second thought, maybe Old Scratch would be more helpful.*

They filed off into the darkness; there was a dull jingle of harness padded with scraps of leather and cloth, a surprisingly muted drum of hooves, fading as they split into small parties and rode east through the canyon mouth and into the valley plain. The ones with the explosive would dismount and crawl in like leopards when they got closer. There was no use in worrying about it, and sneaking around in the dark with hostile intent was something well within the nomad warriors' area of expertise. Now they could only wait.

He looked up; the sky was dense with stars through the clear cool high-desert air, more than he'd ever seen before. They wheeled above as the others waited in companionable silence; a quiet murmur told him that Sandra was praying—which couldn't hurt and might possibly help. Some of the more robust psalms would fit in right now, and he wished he had enough faith in the stern Lutheran God of his ancestors to take comfort from reciting them.

Or even going Ho-la, Odhinn, he thought, his teeth white as he grinned in the darkness. *Old One-Eye would be a natural for help in a setup like this . . . except that he loved to get heroes killed so he could stockpile them in Valhalla.*

Adrienne stood by her horse, stroking its nose to calm it as the beast caught the fear-scent in the humans' sweat.

Always the hardest, waiting, Tom thought. *Abstractly, I couldn't object if I died—I've lived better than most human beings, and seen more.* He met her eyes, and she winked and shaped a kiss. *Concretely, I* would *object. Got too much to live for right now. Maybe that's why armies prefer teenagers!*

Tully broke the quiet at last, when Sandra murmured an *amen* and crossed herself.

"Anyone want odds on how many will pocket the explosives instead of setting 'em as directed?" he said sourly. "Or possibly just throw them away?"

Adrienne shrugged. "Hopefully enough will use it the way they've been told. As to anyone who wants to keep the stuff . . . they're going to get an awful surprise when the detonators go off, aren't they? A very *brief* surprise, if a pound of plastique goes off in a hip pocket."

Tom snorted slightly. It was grim humor, but that was the only type you were likely to get in a situation like this.

"It's the ones who'll try and use little balls of it in their muskets that worry me," he said lightly, checking his watch. The Indians should be nearly at their targets by now. Give them time to set the charges and get out. . . .

"*That*'ll be a surprise, you betcha," he went on easily. "You know, it would be interesting to see what *did* happen if you set fire to a pellet of Semtex under a wad and lead ball. I'd rather someone else did the experiment, though!"

Simmons crushed out a cigarette and said something to

Kolo in the Yokut's language; both men chuckled. Adrienne went over to the Scout and his tracker. "Godspeed and good luck," she said, shaking their hands. "See you again when all this is over."

They nodded and mounted, vanishing into the night. She took a long breath and looked at Tom.

First time I've ever gone into action with someone I loved, the big man thought. *Got some of the same drawbacks as doing it with people who you just* like *a lot, only worse.*

He put a fighting grin on his face, and shoved down absurd thoughts about talking her into going off somewhere else on an urgent mission.

"If we pull this off, we're heroes," he said. "Thanks of a grateful nation. I won't have to sweat when I finally meet your dad."

"If we don't pull it off, we're goats, of course," Tully said, checking his machine pistol.

"I don't think that would be our worst worry," Tom replied.

Adrienne threw her arms around him. He could hear Tully murmuring to Sandra, but the moment was too intense for him to pay attention. Then he felt Adrienne stiffen.

He did too, at the sound from the valley behind them. Engines, many engines—the transports were beginning to warm up their turbines. Turning, he could see the exhausts, streaks of red fire in the night. The landing lights of the airstrips came on, harshly brilliant across the miles of distance.

"Looks like we didn't allow quite enough time," he said grimly, pulling down his night-sight goggles; the dimness sprang into silvery light. Adrienne did likewise and vaulted into the saddle.

"Let's go," she said.

They poured down the wash and out onto the plain, riding at a hand gallop; they *might* be seen, but they *would* fail if they didn't hurry.

Damn, Tom thought, wishing he had a jeep or a motorbike. The great muscles of the gelding flexed between his legs, and the chilly wind cuffed at his face. *You* feel *faster on a horse, but you* aren't *really.*

Closer, and they could see the first heavy transport taxi out on to the runway and halt with the rear ramp lowered. A column of men were coming down the dirt track from the camp; they were insect-tiny in the distance, but it was getting close to ride. . . .

"Down!" Adrienne said, echoing his thought and throwing up a hand.

They all dismounted, all except One Ocelot. He took the reins of the horses as they swung down, then turned south and rode fast, leading them. Tom felt a moment of envy, despite the Zapotec's slim chance of making it anywhere near home. *He* was out of it, with nothing to worry about but his own survival.

"All right," Tom said. "Let's go."

"We couldn't possibly pull this off if they weren't so short of manpower," Adrienne said, settling into a steady jog-trot beside him.

She was carrying one of the P90 machine pistols slung across her back. So were Tully and Tom; any fighting was probably going to be at close range. Sandra Margolin carried an O'Brien rifle. That was the weapon she was familiar with, and you didn't change in midstream.

"That's not the half of it," Tom said—thinking of personnel-detection radars, sonic sensors, drones, robot perimeter-guard guns. "They're running so tight they can't afford to take basic precautions. Everything has to work to ten-tenths or they get a chain of disasters."

Then he laughed.

"What's so funny?" Adrienne said, her eyes fixed grimly ahead. At least one of the transports was going to get off the ground and under way.

Well, we're in exactly the same situation, for starters.

"I was remembering our last date to go running," he said aloud, and she laughed in turn . . . until the first Hercules closed its ramp and accelerated down the runway, dust boiling in the lights as its wheels cut the dirt. It lifted into the night and vanished; they could see its silhouette black against the stars as it wheeled overhead, and its riding lights blinking. Turbine throb echoed in their bones, and then another taxied out on to the strip, and men began to board.

Her lips moved then, in a silent curse or prayer. That was a hundred armed men headed toward the heart of her nation and another hundred filing up the ramp and being handed full magazines.

His country too, he supposed, if he lived and settled down here afterward; well, his great-grandparents had left Norway, hadn't they? Daring the ocean and the Sioux for a chance at land of their own.

I'll worry about that later.

What he *wasn't* worried about was the increasingly brilliant haze of light ahead—they were running parallel to the northwest-tending dirt runway now. All those landing lights and searchlights would just kill the defenders' night-sight and wouldn't show them anything more than a few hundred yards away. His head turned north toward the ranch house. It was lit too, but more softly; at half a mile, its windows shone a gentler yellow into the night.

Was the Batyushkov or this Giovanni Colletta there, watching? Frightened, or exhilarated, or murmuring: "The die is cast"? Odd to be fighting a man and never even have seen his picture.

He might well be relaxing, sighing in relief, thinking *I've done it!* Tom smiled grimly. You shouldn't feel the after-action buzz before the fat lady sang. Doing otherwise was an invitation to being the last casualty of an op and having your friends shake their heads over a beer and talk about how poor X nearly made it back.

"Over to you," Adrienne said when they came to the edge of the lights. "Your area of expertise, Tom."

"Right," he said. "Everyone slow down. Take it at a brisk walk and look like you own the place. Sandy, catch your breath."

She was in hard good condition—all of them were, after crossing the Mohave—but she didn't have as much practice running under a load as the rest of them. He made himself wait until her face was less red and the desperate whooping of her panting had subsided. That despite the crackling tension that he could feel radiating from Adrienne as the next C-130 took off; they were closer to the runway now, and the four big props kicked a torrent of dust.

That made it natural to bend their heads and hold their hands over their eyes. *Not only would this be impossible if the Bad Guys could set a proper perimeter guard,* Tom thought. *It would be impossible if they had any warning we were coming.* The Batyushkovs and Collettas knew that any tall blond white men around here were on their side, and they were keyed up getting the Zapotec mercs onto the C-130s.

It was a mistake to get too focused on what you had planned, but it was a mistake everyone made. Tom licked sweat off his lips and hoped they'd go on making it at least a *little* longer.

The graveled surface of the road down from the camp crunched under the tread of soldiers' boots, coming down in platoon columns. Behind them the searchlights from the guard towers played along the track, showing the endless rows of men in gray uniforms and peaked caps—a battalion was a lot bigger from ground level than you'd think, when you said *eight hundred men.* They marched in the rather stiff Russian style, swinging their free arms up across their chests from the elbow; from the look of it, the lieutenants and a couple of NCOs in each platoon were the men Batyushkov had brought in. A bit older than you'd expect men in junior positions to be, and a lot of them had Red Army medals jingling on their chests—Russkis were strange that way, wearing decorations on combat fatigues.

The armored cars were spaced out along the north side of the road, at two-hundred-and-fifty-yard intervals, ten or twenty yards back from the verge; they and the thin scatter of men between them kept the business ends of their weapons pointed at the marching troops—but fairly casually, in the way of men taking a routine precaution they don't think will be really necessary. *They* were probably feeling relieved too—they'd gotten the wild men trained and on their way without a major mutiny.

The air was full of the sound of boots, of engines, rank with the stink of burnt kerosene.

The six-wheeled car Adrienne had called a Catamount was in the center; not far from it two senior officers were taking the salute of the troops passing by, returning the salute as each company did an eyes-right. One of the pair made the gesture in Russki fashion; he was tall and blond and wore a beret. The other was shorter and darker, wearing a Fritz helmet with a gray cloth cover, and *he* used the American style.

"Major Daniel Mattei," Adrienne said softly, indicating him with a slight tilt of her head. "West Point, class of 1988, believe it or not. He's commander of the Colletta Domain's militia and the Prime's household troops. A Family member, collateral. I don't know the blond. Tom . . . that was the fourth plane."

They were still too far away to really distinguish features. One of the men by Mattei did look over his shoulder toward them, but casually. With just a *little* luck, the Collettas would think they were Batyushkov men, and the Batyushkovs would think the same in reverse. Everyone being in the same uniform, with minor variations, helped a lot—and the uniform was the same gray fatigues Tom and the rest were wearing.

Still, they were going to need a distraction real soon now. And that *was* the fourth plane of eleven. Four hundred and eighty men; they probably intended to put the armor on the last two, to land after the infantry had seized enough ground. The whole thing was sort of pointless if they all got off. . . .

"Sandra," he said, without turning his head. "When the balloon goes up, you hit the deck and try for those two guys. Got it?"

"Go flat, take out those two," she said. "Got it, big man."

She was an excellent shot—as a hunter; he'd seen that. Whether she could actually pull the trigger when a human was in front of the sights was another matter, but it would sure help.

"Roy. On the count of three. One."

He took a long deep breath; worry and thought went away as he exhaled. The commander of the Catamount was sitting on the turret, his left elbow hooked over a pintle-mounted Bren gun.

"Two."

The details of the armored car came clear; six equally spaced wheels, a wedge-fronted box with a slab-sided turret. The driver was at the front in the center, three armor-glass windows in a semicircle around his position, with movable steel shutters and vision slits to cover them at need. Engine and transmission at the rear, turret in the center . . . and the Colletta tommy gun on the side of the hull.

"Three!"

Tully pulled a box the size of a paperback book out of a pouch. It had a handgrip in the center, and above it a covered button. His thumb flicked up the cover; he squeezed the grip safety and mashed his thumb down on the button.

Things seemed to move very slowly after that.

✱ ✱ ✱

Jim Simmons waited patiently, the rifle snuggled against his shoulder. Fire and thunder woke in the night to the northeast, toward the mercenaries' camp. He didn't turn his head; no point in looking at a bright light.

He was flat on the dirt on one side of the runway; the wind from the propellers of the last Hercules had blown off his hat. The *crack* of his rifle was lost in the greater chorus of shouts, shots and screams that broke out closer to the ranch house, where the troops were marching down to embark. Somewhere a dog was barking, which was just what was needed to add the final touch of lovely chaos. Not that a dog could have smelled anything besides the stink of fuel burning. The spent cartridge spun away to his right and tinkled on a rock.

And two hundred yards away, where the two runways met and the control shack stood, a guard crumpled. The man

beside him glanced over sharply; he'd have heard the splitting *twick* of the bullet, perhaps even the flat smack of its
impact on flesh. Simmons shifted the crosshairs—two hundred yards was a clout shot, even in the bad light—and
stroked the trigger again.

Crack.

The second man dropped, shot cleanly through the upper
breastbone, blood splashing on the plank wall behind him.
The impact wasn't quite dead center, and the force of the
blow turned him around and slammed him face-first into
wall. He slid down it, smearing the blood.

"Go!" Simmons said crisply, snatching up the rifle as he
bounced to his feet.

He dashed forward, running across the blunt nose of the
next transport taxiing into position for takeoff. Kolo went
before him, running with an elastic bounding stride and
howling like a wolf every time his feet hit the packed dirt.
He gained with every stride too, carrying nothing but the
knives in his belt and the tomahawk in his hands. Simmons
followed, eyes flicking over the windows in the long shed.

Motion, left two. He halted, the butt swinging smoothly
up to his shoulder; crosshairs on the window . . . target back-
lit by lights in the room behind . . .

Crack. Glass shattered away from the .30-06 round.
Crack. Just in case the bullet had been deflected by the glass
or the frame.

He ran forward again. A dozen paces and Kolo was nearly
at the door; it opened, and someone was standing there with
a machine pistol in his grip—

Simmons halted again, and the rifle made the same
smooth transit to his shoulder. *This is going to be a little
more tricky. . . .*

But Kolo was already diving to one side, not to escape the
stubby muzzle that tracked him, but to give the Scout a clear
shot. The crosshairs leveled on a face—it had to be a head
shot, to make sure the man didn't have enough time to fire.

Crack. The youth with the Uzi toppled backwards, a
round blue hole in his forehead and the back blown out of his

head. *Crack. Crack.* To discourage anyone thinking of following him out.

He pounded forward again. Kolo waited until he was nearly there, then dove through the open doorway. Simmons hurdled the body lying there.

"Eddie?" someone called, from a door to the right down the corridor. "Eddie?"

Kolo went through; Simmons followed just quickly enough to see his hand chop forward. The hatchet moved in a blur, and the technician in the swivel chair behind the radio spun with the blade sunk three inches deep between his eyes, the .45 flying from his hand. His boot heels drummed on the plank floor as he pinwheeled across the room, the chair rattling on its casters. Simmons stopped the chair with a slight grimace of distaste at the huge spastic yawn on the dead man's face and pushed the sprattling body out on the floor. Then he set his rifle against the table and sat down before the shortwave set himself. It was a powerful unit, and there was a relay station on Mount Whitney; it would reach the coastal valleys without a problem. His fingers twisted the dials to the frequency that would be listening twenty-four hours a day, and he flipped the transmission switch:

"Climb Mount Etna. Climb Mount Etna. Climb Mount Etna." That code had been John Rolfe's idea, and for some reason the ghastly old bugger had thought it was hilarious. "Climb Mount Etna. Climb Mount—"

Something very heavy struck James Simmons on the point of the left shoulder. Cold flashed along his side; he clawed at the radio with his right hand, but still fell out of the chair. His legs buckled as he tried to rise, and then he was on his back, half under the table, mouth opening and closing as he tried hard to breathe.

Kolo was fighting with two men, shrieking like a mechanical saw going through a millstone as he leapt and slashed. A third lay curled around himself in the entranceway, trying to hold his rent stomach closed and screaming. The other two were close to Kolo, too close to shoot, trying to hit him with the butts of their rifles or stab with their bayonets. The Yokut moved between them as if they were in slow motion and he in real time, and red drops trailed from his knife. One man folded over with the blade buried in his gut; the other staggered back, firing blindly, blood flooding across his face from a cut that stretched from the corner of his mouth across an eyeball.

Two of the rounds punched home into Kolomusnim's torso, and he dropped limply, the war scream cut off.

The room was suddenly empty except for the crackle of the radio speakers and the moans of the wounded. Simmons tried to breath again, but his insides felt *wet.* There were voices in the corridor outside, shrill with alarm. He fumbled behind himself, and found the toggle of the explosive charge.

Supposed to throw it in when we left, he thought, as he doggedly fought to close the numb fingers. *So damn cold. Mother—*

One last sharp tug.

❋ ❋ ❋

"Three!" Tom said.

Tully's thumb came down on the button. Half a mile away, the Semtex exploded where the Nyo-Ilcha warriors had crawled through the night to pack it around the bases of the watchtowers.

The light from the flashes came a fractional second before the sound, a multitude of thudding, snapping barks. Sound and flashes rippled like a strobe light, the explosions overlapping but distinct. The towers were thread-thin at this distance, the three he could see; their searchlights went out all at once, lowering the ambient light by about half. The blockhouse at the top of one tower seemed to fall straight down; the shock must have blown the four heavy pine logs away from the cross braces, and they'd opened out like someone doing splits. The other two shook, trembled, and then fell inward like hammers—which was exactly the effect the logs of the blockhouses at their summits would have on the machine gunners inside, and any Zapotecs in the tents beneath, when they hit the ground. Dust billowed up, cold under the starlight and the distant floods.

"Well, well, Good Star's men *did* place all their charges," Tom said quietly, as he began to walk briskly toward the armored car.

Behind him Sandra Margolin dropped to her belly in the dirt. Of the three of them, she was the mostly likely to make someone twig that instant too soon—nobody was going to miss the fact that she was a woman, not even in fatigues and not even for the half second that the rough baggy clothing might fool someone looking at Adrienne's taller, sleeker curves.

Besides . . .

Crack.

The shot came from behind him, and the tall blond man in the beret a hundred yards ahead staggered, clutching at his arm.

Tom could have placed the location of the shooter easily from the sound alone, but he was expecting it. Everyone else was staring off toward the tent camp, and the chorus of screams and shouts there. And the high shrill whoops, and the flat banging of muskets. Some of the Russian officers and noncoms marching toward the transport aircraft with their Zapotec trainees had hit the ground and had their personal arms out, and they were bellowing at their charges to do the same. Tom was worried about *their* reflexes; they'd been there when it hit the fan before.

Less worried about the Colletta household troops manning the armor or lining the road. This was their first taste of the devil's stew, mostly.

Crack.

The blond went down with limp finality, but the smaller man beside him had hit the dirt with commendable speed.

Good girl, Tom thought; she'd gotten one definitely at least.

"Good girl!" Tully said. "Didn't freeze, and kept on thinking."

The armored car loomed up, massive and shadowed—most of the light was coming from the landing lights of the airstrip behind him, and they were placed low and pointed straight up. The commander was still out of the turret hatch, his head cocked as he listened to something on the headphones he held in one hand rather than wearing. Now he was looking back a little, at the group of figures in gray field uniforms approaching him, but the light welling up out of the turret would make them indistinct. It made him very clear to Tom, down to the Colletta flash on his shoulder.

Tom began shouting: in Russian, keeping his voice deliberately blurred. The commander of the Catamount probably didn't know Russian very well, and wouldn't expect to understand what this tall blond man was shouting. He *would* recognize the sound of the language and immediately assume it was one of his lord's Batyushkov allies.

Five yards from the vehicle, Tom began to run. Adrienne and Tully were both at his heels, but he left them behind; people were usually surprised at how suddenly Tom Christiansen could accelerate, although not those who'd seen him as a running back at Ironwood High. His legs were long enough that he walked quickly even without taking fast strides, and when he did . . .

Three paces, and he was moving fast enough to leap, reaching for one of the U-brackets welded to the car's hull. The commander started to drop down into the turret; unfortunately, he also tried to reach for the pintle-mounted machine gun beside the hatch and to shout something into his throat mike, all at the same time. The net result was that he did nothing for a crucial second and a half.

Tom's hand clamped on the bracket. His shoulder muscles crackled as he heaved, combining with the thrust of his legs to throw him up onto the flat deck of the fighting vehicle in a single six-foot bound. The muzzle of the machine gun swung toward him; there was nothing wrong with the other man's instincts, although he wasn't going to acquire the experience he needed to use them properly. Tom grabbed the gun in his left hand and wrenched it brutally away; that turned the weapon into a long lever at the end of Tom's even longer arm, a combination that slammed the man holding it into the side of the hatchway with enormous force. He gave an agonized wheeze as it rammed into his body just below the ribs like a blunt axe, but his hand scrabbled at his belt and the holstered .45 anyway.

The determination was admirable, but futile. Tom's right hand closed on his throat and rammed his head sideways into the upright hatch cover. Bone hit steel with a sound like heavy dense wood splintering under an iron maul. Wetness spattered Tom's wrist; he ignored it and surged the man's body up in a straight lift and threw it aside. It tumbled limply on to the rear deck of the Catamount, then slid over the side like something made of jelly.

Adrienne was right behind him. As the body cleared the hatchway she went into it head first . . . except that her right hand went before it, with the FN FiveSeveN pistol, and her left to brace her against something in the interior. Tom caught her by the rear loop of her webbing harness, taking some of the weight.

The little weapon yapped shrilly, three times, hard to hear amid the growing clamor—the burble of the idling diesel would have been enough to cover it. He was profoundly glad it was her doing this part and not him; he was anything but a pistol artist, particularly not in the strait confines of an AFV's turret.

"Clear!" she called, and wiggled backward.

He helped, then popped the gunner's hatch, reached in and pulled out the body of the man who'd occupied that position; it required a bit of shoving and shaking, as well as strength, to prevent the limp weight from catching on things. The dead gunner had a hole in the back of his neck. Most of the front of it missing in a ragged hole that was still pumping out blood, and the body dripped fluids as it came free. Tom threw the corpse away with unnecessary violence.

While he did, Tully was running around to the front of the armored car and leaping up the slope of the wedge-shaped glacis plate. The hatch over the driver's compartment was open, and the central window was spattered with brains and bits of matter. Tully dragged the body out; using both hands and his back, but not taking too much time about it. He was five-six and scrawny, but his strength in a tight spot was surprising.

The whole business had taken perhaps forty-five seconds from the moment Tom made his move.

Now he slid into the hatchway himself, feet first. It was well enough lit inside, and the surfaces were mostly painted or enameled white for better visibility anyway. And it was more spacious than any APC he'd ever ridden in, too. The Commonwealth didn't need to design its fighting vehicles to resist modern weaponry, only small arms at most. This was essentially a big overpowered cross-country amphibious truck with a turret on top. Tom took the gunner's position to the left of the breech of the Bofors gun and the big carousel of ammunition beneath it, ignoring the tackiness and the smell, and wiping off the control surfaces with a handkerchief and the sleeve of his tunic until they were clean enough for government work.

Adrienne had given him a rundown on the fighting machine, and a glance was enough to fix the needful details in his mind's eye. Most of the middle of the turret was taken up with the cannon's workings; an automatic loader cycled rounds up to the breech, presenting the five-round clips to the action; the spent casings ejected out a port in the side of the turret. The gunner's couch-style seat was leather cushioned, with a screen and control yoke before it—there was a backup set of optical sights, and manual wheels for elevation and traverse, but New Virginia had bought state of the art otherwise. Everything stabilized, and a laser rangefinder tied into the sighting screen with feedback through the ballistic computer. The screen showed everything out front, a compressed 180-degree display from a wide-lens pickup right over the gun's barrel and two more at either front corner of the turret; in the center of it was a circle with diagonal arms just touching its perimeter. Place the pipper over the target, and the gun would automatically adjust so the shells hit right there. Another circle, smaller and to the left, gave the point of impact for the coaxial machine gun. The controls were computerized simplicity, a horizontal bar with upright hand-grips at each end. Twist left like you did with a bicycle's han-dlebars and the turret rotated left; twist right for the other direction. Pull back and the gun went up; push forward and it depressed; button under the left thumb for the co-ax, and a foot pedal for firing the main gun. Dial on the control panel to select type of ammunition and fusing.

The screen had magnification up to twelve times, too, and full light amplification. The scene outside was as clear as an overcast noon.

He pulled on the intercom headset as he ran through the controls once more, touching everything so his hands and feet would know what to do. That wouldn't make him an expert, but he didn't have to refight the Battle of 73 Easting, either.

"I've got the unit push for the Colletta troops," Adri-enne's voice said in his ear. "Tully, you've got the closest thing to the local accent, male variety. I'm switching you live. Sound hysterical."

"No problemo," Tully said.

"Switching . . . *now.*"

He went on with a thickening of his native Arkansas, in a voice shrill with fear and excitement:

"We're under attack! The Injuns are attacking! The strike force are joining them! They're breaking into the bunkers and taking the ammuntion. I say again, we're under attack! Open fire on any strike force or Indians you see!"

He repeated himself and then squealed: "*No! God, no! Help*—" and then let loose a bone-chilling scream of agony, dying off in a gurgle and a *click* as the exterior link was cut. Then a hoot of laughter . . . Roy had a rather gruesome sense of humor, when you came right down to it.

As Tully spoke, Tom settled his big hands on the control yoke and felt the quiver of the feedback. A twist, and the lower pip of the screen slid over the dirt road, still full of the startled mercenaries. His left thumb jabbed down again and again, and a streak of tracer lashed out like a finger of red arching fire as the co-ax stuttered long bursts into the packed rows of men. Adrienne was firing the pintle-mounted gun above, standing in the commander's position with her head and shoulders out of the turret.

"Yes!" Tom shouted.

The rest of the Colletta troopers were firing at the mass of Zapotecs and their Russian cadre too!

And the Russians, at least, were shooting back. With empty weapons their students just hugged the ground, or less wisely jumped up and ran and were cut down. Both the lighter armored cars were firing as well; just then the landing lights on the airstrip went out, and the light level outside fell to something approaching full night. It didn't affect the armored car's screens at all, save for an imperceptible flicker as the intensification went up; probably someone at the Colletta HQ wanted to put the Zapotecs at a disadvantage. Behind them the control shack for the airstrip went up in a blast that flung its plank walls away as black confetti in front of orange-red flame.

"Good show, Jim!" Adrienne called, and whooped.

Tom ignored that, and the Indian mercenaries. The ones left on the ground were doomed anyway, and he didn't much like shooting at effectively unarmed men. Instead he lifted his thumb and kept the turret swinging; it had a nice fast traverse. A few seconds later the main sighting pip slid onto the side of the Cheetah on his right. That was lashing the road with both weapons, a heavy machine gun and a belt-fed grenade launcher beside it . . . and both of those would rip the thin armor that surrounded him the way a machete would open up a soda can. The grenades arched out almost slowly enough to see, bursting with bright snaps in rows like firecrackers.

The Cheetah spurted forward onto the dirt road, its turret whickering spiteful flames in the darkness. Tom's foot came down on the firing pedal.

BADUMP! BADUMP! BADUMP!

The 40mm automatic cannon cycled through three rounds

as it pistoned back and forth, and a massive blade-shaped muzzle flash belled out from its muzzle. The twelve-ton weight of the Catamount surged back on its suspension as the massive recoil was transmitted through the trunnions to the turret and hull, like three hard punches in succession.

Those shells were fused for contact; each punched into the little vehicle and exploded, one in the turret, one in the fighting compartment and one in the fuel tank between the engine and the turret basket. That was enough to rip the Cheetah apart along the seams of its welds; fractional seconds later the belts of grenade ammunition went off; the contents of the tank sprayed out into a finely divided mist of hydrocarbon mixed with air and then *they* exploded—the original meaning of a fuel-air bomb. Tom grunted as the big armored car rocked back on its wheels, and Adrienne yipped in involuntary alarm; the Cheetah's turret went flipping up into the air like a steel tiddlywink. Most of the rest of it was converted into the equivalent of fragments from an enormous grenade. Some of them went *pting!* off the hull of the Catamount.

He didn't think they'd have to worry about the Colletta riflemen between them and the armored car, much.

"Goose it, Tully!" he called, reversing the controls and swinging the turret northwest with a wrenching suddenness that made the servos whine in protest.

Jesus, I was a Ranger, not a tanker—

The armored car was moving before the first syllable was out of his mouth; Tully threw it into reverse and swung the wheel hard right. All four of the first two pair of wheels were steerable; the Catamount had a tighter turning radius than many much smaller civilian vehicles. That turned the bow back toward the remaining Cheetah at the other end of the line considerably faster than the turret could have done alone.

Someone there had realized what was happening. The little car was scooting away, its turret reversed to fire behind it and the twin bars of tracer swiveling toward him. They were throwing .50 caliber hardpoint bullets, each the size of a thumb and moving at better than three thousand feet per second. If they hit the thin armor of the Catamount, they'd be moving at least half that when they went through *him*, or Adrienne or Tully.

But driving straight away from him was a bad idea. Zero-deflection shot . . . His foot came down on the firing pedal.

BADUMP! BADUMP! BADUMP!

"Tom, the transports!" Adrienne called urgently from where she rode with her head and shoulders out of the commander's hatch.

As she spoke he heard thumps on the roof of the turret, and the gunner's hatch popped open. He looked up, and saw Sandra Margolin's pale, strained face; she climbed down across him—which would have been interesting, under other circumstances—and then dropped to crouch on the floor of the turret basket. She even muttered an apology as she did it. He checked quickly to see that she wasn't in a position where she'd be in the path of the gun breech or loader.

Adrienne went on sharply: "Tully, Sandra's here. Get us out on the runway. *Now.*"

Tully did, straightening the wheels and hitting the accelerator. The engine was a three-hundred horsepower turbocharged diesel, and the twelve-ton vehicle had acceleration like a jeep. It had a lot more inertia, though, and Tom braced himself with a foot and a hand as it bounced over the ditch on the side of the road, over several bumpy objects—he resolutely didn't think of them as human bodies, probably still alive until a dozen tons rolled over them—and across the strip of dirt. The fence beside the runway was chain-link, with barbed wire on top.

"Close the hatch!" he called to Adrienne as the fence loomed up in the field of the gun screen; you could get decapitated by something like that, if you weren't careful.

She dropped down, pulling the hatch after her; the Catamount lurched as they struck the wire. Some of it broke in a shower of sparks; one of the thick timber posts snapped across and tumbled out over the dirt runway, dragging open a section like a huge door. The Catamount swayed to one side as Tully cut a sharp turn—he wasn't used to driving something this heavy or overpowered either, but Jesus, Odhinn and Almighty Thor witness he was doing a good job!—and hit the gas. The Catamount surged forward like its namesake, going after the sixth transport. The big plane had its ramp up, and the rising scream of its engines came even through the closed hatch.

Tom Christiansen had ridden in a lot of C-130 transports, a couple of them into places where they thought there might be hostiles waiting near the landing fields with heat-seeking missiles. He could imagine *exactly* the fear and confusion aboard the big aircraft, the dim light and crowding and the mind-numbing noise.

And he could imagine exactly what the hundred-odd men packed into it cheek to jowl were about to experience.

The aiming pip slid across the flat rear of the Hercules, eight hundred yards away to the west. It tilted as the nose left the ground. . . . And Tom's foot hit the firing pedal.

BADUMP! BADUMP! BADUMP! The first burst of three rounds hit the thin aluminum of the closed ramp like a giant blade. The ramp dropped open as the shells cut the couplings, shedding great rooster tails of sparks as it dragged on the ground.

BADUMP! BADUMP! BADUMP! Flashes as the shells exploded in the troop compartment. Tom's lips writhed back from his teeth in a grimace of horror.

BADUMP! BADUMP! BADUMP!

He hit something vital this time, the control cabin or the hydraulics. The huge aircraft stopped accelerating away; it tried to turn sharply left while it was traveling faster than a race car, and then pitched over onto one wing as it overbalanced. There was an explosion of sparks, probably from one of the props beating itself to death against the ground, then a real explosion—vaporized kerosene from one of the wing tanks hitting something white-hot. Tom flung his hand up in a reflex action, even though there was nearly a thousand yards of space and a quarter-inch of armor plate between him and the holocaust that followed. A towering ball of flame enveloped the Hercules, and engines and part of a wing flipped out of it. The armored car rocked back, harder than it had from the recoil of its own weapon, then surged forward as Tully hit the brakes. The frame of the C-130 showed again for a moment, and then the stored munitions on board went off; bits and pieces flew into the air, trailing fire and white smoke through the night.

"Jesus," Tom whispered. "A hundred and thirty men. *Jesus!*"

"Tom!" Adrienne said sharply.

"Yah," he replied, scrubbing a hand across his face.

Tully gave a rebel yell and swung the car around in a tight leaning circle—not *quite* on one side's wheels—and they raced back down the airstrip. Tom turned the turret ninety degrees, waiting as the motion dragged the sighting pip across the remaining five C-130s. Those were empty of troops, and probably abandoned by their three-man crews at this point. It wasn't necessary to destroy them either, just to put a couple of shells into their noses. They wouldn't be going anywhere after that.

BADUMP! BADUMP! BADUMP!

The screen let him see how the bows of each peeled back as the shells hit and exploded—at less than a hundred yards, he was putting them right through the windscreens into the control cabins of each. Some of them caught fire, in a low-intensity way, but none of them blew up.

The big fuel store *did* blow up when he put a couple of rounds into it; the huge pyre reached into the night, like the funeral of Giovanni Colletta's bloodthirsty ambitions. It also cast a good deal of light; someone opened up with a light machine gun, and the bullets beat on the hull like iron hail on a bucket. He backtracked along the chain of tracer rounds and discouraged them with a couple of rounds.

"Well, now, do we go help Good Star, or do we just drive out into the desert and watch the lovely fireworks until it's time to meet up with Jim and Henry?" he said.

"Neither," Adrienne said tautly. "Nearly half of them got off the ground. There's still a chance they could pull it off— or at least kill a lot of New Virginians."

"Damned right," Sandra called from the bottom of the turret, where she sat with her arms around her knees. "But what the hell can we do about it, Adri? This thing can't fly."

"No, but those Mosquitoes can," she said. "Tully, get us over there."

Tom opened his mouth to object, then slowly closed it. He knew exactly how *that* conversation would go: she'd say she was going, and he could come or stay as he pleased. And he'd get into the cockpit right beside her. Why bother having an argument?

The fact is, he thought, while his eyes stayed on the screen, *you're doing this from love of country, and I'm doing it for love of you, my Valkyie. I don't love this country—not much, and not yet. I may come to, warts and all, if I live here and my children are born here. But you do, and so I have to follow.*

CHAPTER TWENTY-THREE

Owens Valley/Rolfeston
August 2009

The Commonwealth of New Virginia

Tom's thumb came down on the firing button. The Catamount's turret vibrated as the rasping growl of the machine gun rattled inside it. The third Mosquito shuddered and splintered as the rounds plowed home in the cockpit; he lifted the button after only a few seconds.

"Don't want it on fire, not when we're taking the other two," he said. "All right, everyone, go!"

The other three left the turret; Tom traversed it and punched up the menu. *Right,* he thought, and scanned down to: LOCK ON TARGET.

The servos whined slightly as he settled the firing pip on the distant shape of the ranch house. Then he touched:

FIRE.

ALL ROUNDS.

TIME DELAY—8 MINUTES.

As the little sign at the bottom of the screen turned to 7:59, he was already boosting himself out of the gunner's hatch and leaping down, just in time to see Sandra running up the ramp and swinging into the copilot's seat of the second Mosquito. Tully was already inside, with Adrienne leaning over him and pointing things out.

She slapped him on the shoulder, vaulted down and ran to meet Tom as he sprinted for the last fighter-bomber.

"They're both hot!" she called. "Pilots and ground crew must have gone off to join the fight."

"Good," he said, as he swung into the cramped confines. With Good Star's men ramping through the night like a pack of wolves—wolves with the minds of men—he didn't envy them one little bit.

"I wish them joy of it, you betcha!"

The Mosquito's copilot seat adjusted via levers underneath, as awkward as those on most cars; Tom had a lot of experience with that, since seats were never set for someone his height. He buckled himself in as Adrienne went through a quick checklist.

Roy's voice came through the headphones. "OK, Adri, I think I can get this bitch off the ground. Landing may be a little rough; it ain't a Beechcraft."

"Good luck, Roy," he said. "You too, Sandy."

"Good luck to us all," Adrienne said. "We've had more than our share tonight, but a little more wouldn't hurt!" A pause. "Just in case, it's been a privilege to operate with all of you."

He watched carefully as she opened the throttles; he might, Jesus help him, have to fly this thing himself. It had the same mix of basic and cutting edge tech he'd noticed on the *No Biscuit*, although at least the basic stuff was World War Two, rather than Dawn of Aviation. There was a full set of virtual dials on the thin-film display, though; he could track it and use touches to bring up other data. He did; full fuel load, and full ammo. The armament was eight .50 caliber Brownings with six hundred and fifty rounds each—he'd noticed before that the Commonwealth's military design philosophy tended to the Lots and Lots of Great Big Guns school of thought.

The big piston engines roared, each driving the four paddle-shaped blades into a blurred circle; this design had been a hot ship in its time, faster than most single-seat fighters—but that day had been when his grandfather was popping pimples, reading comics about Superman whupping Nazi butt and worrying about growing hair on his palms. The top speed was about the same as that of a fully loaded C-130J transport.

There are two possibilities: we will catch them or we won't, Tom thought, as they taxied out past the Catamount; he felt a moment's illogical sadness. It *was* only an inanimate object after all, but it had served them all well.

As the thought ran through his mind, the Bofors gun in the boxy turret opened up; without his night-sight goggles on, the huge flame of the muzzle flash was surprising, and the red dots of the shells seemed to float away as he and Adrienne gained distance.

Good luck, he thought toward the vehicle, with a wave as they passed and gathered speed.

The tailweel lifted, and suddenly he could look straight ahead, into the darkness. A minute more, and the Mosquito lifted; Adrienne shot the throttles forward to near the redline and banked northward, to give them time to reach altitude— the twelve-thousand-foot wall of the Sierras was only about six miles to the west.

"Gotcha," Tully's voice said. "Radar positive. I'll follow to your right and rear."

Tom busied himself with the map display; it didn't have GPS, but the inertial system was good. "We should hit Rolfeston just around dawn," he said, and looked down.

There were a *lot* of fires around the little settlement, but not many of the distinctive fire-hose flashes of automatic weapons. That was probably good. He could relax enough to be aware of his surroundings; the rubber taste of the face mask, the stink of blood and dried sweat from his fatigues and Adrienne's, even the crystal light of the stars outside the canopy on the ice-clad peaks to their left.

It was getting cold, too; he turned up the heater a bit with a tap of one strong index finger. The adrenaline rush of combat died down, leaving the heavy feeling and slight nausea it always did. Work was the best cure for that. . . .

"Where are the sights for air-to-air work?" he said after a

minute of flipping through the display menus. The ones for ground-strafing work were excellent.

Adrienne sighed; it sounded a little odd through the face mask. Then she reached over and flipped up a wire ring with a cross in the center.

Tom felt his mouth drop open for an instant; luckily the oxygen mask concealed it. "Isn't that a bit . . . basic?"

She shrugged, and sounded a bit embarrassed when she replied: "Well, Tom, we never thought these things would have to shoot down aircraft. The Commonwealth has the only aircraft in the world, and we weren't planning on any civil wars."

"Nobody does," he said gently; there had been an aching bitterness to the her words.

"Giovanni Fucking Colletta did," she growled. "Sorry."

"You've got a right to be angry," he said. "I'm in this fight because of you, and because I don't want Giovanni Fucking Colletta in charge of the Gate. I know it's more personal for you."

She glanced over at him; he thought she was grinning but couldn't be sure. "You know, Tom, one of the things I like about you is that you don't try to soft-soap me."

The Mosquito banked left, turning west now that it was above the highest peaks. "We're going to get there just around dawn," she said. "And so are they. We may not have to worry about air-to-air, goddamn it." A moment, and then: "Ah! I'm getting broadcast."

The voices in his ears were a chaotic babble to Tom; he didn't know the names, or the call signs, or the background; the transmissions were from everything: militia communications, domain radio stations, ham radio enthusiasts, CB transmitters.

Adrienne did know; she gave him a running summary. "Nostradamus is down," she said. "Giovanni—"

"Fucking Colletta," Tom finished for her.

"—broke into scheduled programming on all channels and started to announce that he'd been forced to take action by a Rolfe conspiracy and that all Settlers should remain calm and ignore 'unlawful orders,' quote unquote. Then . . ."

She whooped, and Tom winced. "Then Grandfather came on, and said, 'Giovanni, your father would have known better than to try and pull the wool over a Rolfe's eyes,' and the whole system went dead the next instant. He must have been working on that ever since my report—he couldn't get the Collettas out of the system, but he *could* keep them from using it."

Tom grinned himself. *The old bastard has style, at least.*

Adrienne went on: "There's fighting at the Gate complex—the Gate Security Force is split—no communications in the last hour, but a militia patrol from Rolfeston was fired on by the GSF checkpoints. . . . Rolfeston's mayor has proclaimed martial law, and called out the town's militia units to fight for 'Our Founder and the legitimate Commission' . . . good . . . Colletta and Batyushkov militia units moving toward the Gate . . . bad . . ."

She gave another whoop.

"Adri, could you not *do* that?" Tom asked. "And what's happening?"

"Karl von Traupitz tried to declare for the Collettas and send men over the Vaca hills against the Rolfe domain," she said. "But his son Siegfried's got control of the domain's militia HQ and is telling everyone to disregard his father's orders! They're fighting each other—the Rolfe domain's safe, and the militia's massing at Napa. . . . The Pearlmutters are sending *theirs* against Colletta Hall from the north. . . ."

"It's certainly no smooth coup," Tom said.

"Chaos and Old Night," Adrienne said. "But if we lose the Gate, the wheels could still come off. It's still too close."

❊ ❊ ❊

"They're landing them on the road," Tom said incredulously.

There was a two-lane highway along the coastal plain; the Hercules transports were dipping down toward it, the section nearest the Gate complex. The first had already landed and run itself off the roadway and into the long grass and trees; one wing hit an oak and the plane spun sideways, but slowly. The ramp dropped, and ant-tiny figures spilled out, deploying as they ran. Darkness covered the Gate area, although the lights of Rolfeston to the north were bright. And muzzle flashes lit up the ground around the big warehouse complex, and came from within it; fires burned, and the little stick-doll figures of dead men lay amid the planters and parking lots and burning trucks.

"He must have planned on combat-lossing the transports," Tom said half-admiringly. "He'd own a whole world if he won."

"He's not going to," Adrienne said. Her hand reached out and brought the ground-attack screen live. "I'll bring us in. You fire."

"Wilco," he said. Then: *"Jesus!"*

Someone was firing at them from the ground, someone with a heavy automatic weapon; twenty millimeter at least. He felt the plane lurch as Adrienne stamped on the rudder pedals and whipped the yoke left; but he also felt the thudding shudder as the heavy rounds struck and exploded.

"Right engine's out," he said, stabbing the control that feathered it; the prop stopped, and flames blew back into the night.

Then his right leg felt cold and hot at the same time. He looked down and saw his hand come away from it glistening wet.

"I'm hit," he said calmly.

Adrienne looked over at him, cursed sharply and whipped her eyes back to the control panel. "We're losing hydraulics . . . fuel's dropping fast; we must be spraying like a waterbomber. . . . I'm going to have to take her down, Tom."

"Yah," he said mildly; it didn't seem all that important, and the world was turning gray at the edges. There was something he wanted to say, but he couldn't.

Blackness.

✸ ✸ ✸

Adrienne Rolfe shook her head, feeling a desperate urgency she couldn't put a name to. Where was she? What was it she had to do?

Then the pain in her head reminded her. She was hanging down from the harness that held her to the pilot's seat of a Mosquito; the plane had pancaked, slid and then run into something that didn't *quite* turn it over. Bits and pieces of the landing came back to her, and why she could hear shooting. And flame-light licked through the canopy; there were slow fires in both the engines, and fuel dripping over her feet and calves.

"Got to get *out*," she muttered.

Tom was hanging limp beside her. She hit the catches of the canopy, but nothing happened. She undid her restraints, slid, and nearly passed out as a wave of fire-shot gray swept across her vision. Tears slid down her cheeks as she sobbed in breath, brought both legs up and kicked, kicked. Every impact seemed to jar small bones loose from the inside of her skull.

At last the side of the canopy gave a protesting squeal and the flap came up; a Mosquito had two, one by each seat. Noise flooded in from the outside; gunfire mostly, the boom of a heavier weapon now and then, explosions, screams, and the crackle of fire. Not far away a Catamount armored car lay on its side, the long auto-cannon bent like a pretzel.

"This is going to be tricky," she said, and winced at the croak that came out, and what it did to her throat. Her brain felt like hot sand had been stuffed up her nose until the whole front of her head was heavy with it; a touch showed that the nose was broken, swollen . . . and possibly something else there too.

"Oh, shit. Oh, shit," she gasped, waiting as the wave of pain in her face receded . . . a little.

When she unbuckled Tom, he was going to drop straight down into the front of the cockpit. There was only one thing to do; the problem was she didn't know if she could do it.

I have to do it. Therefore I can, right? Right. I'm a Rolfe, God damn it. We can do anything! Pocahontas forever!

She pulled the first-aid kit out from its container and threw it out into the night first. Then she turned and backed until she was underneath Tom, with her buttocks braced against the side of the cockpit to his right and her right hand bent back over her own neck to grab him by the front of his tunic. Her left scrabbled with the release of his restraints.

Click.

Two hundred and twenty pounds of man and another ten of equipment fell on her back and side; she bent and pulled, and the front of her face rapped sharply against the control column. She did scream then, long and shrill. She didn't let go of her grip, pulling and shifting with her shoulders until the big man's weight rested across her upper back.

"And . . . out . . . you . . . go!" she wheezed, straightening. "I've . . . lifted . . . more!"

Not when she was in this shape, though. Her thighs trembled, tensed, straightened an inch more. The small of Tom's back touched the side of the open canopy door. She straightened an inch more, twisting and pushing at his stomach with her left hand. He toppled forward, his boots and legs going out and dragging the rest of him around, and fell to the ground below with a thud. She might just have broken his neck . . . but that was better than burning to death.

"Don't you die on me, you great goddamned Scanahoovian lump, don't you *dare*," she wheezed, and crawled out herself.

Dragging Tom's weight took so much concentration she almost went past the aid kit. That was far enough from the dying aircraft that he wouldn't be hurt if it went up, particularly as a chunk of concrete provided a little shelter. She pulled the knife out of her boot and slit his sopping trouser leg. Blood was flowing but not spurting . . . but flowing fast . . .

She held the edges of the wound together, sprayed and strapped and sealed, her hands wet and slippery. His pulse was rapid and thready, but it didn't seem to be getting any worse, and the bleeding was under control . . . and she didn't have a clue about any other injuries. A injection of painkiller relaxed him and helped to fight shock.

Another hypodermic, this time for her: she stripped off the cover and jabbed it into the meat of her thigh, pressing the plunger with her thumb. A wave of heat seemed to flow from it, driving back the grayness from the edges of her vision. Unfortunately, as things became clearer, so did the pain—the great throbbing mass of pain that was the front of her face, and a dozen others. One was the little finger of her left hand, sticking out almost at a right angle—*Toni Bosco, you are avenged*—she thought half-hysterically, and then she grabbed it and straightened it with a single swift wrench.

"Oh, *shit*," she gasped, as she bound it to the one next to it with tape from the kit.

Dry-swallowing a couple of painkillers was all she could do for the rest of it; and not too many, or it would fight the stimulant that made it possible for her to move. Now she could look around her. . . .

The nearest wall of the Gate complex was blown out, its sheet metal tattered. She could see that quite well. . . .

Because two Hercules were burning on the coastal highway, not three hundred yards from where she lay. Others were wheeled off the roadway, their ramps down, but two had definitely been destroyed as they landed.

Tully, she thought, after a moment when her brain simply spun in place. *Roy Tully, you little gargoyle, you are worthy of Sandy, and I hope you both live through this. And Henry Villers, and Jim Simmons, and Kolo too.*

She looked down at Tom; the square rugged face was relaxed in unconsciousness, looking younger than his years for a change. You could see what he'd been as a fresh-faced farm boy just out of high school and waiting for the bus that would take him to boot camp.

"And I *order* you not to die," she whispered.

The fighting seemed to be mostly *out* from the Gate complex, a U of combat noises and muzzle flashes ringing the buildings. That meant that the Collettas and Batyushkovs in the GSF had some sort of control of the Gate itself, or there would be more shooting from inside the building. Their men and the reinforcements were trying to hold a perimeter, staving off the growing weight of the Commission forces loyal to the Rolfes. Which meant . . .

"They expect help through the Gate," she muttered, unable to frame the thought without speaking it. "Oh joy, oh bliss, oh rapture. They could still pull this off. I'll have to set the self-destruct mechanism going."

Let them get a firm control on the Gate and the area around it, and let the other Families and their Settlers realize that their contacts with FirstSide now depended on the Collettas, and support for the Rolfes might yet evaporate. At the very least, the Collettas and Batyushkovs might escape unpunished, the weight of opinion in the committee forcing amnesty to get the Gate back intact.

She still had her pistol; she drew it and moved out cautiously through the parking lot, moving from one car to another. A dead Gate Security Force trooper lay beyond that, where the glass sliding doors she'd passed through so often lay shattered in a sparkle of fragments. Adrienne stooped beside him, closed the staring eyes and took up the G36. It had a C-mag in it, and a glance at the transparent rear face of the magazine showed it was full—a hundred rounds. She slid the sling over her head, in the assault position that put the muzzle forward and left the pistol grip by her right hand. It also made things easier on her injured left.

Adrienne strode forward through the waiting rooms and into the final corridor that led to the personnel check-through station. A man looked up at her as she walked by; he was kneeling by a row of wounded. Then he did a double take and rose, opening his mouth.

She turned and loosed a three-round burst at point-blank range. The medic toppled backward, and the wounded man he fell on moaned weakly. Apart from that everything was vacant until she turned into the Gate chamber itself.

Someone had used an earthmoving machine to sweep a broad lane clear to the rippling silvery surface; a sense of *wrongness* caught at her, this chaos in the place she'd helped keep so orderly. And men were stepping out of the surface, moving in squads—not uniformed, beyond a rough practicality, but all armed. Something stuck its snout through, the muzzle of a vehicle-mounted cannon. Whatever the plot on FirstSide had been, it had worked—probably a lot better than the Commonwealth half.

Everyone in the room was looking at the Gate; there weren't more than a dozen or so men in the whole huge room, which was a sign of how desperately the conspirators' forces were trying to hold their perimeter until this help arrived.

Tsk, tsk, Giovanni—still operating on a shoestring and not leaving a margin for failure! Of course, the odds of her crashing inside the area the enemy were holding and surviving in shape to walk were pretty astronomical. . . .

Terminals were spotted all around the interior of the Gate chamber. She stepped over to one and punched her thumb down on the pad. The small screen lit, and she felt a wave of relief that almost overrode the pain in her head and hand. They had had to leave the local system up, or the Gate complex's internal power and light wouldn't be functioning.

"Identify," she said, and looked into the retina scanner. Her voice might be off enough not to match the files, but eye and thumb together were enough.

"Identified: Rolfe, Adrienne."

"Code—" She rattled off a string of letters and numbers; ones known only to the two elder male Rolfes, until a scant few weeks ago.

"Acknowledged. Query: Authority?"

"Milady. Cardinal. State."

"Acknowledged. Query: Sequence?"

"Hey, you there! What are you doing?"

"Override B-1!" Adrienne said, as the man turned toward her. "Override B-1! Override B-1, Oasis!"

That had been *her* idea—a personal link into the self-destruct sequence that would blow the charges in the floor—and send a wall of high-velocity concrete back through to the

FirstSide end of the Gate, smashing her grandfather's original short-wave set beyond hope of repair.

She turned, finger clenching the trigger, two fingers and a thumb of her left hand on the forestock to keep the assault rifle from riding up. Cartridges fountained out of it, and the whole hundred rounds spat out in less than ten seconds.

"Self-destruct sequence initiated," the computer said in its flat idiot-savant voice. "Five minutes to detonation."

Then she threw the weapon aside and ran, down the corridor, dodging as bullets chipped tile out of the floor, hurdling a fallen row of waiting-room chairs, out into the night—

Fire, and then peace.

EPILOGUE

Pajaro Valley—former Batyushkov Domain
August–December 2009

The Commonwealth of New Virginia

"Cigarette?" Lieutenant Mordechai Pearlmutter said. He was a slender beak-nosed swarthy young man of medium height. "Blindfold?"

"Get it over with!" Dimitri Batyushkov said; the only other sound beyond the gulls and the distant sea was the muttered prayers of the black-bearded, black-robed priest off near the entrance.

The adobe courtyard was plain whitewash, but the wall behind him had a row of pockmarks across it at chest height, all new, and some splashes. The Prime drew himself up as the row of Pearlmutter militiamen filed in with their rifles sloped; he had asked only one thing, that he not be bound to the post.

The officer—Batyushkov wearily thought a curse at the unseen sardonic face of the Old Man who had picked a damned Yid for this!—drew his .45 as he walked back to where the squad would stand; he would administer the coup with the pistol, one final shot behind the ear, if it was necessary. A noncom walked down the row of young men, most of them pale-faced and grim, one or two nervously excited. He took each rifle and loaded it with one cartridge, his back turned to the soldier so that none could see which held the one blank.

"Ready!" the young Pearlmutter collateral said. The weapons came up to the present.

"Aim!" And they went level, all but one or two steady. It would probably be quick.

The air was sweet; he was not afraid, but it was a hard thing to leave a world so beautiful. *Why was I not content with it?* he asked himself. There was no answer.

"*Fire!*"

✳ ✳ ✳

Colletta Hall:

Giovanni Colletta sat behind his desk, looking at the surveillance screens. The soldiers outside on this bright cool fall day had many shoulder flashes: the Rolfe lion, the Pearlmutter Seal of Solomon, even the Von Traupitz eagle. None wore his . . . and he suspected it would be a long time before the tommy gun appeared on an armed man's shoulder flash.

The door swung open. *Well, I was wrong,* the Colletta thought mordantly.

"Major Mattei," he said.

The soldier saluted and then bowed. "Sir," he said. "I have been ordered to bring you the decision of the Chairman."

"As if I didn't know it," the Colletta said; he could feel the eyes boring into his back, from the portrait above.

Mattei silently drew the pistol at his side and laid it on the desk before his overlord. "Chairman Rolfe says that he allows this—and the survival of the Colletta domain—as a favor to his old friend, your father."

Giovanni felt the hot flush of anger on his cheeks. "He would spare my son anyway! There is nothing to tie him to my actions. Why should I make his political life easier?"

Mattei sighed. "Sir, I am afraid that Chairman Emeritus Rolfe predicted that would be your answer."

Giovanni snorted, turning half away from the man who had commanded the domain's troops. Mattei took up the pistol, and the Colletta had a brief moment of utter surprise as he saw it leveled.

"Which is why he allowed me *two* rounds," Mattei murmured, looking at the body sprawled back in the rich leather of the chair. Was that a glint of amusement in the painted eyes in the portrait on the wall above?

"Two rounds, so that I could perform this last service for you, sir. And for your House."

He raised the pistol to his own temple, then shook his head. Better to be safe, even if it was inelegant; if he had a private horror, it was to be a human vegetable hooked to machines. He sat at the feet of the chair—of the man he had followed for so long. Better that he be found so, to make it plain the Colletta had taken his own life, and his faithful retainer had followed him.

The metal of the automatic tasted bitter and oily in his mouth, but not for long.

✳ ✳ ✳

Rolfe Manor

"Most pleasures fade with age," John Rolfe said quietly, obviously savoring the smoke of the cigarillo. "One of the few exceptions is power—not least because it enables one to punish one's enemies and reward one's friends."

Outside the elegant octagonal office, the rains of winter streaked down on the glass of the windows; a fire crackled merrily in the hearth, and a cat curled asleep on the rug before it. There was a hint of the pleasant odor of burning oak mingled with fine tobacco and the scent of a snifter of brandy nearby.

And all ends well, Tom Christiansen thought, shifting his weight to spare the right leg. *And just how ironic am I being, there?*

John Rolfe waved him to a seat. "I insist," he said, then grinned, a charmingly wicked expression in the ancient seamed face. "Pains in the leg are something I'm thoroughly familiar with. . . . Mr. Christiansen, do you know what my favorite part of a Shakespearian drama always was?"

"No, sir."

"The end, where the duke or prince comes out and plays deus ex machina."

Adrienne chuckled slightly beside Tom on the sofa. "And I'm the raccoon in the background, Grandfather?" she said.

Well, you won't be looking like a raccoon much longer, Tom thought stoutly. The reconstructive surgery was over, and the bruises that covered most of her face would fade. Her hand stole into his, and he gripped it gently. Her grandfather went on:

"Now . . . Mr. Tully, I assume you and this young woman intend to marry?"

"Yes, sir," Tully said, taking Sandra Margolin's hand as she sat nervously in her wheelchair; onc leg was still in a cast, waiting for the last in a series of ceramic-and-titanium implants to bond with the bone.

"The young heal quickly," John Rolfe said. "In heart not least. And your marital intentions are very convenient. So much so that I would have had to insist. . . ."

The ancient eagle eyes turned on Salvatore Colletta II: "Young Salvo, we're tying up loose ends right now, and this young lady is—albeit on the wrong side of the blanket—a cousin of yours. I presume you're not going to be tiresome about a DNA test?"

"No, sir," the Colletta said. "Of course, I will have her enrolled among the collaterals of my House at once."

Since you're on long-term probation and escaped execution only by virtue of your father's extremely convenient suicide and extremely detailed documentation proving you were entirely in the dark, Tom thought mordantly. *I am somehow not surprised.*

"Just so," John Rolfe VI nodded. "It will do the Commonwealth good to have that group . . . diversified. And that will make you, Mr. Tully, a member of the Thirty. Hmmm. Of course, you and your bride will also be eligible for an estate of your own in the Colletta domain. I think the Colletta, all things considered, would find the Owens Valley and its attached silver mine a suitable endowment. Especially in view of the long delay in regularizing Ms. Margolin's status."

"Of course, sir," the second Salvatore said. He surprised them all with a smile. "It doesn't have very positive associations for me, if you'll forgive me for saying so, sir."

Rolfe smiled, a sly expression this time. "And the Tully family will have an Indian princess at its genealogical root, just like the Rolfes."

He trickled smoke through his nostrils. "Now, let me think. . . . I've given the Batyushkov domain to young Siegfried von Traupitz; it *would* be embarrassing for him to inherit from his father, after killing the man. Let his younger brother take the original domain and committee seat, when he reaches his majority."

"That was a good idea. And you should do something for Jim Simmons, Grandfather," Adrienne Rolfe said.

"Seeing as he's dead and has no immediate family, what *can* I do besides a posthumous medal?"

"Something for Kolomusnim's family. Jim's tracker. He'd want that."

"Ah." The elder Rolfe closed his eyes, then sighed. "Very well. I'll arrange for citizenship for the tracker's children, and scholarships, and I'll enjoin Charles to keep an eye on them in matters of patronage, according to their abilities. . . . I suppose you will too? Excellent. Loyalty must run both ways. And for you, Mr. Villers? What would you have of me? My House is in your debt, as well. Although I doubt, to be frank, your underlying devotion to its cause."

The black man met the leaf green eyes levelly. "Well, you gave Good Star a whole country down in Sonora," he said. "You going to promote me to the Families as well?"

The old man grinned like a shark. "I suspect that you wish me to do so, Mr. Villers, only in order that you may throw it back in my face."

Henry Villers's own face fell a little. Tom smiled to himself; there were no flies on John Rolfe VI, even if he was slowing down a bit.

I suspect this will be his last hurrah, though, after he's tied up the ends, he thought. John Rolfe VI was enjoying himself, but he *did* look pretty tired. *A fitting conclusion.*

"Well, Mr. Villers, what would you say to a job?" Villers looked startled. "You were a soldier, and a detective, and a very good one, I understand. You ferreted out *our* secret, after all. Now, what would you say to . . . mmm, shall we say a captain's commission? Gate Security must be rebuilt, after all. . . ."

Tom nodded sympathetically as he saw temptation warring with impulse on the other man's face. That wouldn't only make Villers an important man; it would guarantee his children's positions in the Commonwealth, too. Nepotism was an established mode of operation here. He'd have the power to push their careers forward as well, and he'd have a set of powerful patrons backing him while he did it.

"Can I think about it?" he said, with small beads of sweat on the dark brown skin of his forehead. "Sir."

"By all means, Mr. Villers. By all means. Take as much time as you wish. Your father-in-law will need you to run his establishment for a time, in any case."

I wonder what that means? Tom thought.

"And shall I find a reward for you, Mr. Christiansen?" John Rolfe said, after the others had kissed his hand and left.

"You know better, sir," Tom said, and helped Adrienne to her feet. *What a pair of wrecks we are!* "I've found my own."

"Excellent, young man. And now if you will excuse me? There are a few things I must attend to. One or two, before the baptism."

He laughed at Adrienne's expression; Tom had to admit that it *was* sort of raccoon-like, with the rings of dark bruise around her eyes.

"You thought I wouldn't know? Reckless of you to begin so soon, but then we Rolfes never were much for caution."

They bowed over his hand. *"Baciamo le mani,"* Tom murmured.

"Scary," he said when they were outside, and winced a little as his foot caught on a rug.

Adrienne's hand closed on his arm. "Do you want to stay over?" she said. "It's a bit of a drive back to Seven Oaks, in this weather."

"Weather?" he said, looking down at her and grinning. "You Californians call a bit of rain *weather?* Why, back in North Dakota we'd call this a balmy spring evening."

"Yah, you betcha," she said. "And you walked through blizzards to get to school every day, with a rope tied to your waist and a St. Bernard following along behind."

"Skis," Tom said. "That's all we Norski need. Skis, and an axe to beat off the wolves." He looked up; Tully was waiting, standing behind Sandra's chair. "Heck, Roy can drive. Roy! You want to crash at our place?"

"Hell, yes, Kemosabe," the smaller man said. "We can talk about what we'll build out on our place . . . where we're *really* out in the country."

"Sounds good," Tom said. "Let's go. I want to get home." He caught Adrienne's eye and laughed softly. "Nice-sounding word, after all the goddamned adventures, isn't it?"

"You said it."

* * *

Rolfeston: Gate Complex

Sergei Lermontov was sweating slightly, despite the fact that the temperature inside the great metal room was barely fifty degrees. The wreckage had long since been cleared away and the damaged structures removed, but the echoing emptiness of what had been a bustling nexus for so long was a reproach in itself.

Although not so much so as the armed guards, he thought. *And the sentence of death with conditional stay of execution.*

Beside him, Ralph Barnes made a final adjustment to the control console. *A stroke of luck there, that he was the one to interrogate me and take my offer of a new Gate to the Rolfe.*

Like most Americans, Barnes was sentimental about persons he'd come to know *as* persons.

A metal framework outlined the area where the Gate had stood for so long; control cables ran to it, and to a cat's cradle of leads all around it.

"You must understand, sir," he said. "The wave form—"

"Mr. Lermontov," John Rolfe VI said softly.

He sat at his ease in a padded chair, comfortable in his alpaca greatcoat and ascot. The armed men behind him somehow looked entirely at one with his conservative elegance.

"I find myself growing less patient as I grow older," he said. "I'm also content to let you experts handle these matters. Leaders motivate their subordinates, and the subordinates act. A division of labor."

"Blackmailer," Ralph Barnes growled, shooting him a glance from under shaggy brown brows.

John Rolfe arched one of his. "Why, Mr. Barnes, you wrong me," he said, with a slight sardonic smile. "Didn't I shower you with rewards and praise? You are here entirely as a volunteer this time."

"And you said you'd shoot Sergei if he couldn't give you back your toy," Ralph said. "What'm I supposed to do, let you kill him? Besides, Sergei could do it alone. It would just take longer, and maybe something would go wrong and *everyone* would get hurt."

"He helped *break* my toy," Rolfe pointed out reasonably. "It's only just that if he is to live where others died, he make some recompense. And I *do* wish a Christmas present for my grandchildren and prospective great-grandchildren. The Commonwealth can survive without the Gate, but regaining it would be a major boon."

Sergei prayed to a God in whom he'd never believed, and touched the screen.

CRACK!

He winced, then looked up and let himself slump forward in relief, his palms resting on the console and breath shuddering in and out in great gasps. Rolfe might have killed him without rancor, as the price of a sporting wager. . . .

But if I died, it would be in earnest, he thought, and waved the probe forward.

A long boom swung through the gate, with sensors on its end. And a television pickup; it was keyed to a large flatscreen placed where they could all look at it.

The screen flickered, then settled to a clear image. It was raining there, too; as well it might, in midwinter along the Californian coast.

"But where is the Gate complex on FirstSide?" he asked himself; all he could see was long grass. . . .

Rolfe began to laugh; coughed, recovered, laughed again.

Because in the grass was a dead animal, huge and shaggy, almost certainly a giant sloth. Paws braced on it, the sabertooth bared its foot-long fangs and screamed, flattening its ears and bristling its orange-and-black-striped fur.

APPENDIX ONE
The Thirty Families

Rolfe
Domain: Napa, Lake County
Motto: "Carpe Diem et Omnia Mundi."
Sigil: Red lion rampant on black background

Fitzmorton (twice)
Alan Fitzmorton—Domain: south Oakland to San Leandro
Rob Fitzmorton—Domain: Sonoma Valley

O'Brien
Domain: Marin County
Motto: "O'Brien Go Braugh!"
Sigil: winged harp

Colletta
Domain: Santa Clara Valley
Motto: "Silence."
Sigil: winged Thompson gun

Hughes
Domain: Healdsburg area

Pearlmutter
Domain: San Francisco peninsula to Palo Alto—"New
  Brooklyn"
Motto: "The Best You Can."

Throckham
Domain: Petaluma

Filmer
Domain: Concord, Contra Costa

Tuke
Domain: Livermore-Amador, Contra Costa

Cooke
Domain: Orange County

Peyton
Domain: lower Santa Ynez valley

Hammon
Domain: Pleasanton, Contra Costa

Hottywood
Domain: southern Santa Clara valley

Ludwins
Domain: western Santa Maria valley

Carons
Domain: Central Santa Clara (between Collettas, Rob
   Fitzmortons)

Von Traupitz
Domain: Suisun valley

Chumley
Domain: western Yolo county
Motto: "Who dares, wins!"

Versfeld
Domain: Santa Monica, east along Santa Monica foothills
Motto: "Look before you trek!"

Bauer
Domain: Carmel, Carmel valley
Motto: "Death Holds No Repose."

Stanislaus
Domain: southern Oxnard valley
Motto: "We Fight for Our Friends."

Morrison
Domain: Lower Salinas
Motto: "Down Styphon!"

Sanders
Domain: Upper Salinas

Sulgrave
Domain: Russian River valley
Motto: "Fortune Is Bald Behind."

Ball
Domain: Orange County
Motto: "Pick Your Man and Aim Low."

Fairfield
Domain: San Leandro (south of Alan Fitzmortons)
Motto: "By This Right."

Fest
Domain: Ventura; northern Oxnard
Motto: "Winter Isn't Coming."

Barklay
Domain: inland Santa Ynez valley, around Solvang
Motto: "How Shall One Fight a Hundred?"

Wyans
Domain: inland Santa Maria valley, around Sisquoc
Motto: "Westward the Course of Empire."

Devereaux
Domain: Paso Robles area
Motto: "Pour Dieu et la Patrie."

Batyushkov
Domain: Santa Cruz, Pajaro Valley
Motto: "Za Nas!"

Some Collaterals:
Di Montevarichi—collaterals of the Rob Fitzmorton line;
  relatives of his wife. Tuscan nobility.

APPENDIX TWO
Pocahontas and the Rolfes of Virginia

In our history, John Rolfe (1585–1622) married the woman nicknamed Pocahontas, whose real name was Matoaka. She was the daughter of the Powhatan chieftain Wahunsonacock, and married Rolfe on April 5, 1614, ensuring peace between the powerful Powhatan confederacy and the struggling English colony at Jamestown for eight more years.

That probably ensured the survival of the first English foothold on North American soil—without that breathing space, it might well have suffered the fate of the earlier "lost colony" at Roanoke, with unguessable consequences for the history of the Americas. Rolfe was also responsible for introducing the already-popular West Indian variety of tobacco to Virginia, sparking the colony's first boom and putting it, for the first time, on a sound economic footing.

Matoaka, christened as Lady Rebecca at her baptism, gave birth to one son, Thomas, in 1615. In 1616 the colony sponsored a voyage to England for the Rolfes, where Lady Rebecca was given a wildly enthusiastic reception, and Virginia gained invaluable publicity. It was badly needed, for while Virginia was beginning to acquire a reputation as a place where an ambitious man could get rich, for most of the newcomers it was a charnel house. In these decades the average life expectancy of an English settler in Virginia was less than two years; tens of thousands died in the Chesapeake swamps—of malaria, dysentery, Indian arrows, hunger, scurvy, overwork and sheer heartbreak. Not until around 1700 would births outnumber deaths among the English settlers in Virginia, nearly three generations after the foundation of Jamestown.

Lady Rebecca died on her way back to Virginia in the year 1617; like so many of her compatriots, she contracted some European disease, probably smallpox—one of the many maladies to which the long-isolated Amerindians were fatally vulnerable. John Rolfe went on to become a member of the Governor's Council and a successful tobacco planter, before being killed at Berkeley Hundred in the surprise Indian attack which began the Powhatan-English war of 1622. His son Thomas inherited his lands and prospered, but the Rolfe name became extinct in the next generation. Through his daughter, however, Thomas—and the Powhatan chieftains—became ancestors of virtually all the First Families of Virginia; Robert E. Lee, for example, was among their descendants; so was Thomas Jefferson's wife.

In the very slightly different history of *Conquistador,* Lady Rebecca did not contract her fatal disease; she lived until 1622, when she shared her husband's fate at the hands of her furious countrymen. She also bore two more sons, John and Samuel—and from them derived the long line of the Rolfes of Virginia. Few made any great mark on history; they were typical of their time and class: horsemen and hunters, owners of plantations and slaves, and growers of tobacco and wheat and corn. Some served on the Governor's Council; others led the colony's militia in time of war. They shared the declining fortunes of the Virginian gentry as the nineteenth century wore on, and lost the last of their wealth in the convulsions of the Civil War and Reconstruction.

None shook the earth . . . until John Rolfe VI, fresh from the Pacific Theatre of World War Two, started fiddling with a shortwave set one April in 1946. . . .

APPENDIX THREE
A Brief Overview and Ethnography of the
Post-Alexandrian World

When Alexander did not die in 323 B.C.E., the history of the world and its peoples turned down an entirely new track.

After recovering from his illness, Alexander spent several years consolidating his vast conquests, and pressing forward with his policy of Graeco-Iranian synthesis and Greek colonization. In 320 B.C.E., the Greek cities of Sicily and southern Italy, pressed by the Carthaginians and Italics, appealed to Alexander, and a new round of conquests began. . . .

Alexander the Great died in August of 280 B.C.E., in the summer capital of Ecbatanta, in the Zagros mountains. He was succeeded by his son Alexander II (by the Bactrian-Persian princess Roxanne), and his dynasty remained in power for a further century and a half. By that time, the empire ruled from Babylon (renamed, of course, Alexandria) stretched from Iberia to the Ganges delta. After roughly A.D. 0, it began to decline and eventually fissured into a maze of quarrelsome city-states and regional kingdoms; by about A.D. 300 the last pretence of political unity was gone. Its ghost continued to haunt men's minds for many generations, and "Alexandros" became alternate title for Zeus, and the term for "ruler" as well.

Twenty-two hundred years after his death, the heritage of the Conqueror still marked the world. Since the Alexandrian empire had been so much larger than Rome's, its legacy was more widespread; half the 600 million or so human beings on Earth in the early twenty-first century spoke languages derived from Greek, in much the same way as French, Spanish and so forth are derived from Latin. The post-Alexandrian linguistic/cultural zone encompassed the whole Mediterranean basin, the Balkans as far north as the Carpathians, Egypt, Ethiopia, the Near East including Anatolia and the Caucasus, parts of the southern Ukraine, most of the settled part of Central Asia (plus Iran-Afghanistan), and northern India all the way from Pakistan to Bengal.

Technologically, the post-Greek zone was the most advanced part of the world prior to the opening of the Gate in 1946; the level is roughly late-medieval, and has shown little change for many centuries. Paper and printing are known, but gunpowder is not.

Languages and peoples

Arabic is limited to the southern coast of Arabia, and to spots along the East African coast. Most of sub-Saharan Africa is much as it was in our timeline in the Renaissance period, with a huge and obvious exception: no Islam or Christianity. Tribal statelets or ancephalous societies cover most of the continent, with some substantial kingdoms in the savanna of West Africa; those have been profoundly influenced by the neo-Greek states of North Africa via the trans-Saharan trade routes. The South Arabian civilizations have been influential down the east coast.

Southern India is inhabited by Dravidian-speaking Hindus who use Sanskrit as a liturgical language, but they have been heavily influenced by Greek culture. Southeast Asia is mostly Hindu but speaks Austronesian-Malaysian languages, except for a Han kingdom in what is northern Vietnam and southeastern China in our time line.

There are vast differences in Central and East Asia. The Alexandrian empire and its neo-Greek successor states remained strong in Bactria—the settled, agricultural part of southern Central Asia—and assimilated the sedentary Iranian peoples. The north-Iranian nomads, blocked and harassed by the Greeks in Bactria, the southern Ukraine and cis-Caucasia, turn east instead of west—in our history they eventually moved as far as central Europe, pushed and followed by the Turkic, Ugrian (Hungarian) and later Mongol-speaking tribes.

In the Alexandrian timeline the migrations went the other way. The northern Iranian nomads first moved east over the

Tien Shan and pushed the Tocharian-speakers of the Tarim Basin[1] and Shansi directly east, into Manchuria, Korea and northeastern China. Then they followed and bypassed them in waves, taking over outer and inner Mongolia, then invading China proper.

Korea–Manchuria–northeast China is held by a number of Selang-Arsi kingdoms, essentially Tocharian, but with substantial influence from the Chinese substrate. The rest of China as far south as the southern fringes of the Yangtse valley is occupied by mixed peoples speaking Iranian languages. Mongolia, Inner Mongolia, Sinkiang and the steppe zone as far as the Tien Shan are inhabited by North Iranian nomads, and farmers in the oasis zones. The Mongol and Turkic peoples were swallowed up by the Tocharian and Iranian migrations.

Europe was always a backwater to the Alexandrian Empire, although Greece remained culturally important. Italy, southern France (roughly Provence), and Spain are post-Greek—small kingdoms and city-states, civilized in a provincial fashion.

In northern Europe, without the Romans to intervene, the Germanics more or less completely displaced the Celts; the destructive passage of the Cimbri through Gaul around 100 B.C., and their settlement in the Garronne estuary, began the obliteration of the western Celts.

The area from Ireland to the mouth of the Danube is oc-

---

[1] Tocharian is the name given to a group of Indo-European languages spoken in what is now Chinese Turkestan/Sinkiang from the Bronze Age through the early medieval period. The Tocharian speakers were the easternmost of the Indo-European peoples, and their tongue (rather oddly) shows a closer kinship to the western Indo-European languages (Celtic, Germanic, Greek, Italic) than it does to the Indo-Iranian group. Recent archaeological work in the Tarim, whose climate is uniquely suited to preserving bodies, has shown that the Tocharians were European in appearance as well—tall, narrow-faced people with light complexions and often blond or red hair; in fact, they looked rather like Central or Northern Europeans. In our history they were overrun and assimilated by Turkic-speaking peoples, the ancestors of the present Uighur population of Sinkiang.

cupied by various Germanic kingdoms and tribes—all barbarians and preliterate save for a narrow fringe along the edge of the post-Alexandrian zone; occasional folk-migrations and conquests along the Mediterranean shore have been of little long-range consequence, since the invaders were invariably absorbed by the higher culture.

In eastern Europe, the Slavs were weakened by their clashes with the Alexandrian empire and its successors; this largely prevented the Dark Age migrations out of the *urheimat* in southeastern Poland/northwestern Ukraine, which in our history carried the Slavic languages deep into the Balkans and far into Asia. Instead, the Balts supplanted the Slavs in a long series of folk-movements, occupying the zone east of the Germanics and stretching to the upper Volga; however, except for a few of their southernmost kingdoms, they remain even more backward than their western neighbors.

New Guinea and Australia–New Zealand are roughly as in our history—prediscovery—except that the New Virginians have begun making settlements there.

North America was neolithic or hunter-gatherer when the Gate opened in 1946. Some early state-level societies had emerged in the Mississippi-Ohio valley, and the Iroquoian peoples had mostly replaced the others in the northeast and middle-Atlantic states. On the Pacific, the Potlatch tribes—the Haida and their relatives—had the most elaborate culture, and had spread further than in our timeline, reaching down the Oregon coast. They had some contact with the Chumash, the most sophisticated of the Californian peoples.

The Aztec and Inca hegemonies had long since fallen apart in 1946, but their areas remained civilized and had advanced into a full Bronze Age, with extensive use of bronze weapons and tools, and both had developed genuine writing systems ultimately derived from the Maya syllabic script. Politically they were chaotic, with many small kingdoms; they remained handicapped by the lack of horses and other draft animals. The Nahuatl and Quechua languages had spread to most of those areas, reducing their linguistic diversity.

All this was thrown into chaos by the epidemics which accompanied the opening of the Gate, and which were renewed and worsened by the beginning of trans-Pacific trade by both the New Virginians and various East Asian peoples in the early 1960s.

By the twenty-first century, the population of the Americas had declined by about 90 percent from its peak in 1946, from around 35 to 45 million to about 3 to 4 million total, with less than half a million in North America above the FirstSide Mexican border. The percentage decline is roughly similar to that which the Americas suffered in the century after Columbus in our history. Losses were worse than that in the areas along the Pacific coast of North America, where the indigenous populations effectively ceased to exist.

There were also ecological upheavals, partly through the inadvertent introduction of new weeds and microorganisms—this begins almost immediately, as the horses brought over for the first expedition to the goldfields scatter grass seeds in their dung. Within a few years, even more radical changes result from John Rolfe's program of deliberately introducing African and Eurasian animals and plants over huge areas. This is comparable to the post-Columbian exchange in our time line, but faster and larger-scale, since it is conscious rather than inadvertent and the New Virginians have much better transportation technology than Renaissance-era Europeans.

Remnants of the western tribes move east, encouraged by the Commonwealth authorites. With them go horses, and via trade, steel tools and trade firearms (replica flintlocks).

By the twenty-first century, there is a horse-nomad culture on the Great Plains and in the southwestern basin and range area; most of them are hunters, in a rather close analogue of the mounted buffalo hunters of our time line's Old West, but some have become herders of cattle and sheep as well. Technology transfer is rather swifter; for example,

most tribes learn to use wheeled carts and saddles with stirrups almost as soon as they adopt the horse.

The higher neolithic farming societies of the central and
eastern parts of the continent collapse back into a simpler
village-based culture under the hammer of the plagues, losing most of their complex social hierarchies. As yet they
have had little contact with the New Virginians, except in the
immediate vicinity of their trading posts and small settlements on the east coast.

By 2009, the New Virginians are dominant all along the
Pacific coast from southern Alaska to Baja, and are steadily
pushing inland as their numbers increase. They have also
colonized Hawaii (the survivors there migrated to Tahiti by
agreement) and are making a beginning in Australasia.

There are surviving Mexica-Zapotec-Mayan city-states
in Mesoamerica, and ditto in Peru, in contact with the New
Virginians, trading with them and learning a good deal. The
New Virginians have trading posts there, and small colonies
on the eastern coasts—at the mouth of the Rio de la Plata,
Rio, the Caribbean, and the Atlantic coast of North America.

APPENDIX FOUR
The Demographics of the Commonwealth of New Virginia

John Rolfe always intended that the new land beyond the Gate should become an autonomous, self-reproducing community, rather than merely a source of wealth. Much of his initial profit, and at his encouragement a good deal of that made by his associates, went into promoting this growth.

The initial immigration got off to a slow start in 1946 (less than 200), but built up rapidly—by 1950, the Settler population was over 15,000. Then immigration remained at an average of around 1,000 to 1,500 a year for the next twenty years or so, but with wide fluctuations: big spikes in the early 1950s, the early 1960s; smaller ones in the early 1980s and the mid-1990s.

The "steady" part of the influx is Americans, usually recruited by chain migration (people sponsoring friends and relatives) or very careful approaches by Commission agents. There were a sprinkling of "involuntaries," people who stumbled on the Gate secret or looked likely to do so—Gate Security usually abducted them to New Virginia.

Punctuating the steady inflow of Americans are bursts of quasi-refugees: in the 1940s Germans, Italians, Dutch from Indonesia, and Balts; French *colons* from North Africa and British settlers from Kenya in the 1950s and early 1960s; Rhodesians later; and Russians and Afrikaners in the 1990s.

By 2009, the population is 150,000, not counting 40,000 or so temporary Gastarbeiter on five-year contracts, who don't have children. The Commonwealth's TFR (total fertility rate) fluctuates between 3.7 and 4; about like the United States at the height of the baby boom in 1957, but stable, and it has been since the 1950s; the death rate is slightly below 8 per 1,000. Median age is around 26. There is a slight surplus of males among adults because of immigration effects—that happens anywhere with substantial immigration.

The shape of the population pyramid is more like that of

Malaysia or other upper-income developing countries than that of the contemporary United States—or even that of the United States in the 1950s, since the baby boom there followed a period of very low fertility in the 1930s. The Commonwealth of New Virginia started out with a fairly high TFR and has maintained it unchanged, so the pyramid slopes out sharply—each age-cohort is about double the size of the one above.

With the continuing trickle of immigration, the annual population increase is about 3 percent.

Note that immigration tends to distort the population pyramid by increasing the percentage of the total in their prime reproductive years—there is a bulge in the 20 to 40 age group. Thus natural increase is higher than would be expected with the TFR and mortality rates, despite the fact that immigrants tend to have a lower TFR than the native-born.

Doubling time for the Settler population is (as of 2009) about 23 years. This is lower than it was in earlier periods because immigration has remained static or declined slightly and is therefore smaller relative to the total population.

Population distribution is about:

Rolfeston (Berkeley)	28,000
New Brooklyn (San Francisco)	18,000
San Diego	19,000
Napa	5,000
Various small towns	15,000
Farm and mine settlements	50,000
Hawaii	10,000
Australia	5,000
Various outposts	3,000

S.M. STIRLING

**From national bestselling author
S.M. Stirling comes gripping novels of
alternative history**

Island in the Sea of Time
0-451-45675-0

Against the Tide of Years
0-451-45743-9

On the Oceans of Eternlty
0-451-45780-3

The Peshawar Lancers
0-451-45873-7

"FIRST-RATE ADVENTURE ALL THE WAY."
—HARRY TURTLEDOVE

To order call: 1-800-788-6262

R922

Discover an American frontier that never was...

Kurt R.A. Giambastiani

"FANS OF ALTERNATE HISTORY HAVE A NEW HERO."
—*Midwest Book Review*

THE YEAR THE CLOUD FELL
0-451-45821-4

THE SPIRIT OF THUNDER
0-451-45870-2

THE SHADOW OF THE STORM
0-451-45916-4

FROM THE HEART OF THE STORM
0-451-45955-5

**Available wherever books are sold or
to order call 1-800-788-6262**

R920